WHEN WE WERE ANIMALS

WHEN WE WERE ANIMALS

A NOVEL

JOSHUA GAYLORD

MULHOLLAND BOOKS

Little, Brown and Company

New York Boston London

Mulholland Books
Hachette Book Group
1290 Avenue of the Americas, New York, NY 10104
Mulhollandbooks.com

First Edition: April 2015

Mulholland Books is an imprint of Little, Brown and Company, a division of Hachette Book Group, Inc. The Mulholland Books name and logo are trademarks of Hachette Book Group, Inc.

The publisher is not responsible for websites (or their content) that are not owned by the publisher.

The Hachette Speakers Bureau provides a wide range of authors for speaking events. To find out more, go to hachettespeakersbureau.com or call (866) 376-6591.

ISBN 978-0-316-29793-6
LCCN 2014958933

10 9 8 7 6 5 4 3 2 1

RRD-C

Printed in the United States of America

For my mother,
who, when as a child I woke from nightmares
and asked her how dark it was outside, replied, smiling,
"Pitch black."

There was a mean trick played on us somewhere. God put us in the bodies of animals and tried to make us act like people. That was the beginning of trouble. . . . A man can't live, feeling himself from the inside and listening to what the preachers say. He can't do both, but he can do one or the other. He can live like we were made to live, and feel himself on the inside, or he can live like the preachers say, and be dead on the inside.

—Erskine Caldwell, *God's Little Acre*

The youth gets together his materials to build a bridge to the moon, or, perchance, a palace or temple on the earth, and, at length, the middle-aged man concludes to build a woodshed with them.

—Henry David Thoreau

All truth is crooked, time itself is a circle.

—Friedrich Nietzsche

I

CHAPTER 1

For a long time, when I was a girl, I was a very good girl.

You should have known me then. You would have liked me. Shy, undergrown, good in school, eager to please. At the dinner table, especially when my father and I went visiting, I didn't eat before others, and I sometimes went without salt because I was too timid to ask anyone to pass it.

They said, "Lumen is quite a little lady."

They said, "She's so quiet! I wonder what's going on in that mind of hers."

I did all my homework. I ate celery sticks as a snack. I went to bed early and knew that the shrieking outside my window had nothing to do with me at all.

——

SOME PEOPLE SAID the moonlight shone stronger there. Other people said it was the groundwater, a corrupted spring beneath the houses, or pestilent vapors from the abandoned mine shaft in the woods. (It's impossible to know exactly what you breathe—I think about that sometimes.) Once upon a time, Hermit Weaper explained to me and some other girls who had wandered onto his property that there was a creature who lived in the lake, and that this creature crept slyly into town once a month and laid eggs in the open mouths of the youth, and that was why we behaved as we did. Lots of people speculated. I didn't. I don't. I don't for the same reason I don't try to guess why houseflies fly the way they do, capricious and bumbling. Some things just are, and there's nothing to be done but smile the world on its way. Some people—though not as many anymore, since faith has become quaint as magic—even thought that the town was evil and being punished by God, like Sodom and Gomorrah, or Nineveh, or Babylon—poor cities! The truth is, nobody knew why it happened this way, but in the town where I grew up, when the boys and girls reached a certain age, the parents locked themselves up in their houses, and the teenagers ran wild.

It's been a long time since I left that place, and now I lead a very different kind of life. My husband is a great admirer of my cooking—even though I never use recipes. There is a playground attendant at the park where I take my son to play. Playgrounds now have rubberized mats on the ground, and the attendant keeps a watchful eye for potential predators—my son is safe, he doesn't even know how safe. I have friendly neighbors who are concerned about the epidemic of dandelions on our lawns. The checkers at the grocery store greet me as they greet everyone else, smiling and guileless. I'm a different person, mostly.

And it makes me wonder if one day I might be able to rediscover fully the child version of myself, before things fouled themselves up, when I was a little girl with commendable manners, when my father and I were two against the world, when my striving for goodness was so natural it was like leaves falling from trees everywhere around me, when I believed sacredness was to be found in many small things like ladybugs and doll toes, when I didn't have a murderous thought in my head, not even one.

———

HERE'S SOMETHING I remember.

I am six years old. I awaken in my bed to the pitchy darkness of night. The familiar glow of my mermaid night-light is gone, and there are sounds coming from outside in the street—screeches like those of predator birds, but human. There are people out there. And also rain. Thunder.

I call for my father. He comes in, carrying a candle in a crystal candlestick. He sets the candle on the table next to me and sits on my bed. His weight dimples the bed, and my small body rolls against him.

"You're dreaming, little Lumen," he says.

"No, I'm not," I say.

"How can you tell?" He is testing me, but his eyes tell me he is sure I will pass.

"I never dream about the night," I tell him. "All my dreams are daytime dreams."

"Is that true?" He seems pleased.

"Yes."

"Well, that's the sign of a pure spirit."

A blinding flash startles the room, a moment of clear sight in the blindness—and a moment later a violent crack of thunder. The earth is tearing itself apart outside. I picture the ground rent with gaping fissures. And the voices, howling crazy at the sky, the thunder, the apocalyptic sundering of the world.

"What's happening?" I say.

"Just a storm," says my father. He is a geologist. He knows about the currents of the earth. "Must've taken down a power line somewhere. The electricity on the whole block is out. Nothing to worry about."

The rain goes clattery against my windowpane. Then the voices again from outside. Feral cries. They sound not afraid, as I am, but rather celebratory—wanton, a word I am aware of.

"Who's out there?" I say.

"Just teenagers," my father says.

"Why are they like that?"

"That's just the way they are."

"Will I be like that when I grow up?"

"You? Perish the thought." It is a pet expression of his. Perish is to outlaw, but parish is also a place for pastors. It is a magical word, and it might protect me. "You'll be different. You're my good girl, aren't you?"

"Yes," and I am his good girl.

"Will you always be my good girl?"

"Yes."

Always is so easy to promise.

"Then there we go," he says and brushes my hair away from my forehead with his fingertips.

The pandemonium continues outside my window, and I reach out to touch the fine, shimmering angles of the crystal candle-stick. That, too, seems magic, like a wand or a gemstone that holds power in its mineral core.

"Where did it come from?" I ask.

"It's old," my father says. "I found it in the credenza. It was a wedding gift to your mother and me."

Outside there are many voices at once, caterwauling in the

rain. They must be running past, because I hear them grow gradually loud then quiet again. I look at the window, expecting maybe faces pressed against the glass, a smear of pale skin against the dark. Yet there is nothing to see but the hazy reflection of candle flame.

My father must see my apprehensive gaze.

He says, "Do you want me to tell you the story of our wedding?"

"Yes. Was my mother's name Felicia Ann Steptoe?"

"It was. Until she married me, and her name became—"

"Felicia Ann Fowler."

"That's right."

"And did she wear long orchid gloves on her wedding?"

"She did."

I have heard this story many times before. It is a catechism between him and me.

"Show me the pictures," I demand.

But he shakes his head. "It's too dark. Tomorrow, when the sun comes up."

"Okay," I say.

Then I hush so he can tell the rest of the story. And he tells it, every detail the same and perfect. And he looks up to the ceiling as he tells it, as though it were a story of shadows narrated by his easy, ocean-smoothed voice.

And as he tells it, my lips form my magic word against the night—perish, parish—repeated intermittently, like the thread that quilts together many pieces of fabric, while outside the animal cries of teenagers join with the thunder to rattle the windowpanes.

———

THAT'S ONE THING. Here's another, from even earlier.

We are playing hide-and-seek in our big house. It is a serious game, because not even the third floor is off-limits. I run from room to room, looking even in places where I know he cannot fit—under couches, behind bookcases.

I climb the steps to the third floor, out of breath but happy. I am closing in, I'm sure of it. He's not in the bathtub, behind the shower curtain. He's not in the guest room crouched behind the desk. But I am warm.

I open the door of another room, one we keep shut, one used mostly for storage. There is a sound coming from the closet, a low, whispery sound. I've found him.

I swing wide the closet door, and there he is—there he is—clutching at a dress that belonged to my mother, and choked with tears!

THIS IS WHERE I tell you that I grew up happy. Motherless, I was treated nicely in school. I was complimented on my hand-writing (which remains picture-perfect to this day—many people believe I use a ruler to cross my Ts), and my diction, which inspired my fourth-grade teacher, Mrs. Markson, to declare that she had never seen a child so full of grace and refinement in all her years of teaching. English was my favorite subject, because I was a good reader—my father having early on in my life en-couraged me in the ritual of reading together every weekend afternoon in the backyard, I in a hammock slung between two oak trees, he stretched on a deck chair beneath the shade of the slatted wooden pergola over the patio. He would, every now and then, call out, "How's the book?"—and then I would be expected to deliver some thoughtful appraisal of whatever I was reading at the time. Positive or negative—it didn't matter, as long as my critique was grounded in some personal, authoritative interpretation. "I'm not sure why they use farm animals as characters instead of people," I might say. "I don't see the advantage in it." And he would nod, satisfied that a position had been taken one way or the other.

But I was also good at math and science, which led me to believe that my left brain and my right brain were perfectly in balance with each other, that I had an ambidextrous intellect, and that someone with my gifts ought to think very hard about what she really wanted to *do* in life, because there would be so very many options open to her.

The only subject I didn't like much was history. I couldn't be bothered to care about the kings and queens and pilgrims and soldiers who lived so long ago and had nothing to do with my little town and its peculiar ways.

But I was a very dedicated student—even in history class—because my father took great pride in my academic successes, and I wanted to please him. It was difficult for him, having to raise a child on his own, and sometimes he seemed stricken, and I certainly didn't want to add to his already considerable grief. So I did the best I could, and my best turned out to be very good indeed.

And of course this: my mostly female teachers seemed to like my father quite a lot. I watched them moon over him, and he was a lesson to me about what women ought to admire. When they praised me in his presence, their words redirected the compliments toward him. "She is a marvelous reader. You can tell she's been raised to think critically." Or: "She's at the top of her class. It's obvious she has a wonderful support system at home."

You can't take these things personally. My father puffed out his chest with pride, and the look he gave me as he received these adulations was payment beyond measure for my hard work.

As a reward for a good report card and as long as it wasn't a full moon, he would take me to the drive-in movie theater. We got there early in order to find the ideal space in the center of the lot. Then, until the movie started, I was allowed to run back and forth over the rows of tarmac dunes constructed to raise the front ends of the cars to a proper viewing angle.

During the movie, we ate from a bag of popcorn on the console between us. Sometimes a young couple in the car next to us would steam up their windows, and I was embarrassed. But if my father noticed, he never let on.

So it was a simple matter to shut myself off from the mortification of witnessing the private acts that might be taking place everywhere around me.

———

THEN IT WAS the sixth grade and I was twelve and I had a best friend named Polly.

Once, we rode our bikes down to the lake. It was Worm Moon, so it must have been March, and we had gotten out of school early. The school always had late starts and early closings on the three days around a full moon. The purpose of the short-ened hours was to give students plenty of time to travel to and from home without having to be caught outside while the sun was down—but Polly and I lived so close to the school that we could use those extra hours to adventure around town.

We pulled our bikes through a thicket of dense brush until we came to a little patch of beach that was unknown to anyone but us. In the summer we would have stripped off our clothes and dived into the murky water, but on this day there was a crispness to the air, and we pulled our jackets more tightly around us. We skimmed stones off the surface of the lake and spoke of many things, including Hondy Pilt, the slow boy in our class who only knew how to say a few words and spoke them in a loud, inarticulate voice, and Rosebush Lincoln, the girl who was rumored to have made him cry by cornering him in the boys' bathroom and making him pull down his pants so she could examine his boy parts. Rosebush Lincoln was in training to be a doctor.

Petey Meechum was also under discussion. Our school had square dancing once a week, and he was the boy who asked us each to be his partner (Polly seven times and me five) more often than he asked any other girl. All the girls wanted to be his square dancing partner, so Polly and I were pleased about our prospects for young womanhood. Petey Meechum's attentions told us we were on the right track, and they boded well for our futures.

"Do you think he writes about us in his diary?" asked Polly.

The "us" signified a political settlement. There had been some tension between Polly and me on this matter, and lately we had come to some vague truce by speaking about the boy's affections as if they were directed in equal measure toward both of us rather than simply toward one or the other.

"Boys don't keep diaries," I said. I wasn't sure if she had been joking. Polly was sometimes wry and sometimes frank.

"I know," she said. "How come you think that is?"

"I don't know," I said. "Maybe they don't care to dwell on things. Or maybe they don't need to write things down because they have naturally good memories."

"I bet Petey has an excellent memory. My mother says he's the marrying kind."

"The marrying kind? How come?"

"I don't know. She won't say. I think it's because he tucks his shirt in again every day after recess."

We sat on the sand, our legs pulled to our chests, and laughed into our knees. On my right, where Polly couldn't see, I traced my initials in the sand with my finger. Then I imposed PM over my initials and put two twigs in a cross over the top. When I stood up, I would have to remember to brush the whole thing out quickly with my sneaker before Polly saw, and if I did then the incantation would be complete.

I had brains, but I was plain-looking compared to Polly, who had powder-blue eyes and pretty blond hair she wore in a pony-tail. Me, I had mud-colored eyes and common brown hair, which was never the right length. Right then it was just below my jaw-line, and it flipped up on the ends—not in a cute symmetrical way but rather with both sides pointing to the right, so that I looked like a cartoon character in a soft wind. Plus I was puny for my age, the smallest girl in my grade, and freckled, and I wore glasses that were too big and round for my face. The only way I was going to win Petey Meechum from Polly was through magic.

But my magic had no time to work, because just then there was a voice behind us.

"You girls!"

We leaped to our feet and saw, emerging from the brush, the large shape of Hermit Weaper, whose cabin was on the other side of the lake past where the road lost its tarmac and became two rutted rows of bare earth in the weeds.

"You girls!" he said again and pointed his finger at us.

We ran for our bikes and began tugging them through the thick underbrush toward the road. He followed us, finger pointing, his craggy face twisted into a furious jack-o'-lantern, spittle

12

launching from between his dried lips, hanging in strings from his chin.

"You get on out of here!" he called after us as we struggled toward the road. We moved as fast as we could, but he followed us still, lurching his way below low-hanging branches. His left leg was crippled by some ancient injury, but to us that simply made his pursuit all the more monstrous—his lumbering sideways lope through the trees.

Then there was a crash behind us, and we looked back to see Hermit Weaper fallen against the base of a tree, pulling himself up to a sitting position. He had stopped pursuing, but we continued to break our way through the trees as though he were right behind us.

"Don't come back!" he cried, straining his voice to reach us as we got farther from him. "Worm Moon tonight. They'll get you sure! You don't stay inside, they'll hunt you down. They'll take your eyes, you hear me? An hour from now, this whole town goes warg. They'll eat your lungs right outta your chest! They'll pop your lungs like balloons and eat 'em right down! You hear me? Don't come back!"

When we reached the road, we got on our bikes and pedaled hard all the way back to my house. It wasn't until we were safely inside that we realized the sun had already set and the streets were quiet. We had lost track of time at the lakeside.

My father said it was too late for Polly to go home. He said she would stay the night, and he called her parents to tell them so.

That night Polly and I huddled under the covers of my bed and speculated about the world of those who were older than we.

We both knew that Hermit Weaper was just trying to scare us back home. But Polly couldn't let go of his words.

She said, "I don't want my lungs eaten." Then she added, "I don't want to eat them, either. I mean, when we're older."

"Don't worry," I said. I reveled in her nervousness, because it made me feel more keen than my friend. "I'm sure we'll acquire a taste for it."

"Ew," she said, and we giggled.

"Would you rather——" Polly started, then rephrased her theoretical question. "Let's say it's a dark alley. Would you rather meet up with Hermit Weaper or Rosebush Lincoln's brother on a full moon?"

Rosebush Lincoln's brother was sixteen.

"I don't know," I said. "I guess the Hermit."

"I'd rather Rosebush Lincoln's brother."

"Don't say that."

"It's true. They don't really hurt people, you know. It's not true what the Hermit said. They don't eat your——they don't hurt anybody. Except maybe themselves. And each other."

I liked it better when we talked of such things in the fairy-tale terms of lung-eating. It was easier to cope with. If you talked about hurt in the abstract, it was a deeper, more echoey well of a thing.

"They could hurt you," I insisted.

"Not on purpose. They're just teenagers. We'll be like that too one day."

I didn't tell Polly that I had already promised my father I wouldn't be like that. She would have taken it as disloyalty. Much later we tried to sleep, but there were the voices outside. I couldn't forget what Hermit Weaper had said. In my mind there was a picture of Rosebush Lincoln's brother, handsome Billy Lincoln, and there was a hollow cavity in my chest, and where my lungs should have been there was nothing at all, and one of my lungs was actually hanging between Billy Lincoln's teeth, half consumed, deflated and bloody, like a gigantic tongue—and I couldn't breathe, because all my breath was caught in Billy Lincoln's grinning mouth.

MY HUSBAND DRIVES us home from the Petersons' party. This is just last night.

It's 12:15, and we are late in relieving the sitter. Jack is itchy with liquor, and he says to me, "You were—you were the sexiest wife at that party."

"Jack."

"No, I'm serious. I'm not kidding around. No one can hold a candle to you."

"I thought the lamb was overcooked. Did you think so? Everyone complimented it, though. Janet prides herself on her lamb."

Then Jack pulls the car over to the side of the road and turns off the ignition.

"Do you want to fool around?" he asks.

"Jack, the babysitter."

"To hell with the babysitter." It's his grand, passionate gesture. He must have me, here in the car, and the rest of the world can burn. "I'll—I'll give her an extra twenty."

The silliness of family men. I chuckle.

He takes offense. "Forget it," he says and goes to start the car. I've hurt him by not being sufficiently quailed by the blustery storm of his sex. It's funny how many ways there are to hurt people. As many ways to hurt as there are species of flower. Whole bouquets of hurt. You do it without even realizing.

"Wait, Jack. I'm sorry."

"Why did you laugh?"

"I don't know. Maybe I was nervous. What if someone sees us?"

"Let them," he says.

So I reach up under my skirt, hook my underpants with my thumbs, and pull them down. He unzips his pants, and I straddle him. While he quakes and gurgles beneath me, I gaze out the windows of the car. The road where we've stopped is indistinguishable from any of the others in the area—a quiet residential neighborhood with sidewalks and shade trees. In truth there is no danger of being caught. The residents of this area are good and decent people. Their lives, after midnight, consist of sleep or the late, late show on television, played at a low volume so as not to wake the children. The streets are empty. The mild breeze dapples the sidewalk with the shadows of leaves in lamplight. But there is no one out there in the dark. No one.

Jack moves under me. I hold his face to my bosom, I kiss the top of his head. In a few moments, he is finished.

He wants to kiss me passionately to show that his love for me doesn't end when his sexual urgency does. He's a nice kisser after all these years.

He rolls down the windows for the rest of the drive home.

On the way, he points to the sky.

"Look," he says. "A full moon."

"I know," I say without raising my eyes. The car drives along in the quiet, fragile night.

"What do you call that one? Octopus Moon? Spanky Moon?"

"Blowfly Moon."

"Blowfly. That's my favorite one!"

I've told him very little about my childhood or the town where I grew up. What little I have told him—for example, that we had names for the different full moons—he finds quaint and charming. He pictures me as a prairie girl, maybe. Or a Mennonite.

His stuff is leaking out of me, a funny, unbothersome tickle between my legs.

In another part of the country, in the small town where I grew up, at this moment, there are packs of young people stalking the streets, naked, their pale flesh glowing, their breath coming fast and angry, their limbs filled with the quivering of strength and movement. Many, tomorrow, will wake torn and bruised.

When we get home, Jack apologizes to the babysitter and gives her extra money. Then he drives her home. While he is gone, I go upstairs, where my son is sleeping. He wakes when I come into the room, reaching toward me, wanting to be picked up.

I look down at him for a few moments, all that wee human greed and desire. I refuse to pick him up, but eventually I do kneel beside his bed and recite to him a rhyme I learned when I was a little girl.

Brittle Moon,
Beggar's Moon,
Worm Moon, more . . .

Pheasant Moon,
Cordial Moon,
Lacuna's bore . . .

Hod Moon,
Blowfly Moon,
Pulse Moon—roar!

Prayer Moon,
Hollow Moon,
Lake Moon's shore.

First you kiss your mommy,
Then you count your fours.
Till you're grown and briny,
Better stay indoors.

He waits eagerly for his favorite part—the part about roaring—and then he roars. He wants to do it again, but I tell him no. I turn on his night-light, which the babysitter has forgotten. Then I leave the room and shut the door behind me. In the upstairs hall, there is only the sound of the grandfather clock ticktocking away.

I have become a mother. I have become a wife.

Soon Jack returns home. We prepare for bed without much talk. I check the locks on the doors downstairs. It is a thing he always asks when I slide into bed next to him. "Did you remember to check the locks?" he asks. And I say, "Yes," and I can see by the expression on his face that he feels safe.

It starts to rain outside, the droplets of water sounding little tin bells in the gutters. Jack begins to snore next to me. The grandfather clock chimes one o'clock.

And what if I were to forget a lock one night? What if I were to leave a door wide open, casting angled shadows in the moonlight? Nothing would happen. In our neighborhood, there is no one out there in the rain, not a single person squalling under the stormy black.

All our skins are dry.

I WONDER ABOUT it sometimes—what kind of girl I might have been, what kind of woman I would be now, if I had grown up somewhere else. California, for instance, where teenagers have barbecues on the beach and bury bottles of beer halfway in the sand to keep them upright. Or New York, where they kiss in the backseats of taxicabs and lie on blankets in the middle of parks surrounded by buildings taller by far than the tallest tree.

Would I now be one of those women on television who are concerned about what the laundry detergent is doing to their children's Little League uniforms? Would I love my husband more or less? My son?

As a teenager, would I have been one of those girls who go to the mall and defend themselves, all giggling, against boys—huddled together like a wagon circle in the food court? Would my great concerns have been college and school dances and fashion?

In my town, expensive clothes were not held in high esteem. Girls bought cheap. Dresses, they tended to get torn apart.

It's impossible for me to make the connection between who I am now and who I was then—as if I died long ago in that town and resurrected somewhere else, with a brain full of another girl's memories.

Except that I miss my father.

They said I had his mind.

Polly admired him as well. She always told me it was okay that I didn't have a mother—that I didn't really need a mother because I had the best father in town. He made Polly and me grilled cheese sandwiches with ham and the tomatoes from the garden that he and I had cultivated with our own hands. Polly liked hers with cocktail toothpicks sticking out of each quarter. He called

19

her Sweet Polly and said that when the time came she would have so many boyfriends she would never be able to choose just one and would have to marry a whole passel of them.

He stood smiling, tall and skinny at the kitchen island. She glowed for him.

———

SUMMERTIMES, POLLY CAME to my house, and my father would greet her at the door.

"Sweet Polly!" he would say. "Lumen's upstairs."

The long, hot days of July, he would turn on the sprinkler in the backyard, and we would put on our swimsuits and play in the dancing water. The sprinkler was on the end of a hose, and it shot a Chinese fan of water in a slow back-and-forth arc that we liked to jump through. The only rule was that every fifteen minutes we had to move the sprinkler to a different part of the lawn to assure balanced coverage. Polly never remembered, but I always did.

We were the same age, but at thirteen it was clear that Polly was developing before I was. Her swimsuit swelled at the chest where mine was loose and puckered. She stood almost a full head taller than I did, and she did cartwheels through the shimmering water, her long limbs a dazzle of strength and nimbleness. When I tried to cartwheel, my body didn't move the way I wanted it to, and I came toppling down into an awkward crouch.

After a while we were tired and simply lay on our stomachs in the grass, liking the feel of the fan of water as it intermittently showered us with cool needles. We lay in single file, our faces just inches from each other, our chins supported on our fists.

"Shell didn't look so good when she came home this morning," Polly said.

Shell was Michelle, Polly's sister, who was fifteen and a half. She'd begun breaching just two months before. The previous night had been the last night of Hod Moon.

"My parents found her sleeping on the lawn this morning," Polly went on.

"With no clothes on?"

"Yeah."

This was something I still could not fathom—the exposure. For as long as I could remember, my father was very careful about knocking on my bedroom door before he entered so that I would not be walked in upon as I was dressing. How did one nude oneself before another person—before the world?

"And also," Polly said, crinkling up her face, "she was beat up pretty bad."

"Really?"

"Yeah. There were bruises and cuts all over her. Plus—"

Polly went silent for a moment. She pulled up some blades of grass and opened her fist to let them fall, but they were wet and stuck to her fingers.

"Plus," she went on, "she was bleeding. You know?"

I said nothing. I was paralyzed—as though I were standing on a precipice, stricken with vertigo, unable even to pull myself back from the edge. This was large, multitudinous. My mind was a color, and the color was red. The needling water on my back felt like it was falling on a version of me that was a long, long way away.

"They put her in the bathtub," Polly said. "I stayed with her when they went downstairs. The water, it turned pink. She says she doesn't remember anything, but I can tell she does. I think she remembers all of it."

For a time, we were both silent. She picked the wet blades of grass off her hand, and I watched her. It was time to move the sprinkler, but I had to know more, and I couldn't break the spell the conversation had put me under.

Finally I mustered the courage to ask a question:

"Did she get pregnant?"

"No," Polly said. "She told me they put her on the pill before she went breach. She said all the parents do it."

I thought about my father. It was difficult for me to imagine him giving me that kind of pill. How would he do it? He could make a joke out of it, bringing it to me on a burgundy pillow, as though I were a princess—and we could pretend it meant nothing. We could pretend my secret and shameful body had nothing to do with it. Or maybe it wouldn't be necessary. I was determined to skip breaching altogether.

"And she said something else," Polly went on.

"What else?"

"See, I was sitting on the toilet next to the tub, and she closed her eyes for a long time, and I thought she was asleep. I was just looking at the pink water and all the dirt that was in it. There were little leaves, and I picked them off the surface. She was so dirty. She came back so dirty."

"What else did she say?"

"So I thought she was asleep, and there was this little twig in her hair and I wanted to take it out for her. So I went to take it out, but when I tried she grabbed my wrist all of a sudden and gave me a look."

"What kind of look?"

"I don't know. I didn't like it."

"Was it angry?"

"No. Not exactly. More just...I don't know. Like a *jungle* look, you know? But it was only for a second, and then she let go of my wrist and smiled at me. That's when she said it. She said it's all right. She said it's nothing to be afraid of. She said it hurts, but it's the good kind of hurt."

"The good kind of hurt?"

"That's what she said."

I didn't want Polly to see that I was confounded by this notion, because she herself seemed to have accepted it as an obvious and universal truth, the potential goodness of hurt. It was important to Polly that she be in the know about all things adult, and she lived by the rule that performance eventually leads to authenticity. So it was difficult to tell what she actually understood and what she was only pretending to understand.

For my part, I squirmed uncomfortably in my ill-fitting swimsuit. These things seemed entirely detached from the books I read, from the math and science I was so adept in the mastery of. I sometimes wondered (as I sometimes still do) if I had gotten off track somehow, if maybe I wasn't as natural as those around me, if perhaps my life were unjoined from the common lives of others.

The way my teachers looked at me, I suspected they could tell I didn't belong. Especially Mr. Hunter, the drama teacher for the high school kids, whose curious and fearsome gaze I was sure followed me wherever I went.

The sprinkler splashed us with its rainy metronome, and there we lay in the growing shadow of my big house, the two of us, blasted through with the abject discomfiture of our tiny places in the world.

We were fourteen by the following summer, and Polly had developed even further, her hips having shaped themselves into curves—which I thought must have been in some way responsible for the new saunter in her walk. There was still no shape to me at all. I wore colorful dresses and put ribbons in my hair as evidence that I was, in fact, a girl. I stood naked before my bedroom mirror and, with the intention of luring out my stubborn and elusive womanhood, recited Edna St. Vincent Millay poetry I had learned by heart. I smeared honey on my chest, believing it might help me grow breasts. Honeybees are industrious — they can build anything. But the poetry seemed not to possess any magic, and my father found the sticky honey-bear bottle on my nightstand one morning and explained that it was bad for my teeth to snack on it in the middle of the night.

Over the previous year, Polly had begun spending more time with Rosebush Lincoln and the other girls from school. She never excluded me, and I made a concerted effort to join together with all the girls when they sunbathed by the lake or got a ride into the next town to go shopping at the thrift stores. But Rosebush always made it clear that I was only to be tolerated because I was allied with Polly, that my visa into the world of Rosebush Lincoln was temporary and most definitely revocable. I was put on notice.

When there's nothing else to do, you can always watch the birds. The finches, their twitchy and mechanical little bodies — they go where they want to go, driven by impulse and instinct. The finch does not dwell in consideration of its nature or the nature of the world. It is brazen and unapologetic. It hammers its little bird heart against the blustering wind, and its death is as beautiful as its life.

—

IT WAS THAT year, that summer, that I followed the other girls to the abandoned mine. What did they used to mine there? I want to say gypsum, because gypsum is a lovely word and a gyp-

sum mine is a pretty thought to have. It was on a different end of
the woods from the lake, and the entrance to it was at the base of
a small overgrown quarry. The parents of our town instructed us
to stay away from the quarry because of lurking dangers, but it
was always beautiful and peaceful to me. In certain seasons there
was rivulet of melted snow that came out of the mountains and
trickled irregularly down the stony sides of the quarry and ran
finally into the mouth of the mine. If you went there alone, you
could just listen to that plink-plonk of water and be tranquil. You
could lie in nests of leaves, all those dying oranges and reds, all
those deep browns that come from what green used to be, shaded
by the old-growth trees that leaned over the lip of the quarry, and
you could be nothing at all.

The mouth of the mine itself was weeded over with sumac
and creeper vine, and there were two sets of mine-cart rails
that emerged from the opening like tongues and ended abruptly
on the floor of the quarry. You could wonder for hours about
where those tracks went. Miles of underground passages beneath
the town, maybe a whole underground city, with tunnels that
opened in your basement! I explored our basement once, looking
for an opening into hidden Atlantis—but all I found were forgotten mousetraps with hunks of dried-up cheese.

It was almost exactly a year after my conversation with Polly
under the sprinklers, and her sister, Shell, was still breaching.

"I don't think she's ever going to stop," Polly said miserably.
"What if she doesn't stop before I start?"

"You? But we're only fourteen."

"It's not unheard of. My parents said it's not unheard of. It's
different for different people. Plus I'm developing early in other
ways."

"Well, I don't think it's going to happen yet."

"It better not. My parents are going to throw a big party for her when she's done. That's how relieved they'll be. They said I'm not going to be half as bad as her."

It seemed as though this were a source of disappointment for Polly.

So when she came to my house on a weekday morning in July, telling me that everyone was going to the quarry and that we should hurry to join them, I followed her. If I didn't follow her, I reasoned, I might be left behind forever—a child who simply misses the chance to grow up.

So we took our bikes, pedaling hard and purposefully. On other days we might have been leisurely about our pace, weaving in lazy arcs back and forth across the empty roads. But that day was different.

Arriving at the quarry, we saw four girls already there—Adelaide Warren, Sue Foxworth, and Idabel McCarron with her little sister, Florabel, in tow. We scrambled down into the quarry, bringing tiny avalanches of white silt pebbles after us.

"Where's Rosebush?" was the first thing Polly said as a greeting to the other girls.

"I don't know," said Adelaide. "Look what we found."

We all gathered in a circle around the thing on the ground. At first I couldn't figure out what it was—a wispy thing like smoke or frayed burlap, it moved with the breeze. Hair. It was a long skein of mousy brown girl hair.

"It was ripped out," Sue said.

"How can you tell?"

"Look."

She reached down, gathered its tips into a bunch, and picked it up. Dangling from the base of the lock was a scabby little flake that I quickly understood to be scalp skin.

Florabel shrieked and started running in circles.

"Shut it," her sister said.

"Whose is it?" Polly asked.

"I don't know," Sue said. "Better be a local girl."

A fierce territoriality is the by-product of uncommon local practices. Whatever happened in our town was manageable as long as it stayed in our town. We were not encouraged to socialize with people from elsewhere. We were taught to smile at them as they passed through. Every now and then some teenager from a neighboring town would get stuck here during a full moon—and the next day that outsider would usually go home goried up and trembling. That's when trouble came down on us—authorities from other places going from door to door, kneeling down in front of us kids trying to get us to reveal something. But for the most part, people left us alone. Ours was a cursed town to outsiders.

Just then there was a sound in the trees above, and we gazed up to find Rosebush Lincoln standing next to her bike on the lip of the quarry.

"I'm here, creeps," she said and let her bike fall to the ground. Strapped to her back was a pink teddy-bear backpack whose contents seemed heavy enough to make it an awkward process to climb down to the floor of the quarry. Once at the bottom, though, she sloughed off the pack and came over to where we stood.

"What's that?" she asked, pointing to the hair that Sue still held in her fingers.

"Hair."

"Uh-huh," Rosebush said. "I know where that came from. Mindy Kleinholt. My brother says she's been going around all week with a new hairstyle to cover the empty spot. Happens."

Rosebush shrugged with a casual world-weariness that made her seem thirty-three rather than fourteen.

Sometimes the thunderclouds gather overhead, and sometimes your haughty cat refuses its food, and sometimes you are
partially scalped in a moonlit quarry. Such things are a matter of
chance and hazard.

Rosebush, whose lack of interest in the hair made everyone
forget it at once, unzipped her teddy-bear backpack to reveal
what she had been struggling to carry: six tall silver cans of beer
connected at the tops with plastic rings. She set the cans on the
ground before us, stepped back, and presented them with an ex-
pansive gesture of her arms.

"Behold," she said. "My brother stole it from the grocery
store, and then I stole it from him."

"It's double stolen," said Adelaide, crouching down in front of
the beer and running her finger in a delicate circle along the top
edge of one of the cans. She was fairylike, always, in her movements. "It's still cold," she added.

"It's iced," explained Rosebush. "We have to drink it before it
gets skunked."

So she passed around the cans to the other girls. I took one
but found it difficult to open, so Polly opened it for me.

"Where's one for me?" Florabel said.

"You don't get one," said her older sister.

"Cheers, queers," Rosebush said, raising hers.

Everyone drank. I lifted mine in imitation of drinking, but I
didn't let much get into my mouth. Just enough to wet my lips
and tongue. The taste was awful, like moldy carbonated weed
milk. The other girls crinkled their noses as well.

Rosebush lectured us.

"You have to drink it fast," she said. "Hold your nose if you
need to."

"I'm going to enjoy mine throughout the afternoon," said Sue.

"Me too," said Adelaide.

"Suit yourselves," Rosebush said and shrugged.

We sat on the stones, holding our cool cans of beer. I stopped pretending to drink from the can, because nobody seemed to be paying attention to whether I was or not. Instead I put my fingers in the icy trickle of water running down out of the hills.

At one point the conversation turned to boys, and Rosebush brought up Petey Meechum.

"We nearly kissed the other day after school," she announced.

"What's nearly?" asked Sue.

"Nearly," Rosebush repeated in a tone that suggested any further calls for clarification were forbidden.

"He once told me I had pretty hands," said Adelaide, then she held them up for the benefit of any admirers.

"Anyway," Rosebush went on, irritated, "Petey Meechum is the kind of boy who puts girls into one of two categories. You're either a potential lover or you're a permanent friend."

At the words "permanent friend," her gaze landed on Polly and me. Polly looked down, submissive. I made my face blank, like cinder block.

"How can you tell the difference?" Adelaide asked.

Rosebush seemed about to attack, but then she shrugged it off, as would a predator that grows bored with easy prey.

"Believe me," she said, "when you're nearly kissed by him, you can tell."

Then she addressed me amicably.

"On a related topic, do you know who I heard was actually interested in you, Lumen?"

"Who?" I asked miserably.

"Roy Ruggle," said Rosebush.

"Blackhat Roy?"

"He's only got eight toes," Polly contributed. It was well known that Blackhat Roy had exploded two toes off his right foot when he was trying to modify a Roman candle with a pair of pliers two years before.

"But he's dark," said Rosebush, "like Lumen. And he's more her height. Also, he never goes to church, and neither does Lumen. You know, I sit right next to Petey in church. He tells me about his grandmother who died. Did he ever tell you about her, Lumen? You can tell by the way he talks about her he knows about pain. To endure suffering—it's the most romantic thing of all, don't you think?"

———

TO ENDURE SUFFERING. I wonder how much people really endure. They talk about heartbreak, and they turn their faces away. But heartbreak is really the least of it, a splinter in the skin. Hearts mend. Most tragedy is overcome with prideful righteousness. The tear on the cheek, like a pretty little insect, wending its way over your jaw, down your sensitive neck, under your collar.

I wonder how much suffering my husband has endured. Or Janet Peterson, with her dry, overcooked lamb. They are easily horrified, easily disgusted. They turn their heads away from the simplest and most mundane adversity.

On the other hand, to be bound by your own fate, to feel the eager lashes of a grinning world all up and down your nerve endings. To bleed—to make others bleed. To know there is no end of things. To become something that you can never unbecome. There are in the world sufferings that are not stage pieces but rather whole lives.

Rosebush Lincoln. I was shut to her that day.

Yet those words of hers, even now, recall to me the lovely, hungry smell of autumn leaves.

———

JUST AS ROSEBUSH Lincoln was extolling the virtues of endured suffering, there was a sound in the trees above the quarry, and we all gazed up to find a boy on the verge — as though we had conjured boyness with our witchy voices and manifested a puerile sprite from the morning dew itself.

"It's Hondy," said Rosebush. "He must've followed me all the way from town."

Hondy Pilt held the handles of his bicycle and stared down at us in his misty and bloated way. He said nothing. Hondy Pilt rarely spoke, and his eyes never looked at you exactly — instead they looked right over your shoulder, which made you feel that you were just some insufficient forgery of your real self and that your real self was invisible, somewhere behind you.

So Rosebush invited him to join us, and for the next hour she forced him to drink beer and she put wildflowers in his hair and she told him to sit a certain way so that she could use his bulky body to prop up her own and gaze at the clouds above.

I felt bad for Hondy Pilt, but he didn't seem to mind being used as Rosebush Lincoln's lounge chair, and I wondered if that was his particular magic — to be still content with the world in all its pretty little injustices.

It wasn't long before Rosebush got a new idea — which was to send Hondy Pilt adventuring into the abandoned mine. We all looked at the mouth of the mine, weeded and overgrown, a dark void chipped out of the earth, like the hollow well of a giant's missing tooth. We had heard stories of our older brothers and sisters spelunking the mine with flashlights, discovering networks of underground rooms, rusted mining equipment, bottomless shafts easily stumbled into. Our parents warned us against the mine, because a boy once lost his way in the maze of passages and never came back out—but every time they tried to board up the entrance, the breachers, who did not like to be disinvited from places, would tear it open during the next full moon.

"I don't know, Rosebush," said Idabel. "I don't think it's a good idea."

"Come on. Hondy wants to do it. Don't you, Hondy?"

She raised him to his feet and wound her arm in his so that they looked like a bride and groom, and the boy smiled at the sky.

"Ro'bush," he said in his indistinct way.

So she led him to the mouth of the mine, and we all gathered around, too—because nobody could stop Rosebush from sacrificing Hondy Pilt to the mine.

"Go on, Hondy," she said. "Go on now."

He looked into the darkness, then at his own feet, then in the direction of the girl at his side.

She encouraged him with sweeping hand gestures.

"Go on," she said. "Bring me a treasure. Find me a gold nugget."

And he went. While we all watched from the mouth of the mine, he moved forward step by step.

"Rosebush," Idabel admonished.

"Shush," said Rosebush, her eyes never leaving her knight errant. In fact, the farther he went into the dark, the more intent she became, her fists clenching themselves into tight balls, her breath coming faster, an expression on her face like some excruciating ecstasy. I could hear her breathing.

He stopped once, turned, and looked back at us, as if to be reassured.

"Warrior!" Rosebush called to him in a strange, whispery voice.

Then he moved forward again, slowly, until his form was lost completely to the dark.

We waited. A caught breeze blustered through the quarry, rustling the dried sumac, blowing strands of hair in a ticklish way across our lips. We used our fingers to tuck the hair behind our ears, and we waited.

Then, from the deep echoey dark of the mine, we heard a hiss, a monstrous, spitting hiss. Then Hondy Pilt's voice, a low, whining complaint, followed by quick movement—a crash, the sound of feet advancing fast in our direction, his voice again, miserable and high—and behind it all that feral hissing.

Then we saw him disclosed from the dark, his panicked bulk running toward us.

And then we believed in monsters, hissing creatures like aged demons unearthed from the dry crust of the world. We ran. The woods came alive with the sound of our shrieks. Birds fled and crickets hushed, and we turned and ran from the mouth of the mine, squealing, across the floor of the quarry and up the opposite slope, our fingers digging into the loose gravel for desperate purchase.

We were halfway up the side of the quarry when we heard a loud cry of pain below. Hondy Pilt had emerged from the mine at full speed and had tripped over Rosebush Lincoln's pink backpack. He now lay curled into a ball and howling on the floor of the quarry. It would get him. He was a goner now—food for the beasts of the earth—and we left him and hid behind the trunks of trees.

Except that then, beyond him, we saw emerge from the mine the monster that had chased him out of its den, hissing and spitting the whole way. It was a possum. Assured that its home was no longer in danger, the creature turned and scurried back into the dark depths of the mine.

Sometimes it happens this way. Your greatest fears in the dark turn out to be nothing more than angry rodents and zealous girls with pink backpacks. Or nothing less.

———

IT WAS ALL discovered. Hondy Pilt's forearm was fractured from his fall in the quarry. He would have to wear a cast for the next three weeks, and Rosebush Lincoln would be the first to sign her name on it in pink marker. We suffered little in comparison. Our palms were covered with tiny abrasions from our quick scramble up the side of the quarry. But it was nothing a coat of stinging Bactine couldn't fix.

Our parents discovered we had been drinking beer, and they intuited that we had been responsible somehow for Hondy Pilt's accident.

The orchestration of blame was intricate and devious—it was decided that I would take the blame for everything.

After we delivered Hondy Pilt back to the hospital in town, Rosebush Lincoln took me aside to have a talk.

"You have to say it was you," she said, her voice casual but uncompromising.

"It was me what?"

"The beer. And Hondy, telling him to go into the mine. It has to be you."

"Why?"

"They won't do anything to you. You're too good."

I didn't say anything.

"Look, Lumen. It was an accident. I like Hondy. I didn't want to hurt him. I'm already in trouble for a million things. My parents'll kill me. They're not nice. They're not like your dad. Please."

So I did it. While I held my hands palm upward over the sink and my father poured hydrogen peroxide on them, I told him it was all my fault.

"Is that right?" he said.

"Yes. I brought the beer. I told Hondy Pilt to go inside the mine."

"Really? Where did you get the beer?"

"I stole it."

"Stole it!" He smiled down at me. "So you're a thief now, are you?"

"Just that once."

I looked down at my palms, the hydrogen peroxide foaming in all the cuts.

"And you made Hondy Pilt go into the mine?" he asked.

"Yes."

"Why?"

It had never occurred to me that someone would ask why I had done the things I claimed to do—just as I had never thought to ask Rosebush why she was Rosebush. Why ask? People are like characters in books. They are defined by their actions—not the other way around.

"I don't know," I said pathetically.

The smile never left his face. He narrowed his eyes at me, trying to puzzle through my gambit.

"So . . . well, all these moral lapses—I guess you should be punished."

"I guess so."

"Let's see." He pursed his lips and tapped his chin with his fingertips. "What time is your curfew?"

What he meant was between full moons. Everyone had the same curfew when the moon was full: sundown.

"Ten o'clock."

"All right, then. Let's make it nine thirty for the rest of the week."

He went back to tending my palms, rinsing away the hydrogen peroxide and bandaging the cuts.

But something wasn't right. The reason he didn't know what time my curfew was was because I was almost always home for the night by eight o'clock, hunched up on one corner of the couch, reading a book. His punishment was absurd—not a real punishment. And that's when it occurred to me: he didn't believe my confession. He was humoring me.

My suspicions were borne out the next day when Rosebush Lincoln confronted me on the street outside the drugstore where they sold colorful ices.

"You were supposed to take the blame," she said.

"I did," I assured her. "I did. I told my dad I did it."

"No, you didn't."

"I swear."

"Then how come I'm the one being punished for everything? How come Idabel's mom told my mom I was a bad influence?"

"I don't know."

"You're a liar." She pointed one long finger at my chest.

"I'm not. I told my dad it was me." I paused. "It's just—I don't think he believed me."

Rosebush Lincoln looked disgusted.

"Oh, that's just great. You can't even convince people you've

36

done something wrong when you *try*. Just stay away from me from now on."

———

AT THAT AGE we didn't know what we did. Or, rather, we understood that it was impossible for things to go any differently. We were too young to change the course of bodies in motion.

My husband, Jack, he's a schoolteacher, but a new kind of schoolteacher, a kind we didn't have when I was a child. He works with kids who are At Risk—as though safety were such a common commodity that you could easily hang a tag from all those young people who didn't possess it. He has one girl—Natalie, who prefers to be called Nat—who sneers and curses and spits sunflower seeds at his shoes while he's trying to have regular, humane conversations with her. She has been sent to the principal's office many times for fighting with boys and other girls. She, too, knows about tearing out hair.

Trying to get her to rationalize her behavior, Jack asks her why she does the things she does.

"I don't know" is her reply. She says it as though the question is an absurd one and has no true answer.

I am curious how she would respond if I had my hands squeezed around her throat. (Would her muscles grow taut, wild?) But I also understand the authenticity of what she says. People like to talk to teenagers about consequences. They like to explain how certain actions may lead to reactions that are un-desired. But this is the wrong conversation to have. Teenagers understand inherently how one thing leads to another—but to them the point is moot, because the action that initiates its conse-quence is just as inscrutable as the consequence itself. The mouth that spits at my husband might as well not be her mouth at all. His shoes might as well be anyone's shoes, the room a room far away in some other nondescript American suburb.

That is the way of the young. They see something we don't: the great machines that turn us, indifferent to our will, this way and that.

So I wasn't angry at Rosebush Lincoln for asking me to lie to my father. And I wasn't angry at her when she shunned me for not having lied well enough. And I wasn't even angry about the things she did to Hondy Pilt. All she did was play her part in a tableau that, as far as I was concerned, couldn't have gone any other way.

Sometimes, when I was a girl, I climbed onto the roof through the gabled window of my second-story bedroom. From the chimney peak, I could see all the way up and down the street. It was as tall as my world got, and it was wonderful. Those summer evenings, I would lie on the sloping shake, securing myself with the soles of my sneakers, watching the stars come out. From my meager height, I beheld the whole entire world as I knew it. And what could be bad about all this?

CHAPTER 2

My name is Lumen. My father says my mother gave me the name because it means light. I am a light, and I light the way. That's what the North Star and guardian angels do. But my name also means this:

$$\Phi_v = I_v \cdot \Omega$$

Φ_v is me, Lumen. Lumen as a unit. I_v is how many candelas. Candela is another beautiful name. I wish I knew someone named Candela so we could be Lumen and Candela, and we would define each other in measurements of light. The mathematics of illumination. Ω is another unit, steradians, but that is an angular measurement—it defines the direction in which a light is shining. If the light is democratic, if it is loving and gentle and good, if it doesn't prefer one angle over another, then the equation becomes even more beautiful:

$$\Phi_v = 4\pi I_v$$

Because there are four pi steradians in a perfect, all-encompassing sphere.

Here I am, now matured to fifteen years of age, and my grades are excellent, the best in school, and I am also smaller than all the other girls in my class, delayed in my growth—stunted, even—and I stay in the library after the final bell rings to look up my name in the large, dusty encyclopedias.

Who could know me? Not my mother, who was dead before I remember. Not my friends, who seem to have found their way into an idea of adulthood. Maybe not even my father, who is generous to a fault and believes so heartily in the errorlessness of me that I wear myself out with being his good daughter. So maybe these books know for certain who I am. They seem so absolute about what they know. They etch my name in perfect symbols. They draw lines to define me, they show how Lumen equates to other delicious little glyphs. I want to be the precision of these equations. Then I could justify who I am.

So yes, there I am in the library, turning the pages of encyclopedias. My ankles itch under my socks. Many of the other boys and girls in my class, Polly included, have gone down to the lake to swim. The boys have tied a rope to a tree branch that overhangs the lake. They swing out over the water and drop in, like dumplings. Once in, they make a game of submarining their way to the girls and grabbing their legs to startle them. Some boys flip the girls head over tail. When this is done, the mandate of the flipped girls seems to be initial outrage followed by affable censure. I have gone to the lake, too, on occasion, but mostly I sit on the shore and watch. When I do go into the water, I wait patiently to be pinched or tumbled by the underwater boys—but perhaps I am prey too meager for their tastes. My hair stays dry.

I love the smell of the encyclopedia. When no one is looking, I bury my nose deep into the crease of the binding and breathe in the book. No one else does this. I do not witness any of the other students sniffing the pages of *Great Expectations* when the paperbacks are handed out in our English class. Me, rather than putting my nose to it, I casually fan the pages with my thumb, which sends into the air the pleasant aroma of wood pulp and ink.

In the library I sit at a carrel, the farthest one in the back corner, and I search through piles of books looking to understand my name. The dictionary does me little good, but I have no hard feelings toward it—I love the way the pages are thumb-notched to make the finding of particular letters easier. If you look at each page individually, it has a unique half-moon cutout at the edge.

In another book I find this, which is the equation for luminance, which I take to mean the quality of luminousness, the quality of me:

$$L_v = \frac{d^2\Phi_v}{dAd\Omega cos\theta}$$

I recognize again my symbol, the superimposed I and O together. One and zero. Something and nothing. On and off at the same time. I look up the Greek alphabet to discover what my symbol is called. It is phi, and it can be pronounced either fee or fye—which are the first two syllables of the giant's song as he is threatening to eat Jack, who went up the bean stalk: Fe-fi-fo-fum, I smell the blood of an Englishman.

Blood. It always comes back to blood. You start with light,

and you end with blood. But not mine. I am fifteen, I sit in the library with my itchy ankles, and I have not gotten my period yet. I am the last of anyone I know. I am afraid of blood, disgusted by it, and maybe my own fear has suppressed my bleeding.

I go back to the equations, which are black-and-white, pure and lovely.

I find another equation. The best one yet:

$$I_v = 683 \int_0^\infty \bar{y}(\lambda) \cdot \frac{dI_e(\lambda)}{d\lambda} d\lambda$$

It's the equation for luminous intensity. That's how much calculation is required to measure the intensity of me. You see how my symbol, the phi, is gone? The candela is still there, but the lumen is nowhere to be seen. Maybe that means you can't measure the intensity of a thing in relation to itself. You have to put it against others and measure the difference between the light given off by each one.

You have to put Lumen in the lake and see how still she stands, skimming the surface with her pale palms, embarrassed at the flatness of her own chest, noiseless and inert amid the raucous clamor of other boys and girls.

———

MANY OF THE people in my grade went breach that year. I stayed home and studied. Many of the girls acquired and lost a series of boyfriends. I listened to old records my father told me he listened to when he was my age. Many of the bodies around me in school seemed to be undergoing some torturous flux—people coming to school not just with red pimples on their faces but also with rips and tears in the overused skin of their arms and necks. They were savaged. My skin remained smooth and unscored.

Polly came to my house one day, the second day of Worm Moon, and showed me a large purplish bruise on her arm.

"How did you get that?" I asked.

"I don't know," she said.

"How could you not know? Does it hurt?"

"It happened, Lumen," she said. "Last night it happened. I went breach."

"You did?"

"Look."

She showed me again her bruise.

"What was it like?"

"I don't remember very much."

They said you remembered the breaches better after you had been through a few of them. Very few people could remember their first.

I looked at the bruise, and she displayed her arm proudly.

"It looks like a hand," I said.

She tried to twist her head around to see it better.

"See?" I said, pointing at the pattern. "One, two, three, four. Like fingers."

"Someone probably grabbed me?"

"Maybe."

"I'll ask around. Maybe somebody else remembers."

"Do you have anything else?"

She blushed. She knew what I was asking.

"I don't think so," she said. "I don't know."

Then I told her something that was a lie.

I said, "I wish I could have been there with you."

I had no desire to go breach. The thought of running wild,

that mortification, made me clammy and sick. But I was trying to be a good and decent friend.

She believed what I told her. Most people my age looked forward to the breach. It meant you had become something else. You were no longer a child. You were a true and natural person.

Clutching my shoulder with her hand, she reassured me.

"It'll happen for you soon," she said.

I looked down at my diminutive frame, my bony, nondeveloped chest.

"I don't think so," I said.

"Sure it will. Probably next month. Then we'll go out together."

I turned away, but in the mirror I caught her glancing apprehensively at my stubborn body.

"It's going to happen soon," she reiterated. "It happens to everyone."

Of course that was the common thinking. It happened to everyone in our little town. But I wasn't so sure it *had* to be that way. Though Polly couldn't see them, my teeth were clenched tight inside my mouth. She didn't know it, but I had made a determination many years ago that I still clung to as though it were a fierce religion. I wouldn't go breach. I wouldn't do it.

My mother hadn't, and neither would I.

I wouldn't.

———

IT WASN'T SOMETHING I could look up in books, so in order to learn more about the process I had to undertake a course of research that involved keeping secret notes on the things I heard from others. Of Polly I could ask questions directly—and she, before her own breach, provided much information from her experiences with her sister and her sister's friends. I could query my father on a few details, but it made me uncomfortable to speak with him about such things. Some of the teachers talked about it in school, but their approach to the topic was more abstract than I would have preferred. Ms. Stanchek, who taught us sex ed, referred to it obliquely and in cultural terms, citing breaching as one of the "many local customs that play a large role in determining how young people are introduced to adulthood." She went on to say, "Some cultures are very protective of their young people and try to keep them shielded from life as long as possible. Other cultures"—and here she winked at us—"drop you right into the cauldron to see if you can float." I wrote down her words verbatim, because her analogy was baffling to me. If you found yourself in a cauldron, whether you floated was not the issue.

Mr. Hunter, who taught English during the day and drama after school, referred to breaching in his discussion of *Lord of the Flies.* "If you want to understand these characters," he said, "think about how you feel when the moon is full. We might be mysteries even to ourselves. Do you know what you're capable of? Do you really know?"

His eyes fell on me, and my stomach went sideways. I looked down, focusing on my pencil tip pressing hard on the white paper. He was an outsider, having moved into our town only around five years ago. He couldn't truly understand our ways, but he liked to speak of them in provocative terms. I liked him and didn't like him at the same time. There was something in him that I needed magic to ward off.

When my notebook on the subject of breaching was filled, about halfway through my sophomore year in high school, I felt that I had a fair understanding of the process—even a larger and more nuanced understanding than many of my peers, who were going through it firsthand. I had filled in the details little by little over the years, assembling the mystery of it as I would a jigsaw puzzle—certain aspects of the picture becoming clear before others.

Here's the way it worked.

As a general rule, when people in my town reached a certain age—anywhere between thirteen and sixteen—they ran wild. When exactly this would happen was a mystery. For some boys it coincided with their voices getting deeper; for some girls it came with the arrival of their first period—but these were rare harmonies. Our bodies are unfathomable. They resonate with so many things—it's impossible to know what natures they sing to.

When people breached, they cycled with the moon. When the moon was full (usually three nights each month), those who were breaching went feral. The adults stayed indoors with the younger children on those nights, because in the streets ran packs of teenagers—most of them naked, as though clothes were something they had grown beyond—whooping and hollering, crying out violent and lascivious words to each other, to the night, to those holed up in houses. They fought with each other, brutally. They went into the woods to engage in acts of sex.

My father referred to the full-moon nights as bacchanals, but a bacchanal, I learned from the encyclopedia, had to do with Dionysus, the wine god, and it refers specifically to drunken revelries. The breachers were almost never drunk—unless they had gotten drunk before the sun went down. Their indulgences came from a place deeper than wine or virtue or vice.

The mornings after the full-moon nights, the breachers found their ways home and were tended to by their parents, who understood that this was the way of the town and there was nothing to be done about it. Sometimes people got hurt, sometimes seriously—and it was accepted that the damage was simply a physical corollary of the deleterious effects of getting older and being alive in the world. My town had a certain secret pride in that it refused to cosmeticize the realities of adulthood.

And of course the breach was temporary—it was just a stage. It occurred only three nights a month, and for each individual it lasted only for around a year. After that time you were a true adult, and the next time the full moon rose you stayed inside with the others and listened to the howls in the distance and were only just reminded of your time in the wild.

Some people called it coming of age—as though you were ageless prior to that time, as though aging were something you enter by going through a doorway. Did that mean that coming of age was the beginning of dying? I looked it up in the encyclopedia—all the cultural and religious rituals associated with coming of age. In Christianity there were confirmations, in Judaism bar mitzvahs. The Apache had a process called na'ii'ees—which was a beautiful word to look at—but that was just for girls, and I never found what the boys' equivalent was. The Amish had their Rumspringa—and this was as close to our breaching as I was able to find. The sober toleration of wildness. The trial by fire. The wide-eyed gaze upon the violent and colorful sins of the world. Some of the articles I read directed me to something that seemed at first to have nothing to do with coming-of-age rites: mass hysteria. Some people believed that such rituals were related to the kind of localized group thought that led to the Salem witch trials. For my part, I never knew how you could tell an illegitimate witch from a real

Jesus or vice versa, so I was always careful to give concession to any magic that might be at hand.

I asked my father why it was called a breaching, and he did not know. It had just always been called that, he said.

I found nothing about it in the encyclopedia, of course, but right where the article on breaching should have been there was instead an article on breeching—which was a rite of passage for boys who grew up in the sixteenth and seventeenth centuries. It was called breeching because it was the first time in their lives that the boys wore breeches, or pants. Up until that point they wore little dressing gowns. I was tickled by the idea of all those mighty men in history, like Louis XIV, growing up in dresses—I had not known such a thing occurred. Breeching happened earlier, though, between the ages of two and five. Still, it was considered a significant moment in the boys' development into men.

So I liked thinking our breaching was related somehow to that antique practice.

Of course the difference in spelling must have been significant. I looked up breach in the dictionary. "A legal infraction." Definitely. "A break or a rupture." Plenty was broken, plenty ruptured. "A fissure made in a fortification." That one stumped me for a while until it occurred to me that the civilized world, the daytime world, is a kind of fortification against nature and night and brutishness—then it made sense.

But it was the fifth definition of the word that intrigued me most. Apparently breach is also the word for what a whale does when it breaks the surface of the water and leaps into the air.

I wrote that in a box in my research notes, and I drew a picture of a whale bursting from the surface of the ocean. It seemed at odds with the other definitions, and yet at the same time not.

When I slept I dreamed of whales, huge seabound creatures, mustering their power, changing their course, diving deep and then swimming up in a straight vertical, from the dark depths of the ocean floor through the murk to where the light penetrates, up farther and farther, their bodies all muscle in the act of violating the logic of their natural home, thrusting themselves upward, crashing through the surface, feeling the unwet open air on their barnacled skin, taking flight for one tiny moment — taking flight.

———

THEN IT CHANCED to happen that my life became joined with the lives of others.

That's how it occurs, just like that, like the passage of midnight, the hand of the clock creeping past the midpoint of twelve. The minute before midnight and the one after are practically the same, except that they are a full calendar day apart. That's what happened to me. One day things were different.

It was in the tenth grade, and it happened, really, because of Blackhat Roy Ruggle. It was during lunch in the cafeteria, and I was sitting at the table next to Rosebush Lincoln's when he approached her. Rosebush was in tears because earlier in the week her father had initiated divorce proceedings against her mother and had gone to live in a house the next town over, and earlier that day she had also received a C on an English paper.

"What is she crying for?" said Blackhat Roy to anyone who would listen. He was gypsy dark, with black hair that was always a little greasy. He was short, but there was an inherent ferociousness in him that you wouldn't want to see any taller. There might have been something handsome about him if it weren't for the nastiness.

Rosebush tried to ignore him.

"No, seriously," Roy went on, declaiming in a loud voice that hushed those within its range. "I want to know. What is she crying for? Is she worried she won't get into Notre Dame? And then what? What's a Rosebush who doesn't go to Notre Dame?"

"Stop it," said Rosebush, hiding her face in the crook of her arm and allowing herself to be comforted by Jenny Stiles, who had the shortest hair of all the girls in school.

"Oh, wait—I get it," said Roy. "See, the last time I got a C, the principal gave me a fucking trophy—so I guess it's all relative. And what she's worried about, see—what she's worried about is that if she gets a C, then that's her first step to becoming like me."

"Cut it out, Roy," somebody else said.

"Stop it," said Rosebush.

But he leaned in close to her.

"Take a look, Rosebush. It's your future talking. After you fail out of school, we'll get married and have a barrelful of kids. We'll feed them cat food and squirrels and pray every night before we go to bed that little Festus won't burn down the neighbor's house. My father's hit the road, so you won't have to deal with him getting drunk and groping you at the wedding. Hey, wait a minute—do you think that's why your dad left? Shame? Do you think he'll give a toast at our wedding?"

"Stop it, stop it, stop it!" cried Rosebush. She stood suddenly, escaped the grasp of Jenny Stiles, and began beating her little fists against Blackhat Roy, who backed away slowly, hands in the air to show he was not fighting back—a cruel, bemused expression on his face.

Then, as I watched, others intervened. Petey Meechum was there first, pushing himself between Rosebush and Roy.

"Stop!" he said to Roy. "Leave her alone, asshole."

There was a sudden stillness as everyone waited for Roy to explain himself. He looked around, and a sourness crept into his face. What he said was this:

"Cunt."

That was another magic word, I realized that day, because of the power it had over people. They cringed as if struck, as if that single syllable were a weapon more powerful than teeth or fists. It was a dangerous word.

Blackhat Roy walked away then, but I heard something else that maybe no one else heard. It was something he said to himself, under his breath, while everyone else was rushing to Rosebush to comfort her.

"She doesn't get to cry," he said.

I didn't understand what he meant, but then again I did. Still, I felt sorry for Rosebush and her gone father and her C.

It was the very next period when I did something I never would have done if I had had the time to really think it through. The class was history, and we were taking a test. Rosebush sniffled miserably over hers. Me, I answered the questions without much difficulty. It was all material that I had put on flash cards for myself earlier in the week, while, I imagined, Rosebush's father had been moving from room to room in his house identifying what was his and what was his wife's.

Blackhat Roy was also in that class, and when he asked to use the bathroom I had an idea. I waited two minutes, then asked if I could use the bathroom as well.

Outside the room, I turned left down the empty hallway toward the boys' room rather than right toward the girls'. I could smell the smoke coming from the restroom, so I knew he was in there. There was a fire alarm on the wall to the left of the door, and then I watched my hand rise up and pull the red lever down.

51

I ran the other way down the hall so that I could be seen emerging from the girls' room while everyone poured into the hallways amid the screeching bells.

Funny. Sometimes the whole world moves just for you.

But why did I do it?

For one thing, it saved Rosebush. The history test, having been compromised, would need to be rescheduled. But that wasn't really why I did it. Not really.

What happened was this. The principal called Blackhat Roy into his office and accused him of pulling the fire alarm. No one thought to accuse me of anything, even though I was also out of the classroom at the time the alarm went off. I was Lumen Fowler. I was a good student. I was childlike of stature, and I was unimpeachable.

They couldn't prove Roy had done anything, but they didn't need to. In the process of being accused, he grabbed a glass paperweight from the principal's desk and threw it through the window of the office onto the lawn outside, where it almost struck a fourth grader passing by. That was enough to get him suspended for two weeks.

Rather than simply being subject to them, I had wanted to know what it felt like to *be* one of the forces in this world.

—

BUT PETEY MEECHUM saw. The next day he found me tucked into the back carrel of the library, where I liked to be with my books.

"You did it," he said. "I saw you."

I panicked. I gathered my books, stuffed them quickly into my knapsack.

"Why did you?" he said. "I just want to know. Did you know he'd get in trouble?"

"I don't know," I said, trying to get around him. I didn't like being cornered.

"Wait a minute," he said as I pushed my way past him. "I won't tell anyone," he called after me. "I just—I didn't know who you were."

Of course we had known each other for many years, but he meant something bigger. See how easy it is to become someone else? It happens all of a sudden—just like that. A ticktock of motion.

So who am I now?

———

THE YEAR THAT Polly went breach, I had not yet figured out that life sometimes requires contingency plans for the loss of those close to you—that the more people you have buffering you against solitude, the less catastrophic it is when one of them disappears. Among people my age, I only really had Polly—and when she went breach, I no longer had her. She didn't turn on me. It's not that. She had simply been initiated into a corps I wasn't part of. More frequently than not, our casual conversations in the school hallways (usually on the topic of test scores and the relative fairness of teachers) were interrupted by other students who shared giddy stories with Polly about what outrageous things had occurred during the most recent full moon. These others acknowledged me always with a curious, questioning look in their eyes, as if they were too embarrassed to admit they didn't know my name.

As it turned out, though, Petey Meechum, who had also not

yet gone breach, had taken a strange interest in me after the day I had run away from him in the library. Except he liked to be known as Peter now, in the same way that Rosebush, perhaps as a result of her parents' divorce, was demanding that she be called Rose. Apparently we were outgrowing the names of our childhoods. I was always Lumen. There was no evolution in my name. Well, there wasn't until later, after I had left the town behind—and then I started calling myself Ann. Ann Fowler. I'm sure there are hundreds of Ann Fowlers in this world. You would have no reason to single me out. My husband, he believes Ann is my only name and that I have no middle name. He knows no Lumen. It is a secret I keep from him, because when he comes home he tells me about the troubles of his day at work—and Ann Fowler is a remarkably good wife.

So it was Peter Meechum who frequently came to my house to study in the afternoons. Unlikely as it was, popular Peter Meechum came to me for help with geometry. Golden-haired Peter. Peter, whom all the girls ached for in school, and somehow he had delivered himself to me. Peter Meechum in my very own home, where I would make us a snack of carrot and celery sticks and French onion dip. I would pour him a glass of orange juice, and he would drink it all in one long gulp—and then I would pour him another, and he would make that one last awhile.

I wondered how long it would be before he discovered any number of other taller, prettier girls to help him with math. But somehow one of my childhood incantations had borne him to me, and I relished it with the desperate appetite of someone fated to die the very next day.

"It's an offense to my masculinity is what it is," he would say dramatically. "My having to be taught math by a wee girl."

He said it in a way that made me not mind being called a wee girl.

"We'll have to compensate," he went on. "After you explain tangents, you have to promise to let me beat you at arm wrestling."

"Tangents are easy," I would say. "It's just relationships. Angles and lengths. If you have one, you also have the other. I'll show you."

In my room, sprawled out on the carpeted floor, I drew diagrams for him on blue-lined notebook pages.

"How do you draw such straight lines without a ruler?" he asked. "Your triangles are amazing."

He ran his fingertips lightly over my triangles, as though geometry were a tactile thing.

"They're perfect," he said.

"They're not perfect."

He eyed me.

"Maybe you don't know what perfect is," he said. "Those right there—that's what perfect looks like."

That was something about Peter. His language made things happen. Things became funny when Peter laughed, and they became ridiculous when he labeled them so. He seemed, somehow, to belong prematurely to that category of *adults*—people who drove the world ahead of them, like charioteers, rather than being dragged along behind.

The truth is, I was in love with him—Petey Meechum, who was now Peter, who held a carrot stick in the corner of his mouth like a cigar while he was lying on his stomach on the floor of my room complimenting my triangles.

He sighed heavily and rolled over onto his back. He raised his arms toward the ceiling and used his splayed hands to make a triangle through which he peered, squinting, at the overhead light.

"After I graduate high school, I'm leaving," he said.

"Where are you going?"

"New York."

I didn't ask why New York. He would tell me without my prompting him.

"It's like a city on fire," he went on. "The streets are always smoking from underground furnaces."

"Steam," I said. I couldn't help myself.

"What?"

"It's not smoke. It's steam."

"How do you know?"

"I looked it up once. I saw it on TV and wondered what it was. There's a steam-heat system under Manhattan. Sometimes it leaks."

His hands fell to his chest, and he was quiet. I felt bad for knowing more about his dream city than he did.

"What will you do in New York?" I asked, trying to resuscitate his vision.

"Lumen, don't you ever feel like you want to leave?"

"What do you mean?"

"I mean this place. This weird little town with its weird little traditions. Other places aren't like this, you know."

"Every place has its own ways," I declared reasonably.

He rolled over again, back onto his stomach, and there was something beseeching in his tone when he spoke again.

"But don't you ever just want to get out? To go somewhere else? To be somebody else—even just for a little while?"

I looked down at the triangles in my notebook. The secret to drawing straight lines is that you use your whole arm, not just your hand and wrist. My father taught me that.

"I like it here," I said.

"What do you like about it?"

I wasn't prepared for follow-up questions. Part of me always resented having to justify my likes and dislikes. Other people didn't have to. No one ever asked Blackhat Roy what it was he liked about hunting knives. Everyone just knew he kept a collection of them, all oiled and polished, in his bedroom.

"Come on," I said to Peter. "You have to understand tangents. They're going to be on the test tomorrow."

———

"I NEVER SEE you in church," he said on another afternoon.

My father and I were not churchgoers—but we had frequently driven by when services were being let out, and I wished sometimes to be among those enlightened folk who had occasion to dress in finery in the middle of a plain Sunday morning.

Peter had taken to removing his sneakers when we were studying together. He tucked the laces neatly inside and set them side by side by the door. I liked seeing them there—that one touch of alien boyness that transformed my bedroom into something less than familiar.

"My father never took me," I said.

"Do you believe in God?"

"Kind of."

"You kind of believe in God, or you believe in a kind of God?"

I didn't know what to say. How do you tell a boy who takes off his shoes in your bedroom that God is a thing of the mind—but a very, very lovely thing of the mind? I stuttered along for a few moments before he let me off the hook.

"You know, I didn't used to believe in God."

"You didn't?"

"Huh-uh. For a long time I didn't. And then one day I did. Just like that. Does that ever happen to you? You're going along, minding your own business, seeing things the way you've always seen them—and then all of a sudden those things look different to you?"

The way he was looking at me made me wonder if he was talking about something other than God. Or if maybe God and the way he looked at me with those voracious boy-eyes were related. I wanted more of it. His boy-eyes—his godliness, which I felt deep down, like a surge.

Then he leaned back, as though something had clicked shut all at once.

"Never mind," he said. "I'm just feeling philosophical today. If you can help me pass this geometry test, I'll give you a present."

"What present?" I pretended to shuffle through the pages of my textbook, because I didn't want to show him that I was out of breath.

"I don't know—I'll build you a house on the lake."

"On the east shore, so I can watch the sunsets?"

"Sure. And another on the west shore so you can watch the sunrises. And a canoe to go back and forth between them."

"Just a canoe?"

"Come on, I already built you two houses."

"Fair enough."

———

IN SCHOOL, ROSE Lincoln leaned over to my desk during history.

"I heard you're tutoring Peter," she said.

I said nothing.

"Well, is it true?"

I shrugged. "We just study—" I had meant to say, "We just study together," but the *together* suddenly sounded, in one way or another, too complicit and damning.

"It's okay," she said with a laugh. "You don't have to be embarrassed. It's not like he's interested in you or anything. You know Peter—he's a flirt. The other day he told me I looked nice in yellow. He let Angela Weston give him a back rub in the cafeteria. Carrie Bryce said he brushed her butt when she walked by him in the hall. And you know it doesn't mean anything. I mean, I look so like hell in yellow. It's just the way he is. The reason he likes me is that we understand each other."

I wrote Rose Lincoln's name in my notebook and spent the rest of the period crosshatching over it until it was an ugly blotch of shiny ink that bled through to the other side of the paper—and I thought that would do for a curse.

———

BUT I FEARED that what Rose Lincoln said about Peter and me was true—that I was just a functionary to him.

It was a few weeks later. We were in my bedroom, and he was looking at a framed picture on the wall. The picture was of my mother and father when they were very young and just married. Peter had been spending the afternoons with me in my bedroom, and we had played many games of Parcheesi between studying sessions—but he had made no move to kiss me.

"What's it like not to have a mother?" he asked.

I had learned that afternoons make boys profound—the long, slow crawl of light between the shutters, the lazy dust motes in the doldrums of the air. Boys are affected, unconsciously, by such things. You can see it in their eyes. In the sepia light of dusk, they are traveling.

"It's okay," I said. "She died when I was too young to remember her, so I never really felt the loss of anything."

It was my stock answer when people lamented, unnecessarily, my motherlessness.

"Does your dad talk about her much?"

"I don't know," I said, not knowing what constituted "much." It was true that he used to speak to her frequently at night, after he closed his bedroom door, as though it were his personal version of prayer. If I put my ear up to the door, I would hear him relating the events of the day, the progress of my evolution through girlhood. But he hadn't spoken to her like that in a long time. Once, when I was little, I listened so long at his door that I fell asleep. After having your ear pressed against doors and walls for a while, you don't know exactly what you're listening to—maybe just that low, oceany hum of your own blood. It lulls you. He found me there in the morning, called me his beautiful stray, lifted me in his arms. I clung to him.

"Do you want to see pictures?" I asked.

"Sure."

The old albums were in the attic, and I thought that such a dark, cramped place might inspire kissing. I felt bad about using the memory of my mother in that way, but I reasoned that she also would have wanted me to be kissed.

Peter was quite a bit taller than me, so I had him unfold the attic ladder from the ceiling in the hallway, and up we went. I knew right where the boxes with the albums were, because I had helped my father organize the attic just the previous summer. It had been my job to create all the labels. It was warmer up there in the attic, and Peter and I sat side by side, with our backs propped up against old suitcases, an album resting open half on his lap and half on mine. Our shoulders touched.

"This is my favorite picture," I said.

"That's baby you?"

"That's baby me."

Most family pictures show the mother holding the baby while the father sits proudly by—but this one was the opposite. In it, my father, looking lean and dapper, had me bundled up in his arms. He was sitting in the easy chair we still had downstairs in the living room, and next to him was my mother, perched upon the arm of the chair, looking radiant and aloof, the skirt of her dress draped perfectly over her knees. Her smile was something I couldn't describe, except to say that it seemed to be queenly in the way that queens remind you of situations grander than your own puny life could conceive.

"She looks like you," Peter said.

"Does she?" I was pleased. "I think we have a lot in common. Maybe that's why she died."

"Huh?"

"I mean, I know it's morbid, but I think that sometimes. Maybe she had to die because we were so alike that the world couldn't tolerate both of us in it."

"That's . . ." he said, looking uncomfortable. "That's a really weird thing to say, Lumen."

But it didn't seem weird to me at all, and I was hurt by his response.

"Anyway," I said.

We were quiet for a moment. Then he said:

"So what do you have in common? I mean, other than your looks."

"Well, she didn't go breach—and I'm not going to, either."

He looked at me sideways with suspicious eyes.

"It happens," I went on. "Not very often, but it does happen. My father says she was all lit up—he says she carried the daylight with her. The moon, it couldn't have any effect."

"I never heard of that."

"Well, it's true—whether you've heard of it or not. Some people just aren't the same as other people."

"Hm." I could tell he still didn't believe me. "And how come you think you won't go breach, either?"

"We have the same blood. It stands to reason. Plus I can just tell."

"But your father, he went breach."

"Yes."

"So you could be like him."

"I don't know," I said, shrugging. "I can just tell."

It is always a young girl's dream to have a boy believe in her most colorful fantasies. You paint landscapes with your humble heart, then you seek to populate them with boys who will understand.

But then he underwent a quick change—as though he were brushing off the topic altogether. He clambered around so that he was on his hands and knees in front of me. I sat with my own knees pulled up protectively to my chest.

"Let me see," he said.

"See what?"

But he didn't answer. He was looking at my eyes, examining them. He moved his head from side to side, as though to get multiple angles on the subject of my eyes.

"What are you doing?" I asked.

"Shh."

He kept looking, then he seemed to spot something—as

though he had discovered a minuscule village somewhere in the core of my retina.

"Huh," he said.

"What?"

"You're right. Daylight."

That's when he kissed me. At first I held my breath, unsure about what I should do. Then when I finally breathed, I wondered if I should keep my eyes open or closed. His eyes were closed, so I closed mine. That's when my other senses took over. I could smell his skin and that boy shampoo that smells like mowed grass. He pushed himself against me, and I touched his arm with my hand—squeezed his arm as if it were mine, as if our bodies were forfeit to each other's—and then my hand was even on his neck, where there were little hairs, and I was allowed to touch them. I heard a tiny voice, like that of a squeak-mouse, and then I realized it was my own voice, and I thought how beautiful that sometimes your body knows what to do on its own.

At that time, I had a way of thinking of myself as a castle or a tower, something with many spiraling cobblestone steps that became secrets in themselves, winding around each other like visual illusions. The pleasure was in the climbing, the intricate architectures of thought and purpose. But it was on a rare occasion such as this when I could feel something else, something beneath the foundation of the tower, a rumbling in the earth itself that shook to delightful danger all those lattices of cold, cerebral mortar.

———

I HAD LOST track of time in the attic, and when we climbed down the ladder I was surprised to see that a pale, dry dusk had infiltrated the house while we weren't looking.

"Uh-oh," I said.

"What?"

"Prayer Moon. It's the first night."

Peter went to the window and gazed up at the sky.

"It's still early enough," he said. "I don't live that far away. I can make it."

"No, you can't. The moon's up."

"But look—it's quiet. I can make it. They wouldn't bother with me much anyway."

But my father, arriving home, wouldn't hear of it. He called Peter's mother and told her he would stay in our house for the night. There was plenty of room—such a big house for just my father and me. The couch in the upstairs den folded out into a bed, and I got sheets from the linen closet and made it up.

It was the first time there had been a boy sleeping in the house, and I wanted to assure my father that nothing untoward would happen. I found him in the kitchen while Peter was watching TV in the den.

"I told Peter he shouldn't come out of the den after ten o'clock," I said. "You can check on us if you want. Any time you feel like it."

My father grinned in confusion and shook his head.

"I'm sure everything will be fine," he said. "I trust you, little Lumen."

That was nice to hear, but at the same time I had recently grown irritated by the idea that I was so invariably trustworthy. Hadn't I just spent the afternoon in the attic kissing, of all people, Peter Meechum? Hadn't I kissed right through sunset?

"How come you trust me so much? None of the other parents trust their kids so much."

He smiled again, gently. And again there was something in it I didn't care for. Was it condescension?

"Well," he said, "you've never disappointed me yet. Never once. Such a perfect record earns you plenty of trust. Besides, you're fifteen."

I wasn't entirely sure what the fact of my age had to do with anything, but I had an impression—and he turned to the sink immediately after he'd said it, as though embarrassed.

He made spaghetti and meatballs for dinner, and Peter and I were responsible for the garlic toast. Peter made a big production of spreading the garlic butter on the bread, and I topped it with the ocher-colored seasoned salt.

We listened to music during dinner—as we often did during the moons. That night it was the opera *Turandot*.

"The opera's about a princess," I explained, because I had read the libretto the previous year. "She refuses to marry any man unless he answers three riddles first. If he answers any of them incorrectly, he's put to death."

"I guess she has her reasons," Peter said, and I couldn't tell if he was joking.

"She's a princess of death," I said with great seriousness. "It's her nature."

After dinner Peter and I watched TV in the den upstairs, sitting side by side on the couch that had been made up as his bed. We turned the TV loud so we wouldn't hear anything from outside. After a while we fell to kissing again.

It surprised me how quickly the whole thing became mechanical. I found myself too aware of the way our lips met, mapping out the movements of his tongue in my mouth. First he would kiss me square on the mouth, then take my lower lip between his two lips and leave a cold wet spot on my chin that I wanted to wipe off. Then he would turn his head sideways a little, as though passion were all about angles. (If we had been able to kiss with one of our faces turned completely upside down, I suppose that would have been truly making love.) Then he would leave a trail of ticklish kisses from the corner of my mouth up the side of my face to my ear, the lobe of which he took in his mouth. Then a bite or two on the neck, which I didn't know what to do with. Then the whole thing started over again.

The problem was that I was thinking about it as it was happening, picturing it in my mind as though I were a disembodied viewer standing off to the side—and from that perspective the whole thing looked ludicrous. I kept thinking about my father, who trusted me implicitly, and what he would have seen had he come into the room during that mess. Not disappointment, not exactly. But it would have given him reason to remind me again that I was fifteen years old—which was a repellent thought. Had he come in at that moment, he would have seen his daughter succumbing sloppily to teenagehood—whatever preposterous versions of love or curiosity or risk such a state implied.

Then Peter's right hand slid down from my neck to my chest and rested itself on the embarrassing nodule that was still in the process of becoming my left breast.

He froze suddenly. At first I thought it was because he was disappointed with what he'd found there. He lifted himself a few inches from me, his hand still on my chest, and gave me an intent, querulous look.

That's when I realized he was waiting for me to stop him.

I had been so studious and removed from the whole situation that I had forgotten the role I was supposed to be playing. I was the good girl. The girl being groped and salivated upon in the den of her own home was the good girl. You were safe with her, because she didn't allow anything to get out of control.

"I guess we should stop," I said.

"Okay," he said. "Sorry."

But he didn't seem sorry. He seemed relieved.

He levered himself off me, then we sat and watched TV for a while longer. It was half an hour before midnight when I told him I was going to bed. He said okay and leaned over to kiss me good night.

"I'm glad we went to the attic," he said.

It was a sweet thing to say, and the way he phrased it made me think funny thoughts—as though "going to the attic" were some kind of accepted rite of passage. Passage to the attic. I thought then that I knew something about rites, but I was wrong.

There are so many things about the world that might keep you laughing to yourself in the dark when you can't seem to fall asleep. Then again, alone in my bedroom with a hallway between us, the idea of Peter Meechum once again thrilled all my senses. I put my hand on my breast the way he had done it before, and it gave me little shivers all over.

I wondered why romance was a thing I felt in a truly visceral way only when I was alone. Maybe the cold, logical part of my mind closed doors to real people. Maybe I needed to be taught how to open those doors. And I thought that Peter Meechum very well could be the one to teach me.

We've all of us got an inward brain and an outward brain, don't we? When we are by ourselves in our rooms at night, un-selfconscious and free, we are entirely different. That's when you might learn the most about instinct.

But the moon made its exceptions in our town. Here's another song from my childhood that I sing as a lullaby to my son.

Gather, young lovers,
In wind and in rain.
Cleave to the sky fires
That know not your name.
Unravel the day-screws
That tangle your brain.
Hold fast your white angel,
And cut it in twain.
  Hold fast your black devil,
  And cut it in twain.

And then, cut in two as we all are, can we ever take true account of ourselves? Or do we just lisp ourselves to sleep and dreams of freedom?

———

BUT THE NIGHT when Peter Meechum stayed over was also the night when a pack of breachers stood outside my window howling. It was well after midnight, and I had not been able to fall asleep. I heard them out on the street, mewling in the peculiar way they had, which made me think of lonely cats on backyard fences in the nighttime.

Mine was the only window that faced the front of the house. My father's bedroom and the den, where Peter slept, were both in the back—so they couldn't hear.

Then I heard my name, called snakelike and taunting from outside:

"Luuuuuuuuumeeen!"

It was a girl's voice. It was Polly's voice.

Normally the breachers didn't bother with people who kept

indoors when the moon was out. They weren't malicious—they didn't stalk innocent prey. Normally they kept to themselves. They embattled each other if they battled at all. Some of them just liked to run through the streets—they kept on running until the sun came up. Others took to the woods and were lost in the morning when they woke. But by and large they didn't make assaults on those who stayed out of their way.

So this was something different—my name teased out in that manic hyena voice they all had.

"Luuuuumeen!"

I hadn't been sleeping anyway, so I went to the window and looked down.

There were six of them. They were naked, their skin pale and glowing under the light of the street lamps. They ran around in circles, testing the strength of their legs, the length of their arms. They hopped and ran and yipped and snarled. One of them grappled with another and was tossed into the shrubbery at the edge of our yard. When he got himself upright again, I saw there were perforations all over his skin from the brambles. He would hurt in the morning, but he seemed to feel nothing now.

In the middle of the pack, Polly stood very still, smiling up at my window. I didn't like her smile. I couldn't tell you exactly what it was. Her smile was the stillest on the street, but there was a breeze that blew strands of her hair across her face. She made no attempt to remove them.

When she saw me in the window, her smile widened—she even laughed, seeming to luxuriate in my witnessing her in such a state.

"Lumen," she said, seeming to breathe through her words, "come outside! Please, Lumen. Look at me. I want you to see me!"

The girl who stood in the street was not the girl I knew. Instead, she was some nightmarish inversion of the person who had played in the sprinklers with me years before. This girl was raw, viperous, glutted on nature and night. They all were. Like coyotes, they made mockery, with their bleating voices, of those who needed light in order to feel safe.

And yet they were all too human.

I had never seen Polly without her clothes on before. There was a sickly luminescence to her skin, as of a glowworm or one of those creatures that live so deep underground that they have no pigment at all. Her dropsy breasts—I could see that one was larger than the other, that the rusty nipples were more oval than circular, that they possessed the persistent misalignment of nature itself. There were red blotches on her stomach and legs, as though she were rash-broken, and I could see the freckles and moles that dotted her body—even a patchy birthmark that looked like someone had spilled coffee on her hip. The triangle of her pubic hair was discomfiting in the way it grew partly onto her thighs and up her stomach. While I watched, the breeze blew a chattering of tiny leaves down the street, and one of them got caught in her pubic hair—where it remained as long as she stood there.

Then she started to call my name in various ways, feeling it in her mouth, tasting the varietals with which she might be able to permute my personhood were I down there with her.

"Lumen," she called. "Lumenal...Laminal...Lamen... Lamian...Labian...Lavial..."

It seemed, at first, like a child's game—but the way she said the names made them sound obscene. They were versions of my name—if my name were some vulgar tropical fruit whose juice ran down your chin and whose pulp got stuck between your gnashing teeth.

As Polly continued her catechism, another of the breachers took notice and came to stand beside her. It was Rose. I didn't know if it was just because Rose had a different kind of body or because she cosmetically altered it, but her patch of pubic hair was smaller and shorter than Polly's—and as a result it masked less, and I could see the ugly fleshy nubbins of her vagina.

I wanted to look away. I really did. But there are some things in this life that demand your sight, your vision. This was a scene played out particularly for my delectation. There was no one in the world, at that moment, apart from them and me. We existed on opposite sides of a pane of glass. But it didn't matter—I was in their thrall. And they seemed to be in mine. As though I'd become a lonely Rapunzel at the top of a tower.

The others started to gather, too, standing very still in a group and gazing up at me. They smiled their grisly smiles and called to me in words or moans or hisses. Blackhat Roy was there with his two missing toes, but he stood apart, crouched at the line of trees that was the beginning of the woods on the opposite side of the street. A boy I recognized as Wilson Laramy stood at Polly's side. Without seeming to think, and while still gazing up at my window, he reached blindly to his right, found Polly's wrist, and guided her hand down to his crotch. Without shame, and still repeating the prayerful tautology of my name, her left hand closed around his penis. Casual—it was all so casual. You would think they had no idea what nakedness was.

Then they were all there together, as though by the instinct of pack animals, all casting their lewd voices up at me, their skin spectral and yet hideously biological, bleeding, lurching cadavers regurgitated by the earth and sent wandering down the abandoned thoroughfares of our little town—and here they were, uncharacteristically still, all their unclean gestures pointed in my direction—as though to tempt me, as though to mock me for not being tempted, as though the land itself hated me for existing so dry and tidy above its fecund soil.

And that's when Polly started to laugh, high and hysterical—a harsh, shrieking laugh that had no sense in it. And when she laughed, the others laughed, too, and they started to split off from the group—as though suddenly roused into action. First one ran off down the street, followed by two more. Then another—until the only one left was Polly herself, who, when her laughter died away, licked her lips slowly, her tongue moving between her teeth.

Then she, too, turned to run down the street in the direction the others had gone—and I was left to stare at the empty street, the ratchety shadows of tree branches against the lamplight, the only sounds the ticking of the grandfather clock down the hall, the insistent tapping of a twig against the glass of my window, and the stiff flood of my own pulse in my ears.

—

THE BALD WHITE maggotry of it! The spitting, drooling indecency of it! I couldn't sleep that night thinking about it. I can't sleep this night remembering it. We live in an eggshell. We swim in phlegmy albumen—the world outside tap-tap-taps against our chalky home. I stand beside my marriage bed, staring down at my husband, who snorts with rough sleep. I am forever gazing downward at people who live in dream worlds. The breachers, too. They run through the night, but they run in sleep, they run undercurrents deep in memory. In the morning there is no shame because they were not themselves—or their selves were buried so deep that their waking minds are blameless for their nighttime deeds.

I don't sleep the way others do. I fear sleep—and I fear not sleeping.

Once the pack below had gone, I sat in my room, clutching at myself in the pool of moonlight cast through my windowpanes. My head was crowded with so, many things it ached with fullness—Peter's compulsory kisses, his hot boy-breath, the pressure of his hand over my lung, like a medical examination, the hiss of voices in the street, the exposed reechy bodies of those I see in school every day, Turandot, the princess of death, my father declaring me fifteen—*fifteen!*—his embarrassed eyes focused on the project of scrubbing a pot in the sink.

So much shame. I live in an eggshell.

There is so much shame.

———

THE NEXT DAY, I saw Polly in school. She sat next to me in our biology class. She said she was exhausted and rested her head on my shoulder.

She asked me what was the matter. She said I looked worse than she did.

I told her I hadn't slept well.

She called me poor Lumen, and there was no hissing in the way she said my name.

I didn't like how people could be one thing at night and another thing during the day.

I asked her if she didn't remember the night before—coming to my window, calling my name.

She said she didn't remember a thing.

But I could tell by the way she said it that she was lying, and I told her so.

She shook her head and said in a voice filled with sadness but not apology:

"Oh, Lumen, these things—it's like they happen to different people. Other lives."

So we went on, scribbling away about centrioles and lysosomes and Golgi bodies and other microscopic organelles that committed invisible acts of violence and love upon each other many times every second.

CHAPTER 3

That was the year in my life when everyone I knew went breach, one at a time, little oily kernels of corn popping against the pot lid, until I was the only one left, a hard, stubborn pip in the bottom of the pan, burned black.

Menarche was my magic word that year. Before I went to sleep each night, I whispered the word thirteen times — once for each regular moon and once for the Blue Moon, just in case — hoping that mine would come. My father, he never asked a thing about it. He gave me a fair allowance. It was understood that I would be self-sufficient enough to purchase my own products and take care of myself when the time came. So he remained unaware that I was not bleeding like the other girls were.

At my annual checkup, I lied to the doctor about it. I told him I had my first period six months before. He asked if it was happening regularly. I told him yes, regular. Regular as could be.

Polly seemed particularly taken with her breaching. She painted herself with the new habits of womanhood — the tip of her finger on her lower lip when she was lost in thought, a languorous lean against the school lockers when she spoke with boys, fingernails colored somber browns and oxblood reds.

Peter went breach a few months after we kissed in the attic. I had wondered if I would see a dramatic change in him, but he was the same. I asked him about his breach nights, but he didn't like to talk about them. He said, "You shouldn't be thinking about me when I'm like that." If anything, he became all the more proper and gentlemanly to compensate for whatever it was he did when the full moon rose. I admired his rectitude, but it made me feel lonely, too—as though he were visiting me in some foreign country where I lived all by myself, and we were both pretending that the rest of the world didn't exist.

This truth is, I liked my strange country. But I didn't want anyone feeling sorry for me, as though I were in quarantine. Couldn't they see my aloneness was a freedom rather than a prison?

Once, though, Peter brought me something back from his breach night. He said, "Look. I found it by the river."

He put it into the palm of my hand. It was a little metal heart with a loop at the top, a charm lost from a bracelet.

"It's old," I said.

"How can you tell?"

"It's tarnished."

"See?" he said. "It was waiting there for a long time. Waiting for me to find it and give it to you."

"Thank you."

He smiled.

"I think about you," he said, "at night, when I'm out there."

"What do you think?"

"I guess I think about being near you. I think about how it's like there's a bubble around you."

"A bubble?"

"A big bubble. A block wide. It goes where you go—you're the center of it. And every object gets a little bit better while it's in that bubble with you. It's always very bright where you are."

And I *was* bright just then. I was breathing very hard. The only thing I could do was get myself as near to him as I possibly could, so I leaned in and put my head against his chest and listened to his heart.

———

HONDY PILT WAS an interesting case. He had first gone breach when Peter had, during the same moon, and the next day in school the breachers seemed to have a newfound respect and even admiration for him.

I asked Polly about it.

"I don't know what it is about him," she said. "You just want to follow him. He ran through the woods—I've never seen anyone run like that. I mean, Lumen, he was beautiful."

"Really?"

"I know it sounds stupid, but it's no joke. We followed him, and he took us to this clearing on the side of the mountain. Nobody ever knew it was there. He stood on this rock jutting out over nothing. If he fell . . . but he didn't fall. He put his arms out. Like the sky was his or something. I don't know. I can't explain it."

It was true—there was something different about him, something even I could witness during the day. He had always seemed like someone struggling against invisible forces, but now there was a peacefulness about him—as though he had arrived at a place and recognized it as a true home, as though he had discov-

77

ered a back door into heaven and waited patiently for the rest of us to find him there.

I tried to speak to him. In the cafeteria a couple days later, I brought him a banana as an offering. I had always been kind to him—more than most, I believe. I said hello. I asked him how his day was going. Usually he smiled back and uttered a few guttural words of greeting. That day, though, his eyes didn't even meet mine. He was gazing upward, as though he could see the sky through the ceiling. He reached out and put his big hand over my little one, and he just held it there for a long time. I didn't know what to do, so after a while I took my hand back and left him there smiling to himself.

I had wanted him to share his secrets with me, but instead what I got was consolation. The last thing I wanted was to be pitied by Hondy Pilt.

Amenorrhea. I looked it up. That's what it's called when you don't get your first period by age sixteen. At first I wondered what it had to do with the end of a prayer—where you say, Amen. But then I realized it was probably "men," as in "menstruation," and "a," as in "not"—so "not menstruating," amenorrhea. That's the word I tried to counteract with my magic word menarche.

Where did all that blood go if it wasn't evacuating my body? I worried. Did it collect somewhere? Did I have a sac in my thorax that was growing larger every day with unshed blood? That was crowding my other organs? If not blood, what was my body spending its time in the production of? All flowered fantasies and brain work?

Two months after Hondy Pilt and Peter Meechum went breach, the second, smaller Parker twin went breach. That meant I was the only one in my grade who hadn't. In fact many of the people in the grade below me had already started going. It was something you couldn't hide. Your absence on those nights was noticed.

Polly tried to console me. She said it was a sign of great maturity to breach late. Rose Lincoln was not so kind. She said it was because I was underdeveloped, obviously—that I was repressing my womanhood. "You have to have a grown woman *somewhere* in you scrambling to get out," she explained. "How come you don't want to let her out? You can't stay a girl forever, you know. After a while, girlhood's just a shell for something else."

To Rose Lincoln I was a shell. A dry husk. One of those disappointments like cracking open a peanut only to find there's no nut inside.

I knew I wasn't going to go breach at all. But I hadn't known what it would mean—watching everyone else as though we were on opposite sides of a wide river. I could hear them frolicking in the distance with their puffed-out bodies and their bleeding wombs. I felt that I was waving to them from my exile. Sometimes someone waved back.

So I said my magic word every night, and I looked at myself in the mirror every morning to see if any part of me had grown.

Peter Meechum petted me like a poodle and was in constant care not to corrupt me with his newfound adulthood. I wanted his hands on me, but he was reluctant.

And one day after the last night of the full moon, Polly came to my house and told me that Wendy Spencer had gotten an empty soda bottle stuck up in her the night before. She lurched all the way home with it inside her, and the paramedics had to break it this morning to get it out.

"Can you imagine!" Polly said. "It was *stuck*. How deep must it have gone to get *stuck*?"

"Suction," I said, picking at the cover of my history textbook.

"What?"

"It's not how deep. It's suction. They probably had to break the bottom to let the air in."

"Oh. How do you know that?"

I shrugged.

"I don't know. It just makes sense."

And so that was something else for me to think about when I couldn't sleep.

Something was coming, and it had broken glass for teeth. I was running from it, hiding. But in the middle of the night, when I lay awake in my bed listening to the howling outside, I didn't know which I really and truly wanted: this life or that one.

———

I PLEADED WITH Mr. Hunter not to read my essay in front of the whole class, but he said modesty would get me nowhere in life. I said it wasn't modesty, it was just that I didn't like people reading my writing.

He gave me one of his curious looks, one that I could feel in my belly.

"You've got a toughness in you, Lumen. More spine than all of them put together," he said in a low tone. "Why do you hide it?"

I didn't know what to say. Why was he talking about my spine?

"If you want me not to read it," he said, "tell me not to. Don't ask, *tell*."

But I could say nothing.

So he read it aloud and told everyone to pay attention to the diction and the transitions. He didn't say it was mine, but everyone knew anyway. I hunched in my seat.

"You're an excellent writer," said Rose Lincoln after class. "You're a master scribe."

Later, in math class, when we were all supposed to be working through a sheet of problems, she leaned over and whispered to me.

"How's your boyfriend?"

"What boyfriend?"

"You know, Peter Meechum."

I hadn't thought about him as my boyfriend.

"Things got pretty vicious last night, you know," Rose continued. "He got into a fight with Blackhat Roy."

I had seen the scrapes and bruises on Peter's face, but he was avoiding me in school that day so I hadn't had a chance to ask him about it.

"Why?" I asked Rose.

"Why what, sweetie?"

"Why were they fighting?"

"Come on, Lumen. I know you're a little behind us, but you must've heard *something* about what happens. There is no why. Instinct. Besides, you know how Roy is. He's got a meanness you can't do much about. So Peter did what he had to."

I didn't look at her. I tried to concentrate on the math problem in front of me. But the lines and numbers seemed to wobble and blur.

"Anyway, Peter showed himself a real leader," Rose went on. "Like a warrior-prince, you know? His skin was smeared all over with blood and sweat—you just wanted to lick him. And he deserved something—I mean, for taking care of that little creep Roy. So I let him have me. To the victor go the spoils, right? That's me—I'm the spoils."

I stood up from my desk so suddenly that I knocked my book

and worksheet and pencil to the floor. Mr. Goodwin looked at me curiously. I picked up my things and put them on the desk, then walked quickly out of the room, down the hall, and into the girls' bathroom. I looked at myself in the mirror, my diminutive, ugly little self, and it wasn't until I could see my eyes filling up with tears that I knew I was going to cry. So I shut myself in a stall and unrolled thick wads of toilet paper to cry into. I made no sound. I'm a silent crier when I wish to be.

When I was done, I splashed cold water on my face and waited for the redness to lessen. I was in the bathroom so long that the end-of-period bell rang before I got back to the classroom. When I went in to collect my things, Mr. Goodwin asked me if everything was all right.

I told him yes, everything was fine.

Then, on an impulse, I added:

"I was cutting class."

Mr. Goodwin gave me a confused smile, as though he didn't understand the joke. Then he just shrugged it off.

"Are you coming to math clinic today? A lot of kids could really use your help."

———

LATER, WHEN PETER came to my house to study, I remained conspicuously silent about his injuries. At first he tried to hide them or distract me with questions from the textbook. But the more time passed without my asking about it, the more indignant he became.

Finally he said, "Aren't you going to ask what happened to me?"

I shrugged.

"I figure it happened when you were breaching last night."

"But don't you want to ask how? Don't you want to know if I'm all right?"

"Did you have sex with Rose Lincoln?"

His face changed. Whatever ire he had been fostering toward me was suddenly gone—replaced by twitchy panic.

"What?" he said lamely.

"You had sex with her."

"Who said that?"

"She did."

"Rose lies. She's lying."

"I don't think she is."

He didn't say anything. His eyes searched the room. He was in a panic about being caught. I hated him for making me feel sorry for him. He reached out to me, and I pulled myself back so violently that I banged my shoulder against one of my shelves and a pile of books came tumbling down. I was embarrassed and angry.

"Why did you do it?" I said.

"I didn't—"

"You *did*. I know what breachers do. They run in the woods. They beat one another up. They have sex together. Isn't that what happens?"

"Lumen—"

"I thought you liked me."

"I do. So much you don't even know."

"That's not what liking looks like."

"You don't understand. When you're out there . . . you don't—"

"Yeah, I know. I got it. I'm a girl. I'm a nice girl. I'm the opposite of Rose Lincoln. She's the kind of girl you have sex with, and I'm the kind of girl you do math problems with."

"Stop it. It's not—"

"Yes, it *is*. I know it is. You're a sweetheart with me. So kind, so gentlemanly." I was crying by now. I knew because I could feel the tears on my cheeks. And I was embarrassed, which made the tears come even faster. "I'm like the thing you worship. The thing you put on a shelf and dust every week. Don't take Lumen down from her shelf—you're liable to get your fingerprints all over her. Let's keep her from anything ugly. The ugly's just for grownups. She can't handle the ugly—"

"Stop!"

He said it loud, loud enough to jar everything into sudden silence. My father was downstairs, and I was afraid he'd heard it. I didn't like the idea of dragging him into my pathetic little-girl world. I listened for a few moments to the ticking of the grandfather clock in the hallway. Then I looked to the window. It was the third and final night of Hollow Moon.

"You better go," I said, sniffling and wiping the tears from my face with my palms. "It'll be dark soon."

"I'm going," he said. "But you should know—you're better than me. You're better than all of us."

"Well, maybe I don't want to be better," I said. "Get out. Just get out. You don't want to be a danger to me."

———

THAT NIGHT I stuffed cotton balls in my ears and pulled the blankets over my head. I went to beautiful places in my head. I was part of everything I touched, and the world was glad to have me on its surface. I imagined myself on top of a mountain in Switzerland. I looked out over the wide valleys and saw no towns and no roads and no travelers. There was no one around to be surprised or disappointed about what I was or what I was not.

I was alone and unfearful.

———

IN THE MORNING, as my father and I sat at the kitchen table—he reading the paper and stirring his coffee, I ignoring my unappetizing bowl of whole-grain cereal—I asked him what it was like to go breach.

"It's not something for you to worry about," he said, not looking up from his newspaper.

"You mean because it won't happen to me?"

I forget where it started, this mutual belief that I was unbreachable. Was it something he told me as a child? Or was it something I suggested to him that he picked up on? We had lived so long, he and I, with the consensual reluctance to give up the fancies of childhood—and now I didn't know if this was one of them. Simply put, we did not talk about such things.

"I mean," he said, "because it's not something to worry about. Like the weather. It's going to be what it's going to be, whether you fret about it or not."

I knew this to be true, but I wanted more information.

"But you went through it. Do you remember it? What was it like?"

He sipped his coffee and lowered the cup slowly to the table. Then he folded his newspaper twice and leaned forward to look at his daughter straight-on. His eyes were very large, with pale crescents of fatigue beneath them.

"Do you remember," he said, "when you were maybe five years old, and you asked me about death? You wanted to know where your mother had gone. You asked if you would die and if I would die, and I told you it was an inevitability, and then we looked up the word inevitability in the dictionary?"

"No," I said.

"It was one of those conversations you dread having as a parent. For years before it happens, you lose sleep trying to plan for it. But there it was. You wanted to know what it was like where your mommy was."

He shifted in his seat and cleared his throat. I recognized the symptoms of trying not to tear up. I looked down at my cereal to save him embarrassment.

"Anyway," he went on, "I told you I didn't know what it was like. And do you want to know what you said?"

"What? What did I say?"

"You said—very matter-of-fact, as though you were quite positive about it—you said, 'Wherever it is, it probably has curtains.'"

He laughed. I laughed, too. Though it sounded vaguely familiar, and I wondered if he had told me that story before. And if he had, why hadn't I remembered it? Sometimes we are mysteries to ourselves.

"And," he went on, "that's when I thought, 'That's my girl. Whatever comes at her, she'll be able to handle it.' My little Lumen."

He put his open hand on the side of my face, and I leaned my head into it a little bit.

I went to school, and my head was filled with that story all day. It wasn't until many hours later that I realized something.

He hadn't actually answered my question.

—

AFTER SCHOOL THAT same day, as I was riding my bike home, Peter met me by the side of the road.

"Come on," he said. The way he said it was not nice at all.

"Where are we going?"

"Just follow me."

His parents had given him an old Volkswagen on his sixteenth birthday, and it was parked a little way down a side road. He got in, started the engine, and waited for me to join him.

Sometimes people wonder why they do the things they do. I don't wonder. He was Peter Meechum, whom all the girls love, and I was nobody, whom nobody loved. He had given me a command, and I was particularly good at obeying commands. And I had never been invited into his car before. So I went.

I hid my bike in the trees by the road and got into the car. The interior smelled of rust and oil.

He drove into the woods, then turned off the tarmac onto a dirt road. It was cloudy, and there were no shadows on the ground. Everything looked flat, too close. You could suffocate on the grayness of the world. The road was unmaintained. Weeds grew up between the tire tracks, and deep divots jostled my body about inside the vehicle. A weathered road sign lay in the tall sumac, half buried by hard dirt. It announced that the road was a dead end. But everybody knew it was a dead end. Even I knew where this road led.

I looked at Peter, but his gaze remained sternly forward.

Soon the trees opened up, and the dusty sun shone down on the wide expanse of the quarry. Peter brought the car to a stop and shut off the engine. I wondered if he would force me to walk into the mine just as Rose had forced Hondy Pilt to do the year before. But he said nothing. The only thing to be heard was the wind groaning in the trees.

He opened his door and got out, and I got out, too.

"This way," he said.

I followed him around the rim of the quarry to a small grove where the streamlet from the mountain above collected into three small pools before continuing down into the mine. There was a grassy clearing in the grove, and when you were in it you felt protected and safe. That day, though, it was cold. A sharp breeze made a whistling sound through the grove. I shrugged myself deeper into my coat and crossed my arms over my chest.

"Now what?" I said.

"Lay down."

"How come?"

"Because I'm going to have sex with you."

The expression on his face was determined and dire.

When I didn't move at all, he took me by the shoulders and led me to the place where he wanted me to lie. Then he exerted a slight pressure with his hands, almost nothing, really, and down my body went as if by mystical coercion. Maybe he had magic-spell words, too, that he used to cast conjurations. You cannot always understand boys, the things they do. They act, sometimes, as though in thrall to severe but natural forces. They can be waterfalls or wind gusts.

I sat down at first, then he gave me another little push, and I lay back. The dry autumn grass tickled my neck. I stared up into the gray sky, circumscribed by the tops of needled evergreens. It felt like the sky was particularly low that day—a ceiling you could almost reach up and brush your fingers across.

Then Peter stood over me, looking down at me as though he were a giant and I was a poor little farmer at the bottom of a bean stalk.

"I'm going to have sex with you," he said again.

"No," I said—because that seemed to be the thing I was supposed to say.

"You said I was ugly."

"No," I said again. I wanted to reach up and run my fingertips across the sky. I thought it must be silky and lush. Maybe my hand would sink into it. I was no longer cold.

He kneeled down and leaned over me.

"Take off your pants," he said.

"No," I said. I could hear my voice saying it. It was a charming voice—I was charmed by it. I could hear myself saying it in the space between the trees. My voice there between those leaves that fretted and shivered.

Then Peter was unzipping my pants and tugging them over my narrow hips. When he got them to my ankles, he realized he had to take my shoes off as well, so he wrenched them off without untying the laces. It was a very awkward process, and I felt sorry for him—and I kept laughing inwardly at the girl whose body was being turned this way and that.

He must have gotten my underpants off, too, because I could feel the reedy grass tickling my bare bottom.

So there it was. The whole thing. The low ceiling of the sky above, the ticklish sumac beneath, and me sandwiched between the two, my bare lower half looking like a ridiculously pale chicken leg, I suppose, one sock tugged partly off my foot like a floppy dog ear.

Peter unbuckled his own pants and took them off. His underpants were plaid. He stood over me.

"Are you going to do it?" I asked.

"Do you want me to?"

"No."

"It's happening anyway."

"Okay."

He moved my legs apart and kneeled down between them. At first he just examined me with his eyes. Then he fell on me and started moving against my body. His muscles were rigid, his weight on me like a load of lumber pressing me to the ground. They were lurching movements, spasms of anguished effort. He did not kiss me at all. Before there had been lots of kisses and not much else. This was the reverse of that. So maybe kisses were the opposite of sex. Maybe they were the birth of the death of sex.

I thought, *It is happening. This is happening,* thinking, *All our days add up to one day, and then they become something else. The point on the number line where negative becomes positive. The future the mirror image of your past — everything contingent on this moment here, the great, holy zero. My zero to his one. My nothing to his something.*

It was happening. I was waiting for it to happen. I could feel his movements, rough, even angry, against the skin of my thighs. There was a certain pleasure in not having to do anything — in having everything done for you while you just waited. He struggled away, and I waited and felt the warm, stinging chafe of his efforts.

I waited. I knew to expect the pressure of him between my legs, but there was no pressure. Then everything stopped.

For a moment there was an expression on his face of physical industry — vulgar, beautiful things flitting through a heated boy-mind. But then his eyes met mine, and that strange violent desire drained out of his gaze. Instead of falling on top of me, he stood back up.

"Never mind," he said.

I sat up, suddenly embarrassed by my nakedness.

"What happened?" I said. The sky now seemed very far away, measureless compared to how small I felt.

"Nothing happened," he said. "Never mind. You said no."

He was shifting nervously.

"You couldn't do it," I said. It wasn't an accusation. It was something I was realizing aloud.

"I could have," he said. "I didn't. You said no."

I reached for my pants, which were all balled up in the weeds. I put them on, and neither of us said anything.

We drove in silence back to where my bike was stashed. He stopped and waited for me to get out. But I didn't get out.

"You couldn't do it," I said. I didn't want to cry in front of him again, but I could hear the tremor in my voice. "You couldn't even if you tried. I'm a nun."

"You're not a nun."

"Yes, I am. I'm a nun, and nobody wants a nun. Nobody dreams about nuns."

"You're not," he said, but his voice was tired, unconvincing. He just wanted to be away from me.

It was too late. In the woods, for a moment, he had been an animal, he had functioned by beast logic. Now, again, he was just a boy. Was it just that he wasn't able to be the bad man, no matter how hard he tried? Or was I the one responsible for his transformation? Was I the antidote for breaching?

Did I ensnare what the breaching set free?

———

WHEN I TAKE my son to preschool, Miss Lily, his teacher, takes me aside and tells me that he has been having discipline issues and that the day before it was necessary to separate him from the other children for a while.

As she speaks, I watch my boy run forward to greet his

friends. He seems happy enough. Though I know that signifies nothing. I know how love and hate grow from the same seed.

"I mean," Miss Lily goes on, "I'm sure it's not something to worry about. Usually it's only a form of expression. We just need to work on redirecting it. But, again, I don't see it as a reason for real concern, Mrs. Borden."

She knows me as Ann Borden. I used to be Lumen Ann Fowler. Then I left the town where I grew up and I became Ann Fowler to signify that I was a different person. Then I married Jack Borden and became Ann Borden. A life of vestiges.

"Mrs. Borden?" she says again.

"Oh, yes, thank you."

When I leave, I drive across town to the high school where my husband works. I am a good driver. I obey all the traffic signs. I am always respectful to pedestrians, with their breakable bodies.

I do not use the school parking lot when I arrive. Instead I park around the corner and walk to the side of the main building, where Jack's office has a window that looks out on a large grassy expanse with trees and benches and fiberglass picnic tables. I sit at one of the benches, where I can see into his window. His back is facing me, and I can see that he is hunched over his desk, scribbling away industriously. The hair on the back of his neck is closely cropped. Sometimes he has me do touch-ups with a pair of clippers after he comes home from the barbershop. The skin of his neck is burned slightly from standing in the hot weekend sun, watering the front lawn.

I sit on the bench cross-legged. The advantage of my spot is that it is behind the large trunk of an oak tree, so if he should ever turn to look out the window, I can simply lean back and be completely hidden.

When people enter his office, Jack stands and greets them.

Then he waits for them to sit before he does. His adult colleagues smile a lot when they are in his office — he must be a charming man. When his At-Risk students come in, they sometimes fidget, and their heads swivel twitchily. Jack leans back in his chair in these situations.

I pick at the bark of the oak tree while I watch. Underneath is smooth, supple pulp.

When the students begin to talk, I notice that he nods a lot and listens with his head a little sideways — as though his brain were weighed down with the careful consideration of their words. The students seem to respond well to it.

I try it, there on my bench. I angle my head on the pivot of my neck as though carrying the weight of big thought.

A sparrow whistles overhead.

A little later the tough girl, Nat, comes into his office. She sits with her arms crossed and glares at him. Once I think she sees me watching, but she doesn't say anything about it. I know the look on her face. She wants to rip away at things. I know the tips of her fingers tremble like eager claws.

I pick at the bark of my tree.

At home that evening, I listen to Jack speak of his day. I nod and hold my head at an angle while I'm listening, but I must not be doing it right, because he says, "What are you doing?"

I tell him that I'm just listening.

"You feeling all right?" he asks. "You're acting funny again."

I tell him nothing is the least bit wrong. I ask him if he would like more potatoes.

After dinner I wash the dishes in water so hot it scalds the skin of my hands. I think about Peter Meechum and the quarry. I think about the body of that little girl who was me, lying there in the tall grass. Someone knotted up in confusion, always.

———

THE WEEK AFTER Peter Meechum took me to the quarry, the snow came, and I began to wonder if maybe I was a saint—one of those people whom badness slips right off of. People like to talk about ducks and water, about how the two repel each other. Really, it's that ducks have oily feathers. So maybe my pores leaked holy oil. My father also told me that some places have competitions in which young men try to capture greased pigs. That's me, a holy greased pig, slickering away out of the fumbling hands of evil.

Peter stopped coming to my house, and he didn't look at me in school. He was angry at me for being too good to rape. Saints are nobody's favorite people.

The first snow of the year came on a night when there was no moon at all. It was dark as anything, and so quiet all you could hear was the hum of your own thoughts. The snow came six minutes after two o'clock. It fell faintly in the cones of lamplight, descending like fleets of fairies through the cold sky. I was awake—the only one in town, I was sure—and I was sure that those miniature fallen sylphs were for me and my personal delectation. They came for me, because nature likes a saint. They settled on my windowsill, they collected on the dark grass of my lawn, they danced and whirled in the wind gusts before my eyes. I put my hand to the windowpane to greet it, that first snow. By the time I woke in the morning, I saw that after the snow had come to me, it had visited everyone.

That afternoon I stayed in the library after school reading about saints in order to know better what I was up against. A few saints got teamed up with the divines for some help—like Zita, who compelled the angels to bake bread for her. But as it turned out, the world was for the most part unkind to saints. Some of them were derided, including Saint Pyr, who, as far as I could tell, didn't do much to deserve sainthood. The only thing he ever really did was fall down a well.

Then there was Alice, who suffered a life of agony because of physical ailments. She had leprosy, and she also went blind. The only comfort she received was in the form of communion. But even in that respect she suffered. She could eat the bread, but she was banned from drinking from the Eucharistic cup because of her contagious maladies. But she had visions, and in one of her visions, Jesus came and told her everything was okay.

Lucy had her eyes gouged out, and she carried them around on a tray. But she was honored with a feast, which used to take place on the shortest day of the year, but then got moved to December thirteenth. Girls cooked buns with raisins in the middle to look like eyes and carried them on trays. I promised myself to remember Saint Lucy and her dug-out eyes on the thirteenth of December.

Another saint, named Drogo, was so hideously deformed that no one could stand to look at him. He imprisoned himself in a cell and ate only grain and water. But there was something called bilocation, which meant that he could be in two places at once. Some people said they could see him harvesting the fields even though he was locked away in his jail. I wondered if his spectral self, the one doing the harvesting, looked any better.

I discovered that there was a saint named Illuminata, like Lumen, but I couldn't find anything else about her other than that there was a church dedicated to her in Italy.

Apollonia was treated particularly brutally. The heathens bashed out all her teeth. They threatened to burn her alive, but she didn't give them the chance to do it — she escaped from them long enough to throw herself into the fire of her own accord. She was a saint, though, so she didn't burn. The flames had no effect on her. But the story doesn't end there. Heathens, shown evidence of their wrongdoing, don't fall to their knees to beg the Lord's forgiveness. They remained undeterred. They dragged Apollonia out of the fire and decapitated her.

Here's another interesting case — Saint Etheldreda. She was known, commonly, as Saint Audrey, which is where the word tawdry comes from. See, after she died, women took to selling lacy garments in her name. Tawdries were sanctified things, holy garments. Then the Puritans came along and started looking down on cheap indulgences such as lace, so the word changed its meaning. Which just goes to show how you can't do anything to protect your reputation when Puritans get involved — or heathens, either, for that matter.

My favorite saint, however, must have been Osgyth. She was married to a king, even though she didn't want to be. She bore him a son, as was her duty — but then when her husband was away hunting a white deer, she ran off to the convent to become a nun. The white deer. That was important. Whenever they specified the color of something, it was important. I wondered what the white deer symbolized. Something worthwhile, I hoped, because the king lost his wife in the pursuit of it.

Anyway, she was killed at the hands of Vikings, and at the place where she was killed a spring erupted from the earth and continues to give water to this day. The tears of a saint, flooding the land. You could drink them up.

Like Apollonia, Osgyth had her head cut off. But a moment after she died, her body sprang back up (like her tears from the earth itself!). She picked up her own head and carried it to the nearby convent, where she finally collapsed.

This was not, so it seems, an uncommon occurrence among martyrs. There's a whole category of saints who carried their own heads around after death. There's even a name for them. They're called cephalophoric martyrs.

Walking home through the drifts of new snow, I thought about that image. I thought about it over dinner, when my father asked me why I was being so tacit that evening. I couldn't stop thinking about it that day or the day after that or the next day—or ever.

My virginity, my saintliness, like the new snow you hate yourself for tromping on. What saints do, I realized, is make everyone else aware of their lowliness. You were simply about the regular business of your day until the saint walks by and makes you reckon with your true state as a bristly animal wallowing in its own filth. That's why everyone attacks the saints' bodies—to prove they have them and are anchored by them. But what the stories tell us is that they're not.

Peter Meechum had wanted to prove my frail, chafable, blisterable bodiedness. But there I lay under the afternoon sky—like a floating fairy or an ephemeral saint, smiling with her head removed and looking on from somewhere else entirely.

But what about the saint herself? Does she miss it—that puny tag of a body, with all its feeble, quaking pains and pleasures?

I still see it when I close my eyes—Osgyth, her neck a stump on her shoulders, feeling around blindly on the ground until she finds the toppled loaf of her own head, carrying it with effort across the fields to the convent.

What is a body without a mind? A slave to the feral instincts of ugly nature. An inelegant organ of gristle and stupid mechanics.

But also, what is a mind without a body?

It is a useless curd, lost in the mud. Or a pathetic piece of jetsam, bobbing in the spring-lake of its own tears.

———

NOW IT'S TIME to talk about Blackhat Roy Ruggle, who was no good.

I remember how he was in grade school, runty and dark, the teachers leaning away from him with sour expressions on their faces. I remember him cursing them under his breath, seeming very mature in his primal anger. It never occurred to me as strange, back then, that I equated obscenity with adulthood—as though we all grow inevitably toward the twisted and grotesque. Later, in high school, the administration tolerated him with weary resignation, because it was well known that his father had left when he was only two years old, that his mother was a drunk who survived on state aid, that the two of them lived in a shack with a sagging roof on the edge of town, and that he worked in a scrap yard in order to make money to buy things like cigarettes and booze—things that stank of angry manhood.

He came to school dirty, his clothes torn, his shoes tattered and repaired with duct tape, his hair unwashed. There was no fight he backed away from, no conflict he did not lick his lips at. It made no difference how big or small his opponents were—he gnashed his teeth and spit out vulgarities and burned himself bright and hot into a cindered black punk. Teachers avoided him because they knew their authority wouldn't sway him. Younger kids avoided him because they knew their weakness wouldn't, either.

No one was surprised when he breached early. No one was surprised that his breach lasted longer by far than anyone else's.

He had always been part animal, and he needed no moon to tell him that.

Me, I avoided him—which was not difficult. Our worlds had nothing to do with each other.

Until the day they did.

After the day in the woods with Peter, I had spent the next couple weeks mostly alone. I wore white as much as I could—because it was the color of sainthood and it was the color of the deer that Osgyth's king hunted and it was the color of the snow descending everywhere around me.

In school I saw that Polly spent more time with the boys who had already gone breach. They would often have her pressed in a corner of the stairwell or against the lockers, their bodies flush with hers. Sometimes Polly seemed embarrassed to be squished between these boys and the lockers—but other times she gazed at the ceiling with half-lidded eyes, and I could see that she was lost to them.

"Do you have a boyfriend now?" I asked her in French class.

"Oui et non," she said. "C'est compliqué."

"Are you happy?"

"Personne n'est heureux."

"Some people are. Some people are happy."

My voice pleaded with her to be again the Polly I had known just a year or two before.

But that Polly seemed to be gone for good. This one, the one who got put into reveries by being pressed up against lockers, slammed her book closed and shrugged.

"Not everything is about white picket fences," she said. "Portes blanches."

"Clôtures."

Mrs. Farris, our French teacher, looked over at us. I looked down at the passage I was supposed to be translating. When it was safe again, I looked at Polly. I apologized with my eyes, but with her eyes she told me that I didn't understand, that it was not the business of saints to stand too close to the vulgarity of real life. She told me with her eyes to stay wrapped in my white shrouds.

It was on that same day that I saw Blackhat Roy backed up against a wall in the alcove under the stairs by Peter and some of his friends. Such conflicts were never my concern—I was mostly concerned about avoiding Peter, who was facing Roy and not me. Out of the corner of my eye, though, I saw that Roy had fixed me in his gaze, as though I were more interesting than the group of boys threatening to assault him.

"If you're going to do it," I overheard him saying, "just do it, and shut the fuck up about it."

Even as he said the words, he was watching me rather than them.

I rushed around the corner out of his sight. I didn't know what his gaze meant, but I wanted to get out from under it.

It was later that day that Blackhat Roy spoke to me for the first time in my life. It was at the bike cage, where he leaned against the chain-link enclosure—it bowed with his weight. I walked by, trying to be nothing to him, trying to reduce myself.

"Hey," he said. "Come here."

I went over to where he stood.

I flinched when he reached out to me, but he just tugged at the white ribbon in my hair.

"What are you trying to look like?" he said.

"Nothing." This was untrue. We are all, in one way or another, trying to look like something—but we don't like to be called on it.

"You look like a Creamsicle."

"Creamsicles are orange, not white," I said victoriously. Then I chanced to look down and see that I had worn my orange winter jacket over my white cotton dress and white stockings. "Oh."

He tilted his head to the side and seemed to examine me. Then he leaned forward toward my neck and inhaled deeply.

"You haven't gone warg yet. You're late."

I said nothing. I wanted to run.

"Can you feel it? I remember—I could feel it growing in me before it came. Like a tumor or something. A sick feeling in your stomach. Your guts all rolling around. Then it came, and I wasn't scared anymore. Are you looking forward to not being scared?"

He did not wait for a response from me. He seemed to have something in his teeth, and he rolled his tongue around in his mouth until he got it. He plucked it out with two fingers and held it up to look at. It was a piece of pink gristle from the school meat loaf at lunch. He flicked it away and returned his gaze to me.

"Me," he said, "I'm fourteen months already. Longer than anyone else. Maybe I'll never come out the other end. That happens sometimes, you know. Sometimes you stay breach your whole life."

"I never heard of that."

He shrugged.

"Sometimes," I said, "sometimes people don't breach at all. They just skip it."

"Now we've both never heard of something."

Behind me I was aware that two freshman girls were walking across the parking lot. Roy grew silent, and his hyena eyes watched them until they were out of sight.

He leaned back and wound his fingers around the chain link

101

over his shoulders. This is where I'll admit that I'd never really looked at Blackhat Roy before. He'd always been an abstraction to me, like big human notions such as horror and courage and mortification. But now he was forcing me to look at him, all of him. Some people, when they're breaching, don't quite get back to their regular selves when the full moon is gone. For some, like Roy, their breacher sensibility follows them into the daylight, throughout the month, the entire year. This was the worst kind of breacher when the full moon rose—and between moons, even during the daylight, you could still see the feral radiance behind the eyes.

He had grown bigger—I never really noticed it until now. He was no longer the runty creature I remembered from grade school. He had a thick mop of curly hair that fell down over his wide brow. He was dark, and it looked like he needed to shave. When he drew his hand across his jawline, you could hear a gristly static. His teeth were crooked, and the way his lips curled into a smile made you feel complicit in all sorts of crimes—things you didn't even have names for.

His hands, wrapped around the metal ligatures of the cage, were scarred and dirty and short-fingered. The nails were worn down to almost nothing and one of them was ripped off completely, as though he had paws made for digging, hands for labor or violence.

"How come you didn't save me today?" he said. "How come you didn't rescue me?"

"I don't know."

"How come you didn't keep your boyfriend from attacking?"

I said nothing.

"Is it because you figured I deserved it? Because you thought I must've done something wrong? Is that the reason?"

I shivered, and my throat tried to close up. I didn't know what would happen to me.

"Yes," I said quietly.

"Well, you're right. Did you know it's considered bad manners to take a piss in somebody's locker? I guess we learn through our mistakes."

"I didn't do anything," I said, my voice pleading.

"Didn't you?" His teeth gnashed, and for a second I thought he would use them to rip my throat out. I would have run, but I was pinned in a way that was a mystery to me. "Guess what. I may be rotten, but I ain't the only one. I know it was you."

"What?"

"You pulled the fire alarm that one time. You did it. And I know why. Did you think I forgot about that?"

I didn't know what to say to him, this furious and filthy golem of a boy. What could possibly be shared between us, apart from fear and calamity? I wanted to be away from him—I wanted him back in his cell in the abstract part of my brain, where I could trace him in the safe trigonometric functions of my daily life. But he wouldn't go. Maybe he would do what Peter couldn't. Maybe he would attack. Even here at school, because the boundaries of wilderness and civilization were nothing to Blackhat Roy. I closed my eyes and waited for whatever would come.

"Don't worry," he said after a while. "Probably I won't hurt you. I don't get much joy out of hunting down defenseless animals. Not much."

He unleaned himself from the fence, stretched himself to his full length, and rotated his head quickly in a way that produced an audible crack in his neck. He started away, and I thought everything was over between us—but then, before he had walked very far, he turned back.

"But when you go warg," he said, "then you better watch out. Because I think I'd like to chomp on you a little." He smiled when he said it, as though he wanted me not to fear his threats but to savor them.

I didn't move until he was completely out of sight, then I got my bike from the cage and rode home fast. The icy air blasted my face, but I was not cold. My lungs burned sulfur, and I wanted to cry, but the tears wouldn't come. When I got home, I showered—and in my stomach, I could feel the deep bowl of my guts. They sloshed around as though I had all the violent seas of the world inside me.

CHAPTER 4

Just as the streets of our little town were plowed, another snow came and buried us again. People speculated that we were in for a rough winter. The lake froze early, and it froze wide. That year ice skaters could go farther out than they ever had before. I went skating myself, but I went in the early morning, when nobody else was there. I did spins and twirls, and I thought I must be the most elegant sight, a lone skater in the sunrise. When others began to show up, I glided to the shore and sat on a stone to remove my skates. They would always be surprised to see me. Their thought was to have been the first—but they weren't. Sometimes things work that way.

Peter continued to avoid me. And Polly spoke to me as though I were a child—when she spoke to me at all. As soon as the final bell of the school day rang, I rushed home to avoid any further contact with Blackhat Roy, whose eyes seemed to track me in the halls from one room to the next. I had somehow wandered into his domain, and now I couldn't escape. Once I had lamented being invisible, but now there was nothing I de-

sired more than to be out from under his gaze. He seemed to
know when I came into a room, because his head would swivel
on his neck and those dark eyes of his would nail me to a wall.
Even in the cafeteria, swarming with hundreds of moving bodies, echoing with a constant din—even there, when I walked
through the doors, I could see that dusky, scabrous face of his
looking through the crowd at me, a still-pale petal in an algae-
covered pond.

. So instead of looking things up in the library after school,
where I knew I'd be discovered, I took my books to the deserted
school auditorium and studied there.

I was very much enamored with maps that year. Maybe it
was because my father was a geologist and was always looking at
elaborate technical diagrams that made earthly landscapes look
like strange outlined amoebas on the page. I sometimes thumbed
through his books, tracing the curved lines with my finger. But
really my interest was in conventional maps. I looked them up in
old atlases. I followed their legends, exploring—mistaking, perhaps, the paper on which the world was printed for the actual
world itself. I read books that had maps printed on their endpapers. As the events of the book unfolded, I would turn back
to the endpapers and locate them on the map. I liked how the
linear progression of time over the course of a novel could be
condensed into a single map image, as though it were all said and
done before the book even started—as though all of any person's
life could be reduced to just a legend explaining some fixed map
we could not see.

I drew maps in my notebooks during class. Sometimes simple
maps showing the spatial relationships of the students in a classroom, maybe with arrows illustrating their various kinds of connections. Or sometimes complex maps of the entire school

building, featuring dotted lines that traced my regular routes from class to class.

My father liked my maps. He said they showed a unique mind, the kind of mind that existed above itself and was able to see itself in context. Context, he said, was a very important thing. So I said the word to myself thirteen times that night before I went to bed, and it became one more in my arsenal of magic words.

What I was working on that day, sprawled on the warm wooden floor of the empty stage, was going to be a Christmas present for my father. It was a very large and detailed map of the town and all the places in it that were significant to the two of us. Like the drive-in where we used to see movies but didn't, for some reason, anymore. Like the tree in the cemetery under which my mother lies buried. Or the exact place on the freeway where we almost got into an accident and he had to pull over on the shoulder and tell me how much he loved me, how much more than anything else in the world I meant to him. I know it was a strange one to include, but it made sense in my unique mind, and I believed he would understand.

I made our house the center of the map. I drew it in pencil first and then in fine black pen to get as much detail as possible. You could even see into the upstairs window of the house if you cared to look. And there, framed in the window, was the teensy-tiny figure of a girl standing before an easel, drawing a map.

It was nice there in the musty auditorium, the sound of my scratching pencil echoey in the large space, the heavy, muffling curtains hanging loose over the hard wood. The moving air from the vents ruffled them slightly, and they rippled like vertical oceans. I liked the rows of unpopulated seats staring at me, their lower halves all folded up except one on the aisle that was broken and remained always open, a poor busted tooth in that grinning mouth. There is nothing to fear in such cavernous and sepulchral spaces. You fill them with the riots of your imagination.

Absorbed as I was in my map, I hadn't heard Mr. Hunter enter from backstage and leaped up when he spoke to me.

"What's that you're doing?"

"Nothing," I said and quickly gathered my materials, clutching my map to my chest. "Working. There's no play practice tonight." I knew the schedule, you see. I liked to know in advance where people would be and where they wouldn't be.

He stood with his hands in his pockets, gazing at me with a foreign, unreadable expression. Under a tweed jacket, he wore a button-down shirt that had come a little untucked over the course of the day. He looked younger than my father, but I couldn't tell by how much. He had told us that he grew up in a small town outside Chicago, and I had always wondered why someone from Chicago would come to a town like ours. He had a ragged growth of stubble on his chin, and his eyes always looked like they knew more than he was telling.

"You know," he said, "I've been wanting to talk with you."

"What about?"

"What do you think about trying out for the play?"

"Me? I can't act."

"Everybody can act," he said, shrugging. "Everybody *does* act."

I didn't know what to say.

"The best kinds of actors are the ones who perform so often—so religiously—that they don't even realize they're do-ing it."

"I guess," I said.

He would not take his eyes from mine for a long while, and I found I couldn't take mine off his, either—as though some un-breakable current connected our brains.

Finally he breathed in deeply, stretched, and looked up into the rafters.

"Anyway," he said, "think about it. All acting is just lying. You know how to lie, don't you?"

I said goodbye and rushed out as quickly as I dared. The sun had gone down, and the overhead lamps had buzzed on in the deserted parking lot.

Everybody else believed they could see my very soul. So why did I feel so blind?

———

IT'S TRUE THAT I am a Christmas baby—or at least close enough to count as one. I was born on December 23, Christmas Eve Eve, and so I am one of that breed for whom the celebration of existence gets irrevocably tangled up with garlands and lighted trees and window displays. No one likes a Christmas baby. The occasion requires that people purchase two different kinds of wrapping paper. It is too much celebration altogether, and it makes people queasy with indulgence.

Throughout my young life, my father did his best to make my birthday special—so we never put up a Christmas tree until Christmas Eve, the day after my birthday. There was no talk of the holiday at all until that day.

This year was special, because it was my sixteenth birthday, and sixteenth birthdays put you in a different category from the one you were in before. In the morning, my father told me we could do anything my little heart desired. But actually I was feeling a bit unwell, and all I really wanted to do was stay indoors and make pizza and watch movies on television and pretend that the world outside didn't exist.

"Done and done," he said and made me waffles.

Then he brought me a little wrapped box and dropped it on the table in front of me.

"I've been saving it for you for a long time," he said.

I undid the wrapping paper at the taped seams (I'm not one of those people who tear through wrapping paper willy-nilly, as though ferocity of consumption equaled appreciation of a gift) and set it aside. It was a jewelry box, and inside sat a little silver locket with floral engravings on the outside.

"It belonged to your mother," said my father. To look at it seemed to pain him. "I gave it to her when we were sixteen. Now I'm giving it to you."

Inside there were two pictures that kissed when the locket was closed. One was of my mother and the other was of my father—both when they were my age.

"Her name was Felicia Ann Steptoe," he said, reciting the bedtime catechism from my childhood, "and she wore long orchid gloves at our wedding."

It occurred to me on that day that my mother was actually closer to me than if I had been old enough to remember her when she died. She existed entirely in my own brain—she was that close. She was lovely inside there, always posing, always beautiful. She was happy as could be.

I thanked my father for the present, throwing my arms around him and hugging him so tightly he pretended to choke.

"Now you just relax while I do the breakfast dishes," he said.

"Wait," I said. "I need to know something."

"What's that?"

"What time was I born? I mean, exactly."

"It was in the morning some time. I don't remember."

"Is it on my birth certificate?"

"I'm sure it probably is."

"Can we check?"

"On this day, we seek to indulge," he said, wiping his hands on a kitchen towel.

He went to the closet in his office and thumbed through the file cabinets to find what he was looking for. I followed him and sat in his desk chair, watching.

Eventually he found the manila folder he was looking for.

"Ta-da," he said.

Then he took a pale green document out of the folder and scanned it quickly with his eyes.

"Let's see," he said. "Here it is. Eight thirty-two, ante meridian."

I looked at my watch. It was half past nine.

"Congratulations," he said. "You're officially sixteen years old."

So it was true. I was a year older but still periodless.

I was officially a lot of things. Sixteen was only one of them.

———

THE DAY AFTER my birthday was Christmas Eve, and it also happened to be the first night of Lake Moon. There would be no carolers this Christmas, no midnight masses at the church. This would be a Christmas to stay indoors.

My father and I had much to do, since our preparations for the holiday only began that morning. We got up early and picked out a tree from the Christmas tree farm by the freeway. It was my job to stand back and determine its straightness while he secured it in the metal stand in our living room. We decorated and drank eggnog. We sang along to "Good King Wenceslas," which was our favorite Christmas song—and, as far as I have been able to tell, nobody else's favorite Christmas song in the world.

> *Good King Wenceslas looked out*
> *On the feast of Stephen,*
> *When the snow lay round about*
> *Deep and crisp and even.*
> *Brightly shone the moon that night,*
> *Though the frost was cruel,*
> *When a poor man came in sight*
> *Gathering winter fuel.*

We sat together across our small dining room table, and we drank cinnamon-scented mulled wine that had been heated in a saucepan on the stove. My father put a stick of raw cinnamon in each one—and even though the wine did not taste good to me, I liked to be drinking it with him, watching the steam rise from the crystal goblets set on the red tablecloth I insisted on using for the occasion.

After dinner my father put on a Motown Christmas album, and we danced together to "I Saw Mommy Kissing Santa Claus," and then we lit a candle for Felicia Ann Steptoe and put it in the window, without somberness, to invite her ghost to visit.

There were very few presents under the tree, but they were all labeled carefully nonetheless. We made sure that some of them—both for him and for me—were labeled "From Santa," because Santa Claus was the invisible third guest at our miniature holiday. The truth is, we made our aloneness into a gift and gave that gift to each other, and it was our true and main present to unwrap.

I ate fewer frosted sleigh-shaped Christmas cookies than I normally did, because my stomach was still bothering me. So I went to bed early and turned on the radio to be lulled to sleep by "Have Yourself a Merry Little Christmas"—and also to drown out before I even heard them the sounds that might be coming from outside. This was a holy night, a peaceful night, and I would not indulge those wild creatures in the street—not even for a second.

———

IT WAS WELL after midnight when I woke up. At first I thought it was the cramping in my gut that had woken me—I thought for sure my period had finally come. But then, surfacing into consciousness, I realized that the voice I was hearing in my ears was actually coming from outside, that it was the voice of Polly. She called to me from the pitchy night.

"Lumen! Lumen, help me!"

I got out of bed, drew the curtains aside, and opened the window.

The first thing I noticed was the quality of the air that blew into the house. It was frigid in my lungs, but it made me feel much better than I had been feeling over the past couple days, and I made a resolution to get more fresh air than I had been getting.

Polly was there, standing just below my window in the front yard. Strange, I thought, that the last time Polly came and stood under my window Peter was sleeping in the den two doors down and knew nothing of it at all. Now he was somewhere out there among them.

Polly looked roughed up. There were bruises on her face, little abrasions all over the pale skin of her chest.

She was naked, her legs lost to midcalf in the snowbank. As part of my research, I had been made to understand that breachers did not feel the cold the way other people did. I was told that their blood ran hotter during those nights. A girl of science, a daughter of facts, I hadn't entirely believed it until now. Like a beech tree, Polly's frail white body was planted, unshivering, in the snow, her breath coming in visible puffs between her bleeding lips, her skin varicolored by the string of blinking Christmas lights hung on the eaves of the house. While she may have been hurting from her injuries, it seemed the cold was nothing to her.

"Lumen," she said from the pool of lamplight in the street, "please."

"What do you want?" I called down in a quiet voice. The night below was utterly silent.

"Lumen, I miss you," she said. "Remember how we used to be?"

"What are you doing here?"

"It's Christmas Eve, Lumen. I'm hungry. My mother used to make me pancakes in the shape of elephants on Christmas morning."

Her mind was gone wild, her panicked eyes darting from one thing to another.

"Are you all right?" I said.

She sat down in the snowbank and pulled her knees to her chest, rocking back and forth slightly. She mumbled something I couldn't hear.

"What? What did you say?"

"My turn," she said. "They said it was my turn. Sometimes you bleed others, and sometimes you get bled. That's the way. It hurts, Lumen. Apples and cheese—I used to eat them when they were cut up for me. I used to be pretty."

"Who did it? Who hurt you?"

She looked up at me, confused.

"They did," she said simply. "All of them."

It made me feel sick to see her that way, but also angry. I found myself hating her a little also, despising her for being so frail outside my window. She made life — our lives — seem meager.

I could feel the spite bubbling up in me. It felt strange but good.

And then it was gone as quickly as it came, because below me Polly seemed to hear something that startled her. She stood suddenly and looked around.

"What is it?" I called down to her.

But she was no longer listening to me. Tensed like a threatened cat, she ran a few steps one way, stopped, listened some more, then ran a few steps in another direction and stopped again.

"What's happening?" I said. "Polly."

Her breath was coming faster now, and she ran toward the sidewalk and the street beyond.

"Polly, wait!"

I hurried out of my room and down the stairs as quietly as I could, so as not to wake my father, down the hall.

I opened the front door, and it occurred to me again that the blast of bitter night air was a relief. I was overheated, my heart going like crazy, my pulse driving in my ears, and the air seemed blissful and calming. I wondered, in some still part of my frenzied brain, if this was the same beatified air Jesus was born into so many years ago in his little desert manger.

Polly was no longer in the front yard. Now she stood in the middle of the street, her legs bent in a half crouch, poised to run for her life at any moment. But the street was empty. I leaned out the door and looked, and I saw nothing. She was spooked.

I felt bad about the little flare of intolerance I'd had for her just a few minutes before. She was damaged. She needed help.

"Polly," I called in a whisper, which was as loud as I dared.

She seemed to hear me, because she turned her gaze in my direction for one little moment—a crisis moment of longing and sorrow, regret and fear—then she turned again and ran as fast she could down the street.

"Polly," I called again, louder this time, but she didn't come back.

I took a few steps outside, and then a few more. It's a funny thing, sometimes, what we find ourselves doing. I observed myself as I walked, as though watching the actions of a character on television. *Oh, isn't it interesting what she's doing. I wouldn't have expected that of her.* When I came again into my own mind, I realized I was standing in the middle of the snowy street in my pajamas and my bare feet.

I couldn't see Polly anywhere. It was just me under the hazy, big Lake Moon. I turned this way and that, and the only sound I heard was that of my bare feet shifting against the icy surface of the road.

I wondered about that—my feet—and why they didn't seem to sting from the frozen pavement. I looked back at my house, and it seemed smaller from the outside than it was from the inside—like a puzzle that strained your mind to think about.

In the sudden quiet of the empty night, I thought what a curiously wide place the world was—that you could stand in your nightclothes in the middle of a street and be quite, quite alone.

And then something else happened. It started to snow. They were gentle, quiet little flakes, like the dust or pollen of another season. I raised my arm and saw the snow collect on my skin, glistening along all the fine, light hairs.

You find glory in the strangest places.

I guess I wasn't entirely surprised by what happened next. I guess I wasn't. My body told me I had already known.

They came out from behind the trees in the woods across the street from my house. They had been watching me, you see. They had been there the whole time—that was what had Polly so spooked. They came out slowly, their pale bodies steaming in the cold, their skin taut and waxy against the wooded void.

I did not retreat to the house. I watched myself not retreating to the house. It was a wonder.

They came and stood in a circle around me. Rose Lincoln was there, and she approached and stood so close that I could feel her steaming breath on my cheeks.

"You're lost," she said.

The others smiled. They seemed to have difficulty standing still for long. It was all girls. It was the first time I realized they traveled like that sometimes, separated by sex. It was a coven, a brace, a klatch. Marina Donald stood right beyond Rose, and I could see her fists clenching and releasing, eager for something to throttle. Sue Foxworth was there, too, looking distracted. She scratched at herself and gazed off into the woods as though she were already running through them in her mind.

Rose Lincoln took one long, languorous look up and down my body.

"Is this what you wear to bed?" she asked. My pajamas had pink and purple hearts on them. They were cotton. The bottoms had an elastic waistband. The top had buttons down the front. She reached out with her painted nails and undid the top button, then she undid the next.

She seemed to lose interest before the third. She sighed heavily and looked at the sky, the snow falling lightly through the air.

"You keep yourself separate," she said. "Away from us. How come? Is it because you think you're better?"

I tried to respond. I licked the coldness from my lips.

"I don't . . ."

But what did I mean to say? That I didn't keep myself separate? That I didn't know why I kept myself separate? Her accusation felt strange to me, because I had never seen myself as having any agency in my exclusion from the crowd. I was the one excluded by them—I was the one kept at a distance by everybody else.

Wasn't I?

"That's right, you don't," she replied. "You don't. I know you don't. All you are is what you don't."

Suddenly she reached out with both hands and ripped my pajama top open. The remaining buttons popped and clattered to the icy pavement.

The others in the group closed in more tightly around me. Marina and Idabel McCarron were on either side of me. Their laughter was grotesque as they took off my pajama top and let it fall to the ground. Then I was bare-chested before them. Their nudity was nothing—they seemed not to feel it. How could they not feel it? My chest had never been exposed to anyone before. I was aware of it—my own brute nakedness—and my awareness was an excruciating ache that went all up and down my spine.

"She's so small," Sue Foxworth said. The fact that her voice was not accusatory did not comfort me.

Rose Lincoln got closer. She paid no mind to my bare chest. I tried to back away from her, but the girls behind me did not allow escape.

"It's Christmas," Rose said, her voice almost a whisper in my ear. "Don't you want to tear something down?"

I shook my head.

"No," I said. My voice was tiny and unconvincing. I tried it again, stronger. "No."

"No what?" Rose said. "What are you saying no to? Do you have any idea? Or is it just that saying no makes you feel safe?"

I wasn't hearing her. I shook my head and said it over and over: "No, no, no, no."

I came unfrozen and brought my arms up to cover my chest. Then I turned away from Rose and began to push my way through the bodies, feeling against my bare torso their bony protrusions, their ungainly knobs of skin and cartilage, their joints, their breath and fingers. But I made myself into a dart, and I kept pushing through.

They laughed. I could hear them laugh, but only from a great distance.

Behind me, Rose said, "What are you feeling right now, girl? What's your body telling you? Huh? What are you feeling in your guts? In your lungs? In your muscles? Inside those pink pajama pants?"

That's when I broke through. The bodies fell aside, and I stumbled with the sudden lack of restriction. I fell to the asphalt, coming down hard on my hands. Then I was up again, and I was running. But not toward the house. The house was behind me. I was putting everything behind me. I ran down the street in the opposite direction from the one Polly had run. I could hear their voices laughing as I ran. I wanted them behind me, too.

Except they were following. They ran, too, hooting and hollering as they went. They snarled and called out in obscene ways. I thought I could hear Idabel's high-pitched laugh, hysterical, like

119

a mongrel in the gullies. Some of them barked like dogs and gnashed their teeth together as though they would eat me alive if they caught me.

The snow came harder, but I cared nothing about freezing. It felt good, those pinhead flakes against my bare skin. *It is snowing on my body,* I thought in some calm part of my brain. *Snowflakes are melting against my bare skin. Such a strange feeling—so unlikely!*

I ran. I ran past all the houses with their bright, cheerful Christmas decorations, their strings of lights, their plastic Santa Clauses on the front lawns. I ran past the crèche in the Sondersons' yard, the little baby Jesus nested in hay, overlooked by Mary and Joseph and the three wise men with their gifts from far away.

It made me think of the North Star. I would follow it. I would run to it—I would capture it in my hands. Where might it lead me? Were there new messiahs to be found? Or would it just lead me into the wide open—the deserts of wind and black? And I thought that would be all right, too. Running through space like that, feeling as though your legs would never stop working.

They were still behind me, though more distant now.

At the place where the road turned ahead, there was a trail I knew of. It went up over a hill and down into a little valley and then deeper into the woods. It would take me away. To where I didn't know. I didn't care. Away was the only place I wanted to be, and I didn't care what it looked like.

I launched my body up over the embankment and onto the trail, and I kept running. The snow felt like a static charge on my skin—the branches of the trees tore at me—the frozen pebbles of the trail dug into my bare feet. It was nothing. This was nothing. I could breathe right for the first time.

Lumen. There was Lumen, and there were the places people

did not go. And Lumen would go to those places. She would leap over fences and crawl through mud. She would climb up on rooftops and call crazy with every little branch of her lungs.

It was a holy night. I ran. My father slept soundly in his bed, somewhere far behind me, and I ran. Elsewhere in the world masses were being performed and stock was being taken of the glories and regrets of life—and it was nothing to me, because I ran.

My sore legs ached with the same splendid vigor. I relished the soreness, as I did my burning lungs.

I was naked in the woods. It was a beautiful outrage.

I had started running in order to escape Rose Lincoln and her pack. Then I was running to put things decidedly behind me, to seek lovely new emptinesses. Then I ran to outpace the nagging of my ticklish brain. Then I just ran.

II

CHAPTER 5

We live on a cul-de-sac. Our house is at the very end. During the days, when my husband is at work, the cul-de-sac becomes a playground. The mothers sit in front of their houses on lawn chairs and watch their children playing in the dead-end street.

Lola King lives next door. She is from New York and has very little patience for the provinciality of our burg. She has befriended me. She brings her lawn chair to my yard and sets it up next to mine. She also brings a pitcher of frozen daiquiris and two frosted glasses and even paper umbrellas to stick in the top. Her husband got into some sort of trouble back East.

"Cocktail time, darling," she says, a cigarette dangling between her lips.

The other neighbors don't approve. Particularly Marcie Klapper-Witt, who lives three doors down from me. She wears sunglasses so we cannot see that her judgmental gaze is always upon us. Lola raises her glass to toast her.

I smile and am delighted.

The children run in circles. They draw on the pavement with

oversize chalk. They shoot at one another with water guns that look like colorful missile launchers. My son is among them, and to watch him is to acknowledge how impossible it is to stay one thing for your entire life. Much of the time I stare at the clouds.

My son is four years old. He will not run wild and naked in the streets when he becomes a teenager. He will not hack away at the old, tired physical world just to watch it bleed. He will drink to excess with his friends. At most, he will urp up his dinner, drunkenly, on front lawns and then escape in shame. He will fumble awkwardly at the apparatus of girls' bodies. He will be stubborn and recalcitrant. He will slam doors. But he will not run savage through the night, coyote-like, enamored of his own power to sunder and tear. He will not drink hot blood. This town is a very safe town. We have a neighborhood watch, a community league, and I am on the PTA.

But he does bite, my son. He has a problem with biting. According to the other mothers, he is too old to be biting.

Marcie Klapper-Witt brings my son before me one day. She has his arm clasped in her fist, up by his shoulder. His elbow is bleeding, and he is crying.

"Mrs. Borden, your son bit my daughter," says Marcie Klapper-Witt.

"He did?"

"Yes, he did."

"But his elbow is bleeding."

"Fancy pushed him down after he bit her. To get him off her."

Fancy Klapper-Witt wears a tiara everywhere she goes. Her favorite thing is posing for pictures.

"Did he hurt her?" I ask.

"He *bit* her. He's really too old to be biting. You should look into that, Mrs. Borden. They won't let him into kindergarten."

"I'm very sorry, Marcie," I say. "It won't happen again."

Lola smiles up at the other woman.

"Cocktail, Marcie? It takes the edge off."

But Marcie Klapper-Witt marches off without saying another word.

I lean forward to talk to my son.

"Marcus, did you bite Fancy Klapper-Witt?" I ask.

He nods.

"Do you hate her?"

He shakes his head.

"Do you like her?"

He nods.

"Do you like her so much you want to eat her all up, like the wolf in Little Red Riding Hood?"

He nods.

"That's what I thought."

He sniffles. The tears have made streaks through the layer of dust and grime on his face. The blood from his elbow is smeared across his forearm.

"Does your elbow hurt?"

He nods.

"Here," I say. "Look."

I use my thumb to take some of the blood from his elbow and paint it in two horizontal bands across his cheeks.

"Now you're a warrior, Marcus," I say. "Do you want to see?"

He nods.

The tray Lola brought the daiquiris on has a mirrored bottom, so I hold it up for him to see.

He is pleased by this and goes off to play again.

Lola turns to me.

"No Neosporin?" she asks.

"What?"

"For his elbow. Aren't you worried about infection?"

I shrug.

"Bodies can withstand a lot of damage," I say. "If you lean on them, you're surprised how much they can take."

Lola laughs and clinks my glass with her own.

"Darling," she says, "you are a shooting star among drudges. You're just so *ethereal*."

I can feel my mouth grinning, though I am embarrassed.

"Well," she goes on, "that little Fancy bitch had it coming. I guarantee it won't be the last time in her life that some man tries to take a bite out of her."

I stare at the clouds and listen to the cicadas make their repetitious song, and when the sun starts to go down, all the mothers gather their children into their houses. Lights come on in windows all up and down the street.

Lola calls her own children to her.

"Come on, brats! Assemble!"

Then she, too, goes indoors.

I'm the only one left outside when my husband comes home. He parks in the driveway and climbs out of the car. Our son is asleep on the lawn, curled up on the grass like a house cat.

"What are you doing out here?" Jack says.

"Enjoying the evening," I say.

"Aren't you cold?"

"Not to speak of."

"Do you want to come in now?"

"I suppose so."

But the answer to his question is really much more complicated than that.

———

THEY WERE WRONG, all of them. You do remember some things—fragments that gnaw at you—the sense of becoming another animal altogether. That Christmas Eve, I remember myself in the woods—a delicious kind of lostness that was dizzying and joyful. I was alone, I believe, the entire night. I felt large, bigger than the trees that towered over me. Wider than the sky at its widest. I was the center of all I observed. There was nowhere to get back to because I carried all of myself with me. I was my own home.

But I did return to the house. Somehow I did. I woke in the backyard at dawn. I was naked, curled at the base of a rhododendron shrub, the powdery snow melted into a fragile, concave nest around my body.

I was cold. I was starting to feel the cold again.

I crouched there, trying to assess the situation. My mind was still muddled, and part of me still felt bold and unapologetic. But that part was quickly diminishing.

It was still very early. No one was out. I sprinted across the lawn, around the side of the house, and in through the front door, which was still unlocked. Inside I stopped and pressed myself against the wall, breathing hard. I listened, but the house was still quiet. The heat ticked on, and the wall vents rattled faintly. My father had not woken up. I crept up the stairs to my room, where I got a robe out of my closet and wrapped it around my body.

Lying on the bed, I tried to sleep, but my muscles ached and my head was spinning—and I didn't want to sleep, because I felt the opposite of tired.

So I took a bath in the bathroom down the hall. I made the water as hot as I could bear it, thinking to sweat out whatever was still in me from the night before. I was meticulous. I pried out all the dirt that had collected under the nails of my toes and fingers, I scrubbed the soles of my feet raw trying to get rid of all the yellowed mud caked in the creases. I picked pine needles from my hair, and they floated like miniature felled trees on the meniscus of the tub water. Sap knotted my hair in places, and I had to wash it three times in scalding water before I could dig out the coagulants with a plastic comb.

There was a knock on the door.

"Merry Christmas, little Lumen!"

"Merry Christmas," I called back.

"You're up bright and early. Ready for presents?"

"I'll be down in a minute."

I stood, dripping dry on the bathmat. Wiping the mirror clear of condensation, I looked at the girl I saw there. Judging by her looks, her scrubbed pinkness, you would never know where she'd been.

Back in my bedroom, I dressed in red and green, as was the tradition with my father and me. I avoided looking at the windows, because I did not want to think about the snow and the trees and the clear sky of morning. I wanted to be inside and think inside thoughts. I wanted to feel the comfort of walls around me—and to speak the delicate languages of family and society and tradition.

Downstairs, my father and I took turns opening presents. He was eager to see me excited, and so I was excited for him.

He took many pictures of me, but I vowed never to look at them.

It hurt too much to think how completely the girl in those pictures was not me.

———

THE LAST GIFT I gave him was the map I had drawn for him.

Until this very moment, I have never told anyone about it—not even my husband. Sometimes you hide away a memory because it is so precious that you don't want to dilute it with the attempt to recount it. Sometimes you hide a memory because the disclosure of it would reveal you to be a different person from the one others believe you to be. And sometimes you may hide a memory because it inhabits you in some physical way, because its meaning is inexpressible and dangerous. That is this memory—evidence, baleful proof—just the recollection of him opening my gift.

He unrolls it on the ground, kneeling before it like a supplicant, head bowed, prayerful and quiet.

What he says is, "You did this," and his voice is full of wonder and admiration. He does not bother to thank me. It is a gift beyond thank yous.

Using his fingertip, he travels from one place to another on the map, and at each location he pauses to examine the detail. It is as though he lives, for the moment, in that map, as though he and I are travelers on a different plane.

That plane is a place where you can redraw yourself from scratch.

The pen lines are so perfect, so straight and lovely—who would ever want to cross them?

———

I HAD TWO visitors later that day. The first was Polly. We stood, shivering, on the sidewalk, because I did not want her in my

131

house. The space inside those walls was suddenly precious to me.

"Are you having a good Christmas?" she asked.

"I guess." I shrugged.

"Did you get good presents?"

Her face was still splotchy with bruises.

"Are you okay?" I said.

"Oh, this'll go away. It happens."

"Come on," I said. "Let's walk."

"Where?"

"I don't know. It's Christmas."

"It's cold."

"It's not so cold."

In truth it was very cold indeed, but I liked the punishing feeling of the icy wind. So we walked slowly down the middle of the street. There were very few cars out, but when one came we stepped aside and let it pass.

We said nothing for a few minutes. She seemed to be waiting for me to confess something, but I didn't feel like confessing.

Eventually, she said, "So?"

"So what?"

"So last night."

"Yeah."

"It finally happened."

"Uh-huh."

"Everyone was wondering if it was ever going to happen for you. Are you relieved?"

"I don't know."

"Do you remember any of it?"

"Not much."

"We tried to look for you, you know. But we couldn't find you. You're fast. I never knew how fast you were."

I said nothing. The swiftness with which I had run naked through the woods was an unfathomable topic for me.

Polly, observing my reluctance to speak, stopped in the road and turned to face me. In some dim part of my mind, I found myself enthralled by the abrasions on her skin. I could wander free on the landscape of her injuries.

"Hey," she said. "Are you all right? I know it's a big deal. It's scary. I remember my first time."

I remembered her first time as well. She hadn't seemed scared at all. She had seemed proud and gloating.

"Do you remember," she said, smiling, "how you used to say it wouldn't happen to you? I mean, you were so convinced that you were different. I bet that seems silly now, doesn't it? All that worry for nothing."

"I guess so."

"You get used to it. You do. You begin to look forward to it, even. Look, we're young. We're only going to be young for a little while. Then we'll be old forever. We might as well enjoy it, you know?"

A car came, and we stepped out of the road into a snowbank.

"You know," she said, "I kind of envy you that you're just starting. But it'll be better now. We'll be together. It's like you moved away for a while—but you're back now."

The thought that I had traveled so far by accident the night before made me sick.

"It feels wrong, Polly," I said. "It just feels wrong."

"But it's not," she said. She took my shoulders and gave her head a maternal shake to reassure me. "It's not. Don't you see? It's the most natural thing in the world. It's only beautiful. That's the only thing it is."

She shivered, then put her arms around me.

"Come on," she said. "Hug me. It's cold. Let's just forget about everything up till now. The past is dead and buried. That's what the breach is all about, right?"

I put my arms around her. Beneath the perfume of her shampoo, her hair smelled like something else—the fecund tang of earth and rot.

———

MY SECOND VISITOR of the day was Blackhat Roy. I saw him coming from down the street, and I rushed to meet him outside so my father wouldn't see him at the door.

"What are you doing here?" I said.

"Heard the news," he said. "You're out. You're fair game."

"I'm not out." In the daylight you scoff at the shadows you cowered from the night before. I had my mother's blood. I knew I was different. I had faith that I was still not like the others. "I was helping my friend, and I was attacked. I ran."

"Spent all night running away?"

"Go away."

He sniffled from the cold, wiped his nose with the back of his hand.

"I saw you," he said.

"When?"

"Last night. In the woods."

"You didn't. I remember. I ran away from everybody."

"Fuck everybody. It was just me. And you saw me, too."

"No, I didn't."

"The way you looked at me," he went on, ignoring my denials, "I've never seen anything like that before. You didn't just want to tussle—it was like you wanted to rip me to pieces."

He seemed delighted by the fact. The way he said it made it seem lascivious.

"No," I said again. "I was just running. But I'm not doing it again."

"You want to know the truth? I stayed out of your way. I'm not scared of much, but last night I was a little scared of you."

He smiled when he said it, a smile of filth and gloating. So what was that churning I felt in my belly when he winked at me?

"See you on the wild side, girl."

I went back in the house and shut the door on him.

In the kitchen, my father was making ginger tea, which was our favorite.

———

WHAT WAS I?

Defective, for one thing. I had grown wrong somehow. My atoms and molecules were failing to adhere to one another the way they should have. My organs were stunted, dwarflike. My body was one pale refusal.

It didn't matter that everyone else was doing it. Their doing it was native—my doing it was criminal.

Even in this I had failed. Everyone was relieved that I had finally gone breach—they felt that they could talk to me now, that I was one of them, joined together in their wild union. But I wasn't one of them after all. I was still different. They welcomed what I feared. They jumped when I cringed. They howled while I whimpered.

Not that I was looking to be like the others. But to be *between* was too much to bear. To be defined by betweenness is not to be defined at all. It is to live your whole life at dusk, which is neither day nor night and therefore an hour of sad nothing caught between one kind of life and another.

This was my inheritance from my mother.

If I was truly out, as Blackhat Roy had said, why wasn't I glad? And if I hadn't fully gone breach, then what had caused me to blister myself with running?

And that was something else, something my brain burned to think on. If I was still as breachless as my mother's blood had made me, then the night before—when I had stripped myself bare and woken in the melted snow at dawn—who was the girl who had done that? What was she driven by?

What excused her actions if those actions were not to be excused by instinct and biology or the horrible magic of this place?

———

NOT EVERYONE IN our town acquiesced to the breaching so easily. It was difficult, sometimes, for parents to accept that their children could behave in such a way. Sometimes they even tried to delay the breaching or prevent it. There were urban myths about ways to keep your child from breaching. Giving them high doses of thiamine was one. Another was to make them sleep in a fully lighted room throughout their teenage years. For a while, before I was born, I even heard that some parents had begun to believe that if they kept their children shaved, completely hairless, the breaching would not set in. So for a period of five years or so, according to my father, there were a bunch of bald, eyebrowless teenagers walking around.

I was fascinated by the idea. I liked to close my eyes and picture it. And I wondered about these parents. What did they believe? That savagery was something you donned as though it were a pelt?

Other parents believed it was the town itself, our pinprick location under the moon, that was the cause of the breach. Sometimes parents would send their children away for the breach year to live with relatives in safe-sounding places such as Florida or Colorado or Arizona. And moving away did seem to work—insofar as the children did not see fit to run wild over the warm, sandy streets of Scottsdale. Sometimes, if they could afford it, the whole family would relocate and then return when the coast was clear.

So that worked—kind of. Except not really, because when they returned, the breachers seemed different, odd. It wasn't just that they no longer *belonged* to the town—though there was that. It was something else. I remember studying Caroline Neary when she came back after a year of living with her aunt in San Francisco. It was her eyes. She seemed scared. Not of anything outside—but of something else. I think I knew what she was scared of. There was something trapped in her—something grown too big to fit in her body, something stretching her at the seams because it wanted to get out but couldn't. She moved out of our town the minute she graduated from high school—and we all thought she would be better off for it. But then we heard the distressing news, just a few years later, that she had impaled herself on a picket fence by jumping out the second-story window of her pleasant suburban home in the middle of the day on a Saturday.

So I suppose whatever was trapped inside Caroline Neary eventually got out after all.

There were other parents who, when the breach was upon their children and they knew they couldn't escape it, tried to keep it at least *contained,* usually with disastrous results.

When we were in the sixth grade, Polly and I had heard about Lionel Kirkpatrick, whose parents, unwilling yet to see their precious boy go breach, had locked him in the basement to keep him from running wild. Over the course of the night, Lionel had ravaged the space, trying to get out. It cost the Kirkpatricks ten thousand dollars in repairs, including a new water heater, because Lionel had somehow toppled the existing one and flooded the basement. In the morning, they found him asleep, curled on top of a pile of boxes, a castaway on an island in two feet of water.

Another thing, from just the previous year: Amy Litt had gone breach and had come to school one morning with bandages all over her fingers. She, unashamed, explained to us that it was like the Bible story of Noah. Her father had found her sleeping naked in the street one morning after breach. He was a righteous man, and he felt a curse had befallen him for having accidentally seen his own daughter without clothes. So the next night he had shut her in the basement, just as Lionel Kirkpatrick's parents had done to their son. Except Amy Litt's destruction was of a more self-directed variety. All she had wanted was out. When her father had gone down to check on her in the morning, he found the concrete walls smeared with blood and his daughter huddled in the corner, shivering with pain. She had ripped all her fingernails out in trying to claw her way to freedom.

The Kirkpatricks restored their basement, and nine of Amy Litt's nails eventually grew back—so these unfortunate occurrences, like most things, were reversible with time. But they served as admonitions to the parents of our town not to stand in the way of the natural course of events, no matter how ugly or shameful.

I know this now—and I raise my child to understand it as

well. Some parents in our neighborhood do everything they can to keep their children away from violent images. And then, when something terrible happens, like murder or rape or genocide — well, then a conversation has to be had with these young innocents to explain that, yes, goodness is sometimes a fiction, like Santa Claus, and that humanity is, underneath all the cookie baking and song singing, a shameful and secret nastiness. Me, I'm going to raise my son differently. What he will be made to know is that there is violence in everything — even in goodness, if you're passionate about it.

But he already knows that. It's why he pulls hair, why he bites what he loves.

———

BUT THOSE WERE parents who had intervened against the wishes of their children. Their stories were different from mine. I was a half-breed. I wasn't some wild creature. I was good. I was daylight and homework and logical answers. I was no tide to be puppeted by the moon. I had my mother's blood. Maybe the night before had been an aberration. You didn't have to give in to every impulse that stirred your blood. You could be better.

I decided, whatever I had become, not to go outside the next night. I was determined not to yield to whatever disease was growing inside me.

When it got dark, I found my father reading in the living room.

"Good night," I said.

He looked at his watch.

"It's early," he said.

"I know. I'm worn out."

"Good Christmas, Lumen?"

"Good Christmas, Dad. Good Christmas for you?"

"Great Christmas. Among the best."

He was a sweet, oblivious man. He was the kind of man you wanted to be good for. How could you want to damage such a man with the truth of things?

So I had to hide it from him—whatever it was. Up in my room, I shut my door and put my desk chair in front of it. I had seen people do this in movies, though my door didn't seem any more secure for it. Through my window, I could see the moon through the tree branches, low on the horizon.

My skin was itchy all over. I was feeling ragged and burned. There was a fan in my closet that was meant for the hot summer months—but I got it out and plugged it in and sat in front of it with my eyes closed, the air making me feel like I was moving at high speed, on my way to someplace grand and dramatic.

Once, when I was much younger, I had asked my father what my mother had done all those nights when everyone had gone breach around her. He laughed and took me onto his lap, and this is what he said: "Do you want to know what she did? She sewed rag dolls. She was the most amazing seamstress, your mother. The dolls she made, they were exquisite. She became known for them all over town. Children would come by her house and stand beneath her window, and she would throw dolls down to them."

I always loved that story, and it wasn't until I was older that I began to wonder why none of my mother's rag-doll creations were still around. And then, later, my father's story became even stranger to me because of its resemblance to something I read in *Little Women*. Still, I treasured the image of my mother sitting beneath a lamp at night sewing dolls, and I wondered what comparable thing I could do.

I put my headphones on and listened to some music at volume level seventeen—I normally wouldn't allow myself any volume over ten for fear of ruining my eardrums. But there was a bustle in my head that needed drowning out.

On the wall over my bed there was a mismatched seam in the wallpaper, and tonight, for some reason, it bothered me. I picked at it without thinking, digging my fingernails underneath it until I had ripped away a whole flap. My hands wanted something to do. I made myself stop and reaffix the flap with white glue. But then I found myself winding my fingers around strands of hair and tugging them out of my scalp.

To keep my hands occupied, I opened my sketch pad and started to draw a map. It was a map of a place I didn't know. Sometimes those were the best ones. You started with a river and grew a town up around it. You discovered the place as you created it. Sometimes there were surprises.

But tonight, for the first time, I was irritated by my little fictional operettas. The music in my ears seemed mechanical and false. The map emerging under my artless hands seemed flat, predictable. I began to wish I knew how to paint scenes rather than just maps. I wanted to paint like Edward Hopper. I wanted to show the depth of the dark by delivering just a small, broken segment of light. I wanted to look into windows from the outside.

I was hot, and there was nothing the fan could do about it. My skin itched, the kind of itch that made diving into a thorny shrub sound like a delicious dream.

It was only nine o'clock. I went to the window. It was safe, I imagined, just to look. I renewed my resolution not to set even one foot outside. The moon was still low. I could see it superimposed over my reflection on the pane of glass, yet still very far away. I pressed my forehead to the glass and used my hands as a visor in order to see more, to get closer, but my breath quickly fogged the view.

I unlocked the window and slid it upward. It was just something I did. It required no thought or bargaining.

I knew a rhyme that had always seemed powerful to me. If I spoke it aloud, maybe I could still be saved, even with the window open. So I leaned as far as I could out the window into the night and repeated the rhyme over and over.

There was a crooked man, and he walked a crooked mile.
He found a crooked sixpence upon a crooked stile.
He bought a crooked cat, which caught a crooked mouse.
And they all lived together in a little crooked house.

I leaned out the window, and the air sighed upon my itchy skin.

Were these, then, the pathways to damnation—and was this why they were so difficult for people to resist?

There was a crooked man, and he walked a crooked mile.

My window was in a dormer, and I crawled through until half of me was lying on the downward slope of the roof.

But my legs were still inside the house. Inside the little crooked house. No walking a crooked mile tonight—not without those little crooked legs.

You could breathe the night. I never knew that before. The air tasted different when it was uninfused with light. It went deeper in you. You could want it—just that.

And it was cold. There was a high-contrast sharpness to everything. It was a wakeful night—so wakeful that daytime consciousness seemed a blur.

He bought a crooked cat, which caught a crooked mouse.

Yes, the crookedness of things. I could see it now.

You could get sick to death of delicate symmetry. You could want other things, and that wanting could be ambrosial all on its own.

You could even become angry at your own prohibitions — you could begin to suspect the origins of all the tinny moralities that point you in all the directions of your life.

It occurred to me that I would like to feel the moonlight on my bare skin. The thought occurred to me, and I studied it in the cool, rational part of my brain — but while I was studying it, I noticed that my fingers had already begun the process of undoing the buttons on my pajama top. I watched them, curiously, from the rational distance of my brain — I wondered who they thought they were, those fingers that had spent so much time doing my bidding in the past.

Those little crooked fingers, they run their crooked way.

You could sometimes want to run. You could sometimes want to run out your window, off your roof, down the street, deep, deep into the unlit heart of an emptied town.

———

I DARTED FROM yard to yard, looking in windows. Squares of light. Actions playing out in them. Like television screens hung randomly along the street. Sometimes you could see a television screen inside the television screen of the window. Layers of lit life in the distance. And here was I — shrouded behind the curtains of night, lost in the muffled dullness of a noiseless winter. And it was okay. It was better than okay. It was glorious.

I could leap. Fences were nothing to me. Rules were for those small enough to live inside them. I was large.

It was possible, I saw now, to be a grotesque, to be huge and free, to wander the streets in utter freedom despite your atrocity, as long as you did it when everybody else was sealed inside their little lit boxes.

Now it made sense—why monsters came out at night.

CHAPTER 6

I scrubbed myself clean in the morning, coating my skin with lotion that smelled of lemons.

I didn't tell my father. I decided to keep it from him as long as I could. I dreaded being found by him curled naked on the back porch or befouled with mud.

The second night was more lucid than the first. I stayed by myself for a long time. In the distance I could hear the others, roaming the streets in packs. When their voices got louder, I hid. I watched them pass by, tangled around each other and caught up in their passions. I did not want to be joined with them.

In front of the church, I watched from a copse of trees as a group of breachers knocked apart a manger scene left over from Christmas. I waited until they were gone, then I put everything back aright.

As I put the baby Jesus back in his little nest, I stood back and looked at it.

It had nothing to do with God. It was just glowy and sweet, and it spoke of aching desire and a longing for peacefulness.

I wished the scene had been baked in an oven so I could eat it.

———

ATTACK THE NIGHT.

I was hungry for things I didn't know the names of, and the full moon was a strange kind of manna. It emptied you of yourself, and you were relieved.

Such release—you have no idea. Everything absolved. A world where signs meant nothing, where everything was permitted. The claustrophobic restrictions of life falling like clipped fingernails at your feet.

I ran the woods, and I was unstoppable. I thought nothing of school deadlines and frowning fathers. I was entire and alone—blissfully alone. There was nothing outside my skin that mattered—except maybe the odor of tree sap and the brittle ice that depended from tree branches. I wanted to go farther. I wanted to run all the way out of town—through the streets of large cities, leaping from the hood of one taxicab to another, laughing and indifferent.

You could nuzzle your face against the warm world. The undersides of everything. This is how you knew love. There was no ugly. All was beautiful. The bodies, dark or pale, bruised or unspoiled—they were beautiful. The violence was delicious in the way foreign food sometimes is—surprising on the tongue, fresh and sharp. My daytime resentments sloughed away, and I would have gladly merged my life with the lives of others—put my body, all uncovered, against theirs.

Except that I was afraid. Still afraid of myself. And of the others.

Later that second night I watched them from a distance. I ran across them, finally, in the middle of town, and I climbed a dumpster to the rooftop of the Sunshine Diner to observe them. There were so many of them, at least thirty, making loud noises in the square.

They seemed to run in packs, mostly. Like social cliques at school during the daytime. When these packs crossed paths during the full moon, there were fights. Sometimes the fights turned into revelry. Below me I could see some girls, locked into combat on the wide lawn, pulling at each other's hair, biting, choking, shrieking. But they soon grew tired, and their violence became pathetic, little compulsory slaps as their chests heaved with exhaustion. Even kisses.

Elsewhere, near the gazebo in the middle of the square, a pale pink knot of breachers, most of whom I knew, were locked together in various manifestations of sexual congress. Girls, boys, it made no difference. You were skin, and they were skin, and you buried yourself in the skin of others as they buried themselves in yours. Some of them cried, and some of them howled—and whether the crying and howling was pain or pleasure, you couldn't tell, and maybe they couldn't, either. Such are the ambiguities of primal youth.

I could name almost everyone I saw—because I was the kind of girl who knew everybody's name, even though I was allied with none of them. There was Ellie Wilkins, Carl Bodell, Frenchie Lassister, the twins Margot and Marina Anderson, Wally Kemp, Gary Tupper, George Ferris, and also George Dodd. Mildred Gunderson, Marcel Judd, Theo Kaminer. Cameron Mayer, whom most people just called Monkey. Adelaide Warren and Sue Foxworth and Florabel McCarron (who had started breaching so early that she was picked on by the others and had to be hospitalized after her first full moon). John Stonehill, Joel Phelps, Barbara Montgomery. Worth Loomis. Sylvia Hitchcock.

Rose Lincoln was there, too, looking like a matriarch overseeing the soldiery of her empire. She walked among them, her head held high and regal, her pale body indifferent to the bodies around her.

Peter Meechum was there, the king to Rose's queen. He lay atop the gazebo roof, stargazing, while Bessie Laurent nestled against him, her hand moving with a lullaby rhythm between her legs. He paid no attention to her. And that was good, because I was quite sure I loved him — and that I could with very little remorse bite the tongue right out of Bessie Laurent's mouth. That was the kind of clarity you could have on nights like these. All the fine-tuned complications of the day give way to the big absolutes: love, hate, life, death, good, evil, boy, girl, angel, fiend.

Blackhat Roy was there, too. He was relegated to the margins.

I watched them from the safe distance of the diner roof. I watched them, because these were my people. These were the people I had been born to. This was my heritage on true display.

Then, in the distance, there was the sound of a car engine. Headlights on the horizon.

Sometimes people came from the outside. Travelers. We were a long way off the main freeway through the state, so it didn't happen often. But sometimes it did.

Some of the breachers below scattered by instinct. Others stayed. Blackhat Roy stayed, drawn by curiosity nearer the road, to the base of a granite monument in the shape of an obelisk. Peter stayed, raising himself up on his elbows. Rose Lincoln leaned against a tree trunk and crossed her arms, waiting.

The car drove once around the square, its windows rolled

down. We could hear loud, overlapping voices coming from inside, the voices of teenagers like us.

Unlike us.

"This is it? I don't get it."

"I thought you said we were gonna find a liquor store."

"This place doesn't seem so scary. Why's everybody always warning us about it?"

"Fucking Mayberry."

"Aren't there supposed to be ghosts or vampires or something? What the fuck?"

Then they must have spotted the breachers who had made no effort to hide themselves. The car stopped at the edge of the town square, and one of the boys got out and said, "What the hell is this?" and the others also got out and began to laugh and point. "They're naked!" they said, and, "What are they? Hippies? Is this what we're not supposed to see? Hippie bullshit?"

I watched from my perch on the roof. Blackhat Roy, his body covered in soot, moved closer to them. He cocked his head slightly as if considering the visitors.

It was one thing for the breachers to attack one other. That was accepted. That was the nature of the place. It was our nature. But this was something different. Outsiders, the few we got, were usually left alone. It was a precarious balance that worked out most of the time. On the one hand, breachers normally preferred to roam the dark woods rather than the overly bright downtown streets. On the other hand, most residents from neighboring towns stayed away from us during the full moon out of a superstitious fear of the town's reputation. But sometimes there were exceptions in both cases—the habits of breachers were broken, and the mythologies of the town were forgotten by the outsiders.

I might have warned them. I might have called down to them to get back into their car and drive away. But I didn't. I didn't want to.

The five of them were out of the car, some still pointing, some laughing with gaudy, wide mouths, some revolted. That's when the other breachers emerged from around corners and from the dark of alleyways. They came out, naked all, and surrounded the travelers.

Two of the five were girls, and they didn't like what was happening. They got back into the car and begged the three boys to take them home. But the boys continued to laugh. "A town full of retards," one said.

"Please!" the girls said from inside the car. "Please come on!"

But then something strange happened. From my height, I could see that the breachers, led by Peter Meechum, who had hopped down from the gazebo roof, were closing not around the travelers but around one of their own, Blackhat Roy.

It was a sign of dominance, territoriality. I understood it instinctively. Instead of attacking the interloper, attack one of your own. Put on full display the untamed wildness of your power.

By the time Roy saw what was happening, it was too late to run. I could see, even from my height, the panic in his eyes. His head turned around, wondering from which direction the first attack would come.

"It's gonna hurt, Roy," I could hear Peter saying. "You know it's gonna hurt."

But then something occurred to Blackhat Roy. Instead of defending himself, he turned on the travelers, the boys laughing and pointing from their car.

"What do you fucking know about hurt?" he said to the boys. "You and yours. I'm gonna teach you something about hurt."

Roy advanced on one of the boys, going up close and sniffing his neck as a dog might. Then he said something to him, low in his ear, and I couldn't hear what it was. But the boy wasn't laughing anymore, and he was no longer hypnotized by the naked bodies all around him—he just wanted to get away.

Roy wouldn't let him. He grabbed the boy and flung him to the ground, then seized him by the arm and dragged him into the middle of the park. The crowd of breachers separated to let him through—Roy was giving them something to be hungry for.

"Tear him," Marina Anderson said, breathless, to Blackhat Roy. "Rip him."

"Rip him," the others started to say. "Bleed him."

The other two boys tried to run to their friend's aid, but the breachers fell on them, too, beat them and tore off their clothes and rubbed themselves lewdly against the whimpering boys.

Then they came back to the car for the two tearful and screaming girls.

I watched.

I was stirred.

The breezes blew, and I wondered how much awfulness had to be released from one location before you could smell it on the wind.

The girls had locked themselves in the car, but they didn't have the key to start the engine. I could hear their muffled shrieks as the breachers stalked around the vehicle, trying all the doors, pressing their hungry faces against the glass. Blackhat Roy slapped a bloody handprint on the windshield. It was impossible to know whose blood it was.

"Open your eyes," he called to the girls. "Open your goddamn eyes!"

The breachers rocked the car back and forth, some climbing up the hood and onto the roof. The girls screamed.

Finally someone brought a cinder block from the alley and threw it through the windshield. Then it was just a matter of reaching in and dragging the girls out by their fragile, flailing limbs.

———

IN THE PAST, the infrequent attacks on outsiders hadn't been so bad. They could be explained away, mollified with sympathetic fictions. A troubled local youth gone off his medication. A traumatized girl, escaped from her abusive foster home, taking out on innocents what had been perpetrated on her for years. In the daylight, the breachers could be brought forward to apologize, which they did with all true sincerity. They had not meant it. They were full of regret.

Truth be told, even during the full moon, breachers could sense the difference between themselves and others. In general, there was no joy in preying on those who did not stink of nature and violence. The outsiders usually came away with maybe a bruise or a busted lip. Maybe not even that. Sometimes just the uneasy fright of witnessing a naked figure running across the road in front of your car and howling at you as it passed.

The sheriff from the next town over might visit our mayor. There may have been jolly slaps on the back, amicable chuckling, head shaking with regard to the moral abandon of teenagers these days. What was to be done? Mutual shrugs. It was a brutal time we were living in. Sad nods. But the children would survive and be better for it, as the two men had. Reassured stares skyward.

This time, though, it was different. I had seen it. Had just one breacher been there, or two, they might have made a display of animalistic defiance and run off. But it wasn't just one breacher, it was a whole pack. Violence, I discovered, could be contagious. It fed off itself until it had lost its purpose. The result was five teenagers mauled in our town square on the day after Christmas.

The attacks were just too brutal to be ignored. Two of the boys and one of the girls were hospitalized. One of the boys had had his eye gouged out and would have to wear a glass eye for the rest of his life. One of the girls was a cheerleader and had promised her parents and her pastor that she would remain a virgin until the day she married. Someone had to be held responsible.

So our sheriff questioned some of the breachers. It didn't even take a whole afternoon. All we needed was a scapegoat, and we had one readily at hand. The next day everybody knew that Blackhat Roy had been held responsible for the crime and would be sent away to live in Chicago with his uncle.

I hated him. Still, when I thought about him going far away, part of me ached for him.

On certain days in the spring, in late April, say, it is possible to believe what the animals believe—that horror and beauty are hearty allies, and that when you live in the full roiling of your guts it's impossible to make distinctions between them.

———

LATE THAT AFTERNOON, near sunset, Peter Meechum came to me. He came to the front door, rang the bell, and stood there looking mournful and respectable.

"I came to apologize," he said.

"For what?"

"For everything."

I wondered about his willingness to apologize for everything in the world. It was the marvelous kind of stuff that martyrs are made of. He stood there, sheepish and strong, and his smile was just on the final edge of regret, ready to break through to whatever passionate gesture was next. Maybe I was still weak to the fact that he seemed interested in me when there were so many other girls whose doorsteps he could be standing on—but it was more than that. He was wound up, kinetic, and you felt that you could either go along with him or be left behind—and I wanted to go with him.

I invited him in, but he didn't want to be indoors. Instead we walked, wrapped in our winter coats. I kept my eyes on the shoveled sidewalk, paying close attention to whether or not I stepped on the cracks. I wondered if he would try to take my hand, and I left it dangling just in case—but he seemed morose and inattentive.

"You know where I've been all morning?" he said.

"Where?"

"Church."

"Oh."

"It used to make me feel better," he went on, "but it doesn't anymore. I forgot how to be good."

"You didn't forget."

"All the things I've done. The way I've behaved. Do you ever feel like you're two entirely different people? I mean, there's the person you know you should be, the person you want to be, the person everybody else would like you to be. And you can be that person most of the time. It's work. I mean, it's hard—but you can do it. But then there's this other person who does awful things. The sun goes down, the moon comes up—and suddenly you're watching yourself do ugly things. Like you're complacent, at a distance, just watching the happenings of your body as if you had nothing at all to do with them. Do you ever feel that?"

I was silent for a moment. But he didn't give me a chance to answer before he continued.

"No. You wouldn't know about that."

"Maybe I would," I asserted.

"No, you wouldn't. You don't understand."

"I do. I promise."

His smile was generous, but he didn't believe me. I wanted to be something in his mournful life—a comfort or a remedy. Simple fancies, but my chest ached with them.

"Listen," I said. We stopped, and I got in front of him to look up into his eyes. I put my hand on his chest to reassure him. I wanted him to feel the truth of what I was saying. I wanted to press it directly into his heart as though it were soft clay. I could feel the confession spilling out of me, and there was no stopping it. "Listen," I said again, "sometimes...I don't know...sometimes I hate myself. Especially lately. I don't know what to do. I don't know who I am anymore—what I am. My dad, he doesn't know I go out at nights. I can't tell him. I'm not a breacher like other people, I don't think. I can't be. I don't want to be. But I don't know. My mom, she used to make dolls—except now I don't know if she really did. I wish I could make dolls. I wish I were the girl who made dolls instead of the girl who—"

He put his arms around me. "Shh," he said. "It's okay."

He held me and stroked my hair for a few moments until I calmed down. Then, when he let me go and looked me in the face, his expression had changed completely. His mood had transformed—he was elated. Had I done that to him? Did I have that kind of power?

"Come on," he said, taking my hand. "I want to show you something."

He pulled me into the middle of the street.

"Wait," I said. "We're going to get run over."

"It doesn't matter."

He let go of my hand, took me by the shoulders, and turned me around so my back was to him. He put his head over my right shoulder, and I could feel his breath on my cheek.

"Look down there," he said, and I looked at the row of houses and the purple sunset beyond.

"What?" I said.

"No," he said. "You have to look harder."

Just then the street lamps came on overhead with a little click and a buzz. Consecutive pools of light appeared in a bracelet of illumination that fronted all the houses, each of which domiciled any number of lives and dramas and passions and catastrophes. There it was, the way the street arrowed on to the horizon, the way the housefronts glowed rich, organic sepia into the night, the way the parceled land shivered with the deep harmonics of order and structure. I looked, and what I saw was the story of the place, the crystalline symmetry of the houses on their identical plots of land, the swooping curve of the curb and the wispy fans of the sprinklers that came on in the summer with timed precision. I saw the bones and the blood of the town, the infrastructure of copper pipes and PVC and electrical conduits and sump pumps and telephone wires suspended in elegant laurels overhead. I saw everything it took to make this one street, and I saw that street multiplied into a neighborhood and that neighborhood multiplied into a town and that town multiplied into a city and a country and a whole world.

I saw it. He made me see it, and I saw it.

"Think about it," he said. "People *built* this. There used to be nothing here, and now there's this. And the people who built it, were they pure? It doesn't matter. Whatever they were, they overcame it to make something bigger than themselves. Look harder. It's beautiful."

It's become popular for people to talk about suburban dread, the cardboard sprawl that cheapens life, reduces life down to lawn ornaments, manicured shrubs, televisions with extra-large screens, quaint and degraded notions of family life. It's easy to say that life should be grander, more meaningful, heartier — like a meat stew.

But what Peter showed me I'll never forget. It was the land brought to life, the earth made conscious. And it was beautiful. It really was.

"What does it mean?" I asked.

"It means that it doesn't matter what it means," he said. "It means that it'll be okay, Lumen."

———

THE THIRD NIGHT I went into the woods because I was finished with other people and their capricious ways. I wanted my freedom to be mine alone. A wind blew through the trees, and the moonlight lit up all the icy branches, and it was like I was surrounded by stars.

The next morning, when I woke, my body was covered in crystals of ice. I was in the backyard of my house, on the lawn, in a little concavity my hot body had made in the snow. Sitting up, I saw a ghost of myself on the ground.

The sun was up, just visible on the horizon. I guessed it must have been five o'clock. My father would still be in bed.

"You sleep nice."

The voice came from behind me. My body, still moon-driven and instinctive, shot rigid into a crouch. Flee or defend.

Blackhat Roy, still naked, too, sat on the stoop of my back porch. He looked haggard and somehow raw. He was raked with dirt, his hair caked with dry, frozen mud. He scratched at himself casually.

"Your eyelids," he said. "They flutter when you're asleep. You remember what you were dreaming about?"

"You're supposed to be going to Chicago."

"Leaving tonight."

"What are you doing here?"

"Now, me," he went on, "I remember all my dreams. I wish I didn't. Good or bad, it doesn't matter. I wake up in the middle of some fucking fantasyland campfire story, and it takes me a while to get my bearings. You know, what's true and what isn't. Where are you really? In the middle of some horror show with smiling dogs, or maybe an orgy of alien women, or maybe just tucked safe away in your bed. It's a goddamn nuisance is what it is. You ever have that problem? Not knowing for sure what's real?" He scratched behind his ear and picked something from his hair—a bug of some kind—then crushed it between his fingers. "Or have you got it all figured out?"

"You shouldn't be here."

"How come?"

"Why are you here? What do you want?"

"You really want to know?"

Suddenly I didn't like being naked around him. It was too personal, too intimate. Now that the sun was rising over the horizon, it was no longer just nature and breaching. Now there was something else involved—the shame of day. I stood and turned sideways, folding my arms over myself as best I could.

He chuckled, and I was embarrassed about my paltry modesty.

"Let me go inside," I said.

"Who's stopping you?"

I was keenly aware that I would have to pass close by him to go up the porch steps into the house. Taking two steps forward, I watched him to see what he would do—but he made no move. His eyes followed me as I got closer, and, as I put my foot on the first step, I thought his arm might shoot out and he might grab me by the ankle. And what then? Where would he drag me? What dirtiness would he scrape onto me? How would it feel on my skin? Would I hate it?

I bolted, running up the rest of the steps until I had my hand on the knob of the back door. Only then did I turn around to find he had not moved at all—he hadn't even turned around. I looked at his back. There were scars all over it, little white and pink indentations highlighted by dirt and grime.

He had not seized me. He had not dragged me off somewhere, and now I didn't know how I felt about that.

"You shouldn't have attacked those people," I said.

"Is that what you think happened?"

"You attacked them. I saw you."

"If you saw it, then you know better. Sometimes you get tired of being the town garbage. And sometimes, when you're tired like that, you realize that the only way to keep from being the prey"—he turned to look at me—"is to put someone else in your place. Besides, the whole town loves a slaughter. How come I don't get to enjoy myself in the same way once in a while?"

I knew what he said was true, but I had no answer for him.

"You should go home," I said.

"Home," he grunted, turning away again. "Right."

"You act like you're separate from it."

"From what?"

"All of it. What everyone's going through. The breaching."

"Pomp and faggotry," he said. "Girl shit."

"But you're doing it, too."

"Nope," he said simply.

I waited for him to say more, and eventually he did. Though he did not turn around, so I still could not see his face.

"What I do, it's personal. I take responsibility for it. It's me. It ain't some hormones or rite of passage or mass hysteria. I don't fucking cry about it in the morning."

———

BY THE TIME the sun went down, Roy was gone.

I was nervous, because it was the fourth night. Usually the breach went three nights—but the jury was still out on what form of sinner I was. So I thought maybe I would go out again. Maybe for me it was an everyday thing for the rest of my life.

But when the sun went down, I didn't feel the urgent tugging in my chest. I was able to keep my bedroom window closed. And so I knew I would be free of it for another month.

When school started up again after the holiday, things were different. People weren't exactly friendlier. They didn't strike up conversations with me in the cafeteria—but sometimes they gave me a cursory nod as they passed. And I noticed something else, too. When I walked down the hallways, people moved out of my way. Before the winter break I had had to be very conscious

160

of where I walked, because if I weren't careful people would simply walk right into me. But now there was an understanding of presence, a mutual shifting of bodies as they moved through space.

It was as though I had become suddenly *visible*.

In the girls' restroom, I encountered Polly and Rose Lincoln. They were brushing their faces with powder and looking at themselves in the mirror. First they sucked their lips in, then they puckered them out.

Polly still looked pretty beat up, but there seemed to be no animosity between the two of them.

"Lumen!" Polly said when she saw me. "How are you?"

"Fine."

"We didn't see you after the first night," said Rose. She didn't look away from the mirror.

"You didn't try to stay in, did you?" said Polly.

"No," I said.

"It's strange the first couple times, I know."

"Are you okay?" I asked.

"What, this?" Polly said, gesturing to the abrasions showing through the powder on her face. "It's nothing. I didn't mean to frighten you the other night. Sometimes things get a little emotional in the moment. But everybody gets busted up sometimes. Life, you know?"

"One thing you can say about Polly," said Rose approvingly. "She knows how to take a beating."

I didn't say anything.

"You should come with us next time," Polly said. "We'll take care of you. Shouldn't she, Rose?"

"Uh-huh," said Rose.

"I don't know," I said.

"Come on," Polly said. "I know you just started, but mine's almost over. Just for once I'd like to run with you. Don't you want to run with me?"

Rose Lincoln closed her powder case with a snap and turned to us.

"She won't come with us. She's too busy praying at manger scenes."

"I wasn't praying," I protested.

"Where were you the night Roy almost killed those people?"

"I was there."

"No, you weren't."

"Yes, I was. I was watching, and it didn't happen that way. It wasn't just Roy."

"Watching!" Rose Lincoln scoffed. "All you ever do is watch. Well, don't pray over me. I don't need it, and I don't want it."

I didn't know what to say.

"But I wasn't praying," I said lamely.

"Never mind," Polly said. "You'll run with me next time, won't you?"

"I guess."

"Do you promise?"

"Yes."

Promises are easy to make. You utter a word or two, and it's done. But those are magic words, too. They speak of a defined future to which you are required to adhere. They commit you beyond the length of your experience.

What they do is they take away possibility.

Promises are the opposite of hope.

———

MY FATHER SAID, "You look tired. Are you all right?"

"Yes."

"Come here. Let me feel your forehead."

I went to him. He placed his palm on my forehead.

"You feel a little hot. You're sure you're not getting a fever?"

"I'm fine," I said. "You've been cooking. It's probably your hand that's hot."

He looked at me with suspicion.

"Really, I'm okay. Look."

Then I did some dancing twirls, the kind I used to do for him as a girl. He clapped. He was delighted. He was convinced, once again, that everything was just fine.

———

AND THERE WAS something else. Peter started visiting me in the afternoons, as he had earlier in the school year. He looked at me in a new way since I had gone out during the last moon — as though he had never had sex with Rose Lincoln, as though he had never taken me to the woods and been unable to rape me.

One day after school, he showed up on my doorstep with two wooden mallets and a large bag hoisted over his shoulder.

"What's this?" I asked.

"Croquet!" he said. "It's the game of kings."

"Is it?"

So we drove the wickets into the frozen ground of my back-yard, and, bundled in our coats, we hammered our colored wooden balls through them. It felt good — like reclaiming for civilization the very same lawn where I had woken up in shame just a couple weeks before.

Afterward we went up to my room. While I organized my homework into prioritized piles, I could feel his eyes on me.

"I'm something to you now," I said, turning to him.

"You were always something to me," he said. "But for a while you were too much of a something to me. You were all the way up here, and I was all the way down here." He used the full stretch of his arms to make his point.

"So now I'm all the way down there with you?"

"Not quite." He smiled. "But at least you're close enough that I can see you from where I am."

"And where's Blackhat Roy on that scale?"

Peter shook his head. "It's good he's gone. That guy was bad news. Really, Lumen, you don't even know how bad."

He was restless and disinclined to study. While I copied dates from the world history textbook onto note cards, he browsed the books on my shelves. Once, I had to stop him.

"Hey," I said. "Don't open that. Put it back."

He held in his hands a composition notebook he'd plucked from my shelves.

"What is it?" he asked.

"Just notes."

"What kind of notes? School notes?"

"No. Other kinds of notes. Lists and things."

He gave me a teasing smile.

"Like what? What kinds of lists? Give me one example, and I'll put it back."

"I don't know. Like a list of my favorite authors."

"Hm. Interesting."

But he put the notebook back, as he had promised.

For ten minutes he helped me sort note cards into thematic categories. Then, without warning, he leaned over and kissed me. He pushed his chest against mine, and I liked how our breathing became one breathing. With my eyes closed, I could almost forget about everything.

I still held fans of note cards in my hands, and I didn't know what to do with them. When he finally stopped kissing me, I tried to remember where the cards belonged—but my mind was no longer functioning by the logic of categories.

"Is your father at home?" he asked.

"No."

"When will he be home?"

"Six, usually."

Peter looked at his wristwatch.

"That's two hours," he said. He kissed me again, and I dropped the note cards to the floor and wound my arms around his neck. But when he moved against me, we jostled the desk and my purple pencil cup tipped over with a loud clatter that startled me.

"I think we should stop," I said.

"How come?"

"I don't know. It's a big deal."

He backed up and eyed me with a playful smile.

"Okay," he said. "Fair enough. But we're at an impasse, because I think we should keep going."

"You do? How come?"

"The usual reasons, I guess."

"Like what?" I liked this game. "I'm prepared to listen to logic."

He posed himself thoughtfully on the edge of my bed, a prosecutor prepared to make a complex case.

I laughed.

"You know," I said. "I've never done it before."

"Uh-huh," he said. "Acknowledged. And is it your plan never to do it at all, or do you have an intention to one day make love?"

"It's not my plan *never* to do it." I went over to him where he sat on the bed and stood before him. He looked up at me, and I leaned down to kiss him. He put his hands on my waist. Then he backed away for a moment, again with that sly, strategic smile.

"I see," he said. "So it's a matter of situation. Timing, choice of partner, and the like?"

"I guess."

"So in terms of timing—you just started breaching, I understand?"

"Kind of."

"And you know the types of activities breachers participate in?"

"Yes."

"And in terms of choice of partner—would you say that you have a mostly complete sense of the potential romantic partners available to you here in town?"

"Yes."

He grinned—and I grinned, too.

"I don't think I'm being immodest when I say that this is a case that makes itself."

"Maybe," I said. I kissed him again. I wanted badly to be with him, but I didn't know how to say yes to such things. "I just don't think it's a good idea."

"You don't?"

I shook my head.

"Okay," he said, undeterred. "How about a little competition? How about if I can guess the authors on your favorite authors list? How many do you have on the list?"

"Ten."

"Let's say if I can guess three, we'll call it fate. And when fate tells you to do something, you know you better do it."

"What, with unlimited guesses? That bet's stacked in your favor."

"Well, I'd say it's in both of our favors, but okay. How about ten guesses?"

"Three correct out of ten guesses from my list of ten favorite authors?"

"Right."

I narrowed my eyes at him, and he narrowed his at me.

"Okay," I said.

I went to the shelf and took down the composition notebook and flipped to the page that had my list of favorite authors. I inscribe it here for the record:

CHARLES DICKENS
WILLIAM SHAKESPEARE
JUDY BLUME
JACK KEROUAC
EMILY BRONTË
~~C. S. Lewis~~ URSULA K. LE GUIN
TRUMAN CAPOTE
RUMER GODDEN
~~James Thurber~~ V. C. ANDREWS
P. G. WODEHOUSE

"Okay," Peter said, leaning eagerly forward. "Let's see. How about Shakespeare?"

"No fair," I said. "That was an easy one."

"Your predictability is not my problem. How about Mark Twain?"

"Huh-uh."

"F. Scott Fitzgerald?"

I shook my head.

"Really?" he said.

"He's probably number eleven."

"So a good guess."

"Yeah, a good guess." I moved toward him and gave him a kiss. "That's for your good guess." Then I backed away again.

"All right, all right." He rubbed his palms together and stared at the ceiling. After a while he said, "Dickens."

"Because of *David Copperfield*," I said. "Not for *Tale of Two Cities*."

"So I'm right? Two out of four. That leaves me six guesses for the last one. How do you like my odds?"

"I don't like them at all."

"Remember: fate."

"I remember."

"Okay, let's see." He glanced over at my bookshelves.

"Hey, no unfair advantages."

"Sorry."

He covered his face with his hands.

"Ernest Hemingway," he said eventually.

I gave him a look.

"Okay, no critiques on the wrong guesses, please. Oh, I know. Who's that guy who wrote the Buddha book?"

"Hermann Hesse?"

"Yeah."

"No."

"Sylvia Plath?"

I shook my head.

"Kurt Vonnegut?"

"No."

"Oh, wait, I know—*Lord of the Flies*."

"That's not an author."

"What was his name?"

"William Golding. And no."

"Damn it. How many guesses is that?"

"You have one more."

He was quiet for a long time, his face buried in his hands, and I liked how his sandy hair hung tousled over his fingers.

Suddenly he sat up, looking pleased with himself. He reached out for me and pulled me to him so we were sitting next to each other on the bed. Then he leaned in close. I could smell his skin.

"I got it," he said. "Do you believe I've got it?"

"No," I said, my voice almost a whisper.

"Well, I do. I've got it. Are you ready?"

"I'm ready."

He said it slowly, each syllable a victory:

"J. D. Salinger."

I looked at him for a long time, that pristine boy with his acrobatic teetering between glory and shame. Our faces were impossibly close. We shared the heated air—what he breathed out, I breathed in.

"Well?" he said. "That's it, isn't it? I got it, didn't I?"

And I said, "You got it."

We live our lives by measures of weeks, months, years, but the creatures we truly are, those are exposed in fractions of moments.

It was nothing. Three words. Two of them were even plosives, or stop syllables. *You got it.* Nothing at all. It was a flake of a moment, a fingernail of time—but it was there in that narrow margin between one thing and another that I saw who I really was.

He placed his hands lightly on my chest as though to encase my lack of breasts and protect them from harm. Just as you do with newly planted saplings.

The look on his face, beneath features scarred by moonlit nights in the wild, was awfully earnest—and I didn't think that anything Peter Meechum wanted to do could be very bad. It was a legitimate, daylight thing—it was something done all over the world all the time. It had nothing to do with that ugly, lecherous, queasy feeling in my stomach during the three nights of the full moon. This was something else entirely.

As an act, it was cool, somber, polite.

He removed his clothes, and he told me I should remove mine as well. After that, I lay down, and he scooted his body over mine. His chest against me was bony and raw.

"Are you okay?" he asked.

"Yes."

"Are you ready?"

"Uh-huh. Yes."

I didn't know what to expect. There was a pinch, a slight off feeling, as of something being lodged where it shouldn't be. Like a piece of spinach between your teeth. It hurt a little, but not so much. Peter was very careful and considerate.

"Okay?" he said.

"Okay," I said. "You don't have to keep asking."

So he closed his eyes and went about his business. I watched him, a little firebrand of industry, chugging away at his given chore. It made me think of those chain gangs from movies, the prisoners all shackled together, swinging their pickaxes in unison. The idea made me smile, but I didn't want him to think I was laughing at him, so I turned my head and hid my face in the pillow.

His face grew a deep red color, and then I knew he was done, because he fell off me to the side and made sounds that suggested pride and relief.

I felt something leaking out of me, so I went to the bathroom. I took some of the stuff on my fingers to examine it, because it was new to me. It was slippery and a little sticky, and it smelled like pancake batter. I thought about all the invisible, microbial creatures swimming around in it, and it made me a little nauseated, so I washed my hands. But I wished them all well, his little sperms, as I sent them down the drain.

I wasn't on the pill, but I was pretty sure you couldn't get pregnant when you were amenorrheic.

I was suddenly shy again, so I wrapped a towel around myself before I went back to the bedroom. Peter was still collapsed on the bed, all used up.

"You have to get dressed," I said. "Before my father gets home."

"Okay, but kiss me first. Come here."

He held his arms out, so I went to him. He wanted a long kiss, one of those drawn-out ones from before—but it seemed to me that our sex had changed the kind of kisses called for. So I gave him a quick peck and an amiable pat on the bare shoulder. His skin was flushed and clammy.

He stepped into his underwear and his pants.

"Are you getting dressed, too?" he said.

"Yes."

"What are you waiting for?"

"I don't know. I don't want you to see me."

"You are aware we just had sex, right?"

"I know, but still."

"Tell you what," he said, turning to face the closet door. "I promise not to peek. Let me know when you're decent again."

Which I thought was, after all, a very nice thing.

———

AND ALSO: I'M still waiting. With everything that happened after that day—all the things I have done.

When will I be decent again?

CHAPTER 7

My husband closes the door of his office and turns to look out the window while he eats the lunch I packed for him in the morning. He rotates his head in a small circle, meditatively, as though working out some stiffness in his neck. When he takes a bite of his sandwich, he leans forward, then leans back again to chew it, his eyes squinting at the sunlight coming through the window. With his empty left hand, he taps his fingertips together in sequence — which makes it look as though he's counting something, but I don't think he is. Sometimes, between bites, it's almost as though he has forgotten entirely what he's doing. He just sits, his eyes gone far out over the land, his whole body very, very still, until he remembers to take another bite.

I lean back behind the trunk of my tree so that he cannot see me. There's a sandwich of my own tucked in my purse, and I take it out and eat it along with my husband, taking in the same view he sees. I imagine what it must be like to have an office, a desk, a computer to keep track of your appointments, and people visiting you all day, asking you questions and getting you to put your signature on documents.

A man who works for the school walks by with a rake. He waves at me. I smile at him but make no gesture. It is what a ladybug would do, I imagine, smiling indifferently at the world and continuing on her way.

I peek around the tree trunk, and when it is safe, I continue watching Jack. There's one young woman who visits him frequently—she looks like a teacher. During dinner, he usually recounts his day to me in some detail, but he has never told me about her. She wears her hair in a ponytail and speaks in a very animated fashion and does a funny thing where she sits on his desk while she talks. I wonder if they have had sex, locked in his office after hours or suddenly, fervently, in her car in the deserted parking lot under the buzzing lamplight. She is very pretty, and she laughs easily.

Later, when I go to pick my son up at school, the children are all running to and fro on the playground. My son is being chased—or he is chasing, it's impossible to tell—and as I watch, he trips and falls and begins to cry. He sits up and raises his scraped palms to the air. I can see that they are streaked sooty black and pocked with gravel, and they are bleeding a little. Hands are things that never stay undamaged for very long. They go everywhere, and they feel the suffering of all the tactile world. That's why people use fingerprints to identify you—the scarred record of everything you have touched.

My boy cries, as children do when they are in pain.

His teacher, Miss Lily, is suddenly beside me.

"Mrs. Borden," she says.

"Yes?"

"Marcus," she says, pointing. "Your son."

"Oh, yes," I say and go to fetch Marcus and tend to his bloody hands. We wash them in cool water, and I tell him about mountain streams and all the animals that cool their paws in them.

He asks me have I ever been to a mountain stream, and I tell him I have.

He asks me have I ever had my hands scraped like his. I tell him I have, indeed, had that—and much, much worse.

———

WE ALL PREPARE faces to go outside. The world at large does not see us for who we really are, does not see the version of ourselves that's exposed maybe only in front of mirrors in our tiny bedrooms. So we look out our windows, and we dress ourselves for the day, and we put on our masks, and we become the performance of an hour or two—before we can find a place to be alone and breathe again, just for a moment.

Somewhere along the line, we are taught to restrict ourselves for the benefit of the outside world and to be only truly free behind closed doors. Somehow the outside and the inside reverse themselves.

But what if it didn't have to be this way? What if upon stepping outside we shed everything that was not ourselves? We might feel our skin pressed up against all other skins. Discover how meager are the boundaries between our flesh and the flesh of others, the pulpy flesh of trees, the gritty flesh of soil, the tarry flesh of tarmac cooling after collecting a day's worth of sunlight. What if we clambered roughshod over the surface of the earth? Wouldn't the world be our true home?

———

I BECAME, AFTER that first moon, a creature drawn to dark, enclosed spaces. The maps I drew were now heavy with ink, cut through with narrow paths of white. After school, I would sometimes sit in the very back row of the darkened auditorium, watching Mr. Hunter and the drama club rehearse for the school play. I didn't know what the play was—something about union workers in the oil fields.

Mr. Hunter paced back and forth below the stage, trying to explain the significance of the oil. He spoke of the blood of the land—faces gone black with crude, raised to the grimy rain of the stuff. He urged them to think about their own connection to the land, those reveled-in, mucky parts of themselves.

He always seemed to know I was there. He would come to the back and sit next to me, and we would watch the actors declaiming.

"They don't get it, do they?" he said to me. "How can they not get it?"

"They might be a lot of different things," I said, "but they can only be one thing at a time."

He gazed at me with eyes that were accustomed to the dark, and I looked away, embarrassed.

I found myself returning to the quarry—the place where, two years before, Hondy Pilt was chased from the mouth of the mine by a possum. I liked the definition of the place, the artful ridges, the geometrical clefts, the shaved planes of earth—like God's precise fingerprint. I bundled myself up against the cold and lay flat on the frozen earth at its very lowest point.

Once I heard the approach of others and fled to the mouth of the mine, where I watched in darkness a boy and a girl kissing each other on the berm, creating little landslides of pebbled stone. It was an hour before they were through. To keep myself occupied, I felt my way deeper into the mine, one hand flat against the wall, one directly in front of me so I wouldn't run into anything in the pitch black, my feet moving an inch at a time so I wouldn't tumble into an unseen shaft.

I liked it in there. The closeness. The dark. The feeling of being inside out.

What I did was I started mapping the mine.

In our garage, I found an old lantern, which I revived by cleaning the contacts and loading it with fresh D batteries. This was preferable to a regular flashlight for exploring the mine shafts because its light shone in all directions at once. I also carried a penlight in my pocket and held it in my teeth when I paused to inscribe some new part of the map in my notebook. I drew the map as I went. If I reached the edge of a notebook page, I continued on another page and coded both pages with letters and numbers that identified the sequence. I measured distances by my paces and noted those as well on long, straight passages. I drew in features of the mine as place markers. I knew to go left at the overturned mine cart because right was a dead end. I drew a picture of a collapsed wooden frame that looked like a crucifix because it marked the passage to a three-way split in the tunnels. For places where there were no natural markers, I brought along a hammer and nailed ribbons into the ground. The different colors of ribbon meant different things, and I wrote codes on them in marker that referred to the codes in my map notebook.

I carried a baggie of trail mix, too, for when I got hungry. And a stick to scare away possums and rats.

It was cold underground, and damp. The walls were wet with icy water, as though the thaw of spring had not penetrated to this stratum of the earth. I wore a plastic slicker, because sometimes the caverns rained on me, the water droplets echoing loudly in the confines of stone.

I was frightened each time I went—and I thought that I might die. People did die all the time in old mines. There were wide vertical shafts of pure black that seemed bottomless when I listened for the sound of the stones I dropped in them. But it was also peaceful there. And living and dying were not everything to me then.

It was clear that no one had gone deep into the mine in a very long time. The ground up to the first intersection was cluttered with empty bottles, flattened potato chip bags, torn sweaters, tin cans that had been shot through with holes or fashioned into marijuana-smoking devices, even a rotted teddy bear half buried in the packed dirt. But beyond that first intersection the atmosphere was thick with dust, and with my stick I had to brush away spiderwebs that quivered to and fro in the currents of stale air. Once I accidentally dislodged a rock and found a swarm of white spiders that ran off every which way and hid themselves in other fissures of stone.

What was I looking for? What did I seek?

I fantasized about finding some ancient miner who had lost his way in the caverns and never found his way out. He would have set up house somewhere deep underground, a pretty little cave of a living room lit by torches, a patchwork area rug made of discarded miner's clothing.

He would greet me, knowing me on sight, of course, as a fellow dweller of the substrata. We would speak in the secret language that I knew must exist between travelers in the dark.

Sometimes I hummed as I went, and my voice in those caverns was like the sound of my voice in my own head when I closed the flaps of my ears.

I was accustomed to being alone.

I had been spelunking empty caverns my whole life. What I sought were the tunnels that led back underneath the town, the ones that would disclose all the buried truths of the place. There might be whole cities under the surface of the earth, populated by wise men who could see in the dark and who knew, better than I or anyone, how the secret gears of the world worked. And I could speak with them. And they would love me and call me their little light from above, and they would take me in as one of their own.

I had grown sick with questions—and what I searched for was a kingdom of answers.

———

ROUTINE IS IMPORTANT for people like me. It keeps us anchored in reality. It's how we keep from spinning off into the ether.

After I went breach, I did my best to establish a new set of routines to accommodate the disturbances my life became subject to—to diminish their significance by making them normal. Every morning before I brushed my teeth, I examined the sheets of my bed. I knew I would find no blood, but the checking itself became the point. I made my demon disappointment into a simple pattern and so exorcised it. That's how you keep things safe.

Peter started coming over regularly after school, three afternoons a week—three because that is a fairy-tale number and because I liked putting symbols on those days in my calendar to anticipate and memorialize them.

We had sex on those three afternoons every week. We never said much—never said a thing afterward. The act was bigger than words. I was illiterate in the language of bodies, so I abandoned myself to it, and it was lovely not to think so much—simply to feel the firecracker spark of nerves starting in my toes and skittering up my legs.

When it was done, we were diligent about our homework.

I was frequently embarrassed. I knew what we were doing was natural—but not all nature was the same. The stars didn't care about sweat and kisses and panting. They glistened prettily way up there in their heavens. They beatified the sky with their cool, gemlike indifference.

So why shouldn't I?

———

JANUARY'S BRITTLE MOON came.

I didn't want to see anyone else, so I didn't go to the woods. Instead I ran in the other direction, to the center of town. In a parking lot, I found a woman still out after dark. I stood watching her, naked, unashamed. I felt as though I could hurt her. The town, it was mine. The parking lot was mine. She saw me in the distance. What I must have looked like—the tiny, pale-skinned naked girl with her little fists clenched! The woman ran. When she saw me, she ran to her car, fumbled her keys, dropped them to the ground, picked them up again, finally got the car door open, launched herself inside, and closed herself in.

I twitched for wanting to claw at her face. I wondered when was the last time her skin was opened up.

Two thoughts occurred to me simultaneously:

Why was this woman afraid of me?

Why wasn't she more afraid of me?

I went to the town square, where there was a clock tower, a

monument to the soldiers of some war, a gazebo surrounded by grass and trees and shrubbery. It was the place where, last month, the breachers had attacked the girls and boys from the next town.

I trampled over the grass, the frost crystals tickling my toes. The storefronts were all lit up by buzzing street lamps. In the far distance I could hear the low, tidal hiss of the freeway that carried traffic past our little town. But there were no cars going by on the streets around me. No one drove on the three nights of the full moon. Adults lived in dread of running over the wild breachers bounding across dark streets.

Also, they didn't want to see. Once, out of curiosity, I crept up on a house down the block from where I lived. The lights were on in the front room, and I could see someone in there, sleeping on a recliner in front of the television. I put my face against the pane of glass and even tasted it with the tip of my tongue. It was metallic, cold. Then, as though he could sense me there watching him, the man woke suddenly and turned to the window. Our eyes met. I recognized him. We'd never spoken, but I knew him from the neighborhood. He wore a straw hat when he watered his lawn and always smiled at me when I passed by on the way home from school.

Now, seeing me, he looked at his watch and clambered up from the recliner. For a moment he seemed undecided about what to do. I was surprised, standing naked before his window, that I wasn't more self-conscious. But I wanted to see him for what he truly was. I wanted to watch. Finally he came to the window. We looked at each other again, but then his eyes dropped, as if in shame or modesty—and then, very slowly, so as not to incite me, perhaps, he drew the curtains closed.

The nighttime shame of our town. It's what curtains were made for.

Now, in the town square, I reflected on the man's shame.

I decided I wanted to be on top of the gazebo, the way Peter had been when he had looked so kingly during the last moon, so I stalked around it until I found a way up by overturning a trash can and climbing onto the sloped roof. I scraped my belly to pieces hoisting myself over the lip of the roof, but once on top, I lay back and luxuriated in the sting of my cuts.

It was quiet there in the dead center of things. So quiet. I could hear the insistent insect buzz of the street lamps. I could hear the creak of the hanging sign suspended over the barbershop, swinging back and forth in the breeze. I could hear the low mechanical click of the stoplights as they turned from green to amber to red—signs without meaning, because there was no one around to be directed by them.

It was a time to take stock of things, but I couldn't think straight. I wanted to put it all in order, to line it all up. I wanted to go through the list of the people I knew and assess where they fit in my life. I wanted to draw a map and put them all on it. But my thoughts were all bloody or obscene, and it made me want to cry. And I did cry. My mind did weep while my body raged—and there must be something of the mind in the gutters of the body, because I could feel the tickle of real tears creeping down the sides of my cheeks and into the folds of my ears.

I must have slept, because when I opened my eyes again I could hear someone in the gazebo beneath me. It was still deep night, still no one in any direction I could see. I crawled to the sloping edge of the gazebo roof and lowered my head to look.

Hondy Pilt was there, staring right at me, as though he knew that's where I would appear from.

———

"HELLO," I SAID.

"Hello," he said. He never said much, Hondy, but when he did his words were serene and wise-sounding. Even a simple hello.

I swung myself down off the roof of the gazebo, and I sat with my knees to my chest on the bench across from Hondy. For a full minute, we stalked each other with our eyes, as was our habit in those days. Because we were so keenly aware that any human interaction could end in passion or violence, it was important to determine, with muscles rigid and teeth clenched, the direction of the exchange as much as possible before you began it.

He sat pharaohlike, with his palms flat on his thighs, almost completely hairless except for the top of his head and the curls around his lumpy genitals. His skin looked pink in the light of the street lamps, ruddy and young. His stomach bulged a little, and there was a roundness to all the parts of his body. He was a large boy—but my instincts told me I didn't have to defend myself from him, so I relaxed and breathed more deeply.

"How come you're not with the others?" I said.

He smiled up at the serene stars.

"Let me ask you a question," I said. "How long've you been breaching? It's got to be over a year now, right? Are you ever going to stop?"

The street lamps buzzed their electrical buzz.

"Yeah," I said, as though he'd actually answered. I glanced around to make sure no one else was in the vicinity. "You want to know something? I'm not a real breacher. At least, I'm not the same kind as other people."

I watched for his response. Perhaps he would look at me with shock and horror. Perhaps he would march off to unite with the common heart that was not mine.

His gaze came down from the sky long enough to look me in the face.

But the pale gentleness of his eyes did not change. My secret shame, the starry sky, a leaf of newspaper blown down the middle of an empty street—to Hondy they were all of a kind. The progress of the slowly turning earth. We turned with it.

And I suddenly wanted to tell him more, to tell him everything.

"My mother, she never breached. That's how I know. See, I have her blood. So I can't be a real breacher. I'm something else. Something worse, probably—because for me it's not about nature. You understand? It's not natural for me. Even this—being here like this—it's a lie. And my father, he doesn't know. He's been alone for a long time. He misses my mother more than anything. Sometimes that's all he is, the leftovers of my mom. And sometimes I do things with Peter Meechum, who used to be called Petey, and I don't know why he wants to be around me, really, he could have any girl—but there was also Roy Ruggle, who everyone calls Blackhat, and he's gone now, and everyone's happy about it except me, and I don't know why I feel bad for him but I do, and Rose Lincoln used to be called Rosebush, and everybody seems to have a new name except me—I'm just Lumen, which means light, but I think there's something gone rotten in me, Hondy—"

I stopped short. It seemed that the night might crack apart.

"I've gone rotten somehow," I said. "I used to be good. I used to know things. People used to give me prizes for what I knew. Now I don't know anything, and I don't even know what good looks like anymore. Remember we used to send valentines to everyone in class? They had hearts and flowers and shy girls in dresses and boys with straw hats? That's what good looks like to me now. That's how far away. And I don't know what it means, except that I'm rotting out from the inside."

Hondy Pilt shook his head.

"No," he said quietly.

"What?"

"No."

"What do you mean?"

I went over and sat next to him. He looked at the stars.

I wanted to smell his skin, and I did, putting my nose at the place where his arm met his torso. He smelled of powder.

Then my lips were on his chest, but it wasn't like kissing—instead, they were parted slightly, and I brushed them over his skin as though I were reading some truth in the textures of him.

He looked at the stars.

He was so much bigger than I was. I leaned into him, pressed my little body against his. From my memory, a phrase throbbed into my brain like a heartbeat—"more than the sum of our parts"—and I liked it. I wondered what was made in the meeting of our skins. Something large but invisible.

I'd confessed to him.

I reached over and put my hand on his genitals. They were soft and warm. They felt strangely loose, unincorporated.

I wanted to stay there all night, but Hondy Pilt pushed me away. With one hand on my shoulder, he pushed me back as though I were a blanket somebody had thrown over him on a hot night. There was no malice in the act, the same way you don't blame a door for being open or being shut.

Was I an open door or a shut one?

He stood, his attention suddenly caught by something I couldn't see down the street. Some vagary of the night, I supposed—there were so many things I did not see.

———

MY FATHER GOT the map I made him for Christmas framed and hung it in his office, where he could look at it all the time.

Peter Meechum continued making love to me in the afternoons. He said it made him very happy. One time he wondered aloud why I only had sex with him between full moons—which made me the exact opposite of some other girls. He wasn't really asking, so I didn't feel the need to answer him.

And it turned out that January's Brittle Moon was the last breach for Polly. When February's moon came, Polly remained indoors.

"Only eleven months," she said. "I was cheated."

"Maybe you just mature faster than other people," I said to reassure her.

"You're right. Maybe that's what it is."

She smiled, satisfied. She seemed to take it to heart. Suddenly she had no more patience for childish things. Her first order of business was to redecorate her bedroom. She told her parents she could no longer tolerate the pinks and purples. What she required, she told them, were what she called "tasteful blues and creams."

The weeks went on. I hid my full-moon activities from my father, but I think he must have known. Once, there was a long scratch on my neck. He didn't ask about it, but I know he saw.

We all have our fictions. It's not for other people to expose them. And yet I wondered more and more about my mother. I wondered what fictions she might have had. What did she do indoors during the full moons? How did she occupy herself? What stories did she tell herself, all on her own, while the whole town went crazy around her?

———

IN FEBRUARY EVERYTHING was crystals. There were icicles on every eave. I, too, was a brittle stalactite. It seemed that I might not ever grow up, that I might not ever be fully alive. Wandering the mine shafts, I had buried myself. I had shrouded myself with death. I was a premature ghost.

That was also the month that Mr. Hunter asked me to tell him stories.

It was in the middle of a *Hamlet* test. The only sounds in the classroom were the hiss of pens on paper and the occasional creak of a desk as we repositioned ourselves in our seats. I was in the middle of an essay question on the significance of Ophelia's suicide when he startled me by leaning down and whispering in my ear.

"I'm pressing you into service," he said. "Meet me in the auditorium after school."

I couldn't tell you how I finished that test, my stomach tight, my face gone flush, my pen clutched too tight in my fist. I had always been wary of the man, and I was not the kind of girl who received whispered invitations. But I went because I did what I was told to do. Agreeableness was my secret pride.

The auditorium looked empty when I got there, with a high, echoey stillness like that of a church between services. I let the door close softly behind me and waited for my eyes to adjust to the dimness.

"Lumen," he said, and I could make out his form sitting on the edge of the stage. "Come in."

"It's dark."

"I don't want to be bothered."

I walked slowly down the sloping aisle between the empty

seats, which always made me feel like a bride, and when I got to the stage he told me to sit, so I sat on the stage near him, but I kept my distance, my legs dangling over the edge, as his were.

He smiled a strange smile at me, and I didn't know what it meant, and I waited for what would happen next.

"I want you to tell me about it," he said. "The breaching."

"Tell you?"

"Tell me what it's like. You know I didn't grow up here. I didn't experience it myself."

It felt like such a personal thing for him to be asking in such a direct and unapologetic fashion.

"I want to know," he said simply.

"Why me?"

"Lots of reasons," he said. "The main one is that you want to tell it."

I didn't enjoy being fathomed like that.

"I better go," I said.

I stood and started to walk back up the aisle. I wondered what he would do. If he would demand for me to halt or seize me from behind. But he did nothing at all.

I was halfway up the aisle when I stopped and turned and saw him still sitting, unmoved, with a bemused look on his face.

"Where are you from?" I asked from my safe distance.

"East Saint Louis."

"What's Missouri like?"

"Actually, it's Illinois—it's across the river from Saint Louis."

"Oh."

"The mighty Mississippi. It runs brown with mud."

"Oh." Each word I said sounded smaller in the dark.

"Normal."

"What?"

"You asked what Missouri's like. It's normal. Illinois, normal. Saint Louis, normal. East Saint Louis, normal. Partridge Street, with its kids riding bicycles before dinnertime—normal. So much normal you could choke on it."

There was a roughness to him always, as though he were constantly chewing on some bitter root. He was someone who seemed to have little tolerance for things. His demeanor suggested I could stay or go as I pleased. So I stayed.

"It's like a highway," I said, feeling for a moment like I was standing alone, speaking to myself. "The breaching. It's like a long highway in the desert, and you can't see the end of it, and you can see everything for miles in every direction, and there's nothing but you—and maybe that's a good thing, or maybe that's a bad thing, or maybe it's both. But it's just you and your guts in the middle of a desert."

I waited for him to respond, but he said nothing at all. He just leaned forward a little and waited for me to continue.

And that's how it started between him and me.

—

SOMETIMES I TELL myself stories still. During the days, when my husband is at work and my son is at school, I walk through the house tidying things and listening to the tales my voice has to tell.

"There once was a man, just like you and me," I say, "except that at night he liked to remove his head from his shoulders and keep it in a wicker basket beside his bed."

I straighten the pile of coasters on the coffee table and am gone out far in my imagination.

Lola King, who has let herself in by my kitchen door, startles me.

"Who are you talking to, sweetie?"

"Oh," I say. "No one. Just doing some cleaning."

"You're losing it," she says. "Let's us girls have a couple Bloody Marys and go put dirty magazines in Marcie's mailbox. What do you say?"

Lola is lawless. She sees me as the innocent she delights in corrupting. I wonder what she might look like running wild in the woods, naked under the moonlight, tearing at life with her painted fingernails.

She tells me stories about her life before she came here—in New Jersey, where her husband was acquainted with some bad men who sometimes cleaned their guns at her kitchen table. She means to appall me, so I widen my eyes and shake my head slowly back and forth.

We all have stories to tell. Our demons are sunk deep under the skin, and maybe we use stories to exorcise them—or at least know them truly.

———

BEGGAR'S MOON CAME at the end of February. I went into town—but different parts of the town, the places where the others never went. I ran until I was out of breath, my burning lungs heaving for air while I stood naked and alone in the middle of an empty supermarket parking lot. There was an unearthly luminescent glow coming from the supermarket, and I walked toward it until I stood on the sidewalk in front of the massive plate-glass windows. Next to me was a recycling bin filled with empty beer bottles. It gave off an acrid smell that I found comforting. The rear of the store was dark, but they had left the overhead lights on in the front. I pressed my palms to the glass, wanting to feel

the nighttime haunt of a place that the daylight had seen all pop-
ulous.

Surely spirits lingered. Surely they moved slower than bodies,
always half a day behind their corporeal counterparts. I knew this
to be true, because I felt my own spirit still alive somewhere in
the daylight, left behind in the comfort of my bedroom, reading
a book or calculating trigonometry. My spirit was graceful and
true—something to make my father proud.

I felt it alive somewhere. Somewhere else.

There was a sound behind me, and I turned. It was Roddy
Ewell. We knew each other from school. He was in the grade
below me, and he was small, too. I had wondered, the previous
year, if he might ever consider being my boyfriend. Though it had
been a long time since he had crossed my mind at all.

He casted a splay of shadows beneath the humming lamps of
the parking lot—as though his own spirit were manifold and on
the escape.

"I followed you," he said.

"Why?"

"How come you don't run with everyone else? It's not natural."

I turned my back to him and gazed through the plate glass into
the empty store. There was a delicate magic to empty places. I
wished myself inside and wondered what it would take to break
the window with my head.

"Never mind," he said behind me. "I like you. Can we do it?"

"What?" I said, not looking at him. "What did you say?"

"I said, can we do it?"

"Do what?"

"You know."

"Oh, that. No."

"But the moon." He pointed at the sky, though there was no moon to be seen because it was hidden behind clouds.

"No."

"Why not?"

This is what I had learned about breachers—you were either weak or you were strong. How you presented yourself determined what happened to you. Roddy Ewell did not bother to attack, because he assumed I presented no threat. He thought, between the two of us, that I was the weak one.

He should not have thought that.

When I didn't answer, he came up behind me and wrapped his arms around my body. I could feel his penis, erect, against my bottom. I turned myself out of his grasp and shoved him backward.

"Stop it," I said. "You're pathetic."

He cringed, surprised. "What?" he said. This was not going as he had imagined it. My defiance had caught him off guard.

I hated his weakness. I wanted to kill his weakness. I could feel the violence in me twitching all up and down the nerves of my body.

"You're different," he said. "You didn't used to be like this."

For reasons I did not care to explore, this was unacceptable to me. I reached for one of the empty bottles from the bin next to me, and I threw it at him. He flinched, and the bottle hit him in the shoulder then fell and smashed on the concrete.

"Ouch," he said.

"Don't say ouch."

I took another bottle and threw it at him. He knocked it away, but it made a gash on his forearm, and there was blood.

"Ouch," he said. "Stop it."

"Don't say it. I told you not to say it. You don't come to me unafraid. Don't you dare. You think I don't know how to make pain?"

I attacked. I leaped at him, this meager boy, even though I was smaller than he, smaller than everyone. I threw myself at him, and we tumbled to the tarmac of the parking lot, the grit digging into our skin. He held his arms up to defend himself, but it made no difference. I clawed haphazardly, my fingernails digging bloody troughs in the flesh of his arms, his chest, his shoulders.

"Stop!" He sobbed. "Please, please stop it!"

I couldn't hear for all the horror happening in my head. I didn't think. I couldn't tell what was happening. All I knew was ravenous hunger. I wanted to eat that little-boy soul. I wanted to chew it up and swallow it so that maybe he could be a little stronger, or so that maybe the world could.

I could hear my own voice, like a mongrel dog's, grunting and gurgling, and I was surprised. I was blank. The world was white skin and red blood.

I tore at him until he wriggled out from under me. We were both bloodied and raw.

He ran into the darkness, the soles of his feet slapping wetly against the pavement.

I remember nothing else. My mind was truly lost.

I woke the next morning weeping, huddled in a tight ball against the front door of my house. My body shook with the pain of its injuries and the suffocating strength of my sobs. For a long time, I could not stop, and I put my fist in my mouth to hush my cries.

After a while, I had calmed myself enough to go inside.

That was the end of Beggar's Moon.

—

BETWEEN MOONS, I went back to the mine. And I discovered something new in my exploration—a large, hollowed-out chamber, an echoing cistern. Even though its entrance was near the mouth of the mine, I had never noticed it before because it required that I pry loose a collapse of stones and crawl my way through a narrow aperture.

It was a majestic place, a sacramental place. The cave was circular, the dripping walls rising high like a dome in a church. At the very top of the dome was an opening, the size of our kitchen tabletop at home, through which I could see the dusky pink of the late afternoon sky, the overhanging bristles of tree branches.

The floor of the cave was mostly flat, but in the middle was the mouth of a wide shaft, roughly the same size as the opening above, that descended down into pure abyss. I wondered if the shaft and the opening had shared some kind of purpose in the old days of the mine, so symmetrical and aligned did they seem—as though God had poked a gigantic needle into the pincushion of the world. I crept close to the edge of the chasm and felt my stomach do vertiginous tumbles. I stared down into the void so long that I lost track of myself. I hugged a nearby outcropping of stone because I didn't trust myself to stay sane exposed to such nullities. If I leaped in, I might fall forever. I wondered if I would die of fright before I hit the bottom so that my landing might be a curious ghostly bliss.

I thought maybe that's where my previous self had gone, down there in the depthless black, and I spoke to her.

"Lumen Ann Fowler," I said, trusting that my meager voice would carry down the well in the absence of any material to impede it. "Lumen Ann Fowler, Lumen Ann Fowler."

I knew that repetitions of three had power to them. And if you could summon Bloody Mary by uttering her name three times in a mirror, then I reckoned you could summon a lost girl in a similar way.

"It's me, Lumen," I said. "I came looking for you."

I waited, listening to my own breathing in that silent place.

"I know who you are. I remember you. Do you want me to prove it? Your mother wore orchid gloves at her wedding."

I swallowed, and there was grit in my throat. I leaned my head against the outcropping of stone and gripped it tighter.

"It's all right," I said. "You don't have to say anything. We can just be quiet for a while."

It was a home. It was a chapel. A shaft of light shone down at an angle through the opening and lit up all sparkly the grains of dust afloat on the air. This was a chamber of echoes that might as well have been the clattering ossuary of my own mind, and I decided it would be a place of pilgrimage for me.

When the light through the opening above dimmed with impending night, I crawled back out into the mine shaft proper and piled a few stones in front of the entrance to my private citadel so that it would not be stumbled upon by strangers.

Once outside the mine I tried to locate the place in the ground where the cistern opened to the sky, but I never could find it.

As though the avenues of inside and outside used different maps altogether.

CHAPTER 8

Worm Moon was wet with rainfall. You listened to the showers against your windowpanes. You imagined what it must be like to luxuriate in such a torrent, naked, and you thrilled with anticipation. Blackhat Roy came back.

I went to bed early, listening to the thunder, and I fell asleep. But my body jolted itself awake an hour after I lay down. I lurched to the window and opened it and leaped out. It was all very simple when the moon came out. All the considerations and doubts and rationalizations of the daytime were sloughed away. I wanted to be outside, and so I went outside.

It is sometimes a joy to be rained on. The chill of it against your scalp, the tickle of it down the inside of your thighs.

I ran down to the lake to see the ripples on the water and to watch the lightning fork down from the clouds. The others were already there. Some were swimming in the black water, others lay on the muddy earth. I liked looking at the bodies from the shadows of the trees. To look at someone's naked body in the moonlight is to know that person in a new way. Lumpy humanity laid bare. A person stripped of all masks. For surely, I realized, that is what we do. We start with one pure and concentrated version of ourselves, then we modify and mold, we layer defense over pretense over convention. By the time we're done getting dressed in the morning, there is little left of who we really are. It's all just art. Twee and ineffectual art. Cartoon figures drawn in crayon on a paper place mat in a family-friendly Italian restaurant.

Hondy Pilt was there, gazing monklike into the downpour. Sue Foxworth was there. And Adelaide Warren. Rose Lincoln came, too, emerging from the trees with Peter Meechum behind her. Rose's breach had gone on longer than a year. Each full moon was supposed to be her last. But here she was again.

I wondered if she and Peter had been having sex in the rain, and I thought I might enjoy killing her. But such instincts in me seemed to go straight to the brain, where violence takes seed and grows larger over time rather than permitting itself release in the moment. I would say nothing.

Idabel McCarron came up to me and pressed her slippery body to mine. I allowed it, because the sensation was new to me—and, besides, we were all a little rain-drunk.

"Did you hear?" she whispered in my ear. "He's back."

"Who?"

"Look."

She pointed, and just at that moment, emerging from the lake like some mammalian vestige of prehistory, was Blackhat Roy.

He was different—I saw it immediately. He seemed larger, for one thing, a bigger, more solidified version of himself—though after just three months, I don't know if that was possible.

Peter was also seeing him for the first time. He left Rose Lincoln's side and approached Roy. The two stood face-to-face on the lakeshore in the rain. When they were together like that, I could see that Roy still had to angle his head up to meet Peter's eyes. But he was bigger. I swear it. Somehow he commanded more space.

"I thought you were in Chicago," Peter said quietly.

"I'm back."

"Why?"

"You want to hear the whole story? It might cause you grief."

He was different. In my mind, I tried to telegraph to Peter to be careful, because Blackhat Roy was different.

Thunder quaked in the distance. The rain unfurled sideways, like a sheet pinned to a clothesline in the wind. We didn't shield ourselves from it.

"You shouldn't have come back," Peter said. "You don't belong here."

"Really? I would have thought this is exactly where I belonged."

"You terrorized those people."

It seemed that Peter, along with everyone else, had convinced himself of certain fictions about that night.

"Terrorized!" Roy laughed. Then he said the word again, as though he didn't think much of it. "Terrorized."

That's when Peter struck him, his closed fist cutting across Roy's jaw. But Roy didn't move. He put his hand up to his face—as though curious about the pain he found there. Then he raised his voice, because he wasn't just talking to Peter—he was talking to all of us.

"Nobody cares about your noble faggotry. You want dominance? This is how you get it."

And he grabbed Peter's shoulders and kneed him in the crotch. Peter went down, and Roy was on top of him. For several minutes we watched as the two grappled together on the wet earth, the lightning capturing them in gaudy white tableaux, their blood, as they clawed and bit at each other, streaming together with the rain.

Peter stood no chance. There was no fairness in the way Roy fought, no reason, no daylight. He fought as though the choice were pain or death and he had made his decision years before. Peter curled himself into a ball on the shore, but Roy kept after him, crouching over him, biting through the skin of his neck, licking the blood from his lips while Peter whimpered beneath him.

A great foulness, and we all stood and watched. Some, boys and girls alike, rubbed their hands unconsciously between their legs as they observed. We had appetites back then. We knew what we felt.

———

THE RAIN STOPPED. The tree branches overhead continued to drip for a while, but they finally stopped, too.

Once he was through with Peter, Roy walked away. I kneeled over Peter, trying to clean him up, but he hit my hands away.

"I'll kill him," he hissed. "Kill him."

"You're bleeding."

"He's filth."

"Put your hand on your neck. Otherwise you'll get dizzy."

He would not let me touch him, but I tended to him as best I could and made sure he got home in the morning.

Me, I snuck back into my house and was in bed before my father woke. As my bedroom turned pink with early light, I fell asleep and dreamed of boy-skin made slick with blood.

———

THE NEXT DAY I went to Peter's house, but his mother told me he didn't want to see anyone. I asked if I could write him a letter, and she gave me a pad of notepaper and a ballpoint pen.

I wrote:

Peter—

I'm sorry about what happened to you. It doesn't mean any-thing. Sometimes it's a hideous world. Please call me if you need anything.

Love, Lumen

That night I went back to the lake. It seemed to me that things had changed, and I wanted to see how.

Peter was not there. Instead there was Blackhat Roy. Just like that. And so masters and slaves are nothing but the turn of a card.

It was Blackhat Roy, pulling along, as if on a leash, Poppy Bishop, a girl I knew who herself had just started breaching. She was his. She had regressed to infancy, as some do under the in-fluence of the full moon. Her violence was an infant's violence, as was her sensuality. She trailed along behind Roy, sucking her thumb and using her other hand to tug on her earlobe. When she had a tantrum, she became hysterical, striking out this way and that with a toddler's murderous rage. Afterward, when she set-tled down, you might find her curled up, her head in Roy's lap, nursing at Roy's indifferent penis as though it were a binky.

And there were two other new breachers, too. A boy and a girl I recognized from school—from the grade below mine. They held hands like Hansel and Gretel finding their way through the wilderness of mythology, and they were frightened.

I didn't like to look at Blackhat Roy—who seemed to have contempt for everyone around him—and I thought about running off on my own. But I wanted to stay and look at the new members of the brood.

The skin of the two new ones—their names were Ben MacClusky and Mandy Cavell—shimmered pale against the trees. They seemed somehow brighter than the rest of us. As though we all started out luminescent and then faded over time. As though we were all just waiting for our lights to gutter out.

Mandy Cavell was not entirely naked. She wore a pair of white cotton underpants.

Blackhat Roy left Poppy Bishop sucking her thumb atop a rock and approached Mandy Cavell. He said nothing for a moment, instead just walking a slow circle around her while she stood there breathing hard. Then he stopped in front of her.

She would not meet his eyes. Her own gaze had been cast demurely downward, and then Blackhat Roy positioned himself in such a way that his genitals must have been directly in her line of sight.

"Hey," he said. And he had to say it again before the girl looked up at him. "Hey."

"I'm sorry," she said.

"For what?"

She had no answer to this.

"Don't you want to take those off?" Roy said to her.

She shook her head.

"I think you do," he insisted.

She looked at him. Then she looked at the boy next to her, but he was no help. His eyes snapped back and forth between the trees and all the naked girl bodies around him.

"You want to take them off," Roy said again. "But you don't do it. Why not? What's the point of fighting against yourself?"

"It's not nice."

Roy laughed.

"Not nice," he said. "That's true. Nice is one thing it's not."

Mandy Cavell looked around helplessly. I felt for her. She reminded me of some lost version of myself.

"Stop it," I said to Blackhat Roy.

I emerged from the shadows, and everyone looked at me. I didn't like all those eyes on me, but I was feeling hard, and it was a feeling new to me—and I wanted to own it for myself. Somehow Peter's beating the night before had made me romantic for suffering.

"Leave her alone," I said.

Blackhat Roy did leave the girl alone. Instead he came and stood in front of me. I didn't feel like quailing, so I didn't.

"Leave her alone why?" he asked me.

"What do you care if she wants to leave her underwear on?"

"Do you see anybody else out here with diapers?"

"Isn't she supposed to be able to do what she wants? Isn't that what this is all about? Or are you just replacing one kind of conformity for another?"

He looked down at me, and his eyes wanted to gnaw on my bones.

"No," he said. "I'm just showing concern. When the moon's out, you should be able to piss where you want."

Then, without moving, Blackhat Roy let go a stream of urine that splashed against my thigh and ran down my leg. It tickled as it streamed over my ankle and between my toes and made a muddy puddle around my foot. The smell was sharp, and the heat of it in the cold night made a steam that rose between us as our eyes locked.

I made no move. But this wasn't a refusal—not at all. It was an engagement. I stood still, allowing his urine to soak my leg. It went on for an absurdly long time. At first the others laughed. They brayed at this new spectacle. But then, when I refused to run or even look away from his gaze, they got silent again. They recognized that something was happening. They saw that this was not the end of something or a punch line, but really just the beginning.

When he was done, we continued to look at each other. I wondered what his eyes were telling me, then I thought it must be an invitation to violence.

Part of me wanted just to turn and leave—part of me knew that would be the true victory. The animal is no more diminished than when you turn your back on it.

But there was another part of me, and it was hungering to rip and tear. It was wanting to sunder the whole beautiful and ugly world, to play in the exposed guts of all that beauty and ugliness.

It was a desire to kill, and it was ecstatic.

My right arm shot up, my hand like a claw, and it tore across Blackhat Roy's face. Three irregular lines of blood appeared on his cheek where my fingernails had torn him. As we faced each other, saying nothing, the blood began to seep from the cuts, trickling over the ledge of his chin and down his neck.

Everyone was quiet. Tiny waves broke against the lakeshore.

Still, he made no move. A smile spread slowly across his face, and his eyes narrowed.

"Okay," he whispered. "Good."

Then he raised a hand, and that's when I flinched for the first time. But he didn't strike me. Instead he put his hand to his own cheek to wet his fingers with his blood. Then he reached out and drew a bloody fingertip down my chest, making a vertical stripe of his blood between my nipples—like the longitudinal line where they cut you open for an autopsy.

———

HE HAD MADE his point. He returned to his girl, Poppy Bishop, who clung to him.

I left them then. I wasn't in the mood to defend two new breachers—both of whom were bigger than me—from the ravages of the natural world.

I was feeling barbarous, and I hated myself a little.

I found a quiet length of the lake edge and walked into the water to cleanse myself of Blackhat Roy's humors—his blood and his urine. But I had been marked, I knew, deeper than the skin.

I floated on my back. I let myself drift. The night sky was cloudless. So many stars on a night like this. The heavens were crowded. No one bothered to look at the happenings of one small town on one meager landmass on one satellite of one middle-aged star. Maybe no one cared about the moral transgressions of a girl floating on a lake under the moon. Sometimes it was comforting to be nothing at all.

I wanted to run. I needed to run—run like I did on that first night. My muscles ached for it.

But I clenched my teeth and my fists, and I floated. I would hold myself together—I would keep myself contained. Otherwise my body could burst to pieces. It could all break apart. There were shivering hairline fractures everywhere.

—

WHEN I COULDN'T be still anymore, I swam to shore.

Blackhat Roy was there waiting for me. He was alone. He sat on the sandy verge. The claw marks on his cheek had stopped bleeding. They were black in the moonlight.

He watched me emerge from the water but said nothing. He leaned back casually, his palms on the sand. I hated him, but I knew why people followed him. There was some of the follower in me, too.

"Don't touch me," I said.

"Why not?"

"I'll run."

"I'll catch you. You know I'll catch you, right? Are you one of those girls who runs just so you can be caught?"

I went to walk past him up the shore to the woods—but he reached out and caught my ankle. His fist made a shackle, the grip so tight I thought it would snap my bones.

"Let go," I said.

I looked down. His penis was rigid. There was a snarl on his face.

"Let go," I said again, "or I'll hurt you."

But he didn't let go. Instead, he said:

"A hurt is just a different kind of kiss. You want to bite me? Then bite me. Let's make each other bleed."

That's when I attacked. With both my hands made into claws, I swiped at his face below me. I shrieked, primal, pure in a different way, like a banshee, like the true spirit of human pith. There was nothing left of the world beside muscle and blood and bone and thirst.

He pulled my ankle hard, and I fell to the sand. My fingers were wet with his blood and sweat, but I kept striking.

I wanted to hurt. I wanted to hurt everything. I wanted to cause pain.

I thought this must be what evil feels like for those who perpetrate it. Desperate thirst. A craving beyond voices. A will to action that has nothing to do with brains or spirits or codes.

I'd never been so aware of my bones, of my tendons, of how they fit together and stretched—of what a body is really for.

So maybe goodness is a thing of the mind while badness is a thing of the body.

I tore at him, and it felt awful and the awfulness felt good, and the goodness of the awful feeling made me crazy.

He did not move to block me or attack me back. Instead, the skin of Blackhat Roy became the territory of my violence. And he smiled. He did smile. The moonlight showed his teeth, all exposed in a grin.

I struck at him until I was out of breath, until the muscles in my arms ached, until my fingers were bloody and bruised. I found that I knelt over him, that I had climbed on top of him, lemurlike. He lay back, and I straddled his lower belly. If I leaned back, I could feel the tip of his penis against the base of my spine.

I breathed. I sniffled and discovered that I had been crying. When I wiped my forearm across my face, it came away with smeared blood and tears.

Then Blackhat Roy spoke.

He said, "I'm giving you a count of five. If you run now, I won't chase you. If you don't run, something is going to happen. Do you understand?"

I watched the blood trickle down his cheeks. One red rivulet collected in the whorl of his ear. Like a beautiful shell found on the beach—consecrated or defiled by the runoff of savagery.

"Do you understand?" he said. "Nod if you understand."

My head nodded. My neck was sore, the muscles rigid, my skin jittery with popping clusters of nerves.

"Five," he said. "Four."

Yes, something would happen. And my body was unclothed against his. And the night was impossibly loud with the chatter of crickets. The blackest kinds of things were exposing themselves. And, far from turning away, I nuzzled against them. Evil was a body thing. A blanket stinking with sweat.

"Three, two," he said.

I looked to the woods. I could run, but I wasn't running.

Something would happen. And it might be a thing of horror, for I knew that horrors did happen to those who welcomed them.

If you do not flee from the altar, that's when you become wed to the devil.

"One."

I leaped up and ran as hard as I could through the trees. Behind me, I could hear his laughter grow distant and mocking.

———

I HAD MADE a map of our small town, and on the map I had put tiny symbols to mark the houses of all the people I knew so I could see how we stood in relation to each other. I knew where everyone lived. I could have gone anywhere.

But where I ended up was Mr. Hunter's house.

I just wanted to look. It was still before dawn, and all the streets were empty. People were asleep in their beds. And there I was, standing naked and unashamed in the middle of the street under a halo of lamplight, my body dirty and rent from my tangle with Blackhat Roy. I just stood and looked.

His house was so nice. It was a split-level, like so many in our neighborhood, with the bedroom up over the garage. His was painted white with green shutters. There were tall trees all around the sides and back of it. I knew he wasn't married, and I wondered how all the various rooms in the house were outfitted. I imagined walls covered with bookshelves, broken-spined volumes piled to reckless heights. I imagined a little Formica table in the kitchen where he drank his black coffee in the morning.

I stood for a long time just looking at the house, until the black sky began to grow pink at its rim. All of a sudden the street lamps shut off on their automatic timers, and when the reflection of the lights was gone from the glass panes, I could see a figure standing there in a window on the second story, leaning against the frame, gazing down at me. It was Mr. Hunter. He stood still, his head crooked gently to the side, his hands in his pockets. He had not been asleep at all. How long had he been looking out the window—all night?—before I came along and wandered into his view?

I did not run. Aware as I was of my nakedness, I did not make any move to hide myself. Every one of us is a little calamity. That's what I felt at that moment.

He must have known that I could see him now, because as I watched, he raised his left hand and placed his fingertips against the inside of the windowpane.

And me, I responded in kind. I raised my hand in a simple, meager salute. We were both travelers, and our destinations were—both of them—very far away.

208

IT WAS THE opening of garage doors down the block that made me suddenly aware of the time. The sun had risen. My father would be up soon.

I ran. I fled down the streets, feeling the tarmac cold and gristly under the soles of my feet. I leaped over fences and trotted through backyards, never minding the whip and cut of tree branches against my skin. I ran until my lungs burned.

And this was not the gallop of the free absconded from all chains—it was the panicked herding of the damned.

———

I WAS NOT in time.

When I came through the front door, my father was there. He saw me, and he was ashamed. There was no hiding my nakedness.

He looked down at the floor, pretending to have been walking from one room to another when I came in.

"Oh," he said. "I was just—um. Making breakfast. How about waffles? Would you like waffles? Uh—right. Good morning."

Without looking at me, he went to the door of the den and then remembered he was supposed to be going to the kitchen, so he backed out and fled down the hall.

Later, when I came downstairs dressed in the most modest outfit I could find, he was standing over the waffle maker. He stared intently at the steam.

"Ready for waffles?"

I could see him take a testing glance in my direction out of the corner of his eye, to make sure it was okay to look. Then he smiled widely at me—but he had trouble meeting my eyes.

"I was, um, going to use bananas," he said, "but they're still too green."

"I don't mind a green banana," I said, trying to be helpful.

"No, neither do I. But for pancakes and waffles, riper is better. That's a good rule of thumb."

"Okay."

"What kind of syrup? Maple or boysenberry?"

"Boysenberry," I said. It's the kind I preferred when I was little.

He always heated the syrup bottle in a saucepan of water. It was not right, he said, dousing a hot waffle with cold syrup.

He had rules for everything, my father, and the life he lived as a result was just a bit more vibrant, more true.

After we ate, I washed the dishes.

Behind me, I could hear him clearing his throat.

Then he said, "Are you okay?"

I didn't look up from the sink. I scrubbed the plates until every last remnant of impurity was erased.

"I'm fine."

"You know, you could—you could tell me if you weren't."

"I know."

"Do you, um, need anything? A prescription or something?"

"No. I can take care of it."

"Okay. All right."

I thought he would tell me he loved me, but I hadn't heard that from him in a long time. When I was a little girl, he would say it routinely. He seemed compelled to say it. But the declaration had gone the way of tall tale and myth.

As though the love between a father and daughter were only a childish thing. As though womanhood made obscene that which had previously been precious and perfect.

And so did we all fall—and in such a way were a million Edens lost.

———

I WENT TO Peter's house again, and this time he met me at the door. There was a thick wad of white bandage taped to his neck.

"Stitches," he said. "Fourteen of them. Thanks for the note. I didn't really want to see anyone."

In his bedroom, I sat on the edge of his bed, and he swiveled his desk chair to face me.

"Did you go out last night?" I asked.

He chuckled a little. "Did you ever try not to?" he said.

"Where did you go?"

"Down to the railroad tracks. Watched trains go by. Thought about hopping one of them."

"What stopped you?"

"I'm not afraid of running away," he said. "But I won't run away from *him*."

I said nothing.

"And," he continued, "also you."

"Oh."

He looked at me hard, and I blushed.

I put my hand to my neck, a mirror image of the place where he had his wound.

"Does it hurt?" I asked.

"Aches, mostly."

"Can I see?"

"Do you really want to?"

I nodded.

He got up from the chair, took off his shirt, and knelt before me. The bandage was right at the base of his neck, where his shoulder began.

"You do it," he said.

With my finger I tugged at the edges of the tape until they came free, then I folded the bandage back.

The skin was purpled and raw, the laces used to stitch him up blackened with blood and so tight that they pooched the skin up into bumpy ridges. I ran my fingertips over the raised script of his damage to see what might be read there. I had never really thought about stitches as being the same kind of stitches as in sewing—but they were. I thought that flesh must be a pliable and rude sort of fabric, difficult to work with. I pictured an old woman with a thimble pushing a long needle through his worsted, pinched-up skin. Our bodies are craftwork.

I put the bandage back and pressed the tape back into place.

He looked up into my eyes, and I thought he was going to say something, but he didn't. Instead he just leaned forward and pressed his head to my chest. I put my arms around him and stroked his hair.

———

BACK AT HOME, I shut the door of my bedroom, leaned against it, listened to the silence of the house, and felt myself jaundiced, yellowed by life. Strangely, I was relieved to be away from Peter Meechum, whom I loved.

In school the following day, Polly wanted to talk to me about her new adult preoccupations. I found excuses to escape her.

Funny: now that all these people were talking to me, I wanted nothing to do with them. Was it possible, I wondered, to be out of sync with everyone else for your entire life? I felt walled up behind bricks. Like holy people, who are also out of sync. It was called immurement—the practice of walling people up—a fact I had discovered when I had done my research on saints and anchorites.

Even Rose Lincoln seemed more interested in me since I had stood up to Blackhat Roy.

"Did you do all the rest to him, too?" she asked, her dark eyes bright. "It's like a devil got at him."

I was a devil now. It was no surprise. And the worst kind of devil is the kind that believes itself to be holy. Like Satan—the morning light, the angel. One's taste for corruption, it seems, has everything to do with one's memory of goodness. The inversions braid around each other, and it is too hard not to fall.

———

IT WAS THAT same week that Miss Simons, my physics teacher, offered to give me a ride home. She pulled up in her car beside the bike cage. Her hair was still done up, and she still wore her fashionable lipstick.

"Lumen, would you like a ride?"

I told her no, thank you. She had never offered to give me a ride before, and I thought it might have to do with her hearing about me going breach. When you were raised by a single father, sometimes women felt the philanthropic need to step in and have surrogate maternal chats with you.

"Come on. I'd enjoy it. There's something I've been wanting to talk to you about."

"But my bike."

"I'll help you put it in the back."

A previous version of me would have been concerned about being seen getting into a teacher's car. I mused on that while she and I hoisted my bike into the back and I climbed into the passenger seat.

213

"Do you want to know a secret?" Miss Simons said as we pulled out of the parking lot. "I was married once."

She paused and glanced over at me to make sure I appreciated the gravity of that revelation. I didn't know what response would satisfy her, so I said the most innocuous thing I could think of.

"You were?"

"That's right. It was a long time ago, and I was very young. It didn't last long. Fifteen months total. Almost immediately we both knew it was a mistake."

She talked for a little while about her ex-husband, about how he was now an important person on Wall Street, about how she begrudged him nothing, about how she had been single for a long while because she was determined not to make the same mistakes she had made before.

I listened patiently, wondering why I was chosen for these privileged glimpses into the woman's past, until finally, while the car idled at a stoplight, she turned to me with great earnest-ness.

"The reason I'm telling you all this, Lumen, is that—see, I'm fond of your father. Very fond of him, actually."

Oh. So she had a crush on my father. She was asking my advice about how to approach him. Maybe even asking my permission. I was touched by her deference while at the same time determined never to trust her again as long as I lived.

The red light turned to green, and the car glided forward again. We were just around the corner from my house.

"Do you think . . ." Miss Simons began. But she didn't seem to know how to phrase the next part.

I wanted to put her out of her misery. It made me anxious to see adults flounder like that.

"The thing is," I said, "he's still in love with my mother. I've told him he should try to move on, but he just thinks about her all the time."

"No one could ever replace your mother, and that's not what I'm trying to do here."

"I know."

Now I was beginning to be confused by the conversation. But we were pulling up in front of my house, and it seemed important to finish things.

"Anyway," I said. "You're very nice, but I don't think he'd be interested in dating right now."

She looked at me, and she seemed confused. Then something occurred to her.

"Oh," she said. "I'm afraid I've messed this all up. I just wanted to do right by you."

Just then the door of the house opened, and my father emerged. It was a strange thing, because he was not usually home at this time of the afternoon. Also, he did not seem surprised to see me sitting in my physics teacher's car, nor did he come down the path to meet me.

"I asked him," Miss Simons said, "your father. I asked him if I could be the one to talk to you about it."

I felt sick to my stomach in the way that you sometimes do at those moments when you realize the world has been playing tricks on you.

Miss Simons had not been asking my permission to see my father—she was telling me that they had already been seeing each other behind my back. She was not the petitioner but the executioner.

I opened the car door and pushed myself up and out.

As I passed him on the way into the house, my father called after me in a voice that expected no response:

"Lumen. Lumen."

I walked out of his voice. That's what it felt like. I opened the door in the room of my father's voice, stepped outside, and shut the door behind me.

———

THEY HAD BEEN seeing each other since the fall—but I was only told about it after the fact, perhaps as a punishment for my having succumbed to the corruptions of adulthood. Everyone was dirty now. We might as well bare it all. It soon became a habit for Margot Simons to spend evenings with my father and me at our house.

She was maybe ten years younger than my father and very pretty in an angular way. Her lipstick always looked like it had been recently applied, and her brunette hair was trimmed perfectly along her jawline. Her purse rattled with tubes of mascara and clamshells of powder and tortoiseshell combs and an assortment of clips and fasteners to hold her comeliness in place. She wore jeans when she came to our house, and the first thing she did when she arrived was take off her shoes to expose whatever playful color her toenails were painted that day. Her feet were bony, and she folded them up under her when she joined my father and me on the couch for our regular Saturday evening viewings of black-and-white movies.

She would yawn and rest her head on my father's shoulder, and I hated her.

Her attempts at befriending me did not help. She promised she would take me shopping at the mall the next county over. When she said it, my father chuckled uncomfortably and shook his head. He knew I was not a typical teenage girl, one who gets giddy about shopping for dresses at the mall. I glared at him.

One night, after she had left, I confronted him in the kitchen.

"Do you love her?" I asked.

"I don't know. I think I could."

"Will you marry her?"

"Lumen." He leaned forward and touched my hair with his hand, as though trying to incant some long-lost version of himself and me. "I used to hold you on a pillow in my lap. Look at you now."

But when I gave him nothing but a cold look in return, he drew back his hand as though it had been bitten. He looked poisoned, miserable.

"Look," he said, and now there was nothing delicate about his voice. He had rarely in his life used this tone with me, and it had always made me feel criminal. He was explaining something, for better or worse, and whether I liked it or not was beside the point. I shrank back. "I didn't tell you before because I didn't want to hurt you. No one can replace your mother."

"No one's talking about her. Who brought her up?" I was irritated at the way everyone was forecasting the damage I would suffer as a result of my loyalty to my mother. I didn't like being second-guessed.

"I'm just saying I was being careful. But now, now that you're . . . growing up . . ."

And that was it. It was his euphemism for breaching. We are always told that honesty and truth are the shining ideals. But sometimes the truth could be used as a punishment. That's what I learned on that day.

"Go away," I told him.

I wanted to hurt them. I wanted to hurt them all. My father
and Margot Simons. Blackhat Roy and Rose Lincoln. Boring,
bland Polly. Peter Meechum, who seemed ennobled by hurt.
Even my mother, who left me early on rather than staying by my
father's side and being the one single love of his life—even my
mother, the imaginary doll whose enfabulation seemed to grow
more and more childish with each passing day. I wanted to hurt
her, too, for not being real.

———

THE KIND OF geologist my father was was an engineering geologist—which meant that he studied how characteristics of the
natural landscape might affect the man-made structures that are
built on top of it. He was a person who knew how to harmonize
man and nature. He created elaborate three-dimensional simu-
lations on his computer that spun freely in space. When I was
a young girl, I admired them, wishing to be able to create such
pretty artifacts of my own. He also had a whole set of magnifying
lenses that I liked to observe the world through.

Now, though, I tried not to go into my father's office at all. A
border, a line had been drawn between us. Also, I didn't like to
catch sight of the map I had made him, framed and hanging on
the wall. All his creations were so pure and crystalline. Everything I made was corrupt.

I was different now. And he was different, too, though he put
on a show that suggested otherwise.

We were all going on with our lives as though the world had
not been burned to the ground, as though we had not all become grotesques in a pathetic and disgusting circus. Everybody
pretended that everything was just as it had been before.

But I, for one, was made sick by reminders of what the world used to be.

I cleared my room of all its stuffed animals. I boxed them up and put them in the very back of my closet. Harmless animals with big baby eyes and soft, cuddly fur. It seemed like a cruel joke that I was only now beginning to understand.

I sat in the middle of my empty bed then, my knees to my chest and my chin pressed into my knees, and I tried to think of my home as one of my father's computer models—all straight lines and pure white planes. So clean, and everything calculated, accounted for. I could spin it in my mind, floating and free, with nobody but me inside.

———

SOMETIMES YOU WERE impatient for the full moon. Because you were just looking for a reason to run.

I was growing sour to the appurtenances of civilization—the clerks at the stores, the way they smiled politely and bestowed pleasantries on you. The progressive roar of lawn mowers, the tittering of sprinklers.

I went to the mine. It was between moons.

I went to my holy place, the cistern, and I prayed my prayers down into the pit. There were two songs that my father used to sing to me when I was a little girl, and I sang them both down into the void. They echoed and disappeared.

Nothing was the same as it had been.

One day you were one thing, and the next day you were another.

———

EVEN NOW.

I bake snickerdoodles for the meeting of the community league at Marcie Klapper-Witt's house. I pile them high on a cut-crystal platter. Marcie puts them on a long table with other snacks brought by other upstanding members of the community. Fancy, Marcie's daughter, walks up and down the side of the table, sampling the food. She borrows a brownie, takes one bite, and puts the remainder back on the tray. Same thing with the thumbprint cookies, then the cucumber sandwiches. No one watches her.

There is a planter in the shape of a dachshund, and while the girl stands on tiptoes to reach a platter of truffles on the back of the table I take the planter and place it on the ground just to her right. When she moves to continue down the length of the table, Fancy Klapper-Witt stumbles over the dachshund and falls, the tiara tumbling from her head. She begins to cry, sitting there like a pale pork, her hands raised in supplication.

Her mother rushes over, grabs the girl up in her arms, asks her why she moved the doggie planter.

And me? I retrieve the tiara from the floor and deliver it back onto the feathery blond head of the little girl.

Her mother smiles at me gratefully.

My husband, Jack, does not attend these meetings—but I am surprised to see there a woman I recognize. It's Jack's colleague from school—the one who sits on his desk. Her name is Helena, I learn, and she teaches art. Her hands are speckled with dried paint, her fingernails short and scuffed. I don't speak with her, but I put myself in position to overhear her conversations. She has a very melodious voice, and she is absolutely positive about the world. She just recently moved into the neighborhood from California, of all places. She misses the weather there, but she finds the people here delightful.

I follow her from room to room, remaining unobserved. Helena is attentive and careful, much like me. Once, she goes into the kitchen, and I peek at her from around the corner. I see her rinse her glass in the sink — and then, thinking she's alone, she picks something from between her teeth with her fingernail and flicks it into the sink.

I like a woman who pays attention to her teeth.

When the meeting itself gets under way, we all sit around in a big circle in the living room. I stay toward the back, leaning on a windowsill, directly to the right of Helena. She has marvelous ideas about the restoration of the local park. When she is lost in thought, I notice, her lips part slightly and she breathes out of her mouth.

Only once do our eyes meet, and she gives me a small, indistinct smile, as though we were casual compatriots. I wonder if we are.

———

IT WAS THE middle of March, between moons, and our town had its first spell of spring. Afternoons, I would open the window of my bedroom and let the breeze curl the pages of my homework as I finished it. Then, thinking to avoid my father and Margot Simons, I returned to the mapping of the mines. There were too many people aboveground, too many rivalries, too many betrayals, too many suffocating passions — so I went below and found absolution in the pitch black of those lonely passages.

Underground, the air was tight, and the empty spaces felt like a persistent ache — those crumbled walls, those low overhanging beams that were so soft they sometimes turned to wood dust in your grip. I did not mind stumbling upon dead ends, because it meant I could call an end to whatever tunnel it was on my map. I marked cul-de-sacs with special skull symbols. Pretty soon my map was filled with skulls. You could travel in many directions, but there was only one destination.

That was why, one night, I went deeper into the tunnels than I ever had before. I was reckless with voids made out of possibilities.

Getting lost was not a problem anymore. I'd developed a distinct understanding of the dark, a natural sense of how the tunnels were built and which direction they were going. I could feel, in my bones, the elevation of the earth. I could sniff my way north, south, east, and west. I knew the way the breezes blew through those ancient causeways.

But a human body was something I never imagined stumbling upon. Perhaps I was foolish. I don't know.

Still, in the middle of a running life, you sometimes discover death sitting peacefully, just around corners. Waiting for you.

It was the body of a girl.

Where I found her was a dead end, but this was unlike the other dead ends I had found. It wasn't a collapse, it was simply a terminus. The tunnel widened slightly, like a little bulb-shaped room, and then it just abrupted—a round stone room.

I could tell it was a blind tunnel because I knew that the dust hung heavier in the air in caverns that had no outlet. I could feel the end of things in my lungs. I had stopped, leaning one hand against the cold stone and bending double to cough the dust out of me. That's when the dim glow of my penlight fell on her.

Her hair was like wheat. Like dried hay in a barn. Her hair was like that. Like an empty barn on a day when you walk alone down the hill to discover the world for yourself.

Her hair was like hay, and her skin was brittle and dry, like papier-mâché. Her skin was gray—and it was stretched and dried up and petrified by age. It did not give under my touch. When I put my cheek to her cheek, it felt like nothing human. It was the cheek of an old doll. Her skin, her hair—they were kindling for a fire that would burn down the world.

The eyes were closed, the lids glued together by time. The lids were flat and sunken because, no doubt, the eyeballs underneath were shriveled grapes. They did not stare. There was no staring.

Her mouth was the worst thing. And it did not speak.

The skin of her face had dried and shrunk over the bone. Her lips pulled back, exposing two rows of white teeth. Her teeth were dusty. With my finger, I polished them, and they were perfect underneath the dust—rows of pearls. But they looked too big, her grin too wide. And no grin at all, not really. The dead don't laugh. Their mouths are not expressive, they are just hungry. Her jaw hung open, her gaping maw stretched wide, as though she would swallow you. It looked as though she might be calling to me, as though she had something to say. But there was nothing. There were no words. She was dumb as bones.

Hair like hay and her skin like paper. But her mouth was the worst part. It was the start of a dry passageway that went all the way down into the dry sack of her belly. The girl was her own abandoned mine shaft.

She wore no clothes, but her body was half covered by a burlap sack. The burlap was stuck to her. It and her skin and the earth had all melted together and frozen. She leaned, half sideways, against the cave wall. It was an awkward eternity.

She must have been cold. I tried to pull the burlap up to warm her, but it turned to dry shreds in my hands.

I HAD NEVER seen death so up close. She was dried like a mummy in a museum, and I wondered who she had been in life. She was small—young, like me. I wondered if she had had friends like mine or enemies like mine. I wondered if she came here to be alone, as I did. I wondered if this meant that I was now friends with death itself.

The other thing it meant was that I was no longer just a girl. It was the beginning of awful discoveries.

It was the start of everything that came after.

I TOLD MR. HUNTER that I was mapping the mines, but I didn't tell him about the dead girl. When I told him, I watched him closely—expecting that he might scold me or try to persuade me to talk to my father about my self-destructive habits. But he didn't. He leaned forward, in the dark of the auditorium, and he said, "Is it beautiful there?"

"That's not the right word," I said, because it was something other than pretty.

I liked to tell him things, because he seemed to comprehend what things meant even before I tried to explain them. I felt no need to apologize for myself to him. I told him my stories, and his eyes went distant—as though he were recalling some long-ago memory. Sometimes his eyes even glazed over, and he would turn his head away. Sometimes his breath smelled of alcohol.

At dinner one night, I asked Margot Simons about Mr. Hunter.

"What's he like?" I said.

"How come?" she asked. "Have you got a crush on him?"

I held my knife in a grip that whitened my knuckles. I imagined driving the blade between her ribs.

After giving my father a playful glance, she responded to my question.

"We don't see each other that much," she said. "Mostly he doesn't hang around with the other teachers. But I like him. There's something about him. Did you know he didn't grow up here?"

"I know," I said, eager to show off the priority of my alliance with him. "He's from East Saint Louis."

"But," she went on, "he doesn't seem entirely like an outsider. Does that make sense?"

It made perfect sense. But I didn't like that her evaluation of him was so parallel to my own.

"Miss Simons," I said, changing the topic. "Did you know that my mother never went breach?"

"Yes," she said, making her voice hard like a wall. "I knew that."

"So my father told you? He told you she was unique? Isn't it interesting that she was unlike everyone else?"

"Yes, it is," she said again. She did not know the right way to respond. She looked helplessly at my father.

"I thought I might be unique, too," I went on. "I thought it might be in my blood. Do you think things travel that way? From generation to generation? Through the blood?"

My father's fork clattered down on his plate.

"Lumen," he said, "that's enough."

"Sometimes," I said, "sometimes the world isn't as honest a place as you would like it to be."

And then dinner was over all of a sudden. My father asked me to leave the table, and I did. There was a quiver in his voice when he said it, and Margot Simons wore a hard scowl that I knew later would melt into miserableness, and I felt tremendously sorry for her. Her lipstick was smudged at the corners.

I should have been kinder. To my father, to Margot Simons, to Peter Meechum, to everyone.

In English class, Mr. Hunter taught us *Wuthering Heights*. Violent Heathcliff. The smoky moors. Child Cathy tapping at the window, wanting to come in.

He evoked that scene for us. He said, simply, "There is a difference between being inside and being outside," and we knew what he meant. We all nodded our heads, and our eyes grew unfocused.

When you are at a certain in-between age, you believe that adulthood is all about exclusion. You believe that what makes adults adults is that they are legitimized in their suspicions and hatreds. You exercise your own condemnations, and you believe this is the key to growing older.

And what do I believe now—me, a mother and wife, a woman who keeps her past concealed from her adoring husband? Is there something of that mine-dwelling girl left in me, who stalks her husband from makeshift blinds? Or has that girl grown into someone else altogether, naked to hurt, diminished by love?

CHAPTER 9

When my husband goes to work in the morning, I leave our son at the neighbor's and drive to our family doctor. There is nothing wrong with me, but Jack insists that we have regular checkups. So I sit in a cold room wearing a paper smock and smile up at the doctor and the nurses, and I try my best to do exactly what they ask of me. I breathe when they tell me to breathe. I lie back. I answer their questions.

Sometimes I wonder if they will find something awful in me. I imagine the doctor taking me into his office, closing the door, sighing heavily, and diagnosing me with evil growing behind my sternum.

I would assure him that no, it's not growing, it's always been there. The same exact size, the same exact shape. In fact I've learned to live with it, my evil. There is nothing to be afraid of. I am a loving wife and mother, a perfectly normal person.

To the doctors, you are a body tainted by imperfection. The only question they ask is how far you have strayed from the ideal. That's why white and red are the colors of the medical world. White is the pure self, and red is the damage. That is medicine.

But I am declared perfectly healthy.

My doctor says, "You get an A plus for today."

I grin with pride.

Afterward, I pick my son up. He rushes to greet me, clutching at my leg as though I were the only thing standing between him and rude death. I put my palm on the top of his head.

"Mommy," he says to me in his little voice.

He is white and I am red. But one day he will be red, too.

I take him to our neighborhood park, where he likes to fling himself treacherously around the monkey bars. I sit on a bench and look at the cloudy sky through the tree branches overhead.

People like to run around the perimeter of the park, and one of those runners collapses on the bench next to me. Breathing hard, she removes the cap from a bottle of water and upturns it to her lips. The plastic bottle crinkles. I keep my gaze focused on the sky.

"I know you," she says.

Only then do I realize it's Helena, the art teacher who recently moved from California and likes to sit on my husband's desk.

"You were at the community league meeting," she says. She wears tight leggings with a stripe down the side, and I can smell her sweat, sweet and pungent. "You know what? Somebody told me I work with your husband. It's Jack—right?"

"That's right."

"How funny! I teach art."

"No school today?" I ask.

"Part-time," she says. "So what are you doing here?"

"I'm with my son."

"Oh," she says, looking around. "Which one is he?"

"He's over there somewhere."

She laughs. Her teeth are amazing. Her hair is tied up in a ponytail. Her skin is healthy and brown.

"I do ten circuits three times a week," she says. "Trying to get in shape. I'm getting married in August. My fiancé—he's why we moved out here, for his job."

"Congratulations."

"Anyway, your husband, Jack, he's so great with the kids."

"Is he?"

"Such a sweetheart. They all love him. I mean, there are some awful ones, obviously. Like that Nat girl. Im*poss*ible. You don't even know. The nastiest little thing you ever saw. I'm surprised they haven't expelled her yet. Did you know she left a used tampon in one of the teacher's desks? I mean, who does that? Revolting."

"Maybe she's looking for someone to beat her up a little," I offer.

Helena leans back and looks at me for a moment, then she laughs again with all those white teeth of hers.

"I like you," she says. "You're funny."

I smile graciously.

"I better get back to it," she says. "Gotta keep up the stride. But promise me we'll talk again."

"Okay," I say.

And then she's off, running loops around our little park. I watch her without looking like I'm watching her. I wonder what she eats. Probably oats and grains, radishes and kale. I imagine she has many recipes for quinoa. I pick at my fingernails. I suppose if you cut her, her blood would shimmer a bright, healthy color.

———

IT WAS SPRING. The world had thawed, melted, and dried out. Summer was ahead of me, followed by two more years of high school—followed by what? It was impossible to speculate. They said I was destined for so much.

I returned to the mine—I did—to visit my friend Death, who had brittle wheat for hair. I wondered, briefly, if I should report her to the authorities. Then I decided not to. Half buried in the earth, her skin dried to papery thinness, she had been there for many, many years. Whoever might have been looking for her once was looking for her no longer.

I wondered also who she was and if there were some way I could find out. But there was no one I could ask without disclosing what I'd found. And I didn't want to do that.

She belonged to me.

I went to the public library and searched archived newspapers for any clues about who the dead girl used to be. But I had no idea how long she had been there or what she had looked like before she had died. I couldn't even really tell how old she had been.

What I did learn was that girls disappear all the time. They just vanish. I wanted to cut out all the newspaper photos of those lost girls and make a collage of them on my wall. But how much of a memorial did my life have to be?

———

IN MAY PETER began to talk of getting back at Blackhat Roy. "He can't just come back here like that," he said. "He can't just grab whatever he wants. He hasn't earned it," he said. "I'm going to stop him," he said.

In the afternoons we had sex. I closed my eyes and liked the feeling of the sunlight from the window on my skin. Afterward I felt warm and blanketed, and I pressed myself into his arms. He compared me, in abstract terms, to the world at large. "You're the best, truest thing I know. You're not part of all the nonsense. You're above it."

In school, Blackhat Roy seemed to want to tear down to dust all the things that people like Peter spent so much elaborate energy erecting. I began to think of his viciousness and Peter's benevolence as two tides of the same shifting movement.

"You know what?" Roy said. "I've been watching you. Mostly everyone else looks right past you—like you're nothing to worry about. Your smallness, they think that's all you are. But I know different. I've tasted you. You've got some meanness in you, Lumen Fowler, just waiting to get banged out."

He grabbed my arm up near my shoulder, and he squeezed it hard, as though he would drag me to the ground right there in the hall of the school. But then he smiled and let go and walked away. My breath returned, trembling, and for the rest of the day I found my mind was unable to focus.

And yes, it wasn't like Peter Meechum at all—not like him, with his concentrated and generous adoration. Roy was something else. Brutal. Unapologetic but also unwaveringly true. You needn't have worried about social convention around Blackhat Roy. You could drop it all—and sometimes you could almost get the impression, when speaking to him, that you were seeing the world as it actually was.

And there I was, in the emptying hallway of my school, my chest burning—as though Blackhat Roy had persuaded me to open my mouth and swallow a burning ember, as though he had talked me into it somehow.

And now I could feel it, the searing in my lungs and my stomach and other places, too.

———

I WALKED INTO the woods. First I went to the lakeshore, where the sun was low on the horizon and dappled the surface. Then I walked to the quarry, where everything was still but the little rivulet running into the mine. It was wider now, with the season and the melt from the mountains above. There was no one around.

The light grew richer, more full of gold. The sun would set soon. I walked farther, but it was between moons, and I got lost. If I wasn't nosing my way by instinct through the landscape of the moonlit night, then it seemed I was just wandering.

For a long time I went around and around, the sun getting closer to setting, until I climbed to the top of a very high ridge to get a better view. But on the other side of that ridge, I discovered an industrial park—low glass-and-metal office buildings with trapezoidal parking lots between them. I had somehow stumbled upon a back route into civilization. What's more, I recognized the office park. It was in one of those buildings that my father worked.

This was clearly a sign, and I clambered down the opposite side of the ridge and went in search of the meaning of things.

When I found my father's building, I realized the sun was just at the right angle in the sky to show me the insides of the place. I could see him there in his office, bent over his desk, examining some complex paper chart against a spreadsheet on his computer screen. The last time I had visited his office was many years ago when I was too sick to go to school. I must have been eight years old, and he had sat me in the break room with coloring books, and everyone was very nice and seemed to want to talk to me all day.

It would be different now, I thought. His colleagues, they would not know what to say to me now that I had grown into a young woman. People fear those curious interstitial creatures who are neither children nor adults.

So I did not go inside. Instead I sat on the low curb, feeling the coldness of concrete, and watched my father work. I felt alien in that place, watching as the sun went down and the workers began looking at me as they came out of the offices and climbed into their cars. I could smell the oily exhaust of their engines coming alive. I could hear the lonely sound of tires poppling against the surface of the parking lot.

Finally my father came out and saw me. He asked me what I was doing there, and I told him I was waiting for him. He asked how long I had been there, and I told him an hour. He asked what I had been doing—just sitting and watching? Sitting and watching, I replied.

"Sometimes, Daughter," he said, "you are unfathomable."

I liked it when he called me Daughter, and he put his arm over my shoulder, and we walked together toward his car, and for a sliver of a moment I remembered what it was like before things went bad, and I wondered if it would ever be like that again.

———

THAT WAS THE same time that Blackhat Roy Ruggle began parking in front of our house. He had a car now, an old Camaro, once red but now a faded, patchy orange, and it was sitting silent near the woods across the street when I was going to bed that night. I stopped cold when I saw it from my bedroom. I could see the silhouette of Roy's head, backlit by the street lamps, through the rear window. Cigarette smoke rose from the driver's window, and as I watched, his arm reached out and flicked ashes onto the tarmac.

This was the first time. There were others. I meant to confront him, to march out to his car and tell him he did not scare me—but whenever I approached, the Camaro growled to life and sped away.

Sometimes in the morning I found a collection of cigarette butts on the street or a smashed soda cup, the plastic straw twisted into anxious knots. Sometimes I could hear the distinctive sound of his engine pass by without stopping, a high-pitched rumble while approaching and a lower-pitched one departing. I knew this was called the Doppler effect, and in my imagination, I pictured explaining the phenomenon to him, sitting in the passenger seat of the Camaro, maybe drawing a diagram in ballpoint pen on the back of a paper fast-food bag, and him—the all-at-once light in his eyes as he understood—smiling. Sometimes I turned off the light in my bedroom and watched him through a slit in the curtains. He could not have seen me, but he seemed to be looking right at me.

There was nothing I could tell from his dark form.

Maybe he was angry and plotting revenge over something I had done.

Maybe he was sad, like the rest of us.

———

MY FATHER WONDERED where I was going those afternoons and evenings. He did not ask about it directly. It was not his way. Instead he said things like, "Boy, you've been keeping late hours," or "Do you think you'll be home for dinner?"

The house was quieter in those days. We were too aware of each other—like two guarded animals circling each other on a solitary hill. We had sniffed out all the shifts that had occurred in both our lives, and we were keen to them. It wasn't anger or discomfort or fear—just a heightened sensitivity to certain silent currents that seemed to ebb and flow through the house.

We didn't avoid each other. In fact, more frequently than I had in the past, I did my homework downstairs, spread out on the floor, while my father read the newspaper and drank Earl Grey tea. But I was distracted. I couldn't help but be watchful, listening for the fluttering sound of the newspaper pages turning, the sound of his teacup clattering against the saucer as he lifted it and set it down, the sound of his hand running across the scruffy line of his chin while he read.

Sometimes I would listen at the door to his office when he went in there to talk to Margot Simons on the telephone. I couldn't hear particular words, but I didn't need them—I was listening for cadences, certain lilts and tones that might speak to who he really was when I wasn't around to discomfit him.

———

THERE'S SOMETHING ELSE I remember—from a long time before that. When I close my eyes, I can see it still.

My father, he looks the same as ever in my mind, no variations. That magisterial jawline, that long face, those rough hands.

In my memory, he sits on the edge of the couch, and I am caught between his knees. I have a splinter in my finger, and he has fetched the tweezers from the medicine cabinet. He has a monocular magnifying glass wedged magically in his eye — I don't know how he does it. I can't get it to stay in my eye when I try. He switches back and forth between two instruments: the tweezers and the blade of his pocketknife.

I writhe in panic, but his knees tighten around me. They hold my little body still. I am pressed between the muscly levers of his legs, and I am safe.

"Don't worry," he says. "It won't hurt at all. You won't feel a thing. I promise."

He pinches my finger tight.

"Ow," I say.

"Oh, come on," he says. "That doesn't hurt."

He tells me it doesn't hurt, and I believe him, and so it doesn't hurt. He instructs my body on what to feel. And I am relieved, because I relish instruction. How does one know what to make of the world if one is not told?

The vise of his legs, crushing with absolute control my wild little body.

He unpinches my fingers. He tells me the splinter is out. It does not hurt.

His legs release me, and I feel suddenly light — too light, as though I might spin off into the sky like a rogue balloon lost to the thinness of ether.

———

MY HUSBAND IS a good father. When our son gets hurt, Jack is the person he runs to by instinct. I watch the two of them — the way Jack puts his two big hands on the boy's shoulders, creating pacts among males.

When Marcus's teacher calls home to talk about his biting

problem, Jack takes the call. He expresses grave concern. He is apologetic and thankful for the opportunity for social correction. When he gets off the phone, he turns to me, reproaching.

"She says she's spoken with you about Marcus's problems in school?"

"I guess she did," I say. "I don't remember."

"You don't remember? Ann . . ."

He shakes his head and walks out. He has a talk with Marcus later, sitting the boy next to him on the couch. They discuss acceptable modes of expression, ways for Marcus to communicate what's inside of him without hurting others. After it's over, Jack lifts the boy and hugs him tight. I watch from the dining room.

I am concerned that Jack is making our boy too soft. So later that night, after everyone is asleep, I creep into the boy's bedroom and speak rhymes from my own childhood over his slumbering form.

Mary's gone a-breaching,
ho-la-lay, ho-la-la.
Mary's gone a-breaching,
ho-la-lay, ho-la-la.
Mary's gone, and she lost her head.
What might she do with her body instead?
They scored her flesh, and they broke her bones.
Now who will she be if she makes it back home?
Mary's gone a-breaching,
ho-la-lay, ho-la-la.

My husband would not like it if he heard, so I have no choice but to sing my songs to my boy in his sleep. I see his eyes shifting wildly under his lids, and I wonder what animal dreams he's having.

When I go back to bed, Jack wakes briefly.

"Everything all right?" he asks, half asleep.

"You're a good father," I say.

He throws an arm over me and gives me a squeeze. Soon he is asleep again, and I gaze at the stars through the bedroom window.

———

I DREAMED OF the restless dead. Everyone I knew, walking down the street as if in a trance. I ran among them, trying to get their attention, but their eyes were lost to some unknown distance. I tried to speak to them, but they did not respond. I screamed in their ears—my voice was hoarse. Everything was so quiet. I was even deaf to the shuffle of their feet. The only sound was the trickle of water over stone. I looked around to find the source of the sound, but there was nothing to be seen. I closed my eyes and listened harder, trying to recognize it because it sounded so familiar. And then I knew. It was the rivulet that led into the abandoned mine, miles away in the woods. Standing there among the silent zombies of everyone I knew, I could hear it. I could hear the sound of that tiny waterfall, the baby stream of melted ice. What does it mean for something to be inside your skull and miles distant at the same time? I didn't like it. I swallowed, and there was dread in my throat.

When I woke, light was flickering against the wall of my bedroom. I rose and went to the window and saw that the street lamp outside was dying. It stuttered on and off, strobing the street with black and shadowed light.

Parked beneath the street lamp was the faded Camaro, and inside it I could see Blackhat Roy staring right at me, as though he had expected me to come to the window at that very moment.

I froze in place.

While I watched, he brought a hand up in front of his face, opened his mouth, and sank his teeth into the meaty heel of his palm. His head lashed back and forth as though he were a coyote trying to tear away a piece of flesh from its fallen prey—and I could see his face go red from the effort. Finally he stopped and held his hand before his tearing eyes. Then he extended his arm out the car window and held it up for me to see. He had bitten through the skin, and blood ran from the wounds down his wrist and dripped onto the street. In the flickering light, the blood looked black as crude leaked from the earth.

There we were, insomniacs on a moonless night, a pestilent little Rapunzel in her cotton nightdress and her barbarous prince, calling to her with his blood.

———

WE WERE IN the living room watching a Glenn Ford movie, *Blackboard Jungle,* when Margot Simons inadvertently revealed to me a great secret.

She was huddled against my father, and even though there was room for me on the couch with them, I sat cross-legged in the easy chair. The movie is about a rough urban high school, and Margot Simons kept making sly, joking comments to me through the whole thing—about how this school wasn't nearly as wild as our own. I smiled politely in response.

Then, at the end of the film, when the credits rolled, she said, "Huh, that's funny."

"What?" asked my father.

She pointed at the name of the writer whose book the movie was based upon: Evan Hunter.

"Mr. Hunter from school," she said. "His first name is Evan, too."

I thought about all the possible meanings of this connection. I didn't much believe in coincidence. In my experience, harmonies existed everywhere if you were willing to hear them.

You sometimes want answers, and you sometimes go looking for them.

The next day I went to the auditorium after school, even though I knew it was a play rehearsal day. I sat in the back row and watched.

Peter found me there and tried to get me to leave with him, but I wouldn't.

"What do you want to stay here for?" he said. "You're not even in the play. You've got nothing to do with it."

Mr. Hunter could see me talking with Peter, and our eyes met while he directed the students on stage and I shooed Peter away.

"Go on," I told Peter. "I'll talk to you later."

The auditorium emptied out, the students hopping down from the stage, walking past me up the aisles, chatting and ignoring me. I shifted against the hard back of the seat, my skin feeling itchy, as I heard their laughter die out behind the closing doors until all sound had been drained from the auditorium and a great deafness took over. The air was dead still, and I felt flushed. Mr. Hunter stood on the stage at the opposite end of the empty hall, but I didn't make a move toward him. Instead I waited for him to come to the back row, where I sat. Eventually he did.

"Lumen?" he said.

"Everybody lies," I said. "That's what you told me."

"Lumen, are you all right?"

"I think I found out something," I said.

"What did you find out?"

"Are you really—your name, is it really Evan Hunter?" I asked.

He looked confused.

"Evan Hunter," I said. "Born in 1926. He wrote *Blackboard Jungle*. You know what else? He changed his name, too, to write cop books."

"Lumen, there are lots of people with the name—"

"Liar." My hand jumped to my mouth. I had surprised myself with my impudence.

Then he laughed, but it was a terminal kind of laugh, a laugh that meant the end of something.

"Okay," he said and started walking back down the aisle toward the stage. "Come on."

"Where are we going?"

"Come on if you're coming."

He led me behind the stage to the drama office, a little closet of a room with exposed pipes overhead and tall, gray metal cabinets with a fine coating of dust on the tops of them. He sat at the desk and pulled a bottle from a drawer and poured some into a plastic cup. It smelled strong.

"You want?" he said.

I shook my head. Then he downed it in one gulp and poured himself another, then capped the bottle.

"All right," he said with a heavy breath. "You want to talk about the truth of things? Is that what we're doing?"

I said nothing. An awful moment passed, and then another. Finally he shifted and took out his wallet, removed something from it, and slapped it on the desk in front of me. It was a faded photograph showing a skinny teenage boy standing outside the doors of a school. The school I recognized—it was my own.

"Who is it?" I asked.

"Philip Anderson," he said. "Me."

I looked closer at the picture and could see some resemblance in the eyes to the man sitting in front of me. But I realized then that Mr. Hunter must color his hair, because the boy in the picture was blond.

"You're from here?" I said.

He nodded. "Born and raised. When I left for college, I thought I would never come back. I was ready for the real world, you know?" He shrugged. "I managed to stay away for nine years."

"Why did you come back?"

"I don't know," he said, leaning back, his eyes narrowed in thought at the pipes suspended from the ceiling. "I don't think I quite know how to be anywhere else."

"But your name," I said. "How come you changed it?"

He looked down at me, his eyes weighty with meaning. "Sometimes you don't like the person you've become. Sometimes you'd like to try being someone else for a while. You wouldn't understand."

It was quiet then, and he drank and I smelled the spirits.

"Then you breached?"

"I did," he nodded. "When I was your age, I used to breach. Now I do this instead." He grinned and raised his cup.

"You knew my father?"

He nodded. "I was nothing to him. A kid. I've seen him since I've been back. We've talked. He has no idea who I am. Your parents, they were ahead of me in school. They were seniors when I was, I don't know, maybe in seventh grade."

"Wait," I said, my breath catching. At the suggestion of my mother, something inside me fell from a shelf and smashed. "You knew her? My mother?"

The springs in his desk chair creaked. His face seemed to change. He rubbed it, then rubbed hard at his eyes.

"We ran together. Sometimes," he said. "Felicia," and his eyes were now pink, holding on to tears.

"You're lying," I said. "She never breached. You're still lying."

He was sick, this man. And me, I was young and foolish and unkind.

"You look just like her, you know. She had skin like yours. And your eyes."

"She didn't breach," I said again, shaking my head. "Stop lying."

"The moonlight. Sometimes it makes it so you can see right through people's skin. Your mother, her veins are something I remember. Nobody was ever as beautiful. I miss her. We all do."

"Stop it."

"You look just like her," he repeated, and his hand reached out to touch my face.

I recoiled, standing quickly and knocking my chair over.

"You're a liar," I said, my eyes burning. "You fucking liar."

He shook his head.

"Darling," he said, kindly, as I rushed out.

———

BECAUSE THERE WAS nothing to be done, because there was nowhere to go, because there was no one to interrogate or confess to, I ran to the mine. I allowed myself to cry.

People were never what you thought they were. I was ugly and alone, and the world was ugly, too, uglier every day, and there was death in everything, because it didn't matter how many maps you drew, because everywhere was the same place, and you could be fanciful about it but what was the point, especially right there interred in the earth, where it was quiet and where there was nothing to keep your mind from burning itself with running, with hating itself and loving itself, too, because that's what it is to be a teenager, after all, when your little sluglike body aches for things it doesn't understand, glows in its very pores from the effort to explode itself over the world...

So I cried because I could not explode myself, because we are too tiny altogether, too weak and malleable, because our bodies are not even the fingernails on God's hands.

I cried until I howled, my voice a tinny echo in an empty cave. I howled like a beast—I howled like a dying thing—I howled like a little girl. I howled until my throat was dry, and then I blubbered, and it was nothing magical at all. I cried until my tears were useless, until I was numb to all my little tragedies.

III

CHAPTER 10

As a result of that tumorous instinct that grows in some boys, Blackhat Roy treated many of his defeated enemies with the basest kind of contempt in school. In math class, to the mocking delight of a group of jackal boys, he bit Rose Lincoln's pencils in half so that she had to write with one half and erase with the other. He targeted, especially, anyone associated with Peter Meechum. He would have his revenge.

His new girl, Poppy Bishop, continued to trail behind him, because sometimes she liked the way he, upon her request, would attack those she didn't like. But his attentions to her were capricious at best, and sometimes he would turn on her. She took tap dancing lessons, and once, he told her to get up on top of the table during lunch in the cafeteria and dance.

"I don't think I should," she said.

"Do it," he said.

She climbed slowly to the top of the table and shuffled her feet a little. Everyone watched her quietly. Her face went empty.

"That's not dancing," said Blackhat Roy. "Faster. Here, you

need more space?" And he used his arm to clear a wide space on the tabletop, sending people's lunch trays to the floor. "Faster!"

She danced faster, trying to make taps with her sneakers.

"It doesn't sound right," he said. He looked around to the others. "It's usually better. She's not at her best today. You might not know it, but she's got a good body under there. Cute little oval birthmark on her left tit. Poppy, show 'em your birthmark."

She stopped dancing and stood frozen. She crossed her arms over her chest.

Since nobody else would do it, I crossed the cafeteria and made myself as tall as I could in front of Blackhat Roy.

"Stop it," I said. "Leave her alone."

"We're just having some fun. What've you got against fun?"

"Stop torturing people."

"What do you care? You don't even like these people."

It was not the response I was expecting, and I wondered if what he said was true.

One of his friends, Gary Tupper, took me by the arm, saying, "Come on, pocket size, I'll give you a ride to class. Hop on my shoulder."

"Don't touch her," Roy said to him.

"How come?"

In response, Roy punched him in the solar plexus.

It took a minute for Gary to catch his breath and get himself upright again.

"Jesus," he said. "I was just . . ."

But by then it was over. Poppy Bishop had climbed down from the table, everyone in the cafeteria had resumed eating, and Blackhat Roy was long gone.

And still he came to my house sometimes at night. I spotted his old Camaro in different places on my block—not always just in front of my house. One night, approaching a full moon, I went outside to talk to him. I walked down the street to the place where his car was parked—at the corner, under a street lamp. I'd tried before, and he had just driven off when I approached—but not this time. He was waiting for me. I wondered what he would do when I accused him of stalking me. He was rough and humorless, but there was also a fragility in him that fascinated me. Many times in school he looked away from my gaze, and I wondered if he might be ashamed. I was not another Poppy Bishop to him. He did not make me dance or call me names. I wondered what I amounted to in his world.

I approached his car from behind and noticed that the driver's-side window was down. I would demand that he leave me alone, and if he attacked, I prepared myself to fight. Blood could be spilled—we needed no moon to give us permission.

My heart beat hard in my chest, and I leaned down into his window to confront him—but he wasn't there. He wasn't in the car at all. He had just left his scent behind—dry leather and cigarettes and sweat.

I stood suddenly and looked around me. The street was quiet. The night breeze rustled the leaves of the trees. A dog barked in the distance.

He could have been anywhere—hidden behind the trunk of any tree, around the corner of any of these peaceful houses.

I shivered, and I could feel his eyes—as though they had gotten under my clothes somehow and were skittering around on my skin.

I was being hunted.

———

I GOT A D on my geometry test. Mr. Ludlow took me aside. He was a little round man with dandruff on the shoulders of his jacket. His voice was high and gentle, and he frequently spoke of trips he took with his wife to quaint towns with antique stores and tours of houses that belonged to historical figures. Even though he orbited my life only at a great distance, I liked him.

When he spoke to me, he was kindly and solicitous, saying he didn't believe that this grade reflected who I really was as a student. He knew I was better than a D. He asked me whether I was having any problems at home. I wondered if he knew his colleague Miss Simons was eating dinner at my house twice a week. I said no, that I was just tired. I explained that I deserved the grade and didn't blame him for it—because he seemed sad that he had had to write the letter D on my exam. I told him he was a very good teacher and that I would try to do better next time.

He said, "I'll make you a deal. You don't tell anyone, and I'll let you take a makeup next week. I don't want your grade to suffer because of some aberrant exam. What do you say?"

I told him thank you.

"Trust me," he said. "I know exactly the kind of kid you are. You're the kind of kid who doesn't get Ds on exams."

They wouldn't allow me to fall. I plunged downward hard and fast, and they swooped down and fetched me back up before I hit the ground.

Mr. Ludlow said he knew who I was. He would not let me be anyone else.

———

IT WAS LATER that same day that Mr. Hunter wanted to talk to me as well. He let class out twenty minutes early and asked me to stay behind. I did not move from my desk, and when the room was empty he came and stood over me.

He had been distracted since our last conversation. I could smell his breath again. He was just a drunk with odd notions—that was all.

"Lumen," he said, "I want to apologize."

I was stubborn and did not meet his eyes.

"My father's not a liar," I said.

"No, he's not."

"She never went breach."

"No, she didn't."

I accused him with my eyes.

"Then why did you say it?"

At that moment, he looked away again, which made me not trust him. And instead of answering my question, he said this:

"You know something? I knew you a long time ago. When you were just born. I mean, I didn't know you—I knew *of* you. When your mother—when she died, everybody in town brought your father gifts for you. I did, too. I remember I brought you a giraffe. It was purple."

He smiled in memory.

"I have to go," I said and stood.

"I didn't mean to hurt you," he said as I moved toward the door. "I would never—"

But I didn't want to hear it. None of it made any sense to me, and I trusted no one. But here was one thing: I still had that purple giraffe, its fur pale and ratted, its plastic eyes scuffed dull, packed away in a box in my closet because I had thought that I was finished with my childhood.

———

THAT AFTERNOON, ON my bedroom floor, Peter wanted to move me to the bed so we could have sex.

I shook my head.

"We can stay here if you want," I said.

"Here? On the floor?"

And during, I said, "Make me hush."

"What? What do you mean?"

"Put your hand here," and I gestured at my neck.

He caressed my neck with his hand. But he didn't get it. He was too gentle.

"Harder," I said. But he was embarrassed, and the whole thing became awkward.

"I don't want to hurt you," he said.

"I know," I said. "You're nice."

And that night, after I had said good night to my father and climbed the stairs and opened the door to my bedroom, I found Blackhat Roy standing there.

I came close to screaming, but I stopped myself, doubling over and swaying instinctively back from the doorway. But my father was shutting off the lights downstairs, so I lurched into the room and shut myself in there with Roy.

My stomach felt like I had swallowed needles. What was he there for? To kill me, maybe, or rape me, or cut me with a knife? He was an atrocity in this place, where all the safest parts of my identity were hidden.

But he didn't even turn when I came in. He leaned against one of my bookcases, a book open in his hands.

"How did you get in here?"

"Window," he said casually.

"It's the second floor."

He just shrugged.

I saw the book in his hand was my old paperback copy of *The Heart Is a Lonely Hunter.* "Did you read all these?" he asked.

"Get out!" I hissed, trying to keep my voice low. I had backed myself up against the wall, and I was feeling vulnerable there in my pajamas with cats on them. "Get out now!"

That's when he finally deigned to look at me, and his eyes went up and down my whole body.

"Cute outfit," he said.

"Get out."

"I'm going," he said, tossing the book on the desk instead of putting it back on the shelf. "Don't worry. I ain't here to buy. Today I'm just looking."

He moved toward the window to leave, then he turned around once more.

"Nice room," he said. "You could sleep good in here. Cozy. Forget all your worries."

Before he left, I found myself saying, "You can take it if you want."

"Take what?"

"The book. The Carson McCullers. You can take it."

And that's when he flinched as though I had struck him. He crossed the room in two long strides and slammed me against the wall, grabbing my head and holding it in the vise of his two palms. He looked like he wanted to kill me and spoke through gritted teeth.

"Bullshit," he said. "Intellectual clusterfucking bullshit. People cleaning their glasses and discussing themes. Don't fucking mistake me. I ain't here for your classroom handouts."

I stood all hot, unable to breathe, until his anger subsided. Then he let go of me and left. But on his way out the window I saw him look once more at the bookshelves, and I recognized in his expression the ardent pining of a grown man banished from a religion that as a young boy he thought he might be able to truly love.

———

I THOUGHT IF I remembered what it was like to be a good girl, these things would stop happening to me.

The next night, at dinner with my father and Margot Simons, I ate two servings of everything. With great politesse, I passed the dishes to and fro, across the table. I said please and thank you, and I complimented Margot Simons on the corn casserole she had brought in a foil-covered dish.

"Somebody's in a good mood," said my father, and I simply smiled blankly in response. They were pleased, I could tell, though I also caught them giving me suspicious gazes when I wasn't looking.

I helped clean up after the meal. As my father washed the dishes, I dried them and put them in the cupboards where they belonged, arranging them neatly in stacks, making cheerful conversation and chuckling at the stories they told that were supposed to be funny—as if nothing in the world mattered outside these walls, as if there were not grown men speaking drunkenly of my dead mother, as if no pestilent boys were breaking into my bedroom, as if things were not about to change for good.

Afterward I went to the mine. I found my way to the cistern and confessed myself to the inky black of the chasm. I spoke to my mother, because I thought her soul might be down there somewhere in the airy echo of the night, floating free and buoyed on the drafts. I could hear my voice being carried somewhere, and I thought it might be to her.

I told her of many things. Of my two boyfriends, the dark one and the light one, and how they hated each other but both coveted me for some reason. Of my wee body and how I knew it contained some force larger than itself, and how it hadn't yet bled, though maybe that was because it needed that blood for the strange and frightening power it possessed. Of the man who said he knew her, who had gone away and changed his name and then come back just to gaze at me with endlessly suffering eyes. Of my father and his goodness, though not of Margot Simons.

I spoke of many things, and it relieved me. And then I fell asleep, cuddled against a stone outcropping over that depthless shaft.

I guess I knew then why some people speak to God.

———

AND THIS, TOO, is chattering down a well—telling stories to myself in the dark.

My husband and child are upstairs, and they are dreaming of colorful things. But I don't sleep well. I rise from the marriage bed like the ghost of a wife. I creep downstairs, haunted. I pour myself a glass of milk and squeeze chocolate syrup into it. I stir it with a spoon that goes tink, tink, tink on the insides of the glass.

And then I fetch my pages from their hiding place on the top shelf of the pantry, behind the stacked boxes of spaghetti that are no longer used since my husband has become fearful of carbohydrates. I set the stack of pages on the kitchen table, and I add to it, one page at a time. I never knew I had so many words in me. I dust them up, the words, like a good housewife, collect them where they gray the white paper.

But who am I writing to? To Jack? To myself? Who are you?

255

You are not my mother, who wore orchid gloves on her wedding day. You are not my son, to whom one day, as an acknowledgment of his blossomed manhood, I might bequeath his mother's lineage. No, not that. You are not the world at large, from whom I seek forgiveness or solace. Never that. You are not even some version of Lumen herself, not future or former or alternative or lost.

You are no one. And you expect nothing. And your eyes fail you, your head nods in drowsiness. I hope you are happy there in whatever empty, lightless caverns you roam and call home.

Earlier today, this afternoon, there was a commotion at the park. My son runs to the monkey bars, and I notice all the neighborhood mothers constellated in excited chatter at the edge of the playground.

Lola is there, too, sitting apart on one of the benches, stretched out and smoking.

"Did you hear?" she says to me. "The coven caught a bad man."

"Who?"

"I don't know. Some guy. Apparently he was sitting on a bench near the playground, but he didn't have any kids with him. Oh, also he was listening to music on his headphones, and he wore sunglasses. So we called the cops and had him escorted away. Now we are rejoicing."

She flicks the ashes from the end of her cigarette.

Then Marcie Klapper-Witt spots me and comes over.

"Ann," she says, "I'm sure Lola has filled you in on the situation, but I just wanted to let you know that we've taken care of the problem. And we're forming a neighborhood watch to keep an eye on things from now on if you'd like to volunteer. I can order vests—as many as we need."

"But what is he said to have done?" I ask.

"Who?"

"The man."

She shakes her head.

"Ann," she says, "what was he doing in a playground? He didn't have any kids with him. It doesn't take a genius to spot a pervert. You don't know—my husband's cousin is a police officer. The world's not as nice as you think. Jennifer's putting together a petition—and I think it's a good idea that we all sign it—saying that we don't want any adults without children within a thousand feet of the playground."

"A thousand feet," I say dreamily. "That's a lot of feet." Then I say, "Your daughter, she's about to fall."

It is true. Fancy Klapper-Witt hangs upside down by one bended leg from a domed metal latticework. Her frilly blue dress spills over her face, and her polka-dot cotton underpants are exposed.

Marcie Klapper-Witt runs and catches her daughter in the holy safety of her arms.

Later in the evening, after our boy has been safely enveloped between the sheets of his bed, I tell Jack about Marcie and her neighborhood watch and the man in the park.

"Well," he says, "I think a neighborhood watch is a good idea. I'm glad they got him."

"You are?" I am surprised.

"Ann, what's a guy with no kids doing hanging around a playground?"

"That's what Marcie said."

He comes up behind me and puts his arms around me. We are in our nightclothes, preparing for bed, but the gesture is unsexual. His penis, flaccid in his pajama pants, is pressed soft and benign against my bottom.

"It's how you're supposed to feel," he explains, "about your family. I never want anything bad to happen." I can feel his sincere breath on my neck and ear. It tickles, and I writhe out of his grip.

"Nothing's going to happen," I assure him. It isn't a lie. I am quite sure of it. Every day I am quite sure of it.

Nothing is going to happen.

The world will keep spinning within its margins.

He cuddles against me, curled up like a baby in a bassinet, until he falls asleep. I listen to his breathing for a while, so placid and secure, in no way fearful—and then I come downstairs.

I sit at the kitchen table. I drink my chocolate milk. Soon the sun will rise, and the man who delivers papers will toss one from the window of his car onto our front walk. I will fetch it barefoot so I can feel the dew on the soles of my feet.

And in my ankles, and all up and down my calves and thighs, there will be the long-suppressed instinct to run.

CHAPTER 11

Cordial Moon came at the end of May, and I had been waiting for it. The first night, I sat at my window and kept myself from climbing out as long as I could. I wanted to feel the force of it, and I wanted that force to be excruciating. Sometimes these are the games we play with our own minds. I gripped the window jambs, and the tips of my fingers turned white. The smell in the air—I became desperately afraid that I would miss it. It was impossible that that spring nighttime should exist without me in the middle of it. I clamped my jaw on the skin of my upper arm—I bit down hard. I stopped short of breaking the skin—because I wanted the dull ache of compression rather than the sharp sting of pain. I chewed at my skin until it was slobbery wet and bruised purple.

And then, when it was all too much to bear, I flung myself out the window into the night.

Earlier in the day, my father had approached me. Did I need anything? Would I be careful when I went out? Did I want pancakes for breakfast when I returned in the morning? The questions embarrassed both of us. Finally he gave them up and went to read the newspaper in the living room with a mug of coffee. When next we spoke, he was jolly and amiable, everything having been tamped down neatly into place between us.

And now such exchanges seemed all the more ridiculous to me. There was nothing to talk about. There were only wildernesses to breach.

———

DO YOU KNOW what it is to run wild? To lie naked on ordinary ground? To feel against the bare soles of your feet the force of the sunlit day disseminating from the concrete sidewalk? To be neither cold nor ashamed but rather luxuriant in empty space? It is a membership in something greater than yourself, a merging with the populace of insomniacs. There are two worlds, you realize, and you might leap between them and find yourself at home in both.

We are many things all at once. We mistake self-denial for character—or else why not join yourself to every and all custom?

Boys, too. A menagerie of different species, and yet you could love them all. There were the kind boys, like Peter Meechum, who did not peek at you while you dressed, who were pretty and noble, who made love to abstract futures. You could follow them and build skyscrapers on horizons of goodness and truth. And there were awful boys, like Blackhat Roy, who did not fear filth, even the filth you sometimes thought you were, who seemed to see darker truths and did not shrink from them. You could follow them and be on the thrilling, shivery edge of wrong until you died.

Truly was I inexplicable. I wanted others to tell me who I was so I could write it down and know myself true and inscribed. But words were not their medium, so I tried to read their appraisal of me in the bruises on my neck and wrists. My scars would be the palimpsest of my life.

When the moon was out, you could be aware of all the pieces of night—you could see all the things you didn't see during the day, all the subtle little fragments that the world uses to join its wholes. The ladybugs hidden behind the bark of trees, the breath of the daffodils over the dew of a cut lawn, the hum of a power box on a traffic-light post, the gritty taste of rust from old patio furniture, a fawn standing still on a deserted highway. You could see it all—the patterns the lake made and the lightning in the clouds, the patient settlements of dust and the groaning fissures of the earth, the slumber of a whole town and its heartful waiting for dawn. You could fall in love with it all—and you could want, finally and truly, to set a match to it.

I ran to the mine, to the tunnels that twisted this way and that, and I felt my way through them, liking the cool unknown of the inky dark. Maybe I would get lost—I grew out of breath thinking that I could lose myself in those caverns and stay there forever. I could starve to death, pressed tight between worlds, living out my days in darkness, with nothing, with no one.

I could burn the whole world down, because there was some honor in destruction, which was why the Vikings immolated their noble dead.

Then I doubled back to my cistern and uttered no words of prayer or remorse or wishfulness as I watched the sky grow pink with morning through the opening at the top of the cave.

It was not a night for the decencies of language.

———

THAT WAS WHEN everything came apart.

First, it was during the Cordial Moon that Hondy Pilt stopped breaching. So many fallen. So many rescued. He would become, in time, the same person he had been before the breaching. He would fade back into obscurity—no longer a noble leader of wildings under the moonlight, just a lonely explorer in the vast, unpopulated cell of his own mind. And so are we all, I suppose.

I had always wanted more from him. We all did. Maybe we mistook his deep, abiding interest in the universe for an interest in us.

There are times in your life when you project yourself against the sky—you see yourself everywhere, even in the configurations of stars, and you think, "How could anyone fail to notice me there, all my desires and haunted dreams in the nightly patterns of God, who loves me and knows me to be special?"

Me, too. I was guilty of such things.

I was a runner of caverns. I skittered and leaped my way through abandoned mine shafts. I knew where the floor opened up onto bottomless depths. I knew where to duck under the collapsed ceilings. I saw nothing. I moved by feel.

The other thing that happened was that Blackhat Roy followed me into the tunnels. Nobody else would dare. Even in their most primitive states, they feared the dark, the dangers they could not see. Breachers were made for moonlight—they relied on sight, to look and be looked at. Me, I disappeared into the darkness, and they snarled after me. When I emerged again, they crouched and gazed at me through the sides of their eyes. They did not trust me. They did not like outliers. But they did not attack. They knew me to be creatured to some darkness different from their own. I was littler than all of them, but they were afraid.

And Roy followed me all the same. He followed me just to the place where it was lightless and the air was musty with age. I could hear him, breathing hard in the dark, groaning after me, stumbling around. He was an echo in my caverns, an echo in my brain. So I stopped and turned and waited for him. When he caught up, his fingertips reached out tentatively and touched me. I let them rest there on my skin for a few moments, and we held our breath. Then I withdrew, and he was lost again. My bones ached.

He followed me, but it didn't feel like hate. It felt like desperation. It felt like I was large in his mind. That I could ruin him. Ruin myself.

Poor boy! He was tortured by the abstract. Love and peace and relief came from places as far away as Tibet. Maybe he would see them one day, if he became a traveler. How did others locate such things so easily? How did Peter Meechum produce love the same way a magician would draw out an endless handkerchief?

Roy said, in the dark, "I don't know where I am."

So I took him by the hand and led him back outside, where the moon caught him up in its spectral light.

They were out there, the others. They paced back and forth, and their eyes glowed.

———

PETER MEECHUM WAS waiting in my front yard when I came home from school the next day.

"I saw you," he said. He looked angry. He had been pacing back and forth before my gate when I rode up on my bike.

When I did not respond, he came and stood close to me—so close I had to crane my neck to look up at him. His eyes were raw, and his breath was hot. I felt sorry for him—all that fury and nowhere to put it. I thought it must be difficult for him, for boys. They get temperamental when they can't shape the world into what they want it to be. It's easier for girls. Girls are raised knowing that the world is unshapable. So they know better than to fuss.

"I saw you with Blackhat Roy," he said. "What did he do to you?"

"What do you mean?"

"Stop it, Lumen. At the quarry. The mine. I saw you come out with him. He hurt you."

"Everybody hurts everybody."

"No."

He said no, but I wondered how could he not see that.

Cruelty is the natural order of things. Through algorithms of brutality does mankind build its greatest monuments. It's when people begin to see violence as personal that they struggle. It had nothing to do with Peter Meechum. For that matter, it had nothing to do with Blackhat Roy. Goodness and badness had nothing to do with anything.

But Peter let it get to him. He was a believer in the meanings of things. If I was hurt at the hands of Blackhat Roy, well, according to Peter, that was different from my being crushed by a toppled tree. I realized that I once used to think that way, too.

"I'm sorry, Peter." But, in truth, I wondered what I was sorry for. Maybe for him and the conception of the world he carried in his honorable brain.

"But I love you," he said.

"I know," I said. "But why?"

"You know why. Because you're better. You're better than everybody."

I wondered where he had gotten that notion. I wondered, for the first time, if that was the impression I gave — if somehow that was one of the things that kept me separate from others.

"That's just something to say," I told him. "It doesn't mean anything."

"No — it's true," he insisted. "You are better."

"No, I'm not. I'm worse. Your love, it's beautiful — but it isn't true."

He looked appalled.

"But he's a monster," he said.

"I know."

He waited for me to say more, but there was really nothing left to say.

"I'm going in," I said and stepped around him.

But he called after me.

"How can you be that way? You didn't used to be that way."

I had gotten to the front door, had my hand on the knob, but I turned back to him. He looked small there on my lawn. I wished for a moment that I could see him as I had seen him in grade school. I wished to have once more so simple and pure a longing.

I shrugged.

"I used to picture us getting married one day," I said. "You and me. I mean, when I was little. I wrote my name over and over as Lumen Meechum. But it doesn't sound right, does it?"

I looked at him sadly.

"Lumen," he said, and there was a reaching in his voice.

But I didn't reach back. I went inside and shut the door behind me.

———

I WAS LOSING friends, of course. Voids opened up everywhere around me.

Polly and I no longer had much reason to speak to each other. Her disapproval was polite and absolute. I didn't know what, exactly, she disapproved of in my behavior—I didn't know what stories she had been told or whether they were true. But it didn't matter. Her disapproval was right and proper—the common way for two friends to grow apart. It was not for me to get in the way of a natural progression of events.

Peter Meechum was through with talking, but he still watched me from a distance. He was afraid of me, but some part of him must have believed I could still be his. Boys are the most romantic of creatures—their faith is as pure as it is ridiculous.

Rose Lincoln, on the other hand, became increasingly aggressive toward me in school, doing a lispy, babyish impression of the way I speak and throwing old bras at me in the locker room during gym. She didn't like it that I had become the focus of so much boy attention.

I felt for her. I really did. The smallness of her spite was growing pathetic and tiresome to those around her, and there was no other version of Rose Lincoln to fall back on. What happened when your whole identity went out of style? What happened when the boys you used to fascinate were now more interested in some awkward polyp of a girl who had done nothing to invite their affections while you felt yourself growing indistinct against the dusty backdrop of the world? What did you do then?

For one thing, I suppose, you went on the attack.

It happened during gym class on the field, where the girls

were playing softball now that the weather was getting warm. We wore brown shorts and yellow shirts, the school colors. The shorts were tight on some of the girls, who stuck out their behinds with proud vulgarity. On me, the shorts hung like a loose sail in the doldrums, the twiggy masts of my legs pale and meatless.

My team put me in right field, which was okay. It was peaceful out there. Nothing happened, really. You could look at the clouds and listen to the clamor happening elsewhere. You were a placeholder, and nothing was required of you.

If the ball was ever actually hit to me, no one expected me to catch it. My teammates shrugged their shoulders. It was a vagary of the game, a blind spot in the field. Nothing could be done.

But I hated being at bat, hated the moment when our team ran in from the field and I was given a number in the batting order. I couldn't hit. I swung too soon or too late. I had an agile mind, but not a speedy one—not a mind that worked in harmony with my limbs. And if I were lucky enough to hit the ball, it was a strengthless strike, the softball inevitably making a few bounces to the pitcher, who tossed it easily to first base long before I could ever make it there.

On this particular day, Rose Lincoln was on the other team, and she played catcher when my turn at bat came.

I picked up the aluminum bat from the ground, which was muddy from the rain the night before. I stood sideways at home plate and lifted the bat into the air as I had observed the other girls do. But I must have been doing it wrong.

"I guess you can't lean into it," Rose Lincoln said in a voice that only I could hear. "The weight of the bat'll topple you. Don't worry—one day you'll fill out. Maybe by menopause."

The ball came at me. I closed my eyes and swung. The weight

267

of the bat twisted my little body around, and I had to do a dance to stay upright on my feet. I hadn't come anywhere near the ball.

Somebody called the first strike, and Rose Lincoln threw the ball back to the pitcher.

"Seriously," she said. "How old are you?" Then she called behind her to the other girls on my team. "Should we bring out the T-ball thing?" The girls laughed. "It seems only fair."

"Be quiet," I said to Rose Lincoln.

"Sorry—am I breaking your concentration? Let's try a slow one!" she shouted to the pitcher. "Right down the middle."

I gripped the handle of the bat, liking the heft of it, liking the way it made my palms gristly with dirt. When the ball came, I pictured Rose Lincoln's laughing face and swung hard.

Not even close. Strike two. Behind me, I could hear the moans of my teammates. "Come on," they said to the universe, as though I were a small bit of lucklessness they had stumbled upon by pure happenstance.

"I've never seen anything like it," Rose Lincoln said and tossed the ball back to the pitcher. "How do you carry anything with those arms? How do you open jars? How do you brush your teeth? Do you have to take breaks?"

"Be quiet," I said, gritting my teeth.

"What was that?"

"I said be quiet."

"Sorry—you need to speak up. Use your big-girl voice."

"You're pathetic," I said, turning to her. "Pa-the-tic. Did you understand that?"

Her face changed. This was the confrontation she had been nurturing like a seedling between us. Now her fury had a purpose, a mission. She savored her own delicious rage.

I turned my back to her and raised the bat for the final pitch.

Behind me, in a whispery rage, she said, "I'm gonna get you. You're done. Just wait till the full moon. Just—"

At that moment something was decided in me, like a door slammed shut by a wind.

"I'm not waiting," I said.

"What?" she said, a quiver in her voice.

"I said . . ."

But I didn't repeat it. Instead I turned full around and swung the aluminum bat as hard as I ever had.

She was quick, and it's a good thing she was, because if she hadn't gotten an arm up to block the blow, I would have smashed her head in. Instead the bat caught her in the forearm, and I felt a satisfying, liquid crack vibrate through the hollow instrument.

She screeched and fell to the ground.

I raised the bat over my head, prepared to bring it down again—but she shuffled backward, one arm limp and useless, until she was huddled against the chain-link fence.

I advanced and stood over her. She blubbered, and her face was wet with tears. Maybe she believed she would die there.

I dropped the bat, which made an empty-pipe sound, and I advanced until I stood over her.

She turned her face away from me, raised her good arm to ward me off.

Leaning down, I whispered in her ear.

"Does it hurt?"

"Yes."

"I'm sorry."

She gurgled an animal howl of pain.

"Do you want to know how to get through it?" I asked.

She nodded.

"You have to deserve the hurt, Rosebush. Like love."

When I reached out to her, she cringed her eyes closed, as though my touch were death, but I put my hand gently on her head and smoothed her hair.

Suffering is sometimes a boon. All the creatures of the world hold hands in pain.

So I touched her head, and I felt we were both alive together, both girls wriggling, hapless, in the rich loam of girlhood. You can be happy at the strangest moments.

Then the world around us, which had been holding its breath for a number of seconds, exhaled into commotion. The other girls rushed to Rose Lincoln's aid. Mrs. McCandless, the gym teacher, was there. And Mr. Lloyd, the boys' gym teacher. He's the one who took me by the arm so that I could only walk trippingly, and he tripped me to the office, where my father was called and I was suspended from school for one week.

This was fair.

All things are fair.

The world is pretty, and it finds its own balance.

——

MY FATHER DID not know how to express his disappointment in me. His daughter having become a mystery he was afraid to solve, he narrated what had happened rather than ask me about it.

"She provoked you," he said. "The other girls heard. That's why it's just suspension—that and your good standing at the school. The girl's parents aren't bringing charges. I'm helping with the medical bills. You'll apologize, in writing."

So I wrote her a note of apology, which went like this:

Dear Rose,

I'm sorry for hitting you with the baseball bat and breaking your arm.

I remember when you were called Rosebush, and I thought I would like to have a name as pretty as a flower instead of something so scientific and technical as Lumen. I thought you were lucky. My whole life, really, I thought you were lucky. It seemed like you could touch things and make them your way.

Is that true? Can you touch things and make them your way? It wouldn't surprise me. Do you know the story of King Midas? If you don't, I'll tell it to you sometime.

Somewhere while we were growing up, things got strange. I stopped being able to recognize things for what they were, because the closer I looked the more things changed into something else. Do you ever feel this way, or is it just me?

I remember in the third grade you could draw perfect pictures of fashion-plate girls in all kinds of different outfits, and they all looked beautiful, like runway models. I was jealous, because the only thing I could draw were maps, and they weren't pretty at all—just practical and informational.

Also, I miss my mother, even though I never knew her. I wonder what kind of girl I would have been if she had been here. Maybe the kind of girl who wouldn't have ever broken your arm. Maybe the kind of girl who would have been your best friend and brought you flowers and cupcakes when some other girl took to fury and broke your arm with a baseball bat. I could picture that. I can picture lots of things.

So I'm very sorry. Sorry for this and for so much else, stuff that doesn't even have to do with you. There aren't enough sorries in the world for how I am.

Yours truly,
Lumen

I enclosed the letter in a white envelope and put a red tulip sticker, which was the closest sticker I had to a rose, over the back flap.

I wondered if during the next full moon there would be some retaliation for my assault on Rose. But as it turned out, Rose's body had finished its breaching. When June's full moon came, she was not among those who ran. All of a sudden, she had grown up.

I wondered, in my most dreamy states, if I had had something to do with her being weaned from the breach. Had I clobbered her into adulthood? The body had its own magic after all.

The other thing I wondered was this: Would I ever grow up like Rose and like Polly and like all the others before me? Or, having never been a real breacher, would I never fully graduate from breaching?

There were so many beautiful, dark, and lonely ways in the sunken corridors of adolescence—how did everyone else manage to make it through without a map? Were they not tempted, as I was, to linger?

HAVING DISCLOSED MYSELF to Rose Lincoln, I found there were things I wanted to say to Blackhat Roy as well. I had spent too much of my life reacting to people. Now I might be the one other people reacted to. I was ready to be someone who did things.

I rode my bicycle to his home—a place everybody knew about but where nobody went. It was an old house on a dirt road down near the bottling plant. I stood for a long time outside, holding onto the handlebars of my bike, just looking at the place. There was a wraparound porch on the house, but it was filled with rusted sewing machines, stacks of sun-bleached magazines tied together with string, old fishing rods leaning in a huddle against the house, a plastic kiddie car collecting dead leaves, rainwater, and mosquitoes in its seat, chipped wooden frames with no pictures in them, planters spilling over with withered creepers. There was a wooden swing suspended from the porch roof, but seated on it was a stuffed and mounted black boar, its fur coated with dust, its tusks yellowed with age.

I couldn't stop looking into the glass eyes of that snarling boar, even when the screen door slammed open and Roy appeared in the doorway.

"The fuck are you doing here?" he said.

I looked at him, but I found I could say nothing. It was a good question. What was I doing there?

"This is my goddamn home," he said.

Again I said nothing. I gripped the handlebars tighter and gazed at him, at this place. I could not muster a response.

Then his demeanor seemed to relent a little. His body shifted sideways.

"Well," he said in a lower voice, "come on if you're coming."

So I let my bike drop to the ground and followed him inside.

The interior of the house was like the porch—the same disarray of aged artifacts—but what was most remarkable was

273

Roy's comfort with it all, the way he moved through it with a strange kind of ease, as though he were on intimate terms with all the lonely jetsam of the world. He performed a kind of ballet through crusted plates of old food and teetering pyramids of empty beer cans. Where I twitched and fumbled, he shifted. Saying nothing, he led me back to his bedroom, where, pushed up awkwardly against one wall, was a simple iron-frame bed, the mattress, without sheets, skewed a little off the box spring. There was an unzipped plaid sleeping bag bunched up like a quilt on top of it.

On the wall was a framed photograph, crooked, of a man. I wondered who the man was, if it was Roy's father, but when I reached out to straighten it, Roy growled, "Stop. Don't touch anything. You shouldn't've come here."

I turned to him, reminded of my purpose.

"I brought you something," I said. I dug into my bag and pulled out the book. It was *The Heart Is a Lonely Hunter*. I held it out to him.

"Jesus Christ," he hissed. "The fuck do you think you're doing?" His eyes dropped to the book, and I thought I saw something open in them for just a second—but then disdain smeared his features. "What are you doing here, anyway? You come here to make me into a better person? You want to save me? From all this shit? You gonna lift me up? All your fucking decency."

He struck the book out of my hand and sent it flying across the room.

And that's when I did something. I took a step forward and stood in front of him, craning my neck to snarl upward at him.

"What are you doing?" he said, and his voice was different now—surprised—as though he were speaking to a different person entirely.

I dared him. I would dare him.

"It's not full moon," he said.

My hand reached up and slapped him. He did nothing. My hand slapped him again, harder. It would numb itself on his face. It would draw out the taint, but not for me to cure. I wasn't there for purity.

My hand drew back again, but it didn't have time to strike. He grabbed my arm, way up by the shoulder, gripping it with one thick hand, which encircled it completely. He pulled my face to his, but we did not kiss. This was not about kisses. We breathed each other's air, hot and salty.

Then he took me down to the gritty braided rug that covered the wooden floor of his room, still gripping my arm. My choice was to go with him or have my frail limb pulled from its socket. There would be bruises.

He surveyed my body as though he hadn't seen it before. It wasn't the same as before. The full moon had made things different. Now there was clarity in his eyes, and disgust, and worship.

Something swelled in me, in my chest and stomach. Something awful grew there, I knew. I could feel the tears coming. Using all my strength, I turned him over, climbed on top of him, and bit at his neck and arms. He tried to push me off, but I bit harder, digging my fingers into his clothes and skin. I would not release. He must've known I would not release.

"Stop," he said.

But I did not stop. The room stank.

He tried to fling me away, but he only succeeded in rolling over on top of me again. I felt the buttons and zippers of his clothes chafing against my skin. He seized one of my wrists and then another, got them both in his left hand, and held my struggling hands down against the floor above my head.

He had me pinned, and then I felt I could breathe for the first time. I breathed. I licked my lips.

"What are you doing?" he said.

I grunted.

"What?"

"Stop it," I said.

"I'm not doing anything."

"Me. I want you to stop me." And then there were tears. I could feel them on my cheeks. My body shook with fury. I craned my neck to bite his face. I would have gnawed off the skin of his face had I gotten it between my teeth.

With his free hand, he grabbed me by the neck and forced my head back down. For a moment, I couldn't breathe at all—and that felt all right, too. Then he let up.

"*You* stop you," he said.

"I can't. Hurt it."

"Hurt what?"

"The thing that's wrong, inside me. Hurt it. I hate it, and I want it to hurt."

Then maybe he understood. Because he was using one hand to unzip his pants, while I writhed there on the ground, my body convulsed in a furious paroxysm. Like an epileptic, I arched my back and bit at the air with my jaw.

And I couldn't move at all, because his weight was like a sack of iron ingots, pressing me down, and my arms were pinned, and my legs were growing numb, and I said, "Do it, do it," and it was safe because my body was leashed, finally leashed, and I could even feel beautiful and pure and light again because he was beating away all the ugliness in me, hammering it down into a safe little knot that couldn't hurt anyone, and none of it was my fault, it couldn't be my fault, because I had grown wrong and I would pay for it, I would pay for it happily, I would pay for it and breathe again because you had to control wrong things, you had to choke them until they were still and everything was quiet, make me still, make me quiet, make me be still.

And Blackhat Roy pushed himself inside me, deep, to the core of it all, and I thought I must be depthless. He battered my body with his. It hurt between my legs, hurt in a way I could relish in the dark, secret parts of my mind.

Because there was a voice in the room, the low, sickly whine of an animal in pain or in thrall, the throaty mewl of gross instinct, and I heard the voice filling the place and oozing down the walls. It was my voice, I realized. It was a voice to curl all the pages of my books.

This had nothing to do with love or faith or play. It was ugly and selfish. It burned.

And I wept. I knew because I could feel the wetness in my ears. I cried and wailed. I moaned there in the dusty afternoon, and outside the woods went silent and all the tree toads and the crickets muted their song out of dumb respect for me. I was an animal of pain, and the forest listens for such things.

And then he hushed me. I remember it, even now. It's a thing beyond forgetting. He clamped a palm down tight over my mouth, but the sound still came from the organ of my throat, and he didn't know what to do. So with his other hand, he covered my eyes. He blinded me.

And then did I hush truly. Like a horse blindfolded to keep it from spooking, and, too, my breathing, like a horse's, huffing rapidly through my nose, the smell of Roy's sour hand on my wet mouth.

You can only noise yourself for so long. And I felt small again, blissfully, tranquilly small, the ember of my mind cultivated true in the silence and darkness of my bound body. Mute and blind and immobile, the ache of my stubborn muscles, the searing of my bare skin—it was all far, far away, and I was at peace somewhere deep in the lost or abandoned corners of my brain. I was lost and gone, fallen down the deepest of wells, singing myself to sleep while my body burned itself to cinder and ash.

Roy shuddered silently against me.

His breathing slowed. His hands went away, first the one on my mouth, then the one on my eyes. His body rolled to the side. Cool air blew over me, and my skin tingled with the shock of it. I did not open my eyes.

But I was at peace. I was hushed everywhere inside.

———

BECAUSE LUMEN IS also vagina. It refers to anatomy as well as light. The last time I went to the gynecologist, I saw my name on a map of the alien landscape of a woman's insides. The poor woman was only a middle—all splayed open and colorful, with words dangling by black lines from all her secret features.

"There's my name," I exclaimed to the doctor when he came in to examine me.

"Is it?" he said, as though he were speaking to a child. He is a doctor. He doesn't listen to the things I say, so focused is he on the language of bodies.

After I saw my name on the woman map, I went home and did my research, as I used to do as a straight-A student, as my father's good daughter, all those years ago, when encyclopedias were holy magic.

Lumen is just one name for vagina. There are others, many of them crude, which I would not utter but which pulse in my brain and have their own linguistic heartbeats. But Lumen is the best of them all. It makes you think of moons and astronomy and the comforting light of science.

Actually, a lumen is just a tube. It refers to any number of tubes in your body. Your throat is a lumen. And your ears and nose. Your arteries and veins. Your lungs are filled with branching lumens like the roots of a tree growing in your chest. You are made of tubes, and through your body of tubes pass fluids and gases and ephemeral magics that can't be named or quantified.

Our bodies are factories. Food is put in at one end of a tube, it is processed over time, and it is ejected at the other end of the same tube. When it comes out it is something else. Also, the vaginal lumen. A boy puts himself in you. Your body accepts that offering and performs magic on it. Nine months later, out of the same lumen, a miniature human is disgorged.

My name is a processing function.

No. More to the point, a lumen is not the tube itself but rather the space within the tube. That's important. Don't you see how important that is?

That space is the lumen.

So I am Lumen. I am light, and I am space. I am emptiness. I am all the holes of the world. I am hallways and passageways. I am open doors. I am deep, dank wells. Maybe even gaps in time. Maybe I am the empty hiatus between day and night, the held breath of dusk. Or the excruciating nonmoment between an action and its consequence. I am the hiccup on the telephone line when someone delivers tragic news.

I am empty space, and I am the light that illuminates that space.

I am that furious lacuna between prolonged girlhood and the

279

womanhood that refuses to come—when your breasts don't bud and your limbs stay bony and your blood won't come.

I sometimes grow tired of myself. I grow hateful.

I have been in love with punishable things.

———

I MUST HAVE slept, but I don't know for how long. The sun was low on the horizon when I woke. Blackhat Roy sat in the corner. He was looking intently at the cover of the book I brought him, but when he noticed I was awake he tossed it aside.

He said nothing, just watched me while I shifted my clothes back into place. My skin was pinched, my joints aching, my body on humiliating display. All I wanted was to get out of there as quickly as I could, but when I was about to leave, he came over and stood before me.

"Hey," he said.

"What?"

"Just..."

He reached out, and at first I thought he was going to seize me again—but this was something new, something gentle. He moved himself against me, and it was a full moment before I realized he was embracing me.

Feeling bitten, I recoiled and pushed him away.

"Don't," I said.

"Lumen, I—" And he moved forward again.

"Don't you dare," I said and backed away. "Don't touch me."

He looked at me, confused, then down at his own hands as if to discover some unintentional threat there.

I didn't want to explain. I was revolted by tenderness. I simply didn't want to be loved by Blackhat Roy. The idea was unacceptable to me.

He came toward me again, and I clenched up.

"No," I said. "Don't."

"Goddamn it, Lumen," he said, exasperated, "I'm just trying to—is it this?" He gestured all around him, at his broken-down house, his meager life. "I'm just trying—"

He came at me again, more forcefully this time, trying to bind me in his arms. I fought against him, but the more I struggled, the tighter his hold got.

"Stop it," he said. "Lumen, just stop—I'm not doing anything wrong."

And when I finally wrenched myself free of him, my body swung backward, spiraling out of control, my face catching the edge of a plywood shelf, and I fell to the ground.

At first I was numb, dizzy, and then my hand went up to the sudden searing pain on my cheek and came back covered in blood.

"Lumen," Roy said. "I'm sorry. I—"

"Shut up," I said. "Just be quiet for a minute."

I looked at myself in a mirror hanging on his wall, and I was surprised. There was a girl, a long gash on the side of her face, bleeding fluently, something unfocused in her eyes. That was me.

"Goddamn it," Roy was saying behind me, and when I turned I found he wasn't speaking to me at all. He was pacing the floor, his fists pressed tight against his eyes. "Goddamn it," he said again. "I don't know how. I don't know how." He took one of his fists and rapped his knuckles hard against his skull. "She shouldn't be here," he said. "I hurt her. I broke her."

And there was nothing pretty about it, nothing dramatic. This had nothing to do with the rituals of our little town, nothing to

do with breaching or the cycles of the moon. This was something different, horrible in its plainness. His rage, my bloodied
face, his fists, my shame. These were not the primal forces of the
earth working through our polluted souls, not the bright clamor
of youth in the stark urban fields of the modern age. It was just
small and ugly and wrong.

The hospital was closer than my house, so I rode there, my bicycle serpentining across the road in my dizziness. I wasn't sure if
I would make it. By the time I got there, the front of my shirt was
soaked and sticky with blood. I told them I fell. They treated me
immediately, calling my father, giving me six stitches. A plastic
surgeon was called in, since the wound was on my face. Everyone
was very concerned.

The hospital was tidy and clean. It reminded me of civilized
places. Places I didn't belong. Places I was too ashamed to go
back to.

———

AFTER THE STITCHES, I asked the nurse if I could use the
bathroom. I felt funny, and in the bathroom I discovered blood
on the insides of my thighs. At first I thought that maybe Roy had
injured me—but then I realized what it was. I wasn't amenorrheic anymore.

It hadn't been a very long time since I had incanted magic
words to romance my blood into flowing. But now it seemed like
I had traveled a great distance from those fancies. I had grown accustomed to blood of all kinds. This was just a period.

———

I HAVE A treasure. Do you want to know what it is? I could draw you a map to it. First you need to find the place where I live now, in a city in the northwestern quarter of our fair country. In the room where I sleep, there is a dark varnished maple dresser whose origins are unknown to me. On top of that dresser, you will find a jewelry box with many small drawers and hinged doors, like a magician's cabinet. The very bottom drawer pulls out a long way, and you will need to pull it out almost completely in order to discover a packet of white tissue paper tied with a string. Undo the string, unfold the wrapping paper, and there you will find my treasure.

It's a necklace, if you really want to know. It was given to me by my father. I don't wear it anymore—because time has made it into a treasure, and you don't dangle treasures from your neck. Not real ones.

It's not the locket he gave me for Christmas. This he gave me that June, that same June that everything was happening. It was for me to wear at the prom. Ours was a small school, so everyone, even sophomores, went to the prom.

When he gave it to me, it was wrapped in the very same tissue and string (such consistencies are important)—except it was also in a gold foil box with a little bow on top. The box is lost now. You can't save everything. You can't save every little thing.

We were sitting at the kitchen table, and it was just before bedtime, so there were very few lights left on downstairs. We sat in a comfortable pool of kitchen light, surrounded by dark doorways, and we felt safe.

"I just thought you should have something nice," he said. "For the dance."

He was embarrassed, and he stirred more sugar into his mug of coffee for something to do with his hands.

I unwrapped it and held it up to admire it. It was a simple gold chain with a pendant in the shape of a dragonfly. Its wings had little bitty rubies in them, and the whole thing sparkled. It was the most beautiful thing I had ever been given.

"It's perfect," I said, because I wanted him to know he had done a good job of making me happy. He smiled and nodded and sipped his coffee, more pleased than he let on. That was our way, then. He and I, we were timid about the common practices of life now that I'd gotten older. But we helped each other along, and we stumbled through. We knew the quiet codes that stood in place of more overt, gangly expressions of love—and we got by all right.

I remember wondering for a few aching moments if maybe this had been a piece of my mother's jewelry. I pictured her as a girl who would like dragonflies. A wisp of a creature with a name that pointed to darker things.

But then he rose from the table and rinsed his mug in the sink.

"I'm glad you like it," he said. "Miss Simons—Margot—she, uh, she helped me pick it out. You might want to thank her, too."

"Oh," I said. I forced a smile, but he wasn't looking at me anyway. "Yes. Yes, I will."

He came up behind me, leaned down, and kissed me on the top of my head.

"Good night, Lumen," he said. And then I heard the stairs creak with his footsteps as he went up to bed.

———

I DIDN'T WEAR the dragonfly to the prom. That was my statement. I wore a party dress that was a few years old but still fit decently, and I wore the Christmas locket my father had given me—the one with pictures of him and my mother in it. My father and I never exchanged words about it. I saw him glance once at my neck, and that was enough. He distracted himself by taking pictures of me in my dress in front of the living room bookshelves.

If Miss Simons noticed I wasn't wearing the dragonfly, she didn't let it show even a little bit. In fact she stood with me before the mirror in my bathroom and helped me hide with makeup, as much as possible, the sewn-up part of my face. When she was done, I looked like a different Lumen entirely—some future version of Lumen, maybe, the woman I might become.

We both looked at my reflection in the mirror. I thought she was going to tell me how pretty I looked, but instead what she said was, "You're tough, Lumen. Tougher than anyone I know. Don't let them tell you otherwise."

After all, I realized, she wasn't a bad woman. I wanted to give her something in return.

"Thank you," I said.

"You're welcome."

"I mean," I said, "for everything. For the necklace."

She didn't say anything, but she smiled at me in the mirror, a true smile, and she knew.

My father didn't ask if someone was taking me to the dance, because he would not pry so far into my personal life—and the answer would only lead to discomfort whether it was yes or no. Instead he simply asked if I needed a ride to the school, and I told him yes.

When he pulled up in front of the school, I could tell there was something on his mind, so I didn't get out of the car immediately. I waited, and together we watched people arrive, walking through the double doors of the big building, linked arm in arm in their finery.

"Margot and I are going to a dinner party tonight," he said.

"Okay."

"Friends of hers."

"Okay."

"I'll be home by midnight. You'll—you'll be home by then?"

It occurred me that we were talking about a curfew. We hadn't had a conversation about a curfew in years—there had been no need for one. Where was I going to go? I had been a good girl, impervious to trouble. But now things were different.

"I mean," he went on, "there's no moon tonight."

I was embarrassed. We both were. I looked down at my hands.

"I'll be home."

"You'll be home," he said. He did not look at me but nodded to himself, as though confirming a truth that he was ashamed to have questioned in the first place.

"I promise."

I lingered. Suddenly I didn't want to be away from him. We waited and watched the others arrive. He shifted in his seat. I could smell his cologne. I can smell it still.

"Did I ever tell you," he said, a thin smile forming in his beard, "how the coal hole got its name?"

What he referred to was a hollowed space in the wall of our house, under one of the eaves. When the house was originally built, a hidden panel was installed in the wall so that the space could be used for storage. When I was a little girl, I liked hiding myself away in there. I felt safe in that cramped triangle of space, which seemed like it fit me but no other human on earth. When my father saw I liked it, he cleared out the boxes of old photographs he had stored in there and set it up as a hiding place for me, with a light and a tiny bookshelf and an assortment of throw pillows I could arrange however I liked. I would stay in there for hours at a time, and he would bring me crackers and cheese. We called it the coal hole, and it had never occurred to me to wonder why.

"It's from *Silas Marner*," he said.

"I never read it," I said.

"I know. It's about a grumpy old man who has to raise a little girl all on his own. He doesn't know what he's doing. He doesn't know the first thing about children. He's all on his own."

My father paused. He looked away from me and was quiet for a while. I wished I could see his eyes, but I was also afraid of what I'd find in them.

"Anyway," he went on, taking a deep breath, "when she starts to act out, he doesn't know what to do. So to punish her, he shuts her in the coal hole of his house all by herself. Except here's the thing. This girl, she's not like other children. She's got a spirit in her—brilliant, mischievous. And it turns out she *likes* the coal hole. It's no punishment at all to her. Once she discovers it, she climbs in there all the time."

"So . . ." I said, though there was a catch in my throat. "So what does Silas Marner do?"

My father smiled.

"What else is there to do with a girl like that?" he said. "He lets her do what she wants. And he sits back and watches her grow up. And he is amazed."

I leaned over and embraced him, my head against his chest, and I felt small and safe with him as I have never felt with anyone else in my life. He kissed the top of my head and stroked my hair.

"But sometimes a father worries," he said.

287

"I know," I said, and I did not like to think of what I was doing to him by becoming the person I was.

"I know," I said again. "I'll be there when you get home. I promise."

———

I PROMISE.

I don't like to think about it. I don't like to write it. Outside, our neighbor's sprinklers just switched on by automatic timer. It must be nearing dawn. He has told us that early morning is the best time to water your lawn. There is no other sound to be heard. I have been listening to silence for so long.

I promise.

I would erase it if I could. They say you can't hide from truth. But you can't hide from lies, either. You can't hide from anything, really.

So why do we keep trying?

———

HELENA, MY HUSBAND'S pretty colleague who jogs around the park, discovers me behind the school, where I watch Jack through his office window.

"Ann? What are you doing here?"

"Oh," I say and smile too widely in deference to her. "I just came to drop something off with Jack."

"Ugh. I know," she says. "Everybody's been so preoccupied preparing for the parent night tonight. Isn't this a nice place just to sit and contemplate? I like it, but nobody ever comes out here."

"It's very nice."

"Say, what do you think about that woman, Marcie Klapper-Witt, and her brownshirts cleaning up the neighborhood? I'll tell you something—I'm not sure I like it. When people get zealous, I keep my distance. That's my policy. Oh—but you're not close with her, are you?"

"My son bit her daughter," I say, shy and proud.

Helena laughs and touches my arm.

"Ann, I'm making a prediction—you and I are going to be best friends. Mark my words."

I would like to be best friends with Helena, but I'm afraid I don't know how. I don't know if I've ever been best friends with anyone—especially someone like her, who is so merry about life, whom people enjoying being around. I worry that I don't possess the spirit required to uphold the friendship of someone so vigorous. What manner of research is required for such a prospect?

That night, while she and my husband are occupied at the parent event at school, I drop my son off with Lola and walk through the neighborhood. It's empty and quiet, and a dog barks somewhere, and somewhere else a peal of distant laughter escapes from an open window. I am aware of the sound of my own feet shuffling against the sidewalk, so I walk differently—heel, toe—so that I add no noise to the night. When a car comes, I move quickly aside and hide behind a tall bush, compelled by some instinct I shut inside myself a long time ago.

Overhead the night is cloudy, and there are no stars. If it weren't for the street lamps on every block, you could get lost on these lanes. Everything is a jungle when the light is gone. Something in my chest longs for a blackout. And then my eyes would readjust to the night, and then I could see all the helpless residents wandering, lost, feeling their ways. And I could watch them and be unafraid.

At Helena's house, the porch light is on, but all the windows are dark. I would like to get a look at her fiancé, so I put my face to the glass of the front windows, but the house looks empty. I can see the dim outline of the furniture in her living room, but the glare from the street lamps is too great. I go around the side of the house to the back, where one of the kitchen windows is open a crack. There's a fine smell coming from the kitchen, as though many healthful meals have been prepared between those walls, so I lift the window all the way, carefully remove the screen, and climb inside. Once in, I am conscientious in refitting the screen back into the window frame.

I am accustomed to dark, empty houses. I know how to navigate them. You rely on your senses. You trust your widened pupils, your outstretched fingertips, your animal nose.

I go upstairs. In her bedroom, I discover a picture of Helena and her fiancé in a frame by the bed. The picture is taken against the backdrop of some wide, forested valley—as though the only mountains worth climbing are the ones they climb together—and he is a very handsome young man with good eyebrows and an authoritative smile. She wears a baseball cap in the picture, and I wonder if I should get a baseball cap—though I would not know which team logo it should bear.

I lie down on the bed and smell the pillow and try to imagine what it is like to see, every night, the moonlight cast its particular shadow dance over the contours of this room. I imagine what it is like to be pressed under the body of that imposing man in the picture.

In her closet, I find her running shoes, set neatly beside each other, the laces tucked inside. When I put one of them to my nose, I smell nature, ruddy and bountiful. Her toothpaste, I am pleased to see, is the same brand as mine, though all the lotions and shampoos in her shower come in bottles that I've never seen on the shelves of our local grocery store. There is a little nest of her hair in the drain of the shower.

But I am drawn again downstairs, to the kitchen, because that is where I suspect Helena truly lives. The refrigerator is filled with produce, with small cartons of yogurt, with milk on the edge of souring. There are no dishes in the sink. From the smell of it, the ones in the dishwasher are clean and ready to be put away. I run my fingers over the deck of china plates standing there proudly.

In one of the cabinets, I find a jar of wheat germ that announces itself as an excellent source of folic acid and vitamin E. It suddenly feels like a tremendous oversight that I have never had any wheat germ in my house. It is clearly the source of so many good things. Wondering what new splendors might grow from the germ of wheat, I decide to take the jar with me. This will be essential to my friendship with Helena. This is what I have been missing—the key I have been looking for, the one that will unlock more conventional relationships with the world.

Except Marcie Klapper-Witt's neighborhood watch must have seen me when I climbed in through the window of Helena's house—because when I leave by the front door, the police are there waiting for me, their hands poised and ready over their holstered pistols, the lights on their car flashing pretty against the treetops.

CHAPTER 12

The name of my birth town isn't really Pale Miranda. That would be a very fanciful name for a town, and most towns are named in the service of either commerce or heritage. The town where I grew up is of the latter variety, and its real name is Polikwakanda, which is an indigenous name—supposedly from the Abenaki tribe, though I have never been able to find any reference to the word in my research of Native American languages. I don't know what it means, and maybe it means "town where monsters live" or something like that, but the only sense my young girl's tongue could make of the word was Pale Miranda, and so that's how I thought of the place where I was raised—even beyond the time when I was grown old enough to know better.

When I walked into the prom, there were banners everywhere that said, FAREWELL POLIKWAKANDA SENIORS!

Farewell, Pale Miranda.

———

DANCES IN THE town where I grew up were curious events. In other towns, the school dance is an opportunity to break free and go wild for a little while. But because our wildness was routine, because we were reminded of it monthly in cut lips and bruised thighs, our dances were tame. People stood around in compulsory clusters. They talked about dull things. No one tried to sneak vodka into the punch. No virginities were lost underneath the stage or in the backseats of cars in the parking lot. Virginities were simply not things toppled by clumsy, drunken lunging. Instead they were seized and forfeited in clawing battles under full moons while the naked apparitions of your friends looked on, howling. So it was.

When people danced at the prom, they danced slowly, pressed together and rocking back and forth with the sweet romance of dispassion. The tissue streamers wafted to and fro like underwater weeds. The students chatted pleasantly with the adult chaperones. People yawned. They went outside and looked up at the sky because they missed the moon. They sat on curbs and waited.

The previous year, I had gone to the dance with Polly. That now seemed like a very long time ago. We had already started pulling away from each other even then. I remembered seeing her across the gym, laughing at some joke told by a boy who, we had both agreed, was ridiculous. I remembered wondering about the integrity of Polly's personality, because I did not understand how people could go for so long being one thing and then, overnight, suddenly become something else. Such behavior seemed unnatural to me. A year later, though, I knew the difference between unnatural and unliterary. The natural world, it turned out, was not very literary. You could say it had poetry, but it was a rough brand of poetry.

So when I walked into the decorated gym, I entered alone.

What I realized was how far from normal my connections with other people had become. My interactions were based upon spite or jealousy or rage or strange hungers—but whatever they were, they were not dance-going relationships.

Some people said hello to me. Polly made brief conversation—and even Rose Lincoln, whose arm was still in a sling, wished me well in a way that made me think magnanimity was her newly forged weapon.

Somehow, without realizing it, I had become everyone's odd cousin. I existed as a nagging, peripheral figure in their lives—recognized only in specialized circumstances. I had become occasional. To leave a conversation with me was to return to real life.

No one asked me to dance, and I sat for a long time on the bleachers, alone on the dark periphery of the gym, watching the figures of my peers sway back and forth in each other's arms, hating them for all their pretty pretenses.

When a group of boys passed by, I could hear them talking about Mr. Hunter, who was supposed to be one of the chaperones. I hadn't seen him all night, but these boys had observed him walking the grounds of the school, cursing aloud. He swayed as he walked, said one. He was drunk, said another. The boys laughed.

"Where?" I asked.

"What?" they said. They were startled to notice me there in the dark.

"Where?" I said again. "Where was he going?"

"I don't know," said one of the boys, shrugging as though to suggest he wanted no part of whatever freakishness Mr. Hunter and I shared. "Looked like he was going toward the football field."

—

I WALKED DOWN to the field, the crinoline of my pink prom dress rustling against my skin. The field was not lit, but a glow reached it from the school grounds behind me. I was conscious of looking ridiculous out there, where no one was.

I didn't see Mr. Hunter at first, but I found him by the sound of a glass bottle being tapped with steady persistence against a metal rail of the bleachers. He was up in the very top row, gazing out over the field and the stars in the sky beyond.

"There she is," he called out when he saw me. I hiked up my dress and climbed to the top of the bleachers.

"Do you want to hear a story, Lumen?" he said when I reached him. "Now it's time for me to tell you a story. I quit my job. I quit it. I'm leaving. I'm going as far as I can go. Maybe Tibet. Have you ever eaten Tibetan food?"

"You're leaving? But why?"

He shook his head.

"You can't get it back," he said, "once it's gone."

"But you left once before."

He drank from the bottle.

"You have to be dauntless in this life. If at first you don't succeed at quitting, try, try again." Then he looked at my dress and seemed to notice it for the first time. "What are you dressed up as?"

I sat on the cold metal bench beside him, and the folds of my dress creased uncomfortably beneath me.

The moon was overhead, a waxing crescent, and he asked me if I weren't afraid to be alone with him.

"Jesus, girl," he said. "Didn't anybody ever tell you not to hang out with drunk, lying reprobates on emptied-out school property? You're going to stroll yourself into victimhood one of these days. Aren't you afraid?"

"I don't know."

"You should be."

He stood suddenly, wobbly with drink. Leaning over me, he gripped the bar behind me on either side of my head and brought his face down close to mine. I could smell the thick, acrid stench of alcohol. He licked his lips and smiled a threatening smile, and the bleachers tremored under his grasp.

I closed my eyes. I waited for whatever was coming.

There was another sound, and when I opened my eyes, he was standing upright, looking down at me with trepidation, even a little disgust.

"Goddamn it," he said, seething. "Goddamn you! No fear. Not an ounce of fucking fear. You invite—you *invite*—destruction. What's the world to you, huh? A place to die in? You aren't even a girl—you're a... you're a tragedy. There isn't a monster in the world—not a monster in the world till he meets an eager victim."

He reeled backward, and I thought he might fall, but he recovered himself.

"How come?" he said, almost pleading now. "How come you aren't afraid?"

I wanted to tell him that I was afraid. But his fury was wide—he raged against things larger than just me.

"You can't—" he started, then he used his sleeve to wipe his mouth. "You can't rub yourself against death like that. You just can't."

He wanted me to understand. There was a desperation in his eyes. He shook his head, and he collapsed onto the bench again. For a long time he said nothing but just looked out at the scattered stars.

Then he said:

"Your mother, she was the same way."

"You weren't lying, were you?" I said. "I mean, the things you said about running with my mother. Those weren't lies."

He just looked at me for a long time. I wondered what he saw in that frilled pink gown. Whatever it was, he must have deemed it fit.

He drank again and leaned forward, resting his elbows on his knees. "All right," he said then. "Time for another story. Last one. Are you ready?"

"Yes." I held my breath. I clutched at the fabric of my dress, wanting to tear it.

We sat side by side. He looked straight ahead, and I looked straight ahead, and it was no conversation. It was a kind of shared aloneness — words dropped in the void, verbal flotsam for whoever might see fit to collect it.

"She never went breach," he said. "You were right about that. That was a true thing. She was never a real breacher. It was something wrong with her maybe, her genes. Something didn't click like it was supposed to. She didn't feel the drive. No natural love of the night. But this is what you didn't know. She pretended. It was when it happened to your father. She wanted to run with him. So she pretended, and he kept her secret. Nobody knew. She took her clothes off, just like the rest of them, and she ran. You think about it the right way, it's romantic. Her and him — the night."

He paused and sniffed once.

"The problem was," he went on, "she took to it. I mean, eventually she liked it. After your father's year was up, well, she couldn't seem to stop herself. She kept going out. It had bored itself into her some way. It wasn't about instinct for her. It was about taste." He licked his lips and thought for a moment. "That's the difference. It came from a different place inside her. Your father, he tried to get her to stop. Like an addiction. She got pregnant with you, and he thought that might settle her down. But it didn't. She went out anyway, her belly all swollen up. What I heard is that people revered her, almost, like she carried the full moon inside her. I was still too young to go out myself, but I heard."

He paused again briefly.

"She was still going when I went breach," he said. "This was, you know, three or four years later. Everybody knew her secret by then. They'd all gotten suspicious when it went on so long. They figured it out—that she was a pretender. But there wasn't any . . . *disparagement* in it. See, she *chose* the thing that was forced on the rest of us. We—we loved her, even, because she loved us. I'm not saying you have to understand it. I'm just telling you how it was. Your mother, she was—she was *rare*."

I looked over briefly to see his face in the darkness, the glistening orbs of his eyes. I caught a quick glimpse, then looked away again. His story was a private one.

"You," he said. "I saw her in you. Ever since I got back. You want to know the truth? The truth is I don't want to see her anymore. It's been too long. The time comes you have to stop looking at ghosts."

It was a long time before he spoke again. For a while I thought he had forgotten I was there, but I waited patiently—as one does for revelations.

He eventually went on. "Did he . . . your father . . . did he tell you how she died?"

"Car accident," I said.

"Yeah." He shook his head. "That part's not true. But he can't be blamed. Sometimes the lie's necessary. Sometimes the truth is nocturnal. The light hurts it."

He paused again, sighing. I thought he might stop there, but then I realized the story had gone beyond him. The story would get told, as sometimes stories do, one way or the other, regardless of willful human instruments.

"It wasn't any car accident," he went on. "It was the third night of the Lacuna."

The Lacuna was the sixth full moon of the year, the still midpoint around which the rest of the year rotated. June, when the fireflies were out.

"We were down at the quarry. Your mother was there. You were at home, asleep in your crib. She was real still and quiet that night. I remember it. She had this grin, a faraway grin, like she was laughing at some joke nobody else heard. The rest of us, we were at each other one way or another. You know how it is. Foul. But she was a spark, a glistening thing in the middle of us all. She reminded us that we didn't know a thing about love. It was like that."

There was a catch in his voice, barely perceptible. A tiny tremor, the kind that means a massive fissure has quaked open somewhere deep, deep underground.

"That's where we lost her. We hunted for her. We did. The police came the next day. And firemen. But nobody could find anything. Maybe, we thought, maybe she'd come home to us. We liked to think it. Your father thought it. He thought it for a long time."

Then he was quiet, and I wondered if he was done. But after some time had passed, he rose up again, and this time he leaned over and pointed a long, wavering finger right in my face, as though condemning me for reminding him of my lost, moonlit mother.

"But this is what I'll have you know," he said, his voice hard. "She was better than us. Better than all of us. She went after the real thing of what the rest of us were just playing at. And she found it. God help her, she found it."

So there were others who felt the loss of my mother, maybe even more than I felt it, because I had only known the myth of her. Maybe that was what I saw in the eyes of those storekeepers who gifted me with free ice cream or barrettes or jars of maraschino cherries. Maybe in me they saw the reflection of my mother, whom they had lost on the narrow horizon.

And maybe that was the peculiar smell that I breathed in from the purple giraffe I had cuddled to my chest on many nights of my childhood—the odor of loss, which is like sumac and fallen leaves.

"But where?" I said, my voice small. "Where did she go? Where did you lose her?"

There was the quiver in his voice again, and a sound in his mouth like it was chewing on something—but I understood that he was only chewing on his own story, trying to swallow back down what was getting retched up.

"It was that mine," he said.

The mine. Map the mine. Hair like straw. Papier-mâché skin. Gray. A mouth that would swallow you up. I felt sick.

"She just got up and walked away," Mr. Hunter said. "That's how it was. She rose up, and everyone stopped and waited, because it seemed like she might say something—and we listened when she said things. But she didn't say anything. She stood up, and she turned her back on us, and she walked into the mine. See? The dark got her."

Those sunken eyes that looked only inward.

I wanted to run. I wanted to be split from my own skin.

"It was done before we knew it," he said. "When we realized she didn't intend to come back, we went in after her. But those mine tunnels—you've got no chance. There are shafts sunk everywhere that go straight down into nothing. You can't see two feet into the mouth of the thing. She didn't pause or turn around, she just walked forward. And then we couldn't see her anymore."

Sometimes death is a found mother.

And that's how I found mine.

———

THEN I RAN. The moon was not full, but it did not matter. Still outfitted in my papery pink party dress, I ran—I ran through town to the other side, against the headlights of the cars, into the woods, all the way to the quarry and the abandoned mine, where the wind played a shivery kind of music as it dove down into the deepest parts of the earth.

It was between moons—just before the June moon, the Lacuna—when I found my mother. I don't mean her body, which was a thing of brittle ash—I mean her voice, which one day spoke back to me from the void where I had made my meager confessions.

I was sixteen years old, and there was something gone wrong with me. I was sixteen, and I hadn't grown right, and all my friends were no longer my friends, and instead I had people I bit and who bit back. I had a beautiful, sad father and an angry drunken man who saw me as the reincarnation of a perverse angel. There was a pretty young woman with an affection for my father who picked out jewelry for me because my mother was a

301

fantasy told to me in good-night stories. I was sixteen, and my name was light, and my body had been bloodied and torn and repaired. I did well in school. I drew maps. I wondered what my life would become—I tried to picture it. I was sixteen, and I was an animal. I was the wrong kind of animal. I didn't believe as others believed. So there must have been some evil to it. The savagery of nature minus the nature is evil. I was sixteen years old, and I had grown proud of my evil. As though the earth itself had christened me Lumen, as though the heavens had given me their imprimatur. I would take it.

And that's when I discovered my true mother.

———

THE JUNE MOON was called the Lacuna, which the dictionary told me meant "pause." Maybe because it was the halfway point in the year, a moment when time itself held its breath, waited to exhale the remainder of its months. I don't know—but it's true that there was always a kind of holy stillness about that particular moon. It's in that stillness that my mother went away many years before.

There was no light at all—no light anywhere. I ran my fingers along the walls of the caves I knew so well. My dress dragged along packed dirt. I smelled my way.

And maybe, after all, that was growing up—learning to navigate deeper territories, learning how to see in the dark. Or learning not to care that you couldn't see in the dark.

But that seemed wrong, too. The adults around me, they weren't less afraid—they were more. They were afraid of things they couldn't articulate. They had lost the power to utter themselves, and so they cowered in sheetrock houses.

Mr. Hunter. He remade himself but could never make himself unbroken. I felt guilty. I had left him behind, there on his tinny height, no one to say goodbye to.

My father, I loved him. He was a sad man, too. But my whole life he had lied to me.

Still, I didn't blame him. I would sing a song of him. I would write him into a poem. He deserved magic words to keep him safe. Miss Simons was no curse. She was not strong enough to be a curse. She was simply common. But my father and I, we were better. We cultivated ourselves on higher ground.

Maybe he had grown too afraid even to see that.

The adults, they lived in another country—a populace of scrawny fear, as far away as morning is from midnight.

———

I REMEMBER THE way your skin looked in the moonlight.

You.

Peter Meechum.

Blackhat Roy Ruggle.

Hondy Pilt.

Rose Lincoln.

Polly, pretty Polly.

I line you all up in my head, a beautiful processional, slow-motion and smiling. You are of my life.

When I point to you, stand up straight. Let me get a good look at you.

You were pale.

And you were dark.

Your ribs showed through your skin.

You were the one who always had leaves in your hair.

You wore your nakedness proudly—bathing in the moonlight as though your exposure were holy and dreadful.

You, on the other hand, always hid in bushes and behind trees. Was it shame or was it timidity?

You treated your skin before the moon came out. You were ridiculous, but you were lustrous.

You had freckled shoulders.

You had a birthmark on your right calf—I touched it once with my lips when you were sleeping.

I could draw maps of your skin—all of you. I have often, without your knowing it, traveled the topographies of your flesh.

You were brilliant in the moonlight, and I remember you all.

——

I WENT TO visit my mother. Hay for hair, paper for skin. And still just a girl. Of course a girl. It had never occurred to me—when she died she had been just a few years older than I was now. I had thought of my mother as many things: as a queen, as a bride, as a wild woman, as a prophet—but I had never thought of her as simply a girl, like me. In just a handful of years, I would be older than my own mother.

It hurt to think about that.

I could not see her in the dark, so I nestled myself against her. I spoke to her.

I said, "Hello. It's me. It's Lumen, your daughter."

Her silence was profound, mocking.

I said, "Did you wear orchid gloves at your wedding? My dad says you did, but I don't know."

She was preserved in time. I rested my head against her shoulder. Her hay hair tickled my cheek. I smelled her gray skin, and it smelled of nothing at all. Her skin was dusty.

"Did you get lost?" I said. "I got lost, too."

———

SOMETIMES WHEN YOU are looking for something, you find it.

You could call it magic.

If we name things, maybe they'll never get away from us.

———

I SLEPT, MY head in my mother's lap. It might have been five minutes. It might have been an hour. When I woke, I thought it was late. I thought about my father and my promise to be home by midnight. But when I made my way out of the mine, I found Blackhat Roy near the mouth, waiting for me. He said nothing. He looked miserable—tortured. But this boy's wretchedness felt far away from where I was.

"My mother's dead," I said.

"I know," he said. "My father's gone, too."

"I forgot that."

"I know."

"How did you know I was here?"

"People saw you. Running."

"You went to the dance?"

"No. I was looking for you."

I turned and went to my secret place, my cistern. He followed me there, but I didn't care. I had stopped hearing the world. In my head were confused, inarticulate voices. They babbled and boiled, and I drowned in them. My mother was a dead girl. There was darkness and dust and Blackhat Roy. You sometimes go wild, and you sometimes want that wildness shackled.

We faced each other, and the wind whistled up from the pit. While he looked, I undid my prom dress and let it fall to the ground. Then I took off my underwear. We're all of us naked one way or the other.

My mother was calling my name from the deep wells of the earth, and I was rotted from the inside, and my mind was a gemstone mired in murk, and I would torture the impurities out. I would sweat them out, I would bleed them out, I would suffer them out, I would exhaust them out.

For there must be order. There must be balance. For every sin, a punishment. For every shameful act, a suffering. For every impure bite, a pure tooth knocked loose.

Otherwise, what was it all for?

The earth knew, whose days and nights were perfect tides of light.

The moon knew, whose pocky face had waxed and waned by untransgressible law for billions of years.

I knew, who was yet still a girl.

CHAPTER 13

Do you want to know who I am?

Do you want to know what I do?

I live next door to you with my husband and my child.

I have done such things as would shame the devil, yet I keep my front yard tidy, the trash bins lined up neatly on trash day.

I attend the meetings of the PTA. I offer to bake cookies.

At night, after everyone is asleep, I creep downstairs to the kitchen table and write down my memories. They are the stories I tell myself when I can't sleep. Like fairy tales—or the mythos of a lost culture.

I was an excellent student.

I am an excellent member of the community. I never spit, and I always put my waste in the proper receptacles.

Do you know what else I do?

I sometimes walk out into the night. I walk down the middle of the deserted street. Our neighborhood is always silent at this hour—we comprise wholesome families. I feel the chill, as I did not as a girl. Maybe as you get older you grow into new kinds of dis-ease. Maybe death is the ultimate discomfort.

I walk to the park, which is deserted except for four teenagers who scurry away when they see me. The air they leave behind smells of marijuana. On the ground is an empty plastic bag and a box of matches with the name of a bar on it and an illustration of a woman sitting inside a massive martini glass.

The playground equipment is still and skeletal, unhinged as it is at this time of night from the fuss of child life, illuminated by what we used to call a Pheasant Moon.

I am alone. I am in love with my husband and my boy, but I am still alone.

Sometimes you want a hand over your mouth — you want to be hushed. Other times you just want to burn till there's nothing left.

———

WHEN JACK FINALLY comes, he does not speak for a while but instead just paces back and forth outside my cell. I watch him, feeling sorry that he has a wife whom he has to fetch from jail. He is a good man. All the other men in our neighborhood have wives who are properly aligned, who know how to stay in-doors.

"You broke into that woman's house," he says finally, using his hands to show the concreteness of the facts. "You opened her kitchen window, and you climbed in her house when nobody was home. You did these things."

These things and others he knows nothing of. My past is sometimes so noisy in my brain. I can only remain quiet.

"Ann," he goes on. "Ann, Helena and I — we just work together. Sometimes I see her at school. Sometimes we talk. You know there's nothing between us. You know I wouldn't do that, don't you?"

"I know."

"Then why——"

He stops himself. You can see the restraint in his thin, sealed lips. He does not like to ask me why. He fears both the answer and the absence of an answer.

"They said . . ." he continues, almost pleading. "They said you took a jar of wheat germ."

I smile a little to show him that everything will be all right—that things will always be all right—but he does not smile back.

"It seemed important," I say.

Now he approaches my cage and puts his fingers on mine as they grip the bars. He looks at me as though he knows me and understands me and will be my ally forever.

"Ann," he says, "you have to be better. You have to be."

I would like to explain to him that there are worse horrors by far, that we will endure—but I don't. Instead, I just say:

"I know."

———

I STOOD BEFORE Roy—a naked little offering that he did not accept.

He seemed ashamed to see my body. And when he looked at my face, all he saw was the line of stitches.

"I did that to you," he said, swallowing hard.

Absently, I put my hand to the wound. When I brought it away, I noticed that my fingertips were coated with the peach-colored dust that Margot Simons had shown me how to use earlier.

Roy stepped away from me, as though I were difficult to be near. He moved to the other side of the pit and stood before it, gazing at me across that impossible depth. Then he looked down into it. I wondered what he saw there. Maybe he, too, had lost things to the earth. But I was unsettled by something in his eyes that was near to longing.

I was cold, and the gravelly ground bit into the soles of my feet.

"What are you doing?" I said.

"You know something?" he said without looking up. "I liked your room."

"My room?"

"It was a nice room. I wonder if I would have been different if I grew up in a room like that."

His voice was small and hollow. It echoed off the walls of the cistern.

"You grew up all right," I said.

He made a sound that echoed against the walls of the cistern and seemed to come not from him but from the earth itself.

He toed some pebbles into the black pit, and they made no sound at all.

"At the beginning," he said, "I wanted to break you. I really did. But I couldn't. Then, later, I didn't want to break you anymore. I wanted . . . the opposite. But something about me—my hands don't work that way. And I broke you instead. It was an accident."

"Roy," I said. "Roy."

"I hated you for such a long time," he said, looking up at me. He rubbed a hand across his face, and his cheek smeared with ash. That's when I noticed he was covered in it—ashy dust—as though whatever burned in him was smoldering out, leaving his skin desiccated. He smiled a smile that had no smile in it. "At least that I was good at. Hate's simple. It makes sense. You know it, too."

"Roy," I said. "Don't."

He cried now, and his bare frame shivered with his tears.

"You read all those books," he said, shaking his head. "All those fucking books."

I wanted to tell him it meant nothing. I wanted to explain that it was all I knew how to do—that I read books instead of doing real things. I wanted to say to him that I was different now, that I had lost who I was and that I would never get that Lumen back again, that something had gone deranged inside me. I used to think that some people are born so good they are illiterate to the languages of desolation. But we all speak the same tongue.

I wanted to tell him these things, but my heart was going too fast. I was deafened by it, muted by it. I was peaceful in my brain, viewing myself as if from above, wondering at this little monkey of a creature who stood staring.

He gazed into the pit and then back at me, and there was an awful, imploring truth in his eyes.

"Lumen," he said. "Lumen, I did something bad. Really bad. I went to your house tonight. No one was there. I tried to read the book you gave me. But I couldn't. So I wanted to bring it back to you."

He shook his head.

Something was fouled in him, and something was fouled in me, and I watched myself with him, and I could feel my own tears on my cheeks, because I knew what was coming, and I couldn't stop it. I didn't know how to stop things.

311

"Roy," was all I could say. "Don't. Please don't."

"Then help me, Lumen," he said. "Help me." And he put his arms out, palms up, for me to come to him.

It was a moment. I could have become one thing, but I became another. The creatures we truly are are exposed in tiny moments. This was one.

I could have saved him.

I did not save him.

"Help me," he said again.

And I said, "I can't." I said, "I don't know how."

"Lumen," he said.

I said, "Don't be afraid."

But he was. I could see that. He whimpered a little, his wild animal eyes gone all soft.

That's when I turned my back on him. I turned and closed my eyes. I could not bear witness.

I heard a brief shuffle of dirt from beneath his feet. I breathed in the dusty air. I paid attention to my heart, the stubborn beating of my dreadful heart.

When I opened my eyes again and turned around, he'd fallen. Blackhat Roy Ruggle was gone.

———

I WAITED FOR a while, and the earth was quite still. The only sound was my own breathing, and I listened to it. I persisted.

I didn't know what else to do.

I put my prom dress back on, the rustle of the crinoline echoing gaudily in that grim sanctuary. I wiped my face with my gritty hands, and I made my way outside. Walking unhurriedly back through the woods, I was aware of all the voices of the crickets and the tree toads and the owls around me. The air was cold in my lungs, the stars reflected in the still water of the lake as I passed by. I was no part of the things I saw. I was just a traveler across these fields of night, and I was alone.

I smelled the smoke when I was still a great distance from the edge of the woods. What's carried on the air can be carried a long way. I didn't see it until I was almost home, that black plume that rose behind the trees, almost invisible except for the way it blocked out the stars and gave a halo to the gibbous moon. At the same time, I became aware of the flashing lights, blue, white, and red.

I must have looked like an apparition emerging from those trees, my prom dress torn and covered with burrs. But no one noticed. No one was paying any attention, because everyone was looking at the place where my house used to be—where now blackened timbers stood upright and smoked and crackled and released every now and then a dust of ash and ember.

I looked for my father, but I couldn't see him among the neighbors who stood on the street in their nightclothes, shaking their heads and leaning together against tragedy.

When somebody finally saw me, I was seized by a team of uniformed men. Police confirmed that my name was Lumen Fowler, that Marcus Fowler was my father. They wanted to know where I had been.

"Where's my dad?" I said.

They wanted to know if I knew who set the fire.

"Where's my dad?" I said.

Then two paramedics led me to the back of an ambulance, where they put a blanket over my shoulders and performed tests on my pliant body. They told me to stay put there in the ambulance, but when they were gone I found myself wandering away among the vehicles and lights and moving figures. I was a meager ghost. No one saw me—I was nothing to see. I heard their voices. I heard everything. How the firemen had tried to stop him from going inside, how they had told him they'd cleared the house. But he had gone in anyway, saying he knew where I'd be hidden. The coal hole. Saying he was sure I was in there because I'd promised to be home by midnight. I'd promised.

I sat down on the ground, the crinoline bunched up underneath me, and I held out my hands to collect the ash that fell from the sky like flakes of snow.

Margot Simons found me. She tried to lift me, but my legs didn't work right, so instead she sat down next to me on the road. Her face was streaky with soot and dried tears. She put her arms around me.

"It'll be all right, Lumen," she said.

"Yes," I said.

"I'll take care of you," she said. "I'm not going anywhere," she said.

"Yes."

"He loved you," she said. "There was nothing else in the world for him but you."

The ash collected on my palms. Miss Simons tightened her arms around me. She used one hand to brush away the ash that was collecting in my hair.

"You're going to be okay," she said.

I said, "Yes."

CHAPTER 14

Jack drives. It is deep night. No moon at all. There are no streetlights out here. We are in the middle of a great black, the aperture of our headlights opening on the two-lane blacktop scrolling out before us, the margins of the trees flashing past. The only sound is the stable hum of the engine and the groan of the upholstery under us as we shift in our seats.

I glance into the backseat at our son, Marcus. Jack could not find someone to watch him when he came to fetch me from jail.

"He's asleep," I say.

"It's late," Jack says.

"It's late," I repeat, nodding.

I am very much alone, the light in the car strange, the flashes from the oncoming headlights casting shadows that make my husband look like someone I don't know.

He looks at me, earnest.

"It'll be okay," he says. "Helena and her fiancé won't press charges. They won't. I'll talk to them. You'll apologize." He

315

makes his hand into a flat sword and cuts it through the air with each point. "She'll forgive you. It's what people do."

This is true. It requires unrelenting effort to hate. It takes strength, commitment. Most of us are not that ambitious.

"We'll..." he goes on, "we'll schedule an appointment for you. To see a psychologist. It'll be good for you to talk to someone. We'll find someone you can talk to, someone you feel comfortable—"

He stops, looking to see how I will respond.

"I will," I say simply. "I trust you."

He gives me a tentative smile. A solitary car comes from the other direction, and we squint our eyes against its headlights. Then there is a shift in his voice toward gentleness.

"How are you feeling?" he says.

"Sleepy," I say. "But okay. I feel fine."

Then we are quiet for a while. In my mind, I say a little prayer for my father, but it's a prayer I sometimes say over my son in his crib, and sometimes over my husband when he is asleep beside me in our bed. It was one of the traditional lullabies in Pale Miranda—first taught to me by Polly when we were both very little girls. It made everything seem blameless, and it went like this:

Sleep now, baby—
Sleep now, child.
See the moon, so still and mild.
Dream away
From sun's bright noon.
I'll watch you walking on the moon.
And when you're older,
Stout and true,
I will see the moon in you.

None of us is a saint, but the world is still magic.

"Just a few weeks till summer," Jack says beside me.

"It'll be nice."

"We'll have time. Maybe we should go somewhere."

"Yes," I say. "Let's go somewhere. Where do people go?"

My mother, she got lost during the Lacuna, the June moon. My father, he died just before it. Do you know what a lacuna is? It's a space. A hole. A lumen. In music, it's a pause that makes you hear silence as though it were being played by an instrument. In moons, it is the middle of the year — a hiatus. In literature, it's something left out of a manuscript. Here is a lacuna:

Do you see me there? In that empty space — that's where I got lost. It's where I went from that night to this one. It's where my father and Blackhat Roy went. I hope it's bright where they are. Bright as my aching girl-chest, where their hearts, black and white, still do dances.

Next to me in the car, Jack takes a deep breath. Then he speaks, haltingly, as though any word might cause the whole night sky to collapse.

"You know," he says, "you can . . . talk to me."

"About what?"

"I don't know. About things. Anything. Whatever's important."

After a pause, I say:

"I miss my father."

I turn and look at my husband, the way the dim light from the dash makes his face glow with a strange tint. His skin seems almost unreal, his eyes glassy. Then I look at my son, asleep in the backseat. I can see his little chest rise and fall under his striped cotton shirt, his hot breath coming slow between parted lips, his head, hair messy, cocked to one side and leaning against the cushion of his car seat. His hands rest loose on his lap, but I see his tiny fingers twitch slightly around his stuffed pet bunny.

I think of an Easter Sunday, when I was ten.

Every year my father made a special Easter egg hunt for me. He hid them in difficult places, both inside and outside the house, then he gave me clues to those hidden treasures in the form of rhyming couplets written in script on index cards.

That year I was stuck on the last one. The clue said this:

Here lies the measure of all our worth—
Look where sleeps the most precious thing on earth.

I looked in all the places in the house where we kept valuables. I scoured the sideboard in the kitchen, where we kept the china and the silverware. I looked through my father's office drawers, where he kept important documents. I sifted through the dresser where we kept all the things that once belonged to my mother.

While I looked, he watched me, smiling. He refused to help me with any additional hints.

I scowled at him. He gazed back at me with a look I'll never forget.

I finally found the last Easter egg. It was in my bedroom, under my pillow.

"Your father," Jack says now. "You never tell me about him. You never tell me anything about where you grew up, or about your school days, or about what you were like as a girl. You know I'd listen. I love you. I want to hear these things."

I look away from him toward the trees, their briefly illuminated trunks flashing by in the night. I wonder who might be out there.

"Maybe."

———

EVERYONE IN THE neighborhood will know about my breaking into Helena's house and about my being arrested and about the psychological rehabilitation I will undergo. At dinner parties, they will be nice. They are always very nice. They will offer their support. They will tell me they care about me and love me and want what's best for me. Jack will remind me, as he always does, that he loves me.

It's funny, all these people talking about love. They think love is something like a fluffy pillow where you rest your head. They think love is sweet and gentle, all hands and lips and nestling. But they're wrong. I know what love is. Love is angrier than this. It's harsher. It's tasting the world on your tongue and digging your claws deep into the underbelly of life. I know exactly what love is. It's sometimes leaning over your husband while he sleeps, while he conjures in his dreams all the fears and ecstasies he would relish if he were ever able to let himself be truly and wholly alive, breathing in the fermented air exhaled from his pink, undamaged lungs—and it's sometimes wanting to rip out his throat with your teeth.

ACKNOWLEDGMENTS

Special thanks to Josh Kendall and Eleanor Jackson. I owe them considerable gratitude. If you could read the first version of this book, you would see just how much.

ABOUT THE AUTHOR

Joshua Gaylord grew up in Anaheim, California, and currently resides in New York City. Using his own name or the pen name Alden Bell, he has authored three previous novels, including *The Reapers Are the Angels*. He received his PhD from New York University and has taught high school English as well as literature courses at NYU and the New School.

MULHOLLAND BOOKS

You won't be able to put down these Mulholland Books.

WHEN WE WERE ANIMALS *by Joshua Gaylord*

THE DOLL MAKER *by Richard Montanari*

SEAL TEAM SIX: HUNT THE FOX *by Don Mann and Ralph Pezzullo*

WRITTEN IN THE BLOOD *by Stephen Lloyd Jones*

PARADISE SKY *by Joe R. Lansdale*

WHITE CROCODILE *by K. T. Medina*

THE INSECT FARM *by Stuart Prebble*

CROOKED *by Austin Grossman*

THE STOLEN ONES *by Richard Montanari*

THE NECESSARY DEATH OF LEWIS WINTER *by Malcolm Mackay*

HOW A GUNMAN SAYS GOODBYE *by Malcolm Mackay*

THE SUDDEN ARRIVAL OF VIOLENCE *by Malcolm Mackay*

HARD FREEZE *by Dan Simmons*

WHISKEY TANGO FOXTROT *by David Shafer*

THE SILKWORM *by Robert Galbraith*

BROKEN MONSTERS *by Lauren Beukes*

HARD AS NAILS *by Dan Simmons*

Visit mulhollandbooks.com for
your daily suspense fiction fix.

Download the FREE Mulholland Books app.

THE HORMONE DIET

A 3-Step Program to Help You Lose Weight, Gain Strength, and Live Younger Longer

NATASHA TURNER, ND

RODALE

This is a reprint of a book first published in 2009 by Random House Canada, a division of Random House of Canada Limited. The Rodale Inc. direct mail edition with exclusive content published in July 2010.

© 2010, 2009 by Essence Wellness Inc.

Printed in the United States of America
Rodale Inc. makes every effort to use acid-free ∞, recycled paper ♲.

Book design by Terri Nimmo

Photos © Sam Gibbs

Library of Congress Cataloging-in-Publication Data

Turner, Natasha (Natasha S.)
    The hormone diet : a 3-step program to help you lose weight, gain strength, and live younger longer / Natasha Turner.
        p.   cm.
    Originally published : Canada : Random House, 2009.
    Includes bibliographical references and index.
    ISBN-13 978-1-60529-402-5 trade hardcover
    ISBN-10 1-60529-402-0 trade hardcover
    ISBN-13 978-1-60529-385-1 direct hardcover
    ISBN-10 1-60529-385-7 direct hardcover
        1. Reducing diets—Popular works.   2. Hormone therapy—Popular works.   3. Diet therapy—Popular works. I. Title.
    RM222.2T84 2009
    615.5'35—dc22   2010012657

                            2   4   6   8   10   9   7   5   3   1   hardcover

RODALE
LIVE YOUR WHOLE LIFE™

We inspire and enable people to improve their lives and the world around them
For more of our products visit **rodalestore.com** or call 800-848-4735

For my husband,
"Hey Tim," thank you for believing in me.
I am so blessed to share my life with you.

For Mom,
Thank you for your continued reminders to keep things simple,
be positive, make time for others, live life to the fullest, and
to never take it or your loved ones for granted.
Your courage, strength, wisdom, and humor
inspire me—always. I love you.

CONTENTS

INTRODUCTION

If you are looking for a big opportunity, seek out a big problem.
H. JACKSON BROWN JR.

My Story of Hormonal Havoc

Just a few months had passed since I had graduated from college in 1993. I was 22. I arrived home one day from my summer job in tears and feeling overwhelmed. I felt weak and feverish. I couldn't think—my head was buzzing with confusion. I couldn't understand people when they spoke to me. I couldn't seem to process information fast enough to make sense of anything. My best friend, Lise, who was living with me at the time, was talking to me about some mundane household incident and all I could do was stare blankly back at her. She said, "Don't worry, I can tell you're just not getting it. It's okay." I started to cry again. I thought I was going crazy and was certain I had a serious neuro-logical disease.

Later that day, I wound up in the emergency room, where the doc-tors found I indeed had a fever, along with severe anemia. They told me to take some iron and to go home and rest, which was about all I was capable of doing. I would wake up feeling okay, but within minutes the confusion and fogginess in my head would return. I couldn't even watch TV.

When I thought about it as best I could, I realized something had been off for months before my breaking point. I had needed so much sleep—over 16 hours a day—and was too tired to go to the gym, even though I was an exercise fanatic. I was gaining weight—25 pounds, a lot for my small frame—and I felt fat and unattractive. My periods were irregular and I was losing fistfuls of hair. I had chalked it all up to the stress of finishing school and ending a relationship with my boyfriend at the time.

Thank heavens the emergency room doctor who treated me decided to investigate more thoroughly into why I was so anemic and tested my blood to rule out hypothyroidism. Days later, I received a call letting me know my TSH was over 25; a normal level is considered to be less than 4.7, and an optimal level is less than 2. (TSH is a hormone that increases when the thyroid is not functioning well.) I was severely hypothyroid, with extremely low iron levels. Confusion was overcoming me because my brain function was slowing down along with the rest of me. I started taking thyroid medication immediately. Within a week I felt like a completely different person, and I continue to take thyroid medication today.

Looking back, I know I had the telltale symptoms of hypothyroidism as early as age 13. I remember waking up with my pillow *covered* in my hair and being taken to dermatologists for hair loss, but nothing those doctors proposed ever helped. I remember feeling tired all the time and having horrible menstrual issues, including pain, cramping, and irregular cycles. I always had belly fat and would *never* wear a two-piece bathing suit. I hated my body.

Now I know my disease was missed because I seemed to be slim. Because my weight appeared "normal," my doctors did not think of looking for hypothyroidism, a condition commonly found in noticeably overweight people.

Fast forward to 2000. After finishing 4 years of training, I began my practice as a naturopathic doctor. Between patients, I was skipping out to buy cookies or muffins because I craved them so badly. I never used to like these foods, though I sure had to have them now. But within about 20 minutes of the last sugary bite, I would be falling asleep in a "carb coma." Still, I couldn't stop my seemingly insatiable snack habit. At the same time, my periods were becoming more irregular, my breasts were shrinking, my waist was getting wider, and I was losing hair—again.

On a professional hunch, I underwent a thorough investigation involving blood work and ultrasounds. My suspicions were confirmed—I had polycystic ovarian syndrome (PCOS). PCOS is a condition characterized by irregular periods, hair loss, acne, and weight gain; it's also linked to an increased risk of breast cancer, infertility, and diabetes. So I now had not one, but two metabolic diseases. My family doctor, Dr. Tammy Hermant, suggested the diabetes medication metformin, along with the birth control pill, in an attempt to regulate my periods.

Since PCOS is associated with insulin resistance, the underlying cause of type 2 diabetes, insulin sensitizing medications such as metformin are regularly prescribed to treat it. And I was definitely insulin resistant. Besides the high insulin levels detected by my blood work, my cravings, constant hunger, fatigue after eating, and fat gain around my abdomen were obvious signs. But I was truly not interested in taking the metformin. I also had high levels of testosterone and dehydroepiandrosterone (DHEA), which explained my hair loss, dwindling breasts, and bulking waistline. I was also not interested in taking the birth control pill. Given my training, I wanted to figure out how to manage my health—threatened as it was—in a more safe and natural way.

The Genesis of the Hormone Diet Approach

I had already begun to research hormones and hormonally related conditions. I was fascinated by their interconnectedness and the number of bodily functions they influenced. The standard treatment for a seemingly uncomplicated hormonal issue such as hypothyroidism—simply replacing thyroid hormone—was by no means the complete solution. In fact, it was frighteningly inadequate in many cases.

Today, when I see cases of hypothyroidism in my clinical practice at Clear Medicine, I rarely rush to treat the thyroid deficiency right away. (I make exceptions, of course, when a patient's TSH reading is sky-high or the patient already is taking a strong dose of thyroid medication and is still experiencing symptoms.) Instead I start by working to detoxify the patient's liver and digestive system; to balance his or her stress hormone levels with good sleep and stress management; to use foods that level out blood sugar and insulin; to replenish the nutrients needed to make thyroid hormone; and to treat PMS or any other signs of sex hormone imbalance. If the patient is still experiencing unresolved symptoms, *only then* do I address the thyroid.

I believe this approach provides a lasting health fix because each one of these factors influences the thyroid. Jumping right into treating the thyroid would be like building a house on sand. The foundation would constantly be shifting and would require constant repair. Helping a person achieve overall hormonal balance makes specific treatment for the thyroid unnecessary in some cases. While in other cases, body imbalances commonly associated with hypothyroidism, such as low stomach acid (which can reduce nutrient absorption), iron deficiency, high cholesterol, and adrenal (stress) gland fatigue, must be addressed as well.

My multifaceted approach to thyroid treatment has helped me garner a listing as a "Top Thyroid Doctor" on www.thyroid-info.com. But my approach to hormonal balance goes far beyond treating thyroid patients.

Through my years of clinical practice, I have gained a much clearer view of the *real* big picture. Exploring the interrelationship between our hormones and so many functions in the body, I began to realize that a step-by-step approach needed to be followed *in order* to restore total balance and long-term health. I knew that veering from this course would make lasting results next to impossible. I also knew my approach would not necessarily be the quickest, but it would be the most effective.

And so *The Hormone Diet* was born. I have been working on the ideas and treatments described in this book since 2000. In the field of hormones, new information is discovered weekly. I am sure by the time this book hits the press, I will already have more to add.

The Hormone Diet Is for Men and Women of All Ages

The mere mention of "hormones" can conjure images of menopausal women or nefarious food additives. Indeed, many patients come to me seeking to address these specific concerns. But this book is definitely not only for those with hormonal issues. It is not even strictly directed at people seeking to lose weight. I have used the approach outlined in these pages to successfully treat thousands of patients with a broad spectrum of health goals. Some needed to gain much-needed muscle. Others wanted healthier looking skin. Still others wanted to get rid of headaches, improve their sleep, ease their digestion, increase their energy, improve their fertility, or sharpen their memory.

So many of us believe we can get healthy by losing weight. The truth is *we must be healthy to lose weight*. When you complete the steps outlined in Part Two of this book, you will optimize your hormonal balance, lose unwanted fat, and restore your health in the process. Unlike so many other "diet" books lining the shelves these days, *The Hormone Diet* offers a complete wellness plan that addresses *every* cause of obesity. It promotes healthy bodily function from head to toe, inside and out.

Truly Solving Obesity Means Understanding Why We're Fat

Oversecretion of insulin is considered by many experts to be the primary cause of obesity today. Because our body secretes insulin in response to carbohydrates, many experts suggest that simply removing carbohydrates from our diet is the solution. Some researchers go further, suggesting that we should not exercise because it only serves to stimulate our appetite.

I couldn't disagree more strongly. The recommendation to not exercise literally puts lives in danger. Also, if we know that limiting simple carbohydrates reduces insulin and that exercise improves insulin sensitivity, which also reduces insulin—then why not recommend both?

Dieting alone—restricting calories and carbohydrates—does nothing to build metabolically active muscle, a necessary health reserve for our later years. Combine diet and exercise, however, and you will lose the fat and save your muscle. *The number on the scale is by no means your most significant indicator of health.* It does *nothing* to identify how much muscle you have or *where* you carry your fat—both more important factors for wellness than how much you weigh. Instead, the complete Best Body Assessment I have outlined in Chapter 6 will give you clear and easy-to-follow methods for measuring *all* the factors that determine your health and wellness.

The type of exercise we choose is also critical. I would argue that 30 years of regular jogging won't help you attain an optimal body composition, and by increasing physical stress on the body, could potentially accelerate the natural loss of metabolically active muscle we all experience as we age. Doing cardiovascular exercise alone might be just as bad as not exercising at all—we need to add strength training into the mix as well. Strength training and dieting together is *the* answer for achieving a lean, toned body, balancing our hormones and addressing many of the major causes of obesity. I believe you need cardio only once a week! Add in the benefits of sleep, stress management, health-promoting supplements, and an anti-inflammatory detox, and you've got the winning combination I outline later for you in my three-step, 6-week health fix.

As you read on, you'll learn that excess insulin is just *one* of the culprits behind obesity, albeit a big one. Several more of the most common fat-packing imbalances cannot be solved by dieting alone. *These imbalances can prevent successful fat loss even when great diet and exercise plans are in place.* They include:

1. Inflammation
2. Insulin resistance
3. Low serotonin, which leads to cravings, depression, or anxiety
4. Chronic stress
5. Estrogen dominance (a state arising from relative excess of estrogen to progesterone, which is known to cause weight gain and to increase the risk of PMS and breast cancer)
6. Menopause
7. Andropause
8. Hypothyroidism

As a society, we are trained to consult our doctors about the long-term outcome of these imbalances, such as high blood pressure, obesity, diabetes, cancer, arthritis, and heart disease. We are, however, much less likely to consult our doctors for the "less" serious conditions of fatigue, memory loss, low libido, poor concentration, or difficulty managing weight—the first true indicators of potential major health issues that affect a majority of the population today. My hope is that this book will encourage you to *think* and *act* differently about your health.

A Proven Method for Lasting Fat Loss

The guidelines in this book are really quite simple. You'll learn how to sleep soundly, detoxify your body, subdue stress, eat well, take the right supplements, exercise, and enjoy fulfilling sex. As a bonus, I'll teach you about the benefits of safe, natural skin care. Believe me, none of this is rocket science—but they are practices few of us are coordinating well in our busy, stress-filled lives.

The innovative aspect is the *way* I suggest you undertake these steps, the *science* in which they are rooted, and the *effects* they will have on your body. The intricacies and subtleties behind this wellness plan are *vast*. My approach doesn't involve rushing toward an instant cure; it involves gentle preparation, a step-by-step approach, and clever refinements. It makes *The Hormone Diet* perfectly suited to you and to everyone you know, regardless of specific health goals.

If you've tried every diet and they've all failed you, *it's not your fault*. This plan is different and will help you to realize why your past efforts were doomed to fail *unless* they took into account the complex chemicals that are really running the show—your hormones!

More Than Just Another Diet Book

Although this book is written with a slant toward losing fat, it's really about restoring your total health. If you take me up on *The Hormone Diet* challenge, you'll embark on a program that's far more than just an eating plan. It's a total wellness program that differs from other diets. It offers the potential for *lifelong results* because it fixes every reason why we are fat. Before giving a moment's thought to your exercise routine, you will spend the first 4 weeks concentrating on *preparing* your body for lasting weight loss. Only after you have set the foundation for hormonal balance will you begin concentrating on what you do in the gym, which will then restore your metabolism. The preparatory steps are key to addressing *all* potential causes of excess weight and obesity, not just the ones trumpeted by the diet and exercise industries.

How to Use This Book

Read Part One to understand your muscle, your fat, and your metabolism, all of which speak directly to your hormones. Complete your Hormonal Health Profile to discover whether one or more hormonal imbalances have been compromising your health or weight loss efforts.

Use Part Two, the three-step fix, to restore your hormonal balance and total wellness.

Helping You Take Control of Your Health

I am thrilled to have the opportunity to share *The Hormone Diet* with you which, amazingly, became a #1 national bestseller 1 week after its release in Canada. I believe it provides answers to the questions many people are searching for—including why they feel the way they feel and, most importantly, why they can't lose weight.

I wrote this book and founded Clear Medicine because my goal is to bring preventive medicine to anyone who has a desire to achieve better health. When I first began to practice naturopathic medicine years ago, I always had to explain to people exactly what I did for a living. Occasionally, I still do, but today I find people are more aware, as they are looking for answers to support and maintain their wellness.

Someone once told me that the best motivation for living healthily is to develop a chronic disease. Believe me, I've been there, I've witnessed family members in the same position, and I *don't* want this to be your motivation for change. Instead, I wish to inspire you to take *complete responsibility* for your health and to think of managing your wellness with the same eye to the future as you apply to managing your finances. Without your health, all the money in the world means nothing.

Strive for strength and harmony. They are magnificent attributes that will help you in all aspects of your life.

Wishing you perfect balance,

Natasha Turner, BSc, ND
Toronto, December 2009

PART ONE

YOUR HORMONES, YOUR BODY

Life is not a path of coincidence, happenstance, and luck,
but rather an unexplainable, meticulously charted course for one to
touch the lives of others and make a difference in the world.

BARBARA DILLINHAM

CHAPTER 1

THE NEW FORMULA FOR FAT LOSS

Here's what you can expect to learn in this chapter:

- How to set the stage for successful fat loss
- The facts about hormones
- Why dieting can cause hormonal havoc
- How hormones boost metabolic rate and fat burning
- How inflammation causes obesity and hormonal imbalance
- How to control appetite with the help of hormones
- How hormones affect sexual appetite
- The road to safe weight loss

For decades, an endless stream of well-marketed diets and new-fangled exercise programs have been promising an easy path to a leaner, trimmer you. Every year, it seems, we are enticed to drop all "bad carbs" or to purchase the latest piece of home gym equipment and good health and happiness will surely be ours. But the rules of fat loss have changed from what we once thought them to be. No longer can we rely on diet alone to shed unwanted weight. Nor can we simply exercise the pounds away. Certainly, poor eating habits and lack of physical activity are two of the biggies when it comes to explaining escalating obesity rates. But they are by no means the only culprits.

Today's headlines read like a laundry list of previously overlooked factors that can impede successful weight loss—from lack of sleep and excess stress to the chemicals in our soaps. With so many lifestyle influences to consider, all the calorie-cutting and exercise in the world, in isolation, will not provide the golden key to achieving the lasting change we desire.

Until now, the prevailing approach to conquering obesity has been like putting a broken arm in a sling without first resetting the bone. Yes, weight loss happens when we burn more calories—via exercise and basic life functions such as breathing and digesting—than we take in. But there's another absolutely critical, routinely ignored variable that must be integrated into this equation: *our hormones*. These wondrous, unseen chemicals are produced by our bodies to manage everything from breathing to digestion to sexual responses and more. At the same time, our hormones are influenced by a myriad of factors, including exercise, diet, sleep, stress, and even the seemingly innocuous, everyday chemicals in cosmetics.

What Are Hormones?

What are you thinking right now? Do you feel happy or anxious? What did you eat for your last meal? Is it noisy where you are? How deeply or quickly are you breathing? Did you exercise today? How many cups of coffee have you had? Do you like the person beside you at the moment? Have you enjoyed sex lately?

The answer to every one of these questions has an impact on your hormones. As your five senses delicately interact with and respond to your environment, your nervous system is continuously communicating with your endocrine system—a series of glands and tissues constantly at work manufacturing, delivering, and processing a wide assortment of hormones to maintain body balance. Even the emotions you experience have the potential to influence your hormones—and vice versa.

Hormones are essentially tiny chemical messengers that spark communication processes throughout your body. They play an enormous role in influencing almost every aspect of your well-being, including your thoughts and feelings. Whether you feel the need to sleep, warm up, cool down, eat jelly beans, grab a coffee, or have a quickie, your desires and actions can be traced back to your hormonal activity.

Hormones also directly affect your appearance. Besides body composition, the look and feel of your skin and hair are influenced by hormones. If you want to look fresher, stimulate your metabolism, lose fat, feel calmer, sleep better, get stronger, feel sexier, and focus better, gaining control over your hormonal balance is truly the key.

Since hormones control our appetites and stimulate metabolism, achieving and maintaining hormonal balance plays an *essential* role in achieving lasting fat loss. Yes, diet and exercise are important, but so are sleeping well, reducing toxin exposure, maintaining healthy liver function, optimizing digestion, limiting stress, and conquering inflammation. All of these factors can influence our hormonal activity—and weight-loss success—in truly dramatic ways.

Our hormones dictate where we store fat and how we will lose it. Research from the *Journal of the American Medical Association* (April 2007) suggests our hormones also determine our success with different diets. Dr. David Ludwig, director of the obesity program at Children's Hospital Boston, found that people who rapidly secreted large amounts of the hormone insulin in response to consumption of sugar or carbohydrates tended to achieve better weight-loss results on a low-glycemic diet that restricted starches and sugars than they did on a low-fat diet. He also discovered that they carried more weight around the waist (the so-called apple shape) compared with those who secreted less insulin and tended to store their excess fat around their hips (the pear shape).

(continued on page 18)

THE ENDOCRINE SYSTEM

While the nervous system coordinates rapid responses to outside stimuli, the endocrine system controls slower, longer-lasting responses to your environment. The link between these two systems is the hypothalamus, a small, almond-sized gland located in the brain.

Functioning as an endocrine gland, the hypothalamus secretes hormones that stimulate the pituitary gland to release other hormones into the bloodstream. The pituitary is often referred to as the "master gland," since its hormones act on the thyroid, ovaries, testes, and adrenal glands to regulate growth, reproduction, nutrient absorption, and metabolism.

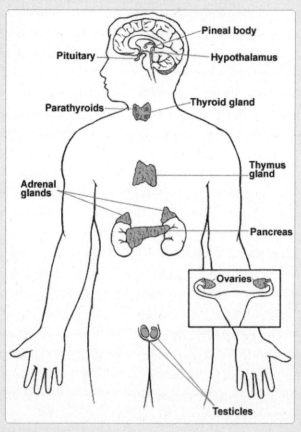

Each of these glands responds to instructions from the pituitary and secretes hormones specific to its unique function in the body. The ovaries and testes, for instance, secrete the sex hormones estrogen, progesterone, and testosterone. The adrenal glands release the stress hormone cortisol and antistress hormone DHEA. The thyroid releases thyroid hormones to manage your metabolic rate.

Many more hormones are produced without the direction of the pituitary gland by other tissues and glands of the endocrine system, including the pancreas, thymus gland, digestive tract, fat cells, adrenal glands, pineal gland, and the brain. Moreover, hormonal messages from other sources are relayed *back to* the hypothalamus to alter our behavior or actions. The hormone leptin is a good example of this type of hormonal control. This substance travels from fat cells through the bloodstream to the hypothalamus to regulate appetite.

Most bodily tissues are targets for one or more hormones released from the pituitary gland. According to Mary Dallman, a professor of physiology at the University of California who studies the effects of stress on appetite and obesity, two predominant endocrine hormones, cortisol and insulin, heavily influence caloric intake by acting on the brain. The stress hormone cortisol, in particular, activates a strong response in the brain to match our perceived stress with a desire to eat comfort foods—the tasty treats we associate with pleasant experiences, often from childhood. Unfortunately, consuming comfort foods, which are typically high in carbohydrates and fat, can cause a resulting spike in our insulin level, leading to the accumulation of belly fat.

Working together, the endocrine, nervous, and digestive systems can either help or hamper your weight-loss and wellness goals. Once you understand these complex systems and get them communicating optimally with one another, you will be well on your way to hormonal bliss and lifelong health.

The pear-shaped subjects fared equally well on both types of eating programs, but they tended to *gain back over half the weight* they lost on the low-fat diet after the study was completed. The apple-shaped people who followed the low-fat regimen also regained their weight, but kept it off after the low-glycemic diet.

Knowing your current hormonal state can help you select the eating plan that will work best for you. In Part Two, I'll tell you about a simple blood test that can provide you with not only a sense of your hormonal profile but also a strong indication of your potential for fat loss and aging well.

Hormonal Imbalance As a Cause of Obesity

The human body is a truly phenomenal machine that naturally strives to remain in a balanced state. When we're cold, we shiver. When we're thirsty or hungry, the brain gives us the appropriate signals to drink or grab a bite to eat. When our hormones and bodily responses are thrown out of balance, stress is the result. The body then miraculously offers a wide range of alerts, which can be as subtle as an increase in thirst or as severe as diabetes.

Consider these alarming statistics:

- An estimated 65 million Americans have metabolic syndrome, a set of underlying risk factors for type 2 diabetes and heart disease.
  - By the age of 30, 1 in 4 people has an associated risk factor, such as abdominal fat or insulin resistance.
  - By the age of 60, 3 out of 4 people have one or more of the associated factors.
- One in 13 people suffers from hypothyroidism. Some sources say up to 30 percent of the population has a thyroid disorder and an estimated 13 million cases may remain undiagnosed each year.

- Forty-three percent of women ages 18 to 59 report experiencing sexual dysfunctions at some point in their life.
- About 75 percent of women experience premenstrual syndrome (PMS).
- Seventy-five percent of menopausal women in North America experience life-disrupting symptoms.
- Andropause, also known as male menopause, affects 30 to 40 percent of aging men.
- An estimated 30 percent of men and 40 percent of women suffer from insomnia, a statistic that increases with age.
- Seventy-four percent of adults are chronically sleep deprived.
- The World Health Organization reports that by 2020 depression will become the number two cause of disability and premature death for men and women of all ages.
- An estimated 80 to 90 percent of all disease is caused by stress.

What's the unifying factor among all these conditions? Every one of them is spurred by an underlying hormonal imbalance. Sadly, the signs and symptoms of hormonal imbalances are so widespread that they barely register as blips on our radar screens. Many of us have hormone-related health conditions that interfere with our quality of life, and we're not even aware of them. In fact, we're so imbalanced, I fear most of us don't even know what "normal" feels like anymore!

At the same time, we are in the midst of an obesity epidemic. More than 61 percent of Americans are overweight (BMI greater than 25), a number that continues to escalate each year. According to National Center for Health 2005/2006 statistics, more than 34 percent of Americans are obese (BMI greater than 30) compared to 32.7 percent who are overweight. Just under 6 percent are extremely obese. Data from the National Institutes of Health (NIH) show obesity and related conditions alone account for more than $100 billion in health-care expenses annually in the United States.

Setting the Stage for Fat-Loss Success

What does hormonal havoc mean to you? Some women might immediately think of hot flashes or the emotional meltdown they experienced before their last period. Men might think back to what it was like being 17, when they could think of nothing but sex, sex, and more sex. Both these situations involve hormones that are out of whack, as do hypothyroidism, infertility, diabetes, stress, insomnia, depression, anxiety, obesity, irregular periods, low libido, memory loss, and a lengthy list of other conditions brought on by hormonal mix-ups.

But maybe you just feel tired all the time. Or you notice fat hanging around that seems impossible to lose. Perhaps your cravings for sweets, carbs, or salt will not let up, your skin is not as bright as it once was, or the texture of your hair has changed. These much subtler signs can also signal a state of hormonal upheaval.

When you complete your Hormonal Health Profile in the next chapter, you will see there are many symptoms of hormonal imbalance. No matter how an imbalance manifests on the outside, the internal reality remains the same—*any and all hormonal imbalance leads to difficulty losing weight, increased risk of obesity and unhealthy aging.* Long-term weight loss and wellness are *next to impossible* until you bring your hormones back into balance.

The New Equation for Fat Loss:

$$\text{Hormonal Balance} + \left(\text{Calories Taken In} - \text{Calories Burned} \right) = \text{Lasting Fat Loss}$$

Boost Metabolism with Help from Your Hormones

One of the primary factors determining body weight is metabolism, the internal furnace that regulates fat burning. Everyone's metabolism is different, which is why some people appear to be able to eat just about anything and remain lean while others seem to pack on pounds easily. But being overweight doesn't necessarily mean you have a slow metabolism, and there are five major factors that affect our metabolic rate.

1. THE THYROID: YOUR INTERNAL THERMOSTAT
   The thyroid controls the metabolic rate of every single cell in the body and also maintains body temperature. Without enough thyroid hormone, all our bodily functions slow down. We feel tired and lethargic, gain weight, experience constipation, feel cold, and are prone to depression.

2. THE RUSH OF ADRENALINE
   A quick release of adrenaline is the body's first response to stress. This hormone provides a short-term metabolic boost because it draws on the body's fat stores to provide that burst of energy we feel in a "fight-or-flight" situation.

3. MARVELOUS MUSCLE
   Muscle tissue is metabolically active at rest, as well as during use. So the more muscle you have, the more calories you'll burn, even while sleeping or watching TV. This metabolic factor is the easiest to control with the right wellness plan. Unfortunately, loss of muscle is a normal part of aging. My three-step plan in Part Two of this book shows you how to slow this process and maximize muscle growth, even as you age.

4. THE THERMIC EFFECT OF EATING
   Thermic pertains to heat. Thermic or "thermogenic" foods literally heat you up and raise your metabolism. The thermic effect happens as your body burns calories, simply by digesting and absorbing the food. Yes, even the very act of eating stimulates your metabolism, especially when you consume protein, which

has the highest thermic effect of any food group. There's another metabolic benefit of protein: Eating it also helps to support metabolically active muscle growth, especially if you are practicing strength training. And strength training helps to increase the thermic effect! A study published in the *Medicine and Science in Sports and Exercise Journal* found the thermic effect of the same meal was 50 percent greater in men who engaged in regular weight training versus those who were sedentary. This certainly helps to illustrate why strength training is so important for optimal calorie burning.

5. YOUR LOVELY LIVER

While your muscle is your primary fat-burning tissue, your liver is your master fat-burning organ. Knowing this, it makes good sense to adopt detoxification and other habits that promote healthy liver function.

All these metabolism factors involve, or are influenced by, your hormones. In each case, an appropriate hormonal balance is the key to ensuring optimal metabolic function.

How Hormones Power Up Your Fat-Burning Pathways

Have you ever thought about all the wonderful things your peroxisome proliferator-activated receptors (PPARs)* do for you? I know—it's a mouthful! You very likely have never even heard of them, but everyone has PPARs, the key regulators of fat burning,

---

* There are different types of PPARs—gamma, delta, alpha—located in different tissues, such as those in the liver (alpha) or the muscle (gamma). Their functions, however, are similar in that they regulate the storage and burning of fat. For the purposes of this book, I have chosen not to differentiate between the types. This subject matter is complicated enough!

blood sugar levels, and the balance of energy within your cells. Naturally present in the liver, fat cells, heart muscles, and skeletal muscles, PPARs are also known to improve cellular response to insulin, a critical factor in successful fat loss. Because the muscles and liver contain fat-burning PPARs, plenty of muscle tissue and optimal liver function are essential to your fat-loss success as well.

After you eat, PPARs react to the presence of fat and sugar in your bloodstream by sending messages to your cells to crank up your fat-burning metabolism. PPARs are also fired up when you exercise. If you are currently overweight and low on lean muscle mass, your PPARs are likely not functioning at their best.

Many factors can interfere with PPARs, but the two biggest influences are *inflammation* and *hormonal imbalance*. Dysfunctional PPARs are also considered key culprits in the development of insulin resistance and obesity. Several pharmaceutical companies are currently investigating drugs that work directly on these receptors to aid fat loss and prevent diabetes.

Since hormones influence PPARs, hormones are directly linked to fat burning and weight loss, right down to the cellular level. For you to lose fat, your hormones have to help open up the PPARs' fat-burning pathways in your liver and muscles. The catch is that this process will not happen successfully until the fires of inflammation are extinguished. Researchers are aggressively searching for ways to tackle inflammation as an underlying cause of disease and obesity. Findings at the Joslin Diabetes Center in Boston, for example, have already led to a clinical trial of an anti-inflammatory agent for treating type 2 diabetes. Six years ago, Dr. Steven Shoelson, a professor at Harvard Medical School, reported that very high doses of aspirin, a known anti-inflammatory, proved effective in improving insulin-glucose tolerance, boosting insulin sensitivity, and lowering blood lipid levels.

All of this is precisely why an anti-inflammatory detox is the essential first step of the Hormone Diet. This may sound like a complicated biology lesson, but my point is simply to let you know that this plan is specifically designed to get your fat-burning PPARs revving!

A FAT-PACKING HORMONAL IMBALANCE

CONDITION 1
The Internal Fire of Inflammation

This concept [inflammation as a cause of disease] is so intriguing because it suggests a new and possibly much simpler way of warding off disease. Instead of different treatments for, say, heart disease, Alzheimer's, and colon cancer, there might be a single, inflammation-reducing remedy that would prevent all three . . . it appears that many of the attributes of a Western lifestyle— such as a diet high in sugars and saturated fats, accompanied by little or no exercise—also make it easier for the body to become inflamed.

Christine Gorman, Alice Park, and Kristina Dell, "The Fires Within" [cover story], *Time* (February 23, 2004)

The last time you suffered through a sinus infection, sprained an ankle, or felt the irritating itch of a mosquito bite, you experienced the effects of inflammation. Infections or injuries trigger a chain of events called the inflammatory cascade. The normal, familiar signs of inflammation, such as redness, pain, swelling, and fever, are the first signals that our immune system is being called into combat mode. Behind the scenes, the body strives to maintain a critical balance between the signals that sustain this protective response and the signals that announce the battle has been won. Eventually, the inflammatory response eases as the body's powerful natural anti-inflammatory compounds move in to initiate the healing phase.

Within a well-balanced immune system, inflammation ebbs and flows as needed. Clearly, a certain degree of inflammation is a basic mechanism of a healthy immune system, just as the proper balance of cholesterol is vital to our cellular health. But, in the same way that surplus cholesterol can block an artery, excessive or persistent inflammation leads to tissue destruction and disease.

Chronic activation of the inflammatory response takes a heavy toll on the body and has recently been recognized as the root cause of most diseases associated with aging. Besides a typical inflammatory illness such as arthritis, the list of conditions spurred by inflammation includes cancer, heart disease, obesity, osteoporosis, Alzheimer's disease, autoimmune disease, diabetes, stroke, and even the wrinkling of our skin.

Inflammation and Obesity
Reducing inflammation is an absolutely vital step in allowing the body to lose unwanted fat. Remember the PPARs, the masters of the fat-burning pathways in our liver and muscle cells? They influence the tight interaction between our insulin sensitivity, inflammation, and weight. A PPAR imbalance contributes to inflammation, obesity, and insulin resistance. Because of this interaction, anti-inflammatory supplements and insulin-sensitizing lifestyle habits, which help to optimize the fat-burning capabilities of our PPARs, can be highly beneficial in the fight against obesity.

Causes of Chronic Inflammation

Widespread inflammation triggers a cascade of problems that seriously weaken the very foundations of our health and well-being. The following are some of the main causes of chronic inflammation.

- **Poor digestive health:** A whopping 60 percent of the immune system is clustered around the digestive tract. Compromises to digestion, including food allergies, bacterial imbalance, deficiency of enzymes or acids, yeast overgrowth, parasites, and stress, negatively affect not only the process of digestion but also our entire immune system. I begin the treatment of every patient by focusing on digestion simply for these reasons. Painful conditions such as gas, bloating, heartburn, reflux, constipation, diarrhea, irritable bowel syndrome, Crohn's disease, and ulcerative colitis are all related to inflammation in the digestive system.

- **An immune system gone awry:** Many experts now view inflammation as a symptom of an immune system in constant overdrive. When the body is stuck in this state, even ordinarily mild stressors such as viral infections, emotional stress, or exposure to household chemicals can cause the immune system to wildly overreact. Allergies, autoimmune disease, and tissue destruction can result when our immune system is working too hard to protect us.

- **Poor nutritional habits:** I discuss this topic in more detail in Chapter 10, Nasty Nutrition, but Dr. Paresh Dandona, a professor of medicine at the State University of New York at Buffalo who specializes in the topic of metabolism and inflammatory stress, found that overconsumption of any macronutrient—protein, carbohydrate, or fat—can contribute to inflammation. He and his team of researchers also identified immediate effects of specific foods on inflammation. Orange juice, for instance, was shown to have anti-inflammatory properties. Red wine was found to be neutral, whereas cream promoted inflammation. The team also discovered that overweight test subjects experienced significant changes in free radical stress indicators and inflammation just *1 week* after starting a more nutritious diet. Considering the long-term health benefits of reducing inflammation, this rapid change is extremely encouraging. You can also expect these benefits within the first 2 weeks of your three-step action plan.

- **Lack of exercise:** Since exercise increases the body's natural production of anti-inflammatory compounds, a lack of exercise can leave us prone to inflammation.
- **Abdominal obesity and insulin resistance:** Preexisting inflammation can also cause both of these conditions. That's right, not only does preexisting inflammation cause both of these conditions, but abdominal obesity and insulin resistance actually cause inflammation! A vicious circle indeed!
- **Estrogen decline:** Menopause appears to be linked to an increase in inflammation, especially due to waning estrogen. Progesterone is also important for keeping the immune system in check.
- **Environmental toxicity, liver toxicity, and fatty liver:** Compromised liver function not only interferes with the body's ability to burn fat, but it also hinders the elimination of toxins.
- **Depression and stress:** Depression in obese men is significantly associated with increased levels of C-reactive protein (CRP), an inflammatory marker in the blood, as shown by a 2003 German study published in the journal *Brain, Behavior, and Immunity*. This research supports the strong link between our emotions, our hormones, and inflammation. In another

study conducted in 2004 and published in *Archives of Internal Medicine*, a similar link was found between depression and higher levels of inflammation (as denoted by CRP) in both men and women. The link, however, was stronger in men than in women. In fact, the men with the most recent bouts of depression showed the highest CRP values.

HORMONES AND DEPRESSION
Patients with major depression are at an increased risk of developing heart disease. The underlying cause is linked to elevated levels of the stress hormone cortisol. Depressed patients often have high levels of both cortisol and insulin. As a result, they experience more heart-harming fat accumulation.

Are You a Hotbed of Inflammation?
Inflammation is a health concern for everyone, but particularly for those who suffer from digestive disorders, allergies, auto-immune disease, arthritis, heart disease, asthma, eczema, acne, obesity, abdominal fat, headaches, joint stiffness, depression, and sinus disorders. The results of your Hormonal Health Profile may help you to assess the presence of inflammation in your body and as a factor interfering with your fat loss. In Appendix A, I also outline all the procedures involved in testing for inflammation, though two blood tests for highly sensitive C-reactive protein and homocysteine are the simplest and best diagnostic tools currently available to assess inflammation.

Your Body Shape and Hormonal Balance

As human beings, we are all unique and each one of us stores fat differently. Are you plagued by love handles, belly fat, or bra fat? Do excess pounds tend to cling to your hips and thighs? The very shape of your body can reveal a lot about what's going on inside of you because hormones also control where your fat accumulates. In Chapter 5 you will learn about healthy body composition and how different hormones contribute to the accumulation of fat in all our favorite places. My most important message to you on this subject is that you can *change your body shape* by bringing your hormones into proper balance.

Hormonal Balance and Appetite Control

As the medical community frantically searches for solutions to the growing obesity epidemic, exciting research in the area of appetite control is building every day. Mounting evidence shows that besides their ability to boost metabolism, many hormones and neurotransmitters (chemical messengers that work within the brain) are involved in appetite control by acting on the hypothalamus gland, the part of the brain that governs feelings of hunger and fullness. By collecting and processing information from the digestive system, the internal biological clock, fat cells, stress-controlling mechanisms, and other sources within the body, the hypothalamus acts as the master switch that tells us to eat more or to put the fork down.

By following my three steps, you can gain control of your hormones, which in turn tames your appetite. Besides what and when you eat, typically overlooked factors such as the amount of sleep you get, your thoughts, and your emotions can influence the hormones that flip the appetite switch one way or the other. Once you understand this guiding principle, you can use it to your advantage for successful weight loss and optimal health.

Hormones and Your Sexual Appetite

Research reveals that 43 percent of women and about 30 percent of men experience a form of sexual dysfunction at some time in their lives. A lack of desire, erectile dysfunction, and inability to orgasm are just a few of the complaints that cause people to lose that loving feeling. These findings are certainly not surprising, though. Many of us are overweight, overtired, stressed-out, and burned-out. No wonder we do not feel up for sex!

Besides all the wonderful weight-loss benefits I've been telling you about, balancing your hormones can also help boost your sex drive and enhance your sexual enjoyment while you trim your waistline. Believe it or not, some of the hormones that control fat storage and the ability to lose weight are the very same ones that influence sexual desire and performance.

Good sex is good for you and for weight loss, too. One of the goals of the *Hormone Diet* is to help you achieve and maintain hormonal balance with the help of more pleasurable sex, more often. This just might be my favorite piece of advice to share.

Dieters Beware: Counting Calories Causes Hormonal Chaos

After everything I've told you so far, you can see why typical weight-loss diets simply do not work. Just look at what happens to your body—and your hormones—when you excessively restrict calories or skip meals.

- You feel hungrier because your body responds to restricted caloric intake by releasing hormones that stimulate appetite.
- Your level of thyroid hormone drops, causing a slowdown in your metabolism.
- Your level of stress hormone increases in response to the physical stress of skipping meals or insufficient carbohydrate intake.
- Reproductive function slows because your sex hormones change due to insufficient caloric intake.
- Growth functions such as cell regeneration and tissue repair are inhibited.

When your hormones are thrown into a state of chaos, your tendency to overeat kicks in. Then, when your caloric intake starts to yo-yo, your metabolism suffers through a dangerous series of highs and lows. The end results of all this havoc include weight gain (exactly what you did *not* want); cravings and mood imbalances; a damaged metabolism; and the loss of precious, metabolically active muscle tissue.

Most important, extreme caloric restriction is not an effective long-term fat-loss solution because it's just not sustainable. The short-term victories achieved with this type of eating are *always* followed with rebound weight gain because, whether we like it or not, hormones will kick in to return the body to status quo. Furthermore, the increase in stress hormones caused by excessive caloric restriction is highly destructive and will actually cause you to want to eat and eat—and eat some more.

Dieting Alone Is Not an Effective Weight-Loss Solution

Stroll through your local bookstore and you'll find volume after volume promising *the* diet plan that will help you melt away unwanted pounds. In truth, medical research reveals that just about every one of today's popular diets offers the same potential outcome as the next. *Sticking* to the diet is actually what yields optimal results. A 2005 study reported in the *Journal of the American Medical Association* found sticking to a diet was a far greater determinant of successful weight loss than the type of diet the person stuck to. When researchers compared popular programs such as Weight Watchers, Atkins, the Zone Diet, and the Ornish Diet, weight loss and changes in cardiovascular disease risk factors were similar among all the diets after a 1-year period.

But most of us can't stick to a diet. In 2007, Traci Mann, an associate professor of psychology at UCLA, led a team of researchers in a comprehensive and rigorous analysis of diet programs using 31 long-term studies. Their results, presented in the *Journal of the American Psychological Association,* weren't encouraging. Mann's team found that most people regained the 5 to 10 pounds they lost, and more. Only a *small minority* of participants experienced sustained weight loss.

The conclusion is clear: *For most people, diets do not lead to sustained weight loss and health benefits.* The UCLA study tells us that most people would be *better off not dieting,* since the practice itself is a predictor of future weight gain! Repeatedly losing and gaining weight is also linked to cardiovascular disease, stroke, diabetes, and altered immune function.

> *We are recommending that Medicare should not fund weight-loss programs as a treatment for obesity. The benefits of dieting are too small and the potential harm is too large for dieting to be recommended as a safe, effective treatment for obesity.*
>
> TRACI MANN,
> associate professor of psychology, *UCLA*

Should we in the health-care profession start recommending against dieting because of its potential health risks? Possibly. Certainly good eating habits are important for weight loss, but exercise is important, too. In fact, people who exercise and basically watch what they eat (rather than follow strict diets) have the greatest weight-loss success. The same UCLA study found exercise to be the key factor leading to sustained weight loss. Dr. Edward Weiss, of Saint Louis University's Doisy College of Health Sciences, goes a step further, suggesting that exercise should be chosen *over* dieting for weight loss if we must choose one or the other.

What's more, Weiss studied two groups of overweight but otherwise healthy adults ages 50 to 60 who followed either a reduced-calorie diet or an exercise program that involved 60 minutes of walking, six times a week. Although both groups lost 9 to 10 percent of their body weight, *those who dieted lost muscle.* Those who exercised did not lose any muscle. Since muscle is so crucial to our metabolic rate, weight gain naturally tends to follow a loss of muscle mass. The loss of muscle mass that naturally occurs with aging is one of the reasons why our metabolic rate decreases as we advance in years.

If we want to optimize weight loss and avoid premature aging, we clearly need to stay away from practices that compromise muscle tissue.

Eating for Hormonal Health

If losing weight is tough, maintaining our goal weight is far tougher. Your odds of losing the pounds and maintaining your optimal weight, however, can be dramatically improved by combining the hormonal benefits of sleep, stress management, detoxification, and exercise with healthy eating. But what is the right diet solution for hormonal balance and good health? I believe the answer lies somewhere between the food selections of a Mediterranean diet and the principles of glycemically balanced eating, or the "Glyci-Med" approach, as I have termed it—the foundation of the *Hormone Diet* nutrition plan.

A Groundbreaking Dietary Approach

Although the Mediterranean diet isn't new, talk of its protective role against many conditions and metabolic syndrome is. Studies conducted over the past 10 years show that the foods of the Mediterranean diet offer protection from a multitude of metabolic disorders including obesity and high blood pressure, as well as heart disease and various types of cancer. It's commonly characterized by daily olive oil consumption and a ratio of monounsaturated to saturated fats that's much higher than in other places in the world. In addition, the Mediterranean diet features the following:

- Daily consumption of unrefined cereals and products (whole grain bread, pasta, rice, etc.)
- Vegetables (2 or 3 servings per day), fruits (4 to 6 servings per day), and fat-free or low-fat dairy products (1 or 2 servings per day). Although intake of milk is limited, cheese and yogurt consumption is relatively high. Feta cheese, for example, is regularly added to stews and salads.

- Moderate consumption of wine (1 or 2 glasses per day), mainly during mealtimes
- Weekly consumption of potatoes (4 or 5 servings per week), fish (4 or 5 servings per week), and olives and nuts (more than 4 servings per week)
- Consumed more rarely are poultry and eggs (1 to 3 servings per week)
- Sweets (1 to 3 servings per week)
- Red meat and meat products are consumed only a few times each month.

Less familiar than the Mediterranean diet are the principles of glycemically balanced eating. The term "glycemic" refers to the presence of sugar in the blood. Glycemically balanced eating means following a diet that focuses on leveling out blood sugar, which in turn prevents the release of excess insulin. Maintaining consistent blood sugar and insulin is one of the most important steps to balancing all hormones in the body and ensuring that your metabolism stays in high gear. Glycemically balanced eating helps you achieve these goals because it means (1) eating frequently and at the right times; (2) eating enough; and (3) consuming protein, fat, fiber, and carbohydrates together at every meal.

You'll find more details in Part Two, but the Mediterranean diet becomes glycemically balanced (to form the Glyci-Med approach) by choosing the right foods at the right times and by tweaking the Mediterranean food selections ever so slightly in this way:

- More vegetables (6 to 10 servings) are consumed than fruits (3 servings) each day.
- Eggs and poultry are eaten more often (3 to 5 servings per week).
- Whey protein and other portable protein sources are recommended, such as a protein bar (1 serving a day).

- Nuts are consumed more often (daily).
- Whole grains are consumed in limited amounts (1 to 3 servings a day, depending on your gender and activity level).
- Potatoes are consumed less frequently (a maximum of once a week).
- Sweets are enjoyed only once a week (rather than 1 to 3 times a week).

Together with exercise, the Glyci-Med dietary approach will help to keep your body at its healthy set point—a body weight that remains consistent, usually within a 5-pound range. Your metabolism will naturally work to preserve your set point with the help of your hormones by either turning up your calorie-burning engines or slowing them down, as needed.

Three Simple Steps to Total Wellness and Fat Loss

STEP 1: RENEW AND REVITALIZE. First, you will revitalize your body and mind as you recuperate from the harmful effects of sleep deprivation and stress. You will cool the fire of chronic inflammation, one of the primary causes of aging, disease, and obesity. Finally, you will maximize the function of your liver—an essential first step for safe, lasting fat loss. By the end of Step 1, you'll have quieted three factors that cause obesity and interfere with weight loss: sleep deprivation, chronic stress, and toxicity—and will have lost 5 to 12 pounds.

STEP 2: REPLENISH YOUR BODY AND BALANCE YOUR HORMONES. Next, you will begin to restore hormonal balance by choosing the right foods at the right times and in the right amounts. You will enhance your efforts by taking the five key supplements we all need in order to maintain health and prevent nutrient deficiencies that can interfere with your metabolism and cause hormonal chaos.

Step 2 also offers targeted fixes for specific hormonal imbalances, *if you need them*. Using the results of your Hormonal Health Profile, the Hormone Diet approach will show you how to take the necessary steps to treat your specific signs of imbalance *in precise order to ensure lasting weight loss, hormonal balance, and health.*

For instance, you will first add extra insulin-sensitizing supplements, if they are needed, to get you back in balance. At the same time, I'll suggest remedies for signs of anxiety, depression, or other brain chemistry imbalances. Your mood and emotional state are directly linked to your total wellness and sleep quality, as well as your cravings and your ability to stick to healthy food choices. By this stage, you'll have successfully tackled two more causes of obesity—insulin resistance and serotonin deficiency. Sound exciting?

Eating regularly and sleeping well help in the war on stress, but if your body is showing signs that it needs extra support to cope, adapt, and refill your energy reserves, subduing excess stress hormones is the next path to follow. Your stress hormones also influence your sex hormones, so the key to restoring your libido and sex hormone balance is tackling excess stress. More specifically, the anti-aging, antistress hormone DHEA increases estrogen and muscle-building testosterone, whereas the long-term stress hormone cortisol can depress progesterone and testosterone. Interestingly enough, an imbalance of estrogen, progesterone, or testosterone interferes with fat loss and muscle building, *even* with the perfect diet and exercise plan. And excess cortisol, insulin, or both can cause abdominal fat, even when you are otherwise thin!

Once your sex hormones are back in balance, you'll feel them work their metabolic magic because each of these hormones influences the master of metabolism, thyroid hormone. By addressing these hormones, you will have removed the last of the possible fat-packing factors—low thyroid, menopause, andropause, and estrogen dominance.

STEP 3: RESTORE STRENGTH, VIGOR, AND RADIANCE. The final step is to address the hormones that maximize strength and renewal—growth hormone, melatonin, and acetylcholine—with hormone-enhancing exercise (and supplements, if you find they are required). These are the hormones that fine-tune your body composition by building muscle, shrinking fat cells, and slowing the effects of aging. This step will revive your metabolism and keep it revving.

This systematic approach is my secret to restoring total hormonal balance. Where other diets may stall, are not sustainable, or simply fail, this key aspect of the Hormone Diet plan will restore your metabolism and keep your fat-loss hormones primed—for life!

If you've never been able to lose those last 5 to 25 pounds, now you will. If you've never dieted but want to feel toned and strong, this is your solution. If you already have good health but want to feel even better, this is the fix for you. If you're on your way to obesity, diabetes, heart disease, or rapid aging, this is the plan that will finally help you restore hormonal balance and turn your health around.

Most of my patients, and readers who have shared their success stories, lose 5 to 9 pounds in their very first week. Although these results provide a wonderful source of motivation, it is the improvement in their overall well-being that inspires them to keep going. Now you, too, can experience what it feels like to be in *perfect balance.*

CHAPTER 2

ARE YOU IN BALANCE?
THE HORMONAL HEALTH PROFILE

If you can uncover the subtle signs and symptoms of imbalance, you can take the right steps to fix it and increase your chances of losing fat and keeping it off. To help you do this, I have created the Hormonal Health Profile.

This easy-to-follow checklist is designed to help you identify hormonal imbalances in the quickest way possible. If you have struggled with weight loss in the past, my bet is that your profile results will be extremely valuable in helping you to figure out why.

With your answers in hand, you will be able to fine-tune your plan by adding specific foods and supplements to address your unique hormone-balancing needs. In some cases, this tool may also encourage you to search out a health-care provider, should you wish to have additional medical treatment to get control of your hormones.

The Hormonal Health Profile
How to Complete It

In the following pages, you'll find a series of checklists of symptoms and conditions arranged into groups. Each numbered group pertains to a specific hormonal imbalance or condition that can, in one way or another, impede your weight loss and increase the negative effects of aging.

As you go through the lists, check off all of the symptoms and signs you are currently experiencing within each group. Add up your total for each group and record it in the box provided at the bottom of the list, or keep track on a separate sheet of paper.

Since more than one hormone can cause similar symptoms, you will find a lot of repetition among the different groups. Just keep going and do your best to be consistent with your answers throughout the entire profile. You want to create the most complete picture of your current state of hormonal wellness.

Next, transfer your scores from each group of questions in the profile to the matching numbered space within the Treatment Pyramid on page 53.

YOUR HORMONAL HEALTH PROFILE

Check off all that apply to you and total your scores in each group.

INFLAMMATION	
Sagging, thinning skin or wrinkling	
Spider veins or varicose veins	
Cellulite	
Eczema, skin rashes, hives, or acne	
Menopause (women); andropause (men)	
Heart disease	
Prostate enlargement or prostatitis	
High cholesterol or blood pressure	
Loss of muscle tone in arms and legs; difficulty building or maintaining muscle	
Aches and pains	
Arthritis, bursitis, tendonitis, or joint stiffness	
Water retention in hands or feet	
Gout	
Alzheimer's disease	
Parkinson's disease	
Depression	
Night eating syndrome (waking at night to binge eat)	

INFLAMMATION (continued)	
Fibromyalgia	
Increased pain or poor pain tolerance	
Headaches or migraines	
High alcohol consumption	
Bronchitis, allergies (food or environmental), hives, or asthma have worsened or developed	
Autoimmune disease	
Fat gain around "love handles" or abdomen	
Loss of bone density or osteoporosis	
Generalized overweight/weight gain/obesity	
Fatty liver (diagnosed by your doctor)	
Diabetes (type 2)	
Sleep disruptions or deprivation	
Irritable bowel or inflammatory bowel disease	
Frequent gas and bloating	
Constipation, diarrhea, or nausea	
TOTAL (Warning score: > 11)	

HORMONAL IMBALANCE 1: EXCESS INSULIN	
Age spots and wrinkling	
Sagging skin	
Cellulite	
Skin tags	
Acanthosis nigricans (a skin condition characterized by light brown to black patches or markings on the neck or underarm)	
Abnormal hair growth on face or chin (women)	
Vision changes or cataracts	
Infertility or irregular menses	
Shrinking or sagging breasts	
Menopause (women); andropause or erectile dysfunction (men)	

HORMONAL IMBALANCE 1: EXCESS INSULIN (continued)	
Heart disease	
High cholesterol, high triglycerides, or high blood pressure	
Burning feet at night (especially while in bed)	
Water retention in the face/puffiness	
Gout	
Poor memory, concentration, or Alzheimer's disease	
Fat gain around "love handles" and/or abdomen	
Fat over triceps	
Generalized overweight/weight gain/obesity	
Hypoglycemia; cravings for sweets, carbohydrates or constant hunger or increased appetite	
Fatigue after eating (especially carbohydrates)	
Fatty liver (diagnosed by your doctor)	
Diabetes (type 2)	
Sleep disruption or deprivation	
TOTAL (Warning score: > 9)	

HORMONAL IMBALANCE 2: LOW DOPAMINE	
Fatigue, especially in the morning	
Poor tolerance for exercise	
Restless leg syndrome	
Poor memory	
Parkinson's disease	
Depression	
Loss of libido	
Feeling a strong need for stimulation or excitement (foods, gambling, partying, sex, etc.)	
Addictive eating or binge eating	
Cravings for sweets, carbohydrates, junk food, or fast food	
TOTAL (Warning score: > 4)	

HORMONAL IMBALANCE 3: LOW SEROTONIN	
PMS characterized by hypoglycemia, sugar cravings, sweet cravings, and/or depression	
Feeling wired at night	
Lack of sweating	
Poor memory	
Loss of libido	
Depression, anxiety, irritability, or seasonal affective disorder	
Loss of motivation or competitive edge	
Low self-esteem	
Inability to make decisions	
Obsessive-compulsive disorder	
Bulimia or binge eating	
Fibromyalgia	
Increased pain or poor pain tolerance	
Headaches or migraines	
Cravings for sweets or carbohydrates	
Constant hunger or increased appetite	
Inability to sleep in, no matter how late going to bed	
Less than 7.5 hours of sleep per night	
Irritable bowel	
Constipation	
Nausea	
Use of corticosteroids	
TOTAL (Warning score: > 7)	

HORMONAL IMBALANCE 4: LOW GABA	
PMS characterized by breast tenderness, water retention, bloating, anxiety, sleep disruptions, or headaches	
Feeling wired at night	
Aches and pains or increased muscle tension	
Irritability, tension, or anxiety	
Difficulty falling asleep or staying asleep	
Less than 7.5 hours of sleep per night	
Irritable bowel	
Frequent gas and bloating	
TOTAL (Warning score: > 3)	

HORMONAL IMBALANCE 5: EXCESS CORTISOL	
Wrinkling, thinning skin or skin that has lost its fullness	
Hair loss	
Infertility or absent menses (unrelated to menopause)	
Feeling wired at night	
Heart palpitations	
Loss of muscle tone in arms and legs	
Cold hands or feet	
Water retention in face/puffiness	
Poor memory or concentration	
Loss of libido	
Depression, anxiety, irritability, or seasonal affective disorder	
High alcohol consumption	
Frequent colds and flus	
Hives, bronchitis, allergies (food or environmental), asthma, or autoimmune disease	
Fat gain around "love handles" or abdomen	
A "buffalo hump" of fat on back of neck/upper back	
Difficulty building or maintaining muscle	
Loss of bone density or osteoporosis	
Cravings for sweets or carbs, hypoglycemia, or constant hunger	
Difficulty falling asleep	
Difficulty staying asleep (especially waking between 2 and 4 a.m.)	
Less than 7.5 hours of sleep per night	
Irritable bowel or frequent gas and bloating	
Use of corticosteroids	
TOTAL (Warning score: > 8)	

HORMONAL IMBALANCE 6: LOW DHEA	
Dry skin	
Heart disease	
Erectile dysfunction	
Andropause	
Feeling wired at night	
Poor tolerance for exercise	
Loss of muscle tone in arms and legs	
Poor memory or concentration	
Irritability or easily agitated	
Loss of libido	
Depression	
Loss of motivation or competitive edge	
Autoimmune disease	
Fat gain around "love handles"	
Fat gain over triceps	
Fat gain around abdomen	
Difficulty building or maintaining muscle	
TOTAL (Warning score: > 6)	

HORMONAL IMBALANCE 7: EXCESS ESTROGEN	
Spider or varicose veins	
Cellulite	
Heavy menstrual bleeding	
PMS characterized by breast tenderness, water retention, bloating, swelling, and/or weight gain	
Fibrocystic breast disease	
Prostate enlargement	
Erectile dysfunction	
Breast growth (men)	
Loss of morning erection	
Irritability, mood swings, or anxiety	
Headaches or migraines (especially in women before their menses)	
High alcohol consumption (> 4 drinks per week for women and > 7 drinks per week for men)	
Autoimmune disease or allergies	
Fat gain around "love handles" or abdomen (men)	
Fat gain at hips (women)	
Current use of hormone replacement therapy or birth control pills	
TOTAL (Warning score: > 6)	

HORMONAL IMBALANCE 8: LOW ESTROGEN	
Dry or sagging skin	
Thinning skin or skin has lost its fullness	
Hair loss	
Dry eyes or cataracts (women)	
PMS characterized by depression, hypoglycemia, sugar cravings, and/or sweet cravings	
Infertility or absent menses (not related to menopause)	
Painful intercourse and/or vaginal dryness	
Shrinking or sagging breasts	
Urinary incontinence (stress or otherwise)	
Menopause	
Fatigue	
Hot flashes	
Poor memory or concentration	
Irritability	
Loss of libido	
Depression or mood swings	
Headaches or migraines	
Fat gain around "love handles" or abdomen (menopausal women)	
Loss of bone density or osteoporosis	
Difficulty falling or staying asleep	
TOTAL (Warning score: > 8)	

HORMONAL IMBALANCE 9: LOW PROGESTERONE	
Dry skin or skin that has lost its fullness	
Spider or varicose veins	
Hair loss	
Short menstrual cycle (< 28 days) or excessively long bleeding times (< 6 days)	
PMS characterized by breast tenderness, anxiety, sleep disruptions, headaches, menstrual spotting, water retention, bloating, and/or weight gain	

HORMONAL IMBALANCE 9: LOW PROGESTERONE (continued)	
Infertility or absent menses (not related to menopause)	
Fibrocystic breast disease	
Menopause (women); andropause (men)	
Prostate enlargement	
Hot flashes	
Lack of sweating	
Feeling cold and/or cold hands or feet	
Heart palpitations	
Water retention	
Irritability and/or anxiety	
Loss of libido	
Headaches or migraines	
Autoimmune disease, hives, asthma, or allergies	
Loss of bone density or osteoporosis	
Difficulty falling or staying asleep	
TOTAL (Warning score: > 6)	

HORMONAL IMBALANCE 10: EXCESS PROGESTERONE	
Acne	
PMS characterized by depression	
Infertility	
Water retention	
Depression	
Frequent colds and flus	
Weight gain or difficulty losing weight	
Current use of hormone replacement therapy or birth control pills	
TOTAL (Warning score: > 4)	

HORMONAL IMBALANCE 11: LOW TESTOSTERONE	
Dry skin	
Thinning skin or skin has lost its fullness	
Painful intercourse	
Heart disease (men)	
Erectile dysfunction	
Andropause (men)	
Loss of morning erection	
Fatigue	
Poor tolerance for exercise	
Loss of muscle tone in arms and legs	
Poor memory or concentration	
Loss of libido	
Depression or anxiety	
Loss of motivation or competitive edge	
Headaches or migraines (men)	
Fat gain around "love handles" or abdomen (men and women)	
Difficulty building or maintaining muscle	
Loss of bone density or osteoporosis (men and women)	
Sleep apnea (men)	
Use of corticosteroids	
TOTAL (Warning score: > 7)	

HORMONAL IMBALANCE 12: EXCESS TESTOSTERONE	
Acne	
Acanthosis nigricans (women)	
Hair loss (scalp)	
Abnormal hair growth on face (women)	
Infertility	
Shrinking or sagging breasts	
Prostate enlargement	

HORMONAL IMBALANCE 12: EXCESS TESTOSTERONE (continued)	
Irritability, aggression, or easily agitated	
Fat gain around abdomen (women)	
Cravings for sweets or carbohydrates (women)	
Constant hunger or increased appetite (women)	
Fatty liver (women)	
TOTAL (Warning score: > 4)	

HORMONAL IMBALANCE 13: LOW THYROID	
Dry skin and/or hair	
Acne	
Hair loss	
Brittle hair and/or nails	
PMS, infertility, long menstrual cycle (> 30 days), or irregular periods	
Abnormal lactation	
Fatigue	
Lack of sweating, feeling cold, or cold hands and feet	
High cholesterol	
Poor tolerance for exercise	
Heart palpitations	
Outer edge of eyebrows thinning	
Aches and pains	
Water retention/puffiness in hands or feet	
Poor memory	
Loss of libido	
Depression	
Loss of motivation or competitive edge	
Iron deficiency anemia	
Hives	
Generalized overweight/weight gain/obesity	
Constipation	

HORMONAL IMBALANCE 13: LOW THYROID (continued)	
Use of corticosteroids	
Current use of synthetic hormone replacement therapy or birth control pills	
TOTAL (Warning score: > 8)	

HORMONAL IMBALANCE 14: LOW ACETYLCHOLINE	
Poor tolerance for exercise	
Loss of muscle tone in arms and legs or poor muscle function/strength	
Poor memory or concentration, decrease in memory or recall	
Alzheimer's disease	
Difficulty building or maintaining muscle	
Difficulty falling asleep or staying asleep, disrupted sleep patterns	
Irritable bowel	
Constipation	
TOTAL (Warning score: > 3)	

HORMONAL IMBALANCE 15: LOW MELATONIN	
Andropause (men); menopause (women)	
Night eating syndrome (waking at night to binge eat)	
High alcohol consumption	
Cravings for sweets or carbohydrates; increased appetite	
Difficulty falling asleep	
Failing to sleep in total darkness	
Difficulty staying asleep (especially waking between 2 and 4 a.m.)	
Sleep apnea	
Less than 7.5 hours of sleep per night	
Use of corticosteroids	
TOTAL (Warning score: > 3)	

HORMONAL IMBALANCE 16: LOW GROWTH HORMONE

Dry skin	
Thinning skin or skin has lost its fullness	
Sagging skin	
Menopause (women); andropause (men)	
Lack of exercise	
Loss of muscle tone in arms or legs	
High alcohol consumption	
Fat gain around "love handles" or abdomen	
Difficulty building or maintaining muscle	
Loss of bone density or osteoporosis	
Generalized overweight/weight gain/obesity	
Failing to sleep in total darkness	
Difficulty staying asleep (especially waking between 2 and 4 a.m.)	
Sleep apnea	
Use of corticosteroids	
TOTAL (Warning score: > 5)	

After you have completed your profile, go ahead and transfer your scores from each group to the appropriate space in the Treatment Pyramid on the opposite page.

Interpreting Your Scores

For each group of profile questions, I have listed a score in parentheses next to the box for your total—the *warning score*. If your score is *the same or higher than* the warning score, you likely have an imbalance. For each of your high scores, refer to the noted sections of the book to learn about the specific imbalance and its impact on your health.

You also have to transfer your scores to the second Treatment Pyramid on page 295 in Chapter 13. It's here that the *treatment solutions* to your imbalances are provided, should you choose to use them as part of your three steps. This pyramid shows how to "tweak" your action plan in order to meet your individual needs, especially if you discover that you have more than one imbalance. The precise order of treatment presented in the pyramid is definitely my *secret to restoring hormonal balance,* as each level builds upon the next.

What Do Your Results Mean?

Even though I have listed a warning score for each group, ultimately it's up to you to decide on a course of action or whether a particular imbalance warrants further investigation. True diagnosis is not something you can do at home. A high score in *any one of the groups* suggests to me, however, that you would benefit from completing *all three steps* of the Hormone Diet. And I am confident you will yield even greater results by *choosing specific treatments* to address your imbalances once you reach Step 2.

As I mentioned, if your profile results reveal that you *do* have hormonal imbalances, you may want to focus on specific sections of the following two chapters. If you wish, you can read both chapters from start to finish. Or, you can focus strictly on the imbalances that apply to you, then get right to the "skinny" on your fat in Chapter 5.

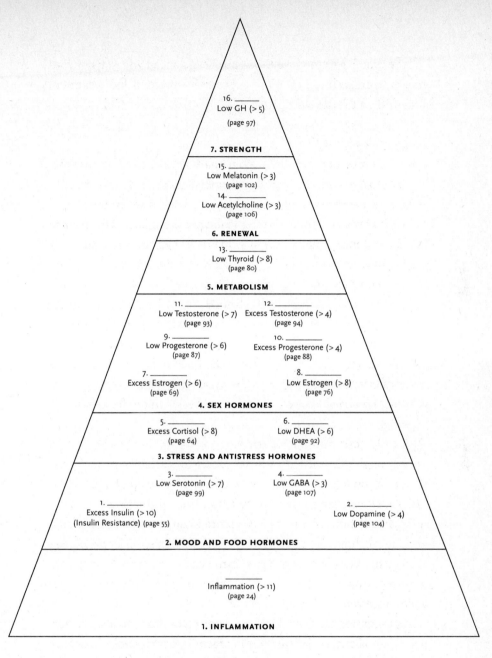

16. _____
Low GH (> 5)
(page 97)

7. STRENGTH

15. _____
Low Melatonin (> 3)
(page 102)
14. _____
Low Acetylcholine (> 3)
(page 106)

6. RENEWAL

13. _____
Low Thyroid (> 8)
(page 80)

5. METABOLISM

11. _____   12. _____
Low Testosterone (> 7)   Excess Testosterone (> 4)
(page 93)   (page 94)

9. _____   10. _____
Low Progesterone (> 6)   Excess Progesterone (> 4)
(page 87)   (page 88)

7. _____   8. _____
Excess Estrogen (> 6)   Low Estrogen (> 8)
(page 69)   (page 76)

4. SEX HORMONES

5. _____   6. _____
Excess Cortisol (> 8)   Low DHEA (> 6)
(page 64)   (page 92)

3. STRESS AND ANTISTRESS HORMONES

3. _____   4. _____
Low Serotonin (> 7)   Low GABA (> 3)
(page 99)   (page 107)

1. _____   2. _____
Excess Insulin (> 10)   Low Dopamine (> 4)
(Insulin Resistance) (page 55)   (page 104)

2. MOOD AND FOOD HORMONES

_____
Inflammation (> 11)
(page 24)

1. INFLAMMATION

THE TREATMENT PYRAMID

CHAPTER 3

YOUR FAT-LOSS FOES:
THE HORMONES THAT PACK ON POUNDS

Losing weight is a cascade of many steps, beginning with the production
of certain hormones and continuing with their action in the brain.
Some people are resistant to these hormones, just as other people are
insulin-resistant. These people never receive the message from the brain
that tells them they're full.

ELVIRA DE MEJIA, assistant professor of food science and
human nutrition, University of Illinois

Here's what you will learn about in this chapter:
• The four hormones that are our fat-loss foes because they interfere with fat
  burning, boost appetite, and cause weight gain
• Three fat-packing hormonal imbalances: insulin resistance, chronic stress,
  and estrogen dominance

Although I could easily dedicate a full chapter to each individual
hormone, I have chosen instead to divide them into two basic
groups: those that are our fat-loss foes and those that are our fat-loss
friends.

This chapter focuses on four fat-packing hormones: insulin, cortisol, estrogen, and ghrelin. When not in proper balance, these substances can absolutely sabotage your fat-loss success.

Besides revealing how individual hormones can either help

or hinder your fat loss, I also wish to explain that no hormone works in isolation. All of these fascinating substances interact with and influence each other, which is why a spike in one hormone typically causes a drop in another. This complex interplay is part of the body's incredible mechanism for coping with an imbalanced state. Too much or too little of any one hormone can interfere with your metabolism, accelerate aging, and compromise your overall wellness.

For your quick reference, I have clearly marked my discussions of each hormone in this chapter and Chapter 4 with the numbers matching the relevant group of questions in the Hormonal Health Profile in Chapter 2 (i.e., as Hormonal Imbalance 1, Hormonal Imbalance 2, etc.). You may choose to concentrate only on the sections that pertain to your specific imbalance(s). Or you can certainly read everything covered in these two chapters and return, if necessary, for a review each time you complete the profile. Choose the option that works best for you—there is a lot of information here to take in!

Hormonal Imbalance 1—Excess Insulin
The Ins and Outs of Insulin

Insulin is an essential substance whose main function is to process sugar in your bloodstream and carry it into your cells to be used. The carbohydrates you eat are broken down into sugar (glucose) through the process of digestion, which begins in your mouth and ends in your small intestine. Once sugar enters your bloodstream from your digestive tract, it triggers your pancreas to release the hormone insulin. Insulin is released in proportion to the amount of sugar in the bloodstream (i.e., more sugar = more insulin).

Once insulin is released, the sugar in your bloodstream can be directed in three ways.

1. **Immediate use as a fuel source.** It is burned off right away, particularly by your brain and kidneys.
2. **Stored as glycogen in the liver or muscles for later use as an energy source.** Just as a glass can hold only so much water, the body's capacity to store glycogen is limited. For this reason, only a finite amount of the carbohydrates we consume can be used in this way. Because most of us consume plenty of carbs daily, our glycogen stores tend to fill up quickly (though exercise is one of the best ways to free up more storage space because it causes the body to draw on glycogen for energy).
3. **Stored as fat.** If all your glycogen storage sites are full and the excess sugar isn't used right away, the body will convert the leftovers to fat, a much longer-term fuel source that's far more difficult to burn off. Now you can see why limiting your intake of high-sugar, high-carb foods is beneficial. In doing so, you'll limit the amount of insulin released and, ultimately, the amount of sugar your body will store as fat.

Insulin and Abdominal Fat

Although insulin plays an essential role in healthy body function, an excess of this hormone will certainly make you gain weight. Not only does too much insulin encourage your body to store unused glucose as fat, but it also *blocks* the use of stored fat as an energy source. For these reasons, an abnormally high insulin level makes losing fat, especially around the abdomen, next to impossible.

Insulin and Appetite

To make matters worse, too much insulin can cause you to consume more calories. According to Dr. Robert Lustig, a pediatric endocrinologist at the University of California San Francisco Children's Hospital whose work was published in the August 2006 edition of the journal *Nature Clinical Practice Endocrinology & Metabolism*, insulin stimulates appetite by working on the brain in two ways. First, it blocks signals to the brain by interfering with the appetite-suppressing hormone leptin, causing us to eat more and become less active. Second, it causes a spike in dopamine, the hormone that signals the brain to seek rewards. Dopamine spurs a desire to eat in order to achieve a pleasurable rush—the same rush we may get from addictive behaviors. No wonder putting down the fork is so tough. We are addicted to food!

Balanced Insulin Does Your Body Good

Maintaining the correct amount of insulin offers tremendous benefits. Insulin is one of the body's main anabolic hormones, meaning it initiates the metabolic pathways that rebuild body proteins while preventing protein breakdown. It also promotes the use of sugar as an energy source. In this manner, the right amount of insulin encourages the growth of your muscles and the refilling of your glycogen stores. We can use these effects to our advantage, especially immediately after exercise—one of the few times when eating carbs and having an insulin spike is beneficial. Right after a workout, it promotes the entry of glucose and amino acids into muscle tissue to support repair and growth.

Insulin may also help prevent further breakdown of muscle tissue after a workout through its enhancing action on testosterone. The male sex hormone testosterone is vital to the growth and maintenance of muscle tissue. In the right amount, insulin prevents the body from breaking down proteins, such as those found in muscle tissue, for energy during times of stress. Without it, your cells would not have access to amino acids, glucose, and fatty acids to survive, let alone to grow, heal, and repair. This is precisely why those living with type 1 diabetes must take insulin by injection when the pancreas fails to manufacture it naturally. The problem of excess fat storage arises only when our insulin level is too high.

Causes of Insulin Overload

There are several reasons for excess insulin, but these are the main culprits:

- Consuming too many nutrient-poor carbohydrates—the type found in processed foods, sugary drinks, and sodas; foods containing high-fructose corn syrup; packaged low-fat foods; and artificial sweeteners
- Insufficient protein intake
- Inadequate fat intake
- Deficient fiber consumption
- Chronic stress
- Lack of exercise
- Overexercising or other activities that compromise muscle tissue
- Steroid-based medications
- Poor liver function and toxin exposure
- Aging

Besides turning you into a walking fat-storage facility, excess insulin will also make you feel just plain *bad*. Heart palpitations, sweating, poor concentration, weakness, anxiety, fogginess, fatigue, irritability, or impaired thinking are common side effects. These symptoms are particularly prevalent in the "crash" you tend to experience following a high-carbohydrate meal or the consumption of a lot of alcohol, both of which cause irregular peaks and valleys in your insulin level.

To make matters worse, our bodies typically respond to these unpleasant feelings by making us think we're hungry, which in turn causes us to reach for more high-sugar foods and drinks. And then we end up in a vicious cycle of hormonal imbalance, not to mention weight gain.

But wait, there's more. Since insulin also influences sodium uptake in the kidneys, an excess of this hormone can cause you to retain water, experience swelling, and look like that famous little dough boy. He's cute, but definitely not anyone's top choice as a physique role model.

Excess insulin can affect men and women in different ways. For men, a high insulin level typically sparks heightened activity of an aromatase enzyme in your fat cells, which causes more of your masculinizing hormone, testosterone, to be converted into the feminizing hormone estrogen. If this trend continues long-term, you'll see increased fat deposits in "female" areas, such as your abdomen and even your chest (as breasts), not to mention a negative impact on your sex drive and erectile function.

Women are just as vulnerable. The same aromatase enzyme boosts conversion of estrogen to testosterone. As a result, high insulin can lead to such lovely effects as increased fat storage in the abdomen, shrinking and sagging breasts, abnormal hair growth, acne, and even male-pattern hair loss. Not good.

A FAT-PACKING HORMONAL IMBALANCE

HORMONAL IMBALANCE 1: EXCESS INSULIN
(Insulin Resistance and Metabolic Syndrome)

When excess insulin is present over a long period, our cells start to grow accustomed to having so much of it around all the time. As a result, our cellular response to insulin becomes blunted and our pancreas is called upon to step up its insulin production in an attempt to maintain a normal blood sugar level. This *decrease* in insulin sensitivity is called insulin resistance.

Imagine insulin as a truck carrying sugars into our cells. The truck enters the cells using a special garage-door opener. If the opener stops working, the truck is stuck in the driveway. Soon after, another truck will pull up behind the first one and they'll both become trapped. Eventually a whole fleet of trucks will be backed up, causing a major traffic jam throughout the body—or chronically high insulin. All of this happens because the garage-door opener (aka the insulin receptor) is no longer responding to the presence of the truck (aka insulin).

Insulin resistance primarily develops in the skeletal muscle cells, but it can also occur in fat cells, the liver, and other tissues. Once our cells become resistant to insulin, losing weight becomes harder than ever. Moreover, physiological changes start to occur in the body, signaling a condition called metabolic syndrome, the clinical manifestation of insulin resistance.

THE INCIDENCE OF METABOLIC SYNDROME

At the 2007 Postgraduate Nutrition Symposium at Harvard University, researchers revealed findings suggesting that inflammation and insulin resistance are *the* major contributors to rising rates of type 2 diabetes and the overall fattening of North America. The diagram on the opposite page, adapted from the Centers for Disease Control and Prevention (CDC), illustrates the current epidemic of insulin resistance and diabetes across the nation.

Medical experts estimate that 40 percent of the US population will be obese by the year 2009. Forty percent! Wow! Simply eating too much (i.e., "super-sizing") or routinely making bad

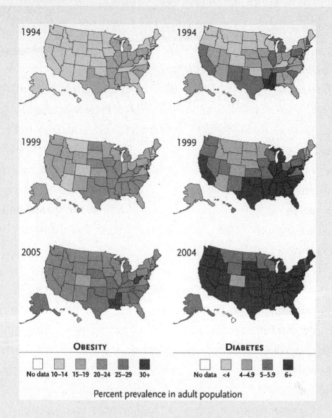

1994			1994		
1999			1999		
2005			2004		

OBESITY

No data | 10–14 | 15–19 | 20–24 | 25–29 | 30+

DIABETES

No data | <4 | 4–4.9 | 5–5.9 | 6+

Percent prevalence in adult population

**THE PROGRESSION OF INSULIN RESISTANCE AND
DIABETES IN THE UNITED STATES FROM 1994 TO 2004**

Source: http://focus.hms.harvard.edu/2007/040607/metabolism.shtml

food choices leads to the consumption of hundreds of excess calories daily. The Centers for Disease Control and Prevention reported that in 2007 23.6 million children and adults in the United States—7.8 percent of the population—had diabetes. Each year, 1.6 million new cases of diabetes are diagnosed in people ages 20 years and older, with the vast majority between 40 and 59 years of age. In addition, an estimated 65 percent of the American population has one or more components of metabolic syndrome (listed below), which is a known precursor to diabetes. Even teens are at risk. A study reported in the April 2005 edition of *Circulation*, an American Heart Association journal, described obesity and insulin resistance as a menacing tag team that dramatically accelerates cardiovascular risk in teenagers.

Insulin resistance is now an epidemic of *massive* proportion, one that is overloading our medical-care systems. We must change our perspective from disease treatment to prevention, the exact objective you can expect to achieve with the help of the *Hormone Diet* three-step system.

ASSESSING YOUR INSULIN SENSITIVITY AND RISK OF METABOLIC SYNDROME

Before you can address a potential problem, you need to gain a better understanding of your current health picture. Your answers to the Hormonal Health Profile may have provided you with a good indication of your insulin sensitivity. In addition, as part of the preparation stage of your three steps (see Chapter 6), I recommend a blood test to assess your insulin sensitivity.

If, in the meantime, you're wondering whether you are insulin resistant or insulin sensitive, take a good look at your waist and pinch your love handles. If you carry excess fat in this area, you may be insulin resistant. If you're naturally lean, your insulin sensitivity is likely in good shape.

A full workup to establish a treatment plan and definite diagnosis for metabolic syndrome includes blood tests, blood pressure readings, and, in some cases, additional exams such as an abdominal ultrasound to assess the liver. Should you wish to talk to your health-care provider about this type of investigation, I have outlined all the tests involved in a complete investigation of insulin resistance. (See Appendix A, "Understanding Blood Tests.")

According to the current medical definition, metabolic syndrome is diagnosed when *three or more* of the following risk factors are identified after a clinical evaluation has been completed:

• Low levels of "good" cholesterol (HDL)
• High levels of "bad" cholesterol (LDL)
• Elevated triglycerides (unsaturated fats)
• Increased waist-to-hip ratio, since fat accumulates around the abdomen and "love handle" areas rather than the hips
• High blood pressure (i.e., above 130/85, according to the National Cholesterol Education Program)
• Elevated blood sugar levels (i.e., greater than 110 mg/dL)

WHAT DOES A DIAGNOSIS OF METABOLIC SYNDROME MEAN FOR YOUR HEALTH?

Metabolic syndrome is associated with increased risk of type 2 diabetes, obesity, high blood pressure, stroke, and coronary heart disease. New research has also uncovered a link between elevated insulin levels and certain types of malignancies, including breast cancer. Furthermore, insulin resistance is associated with higher risk of four of the top five leading causes of death in the United States (as reported by the American Heart Association 2003 Heart and Stroke Statistical Update), including cancer, heart disease, diabetes, and Alzheimer's disease.

On the upside, even severe instances of metabolic syndrome can be improved with better lifestyle habits. Going back to the analogy of a fleet of insulin trucks backed up in the bloodstream, the problem can be alleviated in two ways. First, we can restore the function of the garage door with lubricant so it responds more easily to the opener. Exercise and insulin-sensitizing supplements are highly effective for this purpose. Second, we can lessen the traffic load in the first place by reducing the number of insulin trucks in the fleet. In other words, better nutritional habits lead to an overall reduction in the release of insulin. The three-step plan will give you the tools you need to implement both these solutions, as it has for so many of my patients already. Depending on the results of your Hormonal Health Profile, you may also choose to add supplements, described in Chapter 13, to your program.

Hormonal Imbalance 5—Excess Cortisol
Another Culprit of Unsightly Ab Fat

Our bodies provide us with uniquely designed mechanisms to cope with immediate and chronic stress. Our nervous system drives our immediate stress response, while our chronic stress response is handled by our endocrine system.

Right Here, Right Now: Immediate Stress Response and the Nervous System

Two guys are hiking along a trail in the woods when a huge grizzly bear suddenly appears on the path in front of them. One of the men drops to the ground and starts ripping off his boots and frantically putting on his running shoes. The other man sees what his friend is up to and exclaims, "What are you doing? You can't out-

run that bear!" To which the first man replies, "I know. But I can outrun you."

Fortunately, our bodies are physiologically well-adapted to handle a situation as stressful as crossing paths with a grizzly bear. Our hearts race, breathing becomes rapid and shallow, blood pressure rises, our pupils dilate, digestion slows, and our hands become cold or clammy as bloodflow is directed to our limb muscles in preparation for a speedy getaway. Blood sugars also increase, while a hefty shot of adrenaline sparks the release of stored fats to quickly provide our bodies with the burst of energy we need for a successful escape.

Normally these changes are temporary and are only necessary for those few moments when we're face-to-face with extreme stress. These responses tend naturally to be followed by a period of relaxation, especially after physical exertion (like running away from a bear). Physical exertion also helps to burn up all the sugar and fat our bodies release to help us escape the stress. If there's no physical exertion to burn up that excess fuel, the extra sugars and fats can pose a problem, especially around our waistlines.

Constant stimulation of your nervous system, either through your thoughts or information taken in via your five senses, is one of *the* major causes of hormonal imbalance and weight gain. Your brain responds to stress by encouraging a high intake of fatty and sugary foods—the so-called comfort foods that cause stubborn weight gain. So taking active steps to beat stress and calm your nervous system is *essential* for fat loss.

Here for the Long Haul: Cortisol, Our Long-Term Stress Response

The good thing about short-term stress, such as finding a bear in your path, is that it comes, you deal with it, and it goes. It's the unrelenting stress that comes with worries about finances, a divorce, a job you despise, chronic illness, or generally feeling overwhelmed with your life that can cause lasting damage.

Persistent or chronic stress involves a different physiological process in your body. Under situations of chronic stress—whether the stress is physical, emotional, mental, or environmental, *real or imagined*—your body releases high amounts of the hormone cortisol. For instance, cold, hunger, low blood pressure, pain, broken bones, injuries, inflammation, our sleep-wake cycle, intense exercise, and emotional upsets all cause the brain to activate our stress pathway and increase cortisol production by the adrenal glands (two glands that sit on top of your kidneys and also produce adrenaline).

If you have a mood disorder such as anxiety, depression, post-traumatic stress disorder, or exhaustion, or if you have a digestive issue such as irritable bowel syndrome, you can bet your stress response pathway is in overdrive, cranking up your cortisol. If you routinely have anxiety-provoking or upsetting thoughts racing through your mind, your stress systems will constantly be working overtime.

Mental and emotional stress may be *most* injurious because they're usually not followed by a relaxation response the way most physical stress is. As long as the perceived stressful event remains constantly in your mind, your body cannot fully achieve a relaxed, healthy, balanced state. When prolonged, this state of imbalance leads to permanent physiological changes.

But cortisol, just like insulin, isn't all bad. We need it to survive and to adapt to stressful situations. It also maintains our blood pressure and body temperature, controls inflammation, and allows other hormones (such as adrenaline) to take effect quickly as they provide us with energy by breaking down fat.

HORMONAL IMBALANCE 5: EXCESS CORTISOL

(Chronic Stress or Anxiety)

HOW DOES STRESS MAKE YOU FAT?

Unlike adrenaline, which draws on your fat stores for energy during stressful situations, cortisol consumes your muscle tissue for fuel. Prolonged stress can lead to muscle wasting and high blood sugar simply because your body is struggling to adapt. When these conditions take over, stress becomes extremely destructive to your metabolism, body composition, and wellness.

Another stress hormone called NPY (neuropeptide Y) also plays an important role in controlling your eating habits by working in your brain. Once released, NPY *decreases* your metabolic rate, causes more belly fat storage, and also fuels your appetite for sugary foods and carbohydrates—a triple-whammy for your waistline.

So many side effects of stress conspire to make you fat! Together, high cortisol and elevated NPY impact your metabolism, appetite, and body composition in the following nasty ways:

- Cortisol depresses your metabolic rate by interfering with thyroid hormone
- Cortisol and NPY fuel your desire for fatty foods and carbohydrates
- Both boost abdominal fat storage
- Cortisol depletes your happy hormone, serotonin, causing depression and more carbohydrate cravings
- Cortisol can cause blood sugar imbalance, resulting in hypoglycemia and symptoms of shakiness, irritability, fatigue, and headaches between meals
- Cortisol causes you to eat more than you need to by stimulating appetite-boosting NPY and blocking appetite-suppressing leptin

- Cortisol saps testosterone, which can result in languishing libido and a host of serious health risks
- Cortisol eats away at muscle and slows repair of metabolically active muscle cells
- Excess cortisol leads to sleep disruption, a known cause of weight gain
- Cortisol blunts the growth hormone that helps build metabolically active muscle, aids tissue rejuvenation, and slows the effects of aging
- Cortisol and NPY both decrease cellular sensitivity to insulin, resulting in elevated insulin levels, insulin resistance, and accumulation of abdominal fat

Through a complicated network of hormonal interactions, prolonged stress results in a raging appetite, metabolic decline, loads of belly fat, and a loss of hard-won, metabolically active muscle tissue. In other words, stress makes us soft, flabby, and much older than we truly are!

HOW DO YOU KNOW WHETHER YOUR STRESS IS OUT OF CONTROL?

Since symptoms of stress vary widely, pinpointing whether or not it's the main culprit behind specific health problems can be difficult. The Hormonal Health Profile may certainly help you to assess whether excess cortisol is having negative effects on your health and hormones. And I have outlined specific tests to assess your stress in Appendix A, should you wish to investigate your situation further with the help of your doctor. At this time, there is no lab test for measuring NPY. If you are under severe emotional stress, however, your NPY is likely on the high side. You can assess your cortisol using a salivary cortisol profile test that collects saliva at four different points during the day. When properly balanced, your cortisol should be highest at around 6 a.m. and lowest at night.

I typically see three common patterns of cortisol imbalance in my patients. In some cases, cortisol is elevated at all points of collection. In others, the normal cortisol pattern is reversed so that it's highest in the evening and lowest in the morning. The latter condition is characterized by extreme difficulty getting up in the morning, fatigue during the day, and difficulty falling asleep at bedtime. Low cortisol at all points of collection suggests total adrenal gland burnout.

You must control your cortisol if you want to achieve lasting health and a strong, lean body, which is why thinking positively and managing *all types* of stress are included as the first of the three steps. In fact, all of the steps of the Hormone Diet aim to control cortisol.

Hormonal Imbalance 7—Excess Estrogen
Too Much or Too Little Can Make You Fat

In women, estrogen is produced primarily by the ovaries in response to follicle-stimulating hormone (FSH), manufactured by the pituitary before menopause and by the adrenal glands and fat cells afterwards. Estrogen is the dominant hormone for the first 2 weeks or so after menstruation, when it stimulates the buildup of tissue and blood in the uterus, and the ovarian follicles simultaneously begin their development of the egg. The level of hormone peaks and then tapers off just as the follicle matures before ovulation.

Although estrogen is typically considered a female hormone, a certain amount of it is natural and important for men as well. Excess body fat in men, however, spurs an unhealthy rise in estrogen levels because fat cells are involved in converting testosterone to estrogen. Alcohol consumption and a high-fat diet have also been shown to increase estrogen levels in both men and women. Then there's the natural aging process in men, which tends to bring about a drop in testosterone production and a parallel increase in estrogen. I often say women and men seem to switch hormonal roles with age; men experience an increase in estrogen, whereas women lose it!

The Three Types of Estrogen

Though estrogen is often referred to as a single substance, it's actually made up of three hormones: estradiol, estrone, and estriol. In most cases, the term "estrogen" is used to refer to estradiol (as is the case in this book, unless I note otherwise).

1. **Estradiol** is the strongest and most prevalent estrogen hormone and plays a surprising number of critical roles in the body. This important substance is the primary hormone of the menstrual cycle and dictates the thickness of the uterine wall. Besides controlling vaginal moisture and lubrication, it enhances libido and sexual enjoyment and prevents urinary tract infections and urinary incontinence. It stimulates the cells that build bone and also aids the bone-edifying processes of calcium, magnesium, and zinc absorption. Estradiol supports cardiovascular health by dilating the blood vessels, increasing "good" HDL cholesterol, and lowering "bad" LDL cholesterol. It influences insulin response and aids blood sugar balance. Estradiol also has positive effects on the brain and nervous system, including improving memory, aiding sleep, and protecting nerve cells. This multitasking substance keeps our eyes moist and is also the secret to glowing skin, as it prevents wrinkling by maintaining skin tone, texture, and thickness. It is a potent antioxidant, especially for skin and brain cells.

2. **Estrone** is the second most potent estrogen and is often labeled the "bad" estrogen. It has earned this reputation because an excess is harmful to breast and uterine cells and is also thought to lead to cancer. Before menopause, the ovaries, liver, and fat cells produce estrone. After the onset of menopause, this hor-

mone is naturally produced in the fat cells. Women with excess body fat are, therefore, more likely to be estrone dominant. Regardless of age, estrone dominance is further intensified by high alcohol consumption (i.e., more than four drinks a week for women; more than seven for men), which is also known to boost cancer risk. Furthermore, abnormally high estrone blocks the beneficial effects of estradiol in the body, especially in the brain, and increases the risk of blood clots, toxic fat gain, gallstones, and stress on the liver.

3. **Estriol** is the weakest of the estrogens and is produced when estradiol and estrone convert to estriol. This hormone is often referred to as the "good" estrogen because it appears to block the harmful effects of estrone on breast cells. New research has also found that estriol may have positive effects on autoimmune functions.

Estriol, naturally produced only during pregnancy, is thought to play a crucial role in preventing the mother's body from attacking the fetus as foreign tissue. In a similar manner, estriol may help patients suffering with multiple sclerosis (MS) by preventing an overactive immune system from destroying myelin. A 2002 study by UCLA neuroscientists showed that oral supplementation of estriol decreased the size and number of MS-related brain lesions and increased protective immune responses in patients with relapsing-remitting MS.

Although not as strong as estradiol, estriol still offers significant benefits when used as a supplement during menopause. It is very useful on its own for relieving vaginal dryness and for the treatment and prevention of urinary tract infections. Or, when mixed with estradiol in the form of Bi-est (80 percent estriol, 20 percent estradiol), it aids other symptoms of menopause such as hot flashes and insomnia. Unlike estradiol, estriol does not have the documented benefits on heart health, bones, or the brain, so mixing the two types of estrogen can be beneficial.

A FAT-PACKING HORMONAL IMBALANCE

HORMONAL IMBALANCE 7: EXCESS ESTROGEN
(Estrogen Dominance)

Estrogen balance is essential for achieving and maintaining fat loss. In men and premenopausal women, too much estrogen, a condition called estrogen dominance, causes toxic fat gain, water retention, bloating, and a host of other health and wellness issues. Whereas premenopausal women with too much estrogen tend to have the pear-shaped body type with more weight at the hips, both men and menopausal women with this condition exhibit an apple shape with more fat accumulation in the abdominal area. Researchers have now identified excess estrogen to be *as great a risk factor for obesity*—in both sexes—as poor eating habits and lack of exercise.

Estrogen dominance, a term coined by Dr. John R. Lee, a family physician and author of many books on natural progesterone therapy for menopausal women, can occur in two ways. It may arise when an imbalance of "good" estrogen relative to the "bad" is present, or when the total amount of estrogen is excessive in relation to its natural hormonal opponent, progesterone, which balances estrogen's effects.

Estrogen dominance can also be an issue for men, as testosterone and progesterone naturally decline with age or stress, and estrogen conversely rises. Statistics show that shockingly high numbers of men who live to the age of 65 and older will develop prostate cancer, likely due to estrogen exposure.

CAUSES OF ESTROGEN DOMINANCE

There are only two ways to accumulate excess estrogen in the body: We either produce too much of it on our own or acquire it from our environment or diet. We are constantly exposed to estrogenlike compounds in foods that contain toxic pesticides, herbicides, and growth hormones. Many of these toxins are known to cause weight gain, which serves to fuel the production of more estrogen from our own fat cells. More weight gain then leads to insulin resistance, which, you guessed it, increases the risk of estrogen dominance.

Pharmaceutical hormones such as those used in hormone replacement therapy (HRT) or the birth control pill also increase estrogen, whether we take them actively or absorb them when they make their way into our drinking water. Dr. Richard Stahlhut, a preventive medicine resident at the University of Rochester, writes, "Low-dose exposures to phthalates and other common chemicals [with estrogenic activity] may be reducing testosterone levels or function in men, and thereby contributing to rising obesity rates and an epidemic of related disorders, such as type 2 diabetes."

We are living in a virtual sea of harmful estrogens, and researchers are only beginning to identify the effects of this exposure on health in humans and even other species.

Estrogen dominance has many disturbing causes.

1. **Xenoestrogens:** These harmful compounds mimic estrogen. They make their way into the body from hormones added to foods, especially dairy and beef. They can also be present in pesticides, herbicides, plastics, and even cosmetics.
2. **Stress:** As the body responds to high levels of stress, it "steals" progesterone to manufacture the stress hormone cortisol, often leaving a relative excess of estrogen.
3. **Impaired liver function:** Since the liver breaks down estrogen, alcohol consumption, drug use, a fatty liver, liver disease, and

any other factor that impairs healthy liver function can cause an estrogen buildup.

4. **Poor digestion:** Insufficient dietary fiber, bacterial imbalance in the gut, and other problems that compromise digestion interfere with the proper elimination of estrogen from the body via the digestive tract.

5. **Alcohol consumption:** Research shows that even one alcohol drink can spark an increase in estrogen production.

6. **A high-fat diet:** High intake of saturated or polyunsaturated fat spurs the body's own production of estrogen.

7. **Nutrient deficiencies:** The body requires sufficient intake of zinc, magnesium, vitamin B_6, and other essential nutrients not only to support the breakdown and elimination of estrogen, but also to aid the function of enzymes responsible for the conversion of testosterone to estrogen.

8. **Obesity:** In both men and women, obesity increases the production of bad estrogen, encourages the storage of estrogen in fat cells, and causes a decline in sex-hormone-binding globulin (SHBG). When SHBG drops, more estrogen is left free in the body to bind with tissues in the breasts, ovaries, and fat cells. Obesity also accelerates estrogen production in men because fat cells influence the conversion of testosterone and androsterone into estrogen, which in turn stimulates unfavorable growth of the prostate gland.

9. **Lack of exercise:** One more reason why exercise is so essential for reducing the risk of breast cancer and other malignancies.

10. **Sleep deprivation:** Maintaining habits that prevent sufficient, quality sleep causes a reduction in the hormone melatonin, which helps protect against estrogen dominance.

WHAT DOES ESTROGEN DOMINANCE LOOK LIKE?

If you are a premenopausal woman with estrogen dominance, you likely have PMS, too much body fat around the hips, and difficulty losing weight. Perhaps you have a history of gallstones, varicose veins, uterine fibroids, cervical dysplasia, endometriosis, or ovarian cysts. For all you men out there, low libido, poor motivation, depression, loss of muscle mass, and increased belly fat are big red flags. You may even notice breast development. These symptoms are very similar to those that result from low testosterone, since estrogen dominance is usually accompanied with a low testosterone level.

In both sexes, estrogen dominance is thought to be responsible for many types of cancers. This particular hormone imbalance is currently estimated to be one of the leading causes of breast, uterine, and prostate cancer.

HOW DO YOU KNOW IF YOU ARE ESTROGEN DOMINANT?

Besides checking yourself for the very telling signs and symptoms outlined above, you can further assess your risk of estrogen dominance with your doctor using the tests I have outlined in Appendix A. You can also investigate the Estronex test from Metametrix labs. This test measures the ratio of two critical estrogen metabolites from a single urine specimen. One metabolite, 2-hydroxyestrone (2-OHE1), tends to inhibit cancer growth. Another, 16-alpha-hydroxyestrone (16-A-OHE1), actually encourages tumor development and is associated with estrogen dominance.

Hormonal Imbalance 8—Low Estrogen
Low Estrogen = More Belly Fat for Women

Too little estrogen also has negative impacts on health and appearance. As estrogen levels drop off, especially during menopause, many women find themselves battling that oh-so-lovely shift in body fat from the hips to the waist. Since estrogen helps our cells respond better to insulin, a plunge in estrogen also tends to cause an unwelcome increase in insulin. To make matters worse, the onset of menopause also brings about a decline in the neurotransmitter serotonin. This drop tends to fuel carbohydrate cravings, propelling insulin production even further. Combined with the loss of the cardio-protective benefits of estrogen, these hormonal and body-shape changes definitely contribute to an increased risk of heart disease at menopause.

Estrogen deficiency can affect women at any age. Major causes include the following:

- Aging/menopause
- Premature ovarian failure
- Surgical menopause (removal of the ovaries)
- Smoking
- High levels of stress
- Low-fat diets
- Exceedingly low body fat

The Trouble with Ghrelin

When the digestive system is empty, the stomach and upper intestine produce the hormone ghrelin to stimulate appetite. When you feel hungry and your stomach starts to sound like a grizzly bear, ghrelin is being produced. This hormone does the

SYMPTOMS OF ESTROGEN IMBALANCE

TOO MUCH ESTROGEN (Estrogen Dominance) (Hormonal Imbalance 7)		TOO LITTLE ESTROGEN (Hormonal Imbalance 8)	
Women	Men (Almost always accompanied by testosterone deficiency)	Women	Men
Depression and poor concentration	Prostate enlargement	Vaginal dryness	Loss of bone density
Headaches or migraines	Increased risk of prostate cancer	Memory loss and brain fog	Fatigue
Tendency toward toxic fat gain	Increased toxic abdominal fat	Depression and/or anxiety	Memory not as sharp
Water retention, bloating, puffiness	Breast enlargement	Decreased tolerance for pain	
Weight gain, especially at the hips and thighs	Low sex drive	Increased risk of Alzheimer's disease	
Fibrocystic breasts	Depression	Hair loss	
Uterine fibroids	Erectile dysfunction	Low sex drive	
Low sex drive	Low motivation	Dry eyes	
PMS	Hair loss	Urinary urgency and infections	
Increased risk of breast and uterine cancer	Bloating or puffiness	Thinning and wrinkling of the skin	
Increased risk of autoimmune disease	Increased risk of heart disease and stroke	Increased weight gain at the waist	
Hypothyroidism	Loss of muscle mass	Loss of bone density	
Mood swings	Fatigue	Increased risk of heart disease, high cholesterol, and high blood pressure	
Cervical dysplasia (abnormal PAP tests)	Sleep disruption	Night sweats and hot flashes (which can occur with any change in estrogen level, not just deficiency)	
Heavy periods		Sleep disruption	
Breast swelling and enlargement		Decrease in breast size	
Endometriosis		Increased risk of cataracts	
Ovarian disease		Increased cravings for carbohydrates	
Spider veins and varicose veins			
Cellulite			
Increased risk of gallstones			

important job of letting us know when it is mealtime. But it can also create challenges for us when we attempt to lose weight because it makes us feel hungry when we try to reduce our caloric intake. Research at Oregon Health & Science University has shown that ghrelin activates specialized neurons in our hypothalamus involved in weight regulation and appetite control. Upon reaching the brain, ghrelin also appears to stimulate the release of growth hormone, which in turn promotes the discharge of peptides, especially the stress hormone neuropeptide Y (NPY), which stimulates our desire to eat.

One of the reasons gastric bypass surgery (commonly referred to as stomach stapling) works so well for weight loss is that patients who undergo this procedure lose half of the source tissue that produces ghrelin, and less ghrelin means a lot less of an urge to eat.

Wow, that was a lot of information to process! You have just finished one the most information-dense chapters of the book. Now you can sit back, relax, take a deep breath, and let it sink in before moving on to the next chapter: Your Fat-Burning Friends.

CHAPTER 4

YOUR FAT-BURNING FRIENDS:
THE HORMONES THAT HELP
YOU LOSE WEIGHT

Here's what you will learn about in this chapter:
- The hormones that control your appetite, boost your metabolism, and aid fat loss
- Three more fat-packing hormonal imbalances that interfere with successful weight loss: hypothyroidism, menopause, and depression

So far I have painted a somewhat negative picture of the influences hormones have on your successful weight-loss journey. But there are indeed hormones inside you that actually help curb your appetite and improve your fat-loss prospects.

Your fat-burning friends are hormones that:

1. DIRECTLY STIMULATE METABOLISM
   - Thyroid hormones
   - Adrenaline
   - Glucagon
   - Progesterone

2. STIMULATE FAT LOSS BY SUPPORTING THE GROWTH OF METABOLICALLY ACTIVE MUSCLE
   - DHEA

- Testosterone
- Growth hormone

3. CONTROL YOUR APPETITE AND PERFORM OTHER FUNCTIONS
   THAT FUEL FAT LOSS
   - Serotonin
   - Melatonin
   - Dopamine
   - Acetylcholine
   - Gamma-aminobutyric acid (GABA)
   - Leptin
   - Vitamin D$_3$

So get comfortable. I've filled this chapter with a whole lot of information that can make an enormous difference to your weight-loss efforts and to your quality of life.

1. THE HORMONES THAT DIRECTLY STIMULATE YOUR METABOLISM

Hormonal Imbalance 13—Low Thyroid
Thyroid Hormones: Masters of Your Metabolic Rate

The thyroid is a gland in the front of your neck, just below the Adam's apple. This critical gland produces thyroid hormones that influence every cell, tissue, and organ in your body.

Thyroid hormones regulate our metabolism and organ function, and directly affect heart rate, cholesterol levels, body weight, energy, muscle contraction and relaxation, skin and hair texture, bowel function, fertility, menstrual regularity, memory, mood, and other bodily processes. Normal levels of thyroid hormone are essential to the development of a baby's brain. In fact, women with low levels of thyroid hormone during pregnancy have been shown to give birth to babies with lower IQs.

The Four Types of Thyroid Hormone

1. TSH (THYROID-STIMULATING HORMONE): This substance is produced by the pituitary gland under direction from the hypothalamus. A high TSH suggests that your thyroid gland is not responding properly to signals from your pituitary telling it to make more hormones.

2. FREE T4 (THYROXINE): T4 is the thyroid hormone produced directly by your thyroid gland under stimulation of TSH. It's the major form of thyroid hormone in your bloodstream.

3. FREE T3 (TRIIODOTHYRONINE): T4 is converted to T3 in the cells of the body. T3 is the thyroid hormone that directly influences the metabolism of every single cell, tissue, and organ in your body.

4. REVERSE T3 (rT3): Under periods of stress or with a deficiency of the trace mineral selenium, your body may produce increased levels of rT3. A high level of rT3 is usually a signal of an underactive thyroid.

The levels of T3 and T4 in your body act as negative feedback mechanisms to the pituitary to stop the production of thyroid hormone until it's needed again. So, low levels of T3 and T4 will stimulate increased TSH production. Here's an analogy to make this clearer: imagine the pituitary as the boss and the thyroid as the worker. If the worker starts to slack off, the boss's demands for more work get louder and louder. If the worker is productive, there's less instruction from above.

Thyroid Hormone Imbalance

Like so many other hormones, thyroid hormones must be present in the appropriate balance in order to ensure optimal health. Too much thyroid hormone leads to hyperthyroidism, a condition that throws the metabolism into chronic high gear. Those with hyperthyroidism feel hot and experience a rapid heart rate, weight loss (or weight gain, if they eat a lot more due to increased appetite), irritability, insomnia, shakiness, and digestive troubles. Sufferers can also feel hyper, although fatigue is very common as well. Over time, hyperthyroidism can be extremely detrimental to bone density and muscle mass.

Hypothyroidism is caused by a deficiency of thyroid hormone. This condition affects 1 in 13 people, making it much more common than hyperthyroidism. Without enough thyroid hormone, every system in the body slows down. Those who suffer from hypothyroidism feel tired and tend to sleep a lot. Their digestion slows and weight gain typically occurs. They can also experience extremely dry skin, hair loss, and slower mental processes.

A FAT-PACKING HORMONAL IMBALANCE

HORMONAL IMBALANCE 13: LOW THYROID HORMONE (Hypothyroidism)

An estimated 13 million Americans have underactive thyroid function, only half of whom have been properly diagnosed. Women are five times more likely than men to be diagnosed with hypothyroidism.

WHAT CAUSES HYPOTHYROIDISM?

Hypothyroidism is a complex disorder that can stem from a number of different causes. Factors include the following:

• The thyroid failing to produce enough thyroid hormone. This deficiency is possibly caused by an autoimmune response against the thyroid or other problems with the function of the thyroid gland itself.

- The pituitary gland or the hypothalamus failing to send a critical signal to the thyroid instructing it to produce thyroid hormone.
- Thyroxine (T4) produced by the thyroid may not convert properly to its active form, triiodothyronine (T3), which ultimately influences the metabolism of every cell.
- The adrenal hormones cortisol and DHEA influence thyroid function. A deficiency of DHEA and excessive amounts of the stress hormone cortisol may inhibit thyroid hormone function.
- Toxic levels of mercury, typically resulting from mercury fillings in the mouth or consuming large amounts of mercury-laden ocean fish, may inhibit thyroid gland function.
- High levels of estrogen or a converse deficiency of progesterone inhibits thyroid function. Many menopausal women using estrogen replacement therapy may develop the symptoms of an underactive thyroid. Menopausal women who are already taking medication for hypothyroidism may also need to increase their dosage if they choose to use hormone replacement therapy (HRT).
- The excessive consumption of soy-based foods and beverages may decrease the activity of thyroid hormone in the body.
- Some studies suggest that ingestion of excess fluoride from drinking water and toothpaste may inhibit thyroid gland function. Pesticides in water and occupational exposure to polybrominated biphenyls and carbon disulfide have also been associated with decreased thyroid function.
- Nutritional deficiencies may prevent the proper manufacture or function of thyroid hormone in the body. Iodine and L-tyrosine are necessary for the formation of thyroid hormone, while selenium is necessary for the normal function of thyroid hormone.

Many individuals with decreased thyroid hormone levels also have a zinc deficiency.
- Certain medications may induce hypothyroidism. Lithium carbonate, a medication used to treat manic depression, is one of the most common medications known to cause hypothyroidism. Others include amiodarone hydrochloride (Amiodarone, Cordarone, and Pacerone), interferon-alfa (Infergen, Rebetron, and Wellferon), nitroprusside, perchlorate, and sulfonylureas.

WHAT ARE THE SYMPTOMS OF HYPOTHYROIDISM?

The symptoms of underactive thyroid disease can vary, and not all individuals will present in the same way.

The Hormonal Health Profile may have helped you to determine whether you show signs of a sluggish thyroid; the following are additional symptoms to watch for:
- Frequently feeling cold or having an intolerance for cold temperatures
- Dry skin, brittle hair, and splitting nails
- Lack of or diminished ability to sweat during exercise
- Hair loss
- Irregular menses or heavy menstrual bleeding
- Poor memory
- Depression
- Decreased libido
- Constipation
- Unexplained fatigue or lethargy
- Unexplained weight gain or an inability to lose weight
- Many individuals with hypothyroidism have associated iron deficiency anemia and/or high cholesterol

HOW IS HYPOTHYROIDISM DIAGNOSED?

In Appendix A, I outline the tests you may want to request from your doctor to fully assess the condition of your thyroid. Thyroid disease is diagnosed with blood tests. Four tests—for TSH, free T3, free T4, and thyroid antibodies—should be completed to get the most accurate picture of your thyroid health.

Some important notes on testing: In my practice, I often find thyroid antibodies register as abnormal long before the other three parameters, so these should be assessed. Many health-care providers also share concerns about the currently accepted normal reference ranges for TSH. US health professionals have recently reduced the upper range to 3. However, many integrated health practitioners feel it should be less than 2.0, and I agree.

Ultimately, this discrepancy means that many people suffering with the symptoms of an underactive thyroid may go without proper treatment. If you suspect you have a thyroid condition, make sure your doctor assesses you and your full range of symptoms, *not just your blood work*. Even a modest increase in TSH has been proven to accelerate weight gain and to interfere with a healthy metabolic rate in both men and women.

WHY IS HYPOTHYROIDISM A SERIOUS CONDITION IF LEFT UNTREATED?

A thyroid condition must be treated correctly and quickly to stave off further serious complications. Left untreated, thyroid conditions may lead to an increased risk of cardiovascular disease, infertility, premature ovarian failure, breast cancer, osteoporosis, obesity, goiter, and diabetes.

Adrenaline and Noradrenaline:
Your "Fight-or-Flight" Hormones

When present in the right amounts, adrenaline is very useful in supporting fat loss. It causes the body to free up stored fats and sugars to provide us with the burst of energy we need to escape or face danger, while sparing metabolically active muscle protein. Believe it or not, having a cup of coffee before your workout may offer an extra fat-burning boost simply because caffeine sparks adrenaline production.

Along with adrenaline, noradrenaline (NA, or norepinephrine) is released by nerve cells and the adrenal glands. NA also stimulates energy-expending fight-or-flight responses. Although it's typically not produced in as high a quantity as adrenaline, noradrenaline has very similar effects on physiology, including increasing the heart rate, raising blood sugar, and increasing tension in the skeletal muscles. It also stimulates the brain and helps us to think quickly when we are in tricky situations.

Glucagon: Converting Carbs into Energy

Glucagon works directly opposite to insulin in that it raises our blood sugar. When we exercise, consume protein, or experience a dip in blood sugar, glucagon kicks in to aid fat loss by instructing the body to use stored fat and sugars for fuel. Glucagon release is inhibited, however, when high amounts of sugar and insulin are present in our bloodstream. Another reason to keep that insulin level in check!

Since protein consumption stimulates glucagon activity, eating substantial amounts of meat, dairy, soy, or fish seems like a great approach to weight loss, right? Not necessarily. Your body much prefers carbohydrates over protein for use as an energy source. In fact, we want the body to choose sugar over protein for fuel because the latter process can break down muscle. Excess glucagon can also destroy precious muscle tissue that we work so hard to build and maintain.

The key to maintaining a stable blood sugar level, while also preventing the breakdown of muscle tissue, is to balance protein consumption with low-glycemic carbohydrates, such as fruits, vegetables, and whole grain breads and cereals—carbohydrates that limit insulin secretion. This combination of foods will promote glucagon release while also providing your body with sufficient fuel. If you consume too many carbohydrates or fail to eat enough protein, you will not benefit from the fat-burning effects of glucagon.

Hormonal Imbalance 9—Low Progesterone
Progesterone: Why Too Much or Too Little Makes You Fat

Progesterone is produced by the ovaries before menopause and in small amounts after menopause by the adrenal glands. Opposite to estrogen, progesterone is naturally higher in the second half of the menstrual cycle, when it causes thickening of the uterine wall in preparation for implantation of a fertilized egg. If no implantation occurs, progesterone levels decline, triggering the beginning of the menstrual flow. If implantation does occur, progesterone levels increase steadily during pregnancy. Together with estriol, progesterone helps prevent the mother's immune system from attacking the fetus as foreign tissue. Men also produce progesterone from the testes and the adrenal glands, but in much lower amounts than women.

Progesterone has many beneficial effects. It's a natural diuretic, sleep aid, antianxiety compound, and stimulator of metabolism (because it supports thyroid hormone). It's also considered to be thermogenic because it raises body temperature, just like when we eat protein. Progesterone may help to build bone density, reduce blood pressure, lower LDL cholesterol, improve the appearance and texture of hair and skin, aid libido, and prevent PMS. When balanced properly with estrogen, it's protective against breast and prostate cancer. This multifunctional hormone also aids fertility and helps to balance the immune system, thereby reducing the risk of autoimmune disease.

Progesterone inhibits the enzyme that causes the conversion of testosterone to dihydrotestosterone (DHT), the type of testosterone that contributes to hair loss in both men and women and prostate enlargement in men. As with all hormones, however, more is not necessarily better!

Progesterone tends to decline in women beginning in their 30s and in men after 60. When progesterone is stolen or decreased, estrogen dominance can arise. This imbalance is very common in women in their 30s and 40s.

Progesterone deficiency may arise for many different reasons.

- **Stress:** More stress means lower progesterone, as the body steals progesterone to increase cortisol production.
- **Lack of ovulation:** May occur with conditions such as polycystic ovarian syndrome (PCOS).
- **Low levels of luteinizing hormone (LH):** Released by the brain, LH triggers the production of progesterone.
- **Hypothyroidism:** An underactive thyroid gland.
- **Excess prolactin:** The hormone prolactin stimulates breast development during pregnancy and milk production during nursing. Too much prolactin can suppress progesterone production and can cause infertility and menstrual disorders. Prolactin levels can also increase with hypothyroidism and pituitary disorders.

Hormonal Imbalance 10—Excess Progesterone
Progesterone: Why Too Much or Too Little Makes You Fat
As is the case with its estrogen counterpart, progesterone must be balanced in order to help us maintain a lean body. Progesterone excess is rare, though I often see it in individuals who use progesterone creams or pills. Too much progesterone is troublesome and can cause acne, bloating, water retention, depression, and weight gain.

SYMPTOMS OF PROGESTERONE IMBALANCE

TOO LITTLE PROGESTERONE (Hormonal Imbalance 9)		TOO MUCH PROGESTERONE (Hormonal Imbalance 10)	
Women	Men	Women	Men
Anxiety	Prostate enlargement	Depression	Low libido
Sleep disruption	Sleep disruption	Weight gain and increased fat storage	Weight gain and increased fat storage
PMS	Increased body fat	Water retention and bloating	Water retention and bloating
Hair loss	Hair loss	Poor blood sugar balance, cravings, and increased appetite	Poor blood sugar balance, cravings, and increased appetite
Sluggish metabolism, increased risk of hypothyroidism	Bone density loss/osteoporosis	Increased stress hormones and possibly excess testosterone	Increased stress hormones and possibly excess testosterone
Bone density loss/osteoporosis	Increased risk of prostate cancer	Constipation	Suppression of the immune system; more frequent colds and flus
Autoimmune disease		Low libido	Possible infertility (some suggestion that excess progesterone may interfere with sperm production)
Periods that come too soon or spotting between periods		Suppression of the immune system; more frequent colds and flus	
Infertility or lack of menstruation		Increased risk of breast and uterine cancer	
Headaches, especially before menses		Increased risk of diabetes	
Increased allergies		Infertility	
Night sweats			
Miscarriage			
Water retention			
Swollen, tender, cystic breasts			

A FAT-PACKING HORMONAL IMBALANCE

MENOPAUSE
(Low Estrogen, Progesterone, and/or Testosterone)

According to US census data, there are about 37.5 million women at or near menopause. Menopause, which can begin as early as 40 years of age, is not just about estrogen decline. Supplies of progesterone, testosterone, and DHEA also tend to dry up, right along with the skin, hair, eyes, and libido!

At first I wasn't going to include menopause as one of the conditions of hormonal imbalance and weight gain because it is, after all, a natural and inevitable part of aging. I changed my mind, however, because so many women come through the doors of my office intensely frustrated with the unwelcome changes in their body during this phase of life. One of the biggies, which I mentioned in the previous chapter, is that annoying thickening of the waistline that occurs when estrogen drops. Although some women pass through menopause with few, if any, side effects, others experience life-disrupting symptoms that last for months or even years.

The trying symptoms of menopause stem from an imbalance of estrogen, progesterone, and testosterone. The results of your Hormonal Health Profile will help you discover whether you have specific signs of an imbalance associated with each of these hormones. And, of course, I will provide you with plenty of suggestions to correct specific imbalances to ease your menopausal discomfort in Chapter 13.

The most common symptoms of menopause include:

- Hot flashes
- Difficulty sleeping
- Emotional changes, including depression, anxiety, and irritability
- Headaches
- Heart palpitations
- Poor memory and concentration
- Urinary urgency or incontinence

- Vaginal dryness
- Weight gain around the waist
- Changes in the appearance of your skin and hair

HOW DO YOU KNOW IF YOU'RE MENOPAUSAL?

Clinically, a diagnosis of menopause is made when the menses have been absent for 1 year. But if you've noticed a missed period and are experiencing the symptoms noted above, you may have reached perimenopause. Your doctor can order blood work to determine whether you're menopausal or not. Most doctors will measure levels of FSH, LH, estradiol, and progesterone, though more tests are outlined in Appendix A for your reference.

MORE THAN JUST DISCOMFORT: WHY YOU NEED TO MANAGE MENOPAUSE

After the onset of menopause, a woman's risk of Alzheimer's disease, osteoporosis, heart disease, and cancer significantly increases. But good lifestyle habits (my three steps!), supplements, and bioidentical hormone replacement (BHRT) can help mitigate these risks.

Bioidentical hormones are derived from natural sources outside the body, such as soy and other plants. They function just as effectively as our own hormones, without the potentially harmful side effects of animal hormones or the synthetic hormones used in traditional HRT (such as Premarin). BHRT works wonderfully to restore perfect hormonal balance in menopause. This type of therapy works even better when the foundation for hormonal balance is first set with the help of detoxification, exercise, and good nutrition.

If you wish to try BHRT, be sure to seek out a practitioner who specializes in this area. Regular testing of your hormone levels and proper follow-up are essential when using any type of hormone replacement therapy. Furthermore, high doses of hormones should not be the aim. Instead, the goal should be to replenish hormonal deficiencies and return levels to those we normally experience in middle age, not high school!

2. HORMONES THAT STIMULATE FAT LOSS BY SUPPORTING THE GROWTH OF METABOLICALLY ACTIVE MUSCLE

Hormonal Imbalance 6—Low DHEA
Everyone Digs DHEA: The Antistress, Antiaging Hormone

Produced by the adrenal glands, dehydroepiandrosterone (DHEA) is a precursor to the sex hormones estrogen and testosterone and is one of the most abundant hormones in your body. This hormone with the very long name has a big list of benefits to match. It's known to support healthy immunity (particularly for the prevention of autoimmune imbalances), aid tissue repair, improve sleep, and counteract the negative effects of cortisol. It influences our ability to lose fat and gain muscle. It boosts libido and helps us feel motivated, youthful, and energetic—just a few of the reasons why DHEA is often touted as the antiaging hormone. DHEA naturally declines with age, stress, and illness and is often taken in supplements.

If your DHEA levels are too low, you may experience the following:

* Increased body fat and weight gain
* A decrease in muscle mass
* Loss of a sense of well-being
* Bone density depletion
* Low libido
* Poor ability to handle stress

I support the use of DHEA supplements, but only in low doses and only when a true deficiency has been definitively diagnosed via blood or saliva testing. Taking too much DHEA can trigger an unwelcome increase in testosterone and estrogen, which leads to increased cancer risk, hair loss, anger, aggression, and acne in both men and women.

Women may also experience effects such as a deeper voice, hair loss, and abnormal growth of facial hair.

Hormonal Imbalance 11—Low Testosterone
Testosterone: The Master Muscle-Building Hormone

Testosterone is an androgen—a masculinizing hormone—produced by the ovaries in women, the testes in men, and the adrenal glands in both sexes. Testosterone enhances libido, bone density, muscle mass, strength, motivation, memory, fat burning, and skin tone. In men, it influences sperm production, causes growth of the prostate gland, and is especially important for maintaining motivation and mood.

As with so many other hormones, testosterone levels tend to taper off with aging, obesity, and stress. Exposure to pesticides and toxins also negatively impacts the production of testosterone in the testes. Today, men are experiencing testosterone decline much earlier in life, and overall levels appear to be dropping.

Dr. Antti Perheentupa, a specialist in reproductive medicine at the University of Turku in Finland, presented evidence of this decline at an Endocrine Society meeting in the summer of 2006, reporting that a man born in 1970 has about 20 percent *less* testosterone at age 35 than a man of his father's generation had at the same age. Quite an alarming finding, considering low testosterone has been linked to depression, obesity, osteoporosis, heart disease, *and even death*. Many researchers pin this decline on environmental factors. Dr. Mitchell Harman, an endocrinologist at the University of Arizona College of Medicine, blames the proliferation of endocrine-suppressing, estrogenlike compounds used in pesticides and

> **TEST YOUR TESTOSTERONE**
> Recent studies have found that a decrease in testosterone in men at any age increases the risk of osteoporosis, heart disease, and even death. For this reason alone, having your levels of free testosterone tested in the blood or saliva at least once a year is incredibly important.

HOT HORMONE TIP

SLEEP APNEA DECREASES
TESTOSTERONE LEVELS

Sleep apnea, a disorder characterized by pauses in breathing during sleep, can cause low testosterone and elevate risk of heart disease, diabetes, and depression. If you routinely wake gasping for air, not feeling refreshed, or experiencing headaches, visit your doctor for a referral to a sleep clinic.

other farming chemicals for the downward trend in male testosterone levels. Phthalates, commonly found in cosmetics, soaps, and most plastics (including, ahem, sex toys), are another known cause of testosterone suppression.

Loss of testosterone can lead to andropause, often referred to as male menopause. This condition is estimated to affect about 30 percent of aging men, although actual numbers may be much higher because the widely varying symptoms make a diagnosis difficult. The chart of symptoms of testosterone imbalance (page 96) illustrates how testosterone decline tends to cause an increase in body fat and loss of muscle mass. I should add that these effects can arise *in both men and women, even with dieting and exercise,* when a marked deficiency of testosterone exists.

Hormonal Imbalance 12—Excess Testosterone
Too Much of a Good Thing?

While excess testosterone is not very common in men, it affects about 10 percent of women. A surplus of female testosterone is typically a result of increased production by the adrenal glands and is associated with polycystic ovarian syndrome (PCOS) and hirsutism (excess hair growth). Besides causing acne, facial hair growth, and even male pattern hair loss in women, too much testosterone increases insulin resistance and weight gain (causing the apple body type).

I've had great success returning testosterone to normal levels in patients with PCOS or fertility concerns by using the Hormone Diet approach. The key to lowering testosterone is stress management (i.e., balancing cortisol) and controlling insulin levels through glycemically balanced eating, exercise, and insulin-sensitizing supplements. All of these strategies are included in my three steps.

In some cases, my approach can even restore testosterone to normal levels in men *without* the use of testosterone supplementation. This was the case with 37-year-old Max.

Max had been using testosterone replacement therapy for over 3 years when he came to see me. After we spoke, I failed to find any of the readily recognizable causes of low testosterone. He wasn't overweight, had no history of trauma to the testicles, wasn't reporting feeling overly stressed, had no history of sleep apnea, and had only mildly elevated cholesterol. Of course, my first thought was, Why the low testosterone at his age?

I was especially concerned for him because low testosterone can cause an increase in the risk of heart disease. Even worse, his father had had bypass surgery in his mid-forties; so I investigated the risk factors for heart disease closely. Max's cholesterol was only mildly elevated, his blood pressure was normal, and he was not overweight. Then I tested his homocysteine—it was 20, which is over *three times* the accepted optimal value of 6.3!

I concluded that high homocysteine (a protein known to cause hardening of the arteries), along with his slightly elevated cholesterol, was probably causing obstruction of the bloodflow to the testicles, and the manifestation of this was decreased testosterone production. It was fortunate we found this when we did. In 10 to 20 years he would not only be suffering with low testosterone, but most likely a heart attack as well. And

SKIP THE STATINS AND SAVE YOUR TESTOSTERONE

Some cholesterol-lowering medications, especially statins such as Lipitor and Zocor, may decrease your production of testosterone and bring about the harmful effects of low testosterone. You may be better off selecting natural cholesterol-reducing alternatives to statins, such as policosanols, omega-3 fish oils, garlic, red yeast extract, or coenzyme Q10. These compounds improve cholesterol and cardiovascular health without the potential negative side effects.

HOT HORMONE TIP

guess what? Today Max's testosterone levels are normal—without the use of hormone replacement—and he's the father of twins!

This is a clear illustration of the need for a new, more comprehensive approach to health and hormonal balance—beyond being thin.

SYMPTOMS OF TESTOSTERONE IMBALANCE

TOO LITTLE TESTOSTERONE (Hormonal Imbalance 11)		TOO MUCH TESTOSTERONE (Hormonal Imbalance 12)	
Women	Men	Women (PCOS or Hirsutism)	Men (Andropause)
Muscle loss	Increased abdominal fat, muscle loss	Increased abdominal fat, insulin resistance	Aggression
Decreased libido	Impotence, erectile dysfunction, decreased libido	Acne	Acne
Fatigue	Increased risk of heart disease, fatigue	Irregular periods	Increased hair loss
Bone density loss	Increased risk of death, bone density loss	Increased risk of breast cancer	Possible increased risk of prostate enlargement or cancer
Decreased vitality	Sleep disruption, decreased vitality	Hair loss (scalp)	Increased hemoglobin
Increased body fat	Prostate problems (men treated with natural testosterone have been shown to have improvements in prostate health)	Increased hair growth (face and body)	
Depression and low motivation	Depression	Irritability	
Hair loss	Hair loss	Anger	
Dry skin and poor elasticity	Dry skin and poor elasticity	Decrease in breast size; sagging breasts	
Possibly hypothyroidism	Possibly hypothyroidism		

Hormonal Imbalance 16—Low Growth Hormone
Growth Hormone: In Charge of Growth and Repair

Growth hormone affects just about every cell in the body. Not surprisingly, it also has a major effect on our feelings, actions, and appearance. Because this regenerative hormone tends to decline with age, growth hormone supplements are often promoted as a way to slow the effects of aging.

Growth hormone is released during deep sleep and while we exercise. It's essential for tissue repair, muscle building, bone density, and healthy body composition. When we sleep in total darkness, melatonin is released, triggering a very slight but critical cool-down in the body. As body temperature drops, growth hormone is released and works its regenerative magic. If we sleep with lights on or eat too close to bedtime, the natural cool-down process will not take place, putting us at risk of low levels of both melatonin and growth hormone. At the same time, we lose the important effects of sleep on fat loss.

Once released into the bloodstream, growth hormone has a very short life—only half an hour or so. During that time, however, it makes its way speedily to the liver and many other cells in the body, inducing them to produce another hormone called insulin-like growth factor 1 (IGF-1). Almost every cell in the body is affected by IGF-1, especially muscle, bone, liver, kidney, skin, lung, and nerve cells. Commonly measured as a marker of growth hormone production, IGF-1 is the substance truly responsible for most of the restorative benefits we typically attribute to growth hormone.

The Perils of Low Growth Hormone

Only recently has growth hormone deficiency in adults been recognized as a serious health problem. Adults deficient in growth hormone suffer from the following:

- Premature cardiovascular disease
- Loss of bone density

- Abdominal obesity
- Decreased muscle mass, poor posture
- Thinning or sagging skin
- Depressed mood, anxiety
- Elevated levels of LDL cholesterol
- Slow wound healing
- Fatigue
- Low stamina for exercise
- Poor immune function

A study from the *Journal of Clinical Endocrinology and Metabolism* (April 2007) linked abdominal obesity in postmenopausal women with low growth hormone secretion, elevated inflammatory markers, and increased risk of cardiovascular disease. Test subjects who received supplementary growth hormone showed improvement in inflammatory markers. Researchers at Saint Louis University also found that obese people who received controlled doses of growth hormone lost weight and maintained the energy to exercise.

Even children who lack sufficient sleep are at risk of low growth hormone and obesity. According to data published in the *International Journal of Obesity* by researchers from Université Laval's Faculty of Medicine, the less a child sleeps, the more likely he or she is to become overweight. The risk of becoming overweight is 3.5 times higher for sleep-deprived children than for those who get the 9 to 10 hours of sleep they need.

Should We All Take Growth Hormone?

Boosting growth hormone certainly promises many exciting benefits, including less abdominal fat, more muscle mass, fewer wrinkles, increased bone mass, improved cholesterol levels, and stronger immune system function. But growth hormone supplementation is no panacea for health. Neither is it free of associated risks.

Abnormally high growth hormone can raise blood sugar, contribute to insulin resistance, increase the risk of type 2 diabetes, and cause abnormal bone growth. New research also suggests that elevated IGF-1 may be a risk factor for certain types of malignancies, especially prostate cancer.

3. THE HORMONES THAT CONTROL YOUR APPETITE AND FUEL FAT LOSS

Hormonal Imbalance 3—Low Serotonin
The Comfort of Sweet Serotonin

Though serotonin is typically recognized as a brain chemical, most of this neurotransmitter is produced in our digestive tract. Serotonin exerts powerful influence over mood, emotions, memory, cravings (especially for carbohydrates), self-esteem, pain tolerance, sleep habits, appetite, digestion, and body temperature regulation. Wow! When we're depressed or down, we naturally crave more sugars and starches to stimulate the production of serotonin. Also, when we're cold or surrounded by darkness, serotonin levels drop. Hey, maybe there is a reason for that dreaded winter weight gain after all!

Serotonin is often thought of as our "happy hormone," especially because its production increases when we're exposed to natural sunlight and when we focus on one thing rather than multitask. Production of serotonin is also closely linked to availability of vitamin B_6 and the amino acid tryptophan. So if our diet lacks sufficient protein or vitamins, we run a greater risk of serotonin deficiency. We may experience a dip in serotonin as a result of dieting, digestive disorders, and also stress, since high levels of the stress hormone cortisol rob us of serotonin.

> **SEROTONIN STEPS UP DIGESTION**
> Because it is highly concentrated in the gut, serotonin also has positive effects on digestion. As a result, researchers have now developed serotonin-based medications to ease the painful symptoms of irritable bowel syndrome.

HOT HORMONE FACT

What Happens with a Serotonin Imbalance?

A spike in serotonin rarely, if ever, occurs naturally. An elevated level of this hormone is usually a side effect of antidepressant medications specifically designed to boost serotonin. Too much serotonin can result in **serotonin syndrome**, a rare and life-threatening condition characterized by rapid pulse, headache, nausea, high blood pressure, decreased appetite, sweating, dilated pupils, an overall feeling of edginess, and, ultimately, unconsciousness. If you experience any of these symptoms while taking medications that influence your serotonin levels, see a doctor immediately.

Low serotonin is a far more common concern. In my professional opinion, serotonin deficiency has become an epidemic of equal proportion to obesity. I also believe this parallel is no coincidence.

A FAT-PACKING HORMONAL IMBALANCE

HORMONAL IMBALANCE 3: LOW SEROTONIN
(Insomnia, Anxiety, and Depression)

According to the World Health Organization (WHO), depression is the leading cause of disability as measured by the Years Lost due to Disability (YLD). Both depression and anxiety are linked to elevated cortisol, coupled with an imbalance of our "feel good" hormones, including serotonin, dopamine, and noradrenaline. In some cases, low testosterone in men or decreased estrogen in women can also play a role.

WHY THE EPIDEMIC OF LOW SEROTONIN?

Plenty of sunlight; a healthful diet rich in protein, minerals, and vitamins; regular exercise; and good sleep support serotonin. When we measure our current lifestyle against all the elements necessary for the body's natural production of serotonin, the wide-ranging epidemic of low serotonin is certainly not surprising. Add in *chronic stress* and *multitasking*—two of the main causes of serotonin depletion—and it's a wonder any one of us has been left unaffected by low serotonin.

DEPRESSION, WEIGHT GAIN, AND HORMONAL IMBALANCE:
A CODEPENDENT RELATIONSHIP

When you are depressed, your body naturally craves carbs in an attempt to raise serotonin. Of course, we all understand that excess carb consumption causes weight gain and possibly insulin and leptin resistance. Although antidepressant medications, such as selective serotonin reuptake inhibitors (SSRIs), are effective in raising serotonin in the short term, some evidence suggests these medications actually deplete serotonin in the long term. Plus, weight gain is one of the most common side effects of antidepressant drugs.

Serotonin is just one of a host of neurotransmitters secreted by the brain to regulate mood, attention, and energy levels. Ongoing stress, just like depression, can deplete our serotonin reserves, leading to intense food cravings, particularly for sugar and refined carbohydrates that tend to mimic the soothing effects of serotonin. Persistently low serotonin leads to sagging energy, bouts of depression, worrying, low self-esteem, difficulty making decisions, early morning waking, and compulsive eating.

Researchers from Tufts University have provided scientific support for the close link between anxiety disorders, depression, and higher risk of obesity. A study published in the March 2006 issue of the *Archives of Pediatrics and Adolescent Medicine* discusses the involvement of serotonin in both mood and appetite regulation. The data show that patients suffering from depression (and, therefore, low serotonin) often turn to food, particularly carbohydrates, to temporarily boost their levels.

In light of the clear link between obesity and depressed levels of serotonin (and dopamine, as you'll soon see), the likelihood is that many overweight and obese patients suffer from an imbalance of these hormones. To successfully initiate appetite control and weight loss, therefore, brain chemistry must be addressed along with blood sugar and insulin balance. The catch is that insulin resistance, often associated with obesity, also blocks the activity of serotonin in the brain. Successful treatment, then, must be aimed at restoring the body's response to insulin while also improving serotonin levels and activity within the brain.

Hormonal Imbalance 15—Low Melatonin
Marvelous Melatonin: The Secret to Restorative Sleep

Melatonin is released from the pineal gland and regulates your 24-hour body clock. It normally increases after darkness falls, making us feel drowsy. Acting as a hormone, melatonin influences nervous system function, as well as the endocrine and immune systems. Melatonin production typically peaks between 1 and 3 a.m., while you are asleep in the dark. Exposure to even small amounts of light from, say, the moon or your digital alarm clock, or to electromagnetic radiation from TVs, heating pads, or electric blankets, disrupts this process. Your melatonin production can also be compromised if you regularly take aspirin or ibuprofen, consume caffeinated products, drink alcohol, or smoke.

Because melatonin is a derivative of serotonin, its production is also dependent on adequate protein in your diet, which provides tryptophan, the amino acid building block of both melatonin and serotonin. Melatonin naturally tends to decline with age and menopause, which makes supplementation a helpful, natural option for people over 45 who experience sleep problems.

The Many Effects of Melatonin

Melatonin is a powerful antioxidant that maintains youthfulness, improves sleep, perks up libido, and boosts energy and resistance to infections. It affects your ability to fall asleep and stay asleep, as well as your sleep quality. It also indirectly influences your body composition through its relationship with growth hormone.

Melatonin aids in turning on the body's nighttime repair processes by allowing for a slight, but essential, dip in body temperature. Once the body has cooled sufficiently, growth hormone is released and begins to work its magic, repairing and rebuilding bone, skin, and muscle cells while we sleep. As an added bonus, melatonin decreases cortisol and protects us from the harmful effects of stress. Thanks to its dual effects on growth hormone and cortisol, melatonin helps our metabolic rate by preserving muscle tissue.

When melatonin goes up, serotonin goes down. For example, melatonin levels are known to rise in the winter, when we have less sunlight exposure. The correlative drop in serotonin is thought to be one of the main causes of seasonal depression, also known as seasonal affective disorder (SAD). Increased carbohydrate cravings and weight gain are common symptoms of SAD. Eating more carbs in turn causes the body to step up its production of serotonin. This technique can be an effective way to keep negative moods at bay, as long as it is used in moderation. Unfortunately, we tend to overeat comfort foods (such as chips, cookies, and candy) that pump up serotonin and leave us feeling fat, fuzzy, and even more depressed.

Hormonal Imbalance 2—Low Dopamine
Dopamine: The Pleasure "Rush"

If you are searching for stimulation or, as the song says, you just "can't get no satisfaction," you could probably use a good dose of dopamine. Dopamine is the neurotransmitter that's heavily involved in the pleasure center within the brain. It's released in high amounts during gratifying activities such as eating, sex, and other naturally enjoyable experiences. Being in love, fun social interactions, giving, exercise, and dancing are just a few of the activities that give you a pleasurable dopamine boost.

As a brain chemical, dopamine influences well-being, alertness, learning, creativity, attention, and concentration. Dopamine also controls motor functions and muscle tension, which explains why a deficiency of this hormone is linked to Parkinson's disease and restless leg syndrome (RLS), as well as cognitive changes such as depression, low libido, attention disorders, memory loss, and difficulties with problem solving.

While too little dopamine can leave us craving food, sex, or stimulation, too much can cause addictive behaviors. For instance, Parkinson's patients taking medications to support dopamine levels have been shown to become involved in gambling when their medications were increased. Paranoia or a suspicious personality may arise from too much dopamine, although more of this hormone in the frontal area of the brain relieves pain and boosts feelings of pleasure.

Dopamine isn't released only during pleasurable experiences, but also in the presence of high amounts of stress. So—pleasure and pain are closely related.

Dopamine and Addiction

Many researchers today agree that dopamine is one of the reasons why foods can be addictive. We also know stress stimulates the production of dopamine, which provides us with more energy, drive, and motivation, just as the addictive stimulants chocolate, caffeine (coffee, tea), sugar, and cigarettes can. This means we can become as addicted to stress as we can to stimulants simply because we are searching for a dopamine rush to beat fatigue.

Not surprisingly, almost all abusive drugs and addictive substances influence dopamine production. Alcohol, cocaine, nicotine, amphetamines, and even sugar can mess with our dopamine balance. According to Dr. Nora Volkow, director of the National Institute on Drug Abuse (NIDA), many smokers eat more when they are trying to quit because both food and nicotine share similar dopamine reward pathways. When less dopamine is stimulated as nicotine is reduced, food and sugar cravings naturally kick in to compensate. Fortunately, the Hormone Diet promotes strategies such as eating smaller amounts more frequently, enjoying more sex, not skipping meals, and increasing exercise, all of which can help provide the body with a natural dose of dopamine.

Dopamine for Weight Loss

Besides the many pleasures dopamine brings, this substance naturally suppresses appetite and aids weight loss. Antidepressant drugs such as bupropion (Wellbutrin or Zyban), which act on dopamine receptors in the brain, have been found to help with weight loss. A study at Duke University Medical Center showed weight loss occurred within just a few weeks and remained after a period of 2 years with bupropion use. Many of the study participants who took dopamine also reported feeling satisfied with smaller amounts of food.

Unfortunately, the body tends to work against us when it comes to dopamine production. Researchers at Princeton University found dopamine *decreased* in rats when they *lost weight* on restricted eating programs. With this drop in weight, *the rats' appetites increased and they began to eat more in an attempt to naturally restore dopamine levels.* How does this research translate for us? Supplements such as L-tyrosine, which increases the production of dopamine, may be beneficial to blunt the dopamine drop that occurs with weight loss and may ultimately allow us to sustain better appetite control.

Hormonal Imbalance 14—Low Acetylcholine
Aces for Acetylcholine

Acetylcholine is the neurotransmitter essential to the flow of communication between nerves and muscles. Movement, coordination, and muscle tone are influenced by acetylcholine because it is the messenger molecule that allows your muscles to contract.

The more we exercise, the more acetylcholine we use up. Athletes often have significant reductions in acetylcholine levels following strenuous activities such as running, cycling, and swimming. We can, however, use natural supplements that stimulate the production of choline, the building block of acetylcholine, to vastly improve stamina and even reduce post-exercise fatigue.

Keeping acetylcholine levels high is one of the secrets to maintaining strong, healthy, metabolically active muscle. Acetylcholine also stimulates growth hormone release, thereby improving tissue healing, promoting muscle growth, improving skin tone and bone density, and aiding fat loss (especially abdominal fat).

Besides muscle movement, REM sleep, memory, mental alertness, concentration, and learning are linked to acetylcholine. Healthy digestion and regularity are also controlled by the chemical message acetylcholine delivers to smooth muscle cells along the digestive tract. Acetylcholine declines naturally with aging. Combined with a decrease in physical activity, this drop could be a contributing factor to the constipation that plagues so many people later in life. This depletion is also thought to be one of the major culprits behind age-related memory loss, depression, mood changes, insomnia, and Alzheimer's disease.

Hormone Imbalance 4—Low GABA
Get Mellow with GABA

Gamma-aminobutyric acid (GABA) is a naturally calming, inhibitory neurotransmitter involved in relaxation, healthy sleep, digestion, and the easing of muscle tension, pain, and anxiety. GABA appears to regulate the activity of our stimulating neurotransmitters dopamine, serotonin, and noradrenaline. It calms us down and indirectly helps with fat loss because of its beneficial effects on sleep, stress, tension reduction, and mood. Progesterone supports the activity of GABA, which may explain why many women using natural progesterone (orally or topically in creams) experience better sleep and less anxiety. And, of course, when your mood is better, you tend to make better food choices and take better care of yourself.

Leptin: Your Body Likes It Level

Leptin plays a key role in metabolism and the regulation of fatty tissue. It's released by your fat cells in amounts commensurate with overall body-fat stores. In other words, the more body fat you have, the higher your leptin will be. Leptin acts as a signal to the brain that allows us to determine when we are full or when we should continue eating—*when we respond to it properly.*

Gregory Morton, assistant research professor of medicine at Harborview Medical Center at the University of Washington, has investigated how leptin works on our hypothalamus to influence blood sugar metabolism and the stability of energy in the body. He found a direct relationship between insulin, leptin levels, and body fat stores. In fact, his work has shown that proper leptin signals in the brain effectively reduce our food intake, keep body weight down, and improve insulin sensitivity.

Because leptin levels naturally increase while we sleep, sleep deprivation can cause a significant drop in leptin. This depletion causes us to feel excessively hungry, which in turn leads to overeating.

Along with getting a good night's sleep, we can improve leptin production and our cellular sensitivity to leptin with regular exercise; sufficient caloric intake; consumption of healthy, unsaturated fats; and general weight loss. Good thing these activities are all covered in the Hormone Diet three-step plan!

The Benefits of Just the Right Amount of Leptin

- Lowers body weight
- Lowers percentage of body fat
- Reduces food intake
- Reduces blood sugar
- Reduces insulin
- Increases metabolic rate
- Increases body temperature (in fact, high leptin causes excessive sweating)
- Increases our activity level
- Inhibits the synthesis and release of appetite-stimulating neuropeptide Y (NPY)

Although balanced leptin offers many health-promoting, antiaging benefits, too much of this hormone is not a good thing. Excessive saturated fat and sugar intake and obesity can lead to soaring leptin levels and ultimately to **leptin resistance** (and insulin resistance—in truth, when we have one of these conditions, we most likely have the other, which is why I did not include leptin in the Hormone Health Profile). Under this condition, the brain no longer responds to leptin's appetite-suppressing signals. In the absence of leptin's controlling mechanism, appetite can surge, even when plenty of leptin is present. Leptin resistance is linked directly to obesity, insulin resistance, and inflammation, which means it must be addressed right at the outset of an effective treatment plan to allow for optimal weight-loss results. Unfortunately, the discovery of high leptin in obese individuals has dampened the hope of using leptin as a treatment for obesity, but researchers are still very focused on investigating this option.

Vital Vitamin D$_3$

Vitamin D is made from cholesterol with the help of the liver, kidneys, and skin when we're exposed to natural sunlight. In your body, vitamin D functions as a hormone. Production decreases with age, stress, sunscreen use, low cholesterol, and also when your liver or kidneys are not working well. Suboptimal vitamin D

status is associated with bone disease (osteoporosis), diabetes, cancer, heart disease, inflammation, depression, and autoimmune disease. Some sources suggest muscle weakness, especially in the legs, is also a symptom of low vitamin D.

I have used vitamin D supplements for many years to treat seasonal affective disorder in my patients because it improves the action of serotonin in the brain. The Canadian Cancer Society recently recommended vitamin D supplementation as a protection against cancer of the breast, colon, and prostate. Vitamin D is also intricately involved with the regulation of insulin activity in the body, making it a very useful supplement for diabetics and those at risk of diabetes, including obese individuals. Vitamin D has been proven to improve immune system function and shows promise in the treatment of autoimmune diseases such as multiple sclerosis. All these findings have led me to recommend a daily dose of 2,000 to 5,000 IU of vitamin D to all my patients, even in the summer. It's a vital component of your basic supplement plan, outlined later in Step 2.

**VITAMIN D₃ DEFICIENCY
AND INSULIN RESISTANCE IN
PREGNANCY**

According to a study published in *Diabetes Metabolism Research and Review* (July 2007), more than 70 percent of pregnant women are deficient in vitamin D (< 25 nmol/L). Furthermore, the data reveal a positive relationship between vitamin D status and insulin sensitivity. Researchers now suggest that vitamin D deficiency could be used as a diagnostic indicator of insulin resistance.

Once again, you can sit back, relax, and take a deep breath.

Now that you have a handle on your hormones, the next logical step is to begin imagining the strong, fat-burning machine your body is going to become. You can do this much more easily once you have mastered the topic of the next chapter. It's all about your muscle and your fat.

CHAPTER 5

SKINNY OR FAT ISN'T WHERE IT'S AT: THE FACTS ABOUT BODY COMPOSITION

Here's what you will learn in this chapter:
- All about healthy body composition
- How to read your Hormone Body-Fat Map
- How fat fuels inflammation
- How fat is a hormonal hotbed
- All about marvelous muscle—hard bodies and hormonal wellness

Optimizing your muscle-to-fat ratio is one of the primary goals of the Hormone Diet. In this chapter, I'll explain why your fat and muscle determine a whole lot more than how you look in a tight T-shirt or how much you can bench press. Your balance of fat and muscle tissue dictates many facets of your health, including your hormonal stability, tendency toward inflammation, and potential for aging well. In fact, one of the best ways to slow the aging process is to maintain plenty of lean muscle and keep your body fat low.

Where's the Fat?
In general, fat's stored in two places in your body—as subcutaneous fat under the skin or as visceral fat in the abdominal cavity surrounding our organs.

Fat under your skin tends to accumulate in such lovely spots as the backs of your arms, the love handle above each hip, the sides of your back just under your shoulder blades, and on your belly, buttocks, and thighs. Women tend to have more subcutaneous fat and less visceral fat than men. More subcutaneous fat may be one of the reasons why women also tend to accumulate more cellulite.

Too much fat in any of these storage sites isn't good for us, but visceral fat is especially damaging to our health since it's linked to insulin resistance, heart disease, and diabetes. Fat in the abdominal region is a big red flag telling us the body is likely secreting excess insulin and is subject to inflammation.

Thousands of studies have documented the link between high insulin and abdominal fat. The sad truth is that the more visceral fat we have, the more insulin resistant we become, and the more abdominal fat we store. It's yet another vicious circle that leads to more and more ab fat accumulation.

Cynthia Buffington, director of research at US Bariatric, in an article called "Obesity Begets Obesity" states that "Various studies, including our own, have shown changes in the production (or clearance) of certain hormones in association with increasing body weight and regional fat distribution. Such hormonal changes may promote further weight gain and influence where the fat is distributed on the body," which sums up this concept nicely. The more overweight we become, the more likely our body is to develop its own agenda in order to cope. Packing on pound after pound is like tossing gasoline on the brushfire of hormonal imbalance.

Those of us with more visceral fat will experience more inflammation and higher amounts of the stress hormone cortisol. A study from the *Journal of Psychosomatic Medicine* (September/October 2000) completed by researchers at Yale University found that even slender women with high stress (and therefore cortisol) had more abdominal fat. So no matter what your body type, more cortisol, just like more insulin, equals more ab fat.

Research has also shown that our levels of precious, recuperative growth hormone tend to decrease as we accumulate more fat around the midsection.

Then there's the impact on testosterone. When more belly fat is present, this masculinizing hormone plummets in men and rises in women. Researchers from the University of Virginia Health System found high levels of androgens such as testosterone in obese girls in the early stages of puberty, which increases their risk of more severe health problems later in life.

So hormones can determine where you store fat, and fat stored in specific areas fuels hormonal imbalance—quite a quandary indeed. Of course, where your fat accumulates can have something to do with genetics, which is something we cannot change. But I believe our environment, daily habits, and hormones—factors we *can* control—have a much greater impact than our genetic predisposition. Studies involving twins growing up in different environments provide excellent support for this. If genetics was the determining factor, we would expect both twins to have similar health concerns regardless of their living arrangements, but this isn't the case. Clearly, healthy lifestyle habits are equally, if not more, important in the prevention of the expression of disease-causing genes.

Your Hormone Body-Fat Map

Where you store your fat says a lot about your hormonal state. Take a look at the following Hormone Body-Fat Map to see a clearer picture of the relationship between your hormonal imbalances and fat stores. These are the spots you should pay attention to once you start your three-step fix: Watch them change as you regain hormonal balance. Note that the same storage sites can reveal different information for men and women.

Fat-Storage Site	Hormonal Imbalance: Women	Hormonal Imbalance: Men
Belly or abdomen (apple shape)	Low/high estrogen High testosterone High cortisol High insulin Low growth hormone	High estrogen Low testosterone High cortisol High insulin Low growth hormone
Back of the arm (triceps)	High insulin Low DHEA	High insulin Low DHEA
Hips/buttocks/hamstrings (pear shape)	High estrogen Low progesterone	High estrogen
"Love handles" (above the hips)	Insulin and blood sugar imbalance	Insulin and blood sugar imbalance
Chest (over the pectoral muscles)	High estrogen	High estrogen (often coupled with high insulin and low testosterone)
Back ("bra fat")	High testosterone High insulin	High insulin
Thighs	Low growth hormone	Low growth hormone

Don't Be Frail or Fat—Be Fit!

Once you have a handle on your hormones, appetite, and where your fat is at, you need to form a clear picture of the body you are striving for. Guess what, it won't be the body of all those supermodels who say they never work out. Their oh-so-glam diet of caffeine, nicotine, and lettuce is not the solution for you.

You might be surprised to learn that many of the outwardly beautiful women we see in magazines may actually have a high percentage of body fat. And they could unknowingly be laying the groundwork for many chronic diseases associated with aging because they lack sufficient, healthy muscle.

Being superthin is very different from being superhealthy. The distinction lies in understanding body composition—the ratio of lean to fatty tissue that makes up your total body weight. Your body is composed of many tissues, including fat, bones, muscles, tendons, ligaments, and organs, and also plenty of water. Healthy body composition is determined not by the number on your scale or the size of your jeans but by your percentage of fat versus lean muscle. Keeping the percentage of fat *low* and lean muscle mass *high* is ideal for maximizing your strength, wellness, and hormonal balance.

Excess fat, bone loss, and muscle loss are all factors that can result in altered body composition. The "skinny-fat person" is someone who appears slim but has a high percentage of body fat. In this case, body composition is not altered by excess fat, but rather by an unhealthy deficiency of muscle. Let's look at an example of one of my real patients, since I haven't seen many supermodels in my clinic lately.

I had a 34-year-old male patient

> **DO I LOOK FAT?**
>
> In 1991, researchers V. W. Chang and N. A. Christakis analyzed how adults classified their weight and found we really have no idea! About 28 percent of overweight people judged their weight to be "just about right." The breakdown of this statistic between men and women, however, is truly fascinating. Forty percent of overweight men thought their weight was just about right, whereas 29 percent of women viewed themselves as overweight when they were actually normal weight. If this study was conducted again today, I suspect even more women—and men—would judge themselves to be overweight.

HOT HORMONE FACT

who, at 5 feet 10 inches, weighed only 132 pounds. I measured his body fat and the reading told me it was an unfavorable 22 percent. (The optimal percentage for men his age is 14 percent.) He was certainly not overweight, but he had an alarmingly low percentage of muscle. He had been vegan for over 12 years, which meant his diet probably lacked the protein needed to build and maintain muscle. Moreover, he had never done resistance training, only yoga. When I looked at his basal metabolic rate, I saw that it was a whopping 500 calories below the optimum for someone his age. Based on the rough estimate that to maintain 1 pound of muscle requires about 50 calories a day, he needed to safely gain at least 10 pounds of muscle to safely create a healthier body composition.

We worked together to balance his diet and recuperate his body from stress. Then he began the Hormone Diet exercise plan to build muscle—and his results were remarkable!

Obese versus Overweight

Obesity is a much more common form of altered body composition than the skinny-fat scenario. Not everyone who is overweight, however, is obese. Overweight individuals are classified as having 25 to 30 percent body fat. Obesity is clinically defined as a body fat percentage higher than 30, and although obesity is more common in women, men are more likely to be overweight.

Measuring Body Fat

Body composition is sometimes measured by body mass index (BMI), calculated by dividing weight by height. A BMI in the range of 25 to 29.9 is considered overweight, whereas 30 or more is considered clinically obese. A BMI of 40 or more is considered morbidly obese. These measurements can prove inaccurate for assessing body composition in people who are very short, very muscular, very tall, or who have edema (swelling and water retention). I don't use BMI charts very often, for these reasons.

Instead I use a professional bioimpedance analysis (BIA) machine in conjunction with waist circumference and waist-to-hip ratio measurements. The BIA has been used in thousands of clinical studies as a simple method to assess body fat percentage. It works by sending an electrical frequency through your body. This may sound spooky, but you feel nothing during the test. Different tissues conduct the signal at different rates, so the machine can provide a quick assessment of the amount of fat, water, and muscle in your body.

Typically, the electrical signal travels from your hand to your foot. This method is best because the signal zips through your whole body and can more accurately measure whether more fat is stored in your top or bottom half. The signal can also go from hand to hand via a handheld device or foot to foot while you stand barefoot on a specialized scale. Readings are most reliable first thing in the morning, after you have had some water but no food, since BIA readings are affected by hydration, electrolytes, eating, and exercise.

Although BIA testing is easier, calipers or skin-fold testing may be more accurate. Skin-fold testing is difficult to do on your own, so I recommend you invest in a BIA machine for home to use as an adjunct to your wellness plan. The BIA may not be 100 percent accurate, but it will be a great help in monitoring your progress over time. Check out www.tanita.com for more information on obtaining a BIA machine. Prices may range from $75 to $300.

Acceptable and Optimal Body-Fat Compositions for Men and Women				
	Men		Women	
Age Range	Acceptable % Range	Optimal %	Acceptable % Range	Optimal %
15–20	10–18	13	17–25	20
21–30	10–18	13	17–25	20
31–40	10–18	14	17–25	21
41–50	10–18	15	17–25	22
51–60	10–18	16	17–25	23
61–70	10–18	17	17–25	24
71–80	10–18	18	17–25	25
> 80	10–18	18	17–25	25

HEALTHY BODY FAT PERCENTAGES

Monitoring changes in body fat is especially valuable if you only have about 10 to 20 pounds to lose and you are doing resistance training. This is the method we use at Clear Medicine and it provides a wonderful source of motivation for our patients. In this scenario, the number on the scale may not change much, but you will be able to measure favorable changes in your body composition, such as muscle gain and fat loss.

Significant health problems are associated with obesity, including high blood pressure, osteoarthritis, heart disease, diabetes, stroke, sleep apnea, decreased quality of life, and premature death. Second only to smoking, obesity is a leading cause of preventable deaths.

Sadly, despite the known health risks, most of us are fat and getting fatter!

- According to figures published by the World Health Organization (WHO), by the year 2015 some 2.3 billion adults will be overweight and more than 700 million will suffer from obesity, a pathology seen in growing numbers of children.
- From 1980 to 2000, the percentage of obese Americans more than doubled, from 15 to 31 percent.
- Nearly 50 percent of adults in the developed world are overweight or outright obese.
- Africa has long been regarded as a continent plagued by famine, undernourishment, and starvation. However, as African populations have become increasingly Westernized, the number of overweight and obese people has skyrocketed. Once-undernourished populations have just as high an incidence of obesity as the United States, the current world leader in this condition. Today, more than 25 percent of Egyptians and 40 to 50 percent of South Africans are already obese.

Your Fat Sends Messages—The Hormones Produced by Fat

Over the last decade, scientists have made truly amazing discoveries about fat. Turns out it's not just an annoyance that hangs around making us feel unhappy about our appearance. Fat is now actually recognized as endocrine tissue that constantly sends and receives hormonal signals to regulate body weight, control inflammation, manage our appetite, direct blood clotting, and determine how our cells respond to insulin. Wow!

The worst part? *Fat fuels fat.* That's right—the more fat we accumulate, the greater our risk of obesity. With all the hormonal signals being sent and received from our fat, our fat actually controls how much more fat we store. As a result, we need to take charge of our fat cells to successfully initiate and maintain fat loss. The more fat we have, the more difficult this process; but taking charge is definitely doable and worth the effort.

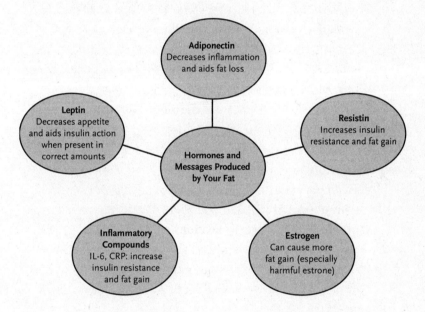

THE HORMONES AND ADIPOKINES PRODUCED BY FAT

In both men and women, fat tissue is a huge source of estrogen production because it contains the aromatase enzyme, which converts testosterone to estrogen. The links between estrogen dominance, obesity, and cancer are undeniable.

Other hormones produced in *and* sent out from your fat cells include leptin, resistin, and adiponectin.

The names may sound alien, but these tiny chemical signals (actually proteins produced by your fat cells) travel to your liver, brain, muscles, and other sites throughout your body. They're vital for keeping appetite under control and for shrinking your fat stores. Researchers have found that adiponectin *increases fat burning and*

SIMPLE, POWERFUL MEASUREMENT: WAIST CIRCUMFERENCE AND WAIST-TO-HIP RATIO

One of the quickest ways to determine whether you are hormonally imbalanced is to measure your waist-to-hip ratio (WHR). Calculating your WHR determines definitively whether the weight around your midsection exceeds that surrounding your hips and thighs.

Measure your waist just above your belly button, at the narrowest part of your waist. Measure your hips around the widest part of your buttocks, while standing with your feet together. A waist measurement of more than 35 inches for women or more than 40 inches for men is pushing into the unhealthy range. Next, calculate your WHR by dividing the measurement of your waist by the measurement of your hips.

If your WHR is greater than 0.9 for men or 0.8 for women, you are also at risk.

For example: Let's say Mary's waist measures 28 inches and her hips are 33 inches. Her waist-to-hip ratio would be calculated as follows: $28 \div 33 = 0.84$. Because 0.8 is considered unsafe for women, Mary is at risk and needs to lose some belly fat. (I suppose she could also try gaining weight on her hips, but I have never had a patient go for this option!)

aids our insulin sensitivity. You can think of adiponectin as the fat factor that leads to its own demise. It's produced by your fat, yet helps to burn it up! Like leptin, adiponectin is definitely a fat-loss friend.

Adiponectin and leptin work in opposition to resistin, a hormone that contributes to fat gain by directly causing insulin resistance in the liver and muscle cells. While adiponectin aids fat burning, resistin actually fuels more fat from fat.

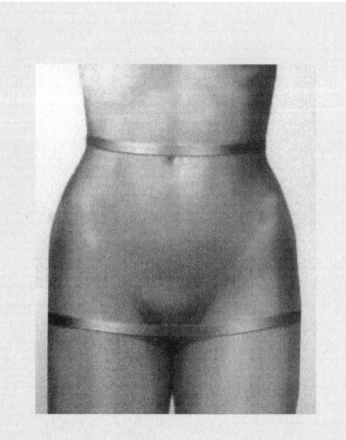

WAIST-TO-HIP MEASUREMENT

Adiponectin also offers us protection against inflammation caused by other compounds produced in the fat cells, called adipokines. Our fat tissues are now recognized as major culprits behind rampant inflammation, one of our major fat-loss foes. Pro-inflammatory compounds like TNF-alpha, IL-6, resistin, and C-reactive protein (CRP) arise from our fat cells and are also known to surge as both body fat and insulin resistance increase. These chemicals directly contribute to arterial damage, insulin resistance, leptin resistance, and heart disease and are typically about 30 percent *more prevalent* in obese people.

When you're fat, your body sets up a hormonal cascade that stimulates more fat, since adipokines create more fat cells, modulate the size of our fat deposits, contribute to inflammation, and influence the distribution of body fat. A 2000 study published in *Endocrine Review* showed abdominal fat in particular produced larger numbers of inflammatory mediators than other types of fat in the body—*ab fat truly is a fire in your belly.* The trouble is that attempting to lose fat while we are inflamed is something like trying to drain a sink with the stopper still in. The hormones that help us to get lean are blocked and fat loss becomes excruciatingly difficult. We absolutely must cool the fire of inflammation first to allow for successful fat loss.

Hormonal Messages Received by Our Fat

While our fat cells do plenty of communicating, they are also continuously receiving hormonal messages that can affect their size, number, distribution, and insulin sensitivity. Here's where the messages received by your fat cells come from.

- **Your fat-loss foes:** Hormones and conditions that increase the size, number, and distribution of your fat cells. These include inflammation, insulin, estrogen, and cortisol.
- **Your fat-loss friends:** The hormones that decrease the size,

number, and distribution of fat cells. These include growth hormone, thyroid hormone, glucagon, adrenaline, DHEA, progesterone, leptin, and testosterone. (Note: Estrogen, when properly balanced, aids fat loss.)

Fat is only one part of your body composition story. Let's talk about the magnificent impact of muscle.

Muscle Is Marvelous for Your Metabolism

Sure, hard bodies look great on the beach and at the gym. Strong, lean muscles are not only important for how you look and feel—they're vital for your enduring wellness. On the most basic level, good skeletal muscle strength and function give you the stability you need to move, walk, run, and avoid falling. Good muscle tone has many additional benefits, even when the body is completely at rest. These include:

- **A major metabolic boost:** With the help of your thyroid hormones, muscle tissue dictates your metabolic rate. Fat is far less metabolically active than muscle, which means the more muscle you have, the more calories your body burns and the fewer calories you need to maintain your weight. As a result, gaining unwanted weight is much easier when you have *less* muscle, simply because you are *less* likely to use all the calories you take in each day.
- **Aiding insulin sensitivity:** Muscle cells are important targets for insulin, since most of our insulin receptors are present within muscle tissue. As we age and naturally lose muscle, the risk of insulin resistance increases. When our cells lose their sensitivity to insulin, more of this hormone must be produced in order for it to do its job, and we become more prone to weight gain.

Use It or Lose It!

Research shows that muscle strength declines by 15 percent per decade after age 50 and 30 percent per decade after age 70. As you might expect, along with this decline in muscle mass comes a 5 percent decrease per decade in our metabolic rate. This process of losing muscle mass, strength, and function with aging is called **sarcopenia.** Scientists have found that sarcopenia occurs not only because we grow older, but also because we stop doing activities that utilize, build, and maintain muscle power. So, the old adage is true—*use it if you don't want to lose it.*

Is Exercise Enough to Keep You Strong?

Sadly, excercise is not enough. Strength peaks in our midtwenties and then begins to decrease. Data collected from over 20 years of studies show that muscle tissue degenerates *even* in people who maintain a high level of physical activity. These findings indicate that other factors besides inactivity contribute to muscle loss. I believe the major culprits are:

- **Poor nutrition:** Insufficient protein, vitamins, and minerals to build and maintain healthy muscle cells
- **Free radical damage:** Damage to muscle-cell mitochondria leads to cell death (less muscle) or dysfunction (weaker muscle)
- **Inflammation**
- **Increased stress hormone:** Can be caused by excessive cardiovascular exercise, excessive caloric restriction, and disease, and also by emotional, environmental, mental, and physical stress
- **Hormone imbalance:** Decline of hormones that maintain muscle mass and strength, including testosterone, DHEA-S, growth hormone, and acetylcholine

Fortunately, the loss of muscle due to aging is partially reversible with the Hormone Diet's three-step approach.

Your muscle restoration program includes strength training, good sleep habits, inflammation control, stress management, glycemically balanced eating, natural hormone replacement (if necessary), and professional-strength supplements.

Lasting Fat Loss Means *Safe* Fat Loss

It appears that the most successful way to slow the aging process is to maintain healthy muscle mass and to eat a highly nutritious, low-calorie diet. But your diet should never involve extreme caloric restriction, no matter what the latest headlines say. *New York* magazine promoted one particular diet as "The Diet to End All Diets" (October 30, 2006) because it promised "the fewest calories your body can stand." Starving is not without its repercussions, as this type of caloric restriction can ravage both your hormonal balance and your metabolism. A weight-loss program that compromises muscle while you lose fat is metabolically harmful and only serves to speed the aging process. Not what you're looking for, I'm sure.

I tell my patients this: Your health reserves lie within your muscles. When faced with an illness, surgery, or other stressful event, your body will naturally tap into muscle tissue for energy to support you during the experience. Always do your best to make sure your reserves are full.

Safe fat loss means losing *only* fat while preserving muscle. A healthy, long-term solution avoids severe caloric restrictions or fad-diet approaches that are unsustainable and always result in hormonally driven rebound weight gain.

Remember, your body and your hormones are programmed to work against you by increasing your appetite and slowing your metabolic rate when you reduce your caloric intake. With a slowed metabolism, you gain weight and feel tired and sluggish. Conversely, using the correct weight-loss techniques will give your metabolism an energizing boost that leaves you feeling brighter and looking your best.

Study after study proves that many of the health complications associated with obesity improve with weight loss. But Dr. Samuel Klein, a professor at the Washington University School of Medicine, raised an important issue in his paper "Outcome Success in Obesity" published in the journal *Obesity Research* in 2001. Although Klein begins by stating that many health improvements kick in after only 5 to 10 percent of initial body weight is lost, he goes on to add: "There is no conclusive evidence that weight loss decreases mortality in obese people." Even though overweight people effectively lower their health risks when they shed pounds, Klein shows that *they still do not appear to live any longer.* Now, you might be thinking, Great, if I'm overweight, I might as well just stay this way. Not so. Klein's study does not tell us that losing weight is pointless; it instead provides us with valuable insight into why the *way* we lose weight is extremely important.

Dr. Klein notes that "Dietary intervention is the cornerstone of weight-loss therapy." Although I agree diet is important, it's just one facet of an effective program. Hormonal balance through sleep, detoxification, supplements, a toxin-free lifestyle, stress management, exercise, and conquering inflammation are just as important as your nutrition habits for safe and lasting weight loss. Finally, safe fat loss means completing a detox at the beginning of your weight-loss journey and again after the first few months, because *the majority of toxins in your body are stored within the fat cells.* While detox takes time and commitment, reducing the negative impact of toxins released during fat loss is critical to your health and your long-term weight-loss success.

You've reached the end of Part One. At this point your brain is surely chock-full with everything you'll ever need to know about your hormones, your muscle, your fat, and your metabolism. Now we're moving on to Part Two, The Three-Step Fix.

PART TWO

THE THREE-STEP FIX

Live in rooms full of light
Avoid heavy food
Be moderate in the drinking of wine
Take massage, baths, exercise, and gymnastics
Fight insomnia with gentle rocking or the sound of running water
Change surroundings and take long journeys
Strictly avoid frightening ideas
Indulge in cheerful conversation and amusements
Listen to music.

AULUS CORNELIUS CELSUS,
Roman encyclopedist, ca. 25 BC–ca. AD 50

INTRODUCING THE THREE-STEP FIX

Winning the War Against Fat

Imagine all the things you do and think in a day. From your smallest tasks to your biggest worries, all your habits, thoughts, and activities influence your hormones and, ultimately, your ability to lose fat. Naturally, the next question is, *What can you do to achieve and maintain the balance you need for the healthy body you want?*

The answer is all laid out for you here in my three-step fix. This three-step plan not only brings back the hormonal balance you need to accelerate fat loss, but it also addresses all potential causes of weight gain that prevent you from achieving your weight-loss goals, including:

- Hormonal imbalance
- Sleep deprivation or poor sleep habits
- Compromised digestion
- Toxicity or inadequate liver function
- pH imbalance (excess body acidity)
- Nasty nutrition and nutrient deficiencies
- Lack of exercise
- Lack of sex
- Toxic body-care products
- Inadequate body temperature regulation

Quite a list of offenders! I hope you now realize that if you haven't been successful at reaching or maintaining your fat-loss goals before, the problem may not be lack of discipline on your part.

The Hormone Diet Three-Step Fix

Because our hormones are so delicately intertwined, this plan is structured to allow each balancing step to set the stage for the next. To achieve optimal results that last, follow the guidelines in the order I have presented them, and move through each stage one at a time.

In the introduction of this book I told you that the Hormone Diet will offer you amazing results because of the precise way it helps you identify and effectively overcome the major fat-packing factors that accelerate weight gain and prevent fat loss. This program enables you to determine why you haven't been able to beat those last stubborn pounds. It then guarantees that you can reap the rewards of your hard work in the gym and discipline in the kitchen.

Now you can put all the science and philosophy you've learned into action. With the help of your Hormonal Health Profile results and the recommendations to come, implementing your action plan and accomplishing your health and weight-loss goals will be easier than you ever imagined.

Tips for the Three-Step Fix

First of all, don't rush. If you invest your efforts wisely now, you'll put an end to yo-yo dieting for good. Also, don't be concerned that I haven't included exercise, beyond walking, until the fourth week of your program (though you can continue working out if you are already doing so). The first two steps build your foundation for enduring, optimal results and prepare your body for the metabolic boost exercise offers.

You have the rest of your life to be lean, fit, strong, healthy, and vibrant. Imagine: After these 6 weeks, you'll never have to search out another "get-skinny-quick" approach again.

At the end of your three steps you can expect wonderful and lasting results such as these:

- Improved digestion
- Less pain and inflammation
- Restorative sleep
- Safe fat loss and increased muscle mass
- Improved strength and stability
- Glowing skin, healthier looking hair
- Better appetite control
- Increased energy and stress recuperation
- Stronger libido, sexual enjoyment, and increased fertility
- Metabolic revival
- Better mood, memory, and concentration
- Protection from many of the diseases of aging
- Slowed aging and illness prevention through maximized immunity and antioxidant defense

Before you begin, I encourage you to focus on achieving great health, feeling good, gaining strength, and building muscle, and *not* on attaining Hollywood's perception of the perfect body. Recall our discussion from Chapter 5. Your goal should be a healthy body that's strong and full of vitality. And remember, healthy weight loss means losing fat—not muscle.

Good luck with your three steps! I hope you find this process as enjoyable and rewarding as so many of my patients have.

The Hormone Diet Quick-Action Steps Guideline

You can skip my explanation of the rationale behind the three steps and begin the process right away with this course-of-action guideline.

Before starting your three-step process:

1. Complete the Best Body Assessment on pages 138 to 143 to determine your baseline health markers. It is not necessary to have any tests done through your doctor to complete your three-step program, but should you wish to visit your doctor for blood tests, consult Appendix A (page 399).

2. Complete the kitchen detox outlined on page 146, and shop for your detox using the shopping list on page 466.

Step 1: Renew and Revitalize

- Complete the bedroom detox and follow the rules for sleeping as described on pages 157 to 163. If you have difficulty sleeping, use the tips on pages 163 to 167 to help you, or select a natural sleep aid from pages 168 to 173.

- Your anti-inflammatory detox diet and detox supplement guidelines are outlined for you on pages 191 to 199. A quick reference chart of foods to enjoy and foods to avoid during your detox, as well as your supplement dosing guide, are on pages 205 to 207. Remember to follow the instructions for coming off the detox (see pages 197 to 199) to a T! Use the Hormone Diet Daily Wellness Tracker to monitor your nutrition and lifestyle habits as you begin your detox program, and continue to do so throughout your three-step process.

- Begin to implement and practice the strategies for stress survival that are summarized on page 231.

- A note about exercise when you begin your three-step process: If you are not exercising, don't worry about starting now—a simple walk after dinner will suffice. If you are exercising, just keep doing what you are doing.

Step 2: Replenish Your Body and Balance Your Hormones

- After your detox, implement the rules for the Glyci-Med dietary approach as described on pages 252 to 279. Sorry, there are no shortcuts here; I want you to understand and master all the rules of hormonally balanced nutrition.

- Begin taking the basic or advanced supplement plan for hormonal balance as summarized on page 293.
- At this stage you may add supplements, foods, or certain lifestyle habits to address your imbalances as identified by the Hormonal Health Profile. If you have not done so already, complete the Hormonal Health Profile on pages 38 to 51 and fill in your scores on the treatment pyramids on pages 53 and 295. The treatment pyramid on page 53 will identify the pages you should refer to if you wish to understand the impact of your hormonal imbalances on your health. The treatment pyramid on page 295 shows the pages you should refer to for treatment options for your hormonal imbalances. Please note that it is neither necessary nor recommended that you take all of the treatment options listed for a particular imbalance. Read through the options and select the one you feel is best suited to you.

Step 3: Restore Strength and Metabolism
- Read Chapter 14 to understand the importance of sex and exercise to your hormonal health.
- Begin the Hormone Diet workout as outlined on pages 342 to 369.
- Top off your efforts with natural skin care as explained on pages 376 to 384.

Follow-Up (6 to 8 weeks after beginning the Hormone Diet)
- Repeat the Best Body Assessment measurements as outlined on pages 138 to 143 to determine your progress.
- Consult the tips for beating a weight loss plateau, presented on pages 390 to 397, if you feel you need additional help.

CHAPTER 6

LAYING THE GROUNDWORK:
GETTING PREPPED FOR THE THREE STEPS

Here's what you can expect to complete by the end of this chapter:
- Your Best Body Assessment
- A kitchen mini-makeover
- Shopping for your detox

This chapter will give you the guidance needed to fully assess your body and risk factors for hormonal imbalance before embarking on your journey to optimal wellness. You'll also establish benchmarks—besides your weight—that will help you to monitor your health improvements and fat loss. First, you'll establish a quantifiable framework for hormonal balance, safe fat loss, and enduring wellness with your Best Body Assessment. The system that follows will provide you with the basic tools needed to manage your risk factors.

So many factors come together to create your total health picture. Your sleep, energy level, tolerance for exercise, memory, outlook on life, self-esteem, ability to laugh, sex life, quality of friendships, family role, connection to nature, spirituality, and coping skills are all factors that influence your overall health. Changes or disruptions in any of these areas are early warning signs of hormonal, and health, imbalances. You have to pay attention to and be aware of what's going on in your body and life. I've treated far too many patients who dismissed their feelings of fatigue or lack of libido for years. Believe me, taking charge of your health will always result in a better quality of life.

I also encourage you to believe you *are* healthy. Refuse to continue in an unhealthy environment, relationship, or job. Refuse to spend time worrying about your health—worry is simply praying to your fears. Make the choice, take action, and refuse to accept habits and circumstances that prevent you from achieving optimal health. You deserve to be happy and well!

> **THE SCALE CAN TRICK YOU**
> During weight loss, far too many of us fixate on the numbers on the scale. We can avoid this unhealthy trap by understanding that a handful of muscle actually weighs more than the same-sized handful of fat. Remember this concept if you feel frustrated because the number on your scale won't seem to budge. Instead, judge your progress by your Best Body Assessment, by how your clothes fit, and—most important—by how you look and feel.

Your Best Body Assessment

As discussed in Chapter 5, establishing your *body composition* and full range of body benchmarks will help you monitor your progress (and keep you motivated) far better than the number on your scale alone. Most of these variables can be measured easily at home with the right tools. The blood test, of course, will require a visit to your doctor's office. (I recommend you ask your family physician for a complete panel of blood tests at least once a year to continually monitor possible risk factors for disease.)

These are the tools you will need to successfully complete your Best Body Assessment.

1. A daily or weekly journal to record your efforts outside of this book. (I recommend this. It's better to record your habits and assessments more often than at the start and end of your 6 weeks.)
2. Litmus paper pH testing strips from your local health food store.
3. A flexible tape measure.
4. A scale.
5. A watch or heart rate monitor.

6. A bioimpedance analysis (BIA) machine is optional, but you can purchase a scale with a BIA built in. Visit www.tanita.com for information on obtaining a BIA for home use. If you can't afford one, don't worry; the rest of the Best Body Assessment measurements still provide a very good indication of your overall health. You can also visit an integrated doctor (MD, ND, or DC) or even a local health club for a body composition test.
7. If you have high blood pressure, I strongly suggest investing in a BP monitor to use at home daily. Check your local pharmacy.

When you have all the tools you need, complete your Best Body Assessment.

Your Best Body Assessment
1. Determine your body composition.

- Weigh yourself first thing in the morning on an empty stomach and record your body weight
  Start date: _____ End of 6 weeks: _____

- Waist measurement (Remember, this measurement should be < 40 inches for men; < 35 inches for women. Refer to page 120 for a refresher on how to take your waist and hip measurements properly.)
  Start date: _____ End of 6 weeks: _____

- Hip measurement
  Start date: _____ End of 6 weeks: _____

- Calculate your waist-to-hip ratio by dividing your waist measurement by your hip measurement (ideal waist-to-hip ratio is < 0.9 for men; < 0.8 for women)
  Start date: _____ End of 6 weeks: _____

- If possible, measure your body fat percentage via bio-impedance analysis either at home or at a local health club first thing in the morning on an empty stomach. (You may drink water beforehand.)

  Start date: _____ End of 6 weeks: _____

2. Check your body pH.

Acidity in the whole body (outside the stomach) is a major cause of hormonal imbalance. The measure of the acidity or alkalinity of a substance is its pH. The pH scale runs from 0 to 14. A lower pH number means higher acidity, and generally less oxygen is present. A higher pH indicates more alkalinity. A solution is considered neutral, neither acid nor alkaline, when it has a pH of 7. Our body continuously strives to maintain its normal, slightly alkaline pH balance of about 7.0 to 7.4. We experience health problems when the pH of our bodily fluids and tissues is pushed out of its comfortable neutral zone.

Understanding pH

Although the stomach should contain plenty of acid to do its job effectively, a slightly alkaline environment is optimal everywhere else to allow the body's metabolic, enzymatic, immunologic, and repair mechanisms to function at their best. The most common form of pH imbalance outside the stomach is *excess acidity*. This condition has become prevalent today because poor diet, insufficient or excessive exercise, and chronic stress can lead to excess acid in our internal environment. High-protein foods, processed cereals and flours, sugar, coffee, tea, and alcohol are acidifying, whereas vegetables, millet, soy, almonds, and wild rice are alkalinizing.

> **HOT HORMONE FACT**
>
> **REDUCE EXCESS BODY ALKALINITY**
>
> Excess alkalinity in the body is rare but requires treatment with supplements of calcium-magnesium and green food. It can be an indication of insufficient protein intake or endocrine imbalance.

When our body becomes acidic, minerals such as potassium, sodium, magnesium, and calcium may be stolen from our vital organs and bones to combat or buffer the acid. If these mineral losses and metabolic abnormalities continue, we increase our risk of developing a number of conditions, including:

- Obesity, slow metabolism, weight gain, and inability to lose weight
- Chronic inflammation
- High blood pressure
- Diabetes
- Bladder and kidney conditions, including kidney stones
- Weakened immunity
- Premature aging
- Osteoporosis: weak, brittle bones; fractures; and bone spurs
- Joint pain, aching muscles, and lactic acid buildup
- Low energy and chronic fatigue
- Mood swings
- Slow digestion and elimination
- Yeast/fungal overgrowth

These problems are not surprising, since excess acid also interferes with our hormones. For example, in an acidic environment, as much as twice the amount of estrogen may be needed to exert its effects in the body, and neither thyroid nor growth hormone will work at their best.

If you have a health problem, you are likely a walking acid trip. No matter what type of therapy you choose to treat your condition, resolution will not come until your pH balance is restored.

You will enjoy the most dramatic results from the three-step system when your body is slightly alkaline. Acidity decreases your body's ability to absorb the vitamins and minerals from your foods and supplements, interferes with your ability to detoxify, disrupts your metabolism, and makes you more prone to fatigue and mood changes. For all these reasons, I have included pH testing as part of your Best Body Assessment.

Test your saliva or urine using litmus paper strips purchased from your local health food store or from www.thehormonediet.com.

WHEN?
Test your pH first thing in the morning or 1 hour before a meal or 2 hours after eating.

HOW?
Saliva: *Before* brushing your teeth, fill your mouth with saliva and swallow; repeat; *spit directly on* the pH test strip. This three-step process will ensure a clean saliva sample. Measure your saliva pH in the same manner again later in the day, at least 2 hours after eating.

Urine: Collect a small sample of your first morning urine in a clean glass container; dip the pH strip into the container.

In either case, match your strip to the associated color on the package of pH papers to determine your pH.

◄ acidic pH 6.0 ———————————————————————————— alkaline pH 8.0 ►

| 6.0 | 6.4 | 6.6 | 7.0 | 7.2 | 7.6 | 8.0 |

Record your pH measurement here:
    Start date: _____ End of 6 weeks: _____

WHAT'S NORMAL?
If the pH of your saliva stays between 7.0 and 7.4 all day, your body is functioning within a healthy range. If your urinary pH fluctuates

between 6.0 and 6.5 in the morning and 6.5 and 7.0 in the evening, your body is within a healthy pH range. First morning urine should be slightly more acidic, as you eliminate waste accumulated throughout the night.

Continue to measure your pH daily if your values are abnormal; otherwise, testing once a week will suffice.

TIPS TO REDUCE EXCESS BODY ACIDITY

- Most fruits and vegetables are highly alkalinizing. If you follow the Hormone Diet as presented and ensure two-thirds of your plate is occupied by veggies at lunch and dinner, you will get a minimum of 8 to 10 servings a day.
- A nice mug of warm lemon water upon rising and/or prior to meals can cleanse your liver, stimulate the flow of digestive juices, and reduce body acidity.
- Have a daily helping of alkalinizing greens, such as 1 cup of spinach, kale, collards, mustard greens, rapini, watercress, or bok choy.
- Choose millet and quinoa to replace acid-forming grains such as wheat and rye.
- Use either a juicer or a blender to make your own alkaline juices and smoothies at home. Powdered green-food supplements are also very helpful. I use one first thing each morning on an empty stomach. Make blender drinks using alkaline juices, green powdered supplements, and fruits.
- Use olive oil, which is less acid-forming than other vegetable oils.
- Use buffered vitamin C to alkalinize the system and increase your absorption of magnesium.
- The sleep and stress tips that make up Step 1 of your three-step program (especially your breathing/meditation exercise) will improve acid balance and promote alkalinity. Your exercise plan

also helps because of its stress-reducing properties.

• If the above suggestions do not restore your body's pH balance, purchase an alkalinizing product such as Tri-Alkali Powder from Pure Encapsulations or Basictabs from BioMed and take as directed. (See www.clearmedicinestore.com.)

3. Measure your blood pressure.

If you don't have a blood pressure (BP) monitor at home, check it at your local pharmacy or your doctor's office. Optimal BP is 110/70 and shouldn't increase with age. When I find readings of 125/80 or higher with my patients, I begin mild hypotensive therapy, which includes salt restriction and supplementation with potassium and magnesium and the amino acid L-arginine, in addition to the three steps.

Monitor your blood pressure daily if you currently have high blood pressure or are at risk.

Start date: _____ End of 6 weeks: _____

4. Measure your resting heart rate.

You may do this by recording your pulse as soon as you awaken, *before you get out of bed*. Measure your pulse for 15 seconds, then multiply the number by 4 to calculate your number of heartbeats per minute. Note that if your pulse increases from one week to the next, you may be overexercising.

Start date: _____ End of 6 weeks: _____

5. Visit your doctor and request one blood test.

To achieve maximal fat loss, we must identify all the invisible, internal factors that can interfere with metabolism. We also want to get a baseline for *early* identification of disease risk factors. I can't stress enough the importance of annual blood testing—it can mean the difference between life and death.

For the purposes of this fat-loss program, however, I suggest a blood test that will assess your *insulin sensitivity*. Although the Hormonal Health Profile helps to identify many signs of insulin resistance, the blood work will provide definitive proof. We can also use the results of these tests as a major marker to monitor your progress. I recommend taking the test and repeating it after you have completed your three steps and are living your new lifestyle.

Don't stress if you can't get to the doctor or don't want to have your blood drawn. Your waist-to-hip ratio and Hormonal Health Profile (the group of signs/symptoms for Hormonal Imbalance 1) will still provide good insight into your insulin sensitivity. But please make sure that you still keep up with your regular blood tests at your annual physical.

THE BLOOD TEST YOU NEED

- Your *fasting* blood glucose and insulin
  and
- A *2-hour pp* blood glucose and insulin test (This is basically the same glucose and insulin test repeated 2 hours after you have eaten.)

HOW IT'S DONE:

You'll go to the lab first thing in the morning with an empty stomach. The technician will draw a sample of your blood to test your glucose and insulin. You'll then leave the lab and eat a big breakfast (e.g., orange juice, toast, pancakes, etc.). Brace yourself—the perfect meal may actually be a McDonald's breakfast of hot cakes with syrup and orange juice! You'll wait and then return to the lab to have your blood drawn again to test your glucose and insulin levels 2 hours later. Do not exercise during this time span.

This test will reveal exactly what's happening with your glucose and insulin in both the fasting and fed states.

If your insulin is elevated at any point, your risk of diabetes is greater. *In fact, if your insulin is elevated you are considered to be a hyperinsulin secretor, displaying signs of insulin resistance.* More specifically, *abnormal* findings are indicated by the following test results:

Fasting insulin: >7 IU/mL

2 hours after eating insulin: >60 IU/mL

Fasting glucose: >86 mg/dL

2 hours after eating glucose: >100 mg/dL

If you are indeed insulin resistant (or heading in that direction), you're more prone to abdominal fat gain and will benefit most from a Glyci-Med dietary approach such as the Hormone Diet. This two-part blood test will also allow you to be much more proactive about your health, since measuring fasting glucose alone (the typical practice) picks up insulin resistance in the late stage of disease, when diabetes is already full-blown. Insulin is often the first imbalance to present itself; high blood sugar is last.

In my clinical practice, I perform many more tests on each patient (see Appendix A for a summary of the tests). But because a glucose/insulin imbalance can appear with any one of the fat-packing hormonal imbalances, this one simple test is the best starting point to determine how well your diet will work, as well as being a strong indication of your overall wellness.

WHAT IF YOUR BLOOD TEST RESULTS ARE ABNORMAL?

If you find your blood insulin is high after fasting or after eating, you can take extra steps now to enhance your fat-loss results.

Although *all* three steps work to improve your insulin response, you may want to add a supplement to improve your insulin response and accelerate fat loss. Your options are outlined in Chapter 13, under Hormonal Imbalance 1.

Give Your Kitchen a Mini-Makeover!

Before you embark on your detox in Step 1, you may want to take some time to clear your cupboards of foods that impair healthy hormonal balance. The list below covers foods you should never eat—I recommend you remove them from your kitchen immediately to prevent further hormonal disruption. Other nasty foods you have in stock, such as low-fat packaged foods, should be gradually phased out of your home.

CHECK LABELS IN YOUR CUPBOARDS, FRIDGE, AND FREEZER AND IMMEDIATELY REMOVE THE FOLLOWING:

- Products containing artificial sweeteners (aspartame, Splenda, etc.)
- Products containing high-fructose corn syrup
- Vegetable oil, palm oil, shortening, margarine, and cottonseed oil; anything containing partially hydrogenated oils; products containing trans fats
- Processed and packaged foods that contain preservatives and lack nutrients, e.g., prepared pasta side dishes
- Packaged products such as sliced meats that contain sulfites and nitrites

PITCH PLASTICS!

The next step in your mini-makeover is to replace all your plastic food storage containers with glass. Gradually phase out condiments and foods in plastic bottles (or recycle them all now) and try to purchase only products in glass.

Always choose metal, glass, or wood instead of plastic for storing, reheating, and serving foods. Use paper wraps instead of plastic, and never microwave your food covered by plastic wrap or in plastic containers or Styrofoam. Potentially harmful or cancer-causing, estrogenlike chemicals called dioxins can leach into your foods and drinks, especially when heated or frozen.

Avoid water in plastic bottles as much as you can, and never drink water bottled in plastic if it has been heated or frozen in your car. Do *not* refill plastic bottles. Purchase all types of drinks in glass bottles as often as possible, or choose stainless steel as a travel-friendly option.

Shop Before You Detox

At this point, you may want to stock up on the body-cleansing, hormone-enhancing foods you'll be eating while you complete your detox. Don't worry! I guarantee you'll have plenty of tasty choices that will leave you feeling energized and satisfied. Your shopping list is provided on page 466.

We have covered all the prep steps you need to get started. You've completed your Best Body Assessment, rid your kitchen of hormone hazards, and created a detox shopping list. Are you pumped? You're now set for the three-step fix.

HORMONE DIET SUCCESS STORY

Marlene W. (age 54)

My story is simple. I began suffering with symptoms of irrational crying episodes, which alternated with unbearable irritability, where I would lash out at the people I cared about the most, and then I would experience such dark feelings of despondency and depression that I took to my bed and decided to hide from the world.

After a week of this with no change, I knew I had to do *something*.

My family doctor and a referring gynecologist confirmed that menopause was the culprit and offered me antidepressants or hormone replacement therapy. I didn't feel that these were the right options for me, and so, through a network of friends, I found a naturopath that I hoped would offer me an alternative.

Enter Dr. Natasha Turner. From the first day I came into her office, I felt hopeful. She listened to my story and confidently told me that she felt certain she could help. She immediately started me on a regimen of bioidentical hormone therapy and dietary supplements (which she determined after reviewing my blood tests), and she recommended that I follow an *anti-inflammatory diet* she had just written a book about. (The hardest part for me: I should give up my red wine. She said alcohol could interfere with hormone levels.) I left her office and thought about this, and within a few days made up my mind that I had to do this if I really wanted to feel better!

Three weeks later, I returned to her office, and not only had my symptoms vastly improved, but I had also lost 17 pounds! Over the previous 10 to 15 years, I had slowly become quite overweight but had not found the motivation to do something about it. Work, stress, commuting from the suburbs, some inconsistent dietary choices, and lack of exercise were contributors. But now . . . enter motivation!

I continued to follow Dr. Turner's regime and added in some exercise. With her consistent tweaking of my supplements, I really felt she was taking individualized care of me—which also contributed to my motivation. I had decided that I would weigh myself only at my visits with Dr. Turner, and each visit brought a new surprise! I didn't even think of it as a "diet" but saw it as a new beginning, a new lifestyle. And honestly, after the first 3 weeks, I never really found it difficult or felt deprived. I bought *The Hormone Diet* and started reading. I began to have a lot of "aha!" moments and "I didn't know that, but it makes sense" moments. So much of our health can be affected by hormones.

Well, after 10 months and an 87-pound weight loss, I am almost where I should be, and I feel great! I am still having a bit of a challenge following a *regular* exercise program, but I am doing my best. I have had the support of a wonderful husband and a fabulous doctor. Thank you both! And that's why my horrific menopause was the greatest thing that could have happened to me. It was my "reason for change," and it brought me to Dr. Turner and *The Hormone Diet*. The hard part of my story was finding the *right* information to follow; the simple part was following it.

STEP 1
RENEW AND REVITALIZE

YOUR FIRST 2 WEEKS

I am seeking, I am striving, I am in it with all my heart.

VINCENT VAN GOGH

CHAPTER 7

SUPERB SLEEP FOR
HORMONAL BALANCE

These are the hormonal benefits you can expect to enjoy from superb sleep:

- Tamed cortisol and a calm nervous system
- Replenished DHEA, the antiaging hormone
- Reduced insulin and subdued inflammation
- Increased GABA and serotonin, the relaxation and feel-good hormones
- Better testosterone status and protection from the harmful effects of excess estrogen
- Increased melatonin and growth hormone for greater nighttime repair and fat-burning benefits
- Increased thyroid hormone to maximize your metabolism
- Enhanced appetite control through increased leptin and suppression of the appetite-stimulating hormones ghrelin and NPY
- More acetylcholine to keep your muscles moving and your mind and memory sharp

Hectic schedules. Bigger workloads. More hours in front of the computer and TV. There are more reasons why we lack sleep than there are hours in a day. *Along with managing stress, ensuring you routinely get a good night's rest is the most important factor for restoring hormonal balance.* Great quality sleep is absolutely vital for fat-loss success. If you've failed at dieting before, chances are that insufficient or improper sleep was a contributing factor.

According to recent statistics, sleep deprivation affects more than 70 million North Americans. In fact, we're spending $24 billion a year just trying to fall asleep. But that's still only a fraction of the $100 billion we spend annually in our attempts to lose weight.

Are You Sleep Deprived?

Ask yourself the following questions:

- Do you fall asleep as soon as your head hits the pillow?
- Do you rely on an alarm to wake you up?
- Do you feel tired during the day?
- Do you tend to sleep more on the weekends?

If you answered yes to any of the above, you are probably sleep deprived.

Sleep and Your Hormones

Sleep deprivation perpetuates a vicious circle of excess stress hormones, reduced sleep-inducing melatonin, and low growth hormone. Your hormonal state also influences your ability to sleep. For instance, hormonal imbalances, such as the low progesterone often associated with PMS or the low serotonin common with depression, can lead to many frustrating nights of tossing and turning or repeatedly waking in the wee morning hours.

Sleep to Stay Slim

Sleep is an absolutely fascinating innate function that depends on the intricate interplay of environmental signals and various structures and chemicals within your body, beginning with the hypothalamus gland. The hypothalamus regulates your internal clock, also known as the circadian rhythm, which dictates your natural sleep-wake cycle. This gland gathers information about body temperature and light exposure to influence our normal sleep habits and hormone-release patterns.

Body temperature is directly linked to our level of wakefulness arousal—believe it or not, the warmer we are, the more alert we become.

Once melatonin is released, it causes your body to cool down and sink into deeper sleep, which is when growth hormone is released. At this point, more cell reproduction takes place and protein breakdown slows substantially. Essentially, your body rebuilds itself during deep sleep, especially your bones and skin and muscle cells. Since proteins are the building blocks needed for cell growth and for repair from the damaging effects of factors such as stress and ultraviolet rays, deep sleep may truly be "beauty sleep." And remember, the release of growth hormone is also encouraging for fat loss.

Growth hormone naturally declines as we age, but poor-quality sleep and low melatonin can cause its production to drop off even further. Without sufficient melatonin, we lose the rejuvenating and fat-burning benefits of growth hormone and become susceptible to abdominal weight gain.

Sleep and Stress

Not surprisingly, sleep has profound effects on your nervous system. Throughout most of the sleep cycle, the sympathetic nervous system (fight or flight) relaxes while the parasympathetic nervous system (rest and digest) is stimulated. (The reverse is true during the REM, or dreaming, phase of sleep.) Activity also *decreases* in the parts of your brain that control your emotions, decision-making processes, and social interactions.

In addition to calming the fight-or-flight nervous system, sufficient rest and recuperation effectively reduce cortisol. A recent study published in *The Lancet* supports these claims, as it showed sleep deprivation caused stress hormones to rise in the evening and heightened the stress response during waking hours. Meanwhile, another study published in the *Journal of Clinical Endocrinology & Metabolism* in 2001 was one of the first to show that chronic insomnia leads to high cortisol and hyperactivity of our stress-response pathway in the brain.

We know high cortisol fuels appetite and makes us feel hungry, particularly for sugary and carb-laden treats, even when we have eaten enough, causing our blood sugars to spike, our insulin to soar, and, eventually, more unwanted fat to collect around the abdomen. After only a few nights of sleep deprivation, otherwise healthy people appear prediabetic on glucose tolerance tests, in that regulating blood sugar after a high-carbohydrate meal can take up to 40 percent longer than normal. Besides making us feel lousy, even short-term sleep debt can make us fat!

Sleep and Appetite

Sleep helps you to lose weight by influencing the hormones that control your appetite and increase your metabolism. A 2004 study at the University of Chicago was the first to show sleep as a major regulator of appetite-controlling hormones and also to link the extent of hormonal variations with the degree of hunger change. More specifically, researchers found *appetite-enhancing ghrelin increased* by 28 percent, whereas *appetite-curbing and metabolism-enhancing leptin decreased* by 18 percent among subjects who were sleep deprived. Appetite was not the only factor found to increase with lack of sleep. The desire for high-calorie, high-sugar foods also jumped with insufficient slumber.

In the same year, researchers at the Stanford School of Medicine found that subjects who had only 5 hours of sleep per night had less leptin, more ghrelin, and experienced an increase in their BMI, *regardless of diet and exercise.* Boy, even the most committed dieters are clearly fighting a losing battle if they do not get the rest they need.

WHY MEALS MAKE US SLEEPY
Scientists at the University of Manchester were the first to discover that the brain neurons that keep us awake and alert are turned off after we eat. It appears the sugar in the foods we eat tells the brain to stop producing orexin, the peptide that increases both appetite and wakefulness. This insight into the activity of orexin may explain why we tend to crave a nap after a big meal and also why we may have a tough time sleeping if we are hungry.

This is precisely why I have included sleep as the first of the three steps in your program for hormonal health and weight loss.

The Hormone Diet Sleep Solution: Four Steps for Hormone-Balancing Sleep

I love sleep. My life has the tendency to fall apart when I'm awake, you know?

—ERNEST HEMINGWAY

Let's face it, no one feels good after endless nights of tossing, turning, or staring at the ceiling. But besides leaving you feeling less than your best, poor sleep interferes with your hormonal balance, appetite control, and fat loss, *even when* your dietary and exercise routines are right on track. Lack of sleep also contributes to inflammation.

Real lasting changes in your body will occur only when you make total lifestyle adjustments. Correcting sleep problems is the first of these vital adjustments. So, try my simple, four-step plan for a lifetime of sweet slumber—although you may find that you require only the first two steps.

Step 1: Create the Ideal Environment for Hormone-Balancing Sleep

The look, feel, temperature, lighting, and sounds in your bedroom can either help or hinder your sleep. So before you ever hit the pillow, you have to make sure your space is set up to promote healthy sleep.

- **Make your room as dark as possible.** When you hit the hay, you should not be able to see your hand in front of your face. If you must use an alarm clock, turn it away from you. I use blackout curtains and recommend my patients do the same. Your children should also sleep in the dark. If they're afraid of the dark, try turning off the night light after they've drifted off to sleep. Why make your room a den of darkness?

When light hits your skin, it disrupts the circadian rhythm of the pineal gland and, as a result, hinders the production of melatonin. Studies have shown that even a small amount of light can cause a decrease in melatonin levels, which affects sleep, interferes with weight loss, and may increase your risk of cancer.

- **Use low lighting in your bedroom.** Once you settle into bed, avoid using overhead lights and lamps with high-wattage bulbs. My husband and I have replaced our overhead light fixture with a ceiling fan, and we each use our own clip-on or handheld book lights for reading. These are great for lighting only the page, rather than shining in your eyes or illuminating the entire room, which can potentially interfere with your sleep or your partner's.

- **Be aware of electromagnetic fields (EMFs) in your bedroom.** These can disrupt the pineal gland and the production of melatonin and serotonin. They may have additional negative effects, including increased risk of cancer. EMFs are emitted from digital alarm clocks and other electrical devices. If you must use these items, try to keep them as far away from the bed as possible—at least 3 feet away.

- **Turn off the TV, turn on your love life.** A television is another source of hormone-disrupting EMFs. Studies show that you will enjoy better sleep and more of it without a TV in the bedroom. Besides, you're also likely to have more sex when you ban the tube from your sleep space. The reasons why sex is so important for your hormonal balance, appetite control, and weight loss are explained in greater detail in Chapter 14, but basically, the more sex you have, the better your hormonal health. And the better your hormonal health, the more often you will have enjoyable sex. If you must have a TV simply to turn your mind off at the end of the day, use the timer function to make sure the set goes off if you fall asleep. That way you'll never wake from the noise or light from the TV. Also, keep the television at least 6 feet from the bed.

- **Use your bed for sleeping and sex only.** If you have kids, you know how easily your bedroom can become grand central station for the entire family. You should definitely avoid engaging in any other activities in bed, as you may start to associate the bedroom with sleep-robbing chores and tasks, rather than relaxing sleep and intimacy with your partner. Above all, *never* work in bed.

- **Create bedroom "Zen."** In my last two homes, I painted the bedroom in calming, dark, earthy tones. Shades like these help make the bedroom a relaxing place. Over the years I've also realized that clutter is a state of mind. Keeping your bedroom neat and clutter-free can be challenging, especially if you live in a small space. Just remember, the primary purposes of the bedroom are sleep and sex. You'll be amazed how much better both will be if you try to keep your bedside tables and dresser tops clear of clutter.

- **Choose comfortable, soothing bedding.** Several companies now offer organic cotton bedding lines that are free of harmful dyes and toxins. These can be a great investment if you have sensitive skin or simply care about the impact of heavy pesticide use on the environment. Personally, I find all-white bedding very soothing and welcoming after a long day of sensory overload. Whatever your taste dictates, select bedding that pleases your eye and feels good on your skin. You should also make sure your bedding keeps you warm but doesn't overheat you. In winter, you may wish to use a light duvet, whereas a thin blanket with a sheet might suffice for summer. Small changes like these will help create a calming, comfortable environment conducive to restful sleep.

- **Keep your bedroom cool but not cold.** No matter how chilly the weather gets outside, your bedroom temperature should be no warmer than 70°F for sleeping. Remember, your body needs to cool slightly at night to ensure the proper release of your sleep-inducing hormone, melatonin. At the same time, make sure your air conditioner is not blasting all night long in the summer. Research shows that over–air conditioning can cause weight gain.
- **Consider purchasing a white-noise device.** If you live in an apartment building or noisy neighborhood, you're probably familiar with the aggravation of being wakened by sounds. You may even wake when your partner walks around at night or snores. If you find you are easily wakened by sounds, the hum of a white-noise machine or a household fan may help. You can also try wearing earplugs to block out sleep-disrupting sounds.
- **Avoid using a loud alarm clock.** Waking up suddenly to the blaring wail of an alarm clock can be a shock to your body; you'll also find you feel groggier when you are roused in the middle of a sleep cycle. Getting enough sleep on a regular basis should make your alarm clock unnecessary. Sleeping through an alarm or relying on an alarm daily may indicate that you are sleep deprived. If you do use an alarm, you should awaken just before it goes off. If you must use one, I recommend the Bose alarm. It starts off at a moderate volume and slowly gets louder, so you aren't jarred out of your sleep. You can also investigate a sunrise alarm, an alarm clock with a natural light built in that simulates a sunrise. This method of waking has the added bonus of improving your mood and increasing your energy throughout the day.
- **If you go to the bathroom during the night, keep the lights off**. Even brief exposure to light can shut down the melatonin

production that's so crucial for good sleep. If you absolutely must use a light in the bathroom, try a flashlight or night light instead of the bright overhead light. Another option is to use a dimmer switch or a night light fitted with a red bulb, since red light exposure at night appears to have less of a negative impact.

- **Invest in a comfortable mattress.** Your mattress should be comfortable for you and your partner, not too hard or too soft. When my mom starting having hip and shoulder pain, we looked at a number of factors and finally came to the conclusion that her mattress was too hard. As soon as she changed it to a pillow-top mattress, the problem was solved. The right degree of firmness or softness is a personal thing, and your preference may change with age (just like my mom's did). If you need to shop for a new mattress, you may wish to consider the recommendations I've provided in Appendix B to reduce your exposure to toxins through your mattress.
- **Don't sleep with your pets or children.** Doing so may disrupt your precious sleep. Have them sleep in their own beds, instead.

Step 2: Implement the Hormone Diet Sleep-Right Rules

Once you've turned your bedroom into a healthy, sleep-inducing oasis, the next critical step is to start sleeping correctly. You may not have known that there is actually a proper way and time to sleep. It's true!

When, how, and how much we sleep is important. Failing to follow these recommendations can impede the fat-burning and hormone-balancing benefits you should gain from sleep each and every night.

Here are the Hormone Diet guidelines for hormone-enhancing sleep.

- **Sleep in complete darkness.** Again, even a small amount of light can hamper your sleep.
- **Sleep nude** (or at least with loose-fitting nightclothes—but nude is better). Do not sleep in tight undergarments (bras, girdles, briefs, etc.). Tight clothing will increase your body temperature and interfere with melatonin release while you sleep.
- **Establish regular sleeping hours.** Try to get up each morning and go to bed every night at roughly the same time. Oversleeping can be as detrimental as sleep deprivation. How you feel each day is an important indication of how much sleep is right for you.
- **Get to bed by 11 p.m.** Since the invention of electricity (not to mention television and computers), we have begun staying up later and later. This change has resulted in a largely sleep-deprived society. Our stress glands, the adrenals, recharge or recover most between 11 p.m. and 1 a.m. Going to bed before 11 p.m. (in fact, 10 p.m. is even better) is optimal for rebuilding your adrenal reserves. I know this can be difficult to achieve, so I recommend my patients start going to bed 15 minutes earlier each week until they reach their new target time.
- **Sleep 7 to 9 hours each night.** The American Cancer Society has found higher incidences of cancer in individuals who consistently sleep fewer than 6 hours or more than 9 hours nightly. Oversleeping is just as harmful as sleep deprivation. Consistently needing more than 9 hours of sleep every night warrants a visit to your doctor for further investigation, as this may indicate an underlying medical condition such as hypothyroidism or depression, or a deficiency of iron, folic acid, or vitamin B_{12} (though some of us simply require more or less sleep than others). If you awaken without an alarm and feel rested, you're likely getting the right amount of sleep for you.

- **See the light first thing in the morning.** Daylight and morning sounds are key signals that help waken your brain. Turning on the lights or opening the blinds is the proper way to reset your body clock and ensure that your melatonin levels drop back to "awake" mode until the evening. Exposure to morning light has also been proven to be one of the simplest ways to increase your energy for the entire day. It's also been shown to boost testosterone in men and fertility in women by stimulating luteinizing hormone release from the pituitary gland. Enhance this action further by exposing yourself to sunlight and by getting outside during the day. I can't say enough about the benefits of getting outside, even for 10 to 20 minutes in the morning light.
- **Keep household lighting dim from dinnertime until you go to sleep.** Believe it or not, this simple step not only prepares your body and hormones for sleep, but it also helps your digestion.

Step 3: Use These Tips If You Have Difficulty Falling or Staying Asleep

After many years of doing things the same old way, many of us tend to develop and grow accustomed to poor sleep habits. As with any bad habit, you must break the cycle by *retraining* your body and mind to sleep again. Whether you have problems falling asleep, wake up frequently throughout the night, wake too early, or experience poor-quality sleep overall, implement as many of these lifestyle modifications as possible. If your sleep disruption is severe or chronic, you may also want to begin using one or more of the natural sleep aids I have suggested as the fourth step.

- **Avoid stimulating activities before bed, such as watching TV or using the computer.** Computer use in the evening raises dopamine and noradrenaline, our brain-stimulating hormones that should naturally be higher during the daytime. In the evening, engage in calming activities or those that involve focusing on one thing, such as reading or meditation, which make you more serotonin dominant. Choose relaxing reading materials that have nothing to do with your work or career. Stop all your work-related activities at least 2 hours before bed. Allow yourself some downtime. Watching television can also be too stimulating for some people; if you suspect this is true for you, break your bedtime TV habit!

- **Develop a calming bedtime routine.** Breaking bad habits often requires cultivating good ones. Reading something spiritual or listening to soft music can become cues that help train your body and mind to relax. Choose your nighttime reading carefully—if it's too enticing, you may stay up too late reading; if it's upsetting or emotional, you may find falling asleep more difficult. Select books, music, or other soothing stimuli that make you feel good and help take your mind *off* the stresses of daily life.

- **If you cannot sleep, get out of bed and do something else until you feel the urge to sleep.** Tossing and turning in bed only leaves you feeling frustrated. Try getting up for a while, but keep the lights low and the TV and computer off. Staring at the clock will also make your sleepless situation worse, so remove the clock from view while you are in bed.

- **Make a to-do list or try writing in a journal.** If you find you often lie awake in bed with endless thoughts of what you must do or things you have done churning through your head, get out of bed and write down your feelings. You'll be surprised by how much relief this process can provide.

- **Exercise at the right time.** Exercising fewer than 3 hours before bedtime may be too stimulating and can impede your ability to fall asleep. Yoga and strength training are exceptions, as these activities are often less stimulating than cardiovascular exercise. Working out 3 to 6 hours before bed, on the other hand, will help you maximize the benefits of exercise on sleep, since the body actually increases deep sleep to compensate for the physical stress of your workout. Exercise also promotes healthy sleep patterns because of its positive effect on body temperature. After a workout, your body gradually cools down, which naturally makes you sleepy. To relax your muscles and trigger the sleep response after exercise, try a hot bath with Epsom salts. Soak in water as hot as you can stand with 1 to 2 cups of Epsom salts for at least 20 minutes. Place a cold towel around your neck if you feel too warm while in the bath.

- **Exercise your mind, too.** Try the daily crossword or Sudoku. People who are intellectually and mentally stimulated during the day feel an increased need to sleep to maintain their performance. Uninterested or bored people do not sleep as well.

- **Take a hot bath, shower, or sauna before bed.** As it does with exercise, your body will naturally cool down after a hot bath or shower, making you feel sleepier. Take a hot bath about 2 hours before bedtime, keeping the water hot for at least 25 minutes to stimulate the drop in body temperature that makes us tired. Again, add Epsom salts to detoxify your body and relax your muscles. An

> **INFRARED SAUNA FOR DETOX**
> Infrared radiation penetrates about $1/2$ inch into the skin to heat the body without significantly heating the air or our core body temperature. The skin is the largest organ in your body and one of the main detoxification pathways. Deeply heating the skin and subcutaneous fat, and the good sweat that comes with it, is one of the most effective ways to reduce toxin accumulation, eliminate harmful heavy metals, aid weight loss, stimulate circulation, curb cellulite, and enhance health. We have one of these at Clear Medicine clinic, and you can also check the resource section if you are interested in an infrared sauna.

HOT HORMONE FACT

infrared sauna is also a great option for detox, weight loss, and aiding sleep. See the resource section for your options.

- **Avoid napping.** If you are getting enough sleep at night, you shouldn't feel tired during the day. Craving a snooze in the afternoon is a good indication that you are sleep deprived, and in reality, napping will not make the situation better. Staying awake until nighttime is best, but if you have to catch a nap during the day, keep it to a maximum of 30 minutes.

- **Avoid caffeine at any time of the day.** Caffeine may be metabolized at different rates in different people. A dose of caffeine usually takes 15 to 30 minutes to take effect and lasts for 4 to 5 hours. In some people, it may last much longer, making caffeine use in the afternoon a bad idea. If you must have caffeine, limit it to small amounts in the morning only. Caffeine may also negatively affect the natural release cycle of cortisol, which is generally highest in the morning and lowest in the evening. Cortisol release rises slightly at 2 a.m. and 4 a.m., then hits its peak around 6 a.m. If this pattern is disrupted, you may awaken at these times and find you are unable to fall back asleep. Although this may sound inconceivable, cutting out caffeine has amazing effects on your energy—within only a week or two!

- **Avoid bedtime snacks that are high in sugar or simple carbohydrates.** Carbohydrate-rich snacks such as breads, cereals, muffins, cookies, and other baked goods prompt a short-term spike in blood sugar, followed by a sugar crash later on. When blood sugar drops, adrenaline, glucagon, cortisol, and growth hormone are released to regulate blood glucose levels. These hormones can stimulate the brain, causing you to awaken and possibly stay awake. Try to avoid eating for at least 2 hours before going to bed. If you do need to eat something, reach for a protein-rich, high-fiber snack, such as a few almonds and half an apple. Protein provides the amino acid tryptophan. The body converts tryptophan to serotonin and melatonin, hormones that are important for sleep. The sugars from the fruit may also help the tryptophan reach your brain and take effect more readily.

- **Try to avoid fluids in the 2 hours before bedtime.** Keeping drinks to a minimum before bed will reduce the likelihood—or frequency—of sleep-sabotaging trips to the bathroom. Remember, if you must answer the call of nature during the night, try to keep the lights off or as dim as possible. Men experiencing frequent trips to the bathroom due to a prostate concern may benefit from Bell Prostate Ezee Flow Tea, available at most health food stores.

- **Go easy on the alcohol.** Yes, a few drinks can make you feel drowsy, but the effect is short-lived. The body metabolizes alcohol as you sleep, which can result in sleep interruption. Alcohol may cause sleep disorders because it appears to affect brain chemicals that influence sleep. It may alter the amount of time it takes to fall asleep, shorten total sleep time, and possibly prevent you from falling into the deeper stages of sleep—the stages in which your body does most of its healing. One glass of wine with dinner isn't likely to affect your sleep, since it takes about 90 minutes to metabolize 1 ounce of alcohol. One ounce or more within 2 hours of bedtime, however, may unpleasantly disrupt your sleep.

- **Complete your meditation or visualizations (further described in Chapter 9) in the evening.** These are highly effective techniques to reduce or eliminate body tension and anxiety. They can help calm your mind, relax your muscles, and allow restful sleep to ensue. Much like a physical workout, exercise that involves deep breathing or progressive relaxation, such as yoga and meditation, is excellent not only for your sleep, but also for your life.

Step 4: Use Natural Sleep Aids to Ease Sleep Disruptions

When taken properly and for the right reasons, natural supplements can be very effective at improving the quality and quantity of your sleep, with few—if any—side effects. If you have followed all my hormone-balancing sleep tips for 2 weeks and still do not see an improvement in your sleep, natural sleep aids are your next best option.

The most important step in selecting a natural sleep aid is to first determine the cause of your sleep disruption, because different supplements can be more effective than others for specific sleep-robbing conditions. Difficulty falling or staying asleep may result from stress, vitamin or mineral deficiency, excess caffeine intake, certain medications, menopause, anxiety, depression, low melatonin, muscle tension, pain, and a whole host of other reasons too numerous to list. Fortunately, many herbal remedies, vitamins, minerals, amino acids, and hormones are available to assist you in your quest for a good night's rest.

Understand that finding the right sleep remedy for you may be a trial-and-error process. You may also wish to combine a few products to create the perfect "sleep cocktail" for your needs. My favorite sleep remedy is two tablets of a calcium-magnesium combination (about 300 to 500 mg of each in a citrate base for better absorption) and two or three capsules of a product called Seditol (available through my Web site and some health food stores, it's a patented herbal blend of extracts of *Magnolia officinalis* and *Ziziphus spinosa*). Taken at bedtime, it works like a charm to combat the most common cause of sleep disruption—stress! But here's a list of other options you can choose from.

GABA: A FAVORITE CHOICE FOR RELIEVING TENSION, ANXIETY, AND PAIN WITH SLEEP DISRUPTION

GABA is an inhibitory neurotransmitter—a brain chemical that has a calming effect. It's well suited for individuals who experience anxiety, muscle tension, or pain.

Take 500 to 1,000 mg before bed. Alternatively, take GABA 10 to 20 minutes before meals, beginning with your evening meal. The standard dose of 200 mg four times daily can be increased to a maximum of 500 mg four times daily, if needed. The latter dosage should not be exceeded, and you should reduce the dose if you experience loose stools.

TAURINE

Taurine is an amino acid that plays a major role in the brain as an inhibitory neurotransmitter. Comparable in structure and function with GABA, taurine provides a similar antianxiety effect that helps calm or stabilize an excited mind. Taurine has many other uses, including treating migraines, insomnia, agitation, restlessness, irritability, alcoholism, obsessions, depression, and even hypomania/mania—the "high" phase of bipolar disorder or manic depression.

By inhibiting the release of adrenaline, taurine also protects us from anxiety and other adverse effects of stress. It even helps control high blood pressure and improves the action of insulin. You may have noticed it as an ingredient in some of the energizing, high-caffeine soft drinks, as it is used to soften overstimulation.

Take 500 to 1,000 mg a day. Taking the last dose right before bed is often most helpful. Taurine should be taken without food.

TRYPTOPHAN

Tryptophan is an amino acid that is the building block of serotonin. Remember, serotonin is our "happy hormone," essential to mood, sleep, memory, and appetite. Tryptophan is effective for insomnia related to depression or to a deficiency of serotonin.

Take 500 to 1,000 mg at bedtime. Note that tryptophan supplements are available by prescription only and should be taken with 50 mg of vitamin B_6. It's most effective when taken on an empty stomach or with a piece of fruit.

5-HTP: A FAVORITE CHOICE FOR DEPRESSION, ANXIETY, EATING DISORDERS, AND CONDITIONS ASSOCIATED WITH PAIN

A derivative of tryptophan that's also used to create serotonin, 5-HTP has been found to be more effective than tryptophan for treating sleep loss related to depression, anxiety, and fibromyalgia. And 5-HTP appears to increase REM sleep. It also decreases the amount of time required to fall asleep and the number of nighttime awakenings.

Take 50 to 400 mg a day, divided into doses throughout the day and before bed. Take it with food if you experience nausea.

MELATONIN: A FAVORITE CHOICE FOR AGES 50+ (ESPECIALLY THOSE WITH HIGH BLOOD PRESSURE) AND SHIFT WORKERS

Melatonin decreases as we age, as well as during times of stress and depression. New research shows it may also be useful for reducing high blood pressure. Supplements are usually only effective for insomnia in people younger than 45 to 50 when melatonin levels are low. To determine if your levels are deficient, I suggest a saliva test for melatonin. You can request a test kit from www.thehormonediet.com.

Take 0.5 to 3 mg at bedtime. Try opening up capsules and pouring them under your tongue. You can also purchase melatonin in sublingual form for ready absorption.

L-THEANINE: A FAVORITE CHOICE FOR REDUCING ANXIETY AND BOOSTING DAYTIME ENERGY

L-theanine is your best choice for relaxation and tension relief throughout the *day*. A calming amino acid naturally found in green tea, it's known to support relaxation without causing drowsiness. L-theanine works by increasing the production of GABA in the brain. Similar to the effects of meditation, it also stimulates alpha brain waves naturally associated with deep states of relaxation and enhanced mental clarity. L-theanine may increase learning, attention, and sensations of pleasure as well. These effects are likely due to the natural dopamine boost brought on by L-theanine.

Take 50 to 200 mg of L-theanine without food. In very high-stress situations, 100 mg to a maximum of 600 mg can be taken every 6 hours.

MILK PROTEIN HYDROLYSATE CONCENTRATE (CASEIN TRYPTIC HYDROLYSATE OR CASEIN HYDROLYSATE): A FAVORITE CHOICE FOR ANY SLEEP OR STRESS CONDITION

Regardless of whether the stress you experience is physical, emotional, psychological, or environmental, milk protein hydrolysate is documented to prevent the associated rise in cortisol by calming your brain's stress pathway. This product can be used to address all types of sleep disruption and to reduce the harmful effects of sleep deprivation, stress, anxiety, or depression. It's safe to say that this product got me through writing this book!

Take 75 to 300 mg a day. Try opening the capsules and pouring the contents under your tongue for rapid sleep or stress relief.

ASHWAGANDHA: A FAVORITE CHOICE FOR BUSY EXECUTIVES OR PATIENTS WITH UNDERACTIVE THYROID

Ayurvedic medicine practitioners use this dietary supplement to enhance mental and physical performance, improve learning ability, and decrease stress and fatigue. Ashwagandha is a general tonic that can be used in stressful situations, especially insomnia, restlessness, or when you are feeling overworked. Studies have indicated that ashwagandha offers anti-inflammatory, anticancer, antistress, antioxidant, immune-modulating, and rejuvenating properties.

The typical dosage is 500 to 1,000 mg twice daily. Capsules should be standardized to 1.5 percent withanolides per dose.

RELORA: A FAVORITE CHOICE FOR ALL TYPES OF STRESS, DEPRESSION, AND ANXIETY

A mixture of the herbal extracts *Magnolia officinalis* and *Phellodendron amurense*, Relora is medically proven to reduce stress and anxiety. This natural sleep aid is my favorite choice for patients who tend to wake up throughout the night, for highly stressed individuals, and for menopausal women with hot flashes that cause sleep disruption. It can significantly reduce cortisol and raise DHEA within only 2 weeks of use.

In a study published by University of Mississippi professor Dr. Walter Chamblis in the *Journal of Psychopharmacology* (2001), 78 percent of participants reported greater feelings of relaxation and well-being when taking Relora. Seventy-four percent said they experienced better sleep when using the supplement.

Relora can be used to prevent the health conditions associated with stress, including poor immunity, high blood pressure, insomnia, sleep disruption, loss of vitality, and weight gain, especially in relation to metabolic syndrome.

Take two 250 mg capsules at bedtime and one upon rising. It is best taken without food. I find the most effective formula contains a mixture of B vitamins and folic acid as well.

PASSIONFLOWER
Passionflower is the herb of choice for insomnia. It aids the transition into restful sleep without the narcotic hangover sometimes associated with pharmaceutical sleep aids. As an antispasmodic, it is helpful in treating tension and stress. It can also be effective in the treatment of nerve pain such as neuralgia and the viral infection shingles.

Passionflower extracts have been studied for their potential ability to decrease anxiety and prolong sleeping time. They have also been tested in combination with other sedative and antianxiety herbs such as valerian. Findings suggest that passionflower may enhance the effectiveness of these other treatments, and together with valerian it may reduce the stress hormone NPY. It may also reduce muscle spasms and decrease pain in some instances.

Take a 100 mg capsule (standardized extract) twice daily to alleviate anxiety.

VITAMIN B$_6$

Vitamin B$_6$ is useful to help correct abnormally high cortisol release throughout the night. Those who wake frequently, particularly at about 2, 4, and 6 a.m., will benefit most from this supplement.

Take 50 to 100 mg before bed.

PHOSPHATIDYLSERINE

Phosphatidylserine is ideal for nighttime worrying, as it influences the inappropriate release of stress hormones and protects the brain from the negative effects of cortisol.

Take 100 to 300 mg before bed.

SPECIFICALLY FOR RESTLESS LEG SYNDROME (RLS)

RLS is a neurological disorder characterized by severe, uncomfortable sensations in the legs, especially prevalent while lying down. Supplements of folic acid, iron, magnesium, and vitamin E may provide some relief from the unpleasant, sleep-disrupting symptoms of RLS. Supplements such as phenylalanine and L-tyrosine that increase dopamine, involved in motor function and muscle tension, can also be of benefit, but these are best taken in the morning or during the early afternoon rather than at nighttime because they are energy enhancing.

HORMONE DIET SUCCESS STORY

Tara M. (age 37)

I had been involved in the fitness industry for about 10 years when I ran into trouble with my weight. I had competed in several bikini competitions, which I really enjoyed. But when I attempted to slim down again for another show, my body would not respond. In fact, I found I was slowly gaining weight.

I was not only putting on weight, but I was also exhausted and crying at the drop of a hat, despite my training and nutrition efforts. I went to several doctors within a 6-month time span. At this point, I was diagnosed with hypothyroidism. I felt some relief in knowing this, and I was able to drop 8 pounds with the help of the drug Levothyroxine. But then my weight loss came to a standstill, and my energy levels had not improved much at all. Plus, I was still 25 pounds heavier than what I was used to. I couldn't model like I loved or participate in any competitions, and I felt like a poor example of a personal trainer. I kept thinking that people were judging me because I didn't look like I practiced what I preached as a trainer—I even thought about switching careers as a result.

After some time of feeling very discouraged, within the span of 1 week I had two colleagues recommend Dr. Turner to me. I was sure it was fate! I quickly made an appointment with her and started reading *The Hormone Diet* right away. I was really excited for a new approach to my health issues.

Dr. Turner did not disappoint me—in fact, quite the opposite. I was so impressed with her gentle manner. She was easy to speak with and really knew her stuff! She asked me many questions about my current health, and she did several tests to get a full understanding of what was going on. We then started down my road to recovery. She addressed many of the issues discussed in *The Hormone Diet*—she tweaked my prescription and gave me sleep instruction, an easy-to-follow diet, supplements to address my hormone/adrenal issues, and new exercise guidelines.

Within a few weeks, my energy increased and I had a much

more positive frame of mind—and thankfully, I stopped crying at the drop of a hat. I was thrilled—not only was I feeling better, but I also started losing weight and ended up losing 20 pounds in less than 4 months. I feel like me again!

CHAPTER 8

YOUR ANTI-INFLAMMATORY DETOX: LOOK AND FEEL BETTER IN JUST 2 WEEKS

These are the hormonal benefits you will enjoy from the Anti-Inflammatory Detox:

- Improved hormonal balance and fat burning with better liver function
- Relief from the effects of harmful excess estrogen
- Reduced insulin and less inflammation
- Restored serotonin activity and enhanced mood, memory, and focus
- Maximized activity of thyroid hormone, our metabolic master
- Support of the breakdown and clearance of cortisol from the body
- Better appetite control, freedom from cravings, and enhanced fat burning through improved leptin levels

Now that you have worked on establishing better habits for sound, restorative sleep, you're ready for the next process in the Hormone Diet plan—ridding your body of hormone-disrupting toxins and fat-packing inflammation.

Toxins Make Us Fat!

Whether we realize it or not, we are constantly exposed to toxins. Potentially harmful compounds enter our bodies in the form of pesticides, fertilizers, hormone-based food additives, prescription and over-the-counter drugs, air pollution, fumes, heavy metals, and even the skin-care products we use every day. Toxins are also naturally found in our body as the end products of the metabolic process and bacterial waste.

No matter whether we consume them via our foods, inhale them from our surroundings, or absorb them through our skin, toxins can pile up in our systems, especially when our natural toxin-elimination mechanisms are not functioning optimally. Even worse, an accumulation of toxins in the body can interfere with our hormones, neurotransmitters, and nervous system activity, resulting in weight gain and a host of health problems.

Toxins affect many of the hormones that influence our body composition and ability to lose weight, including thyroid hormone, testosterone, estrogen, insulin, cortisol, and leptin. Some toxins can mimic particular hormones, causing abnormal activity. Like a stranger finding your house key and letting himself in, other toxins can sneak in and take the place of our hormones in their normal receptor sites. In this case, the stranger puts his own key in your lock, but cannot open it because the key does not fit. But as long as the wrong key is stuck in the lock, the correct key cannot get in to open the door.

Tons of Toxins

Over 80,000 industrial chemicals have been developed in the past 75 years, including heavy metals, solvents, phthalates, polychlorinated bisphenols, and organophosphates. Exposure to industrial chemicals such as pesticides, dyes, perfumes, flavorings, and plastics, even in *extremely small quantities*, has been shown to significantly increase the body mass of mice—and men, too! Many of these chemicals are endocrine blockers that disrupt our hormones and increase fat storage. I could dedicate an entire book to the full list of chemical offenders, but I've narrowed my discussion here to two of the biggies: bisphenol and phthalates.

Bisphenol-A (BPA)

Research has shown that bisphenol, a chemical commonly found in most plastics (including water bottles), alters fat cells when it interacts with insulin. Bisphenol has been found to spark and accelerate two of the biological mechanisms underlying obesity: an increase in the number of fat cells in the body and the enhancement of their fat-storing capabilities. So the presence of this chemical can influence not only the production of more fat cells, but also their increase in size!

Phthalates

Phthalates are a group of chemical compounds used in many household items, including water bottles, soaps, shampoos, and cosmetics, plastic containers, toys, pipes, and even medicines. Current estimates suggest that more than 75 percent of North Americans have significant levels of phthalates in their urine.

Phthalates offer a fascinating, yet frightening, example of the interrelationship of hormonal balance, reproductive health, and obesity. High exposure to this and other toxins can lead to compromised ovarian function, inhibited sperm motility, and the early onset of puberty. Phthalates, in particular, have been connected to reproductive problems in baby boys, smaller penis sizes, testicular problems in adolescents, and poor semen and testosterone production in men. Researchers at the University of Rochester Medical Center have now linked this phthalate-induced reduction in testosterone to abdominal obesity, insulin resistance, and the onset of type 2 diabetes in men. The study, published in *Environmental Health Perspectives* (March 2007), showed that the highest levels of phthalate metabolites appeared in the urine of men with abdominal obesity and insulin resistance.

We Are Terribly Estrogen Toxic, Too

In Chapter 3, I discussed estrogen dominance as one of the main causes of hormonal imbalance and obesity. Besides the estrogen we produce naturally, we tend to accumulate even more of it in our lifetime, thanks to an abundance of estrogen and estrogenlike compounds in our environment. Because of mounting health concerns, the World Health Organization (WHO) has sanctioned a review of endocrine-disrupting chemicals, especially those with estrogenic activity linked to prostate and breast cancer. A study published in the *Journal of Environmental Health Perspectives* by researchers at the University of Texas showed that even minuscule concentrations of estrogen-upsetting chemicals in our environment are capable of causing endocrine disruption within just 30 seconds of exposure.

Canadian and British researchers have discovered a disturbing proliferation of hermaphrodite fish in the Great Lakes due to the presence of estrogens in the water. These hormones have made their way into the lakes in the form of industrial chemicals, oral contraceptives, hormone replacement therapy drugs, and raw sewage from women who use these products. Scientists initially noticed that certain species of male fish were developing eggs. Just 2 years later, the same fish population was almost completely wiped out because their reproductive capabilities were ravaged. Scary.

On an even more chilling note, what happens to us when we drink this water or eat these fish? Researchers from the University of Pittsburgh School of Medicine may have some insight. They treated cultured breast cancer cells with extracts from the estrogen-laden fish. Once exposed to the fish extracts, the cancer cells grew more rapidly!

Your Body's Natural Toxin-Cleansing Team

Our liver, kidneys, and small intestine are the body's natural cleaning team, working together to package toxic compounds for removal. Over time, the function of these organs, especially the liver, can be compromised by illness, poor nutrition, stress, pollution, or toxic lifestyle habits (e.g., using drugs, alcohol, or tobacco).

When the cleanup process is not being carried out as it should, toxic byproducts cannot be properly neutralized. As a result, toxic compounds from the liver are reabsorbed and stored in the fatty tissues of the body rather than excreted. As you would expect, this toxic buildup leads to a dramatic increase in long-term health risks—and it doesn't leave us feeling our best in the short term, either. Complaints such as headaches, weight gain, acne, PMS, infertility, and poor memory often arise when our detox organs are in need of some support.

Let's talk about *how* the Hormone Diet detox actually works to restore your body balance before delving into the details of your action plan. It tackles toxins and inflammation via the five keys to healthy digestion and by supporting healthy liver function.

The Five Keys to Healthy Digestion

KEY I: REDUCE INFLAMMATION BY REMOVING FOOD SENSITIVITIES

Heartburn, headaches, difficulty getting out of bed in the morning, feeling and looking tired even after sufficient sleep, an inability to lose weight, bloating, and relentless water retention can all be related to food sensitivities or intolerances. Because the connection between the symptom and a specific food can be difficult to pinpoint, those who suffer these discomforts often go on feeling worse and worse as their immune system takes a constant beating.

Many of us with food sensitivities don't even realize how bad we feel until the problematic foods are removed from our diet. Then suddenly getting out of bed becomes easier; our energy, mood, and concentration improve; and joint pain, headaches, and sinus congestion disappear.

During your anti-inflammatory detox, you'll take the most allergenic foods out of your diet for a specific period of time to give your body a break and a chance to calm down and detoxify. Slowly reintroducing each food after a 10-day break can allow you to connect particular symptoms with your food choices.

All that experimenting with different foods may sound like a major inconvenience, but the results can be invaluable. For example, I see little point in eating cottage cheese as a source of low-fat protein if it contributes to chronic sinusitis, abdominal cramping, acne, or digestive upset. Why not go for an alternative source of protein that's just as effective for fat loss, but that still allows you to look and feel great?

Perhaps the possibility of reducing the appearance of cellulite might provide you with more encouragement. Did you ever think that those pesky pockets of cellulite could actually be caused by an allergic reaction? Well, the immune response to food proteins may indirectly contribute to increased amounts of cellulite. A delayed allergic reaction to foods may occur within blood vessels, causing inflammation in the vessel walls and subsequently triggering clotting mechanisms. This increased inflammation in the arteries and capillaries may contribute to poor circulation, a known cause of cellulite and reduced lymphatic drainage. Believe it or not, avoiding food intolerances (and following the other recommendations outlined in later steps of the Hormone Diet) may diminish the appearance of cellulite and stop its formation for good.

The results we have seen at Clear Medicine with patients who have discovered their food sensitivities are remarkable. I recall one patient who had suffered with headaches for 20 years—they were gone after just 2 weeks of avoiding wheat. Another woman had bleeding from the bowel for 2 years—it was gone after a single week on a dairy-free diet. A flight attendant who complained of water retention and swelling so bad that she was unable to wear her shoes at the end of the day shed 14 pounds and her water-retention problem after only 4 weeks of eliminating corn and wheat.

Uncovering food sensitivities is a powerful process that I encourage all of my patients to explore. But what you do with the information is up to you. Once you have determined the effects of particular foods on your health, *you* have to decide whether you want to continue eating them.

KEY 2: REDUCE BLOATING AND AID NUTRIENT ABSORPTION
BY REPLACING ENZYMES OR RESTORING ACID LEVELS

An estimated 30 percent of North Americans have low stomach acidity. Natural aging, a poor diet, and chronic use of certain medications such as corticosteroids, antibiotics, and antacids can impair your stomach's ability to produce acid. Certain medical conditions are also commonly associated with low stomach acid, including hypothyroidism, asthma, eczema, allergies, acne rosacea, adrenal dysfunction, osteoporosis, autoimmune disease, psoriasis, and chronic hives.

The signs and symptoms of low acidity in the stomach or digestive enzymes include the following:

- Bloating, belching, and gas, especially after meals
- Indigestion
- Constipation
- Heartburn or reflux
- Multiple food allergies
- Feeling nauseated after taking supplements
- Weak, peeling, and cracked fingernails
- Redness or dilated blood vessels in the cheeks and nose
- Adult acne
- Hair loss in women
- Iron deficiency
- Undigested food in the stools
- Chronic yeast infections

Even though the removal of allergenic foods during a detox is often all that's needed to eliminate uncomfortable bloating or gas, it's not always the solution. If you continue to wake with a flat stomach but look as if you're 5 months pregnant by the end of the day, take animal- or plant-based enzymes with your meals. And if you're searching for a simple way to check for low stomach acidity, look at your fingernails. Chances are your stomach acid levels are low if you see lengthwise (not sideways) ridges. I, however, recommend a more specific test that's easy to do at home: the HCl challenge. Visit www.thehormonediet.com for instructions on how to complete this simple test that can help you to determine whether you have the appropriate level of hydrochloric acid (HCl) in your stomach for optimal digestion. But don't do this test if you have ulcers.

Hypochlorhydria—Low Stomach Acid Challenge

An estimated 30 percent of North Americans have low acidity. Natural aging, a poor diet, chronic use of certain medications, and past infection with *Helicobacter pylori* bacteria can impair the stomach's ability to produce acid.

Stomach acid, technically known as hydrochloric acid, is essential for proper functioning of the digestive system. It activates digestive enzymes that break down food into small particles for absorption. Low acidity may result in only partial digestion of foods, leading to gas, bloating, belching, diarrhea, or constipation. Gastric cancer is also linked to too little stomach acid, as too little acid creates inflammatory changes in the stomach lining and a condition called chronic atrophic gastritis. Over time, this often leads to cancer.

Normal levels of stomach acid help keep the digestive system free of bacteria, yeasts, and parasites. With low acidity and the presence of undigested food, bacteria are more likely to colonize the stomach or small intestine and interfere with the digestion and absorption of protein, fat, and carbohydrates.

Many vitamins and minerals, including magnesium, zinc, calcium, iron, vitamin B_{12}, and folic acid, require proper amounts of stomach acid in order to be properly absorbed.

Signs and Symptoms of Low Acidity

- Bloating, belching, and flatulence immediately after meals
- Indigestion, diarrhea, or constipation
- Soreness, burning, or dryness of the mouth

- Heartburn
- Multiple food allergies
- Feeling nauseous after taking supplements
- Rectal itching
- Weak, peeling, and cracked fingernails
- Redness or dilated blood vessels in the cheeks and nose
- Adult acne
- Hair loss in women
- Iron deficiency
- Undigested food in the stools
- Chronic yeast infections
- Low tolerance for dentures

ARE YOU CONFUSED?

Are you confused about pH? A healthy acid/alkaline balance of your body is the key to great health. When your body is functioning in top form, the digestive tract alternates back and forth between an alkaline and acid pH. Digestion starts in the mouth (which works optimally at an alkaline pH). Moving downward, digestion in the stomach requires an acid pH. Next, the small intestines need an alkaline pH. Finally, the large intestine works best at a slightly acid pH. If any segment fails to keep its proper pH, then the segment before or after it can begin to malfunction. For example, the stomach works best at a low acid pH. If the stomach can't produce enough stomach acid, then it becomes too alkaline. This, in turn, can cause the small intestines (which should be alkaline) to become too acidic.

As many people get older, the parietal cells in their stomach linings produce less and less hydrochloric acid. This is especially true of those who eat (1) heavily cooked foods, which have no live enzymes; (2) difficult-to-digest foods, such as red meat or fried foods; (3) processed foods, such as those containing artificial preservatives and additives; (4) soft drinks, which contain high amounts of phosphorus, white sugar, and immune-stressing chemicals; and (5) barbecued foods, which cause high digestive stress. (The blackened areas of barbecued foods contain carcinogenic, or cancer-causing, agents.)

TAKE THE HCL CHALLENGE

This simple test can help you determine whether you have the appropriate level of hydrochloric acid in your stomach for optimal digestion. Don't do this test, however, if you have ulcers.

Begin by taking one capsule of betaine hydrochloride (BH) *before* your largest meal of the day. I recommend Betaine HCl from Douglas Labs, which you can purchase through my online store at www.thehormonediet.com.

You should feel a burning or warming sensation in your stomach or upper abdomen within about an hour after the meal; this indicates that you have enough HCl and you're done with the test. You may also feel slightly "acidic," as though you have indigestion, which also means you probably have enough stomach acid.

If you don't feel anything after taking the BH, repeat the process the following day with two pills before your largest meal. If you feel the warming or burning sensation, take only one pill the next day. Keep doing this daily until the warming sensation returns. You can then stop taking the pills. You may choose to continue supplementing at each meal (three times a day) with a digestive enzyme that contains HCl along with enzymes. Good choices include Metagest (made by Metagenics) and Ultrazyme (made by Douglas Labs). These are also available through www.thehormonediet.com; look for them in the digestive aid category.

Note: You should feel something after taking one or two pills— this is normal. If you must increase the dosage beyond this point, your stomach acid level is too low. In that case, your aim is to discover just how low, so keep going.

If you do not feel anything after two pills, take three pills the next day before your largest meal.

If you feel the burning or warming sensation, take two pills the next day and remain at two pills until you feel the sensation return, then drop to one pill the day after that. Remain at one until the sensation returns again, then stop taking the pills entirely.

If you do not feel anything at three pills, keep increasing by one pill each day until you reach a maximum of 10 pills. (Take five before and five after beginning to eat your largest meal.) Keep taking 10 pills until you feel the warming sensation, and then drop down to nine, eight, seven, and so on, as outlined above. Be patient and stick with it. Correcting a hydrochloric acid deficiency may take a few weeks or even months.

Your goal is to gradually grow accustomed to the HCl capsules and then to wean yourself off them once the proper acid level has been restored. This process will ensure that you have just the right amount of stomach acid—not too much and not too little—for excellent nutrient absorption, one of the key secrets to looking and feeling your best every day.

KEY 3: REESTABLISH HEALTHY BACTERIAL BALANCE

The maintenance and protection of our healthy digestive-tract bacteria through proper nutrition and, if necessary, supplementation, is very important to good health. Under normal circumstances, friendly bacteria found in our digestive system live with us in symbiotic harmony, but factors such as poor diet and medications such as birth control pills, antibiotics, and corticosteroids can upset this balance and lead to a host of difficulties.

We now know these live microorganisms are cancer protective, immune enhancing, and anti-inflammatory. Other documented benefits of probiotics include the following:

1. **Relief of all types of digestive system upset.** This includes diarrhea, constipation, gas, bloating, etc.
2. **Less fat storage.** Research completed at the Department of Genomic Sciences at the University of Washington found increased fat storage in rats lacking probiotics.
3. **Hormonal balance.** Bacteria in the digestive tract play a hugely important role in the breakdown of excess estrogen. If you are taking the birth control pill, be sure to use a probiotic supplement regularly to avoid the unfavorable symptoms of excess estrogen including weight gain, especially around the hips and thighs.
4. **Vitamin production and nutrient absorption.** This includes vitamins K, B_{12}, and B_5, as well as biotin.
5. **Prevention of yeast infections.** If you're a woman with recurrent yeast infections, the bacterial balance in your large intestine is compromised and you would likely benefit from a probiotic supplement.
6. **Elimination of bad breath.** Eating plain organic yogurt or taking probiotic supplements for 6 weeks or more can help fight certain chemicals in the mouth that contribute to bad breath and gingivitis.
7. **Inflammation control.** Probiotics are proven to be beneficial for relieving symptoms of inflammation, including arthritis, ulcerative colitis, and Crohn's disease.
8. **Allergy relief.** Allergy-based symptoms such as eczema, seasonal allergies, asthma, and hives have been found to improve with probiotic supplements.
9. **Prevention of colds and flus.** Daycare- and school-age children who take supplements of acidophilus and bifidus are sick less often. Supplementing with beneficial bacteria also stimulates immunity in adults, strengthening our resistance to bacterial and viral infections.

KEY 4: RESOLVE INFLAMMATION AND POOR IMMUNITY BY REPAIRING THE DIGESTIVE-TRACT WALL

The competency of the entire wall of the digestive tract is dependent on healthy food choices, bacterial balance, sufficient enzymes and acid levels, and inflammation control. An imbalance in any one of these important factors may result in an irritation of the digestive-tract wall. When that happens, tiny holes may form, allowing partially digested material, toxins, or bacteria to pass through. In the short term, this problem, also known as *leaky gut syndrome*, causes symptoms of digestive upset, gas, bloating, pain, weakened immunity, and allergic symptoms. In the long term, a compromised digestive tract wall can lead to toxic weight gain, obesity, allergies, depressed immunity, autoimmune disease, attention-deficit/hyperactivity disorder (ADHD), depression, and joint inflammation or disease.

Several supplements can help repair a damaged digestive-tract wall. These include glutamine, deglycyrrhizinated licorice (DGL), aloe vera, plantain, and marshmallow. With the exception of glutamine, these products are known as demulcents because they help coat and heal the digestive-tract wall. Most, if not all, of us can use help to repair our gut wall, which is why I have recommended a gut-healing and detoxifying fiber supplement as part of your detox protocol.

KEY 5: REDUCE NEGATIVE EFFECTS OF STRESS ON DIGESTION

Your digestive system has as many nerves as your spinal cord. (So when you get a gut instinct, go with it!) Unfortunately, this design leaves our digestive system susceptible to the effects of stress. When the "fight-or-flight" nervous system is stimulated, digestive function effectively shuts down, as bloodflow to the area is redirected to our limbs. Chronic stress is known to bring on symptoms of irritable bowel syndrome, such as constipation or diarrhea, and to exacerbate symptoms of inflammatory bowel diseases.

In a study published in the *British Medical Journal* (February 2007), researchers found that irritable bowel syndrome (IBS) patients were significantly more likely to report high levels of stress and anxiety. They were also prone to be driven individuals who would carry on *regardless* of their level of discomfort until they were forced to rest— a pattern of behavior known to worsen and prolong the condition.

Determining which comes first, the emotional state or the digestive symptoms, can be difficult. Those of us who suffer from IBS may learn as children to cope with stressful situations by developing digestive symptoms. Other research suggests that IBS sufferers have difficulty adapting to life situations in general, though that is tough to assess.

One of my favorite supplements for patients experiencing stress or anxiety along with digestive issues is the amino acid 5-hydroxytryptophan (5-HTP). As a precursor to serotonin, 5-HTP can help alleviate both concerns since most of this "happy hormone" is produced by cells around your digestive tract and not, as you might have guessed, in your brain. This connection has prompted researchers to develop new medications that influence serotonin for the purpose of treating irritable bowel syndrome.

The Lasting Benefits of the Five Keys to Great Digestion

The first 2 weeks of the Hormone Diet center on optimizing your sleep, enhancing immunity, reducing stress, conquering inflammation, and improving digestion—all at once. This is good news, considering the astounding number of people who are plagued by these health problems. The steps outlined here offer many other positive benefits as well, including more energy, glowing skin, stronger mental focus, less joint pain and stiffness, and, of course, fat loss.

Moving on from the digestive system, we should now discuss the other primary organ responsible for ridding us of toxins, aiding fat burning, and clearing the body of waste—the liver. Your liver is also a major player in achieving hormonal balance because it controls the production of certain hormones, such as your fat-burning friend

T3 thyroid hormone, and the breakdown of others, such as the fat-burning foe cortisol.

An Unhappy Liver Hinders Detoxification and Fat Loss

Similar to the way it does in our muscles, fat burning in the liver occurs through a complex pathway involving our PPARs (peroxisome proliferator-activated receptors). A 2006 study published in the *American Journal of Physiology—Gastroenterology and Liver Physiology* reported that toxins, including drugs and alcohol, can cause abnormalities in the fat-burning pathways of the liver. This causes less fat burning, and leads to increased storage of fat in the body and possibly *in* our liver cells, too. Over time, excess fat stored in liver cells can be harmful to liver structure and impair its function. In the past, a fatty liver was most often associated with excess alcohol intake. However, rising rates of obesity, diabetes, insulin resistance, high cholesterol, high blood pressure, and elevated triglycerides are now the main culprits behind the greater prevalence of fatty liver disease. According to research from the Mayo Clinic, this condition may affect as many as one-third of American adults. More recently, as of September 2008, experts think that as much as 10 percent of overweight children and half of those who are obese may suffer from fatty liver.

Is It Time for a Detox?

Besides all of these larger issues, there is a very basic reason why I suggest beginning your health restoration and fat-loss program with a liver and bowel detox. The signs and symptoms of hormonal imbalance and ill health are often completely resolved when body detoxification is supported. No more symptoms, no need for further, unnecessary treatment. What could be better?

But here are a few questions you can ask yourself to determine your detox need:

- Do you feel tired or lethargic?

- Do you have difficulty concentrating or staying focused?
- Do you experience frequent colds or flus?
- Do you have joint pain or stiffness?
- Do you have frequent headaches?
- Have you had a change in body odor or taste in your mouth?
- Do you have dark circles under your eyes?
- Does your skin lack luster?
- Are you overweight?
- Do you have acne, eczema, or psoriasis?
- Do you have constipation (less than one bowel movement per day)?
- Do you have gas, bloating, or indigestion?
- Do you look puffy or bloated?
- Do you have high cholesterol or fatty liver disease?

The more yes responses you have, the greater your need for a natural, anti-inflammatory detox!

By following the nutrition and supplement guidelines presented in this chapter, you will successfully complete your body detox in just 2 weeks. I recommend going through this body detox process at least twice a year, preferably in the spring and fall. Your health is absolutely worth the investment. (At this stage, you may also want to refer to Appendix B to discover ways you can detoxify your space.)

Getting Started with Your Body Detox

Stick to this anti-inflammatory diet for 14 days. If you're currently experiencing symptoms (fatigue, headaches, gas, bloating, heartburn, acne, eczema, etc.) and find that they are still present at the end of the 2-week period, you *can* extend your cleanse up to 6 weeks before moving on. Otherwise, on Day 11, you'll begin reintroducing some of the foods you've temporarily removed from your diet.

Before you get started, you should eat up (or get rid of) your current supplies of the foods that aren't allowed during your detox. This will help you to avoid cheating or falling off the wagon. Plan your meals according to the detox rules. Shop for specific foods and supplements, and make sure all of your social commitments involving alcohol are out of the way before you begin.

Since the focus is determining food sensitivities and reducing inflammation during these 14 days, caloric intake is not the crucial matter. You should, however, consume at least three meals per day that contain a detox-friendly protein source (egg, turkey, chicken, etc.). Snacks are optional on the Hormone Diet plan, though at least one is recommended in the afternoon, before strength training, or after a workout. You should also consume a serving of grain products (such as rice, gluten-free bread, millet, or quinoa) or sweet potatoes a maximum of once a day, with each serving no larger than the size of your fist. Limit soy and nuts to one serving a day. Then just make sure you avoid the forbidden foods. Please remember *not* to restrict your calories. If you cut your food intake too much, you'll simply hamper your metabolism by creating (or aggravating) imbalances in your stress and blood sugar hormones.

Foods to Eat, Foods to Avoid

The following food groups *must be removed from your diet* during your body detox because they are inflammatory or allergenic:

- **Dairy products.** Yogurt, cheese, milk, cream, sour cream, cottage cheese, casein, whey protein concentrate. One daily serving of 100 percent pure whey protein isolate or sheep and goat milk cheeses is *allowed.*
- **All grains that contain gluten.** Wheat, spelt, rye, kamut, barley. Note that most breads, bagels, muffins, pastries, cakes, pasta, durum semolina, couscous, cookies, flour, and cereals are off-limits, *unless they are gluten free.* Oatmeal, although gluten free, is *not* allowed on the detox.
- **Corn.** Popcorn, corn chips, corn breads or muffins, fresh corn, canned or frozen niblets.

- **Oils:** Hydrogenated oils, palm kernel oil, trans fatty acids, soybean oil, corn oil, cottonseed oil, vegetable oil, shortening, and margarine. Limit your intake of safflower and sunflower oil.
- **Alcohol and caffeine.** During your detox I recommend you cut these out completely. Too much of either one will elevate stress hormones and contribute to hormonal imbalance.
- **Peanuts and peanut-containing products.** Peanut butter, peanuts in the shell, trail mix containing peanuts, etc. Check labels carefully, as many products list peanuts as ingredients.
- **Sugar and artificial sweeteners.** Table sugar (sucrose) and all products with sugar added must be cut out completely. Foods to avoid include maple syrup, honey (except for the small amount in your homemade salad dressings), rice syrup, foods and drinks containing high-fructose corn syrup, packaged foods, candies, soda, juice, etc., as well as all diet products containing aspartame, etc.
- **Citrus fruit.** Oranges, tangerines, and grapefruit. Lemons are okay.
- **Red meats.** Pork, beef, lamb, all types of cold cuts, bacon, and all types of sausages.

The following anti-inflammatory and immune-enhancing foods are *permissible* during your detox program:

- **Gluten-free grains and starchy grains.** Millet, quinoa, rice, buckwheat, rice pasta, rice cakes, rice crackers, sweet potatoes, squash, potatoes, amaranth. Have just one serving per day (the size of your fist).
- **Vegetables.** Unlimited amounts of all vegetables except corn.
- **Fruits.** All fruits *except* oranges, tangerines, grapefruit, canned fruits, raisins, dates, and other nonorganic dried fruits.
- **Beans.** All beans are allowed.
- **Nuts and seeds.** All nuts except for peanuts; all seeds are fine. Maximum serving is one small handful per day.

- **Fish and meat.** All poultry (chicken, turkey, duck, etc.), fish, and seafood are fine.
- **Dairy.** Feta cheese (made from sheep's or goat's milk), goat cheese (1 tablespoon maximum per day), small amounts of butter (1 teaspoon maximum per day).
- **Oils.** Canola oil, flaxseed oil, hemp oil, avocado oil, small amounts of butter, and extra-virgin olive oil are the only oils you should consume.
- **Eggs.** Both yolks and whites are okay.
- **Milks.** Oat, almond, rice, and soy milks are fine, but avoid those with sugar added.
- **Soy products.** All soy products are allowed unless you have noticed digestive upset (gas, bloating, or other symptoms of indigestion) when you have eaten these products in the past. Selections include tofu, tempeh, soy nuts, soy milk, and whole soybeans. Keep soy consumption to one serving a day at most.

Don't worry—I've outlined a detox diet meal plan later on in this chapter, and I've included recipes in Appendix C.

Your Detox Supplement Plan

While you are on the detox diet, you should also include the supplements outlined in this section. Although they're not a mandatory part of your program, I strongly recommend including them in order to enhance your liver detox. These supplements will boost:

- The breakdown and elimination of hormones in the liver and digestive system
- Antioxidant protection
- Your energy and metabolic rate

The Clear Detox products, originally formulated for use by patients at my clinic, are now easily available through www.thehormonediet.com. These products specifically enhance the breakdown and elimination of excess hormones that are our fat-burning foes. I have also recommended other brands here, but don't feel you have to purchase these exact items. Those with similar ingredients should be fine, provided they are from a reputable company. Ask the staff at your local health food store for advice.

1. **A probiotic supplement.** Recall that replacing healthy bacterial balance in the gut is one of the five keys to healthy digestion. Yogurt naturally contains probiotics, but supplements are more effective as a concentrated source. All probiotic supplements should be refrigerated. During your detox, I recommend a probiotic with at least 10 to 15 billion cells per capsule, while a good maintenance dose is 1 to 2 billion of both lactobacilli and bifidobacteria once a day, without food.

   You can also alternate the use of probiotic supplements—1 month on, 1 month off—after your detox. In most cases, daily supplementation is not necessary unless you are taking a medication that affects bacterial balance. For example, during antibiotic therapy you should take increased doses of probiotic supplements 3 hours before or after your medication and continue to take them for twice the length of time of your antibiotic treatment. Take a probiotic supplement daily if you are on the birth control pill, corticosteroids, or HRT.

   Some people experience bloating when they first begin taking probiotic supplements. If you're bothered by this, simply reduce the dosage and slowly increase it as your body adapts.

   Recommended brands include the following:
   - Ultra Flora Plus (Metagenics): 1 or 2 capsules per day on an empty stomach
   - HMF Forte (Genestra): 1 or 2 capsules per day with food
   - Smooth Food 2 or All-Flora (New Chapter): 2 capsules per day on an empty stomach
   - Clear Flora (Clear Medicine)

2. **An herbal cleansing formula for the liver and/or bowels that contains milk thistle, dandelion, turmeric, artichoke, and/or beet leaf.** These herbs improve the flow of bile, aid liver function, reduce inflammation, improve estrogen and cortisol metabolism, and reduce fatty liver, a factor known to accelerate aging.

   Recommended brands include the following:
   - Clear Detox—Hormonal Health (Clear Medicine)
   - Lipo-Gen (Metagenics)
   - Liver-G.I. Detox (Pure Encapsulations)

3. **One serving per day of a bowel-cleansing formula containing fiber.** Choices include glucomannan, apple, beet, or flax fibers; glutamine; the herbal formula triphala and preferably herbs to coat and heal the digestive tract wall, such as deglycyrrhizinated licorice (DGL), aloe, and/or marshmallow. This type of product will promote healthier, more frequent bowel movements while you detox your liver and digestive system. It will also help maintain the integrity of your digestive tract wall, thereby reducing inflammation and leaky gut syndrome.

   Triphala is a standardized blend of three fruit extracts— *Terminalia chebula, Terminalia belerica,* and *Emblica officinalis*— in equal proportions. It is an Ayurvedic herbal blend commonly used for supporting intestinal detoxification, occasional constipation, and overall colon health.

   Soluble fiber is fermented in your large intestines by your intestinal microflora and will help create an intestinal environment that allows beneficial bacteria to thrive. When taken with appropriate amounts of water, soluble fiber also bulks up the stool to support larger, softer stools and healthy bowel movements. As the bulk moves through your intestine, it helps to collect and eliminate other waste and toxins from your intestinal walls.

   Recommended brands include the following:
   - Clear Detox—Digestive Health (Clear Medicine)

- G.I. Fortify (Pure Encapsulations): one serving of the powder per day mixed in, or followed by, 1 cup of water

Note that as a cheaper, although somewhat less effective, alternative to these bowel-cleansing products you can add ¹/₄ cup aloe vera juice or gel and 2 tablespoons of ground flaxseeds per day to your smoothies.

4. **You may include supplements to reduce inflammation** (see page 293 for your options). My first choice for treating inflammation is a supplement of omega-3 fish oils. Take 4 to 6 g per day with food. Wobenzym, turmeric, or resveratrol are my second-line interventions. I recommend picking resveratrol if you want to kick-start your weight loss. It's touted to be the French Paradox in a bottle, which means that in addition to its anti-inflammatory effects, it may allow you to eat more without experiencing weight gain.

The products listed here are necessary only during your detox, though you can certainly finish your bottles should they happen to last longer than 2 weeks. The exception is the supplements added to reduce inflammation. You should continue these as long as your signs or symptoms of inflammation persist. Fish oils and resveratrol may be taken for a lifetime—I say they should be used this long!

Coming Off the Detox

Once you have avoided certain foods for the first 10 days of your detox, you'll slowly reintroduce them. Often it's the end of a detox that's the most important part because it allows you to make the connection between certain foods and how they make you feel.

Reintroduce each food one by one, one day at a time as I outline in your menu plan on page 203. You will try the least allergenic foods first, followed by the foods with the greatest tendency to cause problems. You won't eat each test food again until you have introduced all the other foods. For example, test rye on Day 11 with 100 percent rye bread or Ryvita crackers. Then you'll stop eating rye again and introduce plain organic yogurt on Day 12. On Day 13, yogurt is avoided again and you'll try low-fat cheese. On the last day of your detox, cut out the cheese again and try wheat by having some whole-wheat pasta or bread.

I recommend you test rye, dairy, and wheat first because they are permitted in the next step of your diet, as long as your body likes them. When you reintroduce these foods, be on the lookout for symptoms that point to an allergy or intolerance. Check the chart I have provided below to see the most common reactions to certain foods. Keeping a food diary at this point can certainly be helpful.

As you move on to the next step in the Hormone Diet, you may, for your own enjoyment, continue adding other foods you've been avoiding since the start of your detox, though I normally do not include sugar, alcohol, or caffeine in the reintroduction process. My feeling is that most of us will continue to consume these foods on our cheat days—regardless of their potential negative effect. But I do recommend avoiding them until you are done with the reintroduction process, and longer, if you wish to continue losing weight.

COMMON REACTIONS WITH REINTRODUCTION OF FOODS AFTER DETOX THAT CAN INDICATE A FOOD SENSITIVITY

Food	Typical Reactions
Rye (try 100% rye crackers or bread)	Gas, bloating, constipation, fatigue immediately after eating the food, fatigue on waking the next day, irritability, anxiety, headaches, water retention (e.g., can't get your rings off, puffiness under the eyes), dark circles under the eyes on waking the next day. You may also notice a gradual decline in your energy over a period of time once you have put rye back into your diet.
Plain organic yogurt	Gas, bloating, constipation, diarrhea, sinus congestion, postnasal drip, constant need to clear your throat; allergies (especially environmental) may worsen.
Low-fat cheese	Gas, bloating, constipation, diarrhea, sinus congestion, postnasal drip, constant need to clear your throat; allergies (especially environmental) may worsen.

Food	Typical Reactions
Spelt (try 100% spelt bread or pasta)	Similar to rye.
Wheat (try 100% whole-wheat bread or pasta)	Similar to rye.
Red meats (try lean cuts of pork and beef on separate days)	Joint pain or stiffness, constipation, indigestion, upset stomach.

Detox Q and A: A Few Common Questions Answered

What can I expect to feel while I am cleansing?

Headaches, fatigue, irritability, and general malaise are common for as many as 4 or 5 days into the diet, as your body is doing a lot of housecleaning. *Allow yourself time to rest if you feel sluggish.* Drink lots of water and take extra vitamin C to reduce detox symptoms. By the third or fourth day, you should feel your energy increasing and mental focus improving. If you typically drink a lot of coffee (more than 4 cups per day), decrease the amounts you consume slowly throughout the first few days to minimize the effects of caffeine withdrawal. Also, drink at least 2 liters of water per day. Reverse osmosis water is best; spring water should be your second choice. Distilled water should be avoided because it may leach minerals out of your body.

If you need encouragement and motivation to keep you on track, remember this: *The more severe your detox reactions, the more you really needed it!*

Will I begin to lose weight during the detox?

I have already mentioned that the very act of eating helps maintain our metabolic rate because of the thermogenic effects of food. Eating is a physical process that requires energy to support digestion and absorption. Of all the macronutrients, protein requires the most energy to digest and absorb. Both Step 1 (the detox) and Step 2 (the Glyci-Med approach) promote the consumption of protein with every meal. When you combine the benefits of protein with reduced water retention and bloating commonly experienced with a detox diet, your weight loss will be off to a good start.

Can I exercise during the detox?

If you usually exercise, continue with your current routine but be aware that headaches, fatigue, or feelings of malaise are common during the first few days of a detox. If you experience these symptoms, allow your body to rest, and select less-intense forms of exercise such as yoga, walking, or Pilates. And be sure to keep drinking plenty of water.

If you are not exercising at this point, now is not the time to dive into an intensive workout regimen. You'll have enough to think about already, so don't try to do too much at once. We'll get you exercising once you reach Chapter 15 at the 4-week mark—when your metabolism will be primed for a shake-up. For now, I would like you to go for a walk after dinner, if only for 15 or 20 minutes.

Can I eat out when doing the detox?

Yes, you can still eat out. Japanese food, seafood, dairy-free risotto, Chinese food, salads, grilled chicken, fish, turkey, vegetables, and potatoes are all fine, but keep an eye out for hidden sugars and unhealthy oils in sauces, soups, and dressings. Don't be afraid to ask your server for specific details about what you're ordering. You should absolutely avoid fast-food restaurants unless you are picking up a salad.

What should I do if I experience constipation (less than one bowel movement per day) during the detox?

Keeping your bowels moving regularly is critical at all times, but especially during your detox, to avoid accumulation and reabsorption of toxins in the bowels. On occasion, dietary changes or reduced intake of fibrous grains can cause constipation. Try one or more of these solutions to help things "move along" if you find you need some help.

- **Increase your intake of flaxseeds.** Add 1 or 2 tablespoons daily to your smoothies, salads, or water. Whether you purchase them ground or grind your own, flaxseeds should be kept in the freezer for maximum freshness. You can also supplement with a nonirritating, psyllium-free fiber powder or capsules such as MetaFiber (Metagenics), G.I. Fortify (Pure Encapsulations), or Gentle Fibers (Jarrow).

- **Increase vitamin C.** Take 3 to 8 g of vitamin C (spread out throughout the day, not all at once). Vitamin C is a great natural laxative in higher doses.
- **Take magnesium citrate.** This supplement can encourage bowel movements because it's a natural muscle relaxant. Take 200 to 800 mg per day. Start with a low dose and increase it gradually. (As with vitamin C, don't take your magnesium all at once.) Magnesium and vitamin C are present in the Clear Detox products, not only to encourage regular bowel movements, but also for their antioxidant and hormone balancing benefits.
- **Take essential fatty acids to help lubricate the bowels**. If you choose a liquid form, 1 tablespoon per day is plenty. Good brands include Nordic Naturals fish oils, Carlson fish oils, Opti EPA (Douglas Labs), or Balanced EPA-DHA liquid (Metagenics). All of these come in liquid form and most are also available in capsules. Liquid forms should be kept in the fridge or freezer. If you choose capsules, take 2 to 4 capsules once or twice a day with food. If you find that fish oil "repeats," put the bottle in the freezer and take it with food, or purchase an enteric-coated formula.

More Tips to Help Your Detox

I have compiled a few tips over the years to help patients get through their detox. The good news is that over 99 percent of people feel better after they've completed this health-promoting process.

Don't be shocked if your emotions run high when you embark on your detox. Food is an emotional thing, heavily tied to many of our social and family activities. Don't get down or beat yourself up if you fall off track. Simply do your best and remember that you are doing this as a favor to yourself. If you manage to cut out *even two* potential offenders during your detox, you'll do your body a lot of good. Maybe next time you'll succeed in cutting out a few more problematic foods.

In the meantime, try these helpful detox tips.

- **Check your dates or clear your calendar.** If you have a party or special event planned, wait until *after* these activities to start your detox. Your liver will probably need the detox even more at that point.
- **Stock your kitchen.** Make sure your fridge and cupboards are filled with detox-friendly foods to make snacking and meal prep easier.
- **Fess up.** Let everyone know you are detoxifying. You'll be surprised by how many people will be interested in what you are doing—they may even want to join you. After your detox, you'll look good and feel even better. Don't be surprised when everyone starts asking you what you have been up to.
- **Recruit other detoxers.** Like any difficult undertaking, detox can be easier when you have a friend or two on board with you from the get-go. A friend of mine detoxes with me every time.
- **Record your feelings.** Get yourself a journal and write down how you feel as you detox. This process will help you notice improvements and can help you track your reactions to certain foods.
- **Pamper yourself.** I encourage you to designate 30 minutes to an hour daily as *your time* on an ongoing basis. But during your detox, try to think of one fantastic thing to do each day and do it—a massage, a facial, a sauna, a day at a pool, a stay at a fancy hotel in your area, a manicure and pedicure (toxin free, of course), a bubble bath, a hike, a yoga class—whatever you need to do to reward yourself for getting healthy.

Walk!

From this point onward, walking should be part of your life. Even a short stroll can be a simple and highly beneficial way to avoid cheating or falling off track with your diet, and to lessen the harmful effects of stress and fatty foods on your body. Studies prove that walking after an unhealthy meal can curb the effects of stress by reducing the amounts of fatty acids, sugars, and stress hormones that are released into the bloodstream and subsequently stored as fat. This gentle form of exercise strengthens nearly every aspect of your body. Numerous studies have shown that heading out for even just a leisurely walk can prevent heart disease and offers excellent stress-reducing effects. Exercise also promotes wakefulness and relaxation and improves the quality of your sleep.

Your Detox Sample Menu Plan

Days 1 to 10

On Days 1 through 10 of your detox, pick and choose from any of the meal suggestions in Appendix C marked "detox friendly" by the symbols ✿☺. But I have outlined menus for the designated days for the reintroduction of specific foods here.

Day 11: Reintroducing Rye

SUGGESTED MEALS

Breakfast: 2 slices 100 percent rye bread with ⅓ of an avocado spread on the bread and 1 whole boiled egg plus 2 more egg whites. Pay attention to how you feel after you have eaten this meal, and the next, containing rye.

Lunch: Sweet Potato, Squash, and Ginger Soup (page 435). (Remove the cheese to make it a ✿☺ meal option.) 3 Wasa crackers

Snack: Your choice

Dinner: Your choice

Day 12: *Reintroducing Yogurt*

SUGGESTED MEALS

Breakfast: Organic apple with 1 cup plain yogurt. Pay attention to how you feel after you have consumed the yogurt.

Lunch: Your choice

Snack: ½ cup plain yogurt and 10 almonds. Pay attention to how you feel after your snack containing yogurt.

Dinner: Your choice

Day 13: *Reintroducing Cheese*

SUGGESTED MEALS

Breakfast: Organic apple with 1 cup low-fat cottage or ricotta cheese. Pay attention to how you feel after you have eaten this meal.

Lunch: Your choice

Snack: 2 slices of low-fat Swiss cheese and veggies. Again, pay attention to how you feel.

Dinner: Your choice

Day 14: *Reintroducing Wheat*

SUGGESTED MEALS

Breakfast: Kashi GOLEAN cereal with soy milk and blueberries. Pay attention to how you feel after you have eaten this cereal containing wheat.

Lunch: Your choice

Snack: Your choice

Dinner: Quick-and-Easy Pasta with Tomato Sauce (page 454). Note: Use the version with ground turkey and *not* the one with cheese during Day 14 of your detox. Pay attention to how you feel after you have eaten this whole-wheat pasta.

Although I haven't specifically included them, you may introduce lean cuts of red meat back into your diet on Days 15 and 16. Definitely introduce beef and pork one at a time on separate days, and pay attention to how you feel after you eat these meats again. Moving forward, you should limit your red meat intake to a few times a month because it's high in inflammatory saturated fats.

While I always encourage you to follow your detox diet as closely as possible, *don't fret if you break the rules a few times.* In most cases, if you're sensitive to the food, you'll still notice some sort of reaction when you reintroduce it into your diet.

Once you've completed your detox and learned how to manage stress as outlined in the next chapter, you'll be ready for the lifelong nutrition plan that will wipe out food allergies, restore hormonal balance, and promote fat loss. Now that's a powerful combination for better health!

THE HORMONE DIET 14-DAY DETOX

Review of Suggested Servings and Allowed Foods
Step 1: Anti-Inflammatory Detox

BENEFITS	Calm Inflammation
	Reduce Allergies
	Reduce Bloating and Water Retention
	Lose Weight
	Increase Energy
	Improve Sleep
	Improve Skin and Digestion

Foods to enjoy	Foods to avoid
Grains and starchy vegetables—one serving the size of your fist daily: Millet; buckwheat; rice and rice products, such as rice pasta, rice cakes, and rice crackers; sweet potatoes; amaranth; quinoa; squash; and potatoes.	**All grains that contain gluten:** Wheat, spelt, rye, kamut, amaranth, and barley. Cut out oatmeal, bread, bagels, muffins, pastries, cakes, pasta, durum semolina, couscous, cookies, flour, and cereals.
Vegetables: All vegetables except for corn.	**Corn:** Popcorn, corn chips, fresh corn, canned corn, etc.
Fruits: All fruits except for oranges, tangerines, grapefruit, raisins, dates, and non-organic dried fruit.	**Citrus and processed fruits:** Oranges, grapefruit, tangerines, canned fruits, and nonorganic dried fruits.
Nuts and seeds—one serving per day: All nuts and seeds are fine except for peanuts. Choices include cashews, walnuts, Brazil nuts, sesame seeds, pumpkin seeds, sunflower seeds, pecans, etc.	**Peanuts:** Peanut butter and any products containing peanuts. Also avoid pistachios.

Foods to enjoy (continued)	Foods to avoid (continued)
Fish and meat: All poultry (chicken, turkey, duck, etc.). Fish and seafood are fine.	**Red meats:** Beef, pork, luncheon meats, cold cuts, sausage, bacon, and lamb.
Dairy—1 tablespoon daily: Feta (made from sheep's or goat's milk), goat cheese. Replace dairy milks with oat, almond, rice, or soy milk.	**Dairy:** Cow's milk cheeses, milk, yogurt, sour cream, and soups and sauces containing dairy.
Soy products: All soy products are fine unless you have noticed digestive upset (gas, bloating, indigestion, or other symptoms) when you have eaten these products in the past. Choices include tofu, tempeh, soy nuts, soy milk, and whole soybeans. Limit soy to one serving per day.	**Alcohol and caffeine:** Coffee, nonherbal tea, sodas, and all alcoholic beverages.
Sweeteners: Stevia, maple syrup, and honey are allowed in small amounts in salad dressing mix only.	**Sugar and artificial sweeteners:** Table sugar, any product with sugar added, rice syrup, maple syrup, high-fructose corn syrup, packaged foods, candies, soda, juice, etc.
Oils: Canola oil, avocado oil, flaxseed oil, butter, and extra-virgin olive oil are the only oils you should consume.	**Oils:** Hydrogenated oils, trans fatty acids, palm oil, soy oil, corn oil, cottonseed oil, vegetable oil, shortening, and margarine. Limit your intake of safflower and sunflower oils.
Eggs: Yolks and whites are fine.	
All beans: Chickpeas, lentils, black beans, etc.	

THE HORMONE DIET 14-DAY DETOX SUPPLEMENT PLAN

When and How to Take It	Supplement
On rising (no food)	Probiotic supplement
	Liver-cleansing formula (Clear Detox—Hormonal Health)
	If needed: anti-inflammatory supplements
With breakfast/dinner	**Optional:** Multivitamin and omega-3 fish oils with breakfast and dinner
Before bed (no food)	Probiotic supplement
	Bowel-cleansing high-fiber formula (Clear Detox—Digestive Health)
	If needed: anti-inflammatory supplement

You may wish to use the following chart (or if you don't like to write in this book, print it from www.thehormonediet.com) to track possible reactions when reintroducing specific foods back into your diet:

FOOD REACTIONS TO WATCH FOR

Food	Reactions to Watch For	Symptoms Noted (if any)
Rye (try 100% rye crackers or rye bread) on Day 11	Gas, bloating, constipation, fatigue immediately after eating the food, fatigue on waking the next day, irritability, anxiety, headaches, water retention (can't get your rings off, puffiness under your eyes the next day), dark circles under your eyes on waking the next day. Or you may notice a gradual decline in your energy over a period of time once you have put the rye back into your diet.	
Plain organic yogurt on Day 12	Gas, bloating, constipation, diarrhea, sinus congestion, postnasal drip, constant need to clear your throat. Allergies (especially environmental) may worsen.	
Low-fat cheese on Day 13	Similar to yogurt.	
Wheat (try 100% whole-wheat bread or pasta) on Day 14	Similar to rye.	
Red meats (try lean pork or beef, introduced on separate days) on Days 15 and 16	Joint pain or stiffness, constipation, indigestion, upset stomach.	

HEALTHY HORMONE TIP

HEAVY METALS

Are heavy metals weighing you down?

Just as acidic body pH has a widespread influence on most bodily processes and your overall wellness, the presence of heavy metals can disrupt your hormones and compromise your health. So investigating your risk of heavy metal toxicity is definitely a worthwhile addition to your body detox program.

What are heavy metals?

Antimony, arsenic, aluminum, bismuth, cadmium, cerium, cobalt, copper, gallium, gold, iron, lead, manganese, mercury, nickel, platinum, silver, tellurium, thallium, tin, uranium, vanadium, and zinc are examples of minerals and metals that are harmful when an overload is present in your body. A priority list called "Top 20 Hazardous Substances," compiled by the Agency for Toxic Substances and Disease Registry (ATSDR www.atsdr.cdc.gov/), includes the heavy metals arsenic (1), lead (2), mercury (3), and cadmium (7) high on the list.

Where do we get them from?

Heavy metals accumulate in our soft tissues, brain, bones, and fat. We can be exposed to them at work, at home, or outdoors through occupational contact, food, or water. Acute exposure may come from inhalation of fumes or skin contact with heavy metal dust, usually in the workplace. Exposure can also happen slowly over time from sources such as old plumbing pipes, lead paint, smoking, dental amalgams (fillings), cookware, a tainted water supply, or consumption of ocean fish and seafood. Heavy metals may also be present in personal-care products. For example, certain lipsticks are known to contain lead, and aluminum is an ingredient in most antiperspirants. As evidenced by recent headlines, even some imported children's toys are a cause for concern.

What happens when we have heavy metal toxicity?

Certain heavy metals interfere with our hormones and, consequently, our metabolism. For instance, mercury, which is often present in large ocean fish, inhibits thyroid hormone and growth hormone. Heavy metal toxicity is also very damaging to our nervous system, cognition, lungs, kidneys, liver, eyes, and other vital organs. Long-term exposure may result in slowly progressing, muscular and neurological degeneration that mimics signs of Alzheimer's disease, Parkinson's disease, muscular dystrophy, and multiple sclerosis.

How do you know if you have heavy metal toxicity?

The best way to assess your risk of heavy metal toxicity is through a stool or urine test, available through Doctor's Data, Inc. You may want to consult an integrated-health practitioner in your area or visit www.thehormonediet.com and look under testing recommendations for more information.

What can you do if you have heavy metal toxicity?

You must seek professional medical attention in any case of heavy metal toxicity, especially since treatment options vary depending on the type of metal toxicity you experience. However, there are a number of herbs and supplements that you may use to support your body's own natural chelation (metal removal) mechanisms.

The two most common metal toxicities I have seen in my practice to date involve mercury and lead. My treatment recommendations include oral chelation with DMSA (also known as 2,3-dimercaptosuccinic acid), which has a strong affinity for removing both mercury and lead. Rectal suppositories of ethylenediaminetetraacetic acid (EDTA) have a strong affinity for lead, but also remove all other metals. EDTA was one of the first chelators developed. Visit www.detoxamin.com or the resource section of www.thehormonediet.com for more information. If you're taking prescription medications or if you have a specific medical condition, consult your doctor before using either of these products.

In conjunction with products designed to remove heavy metals, antioxidants and detoxifying agents should be used. A full heavy metal protocol may include whey protein, vitamin C, chlorella, selenium, zinc, cilantro, a high-potency multivitamin, and a blend of essential amino acids. Fiber supplements and liver support (milk thistle, MSM, and turmeric) should also be used to aid elimination. Regular sessions in an infrared sauna are an excellent complement to any heavy metal detoxification protocol, especially for mercury toxicity.

If you suspect you have heavy metal toxicity, don't try to take care of it on your own. Consult a licensed health-care provider to help assess your situation and, if necessary, supervise detoxification.

HORMONE DIET SUCCESS STORY

Vanessa F. (age 27)

I had been suffering with unexplainable intense stomach cramping, bloating, constipation and diarrhea, fatigue, and hypoglycemia since around 2003. I also exercised regularly but couldn't lose weight no matter what I did. The symptoms continued to get progressively worse over the years. I thought that perhaps it was the coffee or the milk or the exercise. I never would have imagined that it might be gluten sensitivity.

I was hungry all the time, and I even woke up at night to eat. I would feel dizzy and shaky, and as if I was in a constant fog. I tried digestive enzymes, Beano, Gas-X, IBS supplements, Tums, and Pepto-Bismol. Nothing helped. I saw the doctor more than four times, and he finally said that I had irritable bowel syndrome, though I was never tested for anything. I pursued his suggestions and bought a book about the proper way to eat if you have IBS. After all that, I still felt sick.

I tried many different diets, to no avail. I even went to a hypnotist because I thought that stress was causing my stomach pains. That didn't help, either. Luckily, one day my mother was watching a television show about a book called *The Hormone Diet*. The book advised people to do a detox, follow a balanced diet plan, and exercise to lose weight and regulate their hormones. I recognized many of the symptoms that were mentioned, so I decided to pick up the book and give it a try.

I purchased all of the supplies and followed everything very carefully. During the detox I stopped eating wheat, rye, dairy, oranges, corn, caffeine, and alcohol. At day 11 I had to reintroduce rye, and when I did I felt horrible. All of my symptoms came back! The next day was dairy, and I felt slightly off. The third day was wheat, and I felt horrible again. That's when I realized that it was gluten sensitivity all along!

I bought a whole bunch of books on gluten-free eating and later did a gluten sensitivity test from Enterolab. Sure enough, I was right (thanks to Dr. Turner's help!), and the tests came back positive for gluten sensitivity. I was so relieved to finally know what was wrong with me and how to stop the pain. After a long battle, I finally feel healthy again.

I used to be sick every day, and I found it hard to work as a dental hygienist and act happy and caring when I had excruciating pain in my stomach and was in the bathroom every hour. Going out with friends to weddings and parties was even more difficult. Now I just have to bring food supplies and watch what I am eating, and I can have fun!

I'm so grateful for Dr. Turner's book and her incredible work! If I hadn't done the detox, I would never have known that gluten was making me sick. I hope my message will help others get the proper diagnosis so they don't suffer for as long as I did.

CHAPTER 9

STRATEGIES FOR STRESS SURVIVAL

These are the hormonal benefits you can expect to enjoy from subduing stress:

- Controlled cortisol and a calm nervous system
- Replenished DHEA, the antiaging hormone
- Reduced insulin, better craving control, and increased ab fat loss
- Increased GABA, dopamine, and serotonin, our relaxation and feel-good hormones
- Topped-up testosterone and protection from the harmful effects of excess estrogen through balanced progesterone
- More melatonin and growth hormone to work metabolic magic on night-time repair and fat burning
- Maximized effects of thyroid hormone, the metabolic master
- Better appetite control via increased leptin and suppressed appetite-stimulating hormones, ghrelin and NPY

Sleeping well and cooling inflammation through detoxification are critical components in the first of your three steps to hormonal health. But Step 1 would be incomplete without tackling one more major lifestyle change. To achieve true hormonal harmony and create the foundation for lasting fat loss, you absolutely must bring your stress hormones under control. The high levels of cortisol associated with excessive stress interfere with almost every other hormone involved in metabolism regulation, appetite control, and fat burning.

You might think stress isn't a problem for you. If so, hey, that's amazing. Though to really assess the role stress plays in your life, you need to fully understand the various ways in which stress can present itself. It can be immediate and short lived, such as narrowly missing a crash on the highway. Or it can be chronic, lasting days to weeks to months to years as we're faced with a divorce, an illness, loss of a job, or a death in the family. I conducted my own research into stress and discovered a few interesting and often overlooked examples that may surprise you.

The Stress of Loneliness

A powerful study completed by researchers at Northwestern University in 2006 showed just how strongly our social and emotional experiences affect our hormonal balance and overall health. Subjects who went to bed feeling lonely, sad, or overwhelmed exhibited high levels of cortisol and a low mood the

next day. This study was the first to prove that experiences influence stress hormones just as stress hormones influence experiences. Interestingly, individuals who got out of bed with low cortisol reported fatigue throughout the day. We need cortisol, just not too much.

The Stress of Commuting

Millions of North Americans commute to work every weekday. If you're one of them, did you ever imagine your daily commute could be contributing to your ab fat—and not just because of all that sitting? Researchers from Cornell University have found a link between a longer commute to work, whether by car or by train, and greater feelings of frustration, irritation, and stress. The research team measured the salivary cortisol of 208 commuters taking trains from New Jersey to Manhattan. All of the subjects had routinely high cortisol readings, proving that commuting is a stressful aspect of work for many people. For some, commuting can be *the* most stressful aspect. Certainly we need to consider commuting stress to be an important, although often overlooked, part of environmental health.

The Stress of Overexercising

Whether we engage in strength training or aerobic activity, cortisol is released during exercise in proportion to the intensity of our effort. Both high-intensity and prolonged exercise cause increases in cortisol, which can remain elevated for hours following a workout. Numerous studies have proven that this rise in cortisol tends to occur with very strenuous exercise and when we exercise for longer than 40 to 45 minutes. Performing repeated strenuous workouts without appropriate rest between sessions also results in chronically elevated cortisol.

You may already be aware of the adverse effects of high cortisol on your health, mood, body composition, and performance. Chronically high cortisol, which is commonly associated with a decrease in muscle-enhancing growth hormone, DHEA, and testosterone, can cause muscle breakdown and suppress our immune function. Researchers at the University of North Carolina have also linked strenuous, fatiguing exercise to higher cortisol and lower thyroid hormones. Remember, thyroid hormones stimulate your metabolism, so depletion is definitely not a desired effect of exercise! The same study found thyroid hormones remained suppressed even 24 hours after recovery, whereas cortisol levels remained high throughout the same period.

Overexercising can lead to loss of muscle, frequent colds and flus, poor recovery after exercise, and slower gains from your workout efforts. Plus, your risk of illness and injury increases as your metabolic rate slows. Certainly these are not the effects you are looking for when you join a gym.

Poor diet, inadequate supplementation, and lack of rest play a key role in excess cortisol secretion. Experiments measuring cortisol in trained athletes on carb-restricted, high-protein diets found that these athletes had *higher* cortisol. When researchers had the athletes take sugar supplements during their workouts, the cortisol and immune-suppression responses to exercise were lessened.

Bear in mind that most athletes are better conditioned to the stress of exercise than the rest of us—these effects would be worse in someone who's not physically fit to begin with. My point is, if you try to lose weight by slashing your calorie intake, eliminating carbs, and going crazy on the cardio machines, you will do more harm than good. Rather than getting fit and losing weight, you'll crank up your cortisol and damage your metabolism. I cringe when I hear a stressed-out patient mention plans to complete a marathon. The added stress of training for such an event can have disastrous effects.

The Stress of Marital "Bliss"

Professor Janice Kiecolt-Glaser from Ohio State University has made some interesting discoveries about stress hormones and (supposedly) happily married couples. She analyzed cortisol in newlywed couples after they had a 30-minute conversation about a few areas of disagreement in their marriage. The results showed high cortisol and weakened immune-system markers. After a transition period, Kiecolt-Glaser had the couples talk about how they met, what attracted them to each other, and other positive aspects of their relationship. The cortisol levels fell, as expected, in 75 percent of the participants. In the remaining 25 percent, cortisol went up or stayed the same. Even more interesting, when the researchers followed up with the women after the study, those who showed higher cortisol levels were twice as likely to end up divorced. The body does not lie, even when the mind does.

Repair versus Protection Mode

All stress responses require energy from storage sites in your body, whether that energy comes from fat in your fat cells or sugar stored in your muscles and liver. This fuel supports the increase in heart rate, blood pressure, and breathing, as nutrients and oxygen are transported to your vital organs or muscles at greater rates to cope with stress. While your body is busy handling these stress-induced tasks, all nonessential, long-term processes are put on hold.

Basically, our bodies can exist in one of two states: growth, repair, and rebuilding mode or protection mode. The longer the body remains in protection mode, the less time and energy is left over for renewal and regrowth. This redirection of energy makes a lot of sense when we are facing a bear—digestion, immune activity, and reproduction become much less important in moments of life-versus-imminent-death. But what happens when the bear is long gone, yet the high-stress response lingers? We become chronically imbalanced, which leads to muscle wasting, premature aging, fat gain, disease, and even death. Do you need more reason to start ridding your body of stress?

We can't control the infinite number of stressors that surround us every day, but we can control our perceptions and responses. Each one of us has a unique set of physical and mental responses to stress, and these can change over time. I've seen some patients suddenly develop anxiety so severe that they lost the ability to drive and had to take a leave of absence from work. Others have come into my office with physical symptoms of hives, palpitations, or insomnia. Stress always shows its nasty face in one way or another. The trick is to recognize it and refuse to let it take over.

Stress is most often related to feeling out of control. I also strongly believe anxiety is a sign that we are *not making decisions that are in accordance with our values*. It can also be a sign that we are *failing to do something we know in our hearts we should be doing.* For example, I commonly see health-related anxiety in busy executives who go for months or even years without making proper eating and rest a priority. There are three books that I highly recommend to help you gain a stronger understanding of the powerful connection between your emotions, stress, and the origins of illness.

1. *Women's Bodies, Women's Wisdom* by Christiane Northrup, MD (Bantam Books, 2002)
2. *When the Body Says No: The Cost of Hidden Stress* by Gabor Maté, MD (Vintage Canada, 2004)
3. *Anatomy of the Spirit: The Seven Stages of Power and Healing* by Caroline Myss, PhD (Three Rivers Press, 1997)

Adrenal Gland Burnout: Another Consequence of Chronic Stress

If you always feel tense or anxious, your body will remain in a constant state of heightened arousal. Constantly overproducing cortisol and adrenaline day after day because of ongoing stress, multitasking, skipping meals, excessive calorie restriction, insufficient carbohydrate intake, too much protein consumption, lack of sleep, or too much coffee will lead to adrenal gland burnout. At this point, your adrenal glands can't keep up with the constant stimulation and outrageous demands for adrenaline and cortisol production, and they simply shut down.

When your adrenal glands go on strike, cortisol levels plummet, resulting in chronic fatigue, lack of stamina for exercise, more allergy symptoms, sleep disruption, blood sugar imbalances, depression, increased cravings, and weakened immunity. In the presence of these damaging conditions, your risk of autoimmune diseases such as rheumatoid arthritis and lupus also skyrockets.

ARE YOU SUFFERING FROM ADRENAL GLAND BURNOUT?

Give yourself one point for each symptom you're experiencing.

___ 1. Feeling burned out, fatigue especially in the morning, or fatigue in general

___ 2. Poor tolerance for exercise

___ 3. Decreased ability to deal with stress

___ 4. Loss of muscle tone in arms and legs, or muscle weakness

___ 5. Aches and pains

___ 6. Arthritis, bursitis, tendonitis, or joint stiffness

___ 7. Poor memory

___ 8. Loss of motivation or competitive edge

___ 9. Increased pain or poor pain tolerance

___ 10. Hives, bronchitis, allergies (food or environmental), or asthma have worsened or developed

___ 11. Loss of sex drive

___ 12. Alternating diarrhea and constipation or irritable bowel syndrome

___ 13. PMS

___ 14. Depression

___ 15. Autoimmune disease (lupus, rheumatoid arthritis, etc.)

___ 16. Hypoglycemia

___ 17. Cravings for salty and/or fatty foods

___ 18. Inability to lose weight even with dieting and exercise

Total: _____

A score > 6 may indicate your adrenals need some support.

If your adrenals are "shot," the Hormone Diet will recuperate you. When you reach Step 3, which involves exercise for hormonal balance, stick to yoga and strength training rather than cardio until you have come out of your depleted state. You will also need extra supplements to restore your adrenal gland function. Check out your options in Chapter 13 for advanced supplements to aid cortisol balance (Hormonal Imbalance 5).

The Hormone Diet Stress Solution: The Four Elements to Conquer Stress

Being a type A personality, a natural-born worrier, and someone who has developed three hormonal conditions—hypothyroidism, depression, and polycystic ovarian syndrome—after highly stressful periods in my life, I've had my struggles with stress management. I certainly understand how stress makes us sick. (How ironic that I'm now writing a book that touches on how to handle the problem!) I do, however, feel my experiences have helped me be a better caregiver, especially in clinical practice. I hope sharing this information will help you, too.

I've chosen to include stress relief as part of Step 1 because it is such an important factor in the Hormone Diet program. Besides, making stress management a priority now will allow you to start dealing with it sooner rather than later. The recommendations I present in this chapter will take longer than 2 weeks to implement, and even longer to become lifelong habits. Just make sure you practice, practice, practice as often as you can and know that your efforts *will* make a difference.

There are four elements to conquering stress, no matter what the source.

1. RELIEVING STRESS NOW: Identify activities you can do or habits you can adopt to immediately lessen stress and its negative effects on your health. These include deep breathing, meditating, exercising, sleeping well, eating healthfully, getting massages, and even laughing.

2. SETTING YOUR GOALS: You need to develop a sense of *where you are* in your life right now and w*here you want to be.* Lack of direction can create chaos and lead to anxiety or stress. If you find you're drifting, you need to set goals (even small ones) and create the concrete roadmap that will take you where you want to go.

3. VISUALIZING SUCCESS: Once you've created your map, you can use visualization techniques to help reduce stress and turn your goals and dreams into reality.

4. HARNESSING THE POWER OF POSITIVE BELIEF: What you believe ultimately dictates how you think, feel, and experience all aspects of your life. This requires the ability to be positive, express gratitude, gain wisdom, and appreciate the good and the not-so-good in life. Arguably, this is the most important aspect of successfully handling stress and *dis-ease*.

All four elements require commitment, but the first element—involving the actions you can take to reduce stress—is often easier than the second and third. The fourth is by far the most difficult, especially if you aren't naturally a positive person. All of the elements involve personal evaluation, growth, and development, which can feel uncomfortable at first but pay wonderful dividends later on. As the Greek philosopher Socrates put it, a life unexamined is a life not worth living.

Stress-Reducing Element #1: Relieving Stress Now

Poor lifestyle choices can crank up your stress pathway and increase cortisol, even if you aren't actually "stressing" about something. Making sure you don't worsen your stress response by skipping meals, skimping on sleep, drinking more alcohol than is healthy, or eating unhealthy foods is extremely important, yet we all tend to do exactly these things.

When we are stressed, we certainly eat more sweets and fatty foods than normal. Sometimes figuring out which comes first, the lifestyle or the stress, is difficult. Every step of your Hormone Diet system provides you with new tools and habits to help you bust out of the stress cycle for good. Great sleep, balanced nutrition, exercise, supplements to reduce stress (see the supplement options for excess cortisol in Chapter 13) and basic supplements to protect your body from stress (the Hormone Diet supplement plan in Chapter 12) are all essential stress-fighting routines extensively covered elsewhere in this book. Here, I will suggest three specific stress-reducing tools to complement your healthy lifestyle habits: meditation, massage, and laughter.

Meditate

The word may conjure up images of flowing white robes, chanting, or bare-chested yogis, but you can actually leave the crystals, candles, and incense at the door. Meditation is as easy as listening to the sound of your breath or repeating a word or phrase for 10 minutes each day. We now know that meditation may actually reshape the brain, modify our responses to daily situations, and train the mind. Meditation works. It's often recommended by doctors as an essential component of any wellness program.

> In terms of aging, the most significant conclusion [about meditation] is that the hormonal imbalance associated with stress—and known to speed up the aging process—is reversed. This in turn slows or even reverses the aging process, as measured by various biological changes associated with growing old. From my experience with studies on people using Transcendental Meditation, it has been established that long-term meditators can have a biological age between 5 to 12 years younger than their chronological age . . . Meditation alters the frame of reference that gives the person his experience of time. At a quantum level, physical events in space-time such as heartbeat and hormone levels can be affected simply by taking the mind into a reality where time does not have such a powerful hold.
>
> —DEEPAK CHOPRA, a leader in mind-body medicine, from *Ageless Body, Timeless Mind*

Meditation also has amazing effects on your hormones. It lowers the stress hormones cortisol and adrenaline and raises our anti-aging, antistress hormones DHEA and serotonin. Meditation isn't difficult to learn and do, but it does require commitment, patience, and practice.

Think of meditation as the cheapest and easiest sport to play. The only requirement is discipline and the ability to comfortably spend a few moments alone without distractions. Ultimately, blocking off this chunk of time for introspection is the greatest challenge, as many of us would rather spend it zoning out with an episode of *Survivor* than practicing conscious awareness of our internal environment. All too often we attempt to avoid or distort reality rather than embrace it. But once you incorporate meditating into your daily routine, you'll find the journey to enlightenment is accompanied by endless physical, emotional, and spiritual benefits.

HOW TO MEDITATE IN FIVE SIMPLE STEPS

1. **Get comfortable.** Sit or lie in a comfortable, quiet place where you will not be interrupted or distracted. You may want to designate a space at home for this.
2. **Clear your mind.** Close your eyes, rest, and *do nothing.*
3. **Concentrate on your breath.** Focus on the sound of your breathing and how it feels flowing in and out of the edge of your nostrils. I find it useful to imagine my breath washing in and out like waves on the beach. You can also pick a word or a phrase that is soothing or meaningful to you. One patient of mine, an extremely tense 85-year-old man with high blood pressure, picked the word "quiet," which I thought was a great choice. Repeat the word or phrase to yourself each time you exhale.
4. **Practice body awareness.** Check for tension, especially in your jaw, scalp, forehead, shoulders, lower back, and hips— all the way down to your toes—by consciously examining that body part. Relax the areas that feel tight as you continue breathing.

5. **Stay in tune with your breathing or the repetition of your word or phrase.** You'll be amazed at how often thoughts start creeping into your mind. Just acknowledge them and return your focus to your breathing. With practice, the amount of time you'll be able to sit without your mind wandering will lengthen, and you may even find that solutions you've been searching for will appear.

Some forms of meditation may actually involve physical, repetitive motions such as running or cycling. If you want to meditate while engaging in these activities, practice staying focused on your breathing and allow thoughts to flow freely. Using this form of meditation is very helpful for people who have a difficult time sitting still.

Meditation can help you prepare for the second element in coping with stress—realizing and setting your goals. I often find clear ideas come to me after meditating, just after waking up and during or after exercise—moments when my mind is free of chatter. The shower is another time when ideas seem to flow. Who knows, maybe the sound of the water calms my brain waves enough to let me hear my inner thoughts. No matter where they happen for you, these moments can be a rich source of wisdom and clarity about where you need to head next.

Get a Massage

We know that the cortisol and adrenaline we produce when we're under stress are destructive to our body tissues, immune system, and adrenal glands when they are present in high amounts for long periods of time. One of the functions of the liver is to break down stress hormones and sex hormones. Massage, which assists the bloodflow and lymphatic delivery of hormonal waste to the liver, expedites this breakdown process, thereby helping to relieve stress in the body.

A study from the *International Journal of Neuroscience* (October

2005) found that massage therapy decreases cortisol and increases levels of serotonin and dopamine. It also increases endorphin release, which is excellent for treating pain, depression, and anxiety. Massage helps ease activity in the sympathetic nervous system (fight or flight) and increases our parasympathetic response (rest and relax). I've had patients report that their memory is better for 2 to 3 days after a massage. I suspect the improvement can be linked to the reduction of cortisol after a massage, since we know cortisol is rough on our brain cells, especially those involved in memory.

Remember, anything that reduces our fight-or-flight response can help improve weight loss, lessen water retention, and improve appetite control. So beyond simply feeling good while you are on the table, massage has definite physiological benefits.

Laugh

Professor Lee S. Berk of Loma Linda University in California has found that the mere anticipation of laughter has significant hormonal effects. In a recent study, one group of subjects was told they were about to watch a funny movie, while the second group was told that they would be reading magazines for an hour. Those who were told about the movie had 27 percent more beta-endorphins and 87 percent more human growth hormone. In previous studies, Berk found that laughter reduced cortisol and adrenaline and enhanced the immune system for 12 to 24 hours. Watch funny movies and make time for laughter in your life—or just think about doing it!

I once prescribed the movie *Planes, Trains, and Automobiles* to a 65-year-old woman constantly worried about her health and told a diabetic man of 35, "Don't come back here unless you've done something *fun*." I kid you not.

Stress-Reducing Element #2: Setting Your Goals

Whatever you are meant to do, move toward it and it will come to you.
—GLORIA DUNN

Until I reached the ripe old age of 30, I wasn't able to write about my goals. It seemed too overwhelming because I felt I had no idea what my goals were. I've had many conversations about this topic with a wise friend, Paul. He provided the first simple tip to guide me toward identifying my goals and putting them down on paper. Paul sits down at the beginning of every year and draws a circle. Within the circle he draws a hexagon. Each side of the hexagon drawn in the circle corresponds to a section of life.

Paul thinks life should be full and well rounded, like the circle. When it is, the "wheel" rolls along smoothly. When one area is not as full, that side of the circle becomes flattened, like the edge of a hexagon, and the circle of life won't roll. It becomes imbalanced when we fail to equally allocate our focus to all six important areas of our lives. It's a simple visual and it works for me.

So I broke down my goals into these categories and thought about *what I would like to achieve* in each area. Next to each goal I wrote *the benefit of achieving the goal, how I expect to reach it,* and *the disadvantage of not achieving this goal.* For example:

Spiritual
GOAL: TO MEDITATE FOR 10 MINUTES AT THE END OF EACH DAY.

- **Benefit of achieving this goal:** Greater clarity, mental focus, relaxation, improved health, less anxiety.
- **Drawback of not achieving this goal:** Continued anxiety, decreased body awareness, lack of creativity, and more stress.
- **How will I reach this goal?** I will create a small space in my house, free of televisions, phones, computers, and other distractions. This will be my space for calming and centering my thoughts. I will spend 10 minutes in this space before bedtime each day.
- **When will I complete this goal?** By July 30, 2012.

Eventually I was able to write down both short-term and long-term goals. I highly recommend you do the same. Try writing your goals when you go away on vacation or at different milestones during the year, such as New Year's, a birthday, the beginning of a new season, or any time you feel motivated to focus, create a plan, and make changes. You may or may not be able to create goals in all areas, and that's okay. The most important thing is that you just start doing it.

I suggest you get a journal to keep by your bedside or write your goals on a page that you can post in a visible spot in your home. When you write your goals, use positive language. Instead of "I will stop nagging," try "I will provide support and encouragement." I'm no expert in goal setting, but this process has worked well for me and the patients I have shared it with.

A SIMPLE, BUT INFLUENTIAL RELATIONSHIP EXERCISE

Since relationships can be a major source of stress (recall the example of cortisol levels in "happily" married people earlier in this chapter), maintaining awareness of the people in your life is very important. One exercise I find very useful is to write down qualities that *describe the relationships you need or wish to have*—at work, with your partner, or even with your friends. This exercise can be great for couples because it eliminates the need for "mind reading" when it comes to understanding each other's needs and desires within the relationship, thereby helping to eliminate resentment or unfulfilled expectations. The exercise can also provide opportunities for clear reflection on the relationships you currently have, as well as creating a template for the people and connections you would like to draw into your life.

Stress-Reducing Element #3: Visualizing Your Success

There are some people who live in a dream world, and there are some who face reality; and then there are those who turn one into the other.

—DOUGLAS EVERETT

I think Shakti Gawain, author of *Creative Visualization*, is the best author to teach you about visualization. She defines creative visualization as the technique of using your imagination to create what you want in your life. She goes on to explain that the energy of your thoughts and feelings attracts energy of the same frequency. Whatever we spend the most time thinking about is exactly what we will attract into our lives.

This is the Law of Attraction, and it's the key message delivered in *The Secret* by Rhonda Burns and *The Law of Attraction* and *Ask and It Is Given* by Esther and Jerry Hicks. No matter the author you choose, they all communicate a similar philosophy: We have to imagine the way we want our lives to manifest.

> **HOT HORMONE TIP**
>
> **MUSIC TO TRAIN YOUR BRAIN**
> Listen to music to increase alpha brain waves when you visualize. An alpha brain wave state, associated with deep relaxation, has been found to be much more effective than a beta brain wave state, which is more prevalent when we're busy with work or tasks. You can also stimulate more alpha waves by meditating right before you do your visualization exercises.

If we are negative or fearful that a particular event may befall us, that event may be exactly what we attract into our lives. I'll take this a step further and suggest that *when our hormones are balanced, we have a much better chance of achieving the physical and mental state that allows us to think, feel, and be positive. Likewise, being positive sets the groundwork that allows for achievement of hormonal balance.* This approach to living with good health and happy hormones is the very essence of the Hormone Diet.

How to Visualize

1. **Set your goal.**
   For example: I want to be strong, lean, and healthy.
2. **Create a clear picture or idea.**
   Believe you are already strong, lean, and healthy.
   Include as many details as you can; envision yourself moving freely and feeling energized; *see* your flat stomach, strong arms, and toned legs!
3. **Focus on these images often.**

In quiet meditative periods and casually throughout the day, focus on these images clearly, but in a light, gentle way, so they become integrated into your life.

4. **Give it positive energy.**
Make strong, positive statements to yourself. See yourself achieving your goal. Try to suspend doubt and disbelief.

5. **Don't forget to breathe.**
Breathe calmly and deeply.

So you now have two very good stress-relief options: meditation and visualization. One involves trying to think of nothing, and the other involves visualizing everything you would like to achieve, have, feel, or experience in as much detail as possible. Cool.

You're free to choose the option that resonates with you, or you may want to incorporate both. Visualizing your success first thing in the morning and meditating to quiet your mind in the evening are wonderful ways to bookend your day. I know we are all busy, and finding time to do both can be challenging. But I fit in my visualizations when I go to bed at night—just 5 to 10 minutes per night. I fit in my meditation when I'm walking the dog in the morning—while I get my daily dose of serotonin-boosting sunlight, too!

Right now I am using the healing visualizations from "Adam" described in his book *The Path of the DreamHealer* (Penguin, 2006). I highly recommend his books and DVDs for health-promoting visualization exercises that you can use for yourself or a loved one. I also suggest going to one of his group healing presentations. (Visit www.dreamhealer.com for details.)

I have seen for myself the incredible benefits that come from regularly doing these simple but powerful mind exercises. I have witnessed them many times with my patients and see them with my mom, who is living with liver cancer as I write this book.

Stress-Reducing Element #4: Harnessing the Power of Positive Belief

He who has a why to live for can bear with almost any how.
—FRIEDRICH NIETZSCHE

The most powerful example I can share with you about this element comes from one of my patients whose mother was diagnosed with lung cancer. Four weeks after her diagnosis, before her treatment even started, she suddenly developed difficulty breathing and died just a day later. My patient told me the situation had probably worked out for the best because his mother didn't want to go through the process of being ill. What a positive way to look at a truly traumatic event in one's life.

Another patient, a 36-year-old man I was treating for a rare blood-clotting disease that caused his lungs to fill with fluid, provided me with an inspiring example of positive thinking. He was awaiting a lung transplant, constantly struggling for air because of his disease. His lips were often bluish because of the poor oxygen exchange in his body. One fall day, I was giving him acupuncture treatments and looked out the window while he was resting on the table. I sighed, "Ah, soon we're going to look out and there'll be no more leaves on the trees." To which he replied, *"Yes, but then we can see farther."*

This approach to life is by far the most important determinant of your well-being. Believing that everything happens for a reason and trusting that you will be taken care of by the universe, God, or whatever higher power you feel most comfortable with will work wonders to reduce your stress and anxiety. Powerful beliefs will also help you adapt to life and all it has to offer.

No matter what happens—or doesn't happen—to you, you can always take heart in believing the outcome is for a greater good: to teach you a lesson, provide an opportunity for growth, help you gain inner strength, or perhaps allow you to form a special connection with someone.

There are many good sources for ideas on stress-reducing element #4, but I'll limit my recommendations to these top choices:

1. *A New Earth* by Eckhart Tolle (Penguin reprint, 2008)
2. *The Four Agreements* by Don Miguel Ruiz (Amber-Allen Publishing, 2001)
3. *The Seven Spiritual Laws of Success* by Deepak Chopra (New World Library, 1994)

Summary of Instructions for Step 1: Strategies for Stress Survival

Implement the elements for conquering stress that you feel will work for you.

1. RELIEVE STRESS NOW. Meditate and/or visualize for at least 10 minutes each day in conjunction with the recommendations outlined in upcoming steps of the Hormone Diet plan. Get a massage at least once per month.
2. SET GOALS. Write your goals in the six categories: spiritual, mental, physical, financial/material, career, and relationships.
3. VISUALIZE. Spend a few moments each day imagining your success in as much detail as possible.
4. BELIEVE IN THE POSITIVE. Understand the power of positive thinking and the Law of Attraction. You'll naturally be more positive when your hormones are balanced. When you are in a positive state, hormonal balance flows.
5. USE SUPPORTIVE SUPPLEMENTS when necessary to restore your hormonal balance and stress recuperation (see Chapter 13).

STEP 2

REPLENISH YOUR BODY AND BALANCE YOUR HORMONES

YOUR SECOND 2 WEEKS

*A man's health can be judged by which he takes
two at a time—pills or stairs.*

JOAN WELSH

CHAPTER 10

NASTY NUTRITION: EATING HABITS
THAT DISRUPT OUR HORMONES

In the end, the biggest risk to the culture may be the inevitable false or misleading low-carb claims and influx of products that ladle on heapings of calories in exchange for carbs. If enough people are seduced by these foods and fail to lose weight, low carbs will go the way of low fat: a strategy that works when you stick to the rules but fails when marketers rush in with promises no one can keep.

"THE LOW-CARB FOOD CRAZE,"
Time magazine, May 3, 2004

Here's what you will learn in this chapter:
- The nutritional habits that instantly cause hormonal imbalance and result in weight gain
- What, when, and how we eat are all important for good health and fat loss

A discussion of the nasty nutrition no-nos will help you before you jump into the specifics of the Hormone Diet nutrition plan in the next chapter. In today's fast-paced, overprocessed, obesity-plagued society, our failure to pay attention to our food choices is a widespread and serious problem. Every day, we reach for inflammatory foods, fast foods, foods containing high-fructose corn syrup and added sweeteners, hormone-infused foods, and fat- and sugar-free foods—all major culprits of perpetuating hormonal imbalance. We also tend to consume too much alcohol and not enough fiber. In the end, we are left feeling fuzzy, flabby, and fatigued. And then, to make matters worse, our poor food choices at mealtimes are compounded by when or how we choose to eat.

Let's talk about each of these hormone-harming habits one by one. Armed with this information, you can start making changes and feeling better by your very next meal.

Foods That Fan the Flames

I've told you plenty about the perils of inflammation and its serious effects on hormones, health, and weight loss. Well, proinflammatory foods increase inflammation and contribute to your risk of chronic illness, including heart disease, diabetes, and Alzheimer's disease. Here are the foods you should avoid to help keep inflammation in check.

- **Refined sugars and grains.** Foods such as white flour, white rice, and table sugar (sucrose) can trigger inflammation by raising blood sugar and insulin. Junk foods, high-fat meats, sugary treats, and fast foods all increase inflammation in your body. (Many of these foods also contain unhealthy fats that further exacerbate the problem.)
- **Foods containing trans fats.** Margarine; foods made with partially hydrogenated oils.
- **Processed meats.** Lunch meats, hot dogs, and sausages contain nitrites and sulphites that are associated with increased inflammation.
- **Excess saturated fats.** These fats, naturally found in meats, shellfish, egg yolks, and dairy products, can promote inflammation. These foods also contain a fatty acid called arachidonic acid. Although some arachidonic acid is essential for your health, too much of it in your diet will contribute to

inflammation. Choosing omega-3 eggs, low-fat milk and cheese, and lean cuts of meat will lessen the inflammatory fallout.

- **Foods that cause allergies.** Most people with true food anaphylactic allergies are aware of them and make a point to steer clear of the offending food. Those of us with food sensitivities or intolerances, however, may not realize that certain foods cause inflammation, faulty digestion, and even compromised immunity. Another reason why experimenting with the removal and slow reintroduction of foods that commonly cause sensitivities from your diet can be a valuable exercise.

- **Too much omega-6 fatty acid.** Omega-6 and omega-3 are essential fatty acids that cannot be produced in the body. Sixty years ago the average American diet included a 1:2 ratio of omega-6 to omega-3. Today, the ratio is estimated at about 25:1. The optimal ratio is 1:1. We obtain much of our omega-6 from safflower, corn, and sunflower oils, which are commonly used in baked goods and packaged items. (Now they are also commonly used in place of trans fats in trans fat–free products.) Too much of these oils in our diet can turn on the hormonal signals involved in inflammation and even stimulate abnormal cell growth. Studies have shown that breast cancer, colon cancer, and prostate cancer cells grow at a much faster rate in the presence of these oils.

In Chapter 1, you got the scoop on inflammation as a cause of hormonal imbalance. There you saw a study by Dr. Paresh Dandona and his team, from the State University of New York, who found that overconsumption of *any macronutrient*—protein, carbohydrate, or fat—can contribute to inflammation. Well, their study even went as far as to link specific, brand-name foods with immediate inflammatory effects:

A 930-calorie meal consisting of an Egg McMuffin or a Sausage McMuffin and two McDonald's hash browns appears to trigger inflammation within arteries "within an hour."

Fast Food: A Fast Track to Fat

These days, we can barely drive around the block without spotting those famous golden arches. We know it's not so good for us but we, as a society, love our burgers, fries, and sodas. Here are some truly amazing fast food facts.

- Each day, 1 in 4 North Americans visits a fast-food restaurant.
- Americans spent $134 billion on fast food in 2005.
- French fries are the most eaten vegetable in America; tomatoes are the most commonly eaten fruit simply because they are the main ingredient in ketchup.
- The fast-food industry in the United Kingdom is estimated to have grown by 14 percent between 2003 and 2007; the industry is now worth more than $15 billion. The United Kingdom also happens to be the most overweight nation in Europe and has the highest rate of childhood obesity.

Fast foods are highly processed, loaded with fat and sugar, and low in the essential nutrients necessary to support your body's own natural production of the hormones involved in repair, growth, mood, mental function, and metabolism. Fast foods also promote inflammation and insulin resistance because they are practically devoid of fiber.

If you haven't done so already, I recommend you check out two very interesting resources on the dangers of fast food: the book *Fast Food Nation: The Dark Side of the All-American Meal,* by Eric Schlosser, and the documentary *Supersize Me,* by Morgan Spurlock.

We're Already Sweet Enough

Our seemingly insatiable desire for sugar and sweeteners can also take some of the blame for making us fatter. We consume roughly 100 pounds of sweetener per person per year. The average adult consumes about 10 to 14 teaspoons of sugar every day!

HOT WEIGHT-LOSS TIP

YOUR BEST NATURAL SWEETENER OPTIONS
- Date paste
- Raisins
- Honey
- Applesauce
- Stevia (natural herbal sweetener)

Also, natural spices and flavorings such as these:
- Cinnamon
- Vanilla
- Cocoa

Sweeteners come in many forms: table sugar, honey, high-fructose corn syrup (HFCS), fruit juice concentrates, artificial sweeteners, and sugar alcohols (like xylitol). Sometimes we know we're eating them, but many times we don't. Sweeteners are used in the obvious places—cookies, cakes, jams, coffee drinks, juices, sodas—the list is endless. They're hiding out in many other products we use daily: salad dressings, breads, pasta sauces, sports drinks, energy bars, "healthy" breakfast cereals, and more. Table sugar, honey, maple syrup, and corn syrup are all sources of carbohydrates. They also contain calories many of us forget to include when measuring our daily carbohydrate intake, especially when we drink them. Naturally, our insulin surges after consuming these products.

HFCS foods (sports drinks, sodas, and many fat-free foods, such as salad dressings) are particularly troublesome because they influence the hunger and appetite-controlling hormones ghrelin and leptin. Remember, ghrelin tells us we are hungry by stimulating NPY in the brain, and leptin tells our brain we're full. HFCS has been shown to lower leptin secretion *so we never get the message that we're full.* HFCS also fails to shut off ghrelin production the way food should. As a result, ghrelin stimulates more NPY in the brain, causing us to feel hungry even though we have food in our stomach. Furthermore, HFCS foods tend to pack a whole lot of calories into a small serving, resulting in tons of extra calories that end up being stored as fat. The long-term effects of consuming too many HFCS foods or drinks are weight gain and a much greater risk of the signs of metabolic syndrome, including high blood pressure, obesity, and eventually diabetes.

Frequently drinking fructose-sweetened beverages increases the production of fat in your liver, causes fat accumulation, and contributes to fatty liver, while also blocking your fat-burning genes (PPARs). These beverages essentially overload your body with so many calories that it cannot adapt.

WATCH YOUR DRINK CHOICES!
We all know we should limit sugary sodas. But even so-called healthy drinks can give us an unexpected sugar blast.
(Note: 1 teaspoon = 5 grams)
* Hype (8 ounces): 64 grams
* Minute Maid Cranberry Grape (8 ounces): 38 grams
* Tropicana Twister Soda (Orange) (8 ounces): 35 grams
* Sunkist Orange Soda (8 ounces): 35 grams
* Fanta Orange (8 ounces): 34.3 grams
* Sun Drop (8 ounces): 33 grams
* SoBe Adrenaline Rush (8 ounces): 33 grams
† Starbucks Dulce de Leche Frappuccino Blended Crème
    (16 ounces; Grande): 85 grams
† Starbucks Caffè Vanilla Frappuccino Blended Coffee without
    whip (16 ounces; Grande): 67 grams

Sources:
*www.energyfiend.com/sugar-in-drinks/
†www.starbucks.com

Harmful Hormones in Our Foods

Hormones are often used in farming to make animals grow more quickly or to increase milk production in cattle. There are six steroid hormones currently approved by the USFDA for use in food production: estradiol, progesterone, testosterone, zeranol, trenbolone acetate, and melengestrol acetate. Zeranol, trenbolone acetate, and melengesterol acetate are synthetic growth hormones used to make animals grow faster. Current federal regulations allow the use of these hormones on growing cattle and sheep but not on poultry (chickens, turkeys, and ducks) or pigs. Much of the controversy surrounds beef, since hormones are given to more than 90 percent of beef cattle in the United States.

The FDA also allows the use of the protein hormone rBGH (recombinant bovine growth hormone) to increase milk production in dairy cattle. This substance is not approved for use in dairy cattle in Canada and Europe, however, due to concerns for both animal welfare and human health.

The use of rBGH increases insulin-like growth factor 1 (IGF-1) in the milk of treated cows by as much as tenfold. Though IGF-1 naturally occurs in humans and cows, higher than normal levels of this substance have recently been linked to breast and prostate cancers in humans. To date, no studies show that drinking milk with high IGF-1 causes levels of this hormone to increase in humans, but researchers do know IGF-1 can be absorbed into the bloodstream from our digestive tract. Who wants to take the chance?

To make matters worse, heavy milking can make hormone-treated cows more prone to mastitis, a bacterial inflammation of the udder. Residues from the antibiotics used to treat the cows then end up in the milk we drink. You've already learned about the importance of healthy bacterial balance in your gut as part of your detox. Well, antibiotic residues from cow's milk can definitely disrupt this delicate balance in your GI tract.

Our children are more at risk from the effects of growth hormone and other substances in dairy products because they tend to drink a lot more milk per unit of body weight. Many health experts, including Lindsey Berkson, author of *Hormone Deception,* worry that hormones in our food supply could be at least partly responsible for a growing trend toward early puberty.

As mentioned earlier, steroid hormones are also problematic additions to our foods. Both estradiol and progesterone are considered probable carcinogens by the National Toxicology Program at the National Institutes of Health. Even though the FDA has concluded that the amount of hormone residue in food is negligible compared with the amount the body produces naturally, many health experts agree that *any* excess is too much. Estrogen has been linked with breast cancer in women, and testosterone with prostate cancer in men. Progesterone has been found to increase the growth of ovarian, breast, and uterine tumors. Rather than taking chances with our health, we can certainly opt for hormone-free organic meat and dairy products instead.

In 1989, the European Union issued a ban on all meat from animals treated with steroid and growth hormones—a ban that is still in effect today.

The Fat-Free Fake-Out

Have you ever wondered why obesity rates soared just when all those fat-free products started hitting the supermarket shelves? The words "fat free" definitely make for enticing packaging, but we now know they're by no means our golden ticket to weight loss. In most fat-free foods, the fat calories are simply replaced with loads of sugar. So while we thought we were watching fat and cutting calories, we were packing on pounds and sending our insulin through the roof.

Besides getting an insulin surge from fat-free products, we also run the risk of eating and eating until we are truly stuffed. Remember, *fats help us feel full* and actually prevent overeating by stimulating the release of leptin and CCK. Both hormones work on the satiety center in the brain to tell us when we are full. If our meals are devoid of fat, our brains take much longer to get the stop signal. One of my favorite examples of fat-free offenders to avoid is fat-free, fruit-flavored yogurt. Next time you are in the grocery store, check its carb content. Then put it back on the shelf!

I encourage you to carefully look at portion sizes and nutrition labels when considering fat-free products. For example, some foods may be considered fat-free in tiny portions, but if you eat a larger amount, even that small bit of fat per serving adds up. In other cases, the full-fat version and the low-fat alternative contain almost the same number of calories. Low-fat ice cream, for example, has 80 calories per scoop, whereas the full-fat version is only 95 calories. Companies simply add sugar and vegetable gums to low-fat ice creams to make up for the lack of taste and volume.

The Skinny on Artificial Sweeteners

The number of Americans who regularly consume sugar-free products increased from fewer than 70 million in 1987 to more than 160 million in 2000. During the same period, the consumption of regular soft drinks increased by more than 15 gallons per capita annually.

We've seen a dramatic increase in the consumption of artificially sweetened foods over the past 25 years. Yet the incidence of overweight and obesity has also increased markedly during this period. Despite the superficial logic that consuming fewer calories will lead to weight loss, the evidence is very clear that using artificial sweeteners can, paradoxically, *cause weight gain.*

Research shows that specific artificial sweeteners (such as aspartame and saccharin) are linked to cancer, but all artificial sweeteners are known to cause increased cravings and weight gain, and may subsequently contribute to insulin resistance. According to a study by researchers at the University of Texas San Antonio, middle-aged adults who drink diet soft drinks drastically increase their risk of gaining weight later on. The study monitored the weights and soda-drinking habits of more than 600 normal-weight subjects ages 25 to 64. When researchers followed up with the participants after 8 years, they discovered those who consumed one diet soda a day were *65 percent more likely to be overweight than those who drank none.* Drinking two or more low- or no-calorie soft drinks daily raised the odds of becoming obese or overweight even higher. The real shocker? Participants who drank *diet soda had a greater chance of becoming overweight than those who drank regular soda!*

> **AWFUL ASPARTAME**
> When aspartame is broken down in the body, methanol is produced. Methanol, a neurotoxic alcohol, is hundreds of times more potent than the alcohol in alcoholic beverages. As a result of this chemical change in form, aspartame has been shown to cause neurological diseases and symptoms, including headaches, muscle spasms, dizziness, twitching, memory loss, migraines, and even seizures.

Artificial sweeteners appear to be a double-edged dieting sword. They don't allow for the leptin release that normally happens when we eat the sugars that signal to the brain that our hunger is satisfied. Moreover, even though artificial sweeteners don't cause your blood sugar to rise, your body still responds as though there is sugar in your bloodstream by secreting insulin. Between the low leptin and high insulin, your appetite and cravings go haywire. Knowing that high insulin is a stepping-stone to type 2 diabetes and obesity, we cannot overlook the connection to the number of diabetic, prediabetic, and overweight people who use these types of products.

Artificial sweeteners may also disrupt our natural ability to mentally count calories based on the sweetness of the foods we eat, according to research conducted at Purdue University. This disruption may explain why more and more of us seem to lack the natural ability to regulate our appetite and food intake.

Increased consumption of artificial sweeteners and of high-calorie beverages is not the sole cause of obesity, but it may be a contributing factor. It could become more of a factor as more people turn to artificial sweeteners as a means of weight control and, at the same time, others consume more high-calorie beverages to satisfy their cravings.
—SUSAN SWITHERS, associate professor of psychological sciences, Purdue University

Researchers have established that the taste and feel of food in our mouth influences our learned ability to match our caloric intake with our caloric need. For instance, we learn very early on that both sweet tastes and dense, thick foods signal high calorie content. Our natural ability to control how much we eat may be weakened when this natural link is impaired by consuming products that contain artificial sweeteners. These foods and drinks prompt us to eat more because they often have a thinner consistency and texture than regular, sugar-sweetened foods. You may have noticed this textural difference in the past when drinking diet versus regular soda or eating yogurt sweetened with artificial sweeteners.

Beware of One Too Many

Many of us like to enjoy a refreshing cocktail or glass of wine once in a while, but we need to approach these drinks with caution. Alcohol is a known appetite stimulant and frequently causes us to overeat because it also lowers our inhibitions. Just a few drinks, especially those mixed with sugary fruit drinks or soda, can cause a serious insulin spike, resulting in hypoglycemia (low blood sugar). Yes, even healthy people can experience low blood sugar with alcohol consumption.

Even a little bit of alcohol (i.e., more than the recommended four glasses of wine per week for women, seven for men) lowers leptin and raises cortisol. This double whammy leads to disturbed sleep, night waking, and those signature cravings for greasy hangover foods the next day. Over time, chronic alcohol abuse can reduce the body's responsiveness to insulin and cause sensitivity to sugar in both healthy individuals and alcoholics with liver cirrhosis. In fact, a high percentage of patients with alcoholic liver disease are glucose intolerant or diabetic.

In men, alcohol is harmful to the testicles and, as a result, can suppress testosterone production. In a study of normally healthy men who drank alcohol for 4 weeks, testosterone levels declined after only 5 days and continued to fall throughout the study period. In premenopausal women, chronic heavy drinking can contribute to a multitude of menstrual and fertility concerns because alcohol interferes with the hormonal regulation of the reproductive system. Alcohol can increase the conversion of testosterone into estradiol and can contribute to symptoms of estrogen dominance, which boosts breast cancer risk.

Failing to Get Our Fiber

Dr. Robert Lustig, a pediatric endocrinologist at UCSF Children's Hospital, presented a comprehensive review of obesity research published in the August 2006 edition of the journal *Nature Clinical Practice Endocrinology and Metabolism*. In the study, he determined a key reason for the epidemic of pediatric obesity—now the most commonly diagnosed childhood ailment—is that high-calorie, low-fiber Western diets promote hormonal imbalances that encourage children (and adults!) to overeat.

Our current Western food environment has become highly "insulino-genic," as demonstrated by its increased energy density, high-fat content, high glycaemic index, increased fructose composition, decreased fiber, and decreased dairy content. In particular, fructose (too much) and fiber (not enough) appear to be cornerstones of the obesity epidemic through their effects on insulin.

—ROBERT LUSTIG, MD

Changes in food processing over the past 30 years, particularly the removal of fiber and addition of sugar to a wide variety of foods, have created an environment in which our foods are essentially addictive. As Dr. Lustig notes, both excess sugar and insufficient fiber promote insulin production and suppression of leptin activity in the brain.

When and How We Eat

Certainly *what* we eat has an enormous impact on our hormonal health and weight status. But did you know that *when* and *how* we eat also make a huge difference? Eating at the wrong times, in the wrong combinations, and in the wrong amounts can also impede weight loss and play havoc with your hormones. Some of the most common hormone-altering habits I see in my clinical practice include super-sizing; eating late at night; skipping breakfast; restricting calories; eating due to stress; and failing to balance protein, carbohydrates, and fats at meals.

Super-Sizing

Food portions are growing and so are our waistlines. Candy bars are larger. Fast-food restaurants serve bigger meals for just a few cents extra. Even regular restaurants typically serve a lot more food than anyone needs in one meal. Need I say more? Too much food in one sitting (i.e., too many calories) raises blood sugar, sparks an insulin spike, increases inflammation, causes weight gain, and elevates your stress hormones.

Eating Late at Night and Skipping Breakfast

The timing of your meals has very specific effects on your hormones. For instance, eating too close to bedtime raises your body temperature, increases blood sugar and insulin, prevents the release of melatonin, and cuts down on growth hormone release. All these factors interfere with the quality of your sleep and the natural fat-burning benefits of a good night's rest. Furthermore, sleep deprivation leads to more cravings and a greater likelihood of overeating the next day.

Your mom was also right when she told you breakfast was the most important meal of the day. When you skip breakfast, you lose its stimulating benefits on your metabolic rate. You also become more likely to eat unbalanced meals, more calories, and larger amounts of saturated fat throughout the day. Plenty of research shows that those of us who skip breakfast are actually heavier. Missing out on a healthy morning meal also increases stress hormones.

Excessive Caloric Restriction

I've already discussed how excessive caloric restriction messes with your hormones and simply does not work as a dieting strategy. Out-of-control calorie cutting elevates your stress hormones cortisol, NPY, and ghrelin, and decreases leptin. All of these hormonal changes work to perk up your appetite. Insufficient food intake also drops your thyroid hormone and metabolic rate—and depletes your sex hormones, especially testosterone.

Stress-Related Eating

Even when we know what and how much we are supposed to be eating, emotional factors and stress greatly influence our food choices and how much food we consume. High cortisol and NPY brought on by stress cause us to overeat, particularly unhealthy sweet or salty snacks. Giving in to these urges leads to higher insulin levels, more cravings, and weight gain, especially around the abdomen.

Eating can be a very pleasurable experience closely tied to feelings and emotions. Many of us use foods for comfort or to cope with stressful, upsetting situations, especially when we have not developed more effective coping strategies. We also eat when we're bored, feel like celebrating, want to boost our spirits, or want to avoid dealing with anxiety, fear, anger, and resentment. In the very short term, foods can make us feel good. But over the long haul, stress-related eating can leave us with more feelings of guilt and regret, not to mention excess pounds.

Failing to Balance Carbohydrates, Fats, and Protein

This is a biggie! When you eat carbs, the digestive system breaks them down into sugar. Your pancreas then releases a rush of insulin to move the sugar from your bloodstream into your cells. Carbohydrates also trigger the production of serotonin, which creates a "serotonin high" to go with the sugar high for a brief period, until the serotonin is depleted and our blood sugar comes crashing down. That crash makes us crave more carbs, and the destructive cycle continues. These cyclical insulin highs and lows perpetuate further hormonal imbalances, including leptin, sex hormone, and cortisol imbalances.

Eating too many carbs in isolation, like grabbing a muffin for breakfast, is something like letting your car race down the road at lightning speed. By consuming protein and fat together with carbohydrates, we can effectively put the brakes on the sugar entering our bloodstream. Sugar then cruises into our bloodstream in a slow and controlled manner, providing us with consistent energy for a longer period of time and preventing the insulin spike that happens when we eat carbs alone. This glycemically balanced technique, combined with eating often and eating enough, is the guiding principle behind the Hormone Diet nutrition plan to come.

Cooking on High Heat

Grilling, broiling, and frying meat and poultry create damaged proteins called AGEs (advanced glycosylation end products) that trigger inflammation. Research at Mount Sinai School of Medicine showed that diabetics who ate a high AGE-inducing diet experienced a 35 percent jump in inflammation. Those on a low AGE-inducing diet experienced a 20 percent improvement.

In addition to poaching and stewing your meat and poultry, you can also reduce your AGE consumption by choosing fish more often. Broiled fish has about one-fourth the AGEs of broiled steak or chicken.

Poor nutrition habits are a major cause of hormonal imbalance. The Hormone Diet plan is designed to lead you far away from offending foods and egregious eating habits. Get set to clear your cupboards—and your body—of nasty nutrition for good.

CHAPTER 11

THE HORMONE DIET NUTRITION PLAN:
THE GLYCI-MED APPROACH

The hormonal benefits you will enjoy from the Glyci-Med eating style are:

- Better fat burning potential through increased glucagon when you eat the right amounts of protein.
- Enhanced melatonin for better sleep (especially when you consume protein, walnuts, or cherry juice and avoid excess carbohydrates at dinner).
- Maximized growth hormone levels when you consume protein, avoid excess sugar before exercising, and have a meal containing protein and carbohydrates within 45 minutes of finishing your workouts.
- Better testosterone status for muscle building when you consume the right amount of protein, carbs, and fats.
- Elimination of harmful excess estrogen when you consume sufficient fiber and enjoy phytoestrogenic foods such as soy, pomegranate, and flaxseeds.
- Prevention of excess estrogen when you avoid high fat intake and too much alcohol.
- Improved serotonin when you avoid excessive carbohydrate restriction and consume enough protein.
- Better appetite control by increasing the appetite-suppressing hormones leptin and CCK when you eat fats and protein at each meal. Consuming enough fiber will have the same benefits on your appetite because, in addition to raising leptin and CCK, it also leads to less insulin release.
- Eating enough and frequently will also prevent the appetite-stimulating hormones ghrelin and NPY from being released.

- Maximized metabolism due to increased thyroid hormone when you eat enough, and frequently enough, and when you obtain the nutrients needed to make thyroid hormone from your diet.
- Increased acetylcholine for muscle function and memory when you include lecithin and eggs among your food selections.
- Reduced insulin and inflammation when you balance your meals and avoid excess sugar, harmful fats, alcohol, and processed foods.
- Better control of cortisol when you avoid skipping meals, consuming excess protein, and severe caloric restriction.

I want you to feel your best. I also want you to enjoy lasting health. In my view, the best ways to accomplish both goals are to avoid foods your body doesn't tolerate well and to leverage the metabolic and hormonal benefits of Glyci-Med eating. When you make these principles part of your life, you can expect to achieve the sought-after results that have eluded you on so many other diets.

The Hormone Diet plan allows you to take control of your health as you gain insight into the close, often overlooked connections between the foods you eat and how you look and feel. Through your process of detoxing and reintroducing foods, you've surely come to realize that one person's pleasure may be another's poison.

Food is the essential fuel that enables your body to do all the wondrous things it can do. But beyond just providing us with energy, the specific foods we eat directly influence our physiology by communicating with our hormones. Your food choices dictate how you feel and function from one moment to the next. Simply paying attention to how you feel after eating a particular food can provide excellent clues to its hormonal effects. Feeling satisfied, focused, and full of energy after eating tells you that the foods you chose had a positive effect on your hormones. If, on the other hand, your meal leaves you tired, foggy, bloated, and craving sweet treats, then you can bet you've just eaten a hormone-hampering meal. The empowering thing about undertaking my plan is that you can enjoy beneficial changes within days or even hours of eating for hormonal balance.

The Glyci-Med Dietary Approach: Balanced Nutrition for Your Metabolism and Your Hormones

The nutritional solution to creating hormonal balance involves blending the food selections characteristic of a Mediterranean diet with the principles of glycemically balanced eating—an eating style I call the Glyci-Med approach. But before we jump into the sample meal plan, here's an outline of the rules. Understanding these rules and the reasons behind them, rather than just following the menu plan, will give you the power to make healthy choices and stay balanced, no matter where you are or what you're up to. These are the rules that you should follow 7 days a week (you are allowed 1 to 2 cheat meals ☺):

1. **Eat the right foods.**
2. **Eat at the right times.**
3. **Avoid the hormone-hindering foods.**

Do this 80 to 100 percent of the time. That's it!

Sticking to these simple rules will help you stabilize your blood sugar balance and boost the hormones that burn fat and control your appetite. It will also prevent the hormonal chaos that can lead to weight gain and overeating.

Now let's go over each rule.

Rule #1: Eat the Right Foods

- Buy fresh, locally grown produce and go for organic or wild sources of food whenever you can. This rule is especially important for meats, eggs, fish, and dairy products, which tend to contain high amounts of hormones and toxins. When you buy produce, I strongly advise you to choose *organic* strawberries, apples, soybeans (and all soy products), apricots, bananas, red and green peppers, tomatoes, lemons, limes, kiwifruit, peaches, grapes, berries (raspberries, blueberries), spinach, lettuce, carrots, green beans, and broccoli. As these fruits and veggies are typically the most heavily sprayed with pesticides, choosing organic will help cut out a lot of hormone-hampering toxins. A fruit and veggie wash is helpful if you are unable to purchase organic foods, and even frozen organic veggies can be a good choice in a pinch.

- Consume Hot Hormone Foods daily. Hot Hormone Foods help you achieve hormonal balance, feel satisfied, fight disease, and lose fat. They include olive oil, broccoli, flaxseeds, green tea, chia, and avocado. To fully take advantage of all the benefits each food has to offer, follow my suggested serving guidelines listed on www.thehormonediet.com. In general, though, you should

---

HOT HORMONE TIP

Chia is a gluten-free ancient grain that can be added to just about any food. On a per-gram basis, chia is touted to be:

- The highest source of omega-3s in nature—65 percent of its total fat is from omega-3 fatty acids
- The most concentrated source of fiber in nature—35 percent (90 percent insoluble and 10 percent soluble)
- Abundant in the minerals magnesium, potassium, folic acid, iron, and calcium
- A complete source of all essential amino acids
- A great choice for a carbohydrate-conscious eater. The carbs in chia are mostly insoluble fiber, beneficial for digestion

Just $3\frac{1}{2}$ ounces of chia offers an amazing 20 grams of omega-3s, the equivalent of $1\frac{3}{4}$ pounds of Atlantic salmon. (Source: www.sourcesalba.com) And then there are the hormonal benefits. Chia stabilizes blood sugar, manages the effects of diabetes, improves insulin sensitivity, and aids symptoms related to metabolic syndrome, including imbalances in cholesterol, blood pressure, and high blood sugar. Chia is highly anti-inflammatory. This wondrous little grain also contains high amounts of tryptophan, the amino acid precursor of serotonin and melatonin. It actually has very little taste—another fantastic feature that makes it so easy to blend with other foods.

enjoy all of these hormone-enhancing foods as often as you can.

- I don't advocate counting calories because the source of your calories is the more important factor for hormonal balance, but you should try to avoid overeating in one sitting, since they can cause stress on your body. Pay attention to my recommended serving sizes (measured by your hand/fist or by the number of grams of protein, carbs, and fat). If you feel you need specific numbers as a guideline, the average woman should eat a maximum of 500 calories in one meal, while 150 to 200 calories in snacks is a reasonable amount to try to stick to. The average man may have 500 to 600 calories per meal and 200 to 300 calories per snack.

- Drink as much water as possible between mealtimes throughout the day—at least eight glasses. For the exact number of ounces you should drink, multiply your body weight in pounds by 0.55. Then divide this number by 8 to convert it to cups (a cup has 8 ounces). I weigh 100 pounds, so my calculation would be: 100 x 0.55 = 55 ounces. Fifty-five divided by 8 = about 7 cups of water per day. If you don't enjoy drinking water, try livening up the taste by slicing fresh fruit or cucumbers into it. If you like to store cold water in your fridge, I recommend keeping it in a glass pitcher and drinking your water from a glass tumbler or bottle, rather than plastic. But most important, drink your water, as it keeps your liver focusing on flushing fat and your appetite in check!

- For better appetite control, try having soup or salad before your meal. It fills you up quickly and helps you to eat less for the rest of the meal—and the next meal, too.

- To stabilize blood sugar and insulin and increase metabolism, the Glyci-Med style promotes choosing one serving of lean protein, low-glycemic carbohydrates and healthy fats at each meal. The benefits, best sources, and how much to consume are detailed right after Rule #3.

Rule #2: Eat at the Right Times

Eating at the appropriate times throughout the day will help to maximize fat burning and keep hunger at bay.

- Aim to eat every 3 to 4 hours. Most people eat three meals and one snack, while others may prefer four smaller meals; you're free to find the combination that works best for you. Timing your meals in this way will improve your fat loss by preventing excess insulin, allowing leptin to work its magic on appetite control and metabolism, and by balancing the stress hormone cortisol. You should also enjoy your meals at the same time every day.
- Eat within 1 hour of rising and never within the 3-hour period before bedtime. If you must eat before bed, opt for a light meal or snack that's high in protein and low in carbohydrates and fat, such as a protein shake made with berries and water, salad with grilled chicken, or a shrimp and veggie stir-fry.
- For better appetite control throughout the day, try combining your starchy carbs at lunch, dinner, or after your workouts rather than at breakfast. Stick to eggs or whey protein smoothies for breakfast and you'll eat less throughout the day.
- Always eat within 45 minutes of finishing your workout. This meal or snack is the only one of the day that should not contain much fat and should be higher in carbohydrates. For example, have a smoothie made with juice, fruit, and protein powder, but no flaxseeds or oil.
- Never do your weight training on an empty stomach. You will need energy from your foods to perform optimally. You may, however, complete your cardio before eating if your session will be less than 30 minutes.

- Do not eat while you are doing anything else (i.e., watching TV, working, surfing on the computer, etc.). Focus on chewing your food and relaxing while you eat.
- Eat the protein on your plate first to help speed the signal to your brain that you are full.
- If you have alcohol or wine, do so *after* your meal to enhance the hormones involved in appetite control and digestion.

Rule #3: Avoid These Hormone-Hindering Foods

The following list includes some hormone-hindering foods you should reduce or totally eliminate from your diet. Note that you can have white processed foods, white potatoes, sugar or sweets, and a few other items listed below on special occasions or on your cheat day, even though you need to avoid them 80 percent of the time. (My guess is that you'll feel so bad after eating them that you won't choose to do so very often!) The majority of the rest of the foods are *always* a no-no, even on your cheat day.

- Although it is ultimately up to you, I recommend that 80 to 100 percent of the time you avoid any food you reacted to during your food reintroduction at the end of your detox diet.
- Processed meats and luncheon meats, which are high in chemicals linked to cancer—avoid 100 percent of the time. Instead, look for natural options from your local butcher or deli.
- White flour, white rice, enriched flour, refined flour, white sugar, white potatoes—avoid 80 percent of the time.
- Harmful fats—trans fatty acids (hydrogenated oils, partially hydrogenated oils, shortening, margarines) and unhealthy inflammatory fats such as cottonseed oil, vegetable oil, palm oil—avoid 100 percent of the time.

- Peanuts—avoid 80 percent of the time, unless they're organic and aflatoxin free (aflatoxin is linked to cancer).
- Saturated fats in full-fat dairy products and red meats—avoid 80 percent of the time. Also limit your intake of safflower and sunflower oil, which may become inflammatory if consumed in excess.
- Fructose-sweetened foods or foods containing high-fructose corn syrup, because it cranks up your appetite—avoid 100 percent of the time.
- Foods containing aspartame and artificial sweeteners, which cause you to overeat and experience cravings—avoid 100 percent of the time.
- Large fish known to be high in mercury, including swordfish, tuna, shark, sole—avoid 80 percent of the time. (For more information and to download your free seafood guide, visit www.seachoice.org.)
- Farmed salmon, because it is plagued with toxins—avoid 100 percent of the time.
- Foods containing harmful artificial coloring, preservatives, sulfites, and nitrites—avoid 100 percent of the time.
- Raisins and dates, because they are so high in sugar—avoid 80 percent of the time. These fruits are okay, however, when consumed with protein (like in your smoothies, for example).
- Nonorganic chicken, turkey, pork, or beef—avoid as often as you can.
- Nonorganic coffee—avoid 80 percent of the time. If you do consume coffee daily, stick to 1 cup a day, preferably before your workout, and definitely enjoy it before lunchtime to avoid interfering with your sleep. Decaf coffee should also be avoided unless it is organic, Swiss water decaffeinated.

In the midst of the current obesity epidemic, scientists are striving to understand both our struggle to gain control of our appetites and our tendency to overeat. They certainly have their work cut out for them! The chart below outlines just a few of the countless complex factors that influence our need to feed. You'll be pleased to learn that the three steps in this book cover all the factors and habits that are known to help get a handle on your appetite.

Factors That Spark the Desire to Eat	Factors That Encourage Us to Put Down the Fork
Sight and smell of food	Out of sight, out of mind!
Overweight or obesity	Maintaining a lean body
Variety of foods and mixture of tastes—buffets and standing in front of the fridge grazing are our downfall!	Avoiding buffets or grazing in front of the cupboard or fridge; limiting flavors and varieties of foods in one sitting can help keep appetite in check
Cold body temperature	Warm body temperature
Lack of sunlight or bright light exposure	A healthy dose of sunshine or bright light
Internal body clock—we tend to get hungry at similar times each day; appetite increases in the winter	Eating regularly throughout the day and *always* having breakfast
Dehydration	Staying well-hydrated
Jet lag, sleep deprivation, and shift work	Sufficient, good-quality sleep
High intake of carbohydrates and lack of fiber and fats	Consuming a mix of protein, carbohydrates, and healthy fats at each meal and snack
Brain chemistry imbalance (low serotonin and dopamine); a compromised digestive system	Balanced brain chemistry (sufficient serotonin and dopamine); a healthy digestive system
High-fructose corn syrup and artificial sweeteners	Consuming enough fiber and avoiding processed carbohydrates, artificial sweeteners, fructose, and HFCS

Quit Feeling Guilty about Food!

Feeling guilty is counterproductive. The enjoyment of your food and your life is beneficial to your hormone balance! If you feel guilty every time you have a "bad" food, you are only amplifying the negative

It takes time for hormonal messages to reach the feeding centers of your brain. So the idea of whetting your appetite with a few hors d'oeuvres before a meal may have a solid scientific basis. According to a study in the October 2006 issue of the journal *Cell Metabolism*, researchers found that the very first bites of food sparked brain activity in the hunger centers of rats trained to stick to a strict feeding regimen. The findings also revealed that the brain center responsible for telling us when we are full or satisfied appears to turn on as soon as food hits the stomach, rather than when our threshold of intake has been exceeded. So enjoying a healthy appetizer beforehand and eating slowly throughout the meal are two basic habits that can help you avoid consuming too much in one sitting. If you tend to eat quickly, use chopsticks instead of utensils, count the number of times you chew, or practice putting down the fork between bites.

effects of the poor food choice on your body. Instead, enjoy the moment and acknowledge it as a reminder that your *future intention is to choose primarily healthy foods.*

Your Best Choices for the Building Blocks of the Glyci-Med Dietary Approach

When we speak about macronutrients, we usually discuss the three biggies: protein, carbohydrates, and fats. But if we define a macronutrient as something that's needed in higher amounts in the diet, then I believe *fiber* and *water* should also be added to the list. When we eat (or drink) these nutrients in the right amounts and at the right times, we can crank up our metabolism and create the perfect hormonal balance for fat loss. So, let's get into the juicy details of each of these nutrients—the building blocks of the Glyci-Med approach.

1. Wonderful Water

Health experts suggest that water indirectly aids fat loss by keeping the kidneys functioning at their best. Optimal kidney function leaves the liver free to do its job as one of our primary fat-burning engines. If the kidneys are stressed, the liver has to take up the slack, distracting the liver from its fat-burning role. But water can help us lose weight in another way, too, by controlling our appetites.

We obtain water not only from drinks, but also from foods. In a 1999 study published in the *American Journal of Clinical Nutrition*, researchers from Pennsylvania State University showed that eating foods with a high water content satisfies our appetites more than drinking a glass of water on its own or with solid food.

High-water foods include soups, certain fruits, vegetables, and low-fat dairy products. These low-glycemic foods also tend to be low in calories, which means we can eat significant amounts and use them to control hunger. They also balance our hormones because high-water, high-fiber, low-calorie, low-glycemic foods limit insulin release and also stretch our stomachs. The appetite-suppressing hormone CCK is released from that stretched stomach, which sends the message to our brain that we're full. These "big" water foods sure cause a lot of stretch.

Just as our hormones dictate when and what we want to eat, they also control our thirst. If we are dehydrated, the stress hormone NPY increases and tells us to drink. Beware, however: Dehydration can also cause us to reach for a snack instead of a thirst-quenching beverage. So get plenty of water! It's a very easy way to control your appetite and maximize fat burning. But remember, sugary drinks don't count toward your daily water intake and must be avoided.

2. Fantastic Fiber

We obtain fiber from plant foods, which are essentially carbohydrates. So it's no wonder many people experience constipation on a low-carb diet. You need dietary fiber mainly to keep your digestive system healthy, but getting plenty of it offers many other health benefits. Stable blood sugar, lower cholesterol, cancer protection, weight loss, and improved hormonal balance are just a few examples. In countries with diets traditionally high in fiber, diseases such as obesity, bowel cancer, diabetes, and coronary heart disease are much less common. Unfortunately, the average North American adult consumes only 14 to 15 grams of fiber a day, when 30 to 40 grams a day should be our goal.

3. Cool Carbohydrates

Vegetables, fruits, beans, grains, cookies, pastries, bread, pasta, rice, juice, soda pop, and candies are all sources of carbohydrates. Despite their bad rap in recent years, carbs are a crucial part of our diet because they maintain our moods and provide us with the energy necessary for most bodily functions, including muscle actions and brain activity.

Carbohydrates eventually end up as sugar in the bloodstream. As I'm sure you know, not all carbs are created equal. So-called "good carbs," also called complex carbs, are converted to sugar in much smaller amounts and at a much slower rate than "bad carbs," or simple carbs. As a result, good carbs spark less insulin release, whereas bad carbs initiate more by causing a fast and furious rush of sugar into the bloodstream. You can differentiate good carbs from bad by looking at a food's **glycemic index (GI)**, the measurement of how quickly a food ends up as sugar in your bloodstream after consumption.

High-glycemic foods such as white pasta, white rice, potato chips, pastries, cookies, candies, muffins, sodas, bagels, and white potatoes are broken down rapidly. These foods are simple carbs that are also normally low in fiber. As a result, they cause a huge influx of sugar into your bloodstream, followed by loads of insulin release.

Low-glycemic carbohydrates such as berries, green vegetables, and legumes are slowly broken down, allowing sugar to trickle gradually into your bloodstream, thereby limiting insulin release. Most of these foods are also high in fiber, which slows the entry of sugar into the bloodstream. So remember: *Low = Slow = Go for it!*

The **glycemic load (GL)** is a newer measure that builds on the principles of the glycemic index. GL provides an idea of the total glycemic response to a food or meal and also takes into consideration the amount of carbohydrate per serving. On this scale, a low-glycemic load is below 10.

To make it easy for you and so that you do not have to consult glycemic index or load charts, I have provided a list of the best low-glycemic carbohydrate choices, along with their fiber content, on page 264.

Happy Hormone Facts about Carbs

* Consuming the perfect amount of carbs at the proper times and in the right forms helps promote hormonal balance and prevent excess insulin, low leptin, and leptin resistance. This leads to higher metabolism, excellent energy, appetite control, and freedom from cravings.

* Too many, too few, or the wrong types of carbs (high GI) at the wrong times leave you with a hormonal imbalance linked to high insulin, inflammation, aging, weight gain, cravings, erratic fluctuations in energy, foggy thinking, and many other undesirable consequences.

* No matter what all those popular diet books say, cutting carbs completely is not a good weight-loss strategy. Here's what happens when we eliminate carbs:
  * We cause physical stress, which in turn elevates cortisol that can lead to loss of muscle tissue and more abdominal fat gain.
  * Testosterone plummets, leaving our libido flat and our muscles suffering even more.

- Serotonin sags, and we experience cravings, overeating, bingeing, depression, and sleep disruption. No wonder a low-carb diet is associated with irritability, fatigue, and poor performance!
- We adopt an unsustainable way of eating. Remember, your body naturally puts up a fight when you restrict carbs— ghrelin and NPY team up to stimulate your appetite while your sinking thyroid hormone puts the brakes on your metabolism.

So We've Gotta Have Carbs—But When?

You know that infamous 3 p.m. slump? The one that makes you want to reach for coffee and a candy bar? Well, guess what? A balanced breakfast will eliminate it. We know that consuming too many carbs at breakfast increases cravings and caloric intake later in the day. Too many carbs throughout the day will also cause insulin spikes that later leave us yawning, sluggish, and searching for something more. It's best to consume a breakfast that's high in protein for hormonal balance and fat loss.

At the same time, the right type and amount of carbs at dinner can increase serotonin and improve your sleep. Beware, however, of too much sugar (or too many carbs) before bed or after exercise because this prevents growth hormone release, sabotaging the muscle-building and fat-burning benefits we enjoy from these activities.

Carbohydrates: Which Sources Are Best and How Much Should You Have?

The text and tables beginning on page 264 outline the top low-glycemic starch, fruit, veggie, bean, and nut options, as well as your daily suggested number of servings for each. You need to select at least one carbohydrate at each meal. Each table includes serving sizes and fiber content. On most days, your intake of dietary fiber will be very close to your 30- to 40-gram target. You may add a fiber supplement to your diet if you find that you are falling short based on your daily selections from all the categories below.

Rather than using the charts I've provided with your recommended selections and serving sizes, you can also determine you carbohydrate intake by reading labels. Women should consume 25 to 35 grams of carbohydrates per meal; men should aim for 35 to 45 grams. Snack servings should be a maximum of half this amount.

YOUR BEST GLYCI-MED GLYCEMIC LOW-CARB CHOICES
STARCHY CARBS
Most women should choose 1 starch daily; men should choose 2.

Very active people generally need more carbohydrates each day than less active people do. If you are an extremely active person (i.e., someone who exercises intensively with weights and/or does cardio 5 to 6 days a week), you may need 2 (women) or even 3 (men) starches daily. If you begin to experience fatigue or if you can't perform as well during your workouts, you likely need an extra serving. Drop the additional serving, however, if you start to gain weight or experience cravings.

Pasta, Rice, Grains	Suggested Serving Size	Grams of Fiber per Serving
Pearl barley	½ cup	3.0
Brown rice	½ cup	2.0
Buckwheat (kasha)	½ cup	8.5
Ezekiel pasta (Foods for Life)	½ cup	4.4
Kamut pasta	½ cup	6.3
Whole-wheat pasta	½ cup	2.7
Quinoa	½ cup	5.0
Chia*	2 tablespoons	4.5
Wheat bran*	½ cup	12.3
Wheat germ*	3 tablespoons	3.9
Starchy Veggies	Suggested Serving Size	Grams of Fiber per Serving
Sweet potato	½ cup	4.0
Acorn squash	½ cup	4.6
Butternut squash	½ cup	2.8

* Not significant sources of carbohydrates, but excellent sources of fiber.

Breads	Suggested Serving Size	Grams of Fiber per Serving
Ezekiel bread (Food for Life)	1 slice	3.0
Ezekiel tortilla (Food for Life)	1 tortilla	5.0
Kamut	1 slice	4.0
Pumpernickel	1 slice	2.7
Rye	1 slice	1.8
Stone Mills Glycemically Tested Bread	2 slices	4
Whole wheat	1 slice	1.5
Cereals	Suggested Serving Size	Grams of Fiber per Serving
All-Bran	⅓ cup	8.6
Fiber One	½ cup	11.9
40% Bran Flakes	⅔ cup	4.3
Kashi GOLEAN	½ cup	5.0
Oat bran, cooked	½ cup	4.0
Oat flakes	1 cup	3.1
Oatmeal	⅓ cup	2.7
Crackers	Suggested Serving Size	Grams of Fiber per Serving
Ryvita Crispbread (light rye, dark rye, sesame rye, or rye and oat bran)	3 slices	5.0
Ryvita Crispbread (multigrain, sunflower seeds and oat, pumpkin seeds and oat)	2 slices	4.0
Ryvita Snackbread (high fiber)	6 slices	5.0
Wasa Sourdough	4 slices	8.0
Wasa Fiber Rye	4 slices	8.0

FRUITS

Women should choose 2 fruits daily; men should choose 3.

Fruits	Suggested Serving Size	Grams of Fiber per Serving
Apple	1 small	2.8
Applesauce, unsweetened	½ cup	2.0
Apricots, dried	7 halves	2.0
Apricots, fresh	4	3.5
Banana	½ small	1.1

Fruit (continued)	Suggested Serving Size	Grams of Fiber per Serving
Blueberries	1 cup	4.0
Cherries	1 cup	2.3
Goji berries	1 tablespoon	4.0
Grapefruit	½ medium	1.6
Kiwifruit	1 large	3.3
Orange	1 small	2.9
Peach	1 medium	2.0
Pear	½ large	2.9
Pomegranate	½ cup	1.0
Plum	2 medium	2.4
Açaí berries	2 tablespoons	3.0
Prunes	3 medium	1.7
Raspberries	1 cup	3.3
Strawberries	1¼ cups	2.8
Watermelon	1¼ cups cubes	0.6

VEGGIES

Both women and men should choose a minimum of 6 to 10 veggies daily, though you may enjoy unlimited amounts of each.

Vegetables	Serving Size (you may have unlimited amounts)	Grams of Fiber per Serving
Cooked Veggies		
Asparagus	½ cup	2.8
Beets, root only	½ cup	1.8
Broccoli	½ cup	2.4
Brussels sprouts	½ cup	3.8
Carrots	½ cup	2.0
Cauliflower	½ cup	1.0
Green beans	½ cup	2.0
Kale	½ cup	2.5
Okra	½ cup	4.1
Peas	½ cup	4.3
Spinach	½ cup	1.6
Tomato sauce	½ cup	1.7
Turnip	½ cup	4.8

Vegetables (continued)	Serving Size (you may have unlimited amounts)	Grams of Fiber per Serving
Raw Veggies		
Cabbage	1 cup	1.5
Carrots	1 large	2.3
Celery	1 cup	1.7
Cucumber	1 cup	0.5
Lettuce, Romaine	2 cups	1.9
Mushrooms, fresh	1 cup pieces	0.8
Onion, fresh	½ cup chopped	1.7
Green pepper	1 cup chopped	1.7
Tomato	1 medium	1.0

BEANS

Both women and men should choose 1 serving daily.

Beans	Suggested Serving Size	Grams of Fiber per Serving
Black beans	½ cup	6.1
Black-eyed peas	½ cup	4.7
Chickpeas, dried or in hummus	½ cup	4.3
Kidney beans, light red	½ cup	7.9
Lentils	½ cup	5.2
Lima beans	½ cup	4.3
Navy beans	½ cup	6.5
Pinto beans	½ cup	6.1

NUTS

Both women and men should choose 1 serving daily.

Nuts or Seeds	Suggested Serving Size	Grams of Fiber per Serving
Almonds	12 whole	1.6
Cashews	9 whole	0.5
Pecans	10 halves	1.35
Walnuts	7 halves	0.9
Almond butter, smooth or crunchy	1 tablespoon	1.0
Flaxseeds	1 tablespoon	3.3
Pumpkin seeds	1 tablespoon	1.1
Sesame seeds	1 tablespoon	0.5
Sunflower seeds	1 tablespoon	0.5

Fiber information primarily sourced from Harvard University Health, Nutrition Services (May 2004), available at: www.uhs.harvard.edu/assets/File/OurServices/Service_Nutrition_Fiber.pdf (accessed June 24, 2008), which was adapted from J.W. Anderson's *Plant Fiber in Foods,* 2nd ed. (Lexington, KY): HCF Nutrition Research Foundation, 1990).

Reading Nutrition Labels and Making Great Carb Choices

Understanding nutrition labels and the glycemic index will help you be carb-smart when you shop, cook, and eat. Just follow these guidelines.

I. READ NUTRITION LABELS CAREFULLY

- **Read the ingredients.** If the product contains any hormone-hindering ingredients, put it back on the shelf. Do the same thing if the product has sugar listed at the beginning of the ingredients.
- **Check the serving size allocated for the nutrition info.** A serving size of five potato chips doesn't make much sense based on the amount that most of us would really eat in a sitting. Sometimes foods look as though they are a good choice for you, but only because the serving size used to report the nutrition values is completely unrealistic.

- **Check the amount of carbohydrates.** Read the amount listed on the label and measure it against the total amount of carbohydrate you should consume per meal and snack. (Remember, the average woman needs 25 to 35 grams, whereas most men require 35 to 45 grams per meal.) If the product is higher than these amounts, look for something else.

- **Check the amount of protein.** Remember this simple guideline: *If the product contains equal amounts of protein and carbohydrates or more protein than carbs per serving, it is a good choice for you.* For example: Vanilla soy milk has 11 g of carbs and 6 g of protein; plain soy milk has 3 g of carbs and 6 g of protein. In this case, the plain milk is a much better bet. Next, compare it with the amount of protein you should consume per meal and snack (the average woman needs 25 to 30 grams per meal, and men need 35 to 40 grams). This will help you determine your serving size.

- **Check the fat content.** Compare it with the total amount of fat you should consume in a meal or snack (10 to 12 g per meal for women and 12 to 15 g for men). Check the saturated fat content in particular, and aim for little to none.

- **Check the fiber content.** Products that contain less than 2 g of fiber per serving are not great choices. If you have a number of brands to choose from, select the product that's highest in fiber.

- **Check the sodium content.** Products with less than 140 mg of salt are considered to be low-sodium choices. Remember that you should consume only 2,300 mg of sodium per day (about 1 teaspoon of salt). When comparing products, pick the one that's lowest in sodium.

- **Check the calorie content.** Measure the calorie count against the total number of calories you should be having—remember that 400 to 500 calories per meal is a good guideline for women, 500 to 600 calories per meal for men.

2. GET FAMILIAR WITH THE GLYCEMIC INDEX (GI) AND GLYCEMIC LOAD (GL) OF YOUR FAVORITE PRODUCTS

You don't have to remember the exact GI or GL number for each food; you only need to know whether it is high or low on the charts. I just outlined the best glycemic choices along with their fiber content for you in the charts provided in this chapter. Web sites are listed for your reference in the resource section of the book.

4. Protein Power

In much the same way that carbohydrates are broken down into sugar, proteins are broken down into smaller subunits called amino acids. Amino acids are the essential building blocks of hormones, neurotransmitters, enzymes that assist in digestion, and antibodies that fight infection. Protein is also vital for tissue healing and repair. If you are not recovering well after your workouts, for example, you may need more protein in your diet.

Avoiding excess protein is just as important as getting enough. Too much protein can cause stress on your kidneys, exacerbate osteoporosis, and hamper your digestive system. Diana Schwarzbein, a medical doctor and the author of *The Schwarzbein Principle,* suggests that taking in too much protein in one sitting or eating protein without carbohydrates elevates cortisol and fatigues our adrenals.

Happy Hormone Facts about Protein

- Protein is a necessary building block for many hormones, including serotonin, melatonin, growth hormone, thyroid hormone, and dopamine. If we fail to get enough in our diet, we can experience mood disorders, memory loss, increased appetite and cravings, decreased metabolism, sleep disruption, muscle loss, and weight gain.

- Protein also packs a hormonal punch because it stimulates the activity of many of our fat-burning and appetite-controlling hormones when we consume it in the right amounts.
- Protein encourages the release of leptin and glucagon, which work opposite to insulin to encourage fat loss.
- Protein also stimulates the release of peptide YY from the gut, suppressing your appetite.
- When consumed before and after workouts, protein increases growth hormone release to stimulate muscle growth, tissue repair, and fat burning.

Protein: Which Sources Are Best and How Much Should You Have?

Although great carb choices are low in sugar, your best protein bets are those that are low in fat. Protein sources high in saturated fats, such as red meats and full-fat dairy products, increase inflammation in your body. And remember, more inflammation only serves to accelerate weight gain, hormonal imbalance, and insulin resistance. You may also notice, as many of my patients do, that reducing or avoiding these inflammatory foods can alleviate joint pain and stiffness within only a few weeks.

Protein requirements vary depending on gender, lean muscle mass, and activity levels. As a very simple guideline you will select a serving of protein about the size and thickness of your palm at every meal, along with a source of carbohydrates and fat. Do this three times a day at mealtimes, and consume about half that much protein in snacks. If

> **HOW MUCH IS TOO MUCH PROTEIN?**
>
> When the low-carb craze hit its peak, many critics claimed that these diets were too high in protein. Consuming too much protein can definitely cause stress on the body, particularly the kidneys. In most cases, a diet made up of about 30 percent is just right.

HOT HORMONE FACT

you're reading a label, women should aim for 25 to 30 grams of protein per meal and 15 grams per snack. Men should consume 40 to 45 grams of protein per meal and 20 grams per snack.

YOUR BEST GLYCI-MED PROTEIN CHOICES

Both men and women should choose a total 3 servings for meals and $^1/_2$ serving for your snacks daily.

Source	Suggested Serving Size	Special Notes
Fish	Size and width of your palm	Choose organic farmed fish or wild fish as often as possible. Limit your intake of tuna, swordfish, mahi mahi, king mackerel, and other larger fish that often have high mercury content. Avoid nonorganic farmed fish as much as possible, as these typically contain more toxins.
Chicken and turkey	Size and width of your palm	Choose organic whenever possible. Remember ground chicken and turkey are a lower-fat alternative to beef in burgers and chili.
Omega-3 eggs and liquid egg whites	Women: 4 to 5 egg whites or 2 whole eggs. Men: 5 to 7 egg whites or 3 whole eggs.	I recommend always using 1 whole egg and adding in more liquid egg whites rather than throwing out your yolks. (The protein from the whites is better absorbed in the presence of yolk, plus it tastes better!)
Low-fat cottage and ricotta cheese	1 cup = 28 grams of protein (so women should consume 1 cup; men 1½ cups)	Great mixed with yogurt to increase the protein content or eaten alone with fruit.
Fermented soy products	Size and width of your palm; stick to a maximum of 1 serving of soy products per day	If you choose soy-based meat substitutes, pick ones that are low in fat and also free of additives and genetically modified (GM) soy. Tofu, tempeh, soy nuts, and edamame can also be used as sources of protein. I prefer tempeh over tofu because it is a fermented source of soy protein and, therefore, more absorbable.

Source	Suggested Serving Size	Special Notes
Organic pressed cottage cheese (Organic Meadows)	½ cup = 24 grams of protein (so women should have ½ cup; men may have ¾–1 cup)	Excellent for adding texture and protein to soups and chilies.
Scallops	5–7 medium-size or about 15 small scallops provide more than 15 grams of protein	Scallops are almost pure protein.
Shrimp	4 ounces = 23 grams of protein	If you choose shrimp, be aware that it does contain significant amounts of cholesterol (though the effect of this on our cholesterol level is debatable).
Lean cuts of red meat	Size and width of your palm	Again, organic is best. These are high in saturated fat, so keep your intake to only once or twice per month.
Whey protein isolate	25–30 grams for women; 40–45 grams for men	Whey protein isolate is the most bioavailable source of protein. It supports healthy immune system function and is the most useful type of protein to encourage the loss of body fat while maintaining muscle mass. It is also a source of the antioxidant glutathione. A whey protein isolate is easier to absorb than a concentrate and tends to cause less digestive upset for individuals sensitive to dairy. Always choose protein powder supplements that are free of added sugar and artificial sweeteners. Those sweetened with xylitol or stevia are best.
Soy protein powder	Same as whey	Choose fermented soy because it is more easily absorbed. Jarrow makes a very good fermented soy powder that is organic, free of sweeteners and sugar, and does not contain genetically modified (GM) soy.
Rice or bean protein powders	Same as whey	These are good options for vegans and can also be used as an alternative to soy if you are concerned about too much soy in your diet.

5. Fabulous Fats

Consuming excess calories from fat will always contribute to weight gain, but we absolutely need fat and cholesterol in our diet. Fats are essential for maintaining a healthy nervous system, stable mood, and strong heart. They also help keep our skin moist, prevent dry eyes, keep our hair shiny, and help us absorb the fat-soluble vitamins A, D, E, and K. Every single cell membrane in your body is made up of fats. So fats are definitely not all bad, and neither is cholesterol.

Fats for Weight Loss?

Fats also help us feel full and satisfied because of their effects on our appetite-controlling friends, leptin and CCK. They prevent cravings and actually help us to lose weight when we consume them in the right forms and amounts.

Perhaps the most persuasive evidence proving that we need to consume fat to lose fat comes from a team of scientists at the Washington University School of Medicine. Their research showed that *old fat* stored around the belly, thighs, or butt *cannot* be burned off effectively unless we have *new fat* coming in from our diet or our liver. The findings, published in the May 2005 edition of *Cell Metabolism,* revealed that knocking out the fat-producing enzyme from the liver of mice (i.e., making mice unable to produce fats necessary to maintain normal sugar, fat, and cholesterol metabolism) caused the mice to develop fatty liver and show signs of disease even when they were fed a *zero-fat* diet! The mice livers were apparently unable to initiate the fat-burning process and also showed signs of increased inflammation.

> **HOT HORMONE TIP**
>
> **IMFLAMMATORY PROTEIN**
> The inflammatory high-fat proteins you should avoid:
> - Full-fat cheeses
> - Full-fat meat products such as steaks, ribs, and pork
> - Processed meats
> - Deep-fried meats (chicken wings, etc.)
>
> If you must eat these things, enjoy them on your cheat day and remember to go for a walk after your meal!

Happy Hormone Facts about Fats

- Like protein, fats and cholesterol are necessary building blocks for certain hormones, including progesterone, testosterone, cortisol, and estrogen.
- Cholesterol is an essential constituent of healthy cell membranes, a precursor to bile salts needed for digestion, and a component of vitamin D.
- Eating fats also stimulates the production of other hormones, including appetite-controlling leptin and CCK. Both these hormones play huge roles in telling us when to stop eating.

The Right Fats Help You Stay Slim!

Saturated fats, such as those in red meats and full-fat dairy products, increase the appetite by reducing the appetite-suppressing hormones leptin and CCK. Yes, you should limit your intake of these types of fats, but eliminating fat altogether is not the answer either. Instead, choose healthy options such as avocado, olives, olive oil, walnuts, and almonds. These healthful, calorie-rich, nutrient-dense foods will actually keep your appetite in check and your cravings under control.

GET YOUR DAILY DOSE OF OLIVE OIL

A diet rich in olive oil not only prevents belly fat accumulation, but also the insulin resistance and drop in adiponectin typically seen in people who eat a high-carbohydrate diet. According to a study in the *Journal of the American College of Nutrition* (October 2007), this was especially the case when olive oil was consumed at breakfast. I recommend my patients take a supplement called **Glyci-Med Forte** that's rich in olive and avocado oil at breakfast for these reasons. You can learn more about this supplement through my Web site. But here's the really amazing tidbit. Research published in the *British Journal of Nutrition* (December 2003) showed that olive oil, besides helping us lose weight, balance our hormones, reduce inflammation, and keep insulin under control, also breaks down fat cells we already have!

HOT HORMONE TIP

Fats: The Good, the Bad, and the Ugly

Fats are sometimes hard to get a handle on because there are many types and remembering which fats are "good" and which are "bad" can be a challenge. Here's a brief overview.

- Good fats *reduce* inflammation, ease pain, and promote heart health. These include the monounsaturated fats (which always remain liquid at room temperature); olive oil; canola oil; and the fats found in walnuts, Salba, and avocados.
- Bad fats *increase* pain; exacerbate inflammation; cause heart disease, diabetes, and Alzheimer's disease; and increase the risk of cancer. These include marbled meats; deep-fried foods; foods containing sunflower and safflower oils, which can become inflammatory when consumed in excess (baked chips, crackers, etc.); full-fat cheeses; hydrogenated oils; vegetable oil; saturated fats in animal products (meat and dairy); cottonseed oil; shortening and margarines (yes, I believe *butter is better* even though it's a saturated fat—though *olive oil is best*).

Fats: Which Sources Are Best and How Much Should You Have?

In keeping true to the principles of the Glyci-Med style, *olive oil must be consumed daily,* so be sure to select it as one of your servings of fat. When reading labels, keep in mind that women should have 10 to 12 grams of fat per meal; men should have 12 to 15 grams. Men and women should have about 5 grams in a snack.

YOUR BEST GLYCI-MED FAT CHOICES

Both women and men should consume 3 servings daily.

Healthy Fats	Serving Size
Olives	3–5 (women)
	5–7 (men)
Extra-virgin olive oil	1 tablespoon (women)
	1½ tablespoons (men)

Healthy Fats (continued)	Serving Size
Organic canola oil	1 tablespoon (women) 1½ tablespoons (men)
Avocados	⅛–¼ of an avocado, depending on overall size of fruit
Macadamia nuts	3 or 4
Butter	1 teaspoon maximum
Omega-3 eggs	2 yolks (women) 3 yolks (men)
Guacamole	1 tablespoon (women) 1½ tablespoons (men)

The Sample Menu Plan

The following is an example of a 7-day menu plan for the Hormone Diet nutrition program, which encompasses all of the rules of the Glyci-Med approach. When creating your own plan, you may also continue using the daily meal plans outlined in your detox step. The main difference between the two sample meal plans is that the detox meals are free of gluten, dairy, and red meats. You should not choose meals containing these foods during this step (or moving forward) if you noticed reactions to the foods during your reintroduction process.

Eating well does not have to be complicated; it just takes some planning. And I guarantee you will never go hungry!

THE GLYCI-MED PLATE

According to your Glyci-Med dietary guidelines, about two-thirds of your plate at mealtimes should be occupied by carbohydrates: one-third salad and one-third veggies. The remaining third should be your protein. Your fats may fall on top of your carbohydrate selections (as salad dressing, for instance) or be consumed within your protein selections. Add spices to your meals as often as you can. Once a day, include your serving of starchy carbohydrate. I recommend including the starch with your evening meal (to improve your sleep and to maintain consistent energy throughout the day) or after your workout, but some of you may prefer having your starch at lunch.

HOT HORMONE TIP

Day 1

Breakfast: Awesome Omelette (page 428)

Lunch: Lovely Lentil Soup (page 436) and tomatoes with Balsamic Vinegar and Olive Oil Dressing (page 431)

Snack: The Simply Bar (page 458)

Dinner: Veggie Chili (page 446)

Day 2

Breakfast: Antiaging Smoothie (page 425)

Lunch: Super Salmon Salad with 1 slice 100 percent rye bread (page 450)

Snack: Hummus and Veggies (page 460)

Dinner: Baby Spinach with Grilled Ginger Scallops (page 451)

Day 3

Breakfast: Pure Energy Smoothie (page 423)

Lunch: California Avocado and Chicken Salad (page 434)

Snack: Black Bean Dip and veggies (page 459)

Dinner: Beef Fajita with Side Salad (page 453)

Day 4

Breakfast: Anti-Inflammatory Smoothie (page 428)

Lunch: Sweet Potato, Squash, and Ginger Soup (page 435) and tossed mixed greens side salad (page 439)

Snack: Simple Apple Snack (page 462)

Dinner: Anti-Inflammatory Curry (page 447)

Day 5

Breakfast: Dopamine Delight Smoothie (page 426)

Lunch: Zippy Three-Bean Salad (page 437) with tossed mixed greens side salad (page 439)

Snack: Almond Butter Protein Bar (page 461)

Dinner: Sweet Garlic Chicken Stir-Fry (page 448)

Day 6
Breakfast: Super Satisfying Shake (page 426)
Lunch: Antioxidant Chicken Salad (page 433)
Snack: Berry-Apple Ricotta Cheese (page 462)
Dinner: Mediterranean Tilapia (page 445) with baked asparagus and tossed mixed greens side salad (page 439)

Day 7
Breakfast: Serotonin-Surge Smoothie (page 427)
Lunch: Warm Black Bean and Turkey Salad (page 438)
Snack: Simple Apple Snack (page 462)
Dinner: Zesty Chicken Salad (page 440)

Now you have a good idea of what, when, and how much to eat every day, as well as a complete menu of healthy, satisfying meals and snacks to choose from. We are ready to move on to the second part of Step 2—replenishing your body, topping up your energy, and balancing your hormones with supplements.

A Review of the Hormone Diet Nutrition Steps

Eat the Right Foods

- Eat lean protein, low-glycemic carbohydrates, and healthy fats at each meal and snack.
- Avoid eating "starchy" carbs at breakfast; stick to protein for better appetite control and to avoid that midafternoon slump.
- Eat olive oil (extra virgin, cold pressed), nuts, beans, whey protein, and an apple every day.
- Eat fresh, locally grown organic produce, and choose organic or wild sources of meat, fish, eggs, and dairy whenever you can.
- Drink as much water as possible during the day—between meals.

At the Right Time

- Aim to eat every 3 to 4 hours; find the best combination of meals and snacks for you.
- Enjoy your meals at the same time every day.
- Eat within 1 hour of rising and never within the 3-hour period before bedtime.
- Always eat within 45 minutes of finishing your workout. This meal or snack should not contain too much fat and should be higher in carbohydrates, with a bit of protein.
- Never do your weight training on an empty stomach.
- You may complete your cardio training before eating if your session is 30 minutes long or less.

Avoid Hormone-Hindering Foods

Avoid these foods 80 to 100 percent of the time. (Consider eating these foods during your cheat meal only.)

- White flour, enriched flour, refined flour, wheat flour, white sugar, white potatoes, and white rice
- Saturated fats in full-fat dairy products and red meats
- Large fish known to be high in mercury, including swordfish, shark, tilefish, marlin, orange roughy, grouper, king mackerel, and tuna
- Raisins, figs, and dates
- Nonorganic chicken, turkey, pork, and beef; as often as you can, choose organic foods
- Consume coffee or caffeine as a treat (once or twice a week), rather than daily. If you must have it daily, use organic coffee, stick to one cup a day, and have it before lunchtime. Decaf coffee should be avoided unless it is organic and Swiss water processed.

Foods to Avoid 100 Percent of the Time

- Processed meats and luncheon meats
- Trans fatty acids (any hydrogenated oils, partially hydro-

genated oils, shortenings, or margarines) and unhealthy inflammatory fats, including most vegetable oils (such as sunflower and safflower), cottonseed oil, and palm oil
- Peanuts, unless they are organic and (optimally) aflatoxin free
- Fructose-sweetened foods or foods containing high-fructose corn syrup (HFCS)
- Foods containing aspartame and artificial sweeteners
- Farmed salmon
- Foods containing artificial coloring, preservatives, sulfites, and nitrates

Reminder: What Does My Plate Look Like?

At lunch and dinner, ask yourself, Do I have protein, fat, and carbohydrates?

Your plate should be two-thirds vegetables and one-third protein, and it should be topped with healthy fats and spices.

Here's a summary of the foods and serving sizes allowed during Steps 1 and 2 of the program.

Step 1: Anti-Inflammatory Detox	Introduction Phase	Step 2: Glyci-Med Approach
Grains & Starchy Veggies (½ cup or 1 fist-size serving per day)	Rye Whole wheat Ezekiel Bread	**Grains & Starchy Veggies (women, ½ cup or serving size suggested per day; men, 1 to 2 servings per day)**
Rice, rice pasta, rice crackers		100% rye bread or rye crackers like Wasa, and Ryvita
Potatoes		Kamut bread (1 slice) or pasta
Sweet Potatoes		Quinoa
Millet		Amaranth
Quinoa		Buckwheat
Amaranth		Whole wheat pasta
Buckwheat		Ezekiel bread (1 slice)
		Brown rice (basmati)
		Millet, amaranth
		Oatmeal, ⅓ cup cooked; ¾ cup raw oats
		Sweet potato
		Squash

Step 1: Anti-Inflammatory Detox	Introduction Phase	Step 2: Glyci-Med Approach
Allowed		Allowed
Fruits All except oranges, grapefruits, and dried fruit	Oranges Grapefruit	**Fruits (women, 2 servings per day/men, 3 servings per day)** Cherries, 15 Apricots, 3 Prunes, 3 Berries, 1 cup Peach, 1 small Pear, 1 small Apple, 1 small Plum, 1 small Orange, 1 small Kiwifruit, 1 small Grapefruit, 1 whole Watermelon, 1 cup Banana, ½ (in shakes only)
Vegetables Unlimited amounts of all, except for corn		**Vegetables** All except potato, corn and parsnips Beets, carrots—max ½ cup cooked or 12 raw baby carrots
Beans All allowed		**Beans (1 serving per day)** Beans, ½ cup Hummus, ¼ cup Soups, ¾ cup
Nuts (1 handful per day) All except peanuts		**Nuts (1 serving per day)** Walnuts, 8 Almonds, 10–12 Seeds, 2–3 Tbsp Nut butter, preferably almond butter, pumkin seed or organic peanut butter, 1 Tbsp

Step 1: Anti-Inflammatory Detox	Introduction Phase	Step 2: Glyci-Med Approach
Allowed		Allowed
Proteins Unlimited chicken, turkey, shellfish, and fish Eggs, yolks and whites	Pressed cottage cheese Ricotta cheese	**Proteins (women, 3 servings the size of your palm or 3–4 oz; men, 6 oz** Chicken, turkey, shellfish, and fish Ricotta or cottage cheese, ¾ cup for a meal; ½ cup for a snack Egg substitute, ⅔ cup Eggs, women, 2 whole or 1 whole and 4 egg whites Eggs, men, 3 whole or 1 whole and 6 egg whites Red meat (including beef, pork, and lamb) max 1 or 2 times per month Tempeh, 8 oz **Dairy Protein Sources:** Ricotta cheese, cottage cheese, ¾ cup for a meal; ½ cup for a snack Pressed organic cottage cheese, ½ cup for a meal Low-fat Swiss cheese, 2 slices Low-fat Jarlsberg cheese, 2 slices High-protein (20 grams per serving) Greek yogurt, 1 serving
Dairy (1 serving per day, optional) Soy milk, almond milk, goat milk, rice milk, ½ cup Goat's milk or cheese, 1 Tbsp	Yogurt	**Dairy (1 serving per day, optional)** Plain organic yogurt, ¾ cup Plain soy milk (unsweetened), almond milk, ¾ cup Goat's milk, goat cheese, or sheep cheese, 1 Tbsp
		Oils (3 servings per day) Olive oil (daily), 1 Tbsp Avocado, ⅛ to ¼ Mayonnaise, canola or olive oil based, 1 tsp Olives, 5 or 6 Butter, ½ tsp Flaxseed oil, 1 Tbsp Omega-3 egg yolks, 2
		Allowed only 1 or 2 times per week; continue to avoid these if you want to lose weight Sugar Alcohol Coffee (go for organic coffee, preferably before a workout)

CHAPTER 12

REPLENISH WITH SOMETHING EXTRA: BASIC SUPPLEMENTS TO SUPPORT HORMONAL BALANCE AND FAT LOSS

These are the hormonal benefits you can expect to enjoy from the Hormone Diet's basic supplement plan:

- Increased metabolism by replacing the nutrients needed to make thyroid hormone
- Reduced insulin and inflammation
- Improved mood, motivation, and craving control via support of the production of serotonin and dopamine
- Better growth hormone and melatonin for nighttime repair and enhanced fat-burning benefits from sleep
- Increased vitamin D for enhancing mood, insulin activity, and immunity

Now that you've learned everything you need to know to make the Glyci-Med eating style a part of your life, we need to take your nutrition plan to the next level with supplements to support hormonal balance and fat loss. At this point, you may be wondering why you can't simply get all the nutrients you need through your diet. So let's address this question right away.

Why Should You Take Supplements?

Over the past 50 years, our food has grown more and more vitamin deficient. Once upon a time, soils were replete with nutrients, which were transferred into the plants they fed. But as farming techniques have changed dramatically over the last half century, so has the nutrient content of crops. Many of the foods on our supermarket shelves have been transported, frozen, cooked, or processed in ways that strip away much-needed vitamins and minerals. Add in our insatiable desire for foods made with white flour, trans fats, and sugar, and it's no surprise that few of us are getting the nutrition we need from our daily meals.

Then there are the lifestyle factors. Living with air pollution, drinking coffee, taking medications, consuming alcohol, and even exercising—all of these increase our vitamin and mineral requirements. Add the various forms of stress to the mixture, and our need for nutrients is higher still. Some sources say our vitamin C is completely sapped after 20 minutes under stress. A deficiency of any nutrient can cause fatigue, poor concentration, malaise, anxiety, increased susceptibility to infections, and, if left untreated, can eventually lead to a more serious medical condition.

Unless you are ready to leave the city and start growing all your own organic food, the best way to ensure that you're meeting your many vitamin and mineral requirements is through supplementation. Now, taking a raft of supplements every day may not make you feel like turning cartwheels in the street, but simply taking vitamins C and E daily can reduce your risk of Alzheimer's disease by 58 percent. Is it not worth a little bit of effort now to be sharp and active at 85?

The documented health benefits of multivitamins continue to accumulate. In fact, most major health organizations now recommend the use of a multivitamin daily. Certain nutrients such as vitamin D, folic acid, vitamin B_6 and vitamin B_{12} have gained particular attention for their cancer-preventing and health-promoting benefits. Highly promising findings about the effects of vitamin D for cancer protection have prompted the American Cancer Society, American College of Rheumatology, National Council on Skin Cancer Prevention, and the World Health Organization (WHO) to recommend daily use of vitamin D supplements or a multivitamin high in vitamin D.

The Hormone Diet Supplement Plan

I believe supplements are an absolutely vital component of any wellness and fat-loss plan. Seeing patients who have lost a lot of weight without taking the right nutrients to support the cleanup of toxins released from fat cells always gives me cause for concern. Recently, one patient's cellular health showed significant signs of deterioration, even though she had made favorable changes in her body composition by gaining 4 pounds of lean muscle mass and losing 8 pounds of fat within a 3-month period. I'm certain her cells were suffering because her body wasn't able to eliminate the resulting toxins effectively. I immediately prescribed antioxidants and liver detoxification support. I also suggested she do 10 sessions in the infrared sauna to sweat out all that harmful waste! Thankfully, within 4 weeks her readings returned to optimal levels.

All this being said, you don't necessarily have to take a pile of daily supplements to reap abundant health rewards. I consider just five supplements to be essential to the Hormone Diet plan, though I believe there are three categories of supplements needed to *completely* restore hormonal balance and vibrant good health. They are:

1. **Basic supplements or foundation products.** These are the basic products required for the Hormone Diet plan covered in *this* chapter, including an omega-3 fish oil, a multivitamin (complete with 800 to 1,000 IU of vitamin D_3), basic antioxidants, a calcium-magnesium combination, and a whey protein supplement.

2. **Products to correct specific hormonal imbalances.** If you have identified any hormonal imbalances or signs of inflammation through your Hormonal Health Profile or blood work, you need to treat these in order to reach your optimal weight and achieve lasting wellness. Your options to correct specific signs of an imbalance are presented in the *next* chapter. The supplements you need in this category will change as your signs

and symptoms improve. You may no longer need them at all once your optimal balance is restored.

3. **Additional supplements to optimize health and wellness.** These include supplements to increase metabolism, energy, immunity, antiaging benefits, and antioxidant protection. Examples of these types of products are glutamine, creatine, co-enzyme Q10, CLA, alpha-lipoic acid, N-acetylcysteine, lutein, DMAE, acetyl-1-carnitine, turmeric, resveratrol, green foods, and more.

The Basic Supplements for Hormonal Balance

Taking high-quality products is important. Unfortunately, many products on the market fail to contain nutrients at the doses we require, while others have ingredients that can be harmful. To learn about my complete and easy-to-use Clear Essentials—Morning and Evening Packs, or to look for one of the brands I have listed for you here, visit www.thehormonediet.com. When you are ready to shop, there are four essential supplements you should be looking for.

1. A High-Quality Multivitamin

Remember, a deficiency of just one nutrient is enough to slow your metabolic rate and increase your risk of disease, especially if your body is not properly supported during detox and weight loss. A daily multivitamin supports your energy, metabolism, and body "cleanup" during fat loss. Your multivitamin should also provide 800 to 1,000 IU of vitamin D_3.

RECOMMENDED BRANDS
- Clear Essentials—Morning and Evening Packs
- MultiThera 3 (ProThera) or Nutrient 950 (Pure Encapsulations)
- New Chapter Multivitamin
- Other reputable brands include Douglas Labs, Natural Factors, Source Naturals, New Roots, and Allergy Research Group

CHOOSING YOUR MULTIVITAMIN

When taking vitamins, you need to consider a number of factors about yourself and your lifestyle. Your age and gender should ultimately dictate your requirements. Your secondary concern should be dosing frequency, as overdosing on multivitamins can create more problems than it solves. Too much iron, for example, can increase your risk of heart disease. Because men tend to accumulate iron as they age, their multivitamins should be iron-free. Menopausal women, who are also normally less susceptible to iron deficiencies, should choose an iron-free multi that's also high in calcium for bone health. Conversely, women in their reproductive years should take a multivitamin containing iron and high amounts of folic acid (600–1,000 mcg).

I recommend taking your multivitamin twice daily with meals. This consistent routine is easier to maintain and also provides your body with a steady supply of nutrients. The recommended dosage of the nutrients that should be present in your multi are on www.thehormonediet.com.

2. Omega-3 Fish Oil High in DHA

Since each and every cell membrane in our body is made of fat, our dietary fatty acid intake determines the healthy composition of all our cells. When you eat fatty acids such as those in fish oils—eicosapentaenoic acid (EPA) and docosahexaenoic acid (DHA)—your cell membranes become more fluid and more receptive to insulin. The more insulin receptors you have on the surface of your cells, the lower your insulin levels and the less prone to weight gain we become. Healthy

HOT HORMONE TIP

EXERCISE + OMEGA-3S = PERFECT PAIRING FOR FAT LOSS
When Professor Peter Howe and his colleagues at the University of South Australia studied the effects of diet and exercise on the body, they found that fish oil supplements and exercise made a powerful fat-loss combination. During the study, overweight to obese adults with metabolic syndrome and a greater risk of heart disease took omega-3 fish oil daily in combination with moderate aerobic exercise three times a week for 12 weeks. Body fat stores, particularly ab fat, were significantly reduced in the fish-oil-plus-exercise group, but not in those who used fish oil or exercise alone. Fish oils make great sense for fat loss, especially when you are exercising.

cell membranes allow you to enjoy greater wellness benefits and weight loss as you prime your body for better insulin balance.

Saturated fats such as those found in animal products have the opposite effects on your cells. You definitely need to choose your fats wisely for wellness! You can, however, prevent the harmful effects of saturated fats by including a supplement of DHA in your diet. When rats fed saturated fats were also provided with DHA fish oils, symptoms of insulin resistance were vastly improved or prevented entirely.

There are many benefits of omega-3 supplements. One of my favorites is that all forms moisten our skin from the inside out, though a fish oil that is higher in DHA is optimal for fat-burning effects.

Dosage: Take 2 to 4 grams per day with meals.

RECOMMENDED BRANDS
- proDHA capsules or ProEFA (Nordic Naturals)
- Super DHA capsules or liquid MedOmega Fish Oil (Carlson)
- EPA/DHA Extra Strength Capsules (Metagenics)
- Clear Omega (Clear Medicine)

5 WAYS FISH OILS HELP WITH FAT LOSS

1. They stimulate secretion of leptin, one of the hormones that decreases your appetite and promotes fat burning.
2. They help us burn fat by activating our PPARs.
3. They encourage storage of carbs as glycogen (in your liver and muscles) rather than as fat.
4. They are natural anti-inflammatory agents. Remember, inflammation causes weight gain and can prevent fat loss by interfering with our PPARs.
5. They possess documented insulin-sensitizing effects.

3. Whey Protein Isolate Supplement

Whey is fantastic for fat loss, building muscle, and boosting our fat-burning hormones. It is also rich in the antioxidant glutathione, aids immunity, and supports the removal of harmful heavy metals. Available in powder form, whey protein isolate is simple to mix into smoothies and is easily absorbed by the body. Choose a product free of artificial sweeteners and sugar.

RECOMMENDED BRANDS
- Dream Protein
- Proteins+ (Genuine Health)
- American Whey Protein (Jarrow or AOR)

4. Calcium-Magnesium Supplement in a Citrate Base with Vitamin D_3

I recommend the citrate form of calcium because it is most absorbable. I also prefer a product that offers a 1:1 ratio of calcium to magnesium. Many formulations have twice the amount of calcium. Taking your calcium-magnesium combination before bed is a great idea, since it's a natural muscle relaxant and can assist with your sleep. Also, calcium is best incorporated into your bones while you sleep.

Most men and women require 1,000 to 1,200 mg of calcium and a minimum of 600 to 800 mg of magnesium daily. Keep this figure in mind when adding up your calcium and magnesium intake from both your multi and your cal-mag supplements.

ADDITIONAL SUGGESTIONS FOR THOSE WHO ARE 40+
1. COENZYME Q10: I recommend 60 to 100 mg every day for *anyone over 40 years of age* and for those who are taking cholesterol-lowering medications. Coenzyme Q10 is a potent antioxidant that is naturally highest in the heart muscle but

that decreases as we age. CoQ10 supplements can increase your energy and brain power and aid your heart health. They are also fantastic for your skin. CoQ10 also has documented benefits for maintaining the health of muscle cells, which typically deteriorate as we age.

2. SAW PALMETTO AND LYCOPENE: Lycopene is a powerful antioxidant that is abundant in tomatoes and pink grapefruit. Saw palmetto is an herb that has been widely studied for its benefits for prostate health. This combination is very valuable for men age 40 and older when used daily for protection of the prostate gland.

ADDITIONAL OPTIONAL SUPPLEMENTS

1. MIXED VITAMIN E: Mixed vitamin E contains all eight types of vitamin E, especially gamma-tocopherol. Most vitamin E products out there contain only the alpha-tocopherol form of vitamin E, so be sure to look for a mix. Gamma-E is insulin sensitizing (and therefore a good adjunct to support fat loss) and has documented benefits for protection from breast cancer.

> **PROTECT YOUR MUSCLES AND GIVE 'EM A BOOST!**
> Mitochondria are the energy centers within your cells. When they are compromised by aging, stress, or disease, muscle cells can deteriorate and die. Supplementing with coenzyme Q10 not only protects those precious mitochondria from damage, but can also give them a welcome boost of energy.

HOT HORMONE TIP

2. LUTEIN: This antioxidant protects our eyes and can help reduce the risk of cataracts. Today the incidence of cataracts and the surgery required to fix them is skyrocketing. Take 6 mg every day with a meal.

3. CREATINE AND GLUTAMINE: You will learn more in the exercise chapter about these supplements, which are excellent for promoting muscle growth and boosting energy.

4. A GREEN-FOOD SUPPLEMENT: According to a study presented in

the *American Journal of Preventative Medicine* (2007), only about 35 percent of adults met the USDA minimum guidelines for daily consumption of vegetables (three or more servings) from 1988 to 1994. Just 27 percent met the daily guideline for fruit (two or more servings). Even though a national fruit and vegetable campaign was launched in 1991, the results from 1999 to 2002 were not much more encouraging. Overall, a mere 11 percent of adults meet the USDA guidelines for both fruits and vegetables. Apparently we need to develop some new approaches to promote healthy eating!

Simply eating fruits and vegetables aids in the prevention of just about every disease associated with aging, yet most of us fail to include these essential foods in our daily diet. A green-food supplement, or a multivitamin similar to the one I recommend for use with my patients (Clear Essentials, which is mixed with a green-food supplement), can definitely help fill the gaps. These products offer an easy and effective way to increase your intake of greens and have documented benefits for energy, immunity, and bone health.

Your Summary of Instructions for Supplements for Hormonal Balance

Beginning a supplement program can be daunting. Spend your time and money wisely by following my suggestions closely. Don't waste your cash or your energy taking the wrong products in the wrong amounts and wrong combinations.

Achieving better health and aging gracefully require preparation. By staying active, getting hormonally balanced, and filling in nutrition gaps with proper supplementation, you'll be better prepared for what lies ahead in your life. You can even expect to enjoy an energy boost—one of the most common benefits reported by patients of all ages once they begin taking supplements. Happy shopping!

Your Bare Essentials Supplementation Plan

BASIC SUPPLEMENT PLAN	
When to Take It	**Supplement**
With breakfast	Multivitamin
	2–4 grams omega-3 fish oil high in DHA (it's best to begin with a higher dosage)
	Whey protein smoothie
With dinner	Multivitamin
	2 Cal/mag/vitamin D3 combination capsules (or take at bedtime)

Your Deluxe Supplementation Plan

Your deluxe version may include the products in the chart above along with any products listed in the next chapter that you wish to add to address your individual signs of imbalance. Use the Hormonal Health Profile or the blood test results explained in Appendix A to pinpoint any imbalances you may have.

ADVANCED SUPPLEMENT PLAN	
When to Take It	**Supplement**
On rising (no food)	Probiotic supplement
	* Green-food supplement
With breakfast	* Multivitamin, 1 mixed vitamin E (high in gamma-tocopherol), a 60–100 mg capsule of coenzyme Q10, and 1 tablet lutein
	2–4 g omega-3 fish oil high in DHA
	Whey protein smoothie
With dinner	† Multivitamin, 2 cal/mag/vitamin D3 combination capsules, 1 antioxidant combination containing A, C, E, selenium, and zinc

Alternatively, you may choose the Clear Essentials—Morning Pack, which provides all of these nutrients as well as your green-food supplement.

† Alternatively, you may choose the Clear Essentials—Evening Pack, which provides these nutrients.

CHAPTER 13

GETTING BACK IN BALANCE: ADVANCED SUPPLEMENTS AND BIOIDENTICAL HORMONE REPLACEMENT

If you succeeded in completing the Hormonal Health Profile in Chapter 2 without any high scores, congratulations! Your hormones appear to be in good shape and you do not need to include this section of Step 2 in your program at this time. You can move on to Step 3. However, if you wish to add supplements to *enhance* certain hormones or to *address specific signs of imbalance* that were revealed by your profile or blood work—read on.

If you choose to add supplements from this chapter, note that *they are the one aspect of the Hormone Diet you will need to alter from time to time to meet your changing needs.* You will experience plenty of changes in your body—for a number of reasons, such as aging, stress, and so forth. Depending on the number of hormonal imbalances you currently have, you may need to continue modifying your supplement regimen for a number of weeks or months.

This plan is certain to offer you amazing results because of the precise way it identifies and effectively overcomes the major fat-packing factors that prevent weight loss. It enables you to determine why you haven't been able to beat those last stubborn pounds and then leads you to a place where your healthy work in the gym and the kitchen will be most highly rewarded—with the help of your Hormonal Health Profile results, the Treatment Pyramid, and the contents of this chapter.

Create Your Own Treatment Pyramid

Transfer your scores from the Treatment Pyramid in Chapter 2 (page 53) to the appropriate numbered space below.

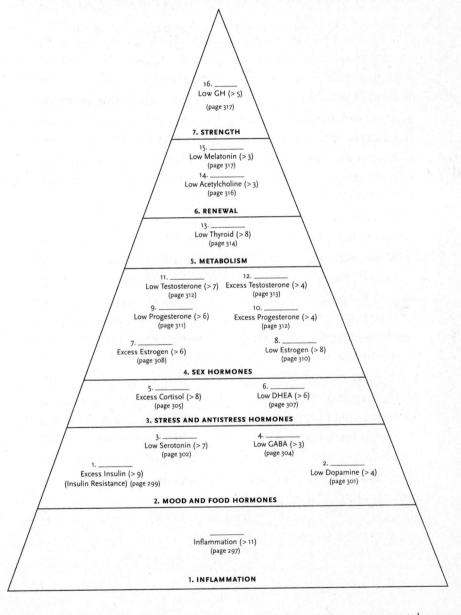

16. _____
Low GH (> 5)
(page 317)

7. STRENGTH

15. _____
Low Melatonin (> 3)
(page 317)

14. _____
Low Acetylcholine (> 3)
(page 316)

6. RENEWAL

13. _____
Low Thyroid (> 8)
(page 314)

5. METABOLISM

11. _____   12. _____
Low Testosterone (> 7)   Excess Testosterone (> 4)
(page 312)   (page 313)

9. _____   10. _____
Low Progesterone (> 6)   Excess Progesterone (> 4)
(page 311)   (page 312)

7. _____   8. _____
Excess Estrogen (> 6)   Low Estrogen (> 8)
(page 308)   (page 310)

4. SEX HORMONES

5. _____   6. _____
Excess Cortisol (> 8)   Low DHEA (> 6)
(page 305)   (page 307)

3. STRESS AND ANTISTRESS HORMONES

3. _____   4. _____
Low Serotonin (> 7)   Low GABA (> 3)
(page 302)   (page 304)

1. _____   2. _____
Excess Insulin (> 9)   Low Dopamine (> 4)
(Insulin Resistance) (page 299)   (page 301)

2. MOOD AND FOOD HORMONES

_____
Inflammation (> 11)
(page 297)

1. INFLAMMATION

Use Your Hormonal Health Profile Results to Create Your Road Map to Hormonal Balance

If your profile revealed *only one* high score, go ahead and address it now with one of the options listed below for the associated hormonal imbalance.

If you have *more than one* high score, start with whichever one appears lowest on the Treatment Pyramid. You will work your way up to the highest imbalance over time. This method is important because correcting a lower-level imbalance may be enough to correct or improve other imbalances noted in the levels above. For example, look at your score in Level 1. If it is high, start to address it now with one of the recommendations listed below. If you do not have a high score in Level 1, move up to Level 2 or keep going up until you reach the next level with one or more high scores. Each level of the Treatment Pyramid builds upon the next, which means that besides starting from the bottom, *you should also address imbalances within the same level at the same time.*

As an aside, taking *all* the supplements I have listed for each hormonal imbalance is *neither needed nor recommended.* Carefully read the information about each product and choose the supplement you feel best suits your needs. You can also visit www.thehormonediet.com for product sources and brand recommendations.

How Long Should You Use a Certain Supplement?

Stick with treatment suggestions for each specific imbalance until you feel your symptoms have improved. The length of time you will need to treat each imbalance will depend on the severity and duration of the imbalance and, of course, your body's response to the treatment steps.

Then, when you feel you're ready, return to your pyramid and address the next high score. But first go back and review the associated group of questions in the profile to identify whether this hormone is still a concern for you. If it is, carry on with the specific treatment suggestions for that hormonal imbalance noted in this chapter.

Don't be surprised if, when you do go back to the profile, symptoms you once had have cleared up. Remember, as you work your way up the pyramid, each level of hormones helps to restore the next.

Keep going through all the levels of the pyramid in this way until you have addressed all your imbalances. After this point, I recommend revisiting the Hormonal Health Profile at least once or twice a year to ensure that you're maintaining balance.

Level 1 Treatment
Inflammation
SUPPLEMENT OPTIONS

1. TURMERIC: Turmeric has anti-inflammatory, antioxidant, anti-aging, immunity-enhancing, and hormone-balancing effects. It works naturally to cut inflammation, pain, and swelling. Turmeric also supports liver function and detoxification. Take 500 to 1,500 mg per day on an empty stomach. Alternatively, take a product that contains turmeric along with a mixture of herbs to cut inflammation, such as Zyflamend (New Chapter) or Inflavonoid (Metagenics).

2. RESVERATROL: A number of studies show this natural red-wine extract assists with weight loss. Have you heard of the "French paradox"—the fact that the French seem to eat and drink what they want but still remain slim? It appears this may be due to the resveratrol from all the red wine they tend to consume. Now we have access to this in a bottle—but not a wine bottle! Data published in the journal *Nature* (November 2006) showed that resveratrol protected mice from the harmful effects of a high-calorie diet, including heart disease, weight gain, and diabetes. Resveratrol appears to act on adiponectin and also possesses natural anti-inflammatory properties. You might recall that adiponectin is produced by our fat cells, but actually helps us lose fat by improving our insulin sensitivity. Resveratrol also provides us with plenty of antioxidant

protection. Take 100 to 200 mg per day on an empty stomach. Resveratrol Extra from Pure Encapsulations is an excellent choice. *Turmeric and resveratrol are both fantastic because they crank up our fat-burning PPARs, too.*

3. WOBENZYM: Wobenzym is the most researched systemic anti-inflammatory enzyme formulation in the world. It is used by Olympic athletes, doctors, and millions of Europeans to help normalize all types of inflammation, speed injury recovery, promote healthy aging, aid surgery recovery, relieve arthritis and tendonitis, and improve circulation. Wobenzym contains bromelain and other enzymes in enteric-coated tablets that pass through your digestive tract and allow the enzymes to enter your bloodstream. The enzymes are distributed throughout your body along with nutrients and oxygen to benefit all your tissues and organs by breaking down inflammatory proteins. Wobenzym rids the blood of these harmful proteins that can damage joints, blood vessels, and other tissues. Take three to eight tablets two or three times a day on an empty stomach. *This is my favorite choice for pain relief.*

4. NATTOKINASE: This enzyme is a by-product of the fermentation of soy. It works like a charm for cutting inflammation and aiding circulation. *I use it specifically for reducing elevated hs-CRP, a blood marker of inflammation.* Take 38 to 50 mg twice a day on an empty stomach for 3 months, then retest hs-CRP.

5. GREEN TEA: Recent research has found that the catechin antioxidants in green tea help to increase fat burning as well as reduce the risk of cancer, high cholesterol, and diabetes. Besides its natural anti-inflammatory effects, green tea may also lower blood sugar by inhibiting enzymes that allow starch and fat absorption in the intestine. Green tea contains theanine, which has a calming yet energizing effect on the body. Typical dosage is 3 or 4 cups of tea per day or a 300- to 400-mg capsule of green tea extract one to three times daily on

an empty stomach. *Green tea is one of my favorite choices for supporting weight loss and cutting inflammation.*

FOODS OR HABITS TO DECREASE INFLAMMATION
- The three steps!

Level 2 Treatment: Mood and Food Hormones
Hormonal Imbalance 1: Excess Insulin

SUPPLEMENT OPTIONS

1. CONJUGATED LINOLEIC ACID (CLA): CLA is naturally present in dairy products and beef. It has anticancer and antidiabetic properties and may be useful in reducing arterial disease as well as osteoporosis. A paper entitled "Dietary Fat Intake, Supplements, and Weight Loss," published in the *Canadian Journal of Applied Physiology* (December 2000), reported that CLA is one of only a few supplements proven to reduce body fat and assist in increasing lean muscle mass without a change in caloric intake. These powerful effects are due to its insulin-sensitizing properties. CLA also shows anti-inflammatory benefits and seems to reduce fat storage in the fat cells while also increasing fat-burning activity in the muscles (it turns on our PPARs). The minimum dosage is 1,500 mg twice daily with food for at least 3 months. Look for CLA from Pure Encap-sulations or for any product containing the conjulite form of CLA, which I feel is highly effective. *CLA is one of my favorite choices for the treatment of insulin resistance and inflammation. It's also my top choice for preserving precious muscle during weight loss.*

2. HOLY BASIL: This important herbal medicine has been found to reduce cortisol and help the body adapt to stress. It also improves blood sugar balance and the activity of insulin in the body. Take two gel caps per day. *Holy basil from New Chapter is my favorite choice for aiding insulin resistance when stress is also a factor.*

3. CINNAMON: Besides adding a nice flavor to cooking and baking, cinnamon has wonderful insulin-balancing effects. A study published in *Diabetes Care* (December 2003) showed that cinnamon may cause muscle and liver cells to respond more readily to insulin. Take 1 to 2 g per day, with or without food.

4. ALPHA-LIPOIC ACID: This supplement improves our cellular response to insulin. It has favorable effects on blood sugar balance, abdominal fat, aging, and all of the complications of metabolic syndrome. Take 200 mg one to three times daily, with or without food. *This is my favorite choice for prevention of long-term complication of high insulin.*

5. MINERALS:

    a) Chromium. As a key mineral involved in regulating the body's response to insulin, chromium deficiency may result in insulin resistance. Chromium polynicotinate, a highly absorbable form of chromium, may help with weight loss because of its positive effect on insulin response. Dosage is typically 200 to 400 mcg per day. Prediabetics or patients with type 2 diabetes often benefit from 800 to 2,000 mcg per day, taken with food.

    b) Magnesium. Most insulin-resistant patients have a magnesium deficiency. Magnesium improves our cellular response to insulin, stabilizes blood sugar, prevents cravings, and reduces anxiety. Take 200 to 400 mg per day, with or without food. *Magnesium is one of my favorite supplements to include when high blood pressure or sleep disruption is a concern.*

    c) Biotin. This mineral is involved in the action of insulin. Take 1 to 3 mg per day.

    d) Zinc. Essential for blood sugar balance and insulin action. Take 25 to 50 mg per day with food.

6. PGX: Kudos to Dr. Michael Lyons, coauthor of *Hunger Free Forever*, and researchers from the University of Toronto, who have developed this water-soluble fiber blend. When con-

sumed before meals, PGX aids weight loss and effectively reduces cholesterol, insulin, and blood sugar levels. It comes in powder or pill form. Begin with 2.5 g once a day before a meal (with water) and gradually increase to 2.5 to 5 g two to three times daily. Use this approach to reduce possible side efects of increasing your fiber intake like gas, bloating, or diarrhea.

FOODS OR SPECIFIC HABITS TO DECREASE INSULIN
- The three steps!

Hormonal Imbalance 2: Low Dopamine
SUPPLEMENT OPTIONS
1. L-TYROSINE: The amino acid L-tyrosine is a building block of dopamine, so supplements can definitely help perk up production of this important mood-influencing hormone. Take 500 to 1,000 mg on rising on an empty stomach. Another dose may be added later in the day, but because L-tyrosine is a stimulating supplement, it should not be taken after 3 p.m. nor by anyone with high blood pressure. This product should be taken for at least 4 to 6 weeks to reach full effectiveness. *L-tyrosine is the best choice if low thyroid hormone or underactive thyroid is also suspected.*

2. D- OR DL-PHENYLALANINE: Like L-tyrosine, phenylalanine is a building block of dopamine. A study published in one German psychiatry journal showed that phenylalanine was as effective as certain antidepressant drugs, though both the D and DL forms have been found to be beneficial for depression. Take 500 to 1,000 mg per day on an empty stomach before 3 p.m. Like L-tyrosine, phenylalanine must be taken for at least 4 to 6 weeks for full effectiveness. *And DL-phenylalanine may be the better choice if you also have body aches and pains.*

3. RHODIOLA: Rhodiola can enhance learning capacity and memory and may also be useful for treating fatigue, stress, or

depression. Research suggests rhodiola may enhance mood regulation and fight depression by stimulating the activity of serotonin and dopamine. Take 200 to 400 mg per day in the morning on an empty stomach for a minimum of 1 month.

4. CHASTEBERRY EXTRACT (VITEX): Chasteberry has been shown to increase both dopamine and progesterone, making it an excellent choice for *women who experience symptoms of depression in conjunction with PMS or irregular menstrual cycles.* Take 200 mg of a 10:1 extract each morning before breakfast for 1 to 6 months.

FOODS OR SPECIFIC HABITS TO INCREASE DOPAMINE

- All proteins (meat, milk products, fish, beans, nuts, soy products). Turkey is high in phenylalanine. In fact, phenylalanine is found in most protein foods, so eat them when you want to feel sharper. Coffee may also stimulate dopamine release.
- Exercise
- Sex
- Massage
- Sources of L-tyrosine to increase the production of dopamine are almonds, avocados, bananas, dairy products, lima beans, pumpkin seeds, and sesame seeds.

Hormonal Imbalance 3: Low Serotonin

SUPPLEMENT OPTIONS

1. 5-HTP: A derivative of tryptophan and one step closer to becoming serotonin, 5-hydroxytryptophan (5-HTP) has been found to be more effective than tryptophan for treating sleeplessness, depression, anxiety, and fibromyalgia. Take 50 to 400 mg per day, divided between two doses throughout the day or all at once before bed. This product should be taken for at least 4 to 6 weeks to reach full effectiveness. *I think this is your best choice, often combined with St. John's Wort.*

2. ZENBEV: Specially formulated from powdered pumpkin seeds,

Zenbev can be taken during the day or in the evening to provide a powerful source of tryptophan, a precursor for serotonin and melatonin. Consume as directed on the label.

3. VITAMIN B$_6$: Vitamin B$_6$ supports the production and function of serotonin in the brain. Take 50 to 100 mg before bed.

4. RHODIOLA: Rhodiola may enhance learning capacity, memory, and mood regulation. It may also help fight depression by stimulating the activity of serotonin and dopamine. Take 200 to 400 mg each day, preferably in the morning.

5. ST. JOHN'S WORT: This herb has been proven effective at easing mild to moderate depression. It appears to work as a natural SSRI (selective serotonin reuptake inhibitor) by preventing the breakdown of serotonin in the brain. It takes at least 4 to 6 weeks to reach full effectiveness. Recommended dosage is 900 mg per day, on an empty stomach. MediHerb and Metagenics make a St. John's wort that is particularly effective.

6. INOSITOL: Naturally present in many foods, inositol improves the activity of serotonin in the brain. As a supplement, it is an excellent choice for alleviating anxiety and depression and supporting nervous system health. I use it in powdered form (Cenitol by Metagenics) and add it to my daily smoothie. Take 4 to 12 g per day. When mixed with magnesium, inositol is very effective at calming the nervous system. *I recommend including this product in all treatment plans for low serotonin, as well as vitamin D$_3$.*

7. Vitamin D$_3$ (2,000 to 4,000 IU) and EPA/DHA (4 to 6 g) taken daily with meals will help serotonin to work more effectively in the brain.

FOODS OR SPECIFIC HABITS TO INCREASE SEROTONIN

- Eating carbohydrates will boost your serotonin. Choose slow-release, complex carbs, including whole grain breads, rice, or pasta to keep you sustained, energized, and balanced. Simple carbs such as white bread and pastries will only give you a momentary boost followed by a crash. Plus they pack on the fat!

- The best food sources of serotonin-boosting tryptophan are turkey, brown rice, cottage cheese, meat, peanuts, and sesame seeds. The grain chia contains tryptophan, too.
- Sun exposure
- Staying warm
- Meditating or focusing your mind on one thing. Avoid multitasking!
- Exercise
- Massage

Hormonal Imbalance 4: Low GABA

SUPPLEMENT OPTIONS

1. GABA is an inhibitory neurotransmitter—a brain chemical that has a calming effect. If you are anxious, have trouble sleeping, and experience muscle tension or pain, this supplement is a good choice for you. Take 500 to 2,000 mg an hour or two before bed. Alternatively, take GABA 10 to 20 minutes before your evening meal. The standard dosage of 200 mg three times daily can be increased to a maximum of 500 mg four times daily if needed. This latter dosage should not be exceeded. *This is my favorite choice for low GABA.*

2. PASSIONFLOWER: This calming herb appears to improve the activity of GABA. An excellent choice for anxiety and sleep disruption—even in children. Take 300 to 500 mg at bedtime.

3. TAURINE: This amino acid plays a major role in the brain as an inhibitory neurotransmitter. Similar in structure and function to GABA, taurine provides a similar antianxiety effect that helps calm or stabilize an excited brain. Taurine is also effective for treating migraines, insomnia, agitation, restlessness, irritability, alcoholism, obsessions, depression, and even hypomania/mania (the "high" phase of bipolar

disorder or manic depression). Take 500 to 1,000 mg a day. Taking your last dose before bed is often most helpful. Taurine should be taken without food.

4. MAGNESIUM: Magnesium has wonderful relaxing effects on tense muscles, racing mind, and overactive nervous system. Take 200 to 400 mg per day.

FOODS OR SPECIFIC HABITS TO INCREASE GABA
- Fish (especially mackerel) and wheat bran may increase GABA
- Relaxation
- Sleep
- Yoga
- Massage

Level 3 Treatment: Stress and Antistress Hormones
Hormonal Imbalance 5: Excess Cortisol
SUPPLEMENT OPTIONS:

1. VITAMIN C: Vitamin C is naturally highest in our stress glands (adrenal glands), so it's no wonder stress can deplete our vitamin C stores. Vitamin C is a potent antioxidant, essential for healthy immune system function and collagen formation in the skin, tendons, and ligaments. Take 2,000 to 6,000 mg spread throughout the day for stress protection and immune support. Make sure that your vitamin C contains bioflavonoids, which enhance the activity of vitamin C in the body.

2. B VITAMINS: Endurance athletes and stressed or fatigued individuals should take extra B vitamins, especially vitamin B_5, which helps the body adapt to stress and supports adrenal gland function. When taken at bedtime, vitamin B_6 is useful in correcting abnormally high cortisol release throughout the night. B vitamins are water soluble and are easily depleted with perspiration and stress. Take 200 to 500 mg of vitamin B_5 and/or 50 to 100 mg of B_6 per day. These are often available in combination.

3. RELORA: This supplement is a mixture of the herbal extracts *Magnolia officinalis* and *Phellodendron amurense*. It is medically proven to reduce stress and anxiety. It significantly reduces cortisol and raises DHEA, sometimes within as little as 2 weeks of use. Relora can be used to prevent health conditions associated with stress, including poor immunity, high blood pressure, insomnia or sleep disruption, hot flashes, loss of vitality, and weight gain, especially in relation to metabolic syndrome. Take two capsules, 250 mg each, at bedtime and one on rising for at least a month. It is best taken on an empty stomach. I find the most effective formulas include a mixture of B vitamins and folic acid, like Relora Plex from Douglas Labs. *Relora is my favorite choice for reducing cortisol; raising DHEA; and relieving stress, low libido, abdominal weight gain, fatigue, and disrupted sleep.*

4. ASHWAGANDHA: Ayurvedic practitioners use this herb to enhance mental and physical performance, improve learning ability, and decrease stress and fatigue. Ashwagandha is a general tonic that can be used in stressful situations, especially insomnia, restlessness, or when you are feeling overworked. The typical dosage is 500 to 1,000 mg twice a day for a minimum of 1 to 6 months. Capsules should be standardized to 1.5 percent withanolides per dose. *Ashwagandha is my favorite choice for reducing cortisol; increasing thyroid hormones; and treating stress combined with a sluggish metabolism, anxiety, poor concentration, and tension.*

5. HOLY BASIL: This herbal medicine has been found to reduce cortisol and help the body adapt to stress. It also improves blood sugar balance and the activity of insulin in the body. Take two gel caps per day for at least a month. *Holy basil is my favorite choice for reducing cortisol when insulin resistance or hypoglycemia symptoms are also present.*

6. HYDROLYZED MILK PROTEIN: No matter whether the stress you are under is physical, emotional, psychological, or environ-

mental, milk protein hydrolysate is documented to prevent the associated rise in cortisol by calming the stress response pathway. Dosage is 75 to 300 mg per day. I love this supplement, and patients consistently report that it "takes the edge off." I use NuSera, a chewable, butterscotch-flavored product, because chewing the product allows it to take effect quickly. *This product can be used in all cases of high cortisol and is often very effective when conbined with other products.*

7. PHOSPHATIDYLSERINE (PS): This supplement is ideal for alleviating nighttime worrying. It curbs the inappropriate release of stress hormones and protects the brain from the negative effects of cortisol, such as memory loss and poor concentration. PS may also reduce the negative effects of cortisol on muscle tissues during exercise. Take 100 to 300 mg before bed.

8. RHODIOLA: This herbal supplement can enhance learning capacity and memory and may also be useful for treating fatigue, stress, or depression. Research suggests rhodiola may enhance mood regulation and fight depression by stimulating the activity of serotonin and dopamine. Take 200 to 400 mg per day in the morning, on an empty stomach, for at least 6 weeks. *Rhodiola is my favorite choice for reducing cortisol and increasing serotonin and dopamine—stress with anxiety, depression, cravings, fatigue, and poor concentration (even ADHD symptoms, too).*

FOODS OR SPECIFIC HABITS TO DECREASE CORTISOL
- The three steps!

Hormonal Imbalance 6: Low DHEA

SUPPLEMENT OPTIONS

1. RELORA: It significantly reduces cortisol and raises DHEA in only 2 weeks of use. Relora can be used to prevent the health conditions associated with stress, including poor immunity, high blood pressure, insomnia or sleep disruption, loss of vitality, and weight gain, especially in relation to metabolic

syndrome. Take two capsules, 250 mg each, at bedtime and one on rising. It is best taken on an empty stomach. I find the most effective formulas, like Relora Plex from Douglas Laboratories, contain a mixture of B vitamins and folic acid as well.

2. DHEA: DHEA should be taken under the medical supervision of a licensed health-care provider. I prefer low dosages of 5 to 25 mg twice daily with meals.

3. 7-KETO DHEA: Unlike straight DHEA, 7-keto DHEA does not convert to estrogen or testosterone, making it a good choice for younger people who, in most cases, would not benefit from increased amounts of these hormones. Also, 7-Keto has documented metabolism-enhancing effects, promotes fat loss, protects us from the harmful effects of excess cortisol, and appears to prevent the decrease in metabolism known to occur when we're dieting. Take 25 to 100 mg twice a day. One hundred mg twice a day has been proven effective for weight loss in clinical trials, according to a report in *Current Therapeutic Research* (2000).

FOODS OR SPECIFIC HABITS TO INCREASE DHEA

- Meditation
- Exercise; weight training
- Sex
- Sleep
- The three steps!

Level 4 Treatment: Sex Hormones
Hormonal Imbalance 7: Excess Estrogen

SUPPLEMENT OPTIONS

1. THE CLEAR DETOX PRODUCTS: There are very few products that support hormonal detoxification, so I formulated my own. Clear Detox—Hormonal Health and Clear Detox—Digestive Health contain all of the nutrients needed to support the breakdown and elimination of excess estrogen, including those listed next. *This is my favorite choice for treating excess estrogen.*

2. INDOLE-3-CARBINOL (I3C): Formulated from extracts of broccoli and other cruciferous vegetables, I3C is known to increase the breakdown and excretion of harmful estrogen metabolites. It may be useful in the treatment and prevention of breast and prostate cancer. Take 200 mg twice a day for 1 to 3 months.

3. CALCIUM D-GLUCARATE: This calcium salt is heavily involved in detoxification and the removal of estrogen from the body. Some evidence suggests it protects against cancers of the colon, breast, and prostate. Take 500 mg twice a day for 1 to 3 months.

4. TURMERIC, ROSEMARY EXTRACT, GREEN TEA, AND MILK THISTLE: Together these herbs support the elimination of estrogen by enhancing the liver detoxification pathways. Look for a product containing a mixture of all these ingredients, such as my detox formula.

FOODS OR SPECIFIC HABITS TO DECREASE HARMFUL ESTROGEN

- Consume weak phytoestrogenic foods such as pomegranate, flaxseeds, pears, apples, berries, organic non-GM fermented soy, wheat germ, oats, and barley.
- Eat yogurt and high-fiber foods to aid the breakdown and elimination of estrogen.
- Choose organic dairy and meat products to reduce your exposure to hormone additives.
- Add plenty of detoxifying foods to your diet, including broccoli, cauliflower, Brussels sprouts, kale, cabbage, beets, carrots, apples, ginger, onions, and celery.
- Avoid alcohol.
- Avoid exposure to xenoestrogens from plastics, cosmetics, and the birth control pill.
- Avoid unfermented soy products.
- Use infrared sauna treatments.
- Exercise.
- Lose fat with your three steps!

Hormonal Imbalance 8: Low Estrogen

SUPPLEMENT OPTIONS

1. BI-EST BIOIDENTICAL CREAM: This topical cream is a mix of 80 percent estriol and 20 percent estradiol. See your MD, ND, or compounding pharmacy. The dosage will depend on your specific condition. I recommend applying the cream to areas of thin skin (wrist, elbow crease, behind the knees, neck, etc.) rather than over fatty tissue (inner thigh, abdomen, back of the arms).

2. PHYTOESTROGENIC HERBS: Black cohosh, *Angelica,* red clover extract, sage, or licorice can be used to support healthy estrogen balance.

    a) Black cohosh can be used to treat hot flashes, night sweats, vaginal dryness, urinary urgency, and other symptoms that can occur during menopause. Take 40 mg twice daily on an empty stomach.

    b) *Angelica* has been used for ages to treat many symptoms of menopause (hot flashes, etc.), lack of menstrual cycle (amenorrhea), and PMS. It is anti-inflammatory and may help to relieve menstrual cramps due to its antispasmodic properties. Take 400 mg on an empty stomach one to three times a day.

    c) Red clover contains high quantities of plant-based estrogens (called isoflavones) that may improve menopausal symptoms, reduce the risk of bone loss, and lower the risk of heart disease by improving blood pressure and increasing HDL cholesterol. Research on the effectiveness of red clover for the treatment of menopause has yielded conflicting evidence—some reports show it is beneficial, whereas others claim it is no more helpful than a placebo. You can try taking 80 mg of red clover per day to see if it does the trick for you. Look for Promensil, which appears to be the most extensively researched product.

d) Sage is an excellent choice to support healthy estrogen balance, especially if sweating and hot flashes are your predominant menopause symptoms. Take 400 mg on an empty stomach once a day.

e) Licorice has phytoestrogenic properties and is an especially great choice if you're feeling burnt out or stressed out. Take 300 to 900 mg per day before 3 p.m. Because licorice is stimulating, it shouldn't be taken later in the day or if you have high blood pressure.

FOODS OR SPECIFIC HABITS TO IMPROVE THE SYMPTOMS
OF LOW ESTROGEN

- Phytoestrogenic foods such as soy products, flaxseeds, fennel, pomegranate, fennel, etc.

Hormonal Imbalance 9: Low Progesterone

SUPPLEMENT OPTIONS

1. BIOIDENTICAL PROGESTERONE CREAM: I prefer a 3 to 6 percent natural progesterone cream. See your MD, ND, or compounding pharmacy. If you're using this product for PMS, apply it on days 14 to 28 of your cycle, when progesterone is naturally highest. For the treatment of menopause symptoms, it may be used for 25 days followed by 5 days off, or it may be applied on a schedule that more closely matches a woman's natural menstrual cycle. *This is my favorite choice for treating low progesterone.*

2. CHASTEBERRY EXTRACT (VITEX): Chasteberry increases progesterone by stimulating the production of luteinizing hormone. Take 200 mg per day, on an empty stomach, for 1 to 6 months.

3. EVENING PRIMROSE OIL (EPO): While flaxseed oil appears to be estrogen enhancing, EPO is touted as a progesterone-enhancing compound. Take 1,000 to 2,000 mg per day with food.

Hormonal Imbalance 10: Excess Progesterone

SUPPLEMENT OPTIONS

1. Option 2, 3, and 4 (the Clear Detox products) listed for excess estrogen (page 309) can be helpful for excess progesterone.

2. Progesterone may also rise when the stress response is chronically overstimulated. Supplements of hydrolyzed milk protein, which decreases stimulation of the stress response pathway, may indirectly help to reduce excess progesterone.

3. Avoid evening primrose oil, since it appears to increase progesterone.

Hormonal Imbalance 11: Low Testosterone

SUPPLEMENT OPTIONS

1. BIOIDENTICAL TESTOSTERONE CREAM: See your MD, ND, or compounding pharmacy.

2. INDOL-3-CARBINOL (I3C): Supplements of this extract from cruciferous vegetables may help to preserve testosterone by preventing the conversion of testosterone to estrogen. Take 200 mg twice daily.

3. TRIBULUS TERRESTRIS: Also known as puncture vine, *Tribulus* may boost testosterone by increasing the secretion of luteinizing hormone (LH) from the pituitary gland. Other studies suggest it boosts testosterone by increasing DHEA. Take 500 to 1,000 mg per day on an empty stomach. *This is my favorite choice because Tribulus also increases DHEA.*

4. TONGKAT ALI (*EURYCOMA LONGIFOLIA*, JACK, OR LONGJACK): Dubbed the "Asian Viagara," longjack has been found to raise testosterone and aid weight loss in men and women. Take 150 to 200 mg per day. Ensure it's a standardized 50:1 extract.

5. L-ARGININE: L-arginine can improve testosterone. Take 3,000 mg per day on an empty stomach, preferably at bedtime. *I include L-arginine and zinc in all treament plans for low testosterone in women and in men.*

6. ZINC: This mineral is needed to maintain testosterone levels in the blood. A deficiency of zinc causes a decrease in the activity of LH, the hormone that stimulates the production of testosterone. Zinc also appears to inhibit the conversion of testosterone to estrogen via the aromatase enzyme. Take 25 to 50 mg per day with food.

7. OATS (AVENA SATIVA): As an herbal medicine, oats are touted to increase bioavailable testosterone in the blood by freeing it from sex hormone binding globulin (SHBG). Take 100 to 250 mg twice a day on an empty stomach.

FOODS OR SPECIFIC HABITS TO INCREASE TESTOSTERONE

- Sleep
- Exercise
- Sex
- Exposure to morning sunlight
- Protein
- Sufficient fat and avoidance of excess carbohydrate restriction
- Cuddling (women)
- Competitive sports (men)
- Success in competitive activities or ventures

Hormonal Imbalance 12: Excess Testosterone

SUPPLEMENT OPTIONS

1. SAW PALMETTO: This herb appears to inhibit the enzyme that supports the conversion of testosterone to dihydrotestosterone (DHT). It may also reduce the risk of prostate enlargement and hair loss commonly associated with DHT. Saw palmetto may improve a woman's breast size if shrinkage has occurred due to excess testosterone exposure. Take 160 mg twice a day on an empty stomach. Supplementing plant sterols also protect the prostate via similar means.

2. OPTIONS FOR HORMONES 1 AND 5: Because high testosterone in

women is usually a result of excess insulin or cortisol, choose supplements that improve insulin sensitivity (Hormonal Imbalance 1) and lower cortisol (Hormonal Imbalance 5) to restore testosterone balance.

3. OPTIONS FOR LIVER DETOX: Support of liver detoxification is also beneficial to aid the breakdown and elimination of testosterone. Therefore, milk thistle, calcium-d-glucarate, and turmeric can be helpful for this imbalance. Clear Detox—Hormonal Health contains all of the nutrients to support the breakdown and elimination of excess testosterone.

Level 5 Treatment: Metabolism
Hormonal Imbalance 13: Low Thyroid Hormone
SUPPLEMENT OPTIONS

1. ASHWAGANDHA: This supplement may increase both thyroxine (T4) and its more potent counterpart, T3. Both ashwagandha and guggulipids appear to boost thyroid function without influencing the release of the pituitary hormone TSH (thyroid-stimulating hormone), indicating that these herbs work directly on the thyroid gland and other body tissues. Good news, since thyroid problems most often occur within the thyroid gland itself, or in the conversion of T4 into T3 in tissues outside the thyroid gland. Take 875 to 1,000 mg twice a day. *Ashwagandha is my favorite choice for supporting the thyroid when stress is also a concern.*

2. FORSKOLIN: Extracted from an herb called *Coleus forskohlii*, forskolin may increase the release of thyroid hormone by stimulating cAMP, a substance that is comparable in strength to TSH, which prompts the thyroid to produce more thyroid hormone. Take 250 mg two or three times per day. *Forskolin is one of the top supplement choices when both weight loss and thyroid support are the goals.*

3. GUGGULIPIDS (*Commiphora mukul*): Guggulipids enhance the

conversion of T4 to the more potent form, T3. Dosage is 500 mg three times a day. *Guggulipids may also lower elevated cholesterol and aid weight loss, so choose this one if you're concerned about high cholesterol or weight loss as well as sluggish thyroid function.*

4. L-TYROSINE: The amino acid L-tyrosine is necessary for the production of thyroid hormone in the body. The recommended dose is 1,000 mg on rising, before breakfast. Do not take this supplement if you have high blood pressure. *L-tyrosine is one of my favorite choices for low thyroid, especially when cravings, low motivation, low libido, or fatigue are concerns.*

5. NATURAL THYROID HORMONE: See your MD or ND for a prescription for natural thyroid. This supplement contains a natural mixture of T3 and T4 thyroid hormone. Using a mix of both will reduce the risk of low T3 in those who fail to properly convert thyroid medication (synthetic T4) to T3. Natural thyroid can be considered as an alternative to synthetic thyroid hormone (Synthroid) or as an adjunct treatment if symptoms of hypothyroidism are still present when using prescription thyroid.

FOODS OR SPECIFIC HABITS TO INCREASE THYROID HORMONE
- Exercise—but do not overexercise!
- Get enough sleep. Sleep deprivation decreases thyroid hormone and your metabolic rate.
- Eat regularly and avoid excessive caloric restriction.
- Consume foods that contain the nutrients necessary for the production of thyroid hormone.
  L-TYROSINE: almonds, avocados, bananas, dairy products, pumpkin seeds, and sesame seeds.
  IODINE: fish (cod, sea bass, and haddock), shellfish, and sea vegetables such as seaweed and kelp. Kelp is the richest source of iodine.
  SELENIUM: brewer's yeast, wheat germ, whole grains (barley, whole wheat, oats, and brown rice), seeds, nuts (especially

Brazil nuts), shellfish, and some vegetables (garlic, onions, mushrooms, broccoli, tomatoes, and radishes).

Level 6 Treatment: Renewal
Hormonal Imbalance 14: Low Acetylcholine
SUPPLEMENT OPTIONS

1. ACETYL-L-CARNITINE: Acetyl-l-carnitine is a potent antioxidant for the brain. It is an anti-inflammatory that provides a source of the acetyl group needed to make acetylcholine, as well as l-carnitine, which assists with fat burning. Take 500 to 1,000 mg per day, preferably in the morning before breakfast. *Acetyl-l-carnitine is my favorite choice for boosting acetylcholine, aiding weight loss, and slowing aging of the brain.*

2. PHOSPHATIDYLCHOLINE (PC): PC provides choline, which is needed to make acetylcholine. Take 1,200 to 2,400 mg per day with food. *PC is my favorite choice for use during pregnancy. It supports development of the baby's brain and nervous system, and I swear the babies in my practice are smarter for it!*

3. DMAE (dimethylaminoethanol): DMAE is an anti-inflammatory and antioxidant that increases the production of acetylcholine. It is useful for both cognitive function and for improving muscle contractions. Take 100 to 300 mg per day with food. As an aside, DMAE may also be used topically to improve skin tone and firmness.

4. L-ALPHA-GLYCEROPHOSPHOCHOLINE (ALPHA-GPC): Glycerophosphocholine plays an important role in the synthesis of acetylcholine. It maintains neurological health and may also help to enhance growth hormone. The standard dose is one or two 500 mg capsules per day on an empty stomach.

FOODS OR SPECIFIC HABITS TO INCREASE ACETYLCHOLINE
- Exercise.
- Consume healthy fats and sources of choline such as

lecithin, egg yolks, wheat germ, soybeans, organ meats (liver, kidney, etc.), and whole wheat products.

Hormonal Imbalance 15: Low Melatonin

SUPPLEMENT OPTIONS

1. MELATONIN: Take 0.5 to 3 mg per day sublingually (under the tongue) at bedtime to aid sleep.
2. CHERRY JUICE EXTRACT: This juice appears to provide a rich source of melatonin and may help us sleep better. Cherry juice is also anti-inflammatory and may help to reduce high uric acid, which is commonly associated with gout.

FOODS OR SPECIFIC HABITS TO INCREASE MELATONIN

- Sleep in total darkness.
- Expose yourself to bright light immediately on rising and during the day; keep the lights dim after dinner.
- Consume protein, particularly sources that contain the tryptophan needed to make melatonin, such as cherry juice, pumpkin seeds, Salba, and walnuts.
- Follow the Hormone Diet habits for healthy sleep.

Level 7 Treatment: Strength
Hormonal Imbalance 16: Low Growth Hormone

SUPPLEMENT OPTIONS

1. OPTIONS FOR HORMONE 14 (ACETYLCHOLINE): Supplements that boost acetylcholine will also enhance growth hormone because acetylcholine is known to stimulate the production of growth hormone (GH).
2. SPECIFIC AMINO ACIDS: The amino acid precursors to growth hormone are L-arginine, lysine, ornithinine, and glutamine. Supplements of these amino acids taken together before bed or after exercise may be useful to support growth hormone production. Aim for the following dosages:

- L-arginine: 2,000 to 3,000 mg per day
- L-glutamine: 2,000 mg per day
- L-ornithine: 2,000 to 6,000 mg per day
- L-lysine: 1,200 mg per day
- L-glycine: 1,000 mg per day
- L-tyrosine: 1,000 mg per day

These amino acids are most effective when combined with vitamin B_3, vitamin B_6, vitamin C, calcium, zinc, and potassium.

FOODS OR SPECIFIC HABITS TO INCREASE GROWTH HORMONE
- Sleep
- Exercise
- Consume sufficient protein
- Manage stress with the three steps!

Remember the Body-Fat Map from Chapter 5? Well, use this chart to find your fat spot(s) and then to pick your solution(s)!

FIND YOUR FAT SPOT(S)

Fat-Storage Site	Hormonal Imbalance: Men	Hormonal Imbalance: Women	Reference "Spot" for Your Solutions
Belly or abdomen (apple shape)	Excess estrogen	Excess estrogen	Hormonal imbalance 7 (p. 308)
		Low estrogen (postmenopausal)	Hormonal imbalance 8 (p. 310)
		Excess testosterone (premenopausal)	Hormonal imbalance 12 (p. 313)
	Low testosterone		Hormonal imbalance 11 (p. 312)
	Excess cortisol	Excess cortisol	Hormonal imbalance 5 (p. 305)
	Excess insulin	Excess insulin	Hormonal imbalance 1 (p. 299)
	Low growth hormone	Low growth hormone	Hormonal imbalance 16 (p. 317)

Fat-Storage Site	Hormonal Imbalance: Men	Hormonal Imbalance: Women	Reference "Spot" for Your Solutions
Back of the arm (triceps)	Excess insulin	Excess insulin	Hormonal imbalance 1 (p. 299)
	Low DHEA	Low DHEA	Hormonal imbalance 6 (p. 307)
		Excess testosterone (more fat in arms in general)	Hormonal imbalance 12 (p. 313)
Hips/buttocks/ hamstrings (pear shape)	Excess estrogen	Excess estrogen	Hormonal imbalance 7 (p. 308)
		Low progesterone	Hormonal imbalance 9 (p. 311)
"Love handles" (above the hips)	Insulin and blood sugar imbalance	Insulin and blood sugar imbalance	Hormonal imbalance 1 (p. 299)
Chest (over the pectoral muscles)	Excess estrogen (often coupled with excess insulin and low testos- terone)	Excess estrogen	Hormonal imbalance 7 (p. 308)
			Hormonal imbalance 1 (p. 299)
			Hormonal imbalance 11 (p. 312)
Back ("bra fat")	Excess insulin	Excess insulin	Hormonal imbalance 1 (p. 299)
		Excess testosterone	Hormonal imbalance 12 (p. 313)
Thighs	Low growth hormone	Low growth hormone	Hormonal imbalance 16 (p. 317)

Remember, you do not need to—and should not—take all of the supplements suggested for each hormonal imbalance. Review the properties of the products in order to *match your specific signs* of imbalance and determine which one(s) will do the trick for you. Also, recall that you may need to change your selections over time as your body responds to the treatments. Fixing one imbalance may be all you need to bring all the others in line. Also, be sure to address each imbalance in the order presented here, and you may not even need to address more than one.

Once your hormones are brought back into healthy balance, you'll be ready to move on to the third and final step in your program. Your body will be ready to respond *wonderfully* to exercise!

Tina R. (age 33)

For the first 30 years of my life I was in great shape, stayed slim, ate well, and exercised regularly. Then my worst nightmare happened—I started losing my hair in handfuls, had little energy to exercise, felt mentally "foggy," fell into a depression, and started gaining weight rapidly despite a low-calorie diet. Blood tests revealed hypothyroidism—something that runs in my family. I was prescribed thyroid medication and hoped for the best—perhaps a one-pill cure-all would bring me back to a point in time where I was symptom free. Unfortunately, that didn't happen. Over the next 2 years I went from doctor to doctor trying desperately to alleviate my symptoms, only to become more despondent. I tried every pill, potion, and diet under the sun and went to every top doctor, acupuncturist, chiropractor, and naturopath in the city. Not only did I fail to lose weight, I felt terrible most of the time, and my zest for life was gone. I thought I would never get my life, my body, or my self back.

The day I walked through Dr. Turner's door, I carried with me my labs tests and a faint glimmer of hope. She assessed my situation and knew immediately that there was an underlying adrenal issue and that my diet, exercise regimen, and medication protocol had to change. Years of burning the candle at both ends had compromised the hormonal equivalent of Mother Nature—my adrenals. I was skeptical, but I figured that I had nothing to lose. I put her plan in motion, starting with her diet, supplement, and exercise recommendations, and lo and behold I started losing weight! Not only that, but my hair stopped falling out, my PMS improved, and my mood swings diminished.

At each visit she would make adjustments, and I would enter the next step of my wellness protocol. I purchased *The Hormone Diet* and added her other suggestions, with great success. Although I'm a "work in progress," I know with *The Hormone Diet* and Dr. Turner's help I will eventually be the best version of myself.

STEP 3

RESTORE STRENGTH, VIGOR, AND RADIANCE

YOUR FINAL 2 WEEKS

Movement is a medicine for creating change in a person's physical, emotional, and mental states.

CAROL WELCH

CHAPTER 14

SEX AND SWEAT: WHY WE NEED BOTH FOR HORMONAL BALANCE

Love is the answer, but while you are waiting for the answer,
sex raises some pretty good questions.
WOODY ALLEN

Here's what you will learn in this chapter:
• Many of us are not enjoying the sex we should
• How sex revs up your fat-burning hormones
• How sex can satisfy cravings and control your appetite
• The benefits of exercise on your hormones for fat burning and metabolism
• The common workout mistakes that slow fat loss and hamper the hormone-enhancing benefits of exercise

Now that you have primed your hormones in Steps 1 and 2, you are set to enjoy the explosive benefits that great sex and exercise have on your hormones, metabolism, and weight loss. If you are not in the habit of getting physical on a regular basis, I hope this chapter will persuade you to change. When I say "getting physical," I mean enjoying two very basic hormone-enhancing, fat-burning, stress-busting activities: sex and exercise. Both involve working up a sweat. Both have wonderful hormone-boosting effects when we engage in them regularly. And, believe it or not, when we do one, we often have more desire to do the other.

Any amount of pleasurable sex is beneficial for you, as is any amount of exercise, when done properly. So, I guess in this sense, every workout counts and every make-out session counts—but doing both a few times weekly is even better! Unfortunately, the majority of us don't exercise, and just as many of us don't enjoy sex as often as we should.

We can come up with a whole host of reasons why we don't exercise: we're too busy, too tired, don't have enough time, not in the mood, don't like it, don't feel well enough, don't know how to do it, don't think we're good at it, can't last long enough, wouldn't know how to start, don't like to do it alone, don't like doing it in public. And I suppose all of these excuses could apply to sex, too.

In my practice, I have at times *begged* patients to begin working out. In some cases I have actually told them not to come back to see me but to spend their money on personal training, instead. One patient in particular was terrific about taking her supplements and was spending plenty of good money doing so. I told her she would probably need *half* the products if she would exercise.

I truly believe there is no better way to change your life than to start exercising. If there's one thing I pray you'll do after reading my book, it's to make exercise a part of your life, if it isn't already. If it already is, perhaps you'll learn something from the second part of this chapter that will allow you to enjoy better results from your efforts. But let's start with sex first. It's always a good attention grabber!

Bringing Sexy Back!

Sex is something we can get by without, whether we are in a relationship or not, but we shouldn't have to. Sex can be a complicated issue because it involves emotions, relationships, past sexual experiences, and physical and spiritual components. It also depends heavily on your current hormonal state, although some experts say your prior sexual functions and relationships are more important variables in determining how much sex you have or how enjoyable it is for you in the here and now.

When a patient comes to see me, I ask two basic questions: How's your energy? and How's your sex drive? When a patient tells me either of these aspects of his or her life has changed, I know immediately that there's a bigger health problem at play. Sadly, I've found that a surprising number of people ignore these changes for years, simply accepting them as normal or feeling too embarrassed to deal with them.

If this scenario sounds familiar to you, I hope to inspire you to think differently and to take steps to get your "mojo" back. You may be one of the millions of adults who experience sexual dysfunction, the incidence of which appears to be at an all-time high. According to an extensive study published in the *Journal of the American Medical Association,* the obesity epidemic is certainly not our only concern at this point. The results revealed that about 43 percent of women and 30 percent of men experience symptoms of sexual dysfunction, including lack of desire, arousal issues, inability to orgasm or ejaculate, premature ejaculation, painful intercourse, lack of enjoyment, erectile dysfunction, and performance anxiety.

If you think sex has fallen away just because you're getting older, are not in a relationship, or haven't done it in a long time, think again. Pleasurable sex is something every adult should enjoy for a lifetime—with or without a partner. And remember, sex doesn't mean intercourse alone. Masturbation (on your own or with a partner) and other forms of sexual play that get your hormones revving are definitely recommended. If you're currently having great sex, keep at it because it's good for you. Have sex all your life, and your body, brain, muscles, and fat cells will thank you for it. Do it over and over—that's right, don't stop.

Are Your Hormones Hampering Your Sex Life, or Is It the Other Way Around?

The answer is both. Sexual dysfunction is a global concern, as shown by the Global Study of Sexual Attitudes and Behaviors (GSSAB). After 13,882 women and 13,618 men from more than 29 countries were surveyed, the researchers concluded: "Sexual difficulties are relatively common among mature adults throughout the world. Sexual problems tend to be more associated with physical health and aging among men than women."

Sexual Issues for Men

An estimated 1 in 5 men currently experience erectile dysfunction (ED). Although psychological reasons play strongly in cases in men 35 years of age and younger, physiological factors are the main cause for men 50 and up. But ED at any age can provide a much bigger picture of a man's health than just what's happening below the belt. We now know, for example, that the state of a man's penis is a very good indication of cardiovascular wellness. Problems in this area are linked to arterial disease, heart attacks, stroke, and diabetes.

Ever since that now-famous little blue pill topped $1.5 billion in sales in 2001, becoming a pharmaceutical smash hit practically overnight, drug companies have been working feverishly to produce second-generation medications to deal with ED. Think about that figure—$1.5 billion! And realize at the same time that about 30 to 50 percent of patients can't even take Viagra because of contraindications such as heart disease. Since this family of drugs hit the market in the late 1990s, the number of American men with health complaints has increased by 50 percent. Evidently sex is an important issue and a great source of motivation for seeking medical intervention. Viagra is certainly working wonders for many people, although in my view it represents a "quickie" solution when a "long-term love affair" with lasting lifestyle change is certainly what's needed. That's right, I mean the three steps.

That Viagra sales, obesity, and stress rates are at all-time highs is no coincidence: The hormonal distress associated with abdominal obesity is a major contributing factor to impotence and erectile dysfunction. All healthy men experience a gradual decrease in testosterone, about 1.5 percent each year after age 30. (This percentage appears to be increasing, however—possibly due to toxin exposure.) Although the link between men's testosterone levels and their desire for sex is not entirely clear, the connection between lower free testosterone and weakened orgasmic function and/or erectile function is definite, according to a 2002 study from the *British Journal of Urology.*

The hormonal changes men naturally experience as they age tend to happen more gradually than the ones women undergo with menopause, although they can still result in symptoms of reduced energy, poor sex drive, declining muscle mass, increased abdominal fat, or irritability. These symptoms may seem uncomplicated, but they are increasingly common in my clinical practice among men in their 30s and 40s and are definite signals of high risk in the field of preventive medicine. Remember, low testosterone in men is linked to heart disease and even death.

Sexual Issues for Women

Drug companies are also scrambling to tap into the sexual dysfunction market for women. Sadly, this market is also huge and, unlike the case with men, the distribution of difficulties is fairly even among women 18 to 59 years of age. About 20 percent of women experience problems with arousal and, as a result, experience poor lubrication. Drug companies are now looking at ways to understand the female brain and develop a means of stimulating the arousal centers. But more pharmaceuticals are not always the answer. The three steps of the Hormone Diet have the potential to create the perfect hormonal balance for both a healthy libido and successful fat loss, especially because of their wonderful ability to calm the cortisol that can crush a healthy sex drive, even under the best of conditions.

Stress is certainly quick to kill that lovin' feeling, but menopause is often no help, either. The natural dip in estrogen, testosterone, and progesterone that are part and parcel of this stage of life can lead to problems in almost all areas of sexual function, including interest, responsiveness, and enjoyment. These same hormones also affect mood, sleep, where we store fat, and how well we lose it. Considering the incredible impact these hormones have on your life, restoring their balance—either with bioidentical hormone replacement therapy or herbal medicines—is extremely important.

Good Sex Is So Good for You

Sexual function is a lot like lean muscle—if we don't use it, we lose it and the health and hormonal benefits that come with it. Guys, if your sex life is in the doldrums lately, you likely have less testosterone as well. The fix is pretty straightforward. Research shows that if we can get you back to enjoying more frequent sex, your testosterone can, ahem, rise again. A group of Italian researchers looked at men with erectile issues and measured their testosterone status before and after treatment (though not with testosterone replacement). Those whose ED treatment was successful had higher testosterone compared with those whose treatments failed to yield improvements. If you needed a strong argument for having sex tonight, now you have one.

Ladies, the same principles apply to you. Women who enjoy more love in the bedroom have increased estrogen and testosterone. When present in the proper balance, these hormones add fire to sexual desire, give us more sex appeal, improve mood and memory, and can even prevent abdominal fat gain. A little precoital cuddling, however, is also very important. Scientists at Simon Fraser University measured the levels of testosterone in women before and after sex, cuddling, and exercise. Although the women's testosterone levels were higher both before and after sexual intercourse, cuddling gave the biggest testosterone boost of all.

Sex Busts Stress

Do I really need to go into detail on the benefits of sex for stress relief? Most of us know that a healthy sex life can help knock the pants off stress. A great orgasm also encourages the release of oxytocin, which makes us feel calmer and more relaxed and can even lower our blood pressure. Orgasms also spark an antiaging surge of DHEA. So having at least two orgasms a week can slow the aging process and indirectly support fat loss, while also offering some protection from the adverse effects of cortisol.

Wait, there's more. Depending on the duration and "energy level" of the session, sex can help you burn calories and improve the fitness of your heart. Sex (including masturbation) improves your sleep and reduces the risk of depression, both of which are essential in preventing fat gain and improving hormonal imbalance. It also causes the release of endorphins, which can help ease pain and boost immunity. Some research even suggests having sex three times a week can slow aging and prevent wrinkling around the eyes. Sounds better than any eye cream I've ever tried.

Sex Can Curb Your Appetite

Sex is a basic human need, just like food and shelter. You won't be surprised to learn, then, that our desire to "get some" is controlled by the hypothalamus, which also regulates appetite, body temperature, and circadian rhythms. I once heard Sam Graci, author of *The Path to Phenomenal Health*, speculate that Mother Nature may start selecting against us when our sex engines cool, simply because of the basic laws of evolution or survival of the fittest. This ideal resonated with me and has certainly motivated me to stay active—and I don't mean in the gym.

Your libido (that's scientific lingo for sex drive) is determined by a set of complex physiological processes that involve delicate interactions between your brain, body, and hormones. For instance, an appetite-suppressing compound in the brain controls sexual arousal as well by stimulating the release of oxytocin. Also involved in sexual responsiveness and orgasm, the hormone oxytocin counteracts stress and depression by combating the harmful effects of cortisol.

Frequent hugs between spouses or partners are associated with lower blood pressure and higher oxytocin levels in premenopausal women. Having regular massages can also help to stimulate oxytocin.

The dose of dopamine we get from sex, which increases steadily to the point of orgasm and then declines, also helps curb our need to feed. Apparently, the dopamine pathways in the brain involved in stimulating desire for both sex and food are shut down by the hormones released immediately after we have an orgasm. Can you imagine better news for appetite and craving control?

So if you remember nothing else after reading this book, I am certain this little snippet of advice will stay with you: *Have more sex.* If you satisfy your sexual appetite, you can satisfy your growling stomach and your need to nibble on candy, too.

There's No Pressure, Though

Perhaps you are like many women and men with a lowered sex drive who find the idea of "jumping" into an active sex life hard to imagine. This can change, however, *if* you want it to. Following the recommendations of the Hormone Diet will help to improve your hormone balance and overall well-being, which will help a languishing libido. But you can also fuel sexual desire further with visualizations or small acts of intimacy. For instance, try thinking of positive words on waking—even if you don't feel positive—like love, joy, peace, strength, happiness, beauty, etc. Next, tailor this simple exercise to help your lowered sex drive by adding words you find sexy—like hot, sensual, sultry, or touchable. You can also slowly bring intimacy back into your life with activities to help you feel close and connected again, such as back rubs, foot rubs, or date nights.

> **SEX KEEPS YOUR HORMONES YOUNG**
>
> Scientists have looked at 100-year-old men and women who have maintained sexual intimacy, love, and function well into their advanced years. Turns out these centenarians living in Okinawa, Japan, and Bama, China, have higher levels of testosterone, DHEA, and estrogen than typical 70-year-olds in the United States!

HOT HORMONE FACT

The Challenges of Sex and Aging

As we age, we tend to have less sex. A good deal of research suggests this decline is caused by hormonal changes that naturally occur with age. But at the same time we know that less sex alters our hormones. It's a real catch-22.

Experiencing both a decrease in the desire for sex and changes in sexual responsiveness is common for both men and women. As we age, women may notice vaginal dryness or discomfort, decreased lubrication, and even pain with intercourse, whereas men may experience more difficulty achieving an erection or erections that are not as firm as they once were. Orgasms may also become less intense for both sexes. All these symptoms are due to the inevitable hormonal shifts that come about as we age. They will occur more rapidly if we stop having sex, because then we lose all the wonderful hormone-enhancing effects sex has to offer.

Natural Help for Sexual Concerns (Besides the Three Steps)

If your sex life is stuck in neutral, you don't have to live with it and you don't necessarily need to turn to pharmaceuticals, either. Here are a few simple tips you can try to get your love life back in gear.

Concern	Helpful Tips for Women	Helpful Tips for Men
Low Libido	For men and women individually, consider the following:	
	Try my supplement recommendations in Chapter 13 for low testosterone, low DHEA, low dopamine, or excess cortisol. If your concern is associated with menopause, look at the suggestions for low progesterone and low estrogen, as well.	Try my supplement recommendations in Chapter 13 for low testosterone, low DHEA, low dopamine, or excess cortisol. You may also wish to consider the options for excess estrogen if you have excess abdominal fat or other signs of estrogen dominance.
	Several supplements can be used to enhance the hormones involved in a healthy sex drive for men and women. Two herbs in particular, maca and ashwagandha, have shown promise for increasing libido in both sexes.	

Concern	Helpful Tips for Women	Helpful Tips for Men
	Investigate other ways to stimulate your sexual interests, including sex toys, books, DVDs, a sex class (tantric sex, etc.), and so forth. I recommend the book *Mating in Captivity* by Esther Perel.	
Vaginal Dryness	Local use of an estriol cream can be very helpful. See your local compounding pharmacy or your MD/ND for a prescription.	
Erectile Dysfunction		Certain herbs and supplements may enhance penile bloodflow: • Ginkgo • L-arginine • Ginseng • Horny goat weed • Magnesium

Get Sweaty: Exercise!

I'm passionate about exercise. Yet despite the well-documented and actively promoted benefits of regular workouts, statistics show that not everyone shares my enthusiasm. Recent research shows that the number-one cause of death in the United States is poor diet and lack of exercise. Believe it or not, these factors kill more North Americans each year than smoking! In other words, failing to exercise is just as harmful as smoking, if not more so.

Recall the hormonal catch-22 we can get into without sex—a hormonal imbalance can cause *and be caused by* a lack of love-making. Well, a hormonal imbalance is unlikely to prevent us from working out (except perhaps depression), but a lack of physical activity sure can bring about a hormonal imbalance. Moreover, too much sex is not an issue for most healthy people, but overexercising or working out incorrectly can cause us more harm than good.

The Benefits of Exercise for Fat Loss

The effects of exercise on your hormones and your weight will vary depending on the type of activities you choose (e.g., cardio, weight training, or yoga) and the intensity and duration of your sessions. But no matter what type of exercise we do, working out is just plain good for us. Here's why:

- CALORIE BURNING: We burn calories while we exercise and, if we do strength training, we burn calories well after the session is completed.

- MUSCLE BUILDING: Exercise can help us build metabolically active muscle. For every pound of muscle you gain, you'll burn an extra 30 to 50 calories, even when you're doing absolutely nothing!

- STIMULATION OF MUSCLE-BUILDING HORMONES: A 2002 study published in the *Journals of Gerontology Series A: Biological Sciences and Medical Sciences* looked at hormonal changes occurring in menopausal women who completed endurance training (40 minutes of cycling at 75 percent maximal exertion) and resistance training (3 sets of 10 reps of 8 exercises) compared with the control group that didn't exercise. Endurance and resistance training both significantly increased estrogen, testosterone, and growth hormone. Only the resistance training, however, increased DHEA. Testosterone will rise higher when you play a competitive sport and even higher still if you win.

- STIMULATION OF OUR FAT-LOSS FRIENDS: Exercise stimulates the hormones that are our fat-loss friends, including thyroid hormone, noradrenaline, testosterone, growth hormone, serotonin, leptin, and dopamine.

- REDUCTION OF OUR FAT-LOSS FOES: It also reduces the hormones that interfere with fat loss, including excess stress hormones that can wear the body down, and excess estrogen, which can increase breast cancer risk. Researchers selected a group of postmenopausal women from Seattle who did not exercise. Half of the women were instructed to begin a moderate-intensity walking program (45 minutes, five times per week); the others were told to do only stretching exercises. The women who walked decreased their harmful estrogen within 3 months.

- MOOD ENHANCEMENT: Exercise stimulates your mood and mental function; decreases anxiety and depression; and reduces pain by increasing dopamine and endorphins, our natural pain killers. According to a 2005 study from the *European Journal of Sports Science*, just 15 minutes of cardiovascular exercise two or three times a week can boost serotonin enough to prevent anxiety and treat depression.
- FAT BURNING AND INSULIN BALANCING: Exercise cranks up our PPARs, the regulators of fat metabolism and insulin sensitivity in our muscle cells.
- APPETITE CONTROL AND REDUCTION OF INFLAMMATION: Exercise has positive effects on fat-cell hormones such as leptin and adiponectin, which control inflammation and influence our appetite.

10 Workout Mistakes That Sabotage Fat Loss

You'll enjoy all the hormonal benefits of exercise I've just shared *providing you perform the right type, frequency, intensity, and duration of exercise*. Here are a few of the top workout mistakes and misconceptions that can *interfere* with our fat-burning results so you can be sure to avoid them going forward.

Workout Mistake #1: Completing Your Cardio Before Your Weight Training

I used to think cardio worked best as a warm-up before doing weights. I now know that saving my strength and completing my weight workout first is a much better plan. You can work out harder and lift more when you avoid fatiguing yourself with cardio first. Plus, you will continue to burn fat should you decide to follow your weight session with some cardio. Just hop on the bike or walk for 3 to 5 minutes, as a warm-up, to loosen up a bit before your weights.

Although I've personally used the weights-then-cardio approach for years, I certainly didn't come up with the idea. A study from the University of Tokyo found that people who did a total-body strength workout before cycling burned 10 percent more fat than participants who only cycled. The author of the study, Dr. Kazushige Goto, also found that less fat was burned and less growth hormone was released by the group that completed cardio first, followed by weights.

At the same time, adding cardio to the end of a particularly taxing weight-training session can cause a spike in your cortisol because the entire workout ends up being too long and stressful. For these reasons, I recommend you do your weights and cardio sessions at separate times. If you do wish to do them together, keep your cardio short. But dividing your workout may actually give you better fat-burning potential; the same study from the University of Tokyo showed that splitting cardio into two sessions maximized the post-workout fat burn. I'm sure the same theory would apply to dividing cardio and weight training into two separate sessions.

If you're still not convinced, I think you'll feel differently once you begin the Hormone Diet exercise plan. Then you'll see that resistance-training workouts can be intense enough that you won't have much zip left for cardio immediately after. Your heart certainly gets pumping when you do your strength training exercises effectively, with little rest in between sets. Resistance training can yield the most amazing changes in your body composition *when you do it properly*. If you want to stand in front of the mirror and love your look, resistance training is the way to achieve your goal. And finally, another great benefit of this approach to exercise is that it keeps your workouts short and sweet.

Workout Mistake #2: Pumping Iron for Hours at a Time

Unless you are an athlete training for a specific sport or event, workout sessions that last longer than 45 minutes are not necessary and may even be harmful. Although exercise is a wonderful long-term stress reliever, working out does put physical stress on your body in the short term. So when your workout is too long, your cortisol goes up, up, up. Cortisol is destructive to muscle tissue, especially when it's present without the muscle-protective hormones growth hormone and testosterone. Keeping your workouts shorter, though still intense, will help prevent excessive cortisol release, which usually starts to happen after about 40 minutes or so of continuous exercise. Compacting your workout in this way will give you the best gains in the shortest amount of time. It also means less wear and tear and quicker recovery.

Workout Mistake #3: Getting Socially Active between Sets

If you are the gym's social butterfly, you need to turn over a new leaf. You don't have time for chatting any more. Most of the workouts outlined for you in Chapter 15 are no longer than 30 minutes, which leaves no time for chitchat during your session. Power through your routine and socialize only after you are done. Studies show this no-nonsense, heads-down approach is the best way to maximize muscle gains and elicit the hormonal response you're looking for.

In a study published in *Medicine and Science in Sports and Exercise Journal* (2005), Kazushige Goto and his team at the University of Tokyo found that a group of test subjects who worked out continuously, with no rest between exercises, had greater increases in growth hormone, noradrenaline, and adrenaline during their workouts and netted greater muscle gains after 12 weeks than those who were instructed to rest between exercises. These findings can help you understand why I recommend completing your exercises in a circuit two or three times before having a rest. I truly don't want to torture you; I simply want you to get the best rewards from your efforts. Give each workout your all and you won't believe how quickly your body will respond.

Workout Mistake #4: Thinking Cardio Is the Best Way to Lose Weight

I know I'll probably ruffle more than a few feathers with this one, but neither running nor continuously training in the "fat-burning zone" is the golden ticket to your best body composition. Shorter workouts with intervals are far more effective than running or using a cardio machine for 40-plus minutes every other day. An interval is a short period of exercise performed at a higher intensity for a specific length of time. Each interval is separated from the next by a short period of rest or lighter activity. To truly take advantage of the benefits of interval training, you must be willing to shake the mindset that endless (and boring!) cardio training is the key to weight loss.

For example, 25 minutes of running can be more effective than 40. How? You burn more fat during and after your workout if you run for 10 minutes at a steady pace, then alternate 1 minute fast and 1 minute slow for the next 10 minutes, and then run at a slower pace for the last 5 minutes to cool down. Even though you're exercising for a shorter period, you'll still net greater fat loss using this method.

A number of studies lend very strong support to the value of interval training. One piece of research by Tremblay and colleagues, published in the journal *Metabolism,* showed greater muscle gains and fat loss in one group of subjects who exercised using intervals at a higher intensity for 15 weeks than a second group who exercised at a steady pace for 20 weeks. Although more *calories* were burned by the steady group, the interval-training group lost much more subcutaneous fat. Moreover, researchers at the University of New South Wales in Sydney, Australia, found 20 minutes of interval training to be more effective in sparking our fat-burning hormones than 40 minutes at a steady pace. How great is this? *More* fat burning with *less* time spent exercising. Clearly, intervals are the secret to shorter workouts with more fat-loss success!

Workout Mistake #5: Having Sports Drinks Before or After Workouts

When you're working out for 30 to 40 minutes, you don't need sugar to get you through your session. The only thing you should be guzzling is water. Consuming so-called sports drinks (i.e., a sugar blast in a plastic bottle) before or after your workout will do nothing but interfere with fat loss and hormonal balance. Too much sugar before or after exercise can also blunt growth hormone release. (An aside: Fatty foods after a workout have also been found to have the same dampening effect on growth hormone.) Sports, energy, and other drinks containing high-fructose corn syrup have no place in your diet at any time.

Workout Mistake #6: Lifting Weights on an Empty Stomach

Your muscles need fuel to reach full force of contraction and strength during exercise. Always consume a blend of protein and carbohydrates before and after your resistance-training sessions. This combination is proven to stimulate more growth hormone release and to encourage more muscle gains.

About an hour before your workout, have a snack that includes the macronutrients you need, such as a slice of Ezekiel bread with almond butter; a bowl of oatmeal with soy milk and blueberries; a Simply Bar (see Appendix C and the Resources section); or a protein shake with flaxseed oil, soy milk, and whey protein. Follow your workout with an Elevate Me! Bar (see Appendix C) or a protein shake made with fruit juice, soy or skim milk, bananas, and whey protein. Do *not* add the fat (flaxseed oil or flaxseeds) to your smoothie after your workouts because it can hamper growth hormone release. Always consume your shake within 45 minutes of finishing your exercise session for the greatest muscle-repair benefits. Remember, this is the one period of the day that you can get away with eating more carbs.

When you do your cardio, on the other hand, you can do it on an empty stomach (although you don't have to), provided you stick to a session that's 30 minutes max. You should still have your smoothie within 45 minutes of finishing your cardio, and it shouldn't contain much fat.

Workout Mistake #7: Believing the More Exercise, the Better for Maximum Fat Loss

I started lifting weights and going to the gym regularly after my first year of college. Ten years later I met a personal trainer who finally told me to stop working out for an hour at a time. In fact, he used to *yell* at me if I ran or exercised on the days I was supposed to rest. For months I couldn't wrap my head around the idea of exercising less. But guess what happened? When I finally followed his advice, *I got in the best shape of my life.*

Overtraining or overuse of cardio is an incredibly common mistake among people who love to work out or are enthusiastic about weight loss. This misguided approach, however, only serves to raise your cortisol and interfere with your ability to build metabolically active muscle. You should train with weights a maximum of four times a week (the Hormone Diet program recommends three) and do your cardio no more than two or three times a week. On the days you are not supposed to work out, don't! When we are trying to maximize the hormonal benefits of exercise, sometimes less truly is more. Stick to your routine, take the time off you need for rest and recuperation, and *trust me,* you will notice greater gains.

You wouldn't believe the results I've seen in my patients who have heeded my advice and gotten away from lengthy stints on the treadmill. Instead, they turned to interval training, yoga, and weights, and now they look amazing! Their body-fat percentages have dropped and they are more toned than ever.

Workout Mistake #8: Thinking Lifting Weights Causes Women to Bulk Up

Ladies, if you've always avoided the weight room for fear of ending up looking like a member of the Russian men's power-lifting team, you need to think again. Most, if not all, women will not bulk up from lifting weights. We women naturally possess only 5 to 10 percent of the testosterone that men do. *Testosterone* is what causes men to build muscle, whereas women are far more reliant on *growth hormone* to build muscle.

Remember, the more muscle you have, the more fat you'll burn, even when you're sleeping. So building more lean muscle mass will absolutely help your fat-loss progress. Using weight training will allow you to build strong, lean muscles without looking too pumped up or masculine, guaranteed.

In fact, exercise for weight loss *must* include resistance training. A comprehensive review of hundreds of studies completed by Miller and colleagues and published in the *International Journal of Obesity* proved this to be the case when *little benefit was found* in subjects who used moderate *cardiovascular exercise and dieting over diet alone.* Meanwhile, it's well documented that people who use a combination of resistance training *and* cardio lose fat while losing *little or no* metabolically active muscle.

Does this mean cardiovascular exercise is a waste? No, cardio boosts your mood, keeps your heart and lungs fit, and helps to maintain body weight, especially after a calorie-reduced diet. But, it's definitely not the answer to lasting fat loss.

Workout Mistake #9: Thinking Heavy Weights Are Just for Guys

Wrong! Ladies, don't be afraid to lift heavier weights. Just make sure you use proper form so you don't run the risk of injuring yourself.

I'm small but can lift a lot of weight and have been doing so since 1999—right about the time I met that trainer who persuaded me to stop overexercising.

Heavier weights tone muscle and boost growth hormone much more than the lighter weights most women tend to use. A 2006 study led by William J. Kraemer, a professor of kinesiology, physiology, and neurobiology at the University of Connecticut at Storrs, found greater gains of growth hormone in women who did fewer repetitions with heavier weights than in those who did higher reps with moderate weight. The study, published in the *American Journal of Physiology—Endocrinology and Metabolism,* showed that women who underwent 6 months of moderate- or high-intensity training and aerobic exercise had higher amounts of growth hormone.

This common workout mistake was the driving force behind the recent setup of the strength training studio at my clinic, staffed by a team of top trainers. Now my patients enjoy the benefits of an integrated approach involving care from an ND, MD, and exercise expert as we guide them through the Hormone Diet program. I want all my patients to learn how to exercise—properly!

Workout Mistake #10: Believing That Yoga Is Just for Girls
Years of weight lifting and running, especially without proper stretching, can shorten tendons and cause stiffness, misalignment, and joint and back pain. With its full spectrum of poses, yoga can bring the body back into its natural alignment, level out imbalances, and strengthen physical weaknesses. If you're an athlete, yoga can improve your performance by increasing your flexibility, relaxation, breathing, and balance. Anyone can improve his or her posture, energy, and endurance with regular yoga practice.

If you think yoga is too easy or too gentle a workout, how wrong you are! We have a yoga studio at Clear Medicine, and when my husband the hockey jock tried it, he couldn't believe how hard yoga was.

This type of workout can be very challenging and can make you feel inadequate if you compare yourself with other practitioners who appear more limber. Just remember, yoga is a solo sport; the only person you should be competing with is yourself. As with all sports or skills, you will definitely see improvements with practice. No matter what your ability level, yoga offers fabulous benefits for calming your nervous system, restoring hormonal balance, *and* strengthening your muscles.

Yoga can also be a terrific stress reliever. Numerous studies, including one completed in 2003 by the Center of Integrative Medicine at Thomas Jefferson University Hospital, in collaboration with the Yoga Research Society, have shown that yoga can lower blood cortisol levels in healthy males and females. It's also known to reduce adrenaline and stimulate our calming brain chemical GABA. Research from Boston University School of Medicine and McLean Hospital published in the *Journal of Alternative and Complementary Medicine* (May 2007) suggests that yoga should be explored as a possible treatment for disorders often associated with low GABA levels, such as depression and anxiety.

If you have excess ab fat or sleep disruption, yoga is one stellar choice of a workout for you. It's also excellent if you have fertility concerns. So leave your gender biases at the door and give yoga a try.

There you have it—all the hormonal benefits of sex and getting sweaty. Now we're ready to make you move—on to the exercise prescription we go!

CHAPTER 15

STRENGTH, STAMINA, AND STRETCHING: THE HORMONE DIET EXERCISE PRESCRIPTION

These are the hormonal benefits you will enjoy from exercise:

- Less inflammation
- Reduced insulin resulting in fewer cravings, better energy, and easier fat loss
- Diminished harmful effects from an accumulation of excess estrogen
- Increased DHEA, your antiaging and muscle-enhancing hormone
- A boost in testosterone for increased motivation and muscle-building benefits
- A dose of dopamine for your mood, motivation, and appetite control
- Tamed cortisol and a balanced nervous system when you exercise properly
- Increased metabolic rate due to increased thyroid hormone
- Increased growth hormone for better growth and repair of skin, bone, and muscle cells
- More of serotonin's beneficial effects on mood, sleep, and cravings
- Increased leptin sensitivity for fat burning and appetite control

Up to this point in my three steps, any exercise other than walking has been an optional component, because I wanted you to focus entirely on understanding and implementing the essentials of hormonally balanced nutrition, sound sleep, stress recuperation, and your anti-inflammatory detox. But now that you've done all the prep work involved in Step 1 and Step 2, your body is absolutely primed for the fantastic benefits of the Hormone Diet exercise plan. I cannot wait for you to experience the incredible body benefits of this approach!

Although reducing our food intake certainly sparks an initial loss of body weight, only the increase in metabolism that happens with exercise will maintain our efforts. The good news is that exercise allows us to enjoy more freedom with our food choices once we have reached our goal. Exercise truly is the more critical determinant of your lasting success than continually cutting your calories.

A weekly exercise routine you can use to stay fit for the rest of your life is outlined in this chapter. I have been using this workout for years, but the program you're about to enjoy also includes the expertise of three wonderful trainers from Clear Medicine: Reggie Reyes, Jason Gee, and Vanessa Bell. I thank them for their generosity and contributions.

GET FIT QUICK WITH THE HELP OF TWO SUPPLEMENTS: CLA AND CREATINE

Exercise is proven to combat the loss of muscle that unfortunately, but inevitably, happens with aging. But here's some good news. According to new research from the Public Library of Science, supplements of creatine mono-hydrate (5 g per day) and conjugated linoleic acid or CLA (3 to 6 g per day) can boost the benefits of exercise even further. Naturally produced by your body and present in meat, creatine is known to supply your muscles with energy. CLA, a naturally occurring fatty acid in beef, helps to preserve muscle tissue while encouraging safe fat loss. When used in conjunction with exercise, these two supplements pack a powerful muscle-building and antiaging punch. Look for Clear Recovery on the Hormone Diet store, which provides a highly absorbable form of creatine.

The Hormone Diet Exercise Philosophy

Before you begin, take a look at the principles behind the Hormone Diet exercise plan that will help you maximize hormonal and fat-burning benefits.

1. **Keep it short and sweet.** All workouts are 30 minutes (or a maximum 40 minutes).
2. **Give every workout your all.** High intensity and maximum effort—to the point where you just can't squeeze out one more rep—are *musts* for effective fat-burning and hormonal

benefits. When you're pushing yourself hard in the gym (or wherever you exercise), just remember that your workout is short and it will all be over soon!

3. **Complete your exercises with little rest between each circuit.** Circuit training keeps your heart rate high throughout your workout. When you use this method, you basically get your cardio workout and resistance training all in one shorter session. Circuit training is also the best type of workout for improving insulin response, boosting testosterone, and stimulating growth hormone. You spend less time exercising but you reap even more benefits.

4. **Work multiple muscle groups with each strength training session (but train each muscle group only once or twice a week).** This approach is designed to increase growth hormone and stimulate more muscle groups at once. It also lets you complete more work in less time and ensures that your muscles get the proper recuperation time they need *between* sessions.

5. **Keep cardio sessions short and use intervals.** Remember, intervals are a series of shorter periods of intense exercise separated by periods of brief rest or lighter activity. This method of training offers the most fat-burning potential and the greatest health benefits. Even cardiac patients can use interval training to improve their fitness.

6. **Use yoga for its hormone-enhancing effects.** Besides challenging and stretching your muscles, yoga can lower blood cortisol levels, reduce adrenaline, and stimulate brain-calming GABA.

7. **Consume the right stuff before and after your workouts for hormonal effects.** Always consume a blend of protein and carbohydrates about an hour before and within 45 minutes after your resistance-training sessions. Limit fat in your post-workout meal. This combination is proven to stimulate more growth hormone release and encourage muscle gains. You can

do cardio on an empty stomach, but eat your snack of protein and carbs (again, no fat) within 45 minutes of finishing your session. Drink only water during your workouts—no sports drinks allowed.

Tools of the Trade

Whether you choose to work out in the gym, outside, or at home, there are a few key pieces of equipment you need to get the job done properly. Most gyms provide these items for you; if you work out elsewhere, you may have to purchase them for yourself. Here's all the equipment required to complete your weekly exercise routine.

a. **A stability ball:** These come in different sizes, so be sure to purchase/use the proper one for your height.

b. **A set of dumbbells:** 3, 5, 8, 10, 12, and 15 pounds for women; 10, 15, 20, 25, and 30 pounds for men.

c. **A support bench:** A weight bench or other stable bench is helpful, but not necessary if you have a stability ball.

d. **A medicine ball:** You can also use a dumbbell.

e. **Options for indoor cardio:** A stationary bike, treadmill, stair stepper, or elliptical machine for home use. (You can also walk, bike, or run outside when weather permits.)

f. **Music:** Listening to your favorite tunes while working out is a great motivator.

The Hormone Diet Workout Weekly Schedule

For maximum health and hormonal benefit, I recommend you exercise 6 days a week. You'll complete three types of workouts each week.

1. Three days a week you'll complete 30 to 40 minutes of strength training.

2. Once a week you'll do cardio (20 to 30 minutes). A second cardio session is optional. If you simply *must* do more cardio, you can do so at the *end* of your weight-training sessions. Don't

overdo it, and don't add more than 15 minutes to your workout.

3. Once a week, preferably twice (but not on your strength-training days), do yoga for 30 to 90 minutes. This is the one workout that may be longer in duration.

One day a week you will rest and do no exercise, though fun activities like in-line skating or a leisurely swim, bike ride, or walk are fine. ☺

Do your best to follow the weekly exercise routine as laid out for you here. The program is specifically designed to keep you working hard during each session and progressing each week, allowing specific muscle groups to recuperate while others are being pushed to develop. A sample schedule of weekly workouts may look something like this:

Monday	Tuesday	Wednesday	Thursday	Friday	Saturday	Sunday
Rest	Day 1 Strength-Training Routine	Cardio Interval Training* Yoga	Day 2 Strength-Training Routine	Yoga†	Day 3 Strength-Training Routine	Cardio (optional 20 minutes of cardio at a steady pace or interval)*

*If you wish to do cardio and strength training on the same day, sometimes it's better to split them into two different workouts (e.g., cardio in the morning and strength training in the afternoon).

†Avoid yoga on the same day as strength training. A yoga class or a yoga DVD at home are both excellent options. As far as the type of yoga is concerned, we prefer Hatha, Ashtanga, or Vinyasa at Clear Medicine, but I'll leave it up to you to decide which you like best.

Selecting the Right Amount of Weight

Time and time again, I see people at the gym who fail to get results, either because they don't lift enough weight to challenge their muscles or because they're lifting too much and using improper form. Choosing the right weight and using correct form are absolutely *essential* to get the results you want and avoid injury.

When you are just starting out, choose a weight light enough to allow you to complete all the suggested repetitions for each exercise without compromising your form. Remember, if your posture is poor or you are swinging your weights instead of lifting them in a controlled manner just to finish the last few reps, you're not doing yourself any favors! In fact, you can really hurt yourself. As your workouts progress, you'll decrease the number of repetitions and increase your weight to the point that you can barely complete the last few repetitions.

Hiring a personal trainer may seem like a daunting or expensive proposition, but don't be afraid to try it, even for just a few sessions, if you feel you need help getting started and someone to show you proper form. (Some trainers will even charge less if you do your session with a partner.) Besides, we're talking about an investment in your long-term health and well-being. I fully believe it's some of the best money you will ever spend and I encourage *all* my patients to do so.

The Hormone Diet Strength-Training Workout

If you've never exercised or have been inactive for a very long time, you can follow the basic strength-training routine for beginners that I have outlined on my Web site under the Book Extras section. Certain to crank up your fat-burning potential, it involves full-body circuit training 3 days a week. Otherwise, you can jump right into the strength-training component of the plan presented here. Remember, every workout counts. Even once a week is better than none, but don't expect great results until you can increase to a minimum of three times a week.

I encourage you to try switching up your workout *even* if you have been exercising successfully on your own. As most exercise experts will agree, the change will challenge your muscles, force your body to adapt, and further your fitness gains.

The exercises are to be done consecutively in sequence with no rest in between sets. Rest for 1 minute at the end of each circuit before moving on to the next. Each workout should take you about

30 minutes, even when you have worked your way up to 3 sets. (By then your fitness level will have improved and you'll be able to finish the exercises faster.) Warm up by riding the bike, walking, or jogging for 4 to 5 minutes before beginning your strength-training session.

You can keep progressing by increasing the weight lifted (while still maintaining form) and by altering your exercise choices. You may also change the order of the circuits within each workout or the exercises within each circuit as a means to keep your body guessing. For more information on these exercises, and for ideas and exercise options that will help you stay challenged, visit www.thehormonediet.com. I promise you'll never get bored. I've been doing this workout for years and years and still love it.

DAY 1 STRENGTH-TRAINING ROUTINE: CHEST, BACK, AND CORE

Circuit Grouping	Exercise	Repetitions	Weight	No. of Times to Repeat Circuit
1	Crunches over the Ball	20	None	2
	Leg Raise with Pulse up to Ceiling	15	None	
	Plank	Hold for 20 to 60 seconds	None	
Rest 30 seconds to 1 minute while setting up for circuit 2				

Crunches over the Ball

Leg Raise with Pulse up to Ceiling

Plank

Circuit Grouping	Exercise	Repetitions	Weight	No. of Times to Repeat Circuit
2	Chest Dumbbell Press on Ball	15	Light first set, moderate second set, heavy third set	3
	Straight-Leg Deadlift (with Dumbbells)	15		
Rest 30 seconds to 1 minute while setting up for circuit 3				

Chest Dumbbell Press on Ball

Straight-Leg Deadlift (with Dumbbells)

Circuit Grouping	Exercise	Repetitions	Weight	No. of Times to Repeat Circuit
3	Dumbbell Fly	15	Moderate first set, heavy second set (for very advanced, add a third set)	2 (3)
	Bent-Over Dumbbell Row (Double or Single Arm)	15		
Rest 30 seconds to 1 minute while setting up for circuit 4				

Dumbbell Fly

Bent-Over Dumbbell Row (Double Arm)

Bent-Over Dumbbell Row (Single Arm)

Circuit Grouping	Exercise	Repetitions	Weight	No. of Times to Repeat Circuit
4	Push-Ups	15	None	2 (3)
	Back Extensions on Ball	15	None	

Push-Ups

Back Extensions on Ball

DAY 2 STRENGTH-TRAINING ROUTINE: LEGS AND CORE

Circuit Grouping	Exercise	Repetitions	Weight	No. of Times to Repeat Circuit
1	Standard Crunch	20	None	2
	Back Extensions	20	None	
	Seated Oblique Twists with Medicine Ball	20 per side	4- to 10-pound medicine ball	
Rest 30 seconds to 1 minute while setting up for circuit 2				

Standard Crunch

Back Extensions

Seated Oblique Twists with Medicine Ball

Circuit Grouping	Exercise	Repetitions	Weight	No. of Times to Repeat Circuit
2	Squats	15	Light first set, moderate second set, heavy third set	3
	Leg Raises with Ball between Feet	15	None, just the ball	
Rest 30 seconds to 1 minute while setting up for circuit 3				

Squats

Leg Raises with Ball between Feet

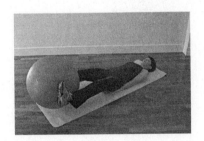 

Circuit Grouping	Exercise	Repetitions	Weight	No. of Times to Repeat Circuit
3	Lunges with Biceps Curl	10–15 each leg	Moderate first set, heavy second set (for very advanced, add a third set)	2 (3)
	Hamstrings Curls with Feet on Ball	15–20	None	
Rest 30 seconds to 1 minute while setting up for circuit 4				

Lunges with Biceps Curl

Note: Your arms will fatigue. When necessary, continue to lunge without the biceps curl.

Hamstrings Curls with Feet on Ball

Circuit Grouping	Exercise	Repetitions	Weight	No. of Times to Repeat Circuit
4	Bent-Knee Dumbbell Deadlift with Calf Raise	15	Moderate first set, heavy second set	2 (3)
	Plank	Hold 30 seconds to 1 minute	None	

Bent-Knee Dumbbell Deadlift with Calf Raise

Plank

Circuit Grouping	Exercise	Repetitions	Weight	No. of Times to Repeat Circuit
1	Ball Pull-Ins with Push-Up	15	None	2
	Side Jackknife	15 per side		
	Side Plank	Hold 20–60 seconds per side		
Rest 30 seconds to 1 minute while setting up for circuit 2				

Ball Pull-Ins with Push-Up

Side Jackknife

Side Plank

Circuit Grouping	Exercise	Repetitions	Weight	No. of Times to Repeat Circuit
2	Standing Hammer Biceps Curls into Shoulder Press	15	Light first set, moderate second set, heavy third set	3
	Lying Triceps Dumbbell Skull-crushers on Ball (or Bench)	15		
Rest 30 seconds to 1 minute while setting up for circuit 3				

Standing Hammer Biceps Curls into Shoulder Press

Lying Triceps Dumbbell Skullcrushers on Ball (or Bench)

Circuit Grouping	Exercise	Repetitions	Weight	No. of Times to Repeat Circuit
3	Standing Shoulder Lateral and Front Dumbbell Raise	15	Moderate first set, heavy second set (for advanced, add a third set)	2 (3)
	Standing Alternating Biceps Curls	15		
	Lying Triceps Dumbbell Extensions (on Ball)*	15		
Rest 30 seconds to 1 minute while setting up for circuit 4				

*Optional. Repeat the skullcrushers from the previous set, but alternate your arms.

Standing Shoulder Lateral and Front Dumbbell Raise

Standing Shoulder Lateral and Front Dumbbell Raise

Standing Alternating Biceps Curls

Circuit Grouping	Exercise	Repetitions	Weight	No. of Times to Repeat Circuit
4	Bent-Over Reverse Dumbbell Fly	15	Moderate first set, heavy second set (for advanced, add a third set)	2 (3)
	Triceps Dips	15	None	

Bent-Over Reverse Dumbbell Fly

Triceps Dips

ADD MUSIC TO YOUR WORKOUTS!

Did you know that just 15 minutes of music a day can improve your immunity and reduce pain? It can also decrease your blood pressure, lower your heart rate, and slow your breathing simply because it helps drop your cortisol and boost your endorphins. Incredibly, researchers in Florida have found that 20 minutes a day of music is enough for patients to report a reduction of more than 50 percent in osteoarthritic pain in just 14 days!

If you are currently exercising without music, you had better get some earphones on ASAP. The newest research from Brunel University in England shows that upbeat music can enhance our aerobic endurance, motivation, and drive. Fast-tempo music will inject vigor into your workouts. Slow-tempo, soothing music, on the other hand, can aid relaxation during cooldown and stretching. In essence, music can make you work harder without realizing it. It offers a pleasant distraction from the discomfort of physical exertion and causes your workout to pass by quicker.

But music does more than make your individual workouts more enjoyable. A 2005 study completed at Fairleigh Dickinson University in New Jersey found that routinely listening to music while exercising made people more consistent with their workouts and boosted weight loss results.

Get the most out of music for your workouts and your overall health. Choose tunes you love to listen to and consider the following:

1. Pick upbeat exercise music to help you work harder and maximize your fitness results.
2. Play soothing music while stretching in your car or while you

(continued)

commute to reduce tension, anxiety, or pain. Relax with chill-out music for 15 minutes at the end of your day. I recommend the Sonic Aid series by Dr. Lee Bartel for relaxation and enhancing brain activity.

3. Bring some music with you for an added mood-enhancing, pain-reducing boost when you go out in the morning for your daily dose of sunshine.

4. Crank up your tunes just for fun or when you feel you need a stress release or mood boost. Even better, dance! Dancing elevates endorphins, raises serotonin, and balances out the sympathetic nervous system by lowering cortisol and dopamine. A December 2005 study published in the *International Journal of Neuroscience* proved that 12 weeks of dance sessions raised serotonin and lowered dopamine (often high when we are stressed). Remember that low serotonin also means more cravings and less motivation. So moving to your favorite tunes is an awesome way to have some fun, burn a few calories, and beat cravings for sugar and carbs!

The Hormone Diet Interval Cardio Training

Sticking to a regular exercise routine can be tough. So choosing an activity you enjoy—one you know you'll keep up with consistently—is always your best cardiovascular fitness option. However, if you want the most bang for your cardio buck, then high-intensity interval training on the treadmill (walking or running), elliptical trainer, stationary bike, or indoor/outdoor track is your secret to success.

Short bursts of intense exercise not only improve your cardiovascular fitness but also increase your fat-burning capacity, even during low- or moderate-intensity workouts. What's more, high-intensity training provides a boost of feel-good and appetite-controlling hormones, which can truly be your secret weapons against unwanted weight gain—especially during the cold, dark winter months when many of us are prone to depression and cravings for comfort foods.

Don't rush into interval training if you have heart disease, high blood pressure, or joint problems, or if you are over the age of 60. If you fit any one of these categories, you should definitely consult your doctor first.

Here are a few examples of interval training to choose from. You'll do cardio at least once a week for 20 to 30 minutes. A second cardio workout is optional.

Four Examples of Interval Training

1. STEADY-PACE INTERVALS OF WALKING, JOGGING, RUNNING, CYCLING, ETC.
- 5-minute warmup at a gentle or moderate pace of the activity of your choice.
- 1 minute at a fast pace or high intensity, followed by 1 minute at a moderate pace. Alternate 5 to 8 times.
- 5-minute cooldown at a gentle or moderate pace.

2. INTERVALS THAT INCREASE IN SPEED OR INTENSITY THROUGHOUT THE WORKOUT
The example I have included here applies to running on a treadmill. A similar approach could be taken, however, by changing the tension or peddling faster on a stationary bike; by increasing the level or moving faster on your elliptical machine; or by walking on an incline on the treadmill while increasing the speed or incline.

- 5-minute warmup at 5.5 mph
- 1 minute at 7 mph
- 1 minute at 6 mph
- 1 minute at 7.5 mph
- 1 minute at 6 mph
- 1 minute at 8 mph
- 1 minute at 6 mph
- 1 minute at 8.5 mph
- 1 minute at 6 mph
- 1 minute at 9 mph
- 5-minute cooldown

3. INTERVALS THAT VARY BY DURATION

Rather than increasing the speed or intensity, as in the example above, your intervals could range in duration—for example, 30 seconds, 60 seconds, 90 seconds, 60 seconds, 30 seconds—with 1-minute, low-intensity sessions between each interval.

4. ADVANCED OPTION: SPRINTING (ONLY 15 MINUTES or so)

- Warm up with a light jog for 5 to 10 minutes.
- Sprint 50 to 100 meters and lightly jog or walk back to your starting point. Repeat 10 times.
- Cool down with a light jog for another 5 to 10 minutes.

You could also use this approach on hills by running (or speed walking) up the hill and lightly jogging down.

A Few Simple Tips to Keep You Active

If you've never exercised before, you must know that getting started is often the hardest part. I am confident that, by now, the first two steps of the Hormone Diet have given you the motivation to make the leap into physical fitness, but here are a few more tips.

- **Schedule your workouts on your calendar.** This habit will help keep you on track and ensure that you make time for exercise.
- **Pick a time that fits with the rest of your daily activities, whether it's first thing in the morning or right after work.** Going home first or working out after dinner, whether you do it at home or at a gym, can make your workout routine much tougher to stick to.
- **Record what you've done during each workout.** Monitoring your progress is a great source of motivation. And reviewing all the hard work you've done feels truly rewarding.
- **Get a friend on board the workout train with you.** It's so much more fun and also gives you a way to fit friend time into your busy schedule. Just make sure you're both working for 30 minutes and save your socializing for afterwards.
- **Hire a personal trainer.** Or enroll in a program like ours at Clear Medicine that integrates your health care with your fitness goals. I believe exercise is medicine. As such, it should be dispensed and explained like any prescription.

Enjoy the changes you see in your body; you'll never look back! And speaking of looks, now that you have your exercise routine in place to take care of all your inner workings, you're ready to optimize your outer appearance—with all-natural, toxin-free skin care.

Mitch A. (age 44)

I was your typical healthy forty-something—or so I thought—until I had my bloodwork done! Like many of us, my poor diet, lack of exercise, and stress levels had caused my cholesterol, blood pressure, and sugars to creep in the wrong direction. My doctor started naming a multitude of prescription drugs to lower my blood pressure and cholesterol levels. I was not only scared—I felt old, too.

The very next week, I went to see Dr. Natasha Turner. She became a partner and supporter, and she made it clear that I could fix my issues if I committed to diet, exercise, stress management, and supplements. Within 4 months, I saw incredible results in how I felt, how I looked, and more importantly, my stats and blood values.

STATS	SEPTEMBER	DECEMBER
Weight	173	162
Waist	37.8	33
Hips	41	38
Cholesterol	298	171
BP	160/100	120/84
Body Fat	20%	15%

It is now 9 months later and I am 20 pounds lighter, in my best shape ever, and my bloodwork is picture perfect. Dr. Turner's program takes commitment, but if I can do it with three young kids and a very active business life, anyone can. The way we eat and live makes us sick, while following a healthier lifestyle can make huge changes to the way you live and feel.

CHAPTER 16

LOOK LOVELY, LIVE WELL:
THE IMPORTANCE OF NATURAL SKIN CARE

Here are the hormonal benefits you can expect to enjoy from choosing natural skin care:

• Protection from harmful chemicals that can mimic estrogen in your body
• Less inflammation
• Protection from the aging effects of other products

Everyone wants soft, supple skin that feels good and looks healthy. To truly make sure your skin looks its best, you must take care of it from the inside out, which, until now, has been the focus of my discussion. So let's start talking about how you can approach your skin from the outside in. You'll be looking fresh in no time.

Skin care is *big* business. On a daily basis we are bombarded with marketing messages about the latest product guaranteed to make us look years younger. But someone once advised me that I should never put anything on my skin that I wouldn't put in my mouth. Think about it—several medications come in cream or patch form because this allows the drug to absorb quickly and easily into the body. This fact led me to realize that I should pay more attention to the products I apply to my skin! After all, the skin *is* our largest vital organ.

That's right, vital organ. Just like the heart, brain, liver, and more,

LET THE SUNSHINE IN
Sunlight, in reasonable doses, enables natural immunity, promotes skin growth and healing, stimulates hormone production (e.g., our happy hormone, serotonin) and contributes to an overall sense of well-being. Getting some sunlight for 15 to 20 minutes a day enables the body to manufacture vitamin D and is responsible for the synthesis of the pigment melanin, the skin's natural sunscreen. Just make sure you don't go overboard. Excess sun exposure is a leading cause of skin cancer and premature aging.

your skin performs several essential biological functions. It blocks viral and bacterial infections from entering your body. It controls your body temperature through sweating. When exposed to sunshine, it supports the production of the vitamin D we need for bone health and insulin balance. Through its intricate network of sensory nerves, it also informs us about our surroundings and allows us to feel a myriad of sensations, including the pleasure of touch. Your skin is crucial for life and for your ability to interact with the world.

Skin consists of three main layers: epidermis, dermis, and subcutaneous tissue (fat). You can almost imagine your skin like a dessert with several layers.

The "Meringue": Your Epidermis

The epidermis is the top layer of skin. It is made up of different types of cells that make the protein keratin—melanin, which is the pigment responsible for your skin color and tone, and immune cells that protect you from infections. As we age, the function of these immune cells of the epidermis weakens, our wounds take longer to heal, and our skin doesn't recuperate from damage the way it once did. Therefore, the benefits of maintaining healthy immune system function are certainly not limited to experiencing fewer colds and flus. (Good thing the three steps offer a completely natural immunity boost.)

Most of your epidermis comprises the cells that make keratin. They begin at the bottom of the epidermis as fresh cells but lose water and flatten out as they move upward. They end up as dead cells on your skin's surface. Eventually these dead cells are sloughed off and replaced by new ones. Somewhat like the meringue topping on a pie, your epidermis is moist on the inside with a delicate but crusty outer surface.

The state of your epidermis determines how fresh your skin appears. *By now, the favorable inner changes you have been making over the past month or so while following your three steps are surely starting to show on the outside, since epidermal cells renew every 4 to 5 weeks.* In fact, most of my patients continue to report substantial improvements in their skin during the first 3 to 6 months after adopting the healthy lifestyle habits prescribed by the Hormone Diet.

The Cream Filling: Your Dermis

Sandwiched between your epidermis and subcutaneous fat is the dermis, the thickest layer of your skin. (Note that some experts view the dermis and subcutaneous fat as one layer.) Nerve fibers, blood vessels, sweat and sebaceous glands, hair follicles, and lymphatic tissue are all found in this layer of your skin.

The dermis is important for your skin's circulation, oil and moisture content, oxygenation, and further protection from invading bacteria or viruses. When your skin fails to produce enough sebum (oil), dryness and wrinkling occurs, whereas overproduction leads to acne and blackheads. You shouldn't be surprised to learn that your sebum and sweat glands respond to your hormones. Testosterone, progesterone, and DHEA are known to increase the production of sebum and are linked to acne breakouts. DHEA, testosterone, and estrogen can also cause or contribute to excess sweating and even body odor.

The dermal layer is also heavily involved in the structural support, elasticity, and resiliency of your skin. If you have wrinkles now, they are rooted within your dermis. A protein called collagen provides skin's structural framework and tone, whereas another called elastin is involved in the suppleness and elasticity of your skin.

Because the dermis is composed of collagen and elastin, your dietary intake of protein and other protein building blocks will affect the health and appearance of your skin. Thinning, wrinkling, and sagging are signs of deficient collagen or elastin production. Estrogen is also an important factor involved in the collagen and elastin production in this layer of your skin.

The Graham Cracker Crust: Subcutaneous Fatty Tissue

This layer of your skin is the one you hope stays in place as you age. Just as the crust is to a tasty pie, subcutaneous fatty tissue is the foundation of firm, fresh-looking skin. Unfortunately, this layer tends to shrink away with aging, which results in sagging and wrinkling. According to an October 2004 report by the American Society of Plastic Surgeons, sun exposure and the loss of fat play far greater roles than gravity in the aging of our faces. Plastic surgeons are now rejuvenating faces by replacing lost facial fat with wrinkle fillers such as collagen and fat cells.

As with the dermis, estrogen also plays an important role in maintaining this layer of your skin. Many women notice thinning and sagging skin as part of menopause. These changes occur because estrogen, which declines during menopause, plays a vital role in maintaining both the elasticity and firmness of your skin.

Your Hormones and Your Skin

Glowing skin; thick, shiny hair; and smooth, flexible nails are all hallmarks of health and hormonal balance. When your hormones are out of whack, visible signs of aging turn up in the look and feel of your hair and skin. Here's a brief summary of just a few of the ways in which hormones affect hair and skin.

Insulin

Foods high in sugar, such as pastries, muffins, white pasta, white rice, and juice, cause spikes in blood sugar and insulin, which can cause inflammation and contribute to wrinkles and aging.

Cortisol

Our long-term stress hormone has documented aging effects on our skin cells. (Anything that beats stress basically beats aging, too.)

Estrogen

As already mentioned, the drop in estrogen production that naturally occurs with age makes our skin thinner and less elastic, which leads to more wrinkling and sagging. As estrogen dips, less collagen and elastin are produced. Estrogen also helps skin stay moist by boosting hyaluronic acid. A 1997 study of 3,875 postmenopausal women concluded that estrogen supplementation helped aging women have younger-looking skin. It also maintained skin's collagen, thickness, elasticity, and ability to retain moisture. According to the Life Extension Foundation, these effects can be enhanced even further with supplements of both estrogen and testosterone.

Testosterone

In both women and men, excess testosterone may result in acne on the face, chest, or back. With age, some women experience an increase in testosterone along with a decrease in estrogen. Meanwhile, men tend to experience the opposite—an increase in estrogen and a decrease in testosterone, which causes the skin to dry out.

DHEA

Dry skin increases with age. Interestingly, DHEA tends to decline with stress, as well as with aging and menopause. DHEA turns on oil production and seems to help combat this problem and improve hydration. It also increases the production of collagen, making skin appear smoother and younger looking. Our skin's natural protective barrier also appears to improve with DHEA.

Melatonin

Both melatonin and serotonin are produced in your skin from the amino acid tryptophan. According to a July 2005 article from the journal *Endocrine,* melatonin is involved in hair growth and protection against melanoma. As an antioxidant hormone, melatonin guards us from UV radiation and appears to play a role in repairing burned skin. New research led by Dr. Russel Reiter, a cell biologist at the University of Texas in San Antonio, also suggests that melatonin supplementation may offer extra protection from skin cancer. Whether it's applied topically or taken internally, melatonin may shield us from environmental and internal stressors.

Progesterone

Ever wonder why pregnant women seem to have that special glow? The secret is the high level of progesterone common in a healthy pregnancy. Progesterone is very beneficial for skin elasticity and circulation.

Growth Hormone

Since growth hormone tends to drop off as we get older, supplements are promoted as a way to "reverse" the effects of aging. Growth hormone is essential for skin-cell repair and the prevention of sagging.

Natural Skin Care

Considering the impact hormones can have on your skin, hormonal imbalances can clearly affect how you look as well as how you feel. We need to choose our skin-care products wisely to ensure they don't disrupt the delicate hormonal balance that keeps us looking our best.

Think about how many different products come in contact with your body every morning before you even leave the bathroom: shampoo, conditioner, body wash or soap, shaving cream, body cream, face wash, moisturizer, toothpaste, deodorant—and the list goes on, especially if you wear makeup or cologne. Before you take your first breath of outdoor air, you've already been exposed to hundreds of chemicals. Imagine how the daily absorption of these chemicals adds up over a lifetime!

This long-term exposure is a definite hormonal health concern. Some of the chemicals found in a variety of cosmetics— including phthalates, acrylamide, formaldehyde, and ethylene oxide—are listed by the US Environmental Protection Agency and the state of California as carcinogens or reproductive toxins. That's serious!

Recall our discussion of phthalates in Chapter 8. This group of industrial chemical plasticizers is used in many cosmetic products from nail polish to deodorants—products that are linked to birth defects, low testosterone in men, and the feminization of baby boys. Unfortunately, phthalates are just one of many examples.

By following the principles of the Hormone Diet, you have made a commitment to ridding your life of hormone-imbalancing habits and toxins. Now that you have optimized your skin's appearance by making so many healthy changes on the inside, natural skin-care products are the absolutely perfect way to round out your three-step plan and get gorgeous from the outside. And guys, this advice is not just for ladies only.

Cleanse and Moisturize

Your cleansing products should be free of sodium lauryl sulfate, a harsh detergent present in shampoos and cleansers. This chemical is highly astringent, which means it strips your skin of natural moisture. It's also used to clean machinery and industrial flooring, if that tells you anything. The skin-care lines Caudalie, John Masters,

Naturopathica, Burt's Bees, and Juice Beauty offer a selection of chemical-free cleansers to choose from.

Contrary to popular belief (prompted by prominent marketing messages), we should avoid using abrasive, scratchy products or brushes to exfoliate our skin. If you really like the feeling you get from such products, make sure the exfoliating ingredient consists of fine particles that won't scratch or damage your skin. Better yet, choose products with natural, fruit-based acids such as lactic acid or alpha hydroxy acid (AHA) to lift off dead skin cells without any abrasive action. Note that you can still overexfoliate, even with these milder fruit acids. Years of abnormally increasing cellular turnover in your skin may accelerate the aging of your skin later on.

If you do choose a mildly grainy exfoliating compound for your body, it should contain natural oils and be free of additives. Alba Organics' Sugar Cane Body Polish is a good choice that's available at most health food stores. The sunflower oil base and added macadamia oil, vitamin E, and honey make it a treat for dry, flaky winter skin. To gently exfoliate and brighten facial skin, try using Environmental Defense Mask from Naturopathica or Juice Beauty's Green Apple Peel twice a week after cleansing.

The moisturizers you use on your body or face should be free of the following: methylparabens, propylparabens, formaldehyde, imidazolidinyl urea, methylisothiazolinone, propylene glycol, paraffin, isopropyl alcohol, sodium lauryl sulfate, and other chemical tongue twisters. I dare you to go into your bathroom right this second and read all the labels you find. No doubt you'll realize almost everything should go directly into the recycling bin. Parabens, in particular, have been identified as estrogenic substances that disrupt normal hormone function and may increase the risk of breast cancer.

Instead, choose products containing pure oils, protective vitamins, and natural scents. Burt's Bees, available in most health food stores and natural pharmacies, makes an excellent line of natural skin-care products for both babies and adults. Two of my personal favorites are Apricot Baby Oil (fabulous on damp skin after bathing) and Milk & Honey Body Lotion. Both of these products smell delicious and include vitamin E and other antioxidants to protect skin cells. I have also discovered Korres, a wonderful natural skin-care line from Greece, whose body lotions and butters are divine. Plus, their lip balm is quite possibly the best I've ever tried.

PERSONAL-CARE PRODUCTS AND THEIR HARMFUL CHEMICALS

Personal-Care Product	Harmful Chemical
Body wash, shampoos, facial cleansers, toothpaste	Sodium lauryl sulfate (a harsh chemical cleanser)
Lipstick	Certain brands may contain lead (which can accumulate and cause lead toxicity)
Most products	Synthetic dyes and fragrances (these increase our risk of allergy and the chemical content of products)
Body wash, shampoo, conditioner, makeup, eye creams, deodorants, body and facial moisturizers	Parabens (methylparabens, propylparabens, etc., are linked to breast cancer)
Nail polish	Formaldehyde (a carcinogen)
Toothpaste	Fluoride (potentially harmful to our thyroid function when present in excess)
Shampoo, lotions, creams	Cocamide DEA (listed in the United States as likely to cause cancer in humans)

Save Face

If preventing aging is your goal, ingredients proven to stimulate collagen production and reduce fine lines, free radical damage, sun damage, and uneven skin tone are a must in your daily skin-care regimen. Look for hyaluronic acid, vitamin C, coenzyme Q10, alpha-lipoic acid, vitamin E, or vitamin A. Applying these nutrients topically has documented antiaging effects. DMAE has also been found to freshen skin and prevent sagging.

The stores are full of skin-care creams that promise wrinkle-free, younger-looking, smooth and toned skin. Realize that little clinical data are available to support these claims. But take heart. Clinical studies have proven a few ingredients to be effective in reducing fine lines and evening out skin tone.

ALPHA-LIPOIC ACID: Lipoic acid is an antioxidant compound involved in healthy blood sugar balance and insulin action. This dual action provides highly protective, antiaging benefits for our skin by reducing the risk of glycation—the abnormal attachment of sugar to our skin cells, causing wrinkling and aging.

Alpha-lipoic acid is both water and fat soluble, making it protective for most tissues in the body. One study reported a 50 percent reduction in fine lines and wrinkles with the topical use of a high-potency lipoic acid cream.

EXTRACTS OF WHITE AND GREEN TEA: A 2003 study from the University Hospitals of Cleveland and Case Western Reserve University found that certain antioxidant compounds in white tea extract are effective in improving skin-cell immunity and offering protection from the damaging effects of the sun. Evidently, a skin cream containing these tea extracts may offer potent antiaging and anticancer benefits.

The Skin Study Center at University Hospitals of Cleveland also found that the antioxidants in green tea can reduce the harmful effects of sunburn. In addition, Dr. Stephen Hsu from the Medical College of Georgia Department of Oral Biology found the polyphenols in green tea help to eliminate free radicals, which can cause cancer by altering cell DNA. As our outer epidermal cells naturally slough off, skin cells from deep within the epidermis make their way to the surface about every 4 weeks. By about day 20, cells are basically hanging out on the upper layer waiting to die. The most abundant polyphenol in green tea, EGCG (also used for its benefits in weight loss), appears to bring dying skin cells back to life when it is applied to the surface of the skin. Besides making us look fresher, these effects of green tea may be very useful for improving skin conditions and for the prevention of scarring. It seems EGCG is the fountain of youth for our skin cells! You might want to look for John Masters's Green Tea & Rose Hydrating Face Serum—I think it's the best, and I received compliments on my skin when first trying it out.

COENZYME Q10: A 1999 study found that topical application of the antioxidant coenzyme Q10 (CoQ10) improved the skin's resistance to the oxidative stress of UV radiation. When applied long term, CoQ10 may reduce the appearance of crow's feet, those nasty lines around the eyes.

DMAE: Dimethylaminoethanol (DMAE) boosts the production of acetylcholine, as well as phosphatidylcholine, a component of cell membranes. DMAE may be the first clinically proven agent to effectively combat facial sagging. Many of Dr. Nicholas Perricone's skin-care products contain DMAE. Visit www.perriconemd.com for more information.

VITAMIN C: Topical use of a product containing stabilized vitamin C can increase the production of collagen in the skin. It can also promote skin-cell growth and aid in cell regeneration, which translates to younger-looking skin and improved firmness. The form of vitamin C used in your skin-care products is important because it has the potential to become unstable and even a potentially harmful source of free radical stress. Ascorbyl palmitate, the fat-soluble form of vitamin C, appears to be the most beneficial and stable type for use in skin-care products. It should be present in significant concentrations to boost collagen production in the skin.

Choose a product that is white or, even better, a colorless serum.

This way you can easily toss your topical vitamin C product if it turns yellow, orange, or brown—a sign it has become oxidized. When this happens, it will do more harm than good.

VITAMIN A: Topical products containing natural forms of vitamin A (retinol, retinyl palmitate, retinoic acid, retinaldehyde) or vitamin A derivatives (called retinoids) have proven to be beneficial for skin damaged by the sun. According to some sources, retinyl palmitate is the best source, since it appears to be less irritating. These products also slow down the signs of aging. *Dermatology Surgery* (June 2004) reported that vitamin A is an effective, well-tolerated treatment for photodamaged facial skin and also reduces fine and large wrinkles, acne, liver spots, and surface roughness.

To avoid overexfoliating the skin, I recommend using a vitamin A cream only once or twice a week. These products should not be applied before sun exposure.

All-natural face care may cost a little more, but getting proven results without harmful toxins is far better than spending a ton on questionable products from your local drugstore or department store. Your local Whole Foods Market, natural spa, or health food store will usually offer the best source of all-natural, age-defying face products, or you can visit the Life Extension Foundation at www.lef.org. You may also visit a compounding pharmacy in your area.

Get Gorgeous

If you use makeup, the products you choose should, like your skin care, be all natural. Dr. Hauschka and Jane Iredale make natural cosmetics from skin-friendly, beautifully colored mineral powders. The products are made in a base of vitamin E and olive oil and actually contain minerals such as zinc, which provides a natural sunscreen.

Don't Forget the "Care" in Your Skin Care

No matter what products you choose, caring for your skin and keeping the effects of aging at bay requires a gentle approach. Consider these suggestions to make the most of your natural skin-care regimen.

- Wash your face with warm, not hot, water, which may damage your skin and accelerate aging.
- Apply your body moisturizer and facial moisturizer immediately after getting out of the shower, when your skin is still damp. In the winter or after shaving, I sometimes follow up my moisturizer with a natural oil to seal in the moisture. The same approach can be used on your face at night after applying your night cream. Evening primrose oil and natural vitamin E can be very soothing and moisturizing without blocking your pores.
- If facial cleanser is part of your routine, use it only at night. In the morning simply wash with water to avoid stripping your skin of its natural moisture.
- I recommend exfoliating twice a week with a product that contains fruit acids or vitamin A. Do not overexfoliate; it can harm your skin and upset your natural cycle of skin-cell regeneration.
- Use a hyaluronic acid serum on your skin after cleansing morning and night to maintain your skin's moisture and boost collagen production. Hyaluronic acid is a smaller building block of collagen that's more readily absorbed into the skin.
- Before applying your moisturizer, use a vitamin C serum once or twice daily to maintain the collagen production in your skin and to prevent free-radical stress.
- Warm your moisturizer before applying by rubbing it between your fingertips. Apply with short strokes or tap it on lightly. Don't stretch, pull, or rub your skin.

Well, it seems the old adage is true: Beauty really does come from within, especially when it comes to your skin. If you want to look (and feel) your best, inside and out, consistently follow these steps: Eat a nutritious diet complete with healthy fats, adequate protein, and low sugar; take your supplements; hydrate; sleep; maintain a healthy digestive system; and manage stress. Without these essential steps, the appearance and even the structure of your skin will suffer, even if you use the very best products available. Here's looking at you!

CHAPTER 17

YOU'RE ALMOST THERE!
A REFRESHER TO KEEP YOU GOING

Do more than exist, live.
Do more than touch, feel.
Do more than look, observe.
Do more than read, absorb.
Do more than hear, listen.
Do more than listen, understand.
Do more than think, ponder.
Do more than talk, say something.

JOHN H. RHOADES

By now I hope you are well on your way to reaching your weight-loss and wellness goals. More important, I hope you are motivated to maintain them. My wish is that this book has provided you with a practical and clear way to improve your health and well-being, not just for a few months, but for a lifetime.

Above all, I hope this plan has taught you to pay attention to early-warning symptoms and to recognize that your health is not defined solely by the number on the bathroom scale. I want you to look good and feel great about every aspect of your life, because you deserve to be happy and well. Take charge of your health and visit your doctor annually for complete blood work. Know your risk factors and continue to track them every year. My mom, who is now living with liver cancer, regrets that she did not take this one simple step.

This chapter gives you a quick, three-section refresher of the Hormone Diet plan. I will leave you with an outline of the perfect hormonally balanced day, a reminder to complete your 6-week check-in, and, lastly, a few final tips to keep you going if your fat loss has stalled.

Refresher #1: Your Hormonally Balanced Day

Reading about hormone-balancing habits is one thing. Making sure they are part of your everyday life is another. Here's an overview of what your hormonally balanced day should look like. Do your best to stick to this regimen 6 days a week. On your cheat day, eat and do whatever you wish—just remember to stay away from the hormone-disrupting foods that are to be avoided 100 percent of the time. Hey, you're even off the hook for shunning sugar on your cheat day, since you only need to avoid it 80 percent of the time!

Note that the specific hormonal benefits of each activity and task are identified in parentheses.

Between 6 and 8 a.m.

Wake up without a loud alarm clock (↓ cortisol). Open your blinds/curtains right away (↑ serotonin, ↓ melatonin, ↑ energy) to set your body clock on "awake."

Take your green-food drink and your probiotics; fit in your workout if you can. Always have breakfast *before* your strength-training workouts. If you aren't working out now, try to head outside for at least 15 minutes of natural sunlight—eat your breakfast outside, walk the dog, etc. (↑ serotonin, ↑ testosterone in men, ↑ fertility/ovulation in women).

Within an hour of waking, eat a breakfast that contains protein, carbohydrates, and fats, preferably a smoothie that includes all three macronutrients (all your meals should illicit this hormonal response: ↑ leptin, ↑ glucagon, ↑ serotonin, ↑ PYY, ↑ CCK, ↓ cortisol, ↓ ghrelin, ↓ neuropeptide Y). Enjoy your cup of organic coffee, if you wish (↑ dopamine, ↑ adrenaline). Take your Clear Essentials—Morning Pack or your multivitamin, vitamin D₃, and omega-3 fish oil (↓ inflammation; ↑ fat burning, energy, and metabolism).

Listen to music, books on tape, motivational material, or whatever you enjoy listening to on the way to work to reduce the stress of driving or commuting. Breathe (↓ cortisol, ↑ serotonin).

9 a.m.
At work, try as much as possible to minimize your exposure to harsh fluorescent lighting; consider earplugs or headphones if you work in a noisy or open office environment (↓ cortisol).

Fill your glass water bottle and grab a cup of green tea a few times throughout the day (↓ cortisol and NPY, ↑ thyroid hormone, ↑ metabolism and appetite control).

Between 11 a.m. and 1 p.m.
Enjoy a lunch that contains protein, good carbs, and healthy fats. Get outside for your dose of sunshine if you didn't get it in the morning, though morning is best (↑ serotonin, ↑ energy, better digestion throughout the day and night).

3 p.m. to After Work
Grab a snack that contains protein, good carbs, and healthy fats. Head for your workout if you haven't done so already (↓ cortisol, ↓ insulin, ↑ growth hormone, ↑ DHEA, ↑ testosterone, ↑ dopamine, and ↑ serotonin). Engage in competitive sports if you want an extra testosterone boost.

Within 45 minutes of finishing your workout, have a snack with protein and carbohydrates or have your dinner (see below). Minimal fat is needed at this time; the meal after your workout is the only one where you can get away with more carbohydrates (↑ growth hormone).

7 p.m.
Have a dinner that includes protein, good carbs, and healthy fats, but limit fat if it is after your workout. Take your Clear Essentials—Evening Pack or your multivitamin and calcium-magnesium.

8 to 10 p.m.

It's time to dim the lights in your house until bedtime (↑ serotonin, ↑ melatonin, ↓ cortisol, better digestion of carbs from your evening meal). If you watch TV or movies, remember that your selections will affect your hormones, so choose accordingly (the right choice should ↑ growth hormone, ↑ progesterone, ↓ cortisol).

If you enjoy alcohol, have it by 9 p.m. Any later and it could interfere with your sleep (because it ↑ insulin, ↑ cortisol, and ↓ melatonin). Consuming one glass right after dinner is best, if you have any at all. Remember, only four glasses per week for women; seven for guys.

Definitely shut down your computer and turn off your TV by 10 p.m., if you haven't done so already (otherwise ↑ dopamine can keep you too stimulated for sleep). Have a hot bath or shower at this time or earlier to improve your sleep, if necessary (↑ melatonin, ↓ cortisol). Showering at night, rather than in the morning, is helpful for your sleep and can sometimes give you more time in the morning.

Enjoy some cuddling, kissing, caressing, or sex (↓ cortisol, ↑ oxytocin, ↑ testosterone, ↑ DHEA, ↑ progesterone). Get to bed 10 to 20 minutes earlier if you want extra time to work your mental magic on your life's plan—visualize or meditate (↑ serotonin, ↑ DHEA, ↓ cortisol, ↓ adrenaline).

11 p.m.

Go to sleep by 11 in total darkness. Remember to create the perfect environment for slumber and follow the sleep rules to maximize your hormonal balance (↑ melatonin, ↑ leptin, ↑ growth hormone, ↑ serotonin, ↑ testosterone, ↓ cortisol, ↓ adrenaline, ↓ insulin).

Refresher #2: Your 6-Week Check-In

Go back to the "get prepped" instructions outlined for you in Chapter 6. Repeat your measurements and check your progress. Feel free to tell me about your results—just visit www.thehormonediet.com. I would absolutely love to hear from you.

From this point on, you should incorporate the following components of the Hormone Diet plan into your life as best you can. Hopefully they'll become regular habits you look forward to using.

- Maintain balance with an anti-inflammatory detox at least twice a year
- Recuperate and rejuvenate with hormone-balancing sleep
- Keep stress in check with meditation, visualization, massage, goal setting, and more
- Eat for hormonal balance and healthy weight maintenance
- Take your basic supplements for hormonal balance and good health
- Exercise and enjoy regular sex
- Look your best with all-natural skin care

Beyond these basic steps, you can continue progressing and modifying your wellness plan by tweaking your supplements to meet your changing needs, hormonal imbalances, or special health concerns. For instance, it's probably been a few weeks since you have looked at the Hormonal Health Profile results you recorded in your Treatment Pyramid. You might want to revisit them if you had more than one imbalance or if you are still experiencing symptoms. Go back to Chapter 13 and look into your next solution.

Most people will have lost 12 to 25 pounds and several inches by this point. Favorable changes will almost always occur in your body fat percentage, too. However, on the off chance that you are not happy with your progress, I encourage you to revisit the signs and symptoms of the fat-packing hormonal imbalances. If you have followed all three steps to a T and you still do not see the results you had hoped for, one of these hormone-hampering conditions or even a medication you are taking could be interfering with your results.

A recap of the fat-packing conditions (and their associated questions in the Hormonal Health Profile):

1. Insulin resistance discussed in Chapter 3 (Hormonal Imbalance 1)
2. Inflammation discussed in Chapter 1
3. Estrogen dominance explained in Chapter 3 (Hormonal Imbalance 7 and Hormonal Imbalance in men 11)
4. Stress discussed in Chapter 3 (Hormonal Imbalance 5)
5. Hypothyroidism covered in Chapter 4 (Hormonal Imbalance 13)
6. Menopause presented in Chapter 4 (Hormonal Imbalance 8, Hormonal Imbalance 9, and/or Hormonal Imbalance 11)
7. Andropause presented in Chapter 4 (Hormonal Imbalance 11)
8. Depression/anxiety discussed in Chapter 4 (Hormonal Imbalance 3)

If you suspect you are experiencing any one of these imbalances, visit your doctor to request the tests outlined in Appendix A. Specific supplements for these conditions (see Chapter 13) will also be helpful.

Refresher #3: Tips for a Metabolic Shake-Up

By now you have been following your Hormone Diet plan for a little over a month and a half. You've actually passed the daunting 21-day mark, the amount of time "they" say is required for your brain to turn a new task or approach into a habit. Now is a good time to take stock and assess your progress. How are you doing? Are you feeling good? Are you happy? Or are you feeling stuck?

Sometimes by week 5 or 6, weight loss may stall. If so, you've probably hit a weight-loss plateau. During such a plateau, weight reduction slows down or stops completely, reflecting the body's natural need to maintain constant equilibrium.

When we change our diet, cut our calories and begin a fitness plan, we typically alter our energy expenditure balance by taking in fewer calories than we burn. At the beginning, this imbalance is beneficial for fat loss, as the body taps into fat stores for fuel. But because our body prefers balance, it gradually adjusts by burning fewer calories in order to protect its reserves. This point is usually when our eating and exercise efforts stop producing the results we are looking for. If you follow my suggestion to wait until the fourth week of your new lifestyle to begin your exercise plan, however, a plateau will be unlikely because you'll enjoy a metabolic boost just at the right time.

Nonetheless, a weight-loss plateau may occur for these reasons:

1. Your body simply needs a "rest" period to adapt to calorie reduction.
2. Your current calorie intake may be in balance with your calorie expenditure.
3. You have reduced your calorie intake too much. Excess calorie cutting prompts your body to respond by slowing your metabolism to conserve calories. Note that you are also at risk of losing metabolically active muscle with excessive caloric restriction.
4. During weight loss, water is generated in the body as a normal part of fat metabolism. This process can lead to water-related weight gain.
5. A hormonal imbalance is interfering with your body's ability to burn fat.
6. For women, fluctuations of a few pounds may also be related to the menstrual cycle or water retention.

What Can You Do to Break Through?

In order to get past the plateau, the best approach is a multifaceted one. The two most important steps are altering your eating habits and changing your exercise program in ways that challenge your body and shake things up. You must also evaluate your lifestyle (honestly) and any negative symptoms you may be experiencing to determine whether one of your fat-burning foes is causing interference. Here are a few ideas to help you power past a plateau.

TAKE L-TYROSINE TO BOOST YOUR DOPAMINE. I spoke of the effects of dopamine on weight loss in Chapter 4. The trouble is, as you lose weight, this fat-loss friend tends to take a dip. It's just one of the ways your body works against you by attempting to maintain the status quo. But you can wake up your metabolism by supplementing with 1,000 mg of L-tyrosine each morning on an empty stomach. Since L-tyrosine increases the production of both dopamine and thyroid hormone, it could give you just the boost you need to push past your plateau.

MIX UP YOUR WORKOUT. Fire up your metabolism (and calorie expenditure) by increasing your activity level. This simple step can "reboot" your metabolism and restart your weight loss. For example, if you usually exercise for 20 minutes each day, try 25 to 30 minutes daily. If you're already exercising for a sufficient length of time, increase the intensity. Do 15 to 20 minutes of interval training instead of 30 minutes at a slower pace. Varying your workout routine can also help. Longer workouts are not always the answer, but 150 minutes per week does seem to be the magic number that sparks weight loss, according to studies.

TRY CARDIO FIRST THING IN THE MORNING ON AN EMPTY STOMACH. If you can manage it, try doing a 30-minute cardio workout (no longer!) first thing in the morning before breakfast. Why? In some cases, this technique may be just the trick your body needs to kickstart your metabolism.

PUMP SOME IRON. Remember, muscle is metabolically active tissue. Muscle mass determines our basal metabolic rate (i.e., the number of calories we burn daily while at rest). The more muscle we have, the more fat we can potentially burn, even while sitting around or sleeping. If your fat loss continues to stall, boost the intensity of your strength-training routine by increasing the amount of weight you lift. A personal trainer may be an excellent investment at this point, even for just a few sessions to get you back in gear and to make sure you are exercising at the right intensity.

DON'T BE AFRAID TO INTENSIFY YOUR WORKOUT (IF YOU ARE HEALTHY). Studies show that you need 150 to 200 minutes of exercise per week for weight loss. For an extra fat-burning boost, pump up the intensity of your cardio sessions with intervals, rather than making your workouts longer.

BE SURE TO REST AND RECUPERATE. Recovery is an essential part of your exercise program. Proper rest allows your muscle fibers to grow and prevents the elevation of cortisol and other stress hormones that can happen when we overtrain. Track your resting heart rate immediately after you wake up for a week or two. An increase from one week to the next could be a sign of overtraining. Remember, excess cortisol tears down the muscle tissue you've worked so hard to gain. Losing muscle will ultimately cause your metabolism to slow down.

MAKE SURE YOU ARE EATING THE RIGHT AMOUNTS AT THE RIGHT TIMES. Some of the biggest weight-loss mistakes are simply not eating enough calories, going too long without eating, or eating meals at irregular times. Skipping breakfast is the worst habit of all! Plenty of research shows that people who skip meals or slash too many calories are *more* obese and have an increased risk of type 2 diabetes and heart disease. If you're following the Hormone Diet eating plan, you should not be going too long without food. The program is designed to help you maintain stable blood sugar and create the perfect hormonal balance for fat loss. Eating the right foods every 4 to 5 hours reassures your body that food is plentiful. It also facilitates calorie burning and prevents metabolic decline.

KEEP A FOOD DIARY. If you feel your nutrition is off track but can't figure out where you're going wrong, try keeping a food journal. You may start to recognize dietary saboteurs, which can help you avoid them and get back on track. Have a professional nutritionist or naturopathic doctor assess your diet, if necessary.

IF YOU HAVE STUBBORN ABDOMINAL FAT, YOU MAY BE INSULIN RESISTANT. Your score from Hormonal Imbalance 1 in the Hormonal Health Profile and/or the results of your blood test from your Best Body Assessment will give you an indication of your insulin sensitivity. If you are insulin resistant, high insulin levels and excess weight will cause an accumulation of abdominal fat and will also impede further weight loss. A Glyci-Med diet is essential to remedy this condition, while supplements and strength training are important for improving insulin sensitivity. Supplement choices include CLA, chromium, alpha-lipoic acid, zinc, and magnesium, but you can review your complete list of options in Chapter 13. Note that this imbalance will take months to improve—trust the three steps and stick with the program!

JOIN A GROUP, GET A WORKOUT BUDDY, OR ASK FOR HELP. Studies show that people who have a support system tend to lose weight and keep it off, as they can share their diet ups and downs with others. Social support from a partner, friend, Web site, trainer, or workout partner can provide essential help and encouragement.

MAKE SURE THAT YOUR WEIGHT-LOSS EXPECTATIONS ARE REALISTIC. Safe weight loss is 1 to 2.2 pounds of fat per week. During the first few weeks of a weight-loss program, more weight may be lost, although most of it is water. After losing this initial weight, people tend to lose an average of 1 pound a week, which is still considered good progress (even a few pounds a month is good). Remember, 1 pound of body fat is equivalent to 3,500 calories, so losing 1 pound per week can mean cutting out 500 calories per day.

GET ORGANIZED. Make time for a good breakfast and travel with your own healthy snacks. Clear your cupboards of problem foods—you can't eat what's not there. Shop with the Hormone Diet eating plan in mind, and be sure you have plenty of healthy choices on hand to make meal and snack prep easy and convenient.

DRINK PLENTY OF WATER. As fat cells begin to shrink, they release toxins that need to be removed from your system by your liver, kidneys, and digestive tract. Studies show that if you don't take in enough water to support these processes, the toxins may interact with your hormones and cause increased fat storage or an inability to burn fat. Water can also help make you feel full and regulate your appetite, as many of us mistake thirst for hunger. To calculate how much water you need, multiply your body weight in pounds by 0.55. Divide the result by 8 to determine the number of cups you need to drink each day.

BE PATIENT AND STAY POSITIVE! A weight-loss plateau may take a few weeks to overcome, but you will get there. Stay focused on your goal and remember all the wonderful health benefits you are already enjoying thanks to the changes you have made to your lifestyle.

BEWARE OF COMMON DIET DEBACLES
- **Fat-free yogurt with added fruit.** Fat-free yogurt typically has 27 g carbs, 4 g protein, and no fat. Too many carbs! Plain yogurt is a much better bet, with 6 g protein, 6 g carbs, and a few grams of fat. Purchase plain yogurt and add your own fruit. If you really must have sweetened or flavored yogurt,

mix it half and half with an unsweetened, plain one to decrease the amount of sugar per serving.

- **Packaged nuts (almonds, peanuts, etc.).** Most of these products contain hydrogenated oils or vegetable oils—no-no foods you need to avoid at all times. Instead, purchase raw nuts from a health food or bulk store.

- **So-called healthy breakfast cereals.** Take Smart Start cereal from Kellogg's, for example. It does offer more vitamins and minerals than other cereals, but it also contains a ton of sugar. The only breakfast cereal I recommend is Kashi GOLEAN or slow-cooked oatmeal. If you choose either of these options, you'll still need to add more protein to your breakfast (e.g., 2 or 3 egg whites) to remain in glycemic balance.

- **Too much fruit.** Fruits contain natural sugars and, just like anything else, too much is rarely a good thing. Aim for a maximum of three servings of fruit per day. At least one of these daily servings should be berries. Other choices include apples, pears, peaches, cherries, or grapefruit. Avoid raisins, dates, grapes, mangos, and melons (though watermelon is okay), and never eat your fruit on its own. Always have it with a food that contains fat and protein, such as a few nuts, some yogurt, or a piece of cheese.

- **Fizzy waters (Perrier, etc).** Although these contain few or no calories, they are very high in sodium, which can cause water retention and bloating. Choose sodium-free options or, better yet, drink pure water with lemon instead.

- **Coffee, lattes, teas, and more and more coffee.** Too much caffeine interferes with fat metabolism. It influences blood sugar and insulin balance and can contribute to an increase in abdominal fat. Although a little caffeine before a workout has been proven beneficial for weight loss, high amounts consumed throughout the day can do you more harm than good. Instead, choose green tea, limit coffee to one a day, and always avoid sweet drinks such as caramel or vanilla lattes that are high in sugar and calories.

STEP UP YOUR STRESS-BUSTING STRATEGY, ESPECIALLY IF YOU HAVE STUBBORN AB FAT. Elevated cortisol inhibits thyroid function. As a result, cortisol is indirectly responsible for lagging metabolism, more water retention, and abdominal fat gain. Try meditation, visualization, or massage to help keep your cortisol in check. If you are under a lot of stress, consider Relora or one of the other supplements that lower stress, improve sleep, and reduce stress-related eating. Take another look at Chapter 13, Hormonal Imbalance 5, for a complete list of options.

GET A BLOOD TEST TO CHECK YOUR THYROID. Remember, your thyroid hormones govern your metabolism. If yours is sagging, TSH, free T3, and free T4 should be tested. Optimally, your TSH should be less than 2.0, not the previously accepted normal reading of 4.7. Note that thyroid problems occur more often in menopause and after pregnancy. You can revisit Chapter 13 for supplements to support a low thyroid hormone (Hormonal Imbalance 13) or talk to your doctor if further medical treatment is called for.

The key to your overall success is consistency. If you experience a setback, don't lose heart. Stay the course. Be kind to yourself, and remember, even if your weight has not budged recently, the healthy lifestyle changes you have made will benefit your body, mind, and soul for life.

If you are a doctor who would like to become certified in the Hormone Diet approach for your patients, or if you would like to become one of our patients, please visit www.thehormonediet.com.

UNDERSTANDING BLOOD TESTS

Visit your doctor at least once per year. *Always request a copy of your blood test results, and keep them in a folder.* Remember, significant changes can occur in your blood work from one year to the next without the appearance of obvious physical signs.

Tests for General Health, Immunity, and Wellness

- LIVER FUNCTION TESTS: AST, ALT, AND BILIRUBIN. These tests are used to identify liver disease and function. Your liver is vital for fat loss and wellness, as you've already discovered. Poor or "sluggish" liver function can interfere with fat loss, cause hormonal imbalances, and increase your risk of disease. The laboratory reference range covers normal values, but lower is better. Liver-cleansing herbs like those in Clear Detox—Hormonal Health, recommended as part of your detox, are essential if your liver enzymes are abnormally elevated. I recommend taking the liver-supportive herbs for at least 1 to 3 months and then retesting your enzymes to see if levels have improved.
- ZINC: Zinc is a cofactor involved in at least 70 different enzymatic reactions in the body. As an essential mineral involved in healthy immunity, blood sugar balance, thyroid function, collagen production, bone density, tissue healing and repair, antioxidant protection, prostate function, and growth hormone

and testosterone production, zinc is vital to good health. Zinc depletion is common with use of the birth control pill, corticosteroids, and diuretics. Its absorption is greatly compromised when your stomach acid (HCl) levels are low. Zinc deficiency causes decreased senses of taste and smell, poor wound healing, white spots in the fingernails, night blindness, low sperm count, hair loss, behavior or sleep problems, mental sluggishness, impaired immune function, and dermatitis. Optimally, your levels should be toward the high end of the laboratory reference range. You may add a supplement of zinc citrate if your zinc is low. Take it with food to avoid nausea.

- COPPER: Excess vitamin C and zinc interfere with copper availability. A deficiency of copper may result in anemia (indistinguishable from iron deficiency); impaired formation of collagen, elastin, and connective tissue proteins; osteoporosis; and arterial wall defects. It makes sense then if you have cardiovascular disease to monitor your copper levels closely. Although deficiencies are harmful, especially for cardiovascular health, it's more common to have excess copper due to medication use, supplements, or from copper leaching into drinking water from pipes. Symptoms of copper toxicity include depression, acne, and hair loss. If you find your copper is low, your multivitamin should provide all that you need. If your copper is too high, take zinc daily to encourage its depletion.

Tests for Glycemic Control, Fat Loss, Diabetes, and Heart Disease Risk

- FASTING GLUCOSE AND INSULIN. Glucose and insulin are implicated in many age-related diseases, such as type 2 diabetes, hypoglycemia, hypertension, heart disease, insulin resistance, and stroke. These tests require a fasting blood level, therefore a 10- to 12-hour fast is required before the collection of a blood sample. The optimal value for fasting blood glucose is less than 86 mg/dL. A value of less than 7 mU/mL is optimal for fasting insulin. Insulin resistance is associated with a glucose reading greater than 100 mg/dL and fasting insulin greater than 10 mU/mL. If your test is abnormal, use the recommendations in Chapter 13 for insulin imbalance in addition to the three steps.

- 2-HOUR POSTPRANDIAL GLUCOSE AND INSULIN. Simply have these two tests repeated 2 hours after you have eaten a very large breakfast (toast, orange juice, coffee, pancakes, syrup). The first sign of insulin resistance is elevated insulin *after* a meal *followed by high fasting insulin.* Insulin tends to be abnormal *long before* blood sugars start to rise typical of the diabetic state. Insulin resistance may be apparent with 2-hour glucose readings of more than 100 mg/dL and insulin levels of more than 60 mU/mL. If your test is abnormal, use the recommendations in Chapter 13 for insulin imbalance in addition to the three steps.

- FASTING GLUCOSE TO INSULIN RATIO. A value of fasting glucose divided by fasting insulin (using readings in US units) of less than 4.5 may indicate insulin resistance in nondiabetic individuals.

- FASTING TRIGLYCERIDES. Triglycerides are a particular type of fat present in your bloodstream that arises from fats or from carbohydrates taken in. Calories you ingest but that are not used immediately by tissues are converted to triglycerides and transported to your fat cells to be stored. Then, your hormones regulate the release of triglycerides from fat stores to help meet your body's needs for energy between meals. Levels greater than 100 mg/dL are associated with insulin resistance. If your test is abnormal, use the recommendations in Chapter 13 for insulin imbalance in addition to the three steps.

- FASTING CHOLESTEROL (TOTAL, HDL, AND LDL). An optimal HDL should be above 60 mg/dL. LDL should be between 80 and 100 mg/dL to be safe, and total cholesterol should be less than 180 to 200 mg/dL. If your cholesterol is too high, the three steps will help to lower your numbers. You might also want to look into supplementing with policosanols, PGX, or red yeast extract as natural alternatives to statins.
- URIC ACID. Normal levels are less than 0.35 mmol/L or 5.0 mg/dL. High levels of uric acid cause gout and are linked to increased heart disease risk; they're also a sign of insulin resistance. If your uric acid is imbalanced, you should consider the additional treatment options for inflammation and insulin imbalance in Chapter 13. Supplements of cherry juice and quercitin may also help to reduce uric acid.
- HBA1C LEVELS. This is an indicator of blood sugar control over the previous 120 days. Ideal levels are less than 4.6. If the number is higher, it indicates your blood sugar control over the previous months has been less than optimal. If your test is abnormal, use the recommendations in Chapter 13 for insulin imbalance.
- FASTING HOMOCYSTEINE (OPTIMAL VALUE: LESS THAN 6.3). Vitamin B_{12} (optimal value: more than 600) and folic acid (optimal value: more than 1,000) are useful tests to do along with this since they are involved in the process of metabolism necessary to reduce homocysteine levels, along with vitamin B_6 and a compound called trimethylglycine. Homocysteine is a protein that, if elevated in the blood, is a proven independent risk factor for heart disease, osteoporosis, Alzheimer's disease, and stroke. Homocysteine has been found to increase with insulin resistance and inflammation. Vitamin B_{12}, found only in animal-source foods, is necessary for the formation and regeneration of red blood cells. It also promotes growth, increases energy, improves sleep and cognition, and helps

maintain a healthy nervous system. Folic acid helps protect against chromosomal (genetic) damage and birth defects. It is needed for the utilization of sugar and amino acids, prevents some types of cancer, promotes healthier skin, and helps protect against intestinal parasites and food poisoning. Take a complex of vitamin B_6, vitamin B_{12}, and folic acid daily for at least 3 months before retesting your levels if your homocysteine is too high.

- HIGHLY SENSITIVE C-REACTIVE PROTEIN. Hs-CRP is a marker of inflammation and a risk factor for arterial disease. Levels tend to increase as body fat increases and with insulin resistance. An optimal value is less than 0.8 mg/L, although the Life Extension Foundation recommends less than 0.55 mg/L for men and less than 1.5 mg/L for women. This test is also important for breast cancer survivors and should be undertaken along with fasting and 2-hour postcarbohydrate challenge (PC) insulin level tests. High CRP or insulin is associated with increased risk of recurrence. If your hs-CRP test is abnormal, use the recommendations in Chapter 13 for inflammation.

- FERRITIN. Abnormally high levels of the storage form of iron (called ferritin) can increase the risk of heart disease in both men and women. It also appears to increase inflammation. Optimal levels should be close to 70 mcg/L in women and 100 mcg/L in men. Low levels of iron are associated with fatigue, hypothyroidism, decreased athletic performance, ADD/ADHD, restless leg syndrome, and hair loss. If your ferritin is too high, you should speak to your doctor about the possibility of donating blood; if too low, use a supplement of iron citrate with 1,000 mg of vitamin C. The citrate form of iron will not cause constipation and the vitamin C aids iron absorption.

- RBC MAGNESIUM. Magnesium is involved in over 300

enzymatic reactions in the body. Therefore, a deficiency of magnesium can result in the physical symptom of fatigue as bodily functions slow on a cellular level. Magnesium controls blood pressure and blood sugar balance. Optimal levels can assist in the prevention of muscle cramps or spasms, headaches and migraines, type 2 diabetes, and heart disease. Your multivitamin and your calcium-magnesium combination should replenish your magnesium levels if your stores are low.

Hormonal Assessments

Hormones are best tested in the morning. Menstruating women should go on day 3 of their cycle to look at estrogen and ovarian reserve and days 20 to 22 of their cycle to investigate progesterone (day 1 = first day of bleeding). Men and menopausal women can test on any day. Note that you can also assess your hormones via saliva or 24-hour urinary hormone analysis. This is argued to be the more accurate way to measure hormones because it looks at the free component of hormones rather than those bound to carrier proteins, as blood tests do. It is the free component of hormones that is biologically active. I use urine, saliva, and blood testing in clinical practice, however, especially when I want to assess the three types of estrogen or when someone is using BHRT, since only looking at blood values could result in overdosing.

- FOLLICLE-STIMULATING HORMONE (FSH) AND LUTEINIZING HORMONE (LH). These hormones are released from the pituitary gland and stimulate the ovaries and testes. High levels are found in menopause, infertility, amenorrhea, premature ovarian failure, or testicular failure. Low levels indicate pituitary dysfunction. If your FSH or LH is elevated you will need to replenish estrogen, progesterone, and/or testosterone. An excess of LH relative to FSH is common with polycystic ovarian syndrome (PCOS).

- DHEA-S. This is a precursor hormone to estrogen and testosterone. An adrenal hormone, it tends to naturally decrease as we age, is protective against the harmful effects of the stress hormone cortisol, is cardio-protective, and is crucial for a healthy body composition. Most antiaging programs recommend the use of DHEA; however, it should not be taken unless a true deficiency has been diagnosed with blood work, and follow-up testing should be completed to ensure an excess is not present. In some cases of PCOS it may be abnormally high, contributing to hair loss and male pattern baldness. Optimal levels should be 300 to 400 mcg/dL for men and 225 to 350 mcg/dL for women.
- CORTISOL. High levels (more than 15 mcg/dL) of cortisol are detrimental to almost every tissue and organ in the body. It causes destruction of muscle; increases calcium loss from bone; accelerates the process of aging; and is linked to memory loss, anxiety, depression, and low libido along with an increase in the deposition of fat around the abdomen. Low levels (less than 9 mcg/dL) indicate adrenal gland burnout. If your test is abnormal, use the recommendations in Chapter 13 for cortisol imbalance.
- CALCULATE THE DHEA/CORTISOL RATIO. The value of this ratio should optimally fall between 15 and 25 (i.e., the value of DHEA divided by cortisol). If your test is abnormal, use the recommendations in Chapter 13 for cortisol imbalance and DHEA.
- FREE AND TOTAL TESTOSTERONE. Many men with insulin resistance, obesity, or sleep apnea have low levels of testosterone, which is known to increase the risk of heart disease. This also influences erectile function, libido, sense of well-being, mood, and motivation. Maintaining testosterone levels is crucial if you want to build muscle and lose fat. Optimal free testosterone levels for men should be in the range of 7.2 to 24 mcg/dL; total testosterone should be 241 to 827 mcg/dL. In women, low

testosterone is damaging to bone density, a healthy libido, and aspects of memory (especially task-oriented memory). If testosterone is too high (often associated with PCOS or insulin resistance), hair loss, acne, increased risk of breast cancer, or infertility may occur. If your test is abnormal, use the recommendations in Chapter 13 for low or high testosterone.

• ESTRADIOL AND ESTRONE. Estrogen values will vary in women depending on their age and point in their menstrual cycle. The optimal value for estrogen is 180 to 200 pg/mL for premenopausal women and 60 to 120 pg/mL for women in their late 40s and older. Men's estradiol should be less than 40 pg/mL. In both sexes, high estrogen encourages fat storage. Elevated levels of estrogen in men are typically found in cases of increased abdominal obesity because the fat cells here encourage the conversion of testosterone to estrogen. High levels of estrogen and low levels of testosterone set the stage for sexual dysfunction and prostate conditions and promote weight gain in men. In women, excess estrogen is associated with PMS, weight gain around the hips, uterine fibroids and other gynecological conditions, and an increase in the risk of certain types of cancers. Before menopause, estrogen is naturally highest in the first half of the menstrual cycle; after menopause, levels are normally consistent and much lower. As estrogen levels decline, more abdominal weight gain can arise as estrogen does affect insulin sensitivity. Lower levels of estrogen are also associated with a decrease in serotonin. Recall from Chapter 3 that low estrogen can cause all of these symptoms: hot flashes, night sweats, urinary urgency and frequency, insomnia, depression, failing memory (especially when attempting to think of a word or name), hair texture and skin elasticity changes, a thickening waistline, vaginal dryness, and a missing "mojo." Low estrogen also increases the risk of heart disease, diabetes,

Alzheimer's disease, and osteoporosis. Evidently, estrogen is not all bad, but must be present in balance—not too high or too low. If your test is abnormal, use the recommendations in Chapter 13 for low or high estrogen.

- PROGESTERONE. Progesterone is naturally highest in the second half of the menstrual cycle and normal values can range widely. Progesterone is protective against anxiety, PMS, fibrocystic breast disease, and water retention. It encourages fat burning and is crucial for fertility. Progesterone is also protective of the prostate gland in men and may help to restore low DHEA levels. Decreased levels are associated with infertility, amenorrhea (lack of menstruation), fetal death, and toxemia in pregnancy. If your test is abnormal, use the recommendations in Chapter 13 for low or high progesterone.

- TSH, FREE T3, FREE T4, AND THYROID ANTIBODIES. These four tests are required to accurately assess the function of the thyroid gland, our master gland of metabolism. TSH should be less than 2.0 to be optimal, not the currently accepted 4.7 reported by most labs. T3 and T4 should be in the middle of your lab's reference range. Thyroid antithyroglobulin antibodies should be negative. Quite often I find elevated antibodies prior to abnormalities in TSH, T3, or T4, which indicates this may sometimes be the first step in the development of thyroid disease. Currently, it's estimated that 1 in 13 people have hypothyroidism, with the majority of cases being missed because of improper testing or interpretation of the test results. There is an increase in the risk of obesity, heart disease, and blood sugar abnormalities in hypothyroid cases. Hypothyroid patients also often have high levels of homocysteine and cholesterol. Also, if you are attempting to conceive, thyroid antibody abnormalities must be corrected to improve your chances of conception. If your test is abnormal, use the recommendations in Chapter 13 for low thyroid.

- REVERSE T3. This is a type of thyroid hormone the body will produce when under stress or when there is a deficiency of selenium. It is chemically similar to T3 (the active form of thyroid hormone) but is inactive and therefore does not have the metabolic benefits of T3. If your test is abnormal, use the recommendations in Chapter 13 for cortisol imbalance and low thyroid hormone activity and take a 200 mcg supplement of selenium daily.

- 25-HYDROXYVITAMIN D$_3$. Vitamin D has proven immune-enhancing, cancer-protective, bone-building, and insulin-regulating benefits. It is also important during pregnancy. Your levels should be over 125. If your vitamin D is low, add a 1,000 IU supplement of vitamin D$_3$ per day to your regime, in addition to your multivitamin and calcium-magnesium supplement. You will receive more than this amount of vitamin D$_3$ from the Clear Essentials—Morning and Evening packs.

- PROLACTIN. Elevated prolactin is associated with abnormal lactation, infertility, and amenorrhea. Prolactin can also be elevated in hypothyroidism when TSH is high. In men, the normal range is 2.17 to 17.7 ng/mL, and in women it is 2.8 to 29.2 ng/mL. If your prolactin is abnormally elevated, you may use the herb chasteberry (*Vitex agnus cactus*) to lower it.

- SHBG. Sex hormone-binding globulin binds with testosterone and makes it less bioavailable. SHBG increases with aging, liver disease, insulin resistance, and low-protein diets. Decreased levels will be found in hirsutism, obese postmenopausal women, and women with diffuse hair loss. If your test is abnormal, use the recommendations in Chapter 13 for insulin imbalance.

- IGF-1. This is a marker of human growth hormone (HGH) status. Because it remains constant in the blood longer than HGH (which tends to fluctuate in response to various stimuli), it is a more accurate indicator of HGH deficiency, and is also more precise for monitoring HGH therapy than is testing HGH directly. An optimal IGF-1 value will range between 200 and 300 ng/mL. Growth hormone is essential for maintaining healthy bones, skin, and hair, as well as strong, lean muscle mass. It tends to naturally decrease as we age; however, conditions such as sleep deprivation, diabetes, hypothyroidism, some cases of osteoporosis, anorexia, and insulin resistance can cause levels to decline more rapidly. If your test is abnormal, use the recommendations in Chapter 13 for low growth hormone.

Optional Advanced Functional Medicine Testing

The following tests are very useful if you can afford them. You may visit www.thehormonediet.com to request kits for the tests and complete many of them at home. Otherwise, I recommend visiting a naturopathic or integrated medical practitioner in your area.

From Metametrix Clinical Laboratory (www.metametrix.com)

URINARY ESTROGEN METABOLITE TESTING

To assess your risk of developing estrogen-sensitive cancers or recurrence of these types of cancer, I highly recommend the Estronex 2/16 test from Metametrix Clinical Laboratory. It measures the ratio of two critical estrogen metabolites from a single urine specimen. One metabolite, 2-hydroxyestrone (2-OHE1), tends to inhibit cancer growth. Another, 16-alpha-hydroxyestrone (16-A-OHE1), actually encourages tumor development. Estronex 2/16 ratios less than 2.0 indicate an increased long-term risk of breast, cervical, and other estrogen-sensitive cancers. It is your biochemical individuality and lifestyle habits that determine which of these metabolites predominates. Luckily, abnormal test results are modifiable with the three-step approach. If your test is abnormal, use the recommendations in Chapter 13 for high estrogen.

IGG ANTIBODY FOOD ALLERGY TESTING

We know that about 60 percent of the population suffers from unsuspected food reactions that can cause or complicate health problems.

Less common but widely recognized immediate food sensitivities, such as the reaction to peanuts or shellfish, are IgE-mediated responses. IgG antibodies are the most common type of immune-related food allergy. They are associated with "delayed" food reactions that can also worsen or contribute to many different health problems. Reactions are more difficult to notice since they can occur hours or even days after consumption of an offending food. Food antibody profiles clearly identify those foods that may be causing health problems. It can help to achieve positive outcomes sooner, especially when combined with the detox diet.

ORGANIC ACIDS TEST

From a single urine specimen, this test can assess the following:
- Fatty acid metabolism
- Neurotransmitter metabolism
- Carbohydrate metabolism
- Oxidative damage
- Energy production
- Detoxification status
- B-complex sufficiency
- Intestinal dysbiosis due to bacteria and yeast
- Methylation cofactors
- Inflammatory reactions

From Doctor's Data, Inc. (www.doctorsdata.com)

COMPREHENSIVE STOOL ANALYSIS

Comprehensive Digestive Stool Analysis uses advanced methods to evaluate digestion, absorption, pancreatic function, and inflammation, in addition to bacterial balance, yeast, and parasitic infection. This profile features exclusive new markers for assessing irritable bowel syndrome, inflammation, colorectal cancer risk, pancreatic insufficiency, and infection. If your results are abnormal, use the recommendations outlined in Chapter 8 on the anti-inflammatory detox, which can improve your symptoms by addressing the five keys to healthy digestion.

URINARY OR FECAL HEAVY METAL ANALYSIS

This test from Doctor's Data looks for the presence of abnormal amounts of metals in the urine or stool, including mercury, lead, cadmium, arsenic, and others. If you have had mercury fillings; flu shots; worked with metals, plastics or ceramics; smoked; or possibly been exposed to contaminated drinking water, invest in this test. Heavy metals influence the function of every cell in the body and greatly increase risks for hormonal imbalance, aging, heart disease, inflammation, and cognitive problems. Search out a qualified integrated medical practitioner to help you with the process of heavy metal detoxification if your results are abnormal. I recommend investigating EDTA suppositories from www.detoxamin.com.

From SpectraCell Laboratories (www.spectracell.com)

VITAMIN AND MINERAL LEVELS IN THE BLOOD CELLS

The FIA (Functional Intracellular Analysis) provides unique insights into the metabolic functions of a variety of vitamins, minerals, antioxidants, and other essential micronutrients, and identifies deficiencies that reflect each person's unique biochemical requirements. SpectraCell's FIA provides you with the next generation of micronutrient analyses based on requirements within your actual cells, rather than just in your bloodstream, for adequate nutritional support for optimal cell function. For example, a more accurate and clinically meaningful determination of folic acid status is gained from measuring its levels within the blood cells, rather than in the serum, which fluctuates daily depending on your intake of foods and nutrients.

The SpectraCell Laboratories report will itemize the supplements you will need to take for at least 6 months to replenish your deficiencies. At that point you should repeat the test.

The Fat-Packing Hormonal Imbalances: A Review of Diagnostic Tests

Should you wish to request further investigation by your doctor for one or more of the fat-packing hormonal imbalances and their complications, I have summarized the tests and the most common expected results to confirm a diagnosis.

EXCESS INSULIN/INSULIN RESISTANCE

Test	Result Indicating Presence of Insulin Resistance
Fasting glucose and insulin	Abnormally elevated glucose and/or insulin
2-hour PC glucose and insulin	Abnormally elevated fasting glucose and/or insulin
Fasting cholesterol panel (total, HDL, LDL)	Elevated total and LDL; low HDL
Triglycerides (TGs)	Often elevated
Uric acid	Often elevated
Homocysteine	Often elevated (> 7)
Hs-CRP	High (> 0.8)
Free and total testosterone (blood or saliva)	Elevated in women; low in men
SHBG	Often elevated
DHEA-S (blood or saliva)	Elevated in women; low in men
Estradiol (blood, saliva, or urine)	Elevated in men
Ferritin	Often elevated
Vitamin B_{12}	Low (< 600)
RBC magnesium	Often low
Folic acid	Often low (< 1,000)
Liver function tests: AST, ALT, GGT	One or more liver enzymes may be abnormally elevated
Zinc and copper	Copper tends to be high and zinc low in insulin-resistant patients.
25-hydroxyvitamin D_3	Often low
Fasting glucose and insulin	Normal or abnormally elevated fasting glucose and/or insulin (abnormal results are more likely in men with this condition)
HbA1c	Often elevated

EXCESS ESTROGEN/ESTROGEN DOMINANCE
(LOW TESTOSTERONE OR ANDROPAUSE IN MEN)

Test	Result Indicating Presence of Estrogen Dominance/Low Testosterone (Men)
2-hour PC glucose and insulin	Normal or abnormally elevated glucose and/or insulin (abnormal results are more likely in men with this condition)
Hs-CRP	High (> 0.8)
SHBG	Elevated
Estradiol (blood, saliva, or urine)	Elevated
Estrone (blood, saliva, or urine)	Elevated
Estriol (blood, saliva, or urine)	Possibly low
Progesterone (blood, saliva, or urine)	Possibly low
DHEA-S (blood or saliva)	Normal or low
Cortisol (blood or saliva)	Normal or elevated
Testosterone (blood, saliva, or urine)	Women: normal, low with stress, elevated with insulin resistance; Men: low
Specialized testing: urinary estrogen metabolite excretions From Metametrix Labs (the Estronex test)	Elevated levels of harmful estrogen metabolites in the urine
Zinc, copper, magnesium	Zinc low, copper high, magnesium low

EXCESS CORTISOL (STRESS)

Test	Result Indicating Presence of Excess Cortisol (Stress)
Fasting glucose and insulin	Normal or abnormally elevated glucose and/or insulin
2-hour PC glucose and insulin	Normal or abnormally elevated glucose and/or insulin
Estradiol (blood, saliva, or urine)	Normal or elevated
Estrone (blood, saliva, or urine)	Normal or elevated
Estriol (blood, saliva, or urine)	Normal or possibly low
Progesterone (blood, saliva, or urine)	Normal or likely low
DHEA-S (blood or saliva)	Normal or likely low
Cortisol (blood or saliva)	Normal or elevated—or suppressed in very late stages of burnout

Test	Result Indicating Presence of Excess Cortisol (Stress)
Testosterone (blood, saliva, or urine)	Women: normal, low with stress, elevated with insulin resistance; Men: low
Hs-CRP	High (> 0.8)
Specialized testing: salivary cortisol profile—4-point collection of cortisol and DHEA throughout the day	Imbalanced pattern or release; elevated cortisol and suppressed DHEA; low DHEA and cortisol in late stages of burnout

HYPOTHYROIDISM

Test	Result Indicating Presence of Hypothyroidism
Fasting glucose and insulin	Normal or abnormally elevated glucose and/or insulin
2-hour PC glucose and insulin	Normal or abnormally elevated glucose and/or insulin
Thyroid panel (TSH, free T3, free T4)	Elevated TSH (> 2) and low free T3 and free T4. One, two, or all of these abnormalities are common.
Reverse T3	Normal or abnormally elevated (when selenium deficiency or stress is a factor)
Thyroid antibodies	Elevated or normal
Homocysteine	Often elevated (> 7)
Cholesterol panel (total, HDL, LDL)	Total and LDL cholesterol are often elevated. HDL may be normal or low.
Ferritin	Often low (< 70)
Vitamin B12	Often low (< 600)
Folic acid	Often low (< 1,000)
Progesterone (blood, saliva, or urine)	Often low
Estradiol and estrone (blood, saliva, or urine)	May be elevated or normal in women; normal or elevated in men
Cortisol (blood or saliva)	Often high
DHEA-S (blood or saliva)	Often low
Prolactin	Often high
Zinc	Often low
Specialized testing: urinary heavy metal analysis (to rule out mercury toxicity as a cause of thyroid suppression)	Often mercury is elevated

LOW SEROTONIN

Test	Result Indicating Low Serotonin
Fasting glucose and insulin	Normal or abnormally elevated glucose and/or insulin
2-hour PC glucose and insulin	Normal or abnormally elevated glucose and/or insulin
Hs-CRP	Often high (> 0.8)
Cortisol (saliva or blood)	Often high (or low in the late stages of burnout)
DHEA (saliva or blood)	Often low
Free testosterone (blood, saliva, or urine)	Often low
Progesterone (blood, saliva, or urine)	Often low
Estradiol (blood, saliva, or urine)	Normal or low
Specialized testing: urinary neurotransmitter analysis from Neuroscience Laboratories	Deficient serotonin; dopamine and noradrenaline may also be imbalanced.

MENOPAUSE

Test	Result Indicating Menopause
Fasting glucose and insulin	Normal or abnormally elevated glucose and/or insulin
2-hour PC glucose and insulin	Normal or abnormally elevated glucose and/or insulin
Hs-CRP	High (> 0.8), especially if overweight
FSH and LH	Elevated
Estradiol (blood, saliva, or urine)	Low
Estrone (blood, saliva, or urine)	Normal, low, or elevated (if estrogen dominant from excess body weight, alcohol intake, or exposure to environmental xenoestrogens)
Estriol (blood, saliva, or urine)	Low
Progesterone (blood, saliva, or urine)	Low
DHEA-S (blood or saliva)	Often low
Cortisol (blood or saliva)	Normal or elevated—or suppressed in very late stages of burnout
Testosterone (blood or saliva)	Often low or may be elevated if insulin resistant

Test	Result Indicating Menopause
Fasting cholesterol panel (total, HDL, LDL)	Possible elevated total and LDL; low or normal HDL
Specialized testing: urinary neurotransmitter analysis from Neuroscience Laboratories	Often serotonin is low; dopamine and noradrenaline may also be imbalanced

INFLAMMATION

Test	Result Indicating the Presence of Inflammation
Fasting glucose and insulin	Abnormally elevated glucose and/or insulin
2-hour PC glucose and insulin	Abnormally elevated glucose and/or insulin
Highly sensitive C-RP	High (> 0.8)
Homocysteine	High (> 7)
Vitamin B_{12} and folic acid	Both often low
Cholesterol panel (total, HDL, LDL)	Possibly elevated total and LDL; low or normal HDL
Uric acid	Often elevated
Immunoglobulin panel (blood) for IgE, IgG, and IgM	Normal or abnormal
Ferritin	Can be high (> 110 in women; > 170 in men)
25-hydroxyvitamin D_3	Often low
Red and white blood count: CBC	Normal; WBC may be suppressed if there is an underlying autoimmune component
Liver function tests: AST, ALT, GGT	Normal or elevated
IgG food allergy testing	Elevated results possible for several different foods
Antigliadin antibodies to rule out celiac disease	Normal or positive
ANA, rheumatoid factor (Rh factor), and thyroid antibodies to assess risk of an autoimmune disease	Normal or positive
Estrogen, testosterone, and progesterone	Imbalanced (maybe high or low)
Cortisol and DHEAs	DHEA low, cortisol may be high or low

TACKLING TOXINS IN YOUR SPACE

When we think about pollution, we usually think about smog, acid rain, CFCs, or other forms of outdoor air pollution. But chemical substances in the air inside our homes also affect our health. Considering that we spend 80 to 90 percent of our lives indoors, household air quality and circulation have huge implications for our well-being. Many studies from both the United States and Canada have shown that exposure to pollution is greater in the home than outdoors. Somewhat unexpectedly, though, researchers found exposure was primarily linked to personal-care products and household cleaners rather than to pesticides or weed killers frequently stored in garages.

Toxin exposure from our environment is a major concern. In fact, the Canadian Environmental Protection Act (CEPA) was developed in 1988 to form strategies to limit our exposure to harmful substances. According to CEPA, we have the potential to be exposed to over 23,000 known chemical compounds through consumer products and industrial processes. Although some are considered safe, others present in many common household products can cause harmful side effects, such as breathing difficulties, fatigue, rashes, headaches, hormonal disruption, compromised immunity (irritated mucus membranes in the respiratory tract, which then increase the risk of viral and bacterial infections), and even increased risk of certain types of cancers. One 15-year study found that women who worked at home had a 54 percent higher death rate from cancer than those who worked outside the home. Given that the National Institute of

Occupational Health and Safety found 884 chemicals out of 2,893 analyzed to be toxic, a high incidence of cancer occurrence should not be surprising.

Your Toxin Solution: Detoxify Your Space

Prevention is your best defense. This involves making environmentally conscious choices and assessing your current living space for possible offenders. To start, purchase a HEPA air filter to clean the debris out of the air in your home. Special filters can also be fitted to your furnace to remove allergens from the air. Next, take a detoxifying tour of your home to create simple solutions to diminish your exposure to dangerous chemicals.

1. Bathroom and Kitchen (Cleaning Products and Kitchenware)

You should choose household and laundry cleaning alternatives that are less toxic than standard products. Examples include Kosher Soap, Citra-Solv, borax, That Orange Stuff, and Nature Clean. For your laundry, consider the nontoxic household products by Seventh Generation (www.seventhgeneration.com). (Note: This site also provides a very useful download, "Guide to a Toxin-Free Home." Click on Living Green to gain access to the document.) Also, purchase personal-care products (shampoos, makeup, lotions, etc.) in glass containers as often as possible—they will be less likely to contain phthalates that leach from plastics.

For cooking, avoid aluminum pots and pans because using these materials has been associated with an increased risk of Alzheimer's disease (and the same goes for antiperspirants that contain aluminum). Limiting or eliminating your exposure to Teflon-coated pans may not be such a bad idea either, as the chemical used to make the nonstick substance is currently being studied for potential health risks.

You can purchase reverse osmosis water systems to attach to your tap in the kitchen for drinking water (see the Resource section). It is much cheaper than a unit for the whole house. I also recommend getting a showerhead from the health food store to reduce your exposure to chlorinated hydrocarbons.

2. Living Room, Den, or Family Room
(Furniture, Carpeting, and TV)

Unfortunately, much furniture and many TVs emit chemicals of great concern, such as flame retardants (PBDEs) or perfluorinated chemicals (PFOAs). PBDEs build up in breast milk and can increase the risk of neurological problems in children, whereas PFOAs have been found to be carcinogenic in animal studies. Chemically conscious furniture companies include IKEA, Herman Miller, and Steelcase. They make an effort to manufacture products low in chemical emissions and toxins. When purchasing a TV, Samsung Electronics or Sony models may be your best choices.

Depending on the source, carpets can possess a sea of harmful chemical pollutants including PBDEs, PFOAs, polyvinyl chloride (PVC) plastic (phthalates), or pesticides. PVC is toxic to the reproductive system and is linked to asthma, as are many of the chemicals previously mentioned. Again, IKEA has made excellent changes in their manufacturing processes to reduce the risk of chemical exposure. The manufacturers Shaw and Interface have also taken some steps to reduce harmful chemicals in their products.

3. The Office (Computers and Other Electronic Equipment)

Many computers and other electronic equipment release harmful chemicals similar to those present in carpets and furniture. Apparently, electronic cables contain the highest amount of harmful PVC (phthalates). If you are concerned, chose Dell. They report a policy to phase out all restricted chemicals. Hewlett Packard, Apple, and IBM also have public policies to phase out "some" or "most" harmful chemicals.

4. Bedroom (Mattress)

In an effort to reduce the number of deaths or injuries caused by mattress fires ignited by cigarettes, a standard was enacted in 1973 calling for preventative measures. This resulted in flame-retardant chemicals such as boric acid/antimony, decabromodiphenyl oxide, zinc borate, melamine, PBDEs, PVC, and formaldehyde being added to mattresses. Unfortunately, these same flame-retardant chemicals are linked to cancer, SIDS, prenatal mortality, reduced fertility, neurological disorders, and other negative effects. You may wish to look for a chemical-free, wool mattress.

Sealy and Serta apparently are in the process of making changes to their mattresses, though they don't yet completely meet safety standards. If you have already invested in a quality mattress but are unsure of the chemical content, an activated carbon blanket can reduce your exposure to toxic mattress fumes (visit www.nontoxic.com).

Other Steps to Reduce Your Exposure to Toxic Chemicals

- Air out your dry cleaning or, better yet, choose a dry cleaner that uses nontoxic products.
- Sleep on white or organic bedding that is free of dyes that can be absorbed through your skin.
- Golf courses are extremely high in pesticides. Take your shoes off at the door after you've played a round to avoid tracking in pesticides. Keep your golf equipment in the garage, away from your kids and pets.
- Don't smoke, and minimize your exposure to secondhand smoke.
- Reduce or stop using pesticides and herbicides for home, lawn, garden, and pet care wherever possible. Try nontoxic alternatives.
- Avoid polycarbonate plastic baby and sports/water bottles

and other products made of polycarbonate that might come in contact with food. These can leach bisphenol A.

- Make sure that PVC plastic "cling" wraps you put in contact with food do not contain phthalates (ask the manufacturer).
- Never microwave foods in plastic containers that may leach harmful compounds. Store foods in glass containers.
- Keep your home well ventilated when vacuuming, cleaning, painting, or doing arts and crafts to clear out indoor air pollutants that get stirred up during these activities, and air out vapors from glues, paints, resins, and lacquers used in craft and home projects.
- If pregnant, avoid pumping fuel, remodeling your home, painting, and hobbies that involve solvents and glues. Be careful to use nontoxic nail and hair products.
- Avoid the use of synthetic chemical air fresheners, fabric softeners, and fragrances.

You may wish to visit these additional Web sites for more information and sources of ecofriendly products.

- www.naturallifemagazine.com: A source of articles on sustainable living.
- http://cleanproduction.org/Home.php: Click on Safer Products Project for a room-to-room tour of the home to learn about specific products and also how products from various manufacturers rank according to whether or not they are adhering to measures to avoid high-risk, hazardous chemicals in their products.
- www.gaiam.com/category/eco-home-outdoor.do: An array of ecoconscious home and outdoor products for those who wish to enjoy a backyard, kitchen, and furniture without the use of harsh chemicals or unsustainable production methods.

APPENDIX C

THE HORMONE DIET RECIPES

- All the recipes serve one person unless otherwise mentioned. Simply double the recipes should you wish to serve two people.
- Choose organic ingredients whenever possible.
- Even though 100 percent whey protein isolate powder is derived from dairy, it's permitted during the detox step (when dairy is not otherwise allowed). If you suspect you are sensitive to dairy, choose an alternate protein powder such as bean, rice, or soy for your recipes during your detox step. After your detox, try reintroducing whey as a "test" food and note how your body responds.
- ✿☺ When you see these symbols next to a recipe, the recipe is compatible with both Step 1 (the anti-inflammatory detox) and Step 2 (the Glyci-Med approach).
- ✿ When you see this symbol next to a recipe, the recipe is suitable only for the Glyci-Med approach because it contains ingredients that are to be avoided during your detox step.
- You are free to add a mixed green salad to any of the meals.
- Please note that the nutrition information for each meal will vary depending on the brands you choose. Visit www.calorieking.com to check the nutrition content of almost any food.
- A note about chia: Should you choose to use this gluten-free, high-fiber, high-omega-3 grain in your smoothies rather than flaxseeds, it will result in a less "grainy" texture because it mixes more completely than flaxseeds do.

BREAKFAST OPTIONS

☼☺ Pure Energy Smoothie

¼	cup raspberries
¼	cup sliced strawberries
¼	cup blueberries
2	tablespoons chia or ground flaxseeds
¾	cup low-fat plain soy milk
4	ice cubes
1	serving whey protein powder (vanilla)

Place all the ingredients except the protein powder in a blender and blend at high speed until smooth. Then add the protein powder and lightly blend it in to stir it into your drink.

Nutrition Information:
Calories 313 | Carbohydrates 30.5 g | Protein 26.8 g | Fat 9.3 g | Fiber 9 g

☼ ☺ Açaí-Avocado Smoothie

¼	cup peeled and sliced avocado, frozen
1	Sambazon Açaí Smoothie Pack, frozen
1	tablespoon chia or ground flaxseeds
	Water to desired consistency
1	serving whey protein powder (vanilla)

Place all the ingredients except the protein powder in a blender, add the desired amount of water, and blend at high speed until smooth. Then add the protein powder and lightly blend it in to stir it into your drink.

Nutrition Information:
Calories 395 | Carbohydrates 40.5 g | Protein 30 g | Fat 12.5 g | Fiber 6.5 g

TIPS FOR MAKING SUPER SMOOTHIES

- Freeze your fruit—including your bananas and avocados (peel and cut them into pieces prior to freezing) or add ice to your smoothies to make them refreshing.
- Blend the ingredients before adding your protein. Do not overblend the protein. Just lightly blend it to stir it into your drink; otherwise you damage the protein molecules.
- I prefer the use of ground flaxseeds over flaxseed oil. However, the seeds do change the consistency of your smoothie. If you don't like the flaxseeds, you may use 1 tablespoon of flaxseed oil instead. Keep your ground flaxseeds or flaxseed oil in a tightly sealed container in the freezer. If your shake tastes "fishy," it is very likely your flaxseeds or flaxseed oil has gone rancid and will need to be tossed out.
- You may add water or ice to any smoothie to thin it out. Do not add more juice or soy milk since this will increase the calorie content of your drink.
- Add 2 tablespoons of lecithin to any smoothie to boost your memory and muscle-enhancing acetylcholine.
- To increase the fiber content of your smoothies, add 1 to 2 tablespoons of wheat or oat bran.
- Add 4 grams of L-glutamine powder to any smoothie to enhance growth hormone, tissue healing, and repair.

☼ ☺ Blueberry-Avocado Smoothie

¾   cup blueberries, frozen
¼   cup peeled and sliced avocado, frozen
1   tablespoon chia or ground flaxseeds
    Water to desired consistency
1   serving whey protein powder (vanilla)

Place all the ingredients except the protein powder in a blender, add the desired amount of water, and blend at high speed until smooth. Then add the protein powder and lightly blend it in to stir it into your drink.

Nutrition Information:

Calories 313 | Carbohydrates 25.5 g | Protein 29 g | Fat 10.5 g | Fiber 9.2 g

☼ ☺ Antiaging Smoothie

½   cup raspberries
½   cup blueberries
½   cup sliced strawberries
¼   cup blackberries
1   cup water
2   teaspoons flaxseed oil
1   serving whey protein powder (vanilla)

Place all the ingredients except the protein powder in a blender and blend at high speed until smooth. Then add the protein powder and lightly blend it in to stir it into your drink.

Note: You may also use 1½ cups of a frozen four-berry mixture instead of adding the four berries separately.

Nutrition Information:

Calories 340 | Carbohydrates 30.4 g | Protein 26.9 g | Fat 11.8 g | Fiber 9.3 g

✿ **Dopamine Delight Smoothie**

½   small banana, peeled and frozen

1   tablespoon chia or 2 teaspoons flaxseed oil

½   teaspoon ground cinnamon

¾   cup soy milk (vanilla or plain)

1   double shot (approx. ¼ cup) espresso (preferably organic)

1   serving whey protein powder (vanilla)

Place all the ingredients except the protein powder in a blender and blend at high speed until smooth. Then add the protein powder and lightly blend it in to stir it into your drink.

Nutrition Information:

Calories 337 | Carbohydrates 26.9 g | Protein 32.7 g | Fat 10.9 g | Fiber 7.9 g

✿ ☺ **Super Satisfying Shake**

½   small banana, sliced, or ½ cup diced pineapple

¼   cup sliced strawberries

¼   cup sliced mango

1   tablespoon chia or ground flaxseeds

1   cup water

1   teaspoon flaxseed oil

1   serving whey protein powder (vanilla)

Place all the ingredients except the protein powder in a blender and blend at high speed until smooth. Then add the protein powder and lightly blend it in to stir it into your drink.

Nutrition Information:

Calories 355 | Carbohydrates 31.3 g | Protein 27.6 g | Fat 13.2 g | Fiber 6.6 g

☼ ☺ **Serotonin-Surge Smoothie**
¾   small banana, sliced
1   tablespoon almond butter
2   teaspoons chia or flaxseed oil
1   teaspoon cocoa powder
¾   cup low-fat plain soy milk
1   serving whey protein powder (vanilla)

Place all the ingredients except the protein powder in a blender and blend at high speed until smooth. Then add the protein powder and lightly blend it in to stir it into your drink.

Nutrition Information:
Calories 389 | Carbohydrates 34.5 g | Protein 33.8 g | Fat 12.5 g | Fiber 8.0 g

☼ ☺ **Testosterone-Surge Smoothie**
1   cup blueberries
½   banana, peeled and frozen
2   tablespoons ground flaxseeds
1   cup plain low-fat soy milk
1   serving whey protein powder (vanilla)

Place all the ingredients except the protein powder in a blender and blend at high speed until smooth. Then add the protein powder and lightly blend it in to stir it into your drink.

Nutrition Information:
Calories 334 | Carbohydrates 33.0 g | Protein 27.0 g | Fat 10.4 g | Fiber 9.5 g

✿ ☺ **Anti-Inflammatory Smoothie**

½   cup blueberries

½   cup raspberries

½   small banana, peeled and frozen

¼   cup diced pineapple

2   tablespoons chia or ground flaxseeds

3   ice cubes

½   cup pomegranate juice

1   serving whey protein powder (vanilla)

Place all the ingredients except the protein powder in a blender and blend at high speed until smooth. Then add the protein powder and lightly blend it in to stir it into your drink.

Nutrition Information:

Calories 343 | Carbohydrates 35.7 g | Protein 29.5 g | Fat 9.2 g | Fiber 10.5 g

✿ **Awesome Omelette**

(Make it a ✿ ☺ meal without the rye toast)

1   tablespoon extra-virgin olive oil

¼   cup diced green bell pepper

¼   cup diced red bell pepper

     A few slices of red onion, chopped

½   cup sliced mushrooms

1   large omega-3 egg

3   large egg whites

2   teaspoons crumbled goat cheese

1   slice rye toast (optional)

1. Heat the olive oil in a small skillet over medium heat. Add the green and red peppers, onion, and mushrooms, and sauté until the vegetables soften.

2. Meanwhile, beat the egg and the egg whites with a wire whisk in a small bowl until blended.
3. When the vegetables are soft, transfer them to another bowl and set aside.
4. Pour the egg mixture into the skillet and cook for several minutes over medium heat until the eggs are set.
5. Spread the vegetables evenly on one side of the cooked egg, top with the goat cheese, and use a spatula to fold the omelette in half over the vegetables. Enjoy with a piece of rye toast—after your detox stage.

Nutrition Information:

Calories 337 | Carbohydrates 31.0 g | Protein 24.0 g | Fat 13.0 g | Fiber 4.6 g

✿ Lovely Leptin Lastin' Satisfaction

½	cup raspberries
¼	cup unsweetened applesauce
½	cup low-fat plain yogurt
½	cup cottage cheese (1% fat)
2	tablespoons chia or ground flaxseeds
3	coarsely chopped walnuts (or 2 cashews)

1. Place the raspberries and applesauce in a blender and blend for a few seconds until smooth.
2. Combine the raspberry and applesauce mixture, yogurt, cottage cheese, and chia or ground flaxseeds in a serving bowl. Top with the chopped nuts and enjoy.

Nutrition Information:

Calories 328 | Carbohydrates 30.9 g | Protein 21.8 g | Fat 13.0 g | Fiber 11.0 g

☼ Eggscetylcholine Pocket

½   cup canned black beans, drained and rinsed

¼   cup salsa

1   large omega-3 egg

2   large egg whites

    Salt and pepper to taste

1   teaspoon extra-virgin olive oil

1   ounce shredded Cheddar cheese

½   whole wheat, high-fiber pita

1. Combine the beans and salsa in a bowl.
2. In another bowl, beat the egg, egg whites, salt, and pepper with a wire whisk until blended.
3. Heat the oil in a small skillet over medium heat. Add the egg mixture and cook for a few minutes, until the egg is almost set.
4. Sprinkle the shredded cheese over the top and stir in the bean mixture. Cook for another minute, until the cheese is melted.
5. Place the mixture in the pita pocket. Enjoy!

Nutrition Information:

Calories 387 | Carbohydrates 39.0 g | Protein 29.1 g | Fat 12.7 g | Fiber 10.0 g

☼ Power Oatmeal

Serves 1

½   cup (for women) or ⅔ cup (for men) slow-cooking oats

15   grams (for women) or 25 grams (for men) protein powder

½   cup (for women) or 1 cup (for men) soy milk

    Berries

½   teaspoon cinnamon

Cook the oats in water according to the package directions. Remove from heat. Stir in the protein powder. Top with the soy milk, unlimited amounts of berries (fresh or frozen), and the cinnamon.

Nutrition Information:

Calories 469 | Carbohydrates 66.1 g | Protein 33.5 g | Fat 8.4 g | Fiber: 11.2 g

LUNCH OPTIONS

☼ ☺ Balsamic Vinegar and Olive Oil Dressing

Serves 4

1–2	tablespoons balsamic vinegar (or apple cider vinegar)
¼	cup extra-virgin olive oil
½–1	teaspoon mustard powder
	Maple syrup or honey to taste
	Sea salt and pepper to taste

Combine the vinegar, olive oil, and mustard powder in a glass jar. Add the maple syrup or honey to your desired sweetness—keep in mind that less is more! Add sea salt and pepper to taste. Cover the jar and shake well to mix. This homemade dressing is good to have on hand and will keep in the fridge.

☼ ☺ Greek Salad Topped with Grilled Chicken Breast

3	cups mixed greens
½	green bell pepper, diced
½	red bell pepper, diced
½	cup halved or quartered cherry tomatoes
¼	cup sliced red onion
1	teaspoon fresh chopped dill
½	teaspoon fresh or ⅛ teaspoon dried basil
3	pitted black olives
1	cup peeled and sliced cucumber
4	ounces grilled boneless, skinless chicken breast, thinly sliced on the diagonal
1	ounce feta cheese, crumbled
2	teaspoons Balsamic Vinegar and Olive Oil Dressing (see above)

(continued)

Mix the greens, green pepper, red pepper, tomatoes, onion, dill, basil, olives, and cucumbers in a large bowl. Top with the grilled chicken slices, feta cheese, and salad dressing.

Nutrition Information:
Calories 420 | Carbohydrates 43.7 g | Protein 30.0 g | Fat 14.0 g | Fiber 7.0 g

✿ ☺ Curried Tuna-Chia Salad

1	can (4 ounces) light tuna in water (about ½ cup drained)
1	tablespoon low-fat mayonnaise (canola oil–based)
¼	teaspoon curry powder
½	tomato, chopped
½	cup peeled and chopped cucumber
½	cup diced green bell pepper
½	cup diced red bell pepper
¼	cup chopped onion
1	dill pickle, chopped
1–2	tablespoons Balsamic Vinegar and Olive Oil Dressing (page 431)
1	tablespoon chia

1. Place the tuna in a small bowl and flake it with a fork. Add the mayonnaise and curry powder to the tuna, combine them well, and then set aside.
2. In a medium-size bowl, combine the tomato, cucumber, green and red peppers, onion, and pickle. Toss with the dressing.
3. Serve on a plate with a scoop of the tuna mixture on top, sprinkle with the chia, and enjoy!

Nutrition Information:
Calories 336 | Carbohydrates 29.0 g | Protein 29.0 g | Fat 11.5 g | Fiber 8.0 g

☼ ☺ **Antioxidant Chicken Salad**

    3   cups baby spinach

    4   ounces grilled boneless, skinless chicken breast, thinly sliced
          on the diagonal

2 or 3 thin slices red onion

    ½   cup raspberries or blueberries

    1   cup strawberry halves

    1   tablespoon Balsamic Vinegar and Olive Oil Dressing
          (page 431)

    ⅛   avocado, peeled and sliced

Combine the spinach, chicken, onion, raspberries or blueberries, and strawberries in a salad bowl. Top with the dressing and avocado.

Nutrition Information:
Calories 335 | Carbohydrates 20.0 g | Protein 32.0 g | Fat 14.0 g | Fiber 8.0 g

☼ ☺ **Goat Cheese, Green Pea, and Spinach Frittata**

    1   large omega-3 egg

    3   large egg whites

    1   ounce goat cheese

    1   tablespoon chopped onion
          Sea salt and pepper to taste

    ½   cup frozen green peas

  1¼ cups frozen spinach

 1–2 teaspoons extra-virgin olive oil

    1   slice whole grain toast (optional in the Glyci-Med stage)

1. Preheat the oven to 350°F.
2. Beat the egg and egg whites in a medium-size bowl with a wire whisk until blended. Mix in the cheese, onion, salt, pepper, peas, and spinach.

(continued)

3. Spread the olive oil in a small ovenproof skillet and add the egg mixture.

4. Bake for 15 to 20 minutes, or until the frittata is fully set. Enjoy with a slice of whole grain toast—if you are not on your detox.

Nutrition Information:
Calories 403 | Carbohydrates 39.0 g | Protein 29.0 g | Fat 14.5 g | Fiber 9.0 g

✿ ☺ California Avocado and Chicken Salad
Serves 4

  Sea salt and pepper to taste
2 large boneless, skinless chicken breasts
1 tablespoon peeled and crushed fresh ginger
2 teaspoons extra-virgin olive oil
4 tablespoons freshly squeezed lime juice
3 tablespoons fresh chopped cilantro
5 cups fresh greens (any kind except iceberg lettuce)
1 avocado, peeled and sliced
2 peaches, peeled and sliced
2 tablespoons chopped red onion

1. Preheat the oven to 350°F.

2. Sprinkle salt and pepper on the chicken and bake until cooked through but still moist (30 to 40 minutes). Remove from the oven and, when cool enough to handle, cut into bite-size chunks, and set aside. (The chicken can be cooked a day in advance.)

3. Combine the ginger, olive oil, lime juice, cilantro, and salt and pepper to taste in a salad bowl and mix well. Add the greens and toss with the dressing.

4. Divide the greens among four plates and arrange the avocado, peaches, and chicken on each plate. Sprinkle with the onion and serve.

Nutrition Information (per serving):
Calories 410 | Carbohydrates 42.0 g | Protein 31.0 g | Fat 13.1 g | Fiber 6.0 g

✿ Sweet Potato, Squash, and Ginger Soup

(Remove the cheese to make it a ✿ ☺ meal)

Serves 4 or 5

1	large sweet potato, peeled and cubed
1	small butternut squash, peeled and cubed
2	carrots, peeled and thinly sliced
	1-inch piece fresh ginger, peeled and sliced
1–2	teaspoons curry powder (optional)
6	cups vegetable stock
1	pear, cored, peeled, and sliced
1	apple, cored, peeled, and sliced
2	large onions, chopped
2	tablespoons extra-virgin olive oil
3	tablespoons apple juice or white wine
1	teaspoon sea salt
	Black pepper to taste
1¼–2½	cups organic pressed cottage cheese

1. Place the sweet potato, squash, carrots, ginger, and, if desired, curry powder in a large saucepan. Add the vegetable stock. Cover, bring to a gentle boil, and then reduce the heat and simmer for about 30 minutes or until all the vegetables are soft.

2. Place the pear, apple, onions, olive oil, and apple juice or wine in a separate saucepan and cook over medium heat until soft (5 to 10 minutes).

3. Add the cooked pear and apple mixture and the salt and pepper to the saucepan with the vegetables, and mix well. Once all the ingredients are thoroughly cooked, purée in a food processor or with a hand blender.

4. Serve topped with ¼ cup (for women) or ½ cup (for men) of the cottage cheese.

Nutrition Information (per serving):

Calories 360 | Carbohydrates 49.0 g | *Protein 24.0 g (*if the cheese is added) | Fat 8.0 g | Fiber 6.0 g

✿ ☺ **Lovely Lentil Soup**

Serves 4

2   tablespoons extra-virgin olive oil

1   sweet potato, peeled and diced

1   large onion, chopped

4   cloves garlic, minced

    1-inch piece fresh ginger, peeled and minced

1   tablespoon curry powder

1   teaspoon cinnamon

1   teaspoon sea salt

1   cup dry red lentils

4   cups vegetable stock

2   tablespoons tomato paste

1. Heat the olive oil in a large saucepan over medium heat. Add the sweet potato, onion, garlic, and ginger, and cook until the vegetables are softened.

2. Stir in the curry powder, cinnamon, and sea salt, and cook for a few more minutes.

3. Add the lentils, vegetable stock, and tomato paste, and mix well. Bring to a gentle boil, reduce the heat, and then simmer covered for 30 minutes or until the lentils are cooked. Remove from the heat and serve.

Nutrition Information (per serving):

Calories 325 | Carbohydrates 44.5 g | Protein 16.0 g | Fat 9.0 g | Fiber 7.5 g

✿ Zippy Three-Bean Salad

(Skip the cheese to make it a ✿ ☺ meal)

⅓	cup canned kidney beans, drained and rinsed
⅓	cup canned black beans, drained and rinsed
¼	cup canned chickpeas, drained and rinsed
1	small red bell pepper, chopped
2	ounces low-fat Cheddar or Colby cheese
	A few slices red onion, chopped
2	cloves garlic, minced
½	teaspoon dried coriander
	Pinch of cayenne pepper, or to taste
	Pinch of ground cumin
2	tablespoons freshly squeezed lemon juice
1	tablespoon extra-virgin olive oil
1	teaspoon apple cider vinegar
	Salt and pepper to taste

Combine all the ingredients in a bowl and enjoy.

Variation: For a bean dip, purée all the ingredients and enjoy with raw vegetables such as sliced bell peppers and carrot and celery sticks.

Nutrition Information:
Calories 395 | Carbohydrates 45.2 g | Protein 26.0 g | Fat 12.0 g | Fiber 9.5 g

✿ Warm Black Bean and Turkey Salad

(Remove the cheese to make it a ✿ ☺ meal)

1	teaspoon extra-virgin olive oil
½	cup diced green bell pepper
½	cup diced red bell pepper
¼	cup chopped onion
1–2	cloves garlic, minced
½–1	teaspoon dried basil
½–1	teaspoon dried dillweed
¼–½	teaspoon dried oregano
	Pinch cayenne pepper, or to taste
3	ounces lean ground turkey
¼	cup salsa
¼	cup canned black beans, drained and rinsed
	Sea salt and pepper to taste
1	teaspoon hot pepper sauce such as Tabasco (optional)
3	cups mixed greens
1	ounce Cheddar cheese, grated

1. Heat the olive oil over medium-high heat in a skillet and add all the veggies, herbs, and spices. Sauté until the peppers and onions are soft.
2. Add the ground turkey and cook until it browns. Drain thoroughly.
3. Add the salsa and black beans and continue cooking until they are warmed through.
4. Add salt and pepper and, if desired, the hot sauce, and mix well.
5. Serve over the mixed greens and top with the cheese.

Nutrition Information:

Calories 383 | Carbohydrates 37.7 g | Protein 29.6 g | Fat 12.6 g | Fiber 8.0 g

✿ India-Style Chicken Pita Pocket with Side Salad

Pita Pocket:

4	ounces grilled boneless, skinless chicken breast, cubed
1	medium stalk celery, chopped
2	cashews, chopped
1	tablespoon low-fat plain yogurt
1	teaspoon Dijon mustard
¼–½	teaspoon curry powder
1	high-fiber whole wheat pita

Side Salad:

2	cups mixed greens
½	cup sliced, peeled cucumber
3 or 4	halved or quartered cherry tomatoes
1	tablespoon Balsamic Vinegar and Olive Oil Dressing (page 431)

1. Combine the chicken, celery, cashews, yogurt, mustard, and curry powder in a bowl.
2. Cut the pita in half, and spoon the mixture into the pita pocket.
3. Toss the salad ingredients together and serve with the chicken pita pocket. (You may enjoy any type of green salad with this dish).

Nutrition Information:

Calories 409 | Carbohydrates 38.0 g | Protein 29.0 g | Fat 14.0 g | Fiber 9.0 g

✿ Zesty Chicken Salad

(Skip the cheese to make it a ✿ ☺ meal)

1½	teaspoons freshly squeezed lime juice
1½	teaspoons apple juice
1½	teaspoons sesame oil
1½	teaspoons tamari soy sauce
2	cups raw spinach
4	ounces grilled boneless, skinless chicken breast, thinly sliced on the diagonal
1	ounce low-fat Swiss cheese, grated
1	medium apple, cored, peeled, and sliced
1	tablespoon finely chopped green onion

1. To make the dressing, combine the lime juice, apple juice, sesame oil, and soy sauce in a small bowl and whisk until well blended.
2. Place the spinach leaves on a plate and add the chicken, cheese, and apple. Sprinkle the green onion on top, toss with the dressing, and serve.

Nutrition Information:

Calories 380 | Carbohydrates 38.6 g | Protein 29.7 g | Fat 12.8 g | Fiber 6.0 g

✿ Easy Caesar Salad

2   cups torn romaine lettuce

4   ounces grilled boneless, skinless chicken breast

1   slice whole grain toast cut into even cubes (for croutons)

2   tablespoons prepared Caesar salad dressing (canola- or olive oil–based)

1   tablespoon grated Parmesan cheese

Assemble the lettuce, chicken, and croutons on a plate. Toss with the dressing, top with the cheese, and enjoy.

Nutrition Information:

Calories 392 | Carbohydrates 34.0 g | Protein 29.0 g | Fat 15.6 g | Fiber 7.0 g

✿ ☺ Marinated Tempe or Tofu

Serves 5

1   package tempeh (you can find tempeh in the freezer at the health food store) or organic extra-firm tofu

2   tablespoons water

⅓   cup apple cider vinegar

⅓   cup tamari

1   tablespoon sesame oil

1   tablespoon canola oil

1   teaspoon black pepper

2   tablespoons ground anise seed

3   teaspoons garlic powder

1. Cut the tempeh into strips or chunks.
2. Mix the water, vinegar, tamari, sesame and canola oils, pepper, anise, and garlic powder in a bowl.
3. Marinate the tempeh in this mixture for 1 to 2 hours, and then grill. Marinated tempeh can be stored in your fridge for up to 5 days to be used as a topping for salads, etc.

Nutrition Information:

Calories 210 | Carbohydrates 10.3 g | Protein 14.6 g | Fat 14 g | Fiber 3.3 g

☼ Egg Salad Lunch
Serves 2

4	large omega-3 eggs, hard-boiled and peeled
1	tablespoon low-fat mayonnaise
1	teaspoon mustard (Dijon or regular)
2	tablespoons diced onion
	Salt and black pepper to taste
3	slices Wasa Crispbread

1. Discard 2 of the egg yolks. Chop the remaining 2 yolks and 4 whites in a medium bowl.
2. Stir in the mayonnaise, mustard, and onion. Season with salt and pepper. Enjoy on the crispbread.

Nutrition Information:
Calories 278 | Carbohydrates 18 g | Protein 26.2 g | Fat 11 g | Fiber 1.3 g

☼ ☺ Roasted Vegetable Soup
Serves 4

4	large carrots, peeled
2	zucchini
2	large tomatoes
2	sweet potatoes
1	large sweet onion
2	leeks, finely chopped
2–3	tablespoons extra-virgin olive oil
	Sea salt and black pepper to taste
5	cups vegetable stock (or more to reach desired consistency)
2	tablespoons chopped fresh basil
1	teaspoon cumin

1. Preheat the oven to 375°F.
2. Wash and chop the carrots, zucchini, tomatoes, potatoes, onion, and leeks. Toss with the olive oil, salt, and pepper and place in a roasting pan with approximately ½ cup of the stock.

3. Bake for 30 to 40 minutes, or until tender. Be sure the vegetables don't burn, and turn them once during baking.
4. Remove from the oven. In small batches, transfer the vegetables to a blender and puree with the basil, cumin, and remaining. (You can do this in a saucepan over low heat if you're using a hand blender.) Let the soup warm for 5 minutes, and then serve.

Nutrition Information:
Calories 298 | Carbohydrates 46.5 g | Protein 6.7 g | Fat 11.3 g | Fiber 8.2 g

✿ ☺ Tomato Soup
Serves 5
(Leave out the Parmesan to make this a ✿ meal)

- 2 tablespoons extra-virgin olive oil
- 1 large onion
- 3 or 4 cloves garlic, minced
- 2 large cans tomatoes or 3 pounds ripe tomatoes, peeled and seeded, then diced
- 1 large red bell pepper, seeded and chopped (optional)
- 4 cups vegetable stock
- ½ cup finely chopped basil
   Sea salt and black pepper to taste
- 5 teaspoons freshly grated Parmesan cheese

1. Heat the olive oil in a large saucepan and sauté the onion. Add the garlic and cook until soft.
2. Add the tomatoes, bell pepper (if using), and stock. Simmer for 30 minutes.
3. Place the soup in a blender (or use a hand blender) and puree. Add the basil and salt and black pepper. Top each serving with 1 teaspoon of the cheese.

Nutrition Information:
Calories 204 | Carbohydrates 27 g | Protein 7 g | Fat 9.3 g | Fiber 5.7 g

✿ ☺ Summer Salad with Honey Mustard Dressing

Serves 1

- 2   tablespoons apple cider vinegar
- 1   teaspoon honey
- 1   tablespoon mayonnaise
- 1   teaspoon Dijon mustard
- ½   tablespoon finely minced onion
-     Pinch of salt
- ½   cup extra-virgin olive oil
- 4   ounces fresh roasted turkey breast
- 4   cups baby spinach
- ½   cup baby mandarin orange slices
- 1   tablespoon roasted pine nuts
- 2   tablespoons or more sliced red onion

1. To make the dressing, combine the vinegar, honey, mayonnaise, mustard, onion, salt, and oil in a small bowl. This dressing will keep up to 1 week in your fridge.
2. To make the salad, toss the turkey, spinach, oranges, pine nuts, and red onion in a medium bowl. Top with 1 tablespoon of Honey Mustard Salad Dressing.

Nutrition Information:

Calories 412 | Carbohydrates 39.8 g | Protein 42.8 g | Fat 11.1 g | Fiber 13.1 g

✿ ☺ Pomegranate, Peach, and Pecan Chicken Salad

Serves 2

(Remove the cheese to make it a ✿ ☺ meal option)

- 2   boneless chicken breasts
- 6   cups mixed greens or baby spinach
- 1   pomegranate
- 1   peach, sliced
- 1   tablespoon chopped pecans
- 2   tablespoons low-fat feta cheese, crumbled

1. Grill the chicken breast and slice it into strips.
2. Mix the greens, pomegranate, peach, pecans, and feta cheese in a large bowl. Top with the chicken and serve with the Balsamic Vinegar and Olive Oil Dressing (page 431), but use apple cider vinegar.

Nutrition Information:

Calories 442 | Carbohydrates 50.7 g | Protein 40.8 g | Fat 11.9 g | Fiber 15.7 g

✿ Turkey Wrap

Serves 1

3	(for women) or 5 (for men) fresh roasted turkey slices (free of nitrites and sulfites)
	Romaine lettuce
2	slices red onion, chopped
1	small tomato, sliced
1	ounce grated low-fat white Cheddar cheese
	Dijon or regular mustard
1	sprouted grain tortilla

Layer the turkey, lettuce, onion, tomato, cheese, and mustard on the wrap, roll up, and enjoy.

Nutrition Information:

Calories 456 | Carbohydrates 31.1 g | Protein 48.5 g | Fat 15.2 g | Fiber 7.1 g

DINNER OPTIONS

✿ ☺ Mediterranean Tilapia

4½	ounce tilapia fillet
1½	teaspoons extra-virgin olive oil
½	tomato, sliced
4	pitted black olives, sliced

1. Preheat the oven to 375°F.
2. Place tilapia in a small, shallow baking dish and brush with olive oil.

(continued)

3. Top the fillet with the sliced tomato and olives and bake in the oven until the fish flakes easily with a fork and is opaque, 10 to 20 minutes.
4. Serve with a side salad tossed with Balsamic Vinegar and Olive Oil Dressing (page 431) and a baked sweet potato or steamed brown basmati rice.

Nutrition Information:
Calories 400 | Carbohydrates 45.8 g | Protein 29.9 g | Fat 13.5 g | Fiber 6.0 g

✿ ☺ Veggie Chili
Serves 4

- 2 teaspoons extra-virgin olive oil
- 1 large onion, chopped
- 1 green bell pepper, chopped
- 4 ounces mushrooms, sliced
- ½ package (or 6 to 8 ounces) extra-firm tofu, cubed
- 1 can (28 ounces) crushed tomatoes, pureed
- 1 can (15 ounces) red kidney beans, drained and rinsed
- 3 or 4 cloves of fresh garlic, chopped
- 2 tablespoons chili powder
- 1 teaspoon dried basil
- 1 teaspoon dried oregano
- 1 teaspoon nutmeg
- ½ teaspoon crushed chiles, or to taste
- 1 tablespoon blackstrap molasses
- 1 tablespoon apple cider vinegar

1. Heat the olive oil over medium heat in a large, heavy saucepan, and sauté the onion, green pepper, mushrooms, and tofu until the vegetables are soft.
2. Add all the remaining ingredients and cook until heated through (10 to 20 minutes) and serve.

Variation: For a nonveggie version, substitute cooked cubed turkey breast for the tofu.

This makes a lot of chili! You can freeze it in individual portions or it will keep in the fridge for up to 5 days.

Nutrition Information (per serving):
Calories 401 | Carbohydrates 43.0 g | Protein 28.0 g | Fat 13.0 g | Fiber 9.0 g

✿ ☺ Anti-Inflammatory Curry

1–3	cloves of garlic, minced
½	cup chopped broccoli
½	cup snow peas
1	green onion, sliced
	Sea salt and pepper to taste
1	red bell pepper, sliced
1½	teaspoons curry powder
2	tablespoons chopped cashews
½	teaspoon peeled and minced fresh ginger
1	small jalapeño pepper, minced
1	teaspoon extra-virgin olive oil
4	ounces boneless, skinless chicken breast, cut into bite-size pieces
¼–½	cup vegetable stock, if necessary for moisture
½	cup cooked brown basmati rice

1. Combine the garlic, broccoli, snow peas, green onion, salt and pepper, bell pepper, curry powder, cashews, ginger, and jalapeño in a bowl. Mix well and let marinate for 10 to 30 minutes.
2. Heat the olive oil in a small skillet over medium heat. Add the chicken and sauté until lightly browned.
3. Combine the vegetables and chicken in a large, heavy saucepan.

(continued)

Simmer covered for 10 minutes or until the chicken is fully cooked, adding the vegetable stock if necessary. Serve over the rice.

Variation: As an alternative to rice, you may have this with one small peeled and cubed sweet potato cooked with the curry.

Nutrition Information:
Calories 465 | Carbohydrates 56.0 g | Protein 29.0 g | Fat 14.0 g | Fiber 5.5 g

✿ ☺ Sweet Garlic Chicken Stir-Fry

2	teaspoons extra-virgin olive oil
1	small zucchini, sliced
1	cup diced red bell pepper
½	cup diced yellow bell pepper
½	cup fresh pineapple, diced
2	cloves garlic, minced
¼	cup vegetable stock, if necessary for moisture
4	ounces boneless, skinless chicken breast, sliced
2	cups spinach
¼	cup cooked brown basmati rice

1. Heat the olive oil over medium heat in a large skillet or wok. Add the zucchini, red and yellow bell peppers, pineapple, and garlic. Cook until the vegetables are tender, adding the vegetable stock if necessary.
2. Stir in the chicken and cook for a few minutes.
3. Add the spinach and cook until it is wilted and the chicken is cooked through. Serve over the rice.

Nutrition Information:
Calories 402 | Carbohydrates 43.0 g | Protein 29.0 g | Fat 12.7 g | Fiber 8.0 g

✿ ☺ **Grilled Halibut with Rice and Broccoli**

Sauce for the Rice and Broccoli:

¼	cup sliced cherry tomatoes
1	tablespoon chopped fresh basil
½	green onion, thinly sliced
1½	teaspoons extra-virgin olive oil
	Salt and pepper to taste

Fish:

1	teaspoon fennel seeds
½	tablespoon freshly squeezed lemon juice
1½	teaspoons extra-virgin olive oil
	Sea salt and pepper to taste
4	ounce halibut fillet
½	cup cooked brown basmati rice
1	cup broccoli, steamed

Note: Be sure to prepare your brown rice and steamed broccoli so that they are done when the fish is ready.

1. To make the sauce, heat the tomatoes, basil, green onion, and olive oil in a saucepan over medium-high heat until the vegetables are soft. Set aside.
2. To make the fish, prepare the grill and place a rack 4 inches above the coals.
3. Toast the fennel seeds in a small skillet over medium heat until fragrant.
4. Combine the lemon juice, toasted fennel seeds, olive oil, salt, and pepper in small bowl.
5. Put the fish in a glass dish and brush the mixture over both sides to coat it evenly. Let it marinate for 15 minutes at room temperature.
6. Place the fish on the hot grill and cook until done through (10 to 15 minutes).

(continued)

7. Meanwhile, reheat the sauce. Serve the fish with the sauce spooned over the rice and broccoli.

Nutrition Information:
Calories 393 | Carbohydrates 38.8 g | Protein 30.7 g | Fat 12.8 g | Fiber 5.0 g

✿ ☺ Super Salmon Salad

4–6	spears of asparagus, steamed and sliced
1	can (4 ounces) wild salmon
¼	cup chopped or sliced tomato
2	tablespoons chopped green onion
1 or 2	cloves garlic, minced
1	tablespoon tamari soy sauce
1	teaspoon extra-virgin olive oil
3	cups mixed greens

Mix the asparagus and salmon together. Add the tomato, green onion, garlic, soy sauce, and olive oil to the salmon mixture. Chill and serve over the mixed greens.

Nutrition Information:
Calories 319 | Carbohydrates 26.0 g | Protein 29.0 g | Fat 11.0 g | Fiber 13.0 g

☼ ☺ Baby Spinach with Grilled Ginger Scallops

Serves 2

1	tablespoon minced sweet onion
2	tablespoons freshly squeezed lime juice
½	cup fresh grapefruit juice
1	tablespoon peeled and grated fresh ginger
3	tablespoons tamari soy sauce
1	tablespoon honey
½	teaspoon Dijon mustard
	Sea salt to taste
1	tablespoon extra-virgin olive oil, divided
8	large sea scallops
1	pound organic baby spinach leaves

1. Put the onion, lime juice, and grapefruit juice in a small skillet, bring to a boil over medium heat, and cook for 1 to 2 minutes.

2. Combine the ginger, soy sauce, honey, and mustard in a small bowl, add to the skillet, and warm through. Remove from the heat and mix in the sea salt and 1½ teaspoons of the olive oil.

3. Heat the remaining 1½ teaspoons of the olive oil in a large skillet. When it's hot, place the scallops in the skillet and sear them by cooking for 30 seconds to 1 minute on each side. Add the sauce and simmer over low heat for 1 to 2 minutes.

4. Meanwhile, pile the spinach leaves on 2 plates. Immediately serve the scallops on top of the spinach, divided between the plates.

Nutrition Information (per serving):

Calories 337 | Carbohydrates 30.0 g | Protein 25.3 g | Fat 10.4 g | Fiber 4.0 g

✿ Carb Craving Shepherd's Pie

Serves 2 (Leave out the spelt flour to make it a ✿ ☺ meal)

2	medium sweet potatoes
1	teaspoon butter
1	tablespoon extra-virgin olive oil
10	ounces lean ground turkey
3	cloves garlic
1	onion, chopped
1	teaspoon sea salt
	Black pepper to taste
¼	teaspoon thyme
1	tablespoon spelt flour (optional)
1	cup vegetable stock
1	teaspoon Worcestershire sauce
1	cup frozen peas and carrots

1. Bake the sweet potatoes, remove the skins, and mash the flesh with the butter (you should have about ½ cup of mashed potato). Set aside.
2. Preheat the oven to 400°F.
3. Heat the olive oil in a skillet. Add the turkey, garlic, and onion and cook until the turkey is lightly browned.
4. Add the salt, pepper, thyme, and, if using, the flour, and mix well.
5. Stir in the vegetable stock and cook until thickened.
6. Stir in the Worcestershire sauce and the peas and carrots, and cover and simmer for 20 minutes.
7. Transfer the turkey mixture to a baking dish and spread the reserved mashed sweet potatoes on top.
8. Put the shepherd's pie in the oven, bake for 15 minutes, and serve.

Nutrition Information (per serving):

Calories 413 | Carbohydrates 43.0 g | Protein 31.0 g | Fat 13.0 g | Fiber 6.0 g

☼ **Beef Fajita with Side Salad**

Side Salad:

2	cups torn romaine lettuce leaves or mixed greens
½	peach, peeled and sliced
2–3	thin slivers red onion
1	tablespoon Balsamic Vinegar and Olive Oil Dressing (page 431)

Fajitas:

1½	teaspoons freshly squeezed lemon juice
1–2	teaspoons chili powder
1–2	cloves garlic, minced
¼	teaspoon dried red pepper flakes
¼	teaspoon ground cumin
¼	teaspoon paprika
	Sea salt and pepper to taste
1	teaspoon extra-virgin olive oil
4	ounces lean eye of round beef, cut into thin strips
½	cup sliced green bell pepper
½	cup sliced red bell pepper
¼	medium onion, chopped
½	tomato, chopped
¼	cup salsa
1	medium whole wheat tortilla wrap

1. Prepare the side salad by combining the greens, peach, and onion. Toss with the dressing just before serving.
2. Combine the lemon juice, chili powder, garlic, red pepper flakes, cumin, paprika, salt, and pepper in a bowl and set aside.
3. Coat a skillet with the olive oil and place over medium-high heat. Add the beef and stir-fry until browned.
4. Add the bell peppers and the onion, and stir-fry until the vegetables are cooked to the desired tenderness and beef is cooked through.

(continued)

5. Mix in the tomato and salsa and stir until heated through.
6. Spoon the mixture onto the tortilla and roll it up. Serve with the side salad.

Variation: Substitute the beef with chicken for a chicken fajita.

Nutrition Information:

Calories 383 | Carbohydrates 39.5 g | Protein 29.7 g | Fat 11.8 g | Fiber 6.0 g

✿ Quick-and-Easy Pasta with Tomato Sauce

Serves 2

	Whole wheat or kamut pasta
1	tablespoon extra-virgin olive oil
½	pound ground turkey
1	onion, chopped
1	bottle (25 ounces) organic sugar-free tomato pasta sauce made with olive oil
2	cups broccoli, steamed and pureed
1	clove garlic, minced
1	teaspoon dried oregano
1	teaspoon dried parsley

1. Prepare the pasta according to the package instructions, making each serving the size of your fist (approximately ½ cup). Cook until it is soft but still firm. (Overcooking pasta raises its glycemic index.)
2. Heat the olive oil in a saucepan and sauté the turkey and onion until the turkey is cooked.
3. Add the tomato sauce, broccoli, garlic, oregano, and parsley and simmer until heated through.
4. Serve the pasta topped with the sauce.

Variation: For a vegetarian option, substitute 1½ cups of pressed cottage cheese for the turkey. Place the cottage cheese on top of the cooked pasta, pour the hot tomato sauce over the cheese, and stir it up. The cheese will melt and you'll have a tasty high-protein, high-fiber meal. Note: Do not use this as your protein source during your detox Day 14 when you will be testing wheat.

Nutrition Information (per serving):
Calories 400 | Carbohydrates 44.0 g | Protein 29.0 g | Fat 13.0 g | Fiber 8.0 g

✿ ☺ Coconut Curry Dish
Serves 2

	Brown basmati rice
2	tablespoons extra-virgin olive oil
1	large onion, chopped
2 or 3	cloves garlic, crushed
2	tablespoons curry powder
2	boneless chicken breasts, cut into strips
1	can low-fat coconut milk
8	cups or 2 large bunches spinach

1. Cook the rice according to the package directions.
2. Heat the olive oil in a skillet and sauté the chopped onion and garlic.
3. Add the curry powder and chicken to the pan. Cook over medium heat for 5 to 10 minutes, stirring frequently.
4. Add the coconut milk and simmer for 20 more minutes.
5. Steam the spinach, drain, and add it to the chicken curry mix. Serve the mixture over a fist-size serving of brown rice.

Nutrition Information:
Calories 362.5 | Carbohydrates 45.1 g | Protein 21.5 g | Fat 14.8 g | Fiber 11.8 g

☼ **Turkey Burger with Mixed Green Salad**

Serves 2

½ pound ground turkey

1 egg white

1½ tablespoons feta cheese

½ teaspoon oregano

Salt, black pepper, and cayenne pepper to taste

1 multigrain burger bun

1. Preheat the grill.
2. Mix the turkey, egg white, feta, oregano, salt, black pepper, and cayenne in a bowl. Form into 2 or more patties.
3. Grill the burgers for 10 to 15 minutes on each side.
4. In another bowl, mix fresh organic greens and toss them with the Balsamic Vinegar and Olive Oil Dressing (page 431).
5. Serve open face on half of the bun with your choice of toppings and the mixed green salad.

Nutrition Information:

Calories 368 | Carbohydrates 19.4 g | Protein 31.3 g | Fat 17 g | Fiber 2.1 g

☼ ☺ **Almond-Encrusted Baked Halibut with Sweet Potato Mash and Baked Asparagus**

Serves 1

1 halibut fillet (about 4 ounces)

½ cup sliced almonds

1 small sweet potato

Asparagus

Olive oil

½ teaspoon brown sugar

¼ teaspoon cinnamon

Salt and pepper to taste

1. Preheat the oven to 350°F.
2. Roll the halibut in the almonds and bake 10 minutes, or until the fish flakes apart.
3. Bake or microwave the sweet potato until it is cooked tender, easily punctured with your fork.
4. In the meantime, coat the asparagus with a small amount of olive oil, and grill or bake as many pieces as you would like.
5. Once the sweet potato is cooked, scoop the flesh into a bowl. Add the brown sugar and cinnamon. Mash and add the salt and pepper to taste.
6. Place the asparagus on a plate and top with the baked halibut. Serve with a fist-size serving of mashed sweet potato.

Nutrition Information:
Calories 430 | Carbohydrates 40.4 g | Protein 34.6 g | Fat 16.1 g | Fiber 10.9 g

✿ ☺ Cajun Shrimp
Serves 2

1½	cups brown basmati rice
2 or 3	cloves fresh garlic, peeled
½	teaspoon cumin seed
½	teaspoon turmeric
½	teaspoon mustard powder
1	teaspoon chili powder
1½	tablespoons apple cider vinegar
¼	cup chopped onion
1	tablespoon olive oil
½	pound uncooked shrimp
2	tablespoons water
	Salt to taste

(continued)

Cajun Shrimp
✿ ☺

1. Cook the rice according to the package directions.
2. Place the garlic, cumin, turmeric, mustard, chili powder, and the apple cider vinegar in a food processor and puree. Remove from the food processor.
3. Place the onion in the food processor and process to a paste.
4. Heat the olive oil in a pan over low heat and sauté the onion paste until golden brown. Add the spice mixture and sauté.
5. Peel and devein the shrimp and add to the pan. Cook for 5 to 7 minutes, stirring often. Add the water and salt and simmer, uncovered, for a few more minutes. Serve over the rice.

Nutrition Information:
Calories 630 | Carbohydrates 100.3 g | Protein 33 g | Fat 13.9 g | Fiber 7.1 g

SNACK OPTIONS

✿ The Simply Bar
A gluten-free, dairy-free, wheat-free, easily digested, high-protein bar that's perfect as a midday snack. It is available in some health food stores or you can visit www.wellnessfoods.ca or www.thehormonediet. com. Choose peanut butter, ginger-flax, or cocoa-coffee flavors—they're the lowest on the glycemic index according to Cathy Richards, creator of the bar.

✿ ☺ Elevate Me! Bar
All-natural, gluten- and wheat-free protein and whole-fruit energy bar. It contains 16 grams of protein and 35 grams of carbs, making it a good choice for a postworkout snack. For women, half a bar would be a snack; men can eat the whole bar. Choose from the flavors that are lowest in carbs: Cocoa Coconut Cluster, All Fruit Origi-

nal, Banana Nut Bread, or Matcha Green Tea with Cranberries. Visit www.prosnack.com.

✿ ☺ Black Bean Dip or Burrito Filling
Serves 4 or 5

1	can (15 ounces) of black beans, drained and rinsed
1	medium onion, chopped
2	cloves garlic, minced
2	teaspoons cumin
1	teaspoon coriander (optional)
½	teaspoon cayenne pepper
½	teaspoon sea salt
2	tablespoons extra-virgin olive oil

Blend all the ingredients in a food processor. Eat as a dip or as a filling for a burrito. You may top the burrito with salsa, 1 tablespoon of guacamole, or 1 ounce of grated low-fat cheese. Store dip in the fridge in a sealed container.

Nutrition Information (per serving):
Calories 208 | Carbohydrates 25.0 g | Protein 15.7 g | Fat 5.0 g | Fiber 4.1 g

✿ ☺ Curried Chickpea Dip
Serves 4 or 5

1	can (15 ounces) organic chickpeas, drained and rinsed
¼	cup extra-virgin olive oil
2	tablespoons freshly squeezed lemon juice
½	teaspoon curry powder
½	teaspoon garam masala spice
2 or 3	cloves garlic, peeled
½	teaspoon sea salt
	Black pepper to taste
1	teaspoon cayenne (optional)
½	cup freshly chopped cilantro

(continued)

1. Purée the chickpeas, olive oil, lemon juice, curry powder, garam masala, garlic, salt, pepper, and, if using, cayenne in a food processor until smooth.
2. Add the cilantro and pulse a few times to combine.
3. Transfer the dip to a bowl. Eat ½ cup as a veggie dip or spread. Store dip in the fridge in a sealed container.

Nutrition Information (per serving):

Calories 245 | Carbohydrates 25.2 g | Protein 24.0 g | Fat 5.4 g | Fiber 4.1 g

✿ ☺ Quick Trail Mix
    3   tablespoons dry-roasted soy nuts
    1   tablespoon dried unsulfured cranberries or cherries

Mix the ingredients together and enjoy!

Nutrition Information:

Calories 203 | Carbohydrates 22.3 g | Protein 13.0 g | Fat 6.9 g | Fiber 3.1 g

✿ ☺ Hummus and Veggies
Serves 4

    Unlimited sliced red, yellow, and green bell peppers; celery sticks; broccoli; carrot sticks; etc.
    1   can (15 ounces) organic chickpeas, drained and rinsed
    2   tablespoons chia
    1   tablespoon plus 1½ teaspoons extra-virgin olive oil
    1–3 teaspoons tahini
    Sea salt and pepper to taste

1. Slice and cut the vegetables for dipping.
2. Place the chickpeas, chia, and olive oil in a food processor and blend until smooth.

Quick Trail Mix ✿ ☺

Hummus and Veggies ✿ ☺

3. Add the tahini and enough water to achieve the desired thickness.

4. Add the salt and pepper to taste and pulse to blend thoroughly.

Variations: Hummus is a very versatile dish; you can add curry, spinach, garlic, roasted red bell peppers, and many other ingredients for different variations on this fantastic snack choice.

Nutrition Information (per serving):
Calories 205 | Carbohydrates 24.0 g | Protein 16.0 g | Fat 6.0 g | Fiber 8.6 g

✿ Almond Butter Protein Bars
Makes 5 bars

2	cups oatmeal
½	cup sliced almonds
¼	cup ground flaxseeds
2	tablespoons lecithin
5	scoops whey protein powder (vanilla)
¼	cup almond butter
¼–½	cup water

1. Combine the oatmeal, almonds, flaxseeds, lecithin, and protein powder in a large bowl.

2. In a separate bowl, mix together the almond butter and water until blended.

3. Combine the almond butter mixture with the dry ingredients and mix well.

4. Place plastic wrap in the bottom of an 8-inch square pan, making sure there is enough to wrap over the top.

5. Place the mixture in the pan and press flat with the overhanging plastic wrap.

6. Put the pan in the freezer for 1 hour and then store in the refrigerator before slicing into 5 bars.

Nutrition Information (per serving):
Calories 225 | Carbohydrates 13.3 g | Protein 17.0 g | Fat 6.0 g | Fiber 5.0 g

✿ **Berry-Apple Ricotta Cheese**

½   cup low-fat ricotta cheese
½   cup strawberry halves
½   apple, sliced
1   tablespoon ground flaxseeds or chia

Mix together the ricotta cheese, strawberries, apple and ground flaxseeds or chia in a bowl. Eat and enjoy!

Nutrition Information:
Calories 219 | Carbohydrates 22.0 g | Protein 18.0 g | Fat 6.5 g | Fiber 5.2 g

✿ **Simple Apple Snack**
(Remove the cheese and use more nuts to make it a ✿ ☺ snack)
1   apple (organic)
1   ounce (or 1 slice) low-fat Swiss cheese
10   raw almonds

Enjoy!
You can change this snack by choosing 5 walnuts, 7 cashews, 8 pecans, or 1 tablespoon of sunflower seeds. You can also increase the amount of nuts you eat and eliminate the cheese (i.e., 12 almonds, 9 cashews, 11 pecans, 8 walnuts).

Nutrition Information:
Calories 165 | Carbohydrates 11.9 g | Protein 9.0 g | Fat 9.0 g | Fiber 4.5 g

✿ Berry-Pecan Mix

½   cup cottage cheese or ricotta cheese (1% fat)

½   cup sliced strawberries

¼   cup blueberries

2   ounces low-fat plain yogurt

1   tablespoon chia (or wheat bran—a fat-free option)

1   tablespoon chopped pecans

Place the ricotta, strawberries, blueberries, yogurt, and chia in a blender and blend until smooth. Top with the chopped nuts.

Nutrition Information:

Calories 252 | Carbohydrates 23.4 g | Protein 17.1 g | Fat 10.0 g | Fiber 4.8 g

✿ Healthy Nacho Snack

12   blue corn tortilla chips

½   cup shredded low-fat Cheddar or Colby cheese

¼   cup canned black beans, drained and rinsed

¼   cup salsa

½   tablespoon guacamole

Place the tortilla chips on a plate. Top with the shredded cheese and the beans. Bake or broil for a few minutes, until the cheese is melted. Use the salsa and guacamole as dips.

Nutrition Information:

Calories 202 | Carbohydrates 22.6 g | Protein 12.6 g | Fat 6.8 g | Fiber 4.1 g

✿ ☺ Tamari Almonds

Serves 8

2 cups raw almonds
2 tablespoons tamari

1. Preheat the oven to 350°F.
2. Mix the nuts with the tamari and bake for 10 to 15 minutes.

Note: Remember, 10 to 15 nuts with your apple is your snack. You have to be careful with nuts because it's not hard to eat too many!

Nutrition Information:

Calories 106 | Carbohydrates 3.6 g | Protein 4 g | Fat 9.1 g | Fiber 2.1 g

A Healthy Tasty Treat

✿ Erin's Healthy Muffins

Makes 24 medium-size muffins

Dry ingredients:

1½ cups organic slow-cooking oats
1½ cups fresh or frozen blueberries
1 cup freshly ground flaxseeds
1 cup whole grain spelt flour
1 cup grated carrots
½ cup crushed walnuts (or almonds or pumpkin seeds)
3 tablespoons dried cranberries or chopped dried organic apricots
4 teaspoons aluminum-free baking powder
1 teaspoon ground cinnamon

Wet ingredients:

- 1 cup organic soy milk
- ½ cup unsweetened crushed pineapple
- 2 omega-3 eggs
- 3 large egg whites
- 4 tablespoons blackstrap molasses
- 3 tablespoons extra-virgin olive oil
- 1 teaspoon vanilla extract

1. Preheat the oven to 350°F.
2. Butter two muffin pans (for 24 muffins).
3. Combine the dry ingredients in a large bowl.
4. Combine the wet ingredients in a small bowl by hand or with an electric mixer.
5. Combine the wet and dry ingredients and mix well.
6. Spoon the batter into the greased muffin pans, filling each cup about two-thirds full.
7. Place in the oven and bake for about 25 minutes.

Nutrition Information:

Don't worry about it. Enjoy your treat—you've earned it!

Your Detox Shopping List

Type of Food	Suggestions
Grain products	Brown rice, basmati rice, rice pasta, rice crackers
	Millet, quinoa, buckwheat or other gluten-free options
Condiments	Tamari (wheat-free soy sauce)
	Almond butter
	Honey (for your salad dressing only)
	Maple syrup (for your salad dressing only)
	Extra-virgin olive oil
	Apple cider vinegar
	Balsamic vinegar
	Hummus—any flavor (just watch for unhealthy oils!) or make your own
	Salsa (ensure no sugar added)
	Cocoa powder (preferably organic)
	Vegetable stock (preferably organic)
	Low-fat mayonnaise
	Tomato paste
	Blackstrap molasses
	Black olives
	Dijon mustard
	Worcestershire sauce
	Organic canola oil
	Sesame oil

Type of Food	Suggestions
Spices	Cinnamon
	Ginger (whole root)
	Ground mustard powder
	Chili powder
	Cumin
	Fresh garlic
	Sea salt
	Fresh ground pepper
	Curry powder
	Basil
	Oregano
	Nutmeg
	Crushed chiles
	Thyme
	Ground turmeric
	Ground coriander
	Anise
	Cayenne pepper
	Dill
Drinks, Milks, and Special Cheeses	Organic unsweetened soy milk (Soy Nice)
	Herbal teas, green tea
	Carbonated water/sodium-free soda water
	Purified water/reverse osmosis water
	Pure fruit juices (not from concentrate, nothing added)
	Goat cheese
	Sheep or goat feta cheese

Type of Food	Suggestions
Vegetables (The detox recipes call for these vegetables—though you can certainly include any vegetable except corn)	Frozen peas and spinach
	Canned tomatoes (large size, preferably organic)
	Sweet potatoes
	Broccoli
	Cauliflower
	Zucchini
	Tomatoes
	Asparagus
	Cucumber
	Baby spinach
	Baby carrots
	Cherry tomatoes
	Mushrooms
	Red and green bell peppers
	Mixed greens
	Red onion
Fruits (All fruits are okay *except for* grapes, melons [watermelon is allowed], raisins, and dates)	Frozen blueberries, strawberries, mango, raspberries, and pineapple
	Bananas
	Lemons
	Dried apricots
	Dried cranberries
	Avocado
	Mango
	Apples
	Peaches
	Bananas
Nuts/Seeds	Raw almonds (unsalted)
	Raw cashews (unsalted)
	Raw walnuts
	Raw pecan pieces
	Soy nuts (roasted)
	Chia and/or flaxseeds
	Sliced or slivered almonds
	Almond butter

Type of Food	Suggestions
Protein	Choose fresh options according to the recipes you wish to try (chicken breasts, ground turkey, scallops, shrimp, tilapia, etc.)
	Liquid egg whites
	Eggs
	Tempeh (usually found in the freezer at your health food store)
	Canned light tuna in water
	Canned wild salmon in water
Beans	Black beans
	Kidney beans
	Chickpeas
	Lentils (red or green—dried)
	Bean dips (or make your own!)
Options for On the Go	The Simply Bar (high-protein bar)
	Elevate Me! Bar (protein/energy bar)

Foods to Add to Your Kitchen—After Your Detox

Type of Food	Suggestions
Grain products	Stonemill bread (glycemically tested)
	Whole wheat pasta
	Rye crackers (Wasa or Ryvita)
	Kamut pasta (Sayoba)
	Whole grain or sprouted-grain tortillas
	100% rye bread (Dimpflmeier bread)
	Kashi GOLEAN Cereal
	Ezekiel bread (Foods For Life)
	High-fiber, whole wheat pita
	Spelt whole grain flour
Dairy products (preferably organic)	Pressed cottage cheese (Organic Meadows)
	Low-fat Cheddar or Colby cheese
	Low-fat cottage cheese
	Plain yogurt

Men's Daily Wellness Tracker

Keep track of your progress by photocopying the tracker and entering the data requested. Be sure to enter all foods eaten for each meal.

Date _____	Bedtime _____	Date _____	Bedtime _____
pH# _____	Hours slept ____	pH# _____	Hours slept ____
	Quality _____		Quality _____

Breakfast Time: _____	Breakfast Time: _____
Food:	Food:

Snack Time: _____	Snack Time: _____
Food:	Food:

Lunch Time: _____	Lunch Time: _____
Food:	Food:

Snack Time: _____	Snack Time: _____
Food:	Food:

Dinner Time: _____	Dinner Time: _____
Food:	Food:

Intake Checklist:	Hot Hormone Foods:	Intake Checklist:	Hot Hormone Foods:
Protein	Olive oil ☐1	Protein	Olive oil ☐1
☐1 ☐2 ☐3	Berries ☐1	☐1 ☐2 ☐3	Berries ☐1
Fats	Apple ☐1	Fats	Apple ☐1
☐1 ☐2 ☐3	Whey protein ☐1	☐1 ☐2 ☐3	Whey protein ☐1
Veggies	Flaxseeds/Salba ☐1	Veggies	Flaxseeds/Salba ☐1
☐1 ☐2 ☐3	Spices: Cinnamon,	☐1 ☐2 ☐3	Spices: Cinnamon,
☐4 ☐5 ☐6	Turmeric, etc. ☐	☐4 ☐5 ☐6	Turmeric, etc. ☐
☐7 ☐8 ☐9	Broccoli	☐7 ☐8 ☐9	Broccoli
☐10	☐2 cups/wk	☐10	☐2 cups/wk
Dairy ☐1	Green tea	Dairy ☐1	Green tea
Nuts ☐1	☐1 cup ☐3 cups	Nuts ☐1	☐1 cup ☐3 cups
Fruits ☐1 ☐2	☐2 cups ☐4 cups	Fruits ☐1 ☐2	☐2 cups ☐4 cups
Beans ☐1		Beans ☐1	
Starchy veg/Grains		Starchy veg/Grains	
☐1 ☐2		☐1 ☐2	

Water	Supplements	Water	Supplements
☐1 ☐2 ☐3	☐	☐1 ☐2 ☐3	☐
☐4 ☐5 ☐6		☐4 ☐5 ☐6	
☐7 ☐8 ☐9		☐7 ☐8 ☐9	
☐10 ☐11 ☐12		☐10 ☐11 ☐12	
☐13 ☐14		☐13 ☐14	

Exercise ☐Strength	Relaxation	Exercise ☐Strength	Relaxation
☐Cardio ☐Yoga	☐Visualization	☐Cardio ☐Yoga	☐Visualization
	☐Meditation		☐Meditation

Date _____ pH# _____	Bedtime _____ Hours slept ____ Quality _____	Date _____ pH# _____	Bedtime _____ Hours slept ____ Quality _____
Breakfast Time: _____ Food:		Breakfast Time: _____ Food:	
Snack Time: _____ Food:		Snack Time: _____ Food:	
Lunch Time: _____ Food:		Lunch Time: _____ Food:	
Snack Time: _____ Food:		Snack Time: _____ Food:	
Dinner Time: _____ Food:		Dinner Time: _____ Food:	

Column 1

Intake Checklist:
Protein
□1 □2 □3
Fats
□1 □2 □3
Veggies
□1 □2 □3
□4 □5 □6
□7 □8 □9
□10
Dairy □1
Nuts □1
Fruits □1 □2
Beans □1
Starchy veg/Grains
□1 □2

Hot Hormone Foods:
Olive oil □1
Berries □1
Apple □1
Whey protein □1
Flaxseeds/Salba □1
Spices: Cinnamon,
Turmeric, etc. □
Broccoli
   □2 cups/wk
Green tea
□1 cup   □3 cups
□2 cups   □4 cups

Water
□1 □2 □3
□4 □5 □6
□7 □8 □9
□10 □11 □12
□13 □14

Supplements
□

Exercise □Strength
□Cardio □Yoga

Relaxation
□Visualization
□Meditation

Column 2

Intake Checklist:
Protein
□1 □2 □3
Fats
□1 □2 □3
Veggies
□1 □2 □3
□4 □5 □6
□7 □8 □9
□10
Dairy □1
Nuts □1
Fruits □1 □2
Beans □1
Starchy veg/Grains
□1 □2

Hot Hormone Foods:
Olive oil □1
Berries □1
Apple □1
Whey protein □1
Flaxseeds/Salba □1
Spices: Cinnamon,
Turmeric, etc. □
Broccoli
   □2 cups/wk
Green tea
□1 cup   □3 cups
□2 cups   □4 cups

Water
□1 □2 □3
□4 □5 □6
□7 □8 □9
□10 □11 □12
□13 □14

Supplements
□

Exercise □Strength
□Cardio □Yoga

Relaxation
□Visualization
□Meditation

Women's Daily Wellness Tracker

Date _____ pH#_____	Bedtime _____ Hours slept____ Quality_____	Date _____ pH#_____	Bedtime _____ Hours slept____ Quality_____
Breakfast Time:_____ Food:		Breakfast Time:_____ Food:	
Snack Time:_____ Food:		Snack Time:_____ Food:	
Lunch Time:_____ Food:		Lunch Time:_____ Food:	
Snack Time:_____ Food:		Snack Time:_____ Food:	
Dinner Time:_____ Food:		Dinner Time:_____ Food:	

Intake Checklist:	Hot Hormone Foods:	Intake Checklist:	Hot Hormone Foods:

Protein
 ☐1   ☐2   ☐3
 Fats
 ☐1   ☐2   ☐3
 Veggies
 ☐1   ☐2   ☐3
 ☐4   ☐5   ☐6
 ☐7   ☐8   ☐9
 ☐10
 Dairy ☐1
 Nuts ☐1
 Fruits ☐1   ☐2
 Beans ☐1
 Starchy veg/Grains
 ☐1   ☐2
	Olive oil ☐1
	 Berries ☐1
	 Apple ☐1
	 Whey protein ☐1
	 Flaxseeds/Salba ☐1
	 Spices: Cinnamon,
	 Turmeric, etc. ☐
	 Broccoli
	     ☐2 cups/wk
	 Green tea
	 ☐1 cup ☐3 cups
	 ☐2 cups ☐4 cups
		Protein
		 ☐1 ☐2 ☐3
		 Fats
		 ☐1 ☐2 ☐3
		 Veggies
		 ☐1 ☐2 ☐3
		 ☐4 ☐5 ☐6
		 ☐7 ☐8 ☐9
		 ☐10
		 Dairy ☐1
		 Nuts ☐1
		 Fruits ☐1 ☐2
		 Beans ☐1
		 Starchy veg/Grains
		 ☐1 ☐2
			Olive oil ☐1
			 Berries ☐1
			 Apple ☐1
			 Whey protein ☐1
			 Flaxseeds/Salba ☐1
			 Spices: Cinnamon,
			 Turmeric, etc. ☐
			 Broccoli
			     ☐2 cups/wk
			 Green tea
			 ☐1 cup ☐3 cups
			 ☐2 cups ☐4 cups

Water ☐1 ☐2 ☐3 ☐4 ☐5 ☐6 ☐7 ☐8 ☐9 ☐10 ☐11 ☐12 ☐13 ☐14	Supplements ☐	Water ☐1 ☐2 ☐3 ☐4 ☐5 ☐6 ☐7 ☐8 ☐9 ☐10 ☐11 ☐12 ☐13 ☐14	Supplements ☐
Exercise ☐Strength ☐Cardio ☐Yoga	Relaxation ☐Visualization ☐Meditation	Exercise ☐Strength ☐Cardio ☐Yoga	Relaxation ☐Visualization ☐Meditation

Date _____	Bedtime _____	Date _____	Bedtime _____
pH#_____	Hours slept_____	pH#_____	Hours slept_____
	Quality_____		Quality_____

Breakfast	Time:_____	Breakfast	Time:_____
Food:		Food:	

Snack	Time:_____	Snack	Time:_____
Food:		Food:	

Lunch	Time:_____	Lunch	Time:_____
Food:		Food:	

Snack	Time:_____	Snack	Time:_____
Food:		Food:	

Dinner	Time:_____	Dinner	Time:_____
Food:		Food:	

Intake Checklist:

Protein
☐1 ☐2 ☐3
Fats
☐1 ☐2 ☐3
Veggies
☐1 ☐2 ☐3
☐4 ☐5 ☐6
☐7 ☐8 ☐9
☐10
Dairy ☐1
Nuts ☐1
Fruits ☐1 ☐2
Beans ☐1
Starchy veg/Grains
☐1 ☐2

Hot Hormone Foods:

Olive oil ☐1
Berries ☐1
Apple ☐1
Whey protein ☐1
Flaxseeds/Salba ☐1
Spices: Cinnamon,
Turmeric, etc. ☐
Broccoli
　☐2 cups/wk
Green tea
☐1 cup ☐3 cups
☐2 cups ☐4 cups

Intake Checklist:

Protein
☐1 ☐2 ☐3
Fats
☐1 ☐2 ☐3
Veggies
☐1 ☐2 ☐3
☐4 ☐5 ☐6
☐7 ☐8 ☐9
☐10
Dairy ☐1
Nuts ☐1
Fruits ☐1 ☐2
Beans ☐1
Starchy veg/Grains
☐1 ☐2

Hot Hormone Foods:

Olive oil ☐1
Berries ☐1
Apple ☐1
Whey protein ☐1
Flaxseeds/Salba ☐1
Spices: Cinnamon,
Turmeric, etc. ☐
Broccoli
　☐2 cups/wk
Green tea
☐1 cup ☐3 cups
☐2 cups ☐4 cups

Water
☐1 ☐2 ☐3
☐4 ☐5 ☐6
☐7 ☐8 ☐9
☐10 ☐11 ☐12
☐13 ☐14

Supplements
☐

Water
☐1 ☐2 ☐3
☐4 ☐5 ☐6
☐7 ☐8 ☐9
☐10 ☐11 ☐12
☐13 ☐14

Supplements
☐

Exercise ☐Strength
☐Cardio ☐Yoga

Relaxation
☐Visualization
☐Meditation

Exercise ☐Strength
☐Cardio ☐Yoga

Relaxation
☐Visualization
☐Meditation

ACKNOWLEDGMENTS

I cannot thank my family and friends enough for putting up with the rigors of my work schedule. Tim, Mom, Simon, Maria, Bruce, Betty, Mari, and the Martin family, I love you. Thank you for your support. Cynthy, Lise, Lorri, Tim Thorney, and PG, you have helped me more than you will ever know.

I wish to thank my patients for enriching my learning and my life in so many ways. I am honored to have the opportunity to care for each and every one of you. A special note to Silvia Presenza, Jeffrey Long, Natalie Shay, and author Caroline Van Hasselt—your support is an incredible source of inspiration for me.

Next, a *huge* thank you to Andrea Ritter for your editing skills, input, and ideas. Thank you for working so hard on such a short timeline. Your contributions have been an immense help in making this book better.

Sandro Sagrati, the value of our friendship and your faith in me is something I cannot begin to measure. You have been instrumental in not only making this book better, but also in continuing to make *me* a better person. Dr. Jan Dorrell, you are a wonderful friend and doctor. I am honored to have had your expertise and contribution on this project.

Thank you to Chantal Richard for your friendship, editing, and encouragement. In front of me is the copy of *On Writing Well* that you gave me years ago along with the note, "I hope this book inspires you as much as it inspires me. You *will* be published someday." All

I can say is thank you. Your belief in me has made a difference.

I wish to thank personal trainer and sports and conditioning coach Reggie Reyes for his input with the exercise component of this program—and for helping with the setup of the training studio at Clear Medicine.

Thank you to my agent, Rick Broadhead. Without you none of this would have been possible. Thank you to Rodale for seeing the potential in this project. A special message of gratitude to Denise McGann for her editorial input and to my publicist, for being instrumental in getting this approach "out there."

A sincere message of thanks to Jonathon Wright, MD, for taking the time out of his incredibly busy schedule to read this book, share his knowledge, and offer his suggestions.

Thank you to Jason Gee, certified strength and conditioning specialist, and personal trainer Vanessa Bell for posing as fitness models and for helping me with the exercise terminology when I was on such a tight deadline. And, to a multitalented osteopath, Sam Gibbs, thank you for your photography skills and for keeping me healthy—I am very grateful.

To Lucia—thank you for your help with this project and my clinic, Clear Medicine.

Lastly, thank you, the reader, for picking up this book. By doing so, you have helped me to fulfill my life's purpose—to inspire others to achieve better health.

RESOURCES

(Please look for the resources for specialized medical testing in Appendix A)

Heavy Metal Detox
   Detoxamin: EDTA suppositories: www.detoxamin.com

Infrared Sauna
   Infrared Saunas: www.saunaray.com

Natural Lubricants
   Hathor: www.hathorbody.com
   O'My: www.omyonline.com

Body Fat/Composition Analyzer
   Tanita: Home body-fat analyzer: www.tanita.com

Natural Skin Care and Makeup
   Naturopathica: Environmental Defense Facial Mask:
      www.naturopathica.com
   Be.Products Company: Skin care made from natural food: www.befine.com
   Caudalie: Toxin free skin care: www.caudalie-usa.com
   Juice Beauty: Toxin free skin care: www.juicebeauty.com
   John Masters: Toxin free skin and hair care: www.johnmasters.com
   Burt's Bees: Natural skin care: www.burtsbees.com
   Alba Organics: Sugar Cane Body Polish, Kukui Nut Organic Body Oil:
      www.albaorganics.com (Unlike the two products listed here, all Alba
      products may not be free of harmful methylparabens and propyl
      parabens.)
   Dr. Hauschka Skin Care: www.drhauschka.com
   Jane Iredale: Mineral makeup: www.janeiredale.com

Supplements

Zenbev: Natural source of tryptophan to boost serotonin, reduce anxiety, sleep disruption, and depression: www.zenbev.com

Wobenzym N: One of the top selling natural anti-inflammatory enzyme formulas in the world www.wobenzym-usa.com; www.thehormonediet.com or www.clearmedicinestore.com

Clear Detox—Homonal Health, Clear Detox—Digestive Health, Clear Essentials—Morning and Evening: www.clearmedicinestore.com or www.thehormonediet.com

Carlson Fish Oils: www.carlsonlabs.com

Nordic Natural Fish Oils : www.nordicnaturals.com, www.clearmedicinestore.com

Jarrow: www.jarrow.com

Genuine Health: (Proteins+, all natural whey protein isolate supplement and Greens+, green food supplements): www.genuinehealth.com

New Chapter: www.newchapter.com

AOR: www.aor.ca; www.thehormonediet.com or www.clearmedicinestore.com

Doctor's Choice: Dream Protein (all natural whey protein supplement): www.thehormonediet.com or www.clearmedicinestore.com

Pure Encapsulations: (G.I. Fortify and Liver-G.I. Detox): www.purecaps.com

Seditol Natural sleep aid containing Magnolia Bark Extract: www.thehormonediet.com or www.clearmedicinestore.com

Glyci-Med Forte: Olive and avocado oil supplement to aid weight loss: www.thehormonediet.com or www.clearmedicinestore.com

Metagenics: www.metagenics.com, www.thehormonediet.com, or www.clearmedicinestore.com

Life Extension Foundation: www.lef.org

Specialty Foods

Green and Blacks: Organic chocolate: www.greenandblacks.com

NewTree: Fine Belgian dark chocolate: www.newtree.com

Cocoa Camino: Organic fair-trade chocolate: www.cocoacamino.com

The Simply Bar: Gluten-free protein bar: www.wellnessfoods.ca; www.thehormonediet.com or www.clearmedicinestore.com

Acai Canada Inc.: Açaí berry products: www.acaicanada.com

Sambazon: Açaí concentrate: www.sambazon.com

Navitas Naturals: Goji Power: www.navitasnaturals.com

Pom Wonderful: Pomegranate juice: www.pomwonderful.com

La Tortilla Factory: Pitas, wraps, and gluten-free products: www.latortillafactory.com

Muzi Teas: Green tea: www.muzitea.com

Mr Pita: Low-carb, high-protein pita: www.mrpita.ca

Organic Meadow: Organic pressed cottage cheese: www.organicmeadow.com

Liberté: Organic yogurt: (this brand has the right balance of protein and carbs): www.liberte.qc.ca/en/home.ch2

Kashi Company: GOLEAN high-protein, high-fiber cereal: www.kashi.com

Dimpflmeier Bakery: 100% rye bread: www.dimpflmeierbakery.com

Food For Life Baking Co.: Ezekiel breads: www.foodforlife.com

Bob's Red Mill Natural Foods: Gluten-free and other grain products www.bobsredmill.com

So Nice: Unsweetened organic soy milk: www.sonice.ca

PROsnack Natural Foods: Elevate Me! (organic whole-food and protein bar): www.prosnack.com

Relaxation Aids

Somerset Entertainment: Sonic Aid (meditation and sleep CD series by Dr. Lee Bartel): www.somersetent.com

Toxin-Free Household Cleaning Products

Nature Clean: www.naturecleanliving.com

Attitude: www.thegoodattitude.com

Seventh Generation: www.seventhgeneration.com

Organic Cotton Bedding and Mattresses

The Guide to Less Toxic Products (provides numerous sources): www.lesstoxicguide.ca

Health Information Resources

Life Extension Foundation: www.lef.org

Mary Shomon's thyroid health Web site: www.thyroid.about.com

SeaChoice: Healthy seafood choices: www.seachoice.org

Harvard School of Public Health: The Nutrition Source www.hsph.harvard.edu/nutritionsource/index.html

Whole Foods Market: Tasty soup recipes!: www.wholefoodsmarket.com/recipes

Slice—Health Inspired Food: www.sliceofhealth.com

Environmental Working Group: Information about cosmetics, seafood safety, etc.: www.ewg.org

Calorie King: Nutrition information database: www.calorieking.com

Glycemic Index and GI Database (University of Sydney):
    www.glycemicindex.com
American Journal of Clinical Nutrition Glycemic Load Chart:
    www.ajcn.org/cgi/content/full/76/1/5#SEC2
International Hormone Society: www.intlhormonesociety.org
Clear Medicine: www.clearmedicinestore.com

INDEX

Underscored page references indicate sidebars. **Boldface** references indicate photographs and illustrations.

Aging
   growth hormone declining with, 155
   inflammatory diseases associated with,
      25
   metabolism slowed by, 124
   muscle loss with, 21, 32–33, 124
   progesterone declining with, 72
   sex and, 328, 330
   of skin, 374, 375, 376
   slowing, 125
   testosterone declining with, 69, 72
Alcohol
   avoiding
      in Anti-Inflammatory Detox, 193
      before bedtime, 167, 388
   estrogen dominance from, 69, 71, 74
   harmful effects of, 148, 244–45
Alkaline juices and smoothies, for
      reducing body acidity, 142
Alkalinity, whole-body
   excess, 139
   normal range of, 139
Allergies, probiotics relieving, 187
Almond butter
   Almond Butter Protein Bars, 461
Almonds
   Almond-Encrusted Baked Halibut
      with Sweet Potato Mash and
      Baked Asparagus, 456–57
   Tamari Almonds, 464
Alpha-glycerophosphocholine, for low
      acetylcholine, 316
Alpha-lipoic acid
   for excess insulin, 300
   in skin-care creams, 380
Amino acids, for low growth hormone,
      317–18
Andropause, 19, 36, 94, 96, 413
Angelica, for low estrogen, 310
Anti-Inflammatory Detox
   determining need for, 190–91
   five keys to healthy digestion in, 180–
      89
   foods disallowed in, 134, 146, 192–93,
      205–6
   foods permitted in, 134, 192, 193–94,
      205–6, 282–83

   foods to add to kitchen after, 469
   getting started with, 191–97
   hormonal benefits from, 176
   kitchen mini-makeover for, 134,
      146–47
   questions and answers about, 199–201
   reintroducing foods after, 197–98,
      198–99, 203–4, 207
   for safe fat loss, 126–27, 126
   sample menu plan for, 203–4
   shopping list for, 134, 147, 466–69
   supplements in, 134, 194–97, 206
   tips for, 201–3
   walking in, 203
   when to repeat, 389
   whey protein isolate powder during,
      422
Anxiety
   step 2 reducing, 36
   supplements reducing, 168–69, 170,
      172
Appearance, effect of hormones on, 15
Appetite, factors influencing, 29, 258
   exercise, 333
   fats, 274, 275
   ghrelin (see Ghrelin)
   insulin, 56–57
   leptin (see Leptin)
   sex, 328–29
   sleep, 156–57
   stress hormones, 67, 68
Apples
   Berry-Apple Ricotta Cheese, 462
   Simple Apple Snack, 462
Apple shape
   from excess estrogen, 72
   insulin secretion and, 15
   low-fat vs. low-glycemic diet and, 18
Arm exercises. See Hormone Diet exercise
      plan, strength training workout in
Artificial sweeteners, 242–44, 257
   avoiding, in Anti-Inflammatory Detox,
      193
Ashwagandha, for treating
   excess cortisol, 307
   low thyroid hormone, 314
   sleep problems, 171

Asparagus
  Almond-Encrusted Baked Halibut
      with Sweet Potato Mash and
      Baked Asparagus, 456–57
Aspartame, 243, 257
Avocados
  Açai-Avocado Smoothie, 423
  Blueberry-Avocado Smoothie, 425
  California Avocado and Chicken Salad,
      434

B
Back exercises. *See* Hormone Diet exercise
      plan, strength training workout in
Back extensions, for legs and core, 353,
      354
Back extensions on ball, for chest, back,
      and core, 352, **353**
Bacterial balance, for healthy digestion,
      186–87
Bad breath, probiotics preventing, 187
Ball pull-ins with push-up, for arms and
      core, 358, **358**
Bathroom, detoxifying, 134, 418
Beans
  Black Bean Dip or Burrito Filling, 459
  Curried Chickpea Dip, 459–60
  Eggscetylcholine Pocket, 430
  Healthy Nacho Snack, 463
  Hummus and Veggies, 460–61
  permitted in Anti-Inflammatory
      Detox, 193
  Veggie Chili, 446–47
  Warm Black Bean and Turkey Salad, 438
  Zippy Three-Bean Salad, 437
Bedroom
  detoxifying, 134, 420
  sleep improvement and, 157, 158, 159,
      160, 161
Beef. *See also* Meats
  Beef Fajita with Side Salad, 453–54
Belly fat. *See* Abdominal fat
Bent-knee dumbbell deadlift with calf
      raise, for legs and core, 357, **357**
Bent-over dumbbell row (double arm),
      for chest, back, and core, 351, **351**
Bent-over dumbbell row (single arm), for
      chest, back, and core, 351, **352**

Bent-over reverse dumbbell fly, 364, **364**
Berries
  Antiaging Smoothie, 425
  Anti-Inflammatory Smoothie, 428
  Berry-Apple Ricotta Cheese, 462
  Berry-Pecan Mix, 463
  Blueberry-Avocado Smoothie, 425
  Lovely Leptin Lastin' Satisfaction, 429
  Pure Energy Smoothie, 423
  Super Satisfying Shake, 426
  Testosterone-Surge Smoothie, 427
Best Body Assessment, 6, 134, 135
  components of, 138–46
  purpose of, 136
  tools for, 137–38
Betaine hydrochloride (BH), for HCl
      challenge test, 185–86
Beverages, fructose-sweetened, 239
BH, for HCl challenge test, 185–86
BIA machine, for measuring body fat,
      116–17, 138
Bi-est bioidentical cream, for low
      estrogen, 310
Bioidentical hormone replacement
      therapy (BHRT), 91, 148, 404
Bioidentical progesterone cream, for low
      progesterone, 311
Bioidentical testosterone cream, for low
      testosterone, 312
Bioimpedance analysis (BIA) machine, for
      measuring body fat, 116–17, 138
Biotin, for excess insulin, 300
Birth control pills, 3
  excess estrogen from, 73
  probiotics and, 186, 187, 195
  zinc depletion from, 400
Bisphenol-A (BPA), 178
Black cohosh, for low estrogen, 310
Bloating, from low stomach acidity,
      182–83
Blood pressure, measuring, in Best Body
      Assessment, 143
Blood pressure monitor, 138, 143
Blood sugar
  carbohydrates increasing, 156
  glucagon increasing, 86
  maintaining, for hormonal balance, 34

PPARs and, 23
stabilizing, 86–87
Blood tests, 134
annual, 137, 143, 385, 399
assessing insulin sensitivity, <u>62</u>,
144–46
for general health, immunity, and
wellness, 399–400
for glycemic control, fat loss, diabetes,
and heart disease risk, 400–4
hormonal assessment, 404–9
thyroid, 397
Blueberries
Erin's Healthy Muffins, 464–65
Body assessment. *See* Best Body Assessment
Body composition
determining, in Best Body Assessment, 138–39
fat vs. lean muscle, 114–16
measurements of, 116–17
menopause changing, 76
monitoring changes in, 117–18
of obese vs. overweight people, 116
of "skinny-fat person," 115–16
stress hormones affecting, <u>67</u>, <u>68</u>
Body fat
hormones produced by, 118–22, **119**
sugar stored as, 56
Body mass index (BMI), 116
Body shape. *See also* Apple shape; Pear
shape
effect of hormones on, 28–29
Body weight
maintaining set point of, 35
metabolism affecting, 20–21
Bowel-cleansing formula with fiber, in
Anti-Inflammatory Detox, 196–97
BPA, 178
Breakfast(s)
Açai-Avocado Smoothie, 423
Antiaging Smoothie, 425
Anti-Inflammatory Smoothie, 428
Awesome Omelette, 428–29
balanced, 263
Blueberry-Avocado Smoothie, 425
Dopamine Delight Smoothie, 426

Eggscetylcholine Pocket, 430
in hormonally balanced day, 386
Lovely Leptin Lastin' Satisfaction, 429
olive oil and, <u>275</u>
Power Oatmeal, 430
Pure Energy Smoothie, 423
Serotonin-Surge Smoothie, 427
skipping, 247, 393
Super Satisfying Shake, 426
Testosterone-Surge Smoothie, 427
Breast cancer
CRP and, 403
estrogen and, 7, 179, 241, 245, <u>261</u>,
333, 378
exercise preventing, <u>74</u>
hypothyroidism and, <u>85</u>
metabolic syndrome and, <u>63</u>
omega-6 fats and, 236
parabens and, 378
polycystic ovarian syndrome and, 3
progesterone preventing, 87
supplements preventing, 109, 291,
309
testosterone and, 406
Broccoli
Grilled Halibut with Rice and Broccoli,
449–50
B vitamins, for excess cortisol, 306

C
Caffeine
avoiding, in Anti-Inflammatory Detox,
193
interfering with sleep, 166
limiting, 396–97
Caffeine withdrawal, 199
Calcium D-glucarate, for treating
excess estrogen, 309
excess testosterone, 314
Calcium-magnesium supplement, 290,
<u>293</u>
Calorie burning
from exercise, 332
from muscle, 21, 22
Calorie counting, avoiding, 254
Calorie restriction, problems with, 30–31,
125, 247
Calories, on nutrition labels, 270

Cancer. *See also* Breast cancer; Prostate
    cancer
  artificial sweeteners and, <u>242</u>, 243
  from estrogen dominance, 70, 71, <u>72</u>,
    75, 119
  exercise preventing, <u>74</u>
  gastric, 183
  from indoor toxin exposure, 417–18
  obesity and, <u>126</u>
  sleep deprivation and, 162
  vitamin D preventing, 109, 285
Carbohydrate cravings
  from high cortisol, 156
  with insulin resistance, 2, 3
  from low serotonin, 76
Carbohydrates
  avoiding, before sleep, 166
  balancing fats and protein with, 248,
    255
  eaten with protein, 86, 87
  in Glyci-Med Dietary Approach,
    261–64, <u>264–68</u>
  for increasing serotonin, 303–4
  insulin and, 5, 6, 55, 56, 58
  on nutrition labels, 269
Cardio exercise
  avoiding overuse of, 338–39
  for boosting metabolism, 392, 393
  in Hormone Diet exercise plan, 344
  interval, 366–68
  problem with, 6
  workout mistakes with, 334–35,
    336–37
Carrots
  Roasted Vegetable Soup, 442–43
CCK, <u>109</u>, 242, 250, 260, 274, 275
Cellulite, 181
Chasteberry extract, for treating
  low dopamine, 302
  low progesterone, 311
Cheese
  Berry-Apple Ricotta Cheese, 462
  Goat Cheese, Green Pea, and Spinach
    Frittata, 433–34
  reintroducing, during Anti-Inflammatory
    Detox, <u>198</u>, <u>204</u>, <u>207</u>
  Simple Apple Snack, 462

Cherry juice extract, for low melatonin, 317
Chest dumbbell press on ball, for chest,
    back, and core, <u>350</u>, <u>350</u>
Chest exercises. *See* Hormone Diet exercise
    plan, strength training workout in
Chia, <u>253</u>, 422
  Curried Tuna-Chia Salad, 432
Chicken
  Anti-Inflammatory Curry, 447–48
  Antioxidant Chicken Salad, 433
  California Avocado and Chicken Salad,
    434
  Coconut Curry Dish, 455
  Easy Caesar Salad, 441
  Greek Salad Topped with Grilled
    Chicken Breast, 431–32
  India-Style Chicken Pita Pocket with
    Side Salad, 439
  Pomegranate, Peach, and Pecan
    Chicken Salad, 444–45
  Sweet Garlic Chicken Stir-Fry, 448
  Zesty Chicken Salad, 440
Chickpeas
  Curried Chickpea Dip, 459–60
  Hummus and Veggies, 460–61
Chili
  Veggie Chili, 446–47
Cholesterol
  function of, 274, 275
  reducing, 95
Chromium, for excess insulin, 300
Chronic atrophic gastritis, 183
Cinnamon, for excess insulin, 300
Circuit training, 344
Citrus fruit, avoiding, in Anti-
    Inflammatory Detox, 193
CLA, 299, <u>343</u>
Cleaning products, nontoxic, 418
Cleansers, face, natural, 377–78
Clear Detox products
  for Anti-Inflammatory Detox, 194,
    196, 201
  for liver detox, 314, 399
  for treating
    excess estrogen, 308–9
    excess progesterone, 312
    excess testosterone, 314

Coconut milk
    Coconut Curry Dish, 455
Coenzyme Q10, 290–91, 291, 381
Coffee, 257, 386
Coldness, from deficient thyroid
    hormone, 21
Colds, probiotics preventing, 187
Computers, chemicals released by, 419
Conjugated linoleic acid (CLA), 299, 343
Constipation
    during Anti-Inflammatory Detox,
        200–201
    from deficient thyroid hormone, 21
Cookware, nontoxic, 418
Core exercises. See Hormone Diet exercise
        plan, strength training workout in
Corn, avoiding, in Anti-Inflammatory
        Detox, 192
Cortisol
    abdominal fat and, 36
    adrenal gland burnout depleting, 217
    assessing level of, 68
    caffeine and, 166
    calorie intake and, 17
    depressing progesterone and
        testosterone, 36
    detoxification and, 176
    excess
        high testosterone with, 314
        Hormonal Health Profile for
            assessing, 43
        hypothyroidism from, 83
        muscle loss from, 393
        preventing weight loss, 397
        review of diagnostic tests for, 413–14
        from stress, 64–66, 67–68, 212,
            213, 214, 215, 223, 247
        supplements for treating, 305–6
    factors increasing
        alcohol, 245
        calorie restriction, 247
        depression, 28
        excess protein, 270
        visceral fat, 112
    fats and, 275
    Glyci-Med Dietary Approach
        controlling, 251, 255

lowering, with
    exercise, 342
    laughter, 224
    massage, 223, 224
    meditation, 221
    yoga, 341
positive functions of, 66
secretion of, 17
sex and, 328
skin aging and, 374–75
sleep and, 156, 166, 173
testing levels of, 405
understanding levels of, 68–69
Cosmetics
    chemicals in, 377
    natural, 382
C-reactive protein (CRP)
    blood tests for detecting, 28
    depression and, 27, 28
Creatine, 291, 343
Crunches over the ball, for chest, back,
        and core, 348, 348
Curry powder
    Anti-Inflammatory Curry, 447–48
    Coconut Curry Dish, 455
    Curried Chickpea Dip, 459–60
D
Dairy products
    avoiding, in Anti-Inflammatory Detox,
        192
    permitted in Anti-Inflammatory
        Detox, 194
Darkness, for sleep improvement,
        157–58, 162
Dehydroepiandrosterone (DHEA). See
    DHEA
Den, detoxifying, 419
Depression
    from deficient thyroid hormone, 21
    heart disease risk and, 28
    inflammation and, 27–28
    as leading disability, 19
    from low serotonin, 99, 100, 101–2
    oversleeping and, 162
    step 2 for reducing, 36
    supplements for, 169, 170
Dermis, 373–74

harmful effects of, 58–59

high testosterone with, 314

Hormonal Health Profile for
assessing, <u>40–41</u>

review of diagnostic tests for, <u>412</u>

supplements reducing, 299–301

factors increasing

alcohol, 244–45

depression, <u>28</u>

low estrogen, 76

low-fiber foods, 246

functions of, 55

glucagon release and, 86

obesity and, 5, 6

PPARs and, 23

reducing, with

exercise, 342

fish oils, 288–89

Glyci-Med Dietary Approach, 251, 255

secretion of, determining best diet
type, 15

Insulin resistance, <u>60</u>, **61**, <u>62</u>

abdominal fat from, 145, 394

blood tests revealing, 144–46

dysfunctional PPARs and, 23

Hormonal Health Profile revealing, 144

inflammation and, 27

with polycystic ovarian syndrome, 3

resistin causing, 121

review of diagnostic tests for, <u>412</u>

visceral fat and, 112

vitamin D and, <u>110</u>

Insulin sensitivity

assessing, <u>62</u>, 144–46

improving, with

adiponectin, 120–21

exercise, 6, 333

muscle, 123

vitamin D and, <u>110</u>

Interval training

benefits of, 336–37

cardio, 366–68

Irritable bowel syndrome, <u>99</u>, 188–89,
<u>210–11</u>

J

Journaling, 164, 202, 226

K

Kitchen, detoxifying, 418–19

L

L-arginine, for low testosterone, 312

Laughter, for stress relief, 224

Law of Attraction, 228

Leaky gut syndrome, 188, 196

Lecithin, in smoothies, 424

Leg exercises. *See* Hormone Diet exercise
plan, strength training workout in

Leg raises with ball between feet, 355, **355**

Leg raise with pulse up to ceiling, for
chest, back, and core, <u>348</u>, **349**

Lemon water, for reducing body acidity,
<u>142</u>

Lentils

Lovely Lentil Soup, 436

Leptin, <u>17</u>, 57, <u>67</u>, 107–9, <u>109</u>, **119**, 120,
121, 123, <u>153</u>, 156, <u>176</u>, 177, 212,
238, 242, 243, 245, 246, 247,
250, 262, 271, 274, 275, <u>289</u>, 332,
333, <u>342</u>, 386, 388

Leptin resistance, <u>101</u>, 108, 122

L-glutamine powder, in smoothies, 424.
See also Glutamine

Licorice, for low estrogen, 311

Light(ing)

effect on sleep, 158, 160–61, 163, 388

morning, 163, 386

at work, 387

Litmus paper strips, for pH testing, 137,
141

Liver

detoxifying, for excess testosterone, 314

fat burning and, 22, 189–90

PPARs in, 23

in toxin removal, 179, 180

Liver function

maximizing, for total wellness and fat
loss, 35

poor

effects of, 27

estrogen dominance from, <u>73–74</u>

Living room, detoxifying, 419

Locally grown foods, 252, 279

Loneliness, stress of, 213

Longjack, for low testosterone, 312

Low-fat diet

estrogen deficiency from, 76

insulin secretion and, 15, 18

Peroxisome proliferator-activated
receptors (PPARs), 22–24, 25
Personal trainers, 338, 347, 369, 393
PGX, for excess insulin, 300–301
pH balance, in digestive tract, 184–85
Phenylalanine, for low dopamine, 301
Phosphatidylcholine, for low
acetylcholine, 316
Phosphatidylserine
for excess cortisol, 307
for improving sleep, 173
pH testing, in Best Body Assessment,
141–42
Phthalates, 178, 377
Pituitary gland, 16, **16**, 17, 83
Plank
for chest, back, and core, 348, **349**
for legs and core, 357, **357**
Plastics, eliminating, for detox, 146–47
Plate arrangement, in Glyci-Med Dietary
Approach, 277, 281
Polycystic ovarian syndrome (PCOS), 3
Pomegranate
Pomegranate, Peach, and Pecan
Chicken Salad, 444–45
Portions, super-sized, 246
Positive belief, for stress relief, 220,
230–31
Poultry. *See* Chicken; Turkey
PPARs, 22–24, 25
Pregnancy, vitamin D3 deficiency in, 110
Premenstrual syndrome (PMS), 4, 7, 19,
75, 87, 154, 180, 302, 310, 311,
406, 407
Probiotic supplements, 293, 386
for Anti-Inflammatory Detox, 195
benefits of, 186–87, 195
Progesterone
cortisol depressing, 36
declining with age, 72
effect on skin, 373, 375
excess, 88
Hormonal Health Profile for
assessing, 47
supplements for treating, 312
symptoms of, 89
fats and, 275

GABA supported by, 107
for immune system health, 27
low, 87–88
Hormonal Health Profile for assessing, 46–47
hypothyroidism from, 83
sleep deprivation from, 154
supplements for treating, 311
symptoms of, 89
secretion of, 17
testing levels of, 407
Prostate cancer, 72, 75, 87, 99, 236, 240,
241, 309
Prostate health, supplements for, 291
Protein
in bedtime snacks, 166–67
eaten with carbohydrates, 86, 87
eaten with carbohydrates and fats,
248, 255
excess, effects of, 270, 271
in Glyci-Med Dietary Approach,
270–72, 272–73
for increasing dopamine, 302
inflammatory high-fat, 274
for metabolism boost, 21–22
on nutrition labels, 269
for skin health, 373–74
weight loss from, 199–200
Protein bars
Almond Butter Protein Bars, 461
Elevate Me! Bar, 458–59
Simple Bar, The, 435
Push-ups, for chest, back, and core, 352, **352**
R
rBGH, in milk, 240–41
Recipes, 422–65. *See also specific recipes*
Red clover, for low estrogen, 310–11
Refreshers
hormonally balanced day, 386–88
metabolic shake-up, 390–97
6-week check-in, 388–90
Relationship exercise, 227
Relora, for treating
excess cortisol, 307
low DHEA, 307–8
sleep problems, 171–72
stress, 397

Sex
  benefits of, 135, 322, 324, 327–29
  centenarians having, 329
  in hormonally balanced day, 388
  television preventing, 158
Sex drive
  changes in, indicating health problem,
    323–24
  effect of hormones on, 29–30
  improving, 329
Sexual dysfunction
  with aging, 330
  in men, 325–26
  natural help for, 330–31
  prevalence of, 19, 29, 324–25
  in women, 326–27
Shellfish. *See* Fish and shellfish
Shopping list, Anti-Inflammatory Detox,
    134, 147, 466–69
Shrimp
  Cajun Shrimp, 457–58
Side jackknife, for arms and core, 358, **359**
Side plank, for arms and core, 358, **359**
Simply Bar, The, 458
6-week check-in, 388–90
Skin
  functions of, 371–72
  hormonal effects on, 374–76
  layers of, 372–74
Skin care, natural, 135, 371, 376–84, 389
Skin-care creams, 379–82
Skin-fold testing, for measuring body fat,
    117
Sleep. *See also* Sleep deprivation; Sleep
    improvement
  effect of eating on, 156
  melatonin and, 97, 154, 155, 158, 162,
    163, 167
  recommended amount of, 162
  for reducing body acidity, 142
Sleep apnea, 94
Sleep deprivation
  contributors to, 153
  estrogen dominance from, 74
  hormonal imbalances from, 154
  incidence of, 19, 154
  overweight and, 98
  signs of, 154

Sleep improvement
  creating environment for, 134, 157–61,
    388
  for difficulty falling or staying asleep,
    163–67
  hormonal benefits from, 153, 389
  Hormone Diet rules for, 161–63
  natural sleep aids for, 168–73, 304
Smoothies
  Açai-Avocado Smoothie, 423
  Antiaging Smoothie, 425
  Anti-Inflammatory Smoothie, 428
  chia in, 422
  Dopamine Delight Smoothie, 426
  Serotonin-Surge Smoothie, 427
  strength training and, 337–38
  Super Satisfying Shake, 426
  Testosterone-Surge Smoothie, 427
  tips for making, 424
Snacks
  Almond Butter Protein Bars, 461
  before bed, 166–67
  Berry-Apple Ricotta Cheese, 462
  Berry-Pecan Mix, 463
  Black Bean Dip or Burrito Filling,
    459
  Curried Chickpea Dip, 459–60
  Elevate Me! Bar, 458–59
  Erin's Healthy Muffins, 464–65
  Healthy Nacho Snack, 463
  in hormonally balanced day, 387
  Hummus and Veggies, 460–61
  Quick Trail Mix, 460
  Simple Apple Snack, 462
  Simply Bar, The, 458
  Tamari Almonds, 464
Sodium, on nutrition labels, 269–70
Soft drinks, artificial sweeteners in, 243
Soups
  Lovely Lentil Soup, 436
  Roasted Vegetable Soup, 442–43
  Sweet Potato, Squash, and Ginger
    Soup, 435
  Tomato Soup, 443
Soy products
  hypothyroidism and, 83
  permitted in Anti-Inflammatory
    Detox, 194

Total wellness program, *Hormone Diet* as, 8

Toxins
    bisphenol-A (BPA), 178
    buildup of, 179–80
    estrogen-disrupting chemicals, 178–79
    harmful effects of, 176–77
    indoor
        detoxification plan for, 418–21
        harmful effects of, 417–18
    phthalates, 178

Trail mix
    Quick Trail Mix, 460

Trans fats, inflammation from, 235

Treatment Pyramid, of Hormonal Health Profile, 39, 52, **53**, 135, **295**, 296, 389

Tribulus terrestris, for low testosterone, 312

Triceps dips, 364, **364**

Triphala, for intestinal detoxification, 196

Tryptophan
    food sources of, 304
    for improving sleep, 169

TSH (thyroid-stimulating hormone), 81
    for hypothyroidism, 3–4
    normal vs. abnormal levels of, 2
    testing levels of, 85, 397, 407

T3 (triiodothyronine), 81, 83
    testing levels of, 85, 397, 407, 408

Tuna
    Curried Tuna-Chia Salad, 432

Turkey
    Carb Craving Shepherd's Pie, 452
    Quick-and-Easy Pasta with Tomato Sauce, 454–55
    Summer Salad with Honey Mustard Dressing, 444
    Turkey Burger with Mixed Green Salad, 456
    Turkey Wrap, 445
    Warm Black Bean and Turkey Salad, 438

Turmeric, for treating
    excess estrogen, 309
    excess testosterone, 314
    inflammation, 297

2-hour pp blood glucose and insulin test, 144–45

U

Urine testing, for assessing
    food allergies, 410
    heavy metal toxicity, 209
    pH level, 141, 142

V

Vegetables. *See also* Salads; *specific vegetables*
    Anti-Inflammatory Curry, 447–48
    Awesome Omelette, 428–29
    Carb Craving Shepherd's Pie, 452
    Hummus and Veggies, 460–61
    permitted in Anti-Inflammatory Detox, 193
    for reducing body acidity, 142
    Roasted Vegetable Soup, 442–43
    Sweet Garlic Chicken Stir-Fry, 448
    Veggie Chili, 446–47

Visceral fat, health risks from, 112

Visualization(s)
    before bedtime, 167
    in hormonally balanced day, 388
    for stress relief, 220, 227–29, 228, 389, 397

Vitamin A, in skin-care products, 382

Vitamin and mineral absorption, stomach acid and, 183

Vitamin B6
    for improving sleep, 173
    for low serotonin, 303

Vitamin C
    buffered, for reducing body acidity, 142
    in skin-care products, 381–82
    stress depleting, 285
    for treating
        constipation, 201
        detox symptoms, 199
        excess cortisol, 306
        heavy metal toxicity, 210

Vitamin D3, 109
    for cancer protection, 109, 285
    deficiency of, in pregnancy, 110
    for low serotonin, 303
    from sunshine, 372, 372

Vitamin E, 285, 291

Vitamin or mineral deficiency. *See also* Nutrient deficiencies
    oversleeping and, 162

Vitamin production, probiotics and, 187
Vitex, for treating
    low dopamine, 302
    low progesterone, 311

W

Waist circumference, for measuring body fat, 116, <u>120</u>
Waist-to-hip ratio
    indicating insulin sensitivity, 144
    for measuring body fat, 116, <u>120</u>, **121**
Walking, benefits of, 203
Warning scores, in Hormonal Health Profile, 52
Water drinking, 254, 260, 395
Weight gain
    from artificial sweeteners, 242–43
    from deficient thyroid hormone, 21
    after dieting, 31, 32, 125
    hormonal changes with, 112
    with hypothyroidism, 1, <u>173–74</u>
    from low serotonin, 99, <u>101</u>
    with polycystic ovarian syndrome, 3
    potential causes of, 131
    from sleep deprivation, 154–55, 156
    from stress, 65
Weight loss. *See also* Fat loss
    from Anti-Inflammatory Detox, 199–200
    dieting alone as ineffective for, 31–33
    dopamine for, 105–6
    effect of hormones on, 14, 15, 18
    fats for, 274
    ghrelin interfering with, 78
    hormonal balance for, 5
    from Hormone Diet, 35, 37, <u>148</u>, <u>149</u>, <u>175</u>, <u>320</u>, <u>370</u>, 389
    insulin resistance preventing, <u>60</u>
    obstacles to, 13–14
    safe weekly amount of, 394–95
    sleep aiding, 156
Weight-loss plateau, tips for overcoming, 135, 390–97
Weight maintenance, keys to, 33–35
Weight on scale, muscle affecting, <u>137</u>

Weight training. *See* Strength training
Wellness Tracker. *See* Hormone Diet Daily Wellness Tracker
Wheat, reintroducing, during Anti-Inflammatory Detox, <u>199</u>, <u>204</u>, <u>207</u>
Whey protein
    in basic supplement plan, 286, 290, <u>293</u>
    in detox, 422
    in smoothies, 424
White-noise machine, for sleep improvement, 160
White tea extracts, in skin-care creams, 380
Wobenzym, for reducing inflammation, 298
Women's Daily Wellness Tracker, <u>472–73</u>
Workouts. *See also* Hormone Diet exercise plan
    eating before and after, 255–56, 271, 337–38, 344–45
    in hormonally balanced day, 386, 387
    lengthening, for boosting metabolism, 392
    mistakes with, preventing fat loss, 333–41
Wrinkles, 374, 375, 380

X

Xenoestrogens, estrogen dominance from, <u>73</u>

Y

Yeast infections, probiotics preventing, 187
Yoga
    benefits of, 340–41
    in Hormone Diet exercise plan, 344
Yogurt, reintroducing, during Anti-Inflammatory Detox, <u>198</u>, <u>204</u>, <u>207</u>

Z

Zenbev, for low serotonin, 302–3
Zinc
    for excess insulin, 300
    for low testosterone, 313
Zucchini
    Roasted Vegetable Soup, 442–43

Dr. Natasha Turner is one of Canada's leading naturopathic doctors and natural health consultants. She is clinic director and founder of Clear Medicine—a wellness boutique in Toronto. As an expert in nutrition and natural health, she is regularly featured in print and on television. Her experience has contributed to the design and development of two commercial weight-loss programs, which have helped to transform an abundance of lives. She also frequently lectures to both the public and health care providers on topics related to healthy hormonal balance. She lives in Toronto.

Visit her Web site: www.thehormonediet.com.